PRAISE FOR PIERCE BROWN'S RED RISING SERIES

LIGHT BRINGER

"For freedom to grow, for wounds to heal, the worlds need light. The sixth installment in the bestselling *Red Rising* series, *Light Bringer* is the long-awaited continuation of a story that has captured the hearts of millions."

—*LitReactor*

"Pierce Brown is releasing another Red Rising book; do fantasy fans even need more reason than that to get hype?"

—*Paste* magazine

DARK AGE

"[Pierce] Brown's plots are like a depth charge of nitromethane dropped in a bucket of gasoline. His pacing is 100 percent him standing over it all with a lit match and a smile, waiting for us to dare him to drop it."

—NPR

"An epic story of rebellion, social unrest, and sacrifice."

—*Orlando Sentinel*

"*Dark Age* proves that Brown has truly become a master. . . . Pierce Brown's ability to craft a riveting story with amazing character development [has] grown far beyond the original Red Rising trilogy. . . . With *Dark Age* he graduates to a whole new level, and let's just say that I'm both excited and scared to see some of these threads come together."

—*The Geekiary*

"Much like A Song of Ice and Fire's George R. R. Martin, Brown is an author who is interested in exploring the consequences of his protagonist's actions. Revolution doesn't come without a price and no one can stay a hero forever. . . . *Dark Age* continues the trend of compelling characters, fast plotting, action, and the feeling that no one is truly safe and no one is who you think they are."

—*The Mary Sue*

IRON GOLD

"Complex, layered . . . mature science fiction existing within the frame of blazing space opera . . . done in a style [that] borders on Shakespearean."

—NPR

"A thoughtful blend of action, intrigue, and prosaic human drama."

—*Publishers Weekly* (starred review)

"The gritty action and emotional punches will thrill fans eagerly awaiting more from [Pierce] Brown."

—*Library Journal*

"This is one you absolutely will have to read."

—*The BiblioSanctum*

"It's not a Red Rising book unless you feel your very existence is being threatened while reading it. *Iron Gold* certainly fits that bill, so Howlers: brace yourselves and pray for your faves."

—*Read at Midnight*

"The mix of political intrigue, action and thematic journeys elevate this book from a simple sci-fi adventure into something more thought-provoking and rewarding."

—*Flickering Myth*

"Pierce Brown's *Iron Gold* ends up being perhaps his best effort since *Red Rising*, and for a book that expands a trilogy, that's an impressive feat."

—*Culturess*

MORNING STAR

"You could call [Pierce] Brown science fiction's best-kept secret. . . . He flirts with volume, oscillating between thundering space escapes and hushed, tense parleys between rivals, where the cinematic dialogue oozes such specificity and suspense you could almost hear a pin drop between pages. His achievement is in creating an uncomfortably familiar world of flaw, fear, and promise."

—*Entertainment Weekly*

"Brown's vivid, first-person prose puts the reader right at the forefront of impassioned speeches, broken families, and engaging battle scenes."

—*Publishers Weekly* (starred review)

"A page-turning epic filled with twists and turns . . . simply stellar."

—*Booklist* (starred review)

"There is *no one* writing today who does shameless, Michael Bay–style action set pieces the way Brown does. The battle scenes are kinetic, bloody, breathless, crazy. Everything is on fire all the time."

—NPR

"*Morning Star* is this trilogy's *Return of the Jedi*. . . . The impactful battles that make up most of *Morning Star* are damn near operatic. . . . It absolutely satisfies."

—Tor.com

"Multilayered and seething with characters who exist in a shadow world between history and myth, much as in Frank Herbert's *Dune* . . . [*Morning Star* is] ambitious and satisfying."

—*Kirkus Reviews*

GOLDEN SON

"Gripping . . . On virtually every level, this is a sequel that hates sequels—a perfect fit for a hero who already defies the tropes. [Grade:] A"

—*Entertainment Weekly*

"[Pierce] Brown writes layered, flawed characters . . . but plot is his most breathtaking strength. . . . Every action seems to flow into the next."

—NPR

"In a word, *Golden Son* is stunning. Among science-fiction fans, it should be a shoo-in for book of the year."

—Tor.com

"The stakes are even higher than they were in *Red Rising,* and the twists and turns of the story are every bit as exciting. The jaw-dropper of an ending will leave readers hungry for the conclusion to Brown's wholly original, completely thrilling saga."

—*Booklist* (starred review)

"Stirring . . . Comparisons to *The Hunger Games* and *Game of Thrones* series are inevitable, for this tale has elements of both."

—*Kirkus Reviews*

RED RISING

"[A] spectacular adventure . . . one heart-pounding ride . . . Pierce Brown's dizzyingly good debut novel evokes *The Hunger Games, Lord of the Flies,* and *Ender's Game.* . . . [*Red Rising*] has everything it needs to become meteoric."

—*Entertainment Weekly*

"[A] top-notch debut novel . . . *Red Rising* ascends above a crowded dystopian field."

—*USA Today*

"Reminiscent of . . . Suzanne Collins's *The Hunger Games* . . . [*Red Rising*] will captivate readers and leave them wanting more."

—*Library Journal* (starred review)

"A story of vengeance, warfare and the quest for power . . . reminiscent of *The Hunger Games* and *Game of Thrones.*"

—*Kirkus Reviews*

BY PIERCE BROWN

Red Rising

Golden Son

Morning Star

Iron Gold

Dark Age

Light Bringer

LIGHT BRINGER

PIERCE BROWN

NEW YORK

2024 Del Rey Trade Paperback Edition

Copyright © 2023 by Pierce Brown
Maps copyright © 2023 by Joel Daniel Phillips

Published in the United States by Del Rey, an imprint of Random House, a division of Penguin Random House LLC, New York.

DEL REY and the CIRCLE colophon are registered trademarks of Penguin Random House LLC.

Originally published in hardcover in the United States by Del Rey, an imprint of Random House, a division of Penguin Random House LLC, in 2023.

ISBN 9780425285992
Ebook ISBN 9780425285985

Printed in the United States of America on acid-free paper

randomhousebooks.com

2 4 6 8 9 7 5 3 1

Book design by Caroline Cunningham

TO TRICIA NARWANI, MY ATHENA

TO MIKE BRAFF, MY VIRGIL

PROGRADE GROUP

CALLISTO
EUROPA
IO
GANYMEDE

THE JOVIAN SYSTEM
KNOWN ORBITAL OBJECTS: 121

In the twelfth year of the Solar War
Commissioned by Sovereign Virginia
Augustus, 755 PCE

◯ -- MOONS

RETROGRADE GROUP

-- KALYKE

THE MOON IO
ORBITAL RADIUS 422,000 KM

In the twelfth year of the Solar War
Commissioned by Sovereign Virginia
Augustus, 755 PCE

INSTITUTE

NESOS

PLUTUS

YELLOW
SEA

DEMETER'S GARTER

DRAGON TOMB

SUNGRAVE

NIGHTMOURN

WASTE OF
KARRACK

DARKFALL

THE MOOΠ EUROPΛ
ORBITΛL RΛDIUS 670,900 KM.

In the twelfth year of the Solar War
Commissioned by Sovereign Virginia
Augustus, 755 PCE

HΛRMOΠIΛ

HERΛKLIOΠ

DISCORDIΛ
SEΛ

ΠYΛD
ISLES

THE DEEP

ΠIXIΛΠ
ISLES

OCEΛΠUS

PSYCHOΠΛS

DRAMATIS PERSONAE

THE SOLAR REPUBLIC

DARROW OF LYKOS/THE REAPER   ArchImperator of the Solar Republic, husband to Virginia, a Red

VIRGINIA AUGUSTUS/MUSTANG   Reigning Sovereign of the Solar Republic, wife to Darrow, Primus of House Augustus, sister to the Jackal of Mars, a Gold

PAX AUGUSTUS   Son of Darrow and Virginia, a Gold

DIO OF LYKOS   Sister to Eo, wife to Kieran of Lykos and mother of Rhonna, a Red

KIERAN OF LYKOS   Brother to Darrow, ArchGovernor of Mars, a Red

RHONNA OF LYKOS   Niece of Darrow, daughter of Kieran, Howler lancer, Pup Two, a Red, lost in the fall of Heliopolis

DEANNA OF LYKOS   Mother to Darrow, a Red

SEVRO BARCA/THE GOBLIN   Imperator of the Republic, husband to Victra, Howler, a Gold

VICTRA BARCA   Wife to Sevro, neé Victra au Julii, a Gold

ELECTRA BARCA   Daughter of Sevro and Victra, a Gold

ULYSSES BARCA Son of Sevro and Victra, killed by Harmony and the Red Hand

DANCER/SENATOR O'FARAN Senator, former Sons of Ares lieutenant, Tribune of the Red bloc, a Red, killed on the Day of Red Doves

KAVAX TELEMANUS Primus of House Telemanus, client of House Augustus, a Gold

NIOBE TELEMANUS Wife to Kavax, client of House Augustus, a Gold

DAXO TELEMANUS Heir of House Telemanus, son of Kavax and Niobe, senator, Tribune of the Gold bloc, a Gold, killed by Lilath au Faran

THRAXA TELEMANUS Praetor of the Free Legions, daughter of Kavax and Niobe, Howler, a Gold

ALEXANDAR ARCOS Eldest grandson of Lorn au Arcos, heir to House Arcos, allied to House Augustus, lancer, Pup One, a Gold, killed by Lysander au Lune

LORN AU ARCOS Former Rage Knight, head of House Arcos, mentor to Darrow of Lykos, a Gold, killed by Lilath au Faran and Adrius au Augustus

CADUS HARNASSUS Imperator of the Republic, second in command of the Free Legions, engineer, an Orange

ORION AQUARII Navarch of the Republic, Imperator of the White Fleet, a Blue, killed in Operation Tartarus

ORO SCULPTURUS Navarch of the Republic, leader of Phobos's astral defense, a Blue

COLLOWAY CHAR A pilot, reigning kill-leader of the Republic Navy, Howler, a Blue

HOLIDAY NAKAMURA Dux of Virginia's Lionguard, sister to Trigg, client of House Augustus, Centurion of the Pegasus Legion, a Gray

QUICKSILVER/REGULUS SUN Richest man in the Republic, head of Sun Industries, a Silver

MATTEO Husband to Regulus Sun, a Pink

THEODORA Leader of the Splinter operatives, client of House Augustus, a Pink Rose, executed by the Vox Populi

CLOWN Howler, client of House Barca, a Gold

PEBBLE Howler, client of House Barca, a Gold

MIN-MIN Howler, sniper and munitions expert, client of House Barca, a Red, killed by the Abomination

SCREWFACE Howler, client of House Augustus, a Gold

CASSIUS BELLONA Son of Julia au Bellona, former Olympic Knight, former mentor to Lysander au Lune, a Gold

THE SOCIETY

ATALANTIA AU GRIMMUS Dictator of the Society, daughter of the Ash Lord Magnus au Grimmus, sister to Aja and Moira, former client of House Lune, a Gold

LYSANDER AU LUNE Grandson of former Sovereign Octavia, heir to House Lune, former patron of House Grimmus, a Gold

ATLAS AU RAA/THE FEAR KNIGHT Brother to Romulus au Raa, Legate of the Zero Legion ("the Gorgons"), former ward of House Lune, client of House Grimmus, a Gold

AJAX AU GRIMMUS/THE STORM KNIGHT Son of Aja au Grimmus and Atlas au Raa, heir of House Grimmus, Legate of the Iron Leopards, a Gold

KALINDORA AU SAN/THE LOVE KNIGHT Olympic Knight, aunt to Alexandar au Arcos, client of House Grimmus, a Gold, killed by Darrow

JULIA AU BELLONA Cassius's estranged mother and Darrow's enemy, Primus of the House Bellona remnant, Princeps Senatus of the Two Hundred, a Gold

PALLAS AU GRECCA Captain of the Bellona chariot team, Bellona client, a Gold

SCORPIO AU VOTUM Primus of House Votum, a Gold

CICERO AU VOTUM Heir to House Votum, Legate of the Scorpion Legion, a Gold

HORATIA AU VOTUM Sister to Cicero au Votum, member of the Reformer bloc in the Two Hundred, a Gold

CIPIO AU FALTHE Primus of House Falthe (the purity-obsessed war masters of Earth), a Gold

ASMODEUS AU CARTHII Primus of House Carthii (the shipbuilders of Venus), a Gold

VALERIA AU CARTHII Daughter of Asmodeus au Carthii, and one of his many heirs, a Gold

RHONE TI FLAVINIUS Dux of House Lune, leader of Legio XIII Dracones (the Praetorian Guard), a Gray

DEMETRIUS TI INTERIMO Lunese, archCenturion of Legio XIII Dracones, a Gray

MARKUS TI LACRIMA Lunese, centurion of Legio XIII Dracones, a Gray

DRUSILLA TI PISTRIS Lunese, decurion of Legio XIII Dracones, a Gray

KYBER TI UMBRA Lunese, legionnaire of Legio XIII Dracones, whisper to Lysander au Lune, a Gray

MAGNUS AU GRIMMUS/THE ASH LORD Former ArchImperator to Octavia au Lune, the Burner of Rhea, a Gold, killed by the Howlers and Apollonius au Valii-Rath

OCTAVIA AU LUNE Former Sovereign of the Society, grandmother to Lysander, a Gold, killed by Darrow

AJA AU GRIMMUS Daughter of Ash Lord Magnus au Grimmus, a Gold, killed by Sevro, Cassius, Virginia, and Darrow

GLIRASTES THE MASTER MAKER Architect and inventor, an Orange

EXETER Valet to Glirastes, a Brown

PYTHA XE VIRGUS Captain of the *Lightbringer*, former co-pilot of the *Archimedes*, a Blue

THE RIM DOMINION

DIDO AU RAA Co-consul of the Rim Dominion, wife to former Sovereign of the Rim Dominion Romulus au Raa, née Dido au Saud, a Gold

DIOMEDES AU RAA/THE STORM KNIGHT Son of Romulus and Dido, Taxiarchos of the Lightning Phalanx, a Gold

SERAPHINA AU RAA Daughter of Romulus and Dido, Lochagos of the Eleventh Dustwalkers, a Gold, killed in battle

HELIOS AU LUX Co-consul of the Rim Dominion, with Dido, former Truth Knight, a Gold

ROMULUS AU RAA/THE LORD OF THE DUST Former Primus of House Raa, former Sovereign of the Rim Dominion, a Gold, killed by ceremonial suicide

GAIA AU RAA Mother to Romulus au Raa and grandmother to Diomedes and Thalia, a Gold

THALIA AU RAA Younger sister of Diomedes, a Gold

VELA AU RAA Sister of Atlas and Romulus, a Legate, a Gold

GRECCA AU CODOVAN Lady of Ganymede, a Gold

THE OBSIDIAN

SEFI THE QUIET Queen of the Obsidian, leader of the Valkyrie, sister to Ragnar Volarus, an Obsidian, killed by Volsung Fá

VALDIR THE UNSHORN Warlord and royal concubine of Sefi, imprisoned for treason against the Republic, an Obsidian

RAGNAR VOLARUS Former leader of the Obsidian, Howler, an Obsidian, killed by Aja au Grimmus

VOLSUNG FÁ King of the Obsidian, father of Sefi, grandfather of Volga Fjorgan, once known as Vagnar Hefga, an Obsidian

VOLGA FJORGAN   Daughter of Ragnar, former colleague of Ephraim ti Horn, an Obsidian

UR THE EATER OF JOY   Named Spear of the Throne of Ultima Thule, an Obsidian

SKARDE OLSGUR   Jarl of the Volk, tribe of the Blood Ram, an Obsidian

SIGURD OLSGUR   Son of Skarde, brave of the Blood Ram

OTHER CHARACTERS

AURAE   A Raa hetaera and companion to Cassius, a Pink

APOLLONIUS AU VALII-RATH/THE MINOTAUR   Heir to House Valii-Rath, verbose, a Gold

THARSUS AU RATH   Brother to Apollonius au Valii-Rath, a Gold

VORKIAN TI HADRIANA   Centurion in the Rath house legions, a Gray

LYRIA OF LAGALOS   Gamma from Mars, client of House Telemanus, a Red

LIAM OF LAGALOS   Nephew of Lyria, client of House Telemanus, a Red

CHEON   Chiliarch of the Black Owls, a Daughter of Athena, a Red

HARMONY   Leader of the Red Hand, former Sons of Ares lieutenant, a Red, killed by Victra

FIGMENT   Freelancer, a Brown, dead

FITCHNER AU BARCA/ARES   Former leader of the Sons of Ares, Sevro's father, a Gold, killed by Cassius au Bellona

EPHRAIM TI HORN   Freelancer, former member of the Sons of Ares, husband to Trigg ti Nakamura, a Gray, killed by Volsung Fá

PART I

CIRCUS

Yea, and if some god shall wreck me in the
wine-dark deep, even so I will endure . . . For
already have I suffered full much, and much
have I toiled in perils of waves and war. Let
this be added to the tale of those.

—HOMER

1

DARROW

Castaway

O UR SUN FLOATS IN darkness attended by moons made of trash.
Long ago, when the planets were reshaped by mankind, the
detritus of their terraforming operations was fused together into moon-
sized spheres by orbital compactors and shoved out toward Sol. Gripped
by the gravity of her mass, most of these trash moons have completed
their centuries-long funeral march into the nuclear fires of the sun, but
several hundred laggards still remain circling their eventual demise.

Tethered to the barren landscape of a forgotten trash moon once
catalogued as Marcher-1632, a shipwrecked corvette named the *Archimedes* hides in the shadow cast by a waste escarpment a kilometer high.
Martian slaves-turned-soldiers-turned-castaways crawl over the ship.
Our welding torches flare against the hull. Our space suits are stinking
bogs. We are marooned two hundred million kilometers from home,
and I stew in sweat, nausea, and discontent.

That bloodydamn Bellona. That arrogant Peerless shit.

I'm going to break his knee if I ever see him again. It should be him
on this hull. I'd tell him to his face, but he took the only relic in the
base's hangar that could still fly and stole off with Aurae, his Pink ac-
complice, while I slept. He recorded a little message telling me to tend
my wounds, and left his mess behind—his crippled ship—for us to repair. The bastard.

More than a decade separated from Olympia's airy sepulchres has
done little to dim Cassius's spectacular talent for condescension. Worst
of all, in typical Cassius fashion, he's taking his damn time. Six weeks

he's been gone on a mission to Starhold—an ecliptic trade post between the orbits of Mercury and Venus—to secure us the helium we need for the *Archimedes*. While here I am: either languishing in the old Sons of Ares base that's hidden in the belly of the trash moon or latched onto the side of his ship like an industrious barnacle welding the days away, knowing time is running out.

Hades, it may already have run out.

Cut off from communication with the outside world, I have no way of knowing the course of the war I began. No way of knowing if Virginia and Victra have managed to weather the united power of the Golds of the Rim and the Core. No way of knowing if Sefi has come back to the Republic or if Lysander has used my defeat on Mercury as a ladder to the Morning Chair.

No way of knowing if the enemy has already burned Mars, my family, my home.

I think of Mars and her highland moors and whispering woods . . .

No. Virginia told me to endure.

I've been imprisoned before. I know I must force away the thoughts of home before they make debris of me. Not for the first time, I try to seek refuge in anger. I want a fight. I need a fight. It's how I'm made—to struggle in eternal vain. But instead of a fight, instead of the forward motion that soothes my restless nature, all I get is the monotone hum of generators and the days congealing together, a litany of endless routine.

I started this war. Others are finishing it. I must escape. Atalantia must die. Atlas must die. Lysander must die. I picture them each groveling before me, my ears deaf, my hand choking the life from them as blood swells in their eyes.

The violent fantasies do nothing to ease my desolation. The anger that once made planets tremble is now toothless. Shorn of my myth by my failure, shorn of my army by my mistakes, shorn of my friends and family by the demands I made on them, I know hate will not return what I have lost or repair what I have broken.

The sun has raged for 4.6 billion years. I have raged for sixteen. No surprise, the sun has more fuel to spare. Even my anger at Cassius feels performative. I can't sustain it anymore, can't feed this endless anger at myself and everyone. Not after what I have done.

I escaped Mercury with my life, but it cost me my Free Legions and what remained of my self-respect. I led children of Mars to a planet far from home promising we could finish the war, only to abandon them to the enemy to save my own hide. My heart is buried with my army in those sands. But my body trudges on, as it does, no matter the ruin it leaves in its wake.

It's been a backward slide since I fled Mercury with my small band of survivors. Cassius rescued barely two hundred of us from Heliopolis, but it was not a clean escape. Harried by Grimmus torchShips, we missed our rendezvous with the Telemanus fleet. Missed our chance home. We barely managed to limp into the base on the Marcher before Cassius took off.

The silence is broken by the chatter of the other welders. One tells a joke. It's funny enough for me to stop flagellating myself. I listen to the other voices. They remind me of the drillboys chattering in the tunnel above my clawDrill back in Lykos. Their bad jokes soothe me, and my mind wanders to the tattered book Aurae left in the helmet of my space suit before she slipped off with Cassius.

The note Aurae left with it said that the book was her path through the darkness of her servitude in the Rim. I was angry after Aurae and Cassius left and nearly used the book as toilet paper. But I've always felt Pinks to be the most oppressed of the Colors, their plight imbuing some of them with preternatural internal strength. Evey and Theodora taught me that. So, more out of respect for them than Aurae, I read the first page. I grew annoyed by the opacity of the writing. It read like a divination book, repeating conventional wisdom in esoteric metaphors. Still, I recall a few lines that seem apt.

The path is made of many stones that look all the same. When you trod upon evil, do not rest or look down because goodness is only a step away. The next may bring ruin, the next joy, but these stones are not your destination, they are but your journey to the path's end.

I mull that over as I weld a new panel onto the hull. Maybe this is just a stepping stone. Maybe this place isn't perdition. Maybe it is a gift.

Truth is I should have died on Mercury. Truth is everything after that hell *is* a gift, even this place. It may be tedious repairing the antique fifty-meter corvette with only hand tools, but labor gives a man purpose, I suppose. Each panel welded a step forward. Each step forward takes me closer to my family. So long as Cassius returns with the helium we need for the reactor, and so long as Harnassus actually fixes the reactor, we will go home.

Maybe I'll read another page tonight.

But I'm a stubborn bastard, so maybe not.

My com crackles. *"Welder twenty-three, do you register?"* I holster my torch and ease back on my security line. *"Welder twenty-three. Ignore your existential dread for a moment and do reply . . ."*

"Welder twenty-three registers. What's what, Thraxa. That rash acting up again?"

Unable to find any suits wide enough for her prodigious thighs, Thraxa's stuck inside the base. Daily, the bellicose woman grumbles that she would have preferred the honorable suicide she intended to commit in Heliopolis to the daily monotony of shift management.

"Sun's on its way in thirty. Be a dear and rein your squad in before you boil in your suits."

I glance over my shoulder to the eastern curve of the trash moon. "A little early, no?"

"Archimedes's mass is speeding up the moon's rotation. We all know you skipped physics, but trust me on this one or by tomorrow your prick will look like a hydra. You're rad heavy as is."

"We can finish the hull this shift," I say.

"Next shift can finish. Aren't going anywhere without helium and the reactor fixed anyway. Call it."

With a grumble, I agree and call my crew to end shift. The welders scurry along their safety lines back to the base as I count heads. When the last is in, I pull myself down the hull, push toward the base, and ease down to the airlock.

At the rim of the airlock, I pause and do something I haven't done in all my welding shifts. I take the time to look out over the craggy horizon. A thin scythe of sunlight carves around the trash moon. It warps the mottled surface outward with heat, inverting expansion calderas until dust and toxic gas spew. The dust and gas coalesce around a scarp of green-black plastic before stretching out behind the moon to form a tail of shimmering particles.

I have seen things a Red miner was never meant to see—unspeakable horrors, impossible beauty. Things that would make the tail of particles seem commonplace. But today I feel a little different. A little more willing to see there's beauty here on this stepping stone. Maybe it's the book. Maybe it's the radiation. Whatever it is, I feel like today I have enough strength to look the other way, past the shadowy shoulder of the *Archimedes* to an expanse of stars in the distance where my eyes settle on a dim, ruddy light.

Home.

Space is empty and silent but my memory is full and rich with the sounds of home. I close my eyes and hear the whisper of the godTrees, the murmur of the Thermic Sea, the beating of griffin wings, Victra shouting at Sophocles, Sevro cackling at his girls, the clink and whir of Pax fiddling around in the garage, the voice of my wife.

For a perfect moment I see the promised dawn, my return to Mars, my home. Then it is gone. The moon has turned toward the sun. The light blazes through my eyelids until it is too much even for my golden eyes to bear. It is time to go down.

2

DARROW

The Book

I F MERCURY WAS A perpetual frontal assault on the nerves, Marcher-1632 is a slow siege on the mind.

The old Sons of Ares base is a claustrophobic, spartan affair. Built inside the Marcher to give early Sons raiders a hidden harbor from which to harass Venusian slavers, the base was abandoned eleven years ago when its garrison joined my fleet in our desperate attack on Luna. Eight months ago, we limped in to find the halls cold and in vacuum. By restarting the base's solar-powered generator we reestablished habitability. We found water stores, calories when we most needed them. But temperatures and gravity remain low, and the hostile radiation beyond the lead-lined walls makes us feel besieged. We look it. We are skinny, pale despite the sun-scars of Mercury on our faces. Nearly all of us are bald and those who can wear beards in remembrance of Ragnar.

Removed from the war, blind to the movements of friends and enemies, cut off from all communication from home, worry is our incessant refrain and routine our only salvation.

I worry over my son as I de-radiate with my crew in the flush, clutching the gravBike key Pax gave me before I left Luna as I used to clutch Eo's wedding band in the Lykos flush. I worry for Virginia as I slump through the narrow, drill-carved halls to the mess. I worry over Sevro—lost when Luna fell to the Vox—as I slurp down the freeze-dried amino mush. The others, as bald as I am, worry to either side. About their own loves. Homes. Lost time. Lost worlds. Together, we make a sea of worry under the dim chemical lights. We try to hide that worry from each other like it's something dark and secret and shameful. Like all lost soldiers, my survivors are tired and quiet except when they are grotesque, flippant, or profane. Sincerity is found only in the awkward silences or the quiet moments when Aurae's lyre fills the mess with songs of the Rim that somehow remind us of our own homes.

Not for the first time, I miss her songs. It's not been the same since she and Cassius slipped away.

I eat quickly, clean my tray, say good night to my troops, and resist the urge to condescend with a joke to get a smile. They know I left their friends to die for my mistakes. And they know I will work them half to death again next cycle. That's my job. If you don't use a machine, it breaks down. Like the Sons of Ares when we phased them in to the Republic military, like this base. But if something is used too much, it breaks apart, like Orion on Mercury. Like Sevro after Venus. Leadership is a tightrope, especially when you're losing.

Checking in at the base's machine shop to get a progress report from Harnassus, I find the Orange Imperator hunched over parts from the *Archimedes*'s reactor with a gaggle of mechanics. He is a simian-shaped man with big knuckles and a drinker's nose. His beard is more prolific than my own and shot through with gray. Spanners and auto-drivers rattle in the background as he comes to speak with me.

"Cadus."

"Darrow. Hear the hull's ready to go," he says.

"Nearabout. Third shift gets the honors of finishing. Won't take them half an hour. You're sure the plating will still be sensor resistant? It'll be stealth that gets us home."

"In theory it will be. So long as we didn't dilute the plating too much thinning it out," he says. "We're on track to finish right behind you."

I brighten. "Really? That test run didn't seem too prime—"

"That's because you're not an engineer. Assuming we get the helium we need, the *Archimedes* will be ready to fly when Bellona returns. If Bellona's not being tortured in a Grimmus sorrow sphere, that is."

"You might be the only one who thinks he intends to come back," I say with a glance for his men.

He shrugs. "We wouldn't be around to doubt him now if he didn't save us on Mercury. But I am worried he is bedblind. We should be warier about that Pink of his."

"Not that it's any of our business, but I don't think they're sleeping together," I say.

He's shocked. "Really? The man's utterly besotted."

"I don't think he has much say in the matter," I reply.

Cassius told me the tale of his escape from the Rim after we landed on the Marcher. He'd been a prisoner of the Rim with Lysander and forced into a series of unfair duels on Io. Impressed by Cassius, Diomedes au Raa falsified his death to protect him after he'd survived the duels. Diomedes hid Cassius in his estate on nearby Europa after accepting his parole—a promise not to flee until the war was done. Aurae, a hetaera of House Raa, helped Cassius escape Diomedes's estate on the *Archimedes*. She claimed to be a sympathizer of the Republic. Together they rushed back to the Core to warn the Republic of the Rim's plan to enter the war. They were too late. She's served as Cassius's crewmember ever since.

"Well even if they're not shagging, just because she looks like a dryad, sings like a Siren, talks like an oracle, and has a bloodydamn alibi doesn't mean she ain't Krypteia."

"If she were Rim intelligence, we'd already be dead," I say. Calling the Krypteia "Rim intelligence" is a compliment. Intelligence work is part of their charge, certainly. But the Krypteia's most insidious duty is maintaining the hierarchy in the Dominion at all costs.

"Unless she's leading the Krypteia to us right now. You have to admit: even for a Raa hetaera, she does have a diverse collection of skills. Medical. Engineering. Not exactly the domains of a courtesan."

My eyes narrow. "You've been talking to Screwface, haven't you?"

He grimaces. "Man does like to talk these days. Sows doubt like it's his job. Might do for you to check in on him?"

I don't know if I have anything left to say that will pull Screw from his depression. A thought comes to me. Maybe he'll be more receptive to Aurae's book than I am. He's a reader, Screw. I clap Harnassus on the shoulder and head for the door. I call back, "Cadus, if you thought Aurae was Krypteia, why'd you make her a lyre?"

Before she left with Cassius, Aurae would play her lyre and sing the songs of her spheres to the troops after dinner. Harnassus never missed a performance.

"It was for the troops," he lies with a blush.

I tell myself I'm checking on Screwface to keep him straight, but it's my own loneliness that inspires the visit. Of all my survivors, he is the only one who shares memories of the Institute. I just want a spark of our days of glory from an old member of my pack.

Taking two thermoses of the diluted caf from the processor, I grab my training pack and Aurae's book from my room and make my way through the base's upper labyrinth toward the coms chamber. I find Screw bathed in computer screens under thermal blankets next to his space heater. He looks more like an animated stack of laundry than the legend he is. It breaks my heart.

Screwface is a man uncelebrated by the public, because his sacrifices have always been in the shadows. Much to his chagrin. A lover of the high life, he envies the fame of Colloway Char or Sevro. When I met him at the Institute, he was ugly, lazy, and a freeloader. He is still a freeloader and would rather amputate his own testicles than pay for a drink. But with three years behind enemy lines and after being carved by Mickey and given a new identity by Theodora to infiltrate the Ash Legions, no one could describe him as lazy.

At first, he was delighted by his deep cover mission. Chronically insecure, when he emerged from Mickey's recovery suite, broad shouldered, ruggedly Roman in the face, with a chin almost as fine and just a little larger than Cassius's, I'd never seen a man finally so at home in his own skin.

"Fit, mate. I look bloodydamn fit to slag an entire ballet troupe. Bellona, what? Ash Legions here I come," he'd said, striking an Olympian pose. He was nude. Epically proportioned. Theodora even applauded.

But now? Now Screwface is ugly again, and he hates it. When Heliopolis fell, he was scalped and lost a leg. He covers the livid scar that starts just above his eyebrows with a wool cap, but the base's stores lack prosthetics, so he's made do with a peg of plastic padded with packing foam against the stump.

My command has ruined the man. *Twice.* Bitterness seeps through his every word, but he was there for me in Heliopolis, before it fell. He helped pull me back from despair. So, I can stomach his bitterness. "Word from Bellona?" I ask, handing him the caf.

He doesn't thank me. "Oh, we're calling the Decapitator of Ares by his real name today?" He pouts. "Alas, no the Chin and the Siren are still wayward."

"Do you always have to bring that up?" I ask.

"Aw, come now. Yesterday's talk was so fun. You had many adjectives for the Feckless Quim. The Avian Turncloak. Even a few adverbs."

"I was—"

"Bitter and drunk?" he asks. "You're all wrath when you're bitter and drunk. Honestly, I think this war would be won if you were that way the whole time, but then I fear it'd just be you and me lording over an autarchy." He chuckles at his rhyme, his lingo inverse to his birth, which was low. "Let's be candid though, everyone's been bitter about Bellona their entire life. Handed all the cards, wasn't the Putrid Adonis?"

"And misplayed them all," I offer.

"Except that dimpled chin. Oh, the dew-dappled valleys it's explored. My kingdom to be a hair on that mentum . . ."

I resist glancing down at Screwface's very dimpled chin. Unlike the rest of us, he still maintains a clean shave.

"Anything on the sensors?" I ask.

"Nil, oh bald and bearded liege." He cups both his hands around the thermos for warmth. The nails of both fingers are bitten to nubs. "Radar and lidar are still slagged. Tried building some filters to strain the soup—you know all this." He chews on a caf stick, swigs his coffee, and cocks his head back. "Routine may be your sanity, but you're driving me mad."

"You haven't left this room in three days," I say and nod to his slop bucket. "Your decor is starting to look very Sevro."

He looks around. "No jade. No golden walls. No silk. I've got about zero in common with that deserter's den."

"Screw, you know he did what he thought was right."

Screw spits on the ground. "I spent three years amongst Atalantia's sociopaths on behalf of the Republic while he was sucking on the tit of Gold royalty. Look at my reward." He removes his cap to show his mutilated scalp. "While we died, Sevro ran home. And I'm here waiting for that Pink to lead the Dustwalkers right to us."

"She's something all right, but she's not Krypteia," I say.

He frowns. "Then what is she?"

I think of Aurae's skills, the book, the way she watches me like a judge sometimes. "A friend, I hope."

"Let's pray you're right. Because they're out there, hunting us. They'll want to cut your head off for destroying the Dockyards of Ganymede. You and Victra. And Dustwalkers never stop till they find their mark."

I share Screw's respect for the Rim's stalker squads, just not his agitated tenor. It'd be almost ironic if they found us and dragged me back to the Rim to pay for my sins. But it isn't because of them or Aurae that Screw shits in a bucket for fear of abandoning the sensor station. Neither is it because of Ajax au Grimmus, who came closest to discovering us when his destroyer, *Panthera,* prowled within fifty thousand clicks of us five months back. Rightfully, Screw is only afraid of Fear himself.

I sympathize, because I am too.

"Atlas isn't hunting us," I say. He looks up at me like Pax would when I'd wake him from a bad dream. "Our trail's cold. In relation to the System, we're smaller than a zooplankton on a krill's back in all the seas of all the worlds put together. Even if Atlas doesn't think we're dead, he won't waste time looking."

"Not when he knows where we want to go, you mean," Screw murmurs. Maybe that was the wrong conclusion to lead him toward. "Shit, boss. Even if Bellona does come back with helium . . . it's a long sail home and we're the bottom of the food chain. If the enemy patrols spot us . . . won't be anywhere to run. Those Rim ships are faster than us. Not that it matters. Most of the lads and lasses think Mars has already fallen anyway."

"I need you to stop encouraging them in their pessimism. You're a Howler. The men look to you to set the tone. So do I. You're the only other one here from the old pack besides me."

"Pack? Two is not a pack, goodman. Two is debris circling a drain." He looks me over. "You're in denial, boss. Afraid to face the facts. Sefi and her Volk abandoned the Free Legions to steal a kingdom on Mars. The White Fleet is gone. Orion is dead. Free Legions are dust. Senate hung us out to die. Virginia didn't send reinforcements to Mercury. Sevro dumped us for his little Gold family. Clown and Pebble pixied out. Our pack's done. Our army's rotting on the pales. I don't blame you. I don't blame me. I don't blame the troops. I blame the mobs that balked and the politicians that connived."

So much for that spark I was seeking. I leave Aurae's book in my bag. Screw doesn't need words. He needs to go home.

"All the same . . . bitch to me, not the men," I say.

"Yeah. Yeah." He sips his coffee. "My bad."

Leaving Screwface no better but also hopefully no worse than when I found him, I head to the *Archimedes*'s sparring chamber via the umbilical that attaches the ship to the base. The white padding of the chamber is stained by years of sweat. Most of it belongs to Cassius and Lysander, but I've made my own marks in their absence. Since Lysander broke my blade, I've been reduced to using the room's practice razors—the very same ones Lysander would have trained with. Fetching one from the wall, I feel silly. Screw's words eat at me more than I'd like.

What's the use in training? The blade in my hand can't fix what's broken.

Much as I hate to admit it, resentment toward Sevro gnaws at me like it gnaws at Screwface. Sevro abandoned me when I needed him most. I could forgive him that. It's harder to forgive his betrayal of the army. He was the first brother of the Free Legions: when he left, doubt crept into the rank and file. Into me. Worse, Sevro's choice indicted my own choice. More than anything I wanted to return to Pax when he was kidnapped. To rescue him. To prove in the end I was there for him. I chose the duty of an Imperator over the duty of a father. Now I'm alone playing with blades.

The silence strangles me.

I almost turn back around. No one will notice if I take a day's leave. No one will dare say I didn't work hard enough. I yawn again. Maybe just a stretch today. Body could use it. Better to face tomorrow rested.

I almost cave. But I know by now that voice of reason is the enemy. Inside me there is a coward who fears discomfort. That coward will offer solace in the form of excuses. But it is the coward who grooms a man for his defeats. The coward who makes him accept them because he is accustomed to finding a good reason to quit. The coward inside can only be killed one way. I toss down my pack and don my training kit.

"Hello, teacher," I say to the sphere's computer.

"Welcome, blademaster three." The computer's voice is feminine and seductive, just the sort Cassius would choose. Ten years ago, I would have marveled at speaking to a computer, but the tech boom of the Republic has made the once-forbidden technology eerily commonplace. Compared with some of Quicksilver's systems, this computer is a troglodyte.

"Martian gravity profile again?"

"No."

"Asteroid combat profile?"

"No. Randomized intervals to a floor of point two and a ceiling of four point five G's. Let's run the system today. We'll finish on Mars." I rub my left forearm hoping it will hold over four G's.

"Affirmative. Duration?"

"Dealer's choice."

"Affirmative, blademaster three. Preparing session one six eight."

I fight back another yawn as the room warms up. I roll out my shoulders. They're stiff from the welding and from countless dislocations over the years. A tightness seizes my left lung as I take a deep breath, a souvenir of the razor Lysander drove into my chest in Heliopolis. I shake out my left arm, which had shattered when my slingBlade clashed with the blade Lysander took from Alexandar's corpse. Aurae, suspiciously versed in medicine, pinned the bones of my left arm back in place and applied a calcium catalyst, but I'll need a carver's work to regain full functionality.

My arm throbs. A good reminder of unfinished business.

A thought comes to me as the room's gravity wells warm up. When I trained with Lorn, he would speak to me as I flowed through the forms of the Willow Way. I miss the metronomic company of his voice, and I'm tired of silence.

"Computer, link to my datapad." I fish out my datapad and Aurae's book from my bag and scan in the first two dozen pages. I instruct the computer to narrate the text, then ease into the winter stance of the Willow Way, blade above my head held with both hands. I pause. "Computer. Voice sample from holofile one three one: Sovereign's Saturnalia Address."

A moment later, Virginia's voice fills the room.

"To those who wrote that we might read, to those who fell so we might walk, to those who came before so we might come after, gratitude."

The sphere begins its program. The gravity shifts are slow at first, alternating orientation as I move through the first branch of the winter stance and sweep the blade diagonally in descending cuts. I grunt in pain as my body warms up and the stiffness dissolves. Soon the only sounds are the whisper of the practice blade, the shuffle of my feet, my breathing, and Virginia's voice.

"The first understanding: The path to the Vale is inscrutable, eternal, and

perfect. It cannot be seen with the eyes, nor felt underfoot. It winds as it wills. It ends where it must. It climbs when it does. It falls when it should."

I flow into the autumn strikes, bending back and lashing forward in attack.

"It stretches deep into the rocks we dig, and back into our hearts. It winds on before and after us, in all directions and none. Though we may walk it, we may never master it. Though we may see the path, we can never know the truth. The path to the Vale is inscrutable, eternal, and perfect. It must be followed at all cost."

Six more understandings follow the first as I pass through the seasons of the Willow Way to fluctuations in gravity. Over the course of the hour, the narration loops a dozen times, playing on when I lay heaving on my back.

"The fourth understanding: The supreme good is the wind of the deep-mines. It flows through rock, around people, and over all lands. The wind is oblivious to obstacles though they shape her path. When you smell rust on her breeze, or hear the echo of tools in the dark, smile and be glad. The path is upon you, and you are upon it. All you must do is walk."

My left arm aches. My lung is tight and on fire, but my mind is blessedly empty as I lay listening to Virginia's voice. The words of the book are, as I first thought, opaque. I do not understand them yet, much less accept them, but they remind me of something I read long ago when I trained with Matteo. Not Dumas, not the Greeks, something that fell between the cracks. The book is familiar, as comforting as the echo of a lullaby from my childhood.

I return to my quarters in a trancelike state. With water scarce, I use a dull knife to strigil off the sweat and dead skin before continuing my nightly rituals. I record a message to my wife as though we'd just been talking and store it with the rest without review. Then I record my message for my son, another chapter in the testimony of an absentee father.

Months ago, I started telling him my life's story, a story I should have told him in person. Even if I can't make it back to him, maybe my story will. Tonight I begin with the day I met Virginia at the Institute and end with Cassius, Sevro, and I howling like wolves as we raced across the moonslit plains with Minerva's standard.

When I've finished, I sit on my bed feeling empty and satisfied. The book said something about emptiness being what we use. Boxes, cups. They are useless to us when full, because we use their emptiness by filling them. I leaf through the book again to find the phrase. Before I can, the base's proximity alarm begins to scream.

They've found us.

I jump from my bed, guilty with joy. At last, a fight, an opportunity, this I know how to do. I dress in sober glee, ready to kill.

Screwface's voice fills my room.

"Battle stations. Battle stations. Proximity warning. Votum torchShip inbound."

3

DARROW

Revenants

ALARMS BLARE THROUGHOUT THE base. I sprint down the corridor and catch a railrifle thrown by Thraxa as she falls into a run beside me. Her mouth is open in a mad-bad grin. She has the only razor on the Marcher and seems not at all interested in sharing it. "How many ships?" I ask.

Her eyes twinkle. "Just one," she says. "Still big enough to glass us. I say we play dead. Let them come in with boarding teams. Kill them all, take their shuttle, ride it over to their ship, commandeer it and . . ."

Ride it home.

My eyes go dark. "We might lose half the men."

"More," she says.

A cabal of two, we share a single mind. Our troops flow around us in the hall. They are so small. They glance up at us, their generals, for reassurance. Thraxa grips me, voice low. "If there's opportunity, we do what we gotta do."

"TorchShip closing! It knows we're here!" Screw calls.

"So much for playing possum," I say. I look at Thraxa's blade, Bad Lass. She shields it from me with her body and we jog on.

In our rush to access the main hall's slide, we nearly collide with engineers streaming up out of their barracks. Most wear only their field chest armor, still scuffed and dented from their trek through the Ladon. I take a chest plate from one and marshal two dozen on me. I send Thraxa to command the two railgun batteries as I head to defend the hangar.

"I should have the blade," I call as we part.

She booms a laugh. "You had your own!"

I did. I miss my wife's gift. I feel naked without it. Rifles are fine, but I hate being at the mercy of the quality of an enemy's armor. Better to be close, where the kill is assured.

"Have they spotted us?" I ask into my com. "Screw?"

Screw doesn't reply. In the hangars, I find Harnassus and several Oranges making a firing line behind a barricade. Harnassus tries to keep the fear from his voice. "It'll be Obsidian berserkers first through the doors," he says as I join him.

"Screw. I need a report," I say into my com. "Are they within range of the base's railguns yet? Screw?"

"They're transmitting a message." A pause. My heart thumps. Railguns prime down the firing line. Then Screw bursts into laughter. *"I'll be damned."* Has he finally snapped? Like Orion? Like Sevro? *"Boss, tell Thraxa to stand down the batteries. Stand down! The torchShip's a friendly. It's the Wayward Chin, and he's brought friends."*

The torchShip extends an umbilical to connect with our base. My troopers flock to the aperture as Colloway Char slinks out. Harnassus, Thraxa, and I wait for Char. Screw didn't bother coming.

Instead of ducking his slender shoulders and making a beeline for me, the best pilot in the Republic slows. Colloway Char is skinny as a rail, the dark skin of his face drawn tight to show every contour of his skull. When he looks out at the men, it's not with his usual weary tolerance, but with stony sovereignty. Char has never favored responsibility. I'd hoped he'd be a leader one day. He began that transformation on Heliopolis after Orion died, but he's completed the transformation in my absence.

"Are you with the Telemanus fleet?" a Red engineer calls to him.

"Has Mars fallen?" shouts a Brown rifleman with rusted mod arms and sunwashed eyes.

Colloway rears on the Brown. "Has Mars fallen? Has Mars fallen?" He sneers. "Where is your faith, Martian? Mars stands. As will she always."

The troops cry out in relief so profound it sounds like a lamentation. Char picks his way through them and tries a salute before I wrap him in an embrace. The top of his head does not even reach the bottom of my chin. I thought I'd gotten skinny, but I can feel his shoulder blades through his jumpsuit. Behind him several dozen Blues and Grays disembark and seek out friends amongst my band. I pull back from Char. Once he's greeted Thraxa and Harnassus, I blurt out: "Virginia. Is she alive? Is Pax?"

He turns on me with the look of a weary castaway who has seen too much to think of the people we once knew back home as anything other than vague concepts. After a moment, he nods.

"Virginia is," he murmurs. "She governs from Agea. Don't know about your son." I hold on to his shoulders to steady myself. Thraxa pats my back. "I saw Virginia issue an address three days ago, Darrow. Victra was by her side. As were Kavax and Niobe, and your brother, Kieran. He's ArchGovernor now."

I sway with so much emotion it hits like grief. I cannot speak.

"Kieran? What happened to Rollo?" Harnassus asks.

"Rollo was assassinated months ago," Char says.

I'm so used to death I don't blink.

ArchGovernor Kieran. Strange. I cannot imagine my reserved, polite brother holding the office Nero au Augustus once occupied. "Tell us more. We've been dark for months. What else?" I demand, drunk already and craving more.

"Not much. System is dark soup. Some new Gold weapon, or maybe one of ours. Rim's? Quicksilver's? Who knows. It's playing havoc with sensors and broadcasts from here to the Belt. False signatures everywhere. Solar flares. Laser warfare on telescopes. Drones with atomics. Add that to the broken hulks spinning everywhere and it's a mess. We're putting up a fight, I think, but it's safe to say we aren't winning the war. Rim came in force."

"Who's in command?" Harnassus asks.

"Helios has the Dust Armada and Dido the Dragon," Char answers.

Thraxa and I glance at one another. The Rim brought two of their three main armadas. Helios is not good news either. He is their best astral commander. A steely veteran more than twice my age and experience. "And Quicksilver? Is he back on Mars?" I ask.

Char frowns. "Soc gossip is he quit the war."

I stare at Char. "Quit the war? He started it with Fitchner."

He seems to resent how little I know. "Sefi's dead too. Blood eagled by Ragnar's father."

I stare at him. Is he even speaking Common?

"He rules the Obsidians, and stole the best of the Volk fleet before fleeing Mars."

Thraxa and I share a glance. She's covered in Obsidian tattoos. "Ragnar's father would be ancient. If he's even alive."

"Imposter," Thraxa sneers. "They fled Mars? Unshorn too?"

Char looks overwhelmed by our inquiries.

"Never mind that," I snap. "What about Sevro?" Thraxa makes a sound of contempt, far more interested in the Obsidians. "Where is he?"

Char doesn't answer. There's distance between us. Blame. "I thought you were dead. They said you were dead—the smugglers that got us off Mercury. Everyone thinks you are dead," he says. "You look halfway there."

I feel a pang of sorrow. Like I've been left behind. Outmoded, forgotten.

"I wasn't sure anyone else made it off Mercury," I murmur. I search behind him. "I don't see Rhonna with you."

"No." A lump forms in my throat. The last time I saw my niece, Lysander had broken her face after shooting Alexandar in the head. I look down. How will I tell Kieran I left his daughter behind? ArchGovernor Kieran.

"Her shuttle didn't make it to the *Morning Star* before the EMP went off," Char says. "She went down in the city. Only reason we escaped is because some of the assault shuttles in the *Star* were shielded from the EMP by the hull. We couldn't make it to orbit, so we hid in the mountains until we hired iron smugglers to sneak us off-planet. We stole the torchShip from the smugglers, who stole it from the Votum fleet. She's more battered than she looks. Half her guns are gone. Her armor's patchy. But she has a Votum transponder and she flies like a bat out of hell. Should be enough to get us home."

"How many are you?" Harnassus asks.

"Two thousand and eleven. All I could get out of Heliopolis. There's room for more on the torchShip. But we're packed pretty tight. Hoping you have food."

"Old MREs," I say. "Lots."

His eyes search the tunnel passages at the rear of the hangar. "Is this all your people?" When I nod, he doesn't look disappointed. He looks angry. I feel the weight of his indictment.

"You were on Mercury for weeks . . ." I begin. "The rest of the legions. The ones who couldn't get out. What happened to them?"

He surveys my face. "Do you care?" It'd have hurt less if he stabbed me.

Thraxa jabs a finger in his chest. "Your ArchImperator asked you a question, Char."

We're two different tribes now. My eyes narrow. How bad does he want our food?

"Butchery." Char looks away, and that common grief indicts my narrowed eyes. "Those who didn't starve to death inside the *Morning Star* or weren't eaten by Atalantia's hounds were impaled by Atlas. From Heliopolis all the way to Tyche. The rest they sent to the Votum iron mines. I saw it from the air. The road they made."

From Heliopolis to Tyche. I should have killed Atlas when I had him in my grasp. Just as I should have killed Lysander. Does no mercy go unpunished?

"No cheer for the hero of the hour or the helium he's purloined?" a patrician voice calls from the umbilical. Thraxa mutters a choice curse. With his golden curls shining in the grim hangar light, the bloodydamn Bellona enters and poses like a gallant razormaster entering the Bleeding Place to the amorous cries of fawning Pixies. When only silence greets him, he sighs his disappointment and waltzes toward me with four canisters of processed warship-grade helium balanced on his shoulders. They're stamped with the Bellona eagle.

Despite the fact that Cassius is offensively handsome, over seven feet tall, built like a highGrav boxer, and resplendent in his gray traveler's cloak, all eyes drift toward the dusky woman behind him. Though she wears filthy crewman overalls and carries a pistol, Aurae is as out of place amongst us rude soldiers as an orchid in a munitions belt, and not just because she and Cassius still have hair.

Aurae is a rare Pink. Not a cheap thrill with angel wings or horns or a silky tail waiting for a client in a Pearl club. Nor a Helen of Troy either—the type of flashing thoroughbred as might be seen on the arm of Atalantia or Apollonius. Aurae is a Raa hetaera. A beauty of shadow and dust with autumnal tragedy written in her features. Her face is long. Her skin is a shade darker than olive. Her thick hair is wavy and blue-black and never seems to be the same color or in the same braid twice. It is impossible to guess her age. Some have guessed forty, some thirty, some twenty. It's her eyes that make that last one impossible. They are wide set, dark pink, and ancient.

My troops may gossip and cast aspersions, but when they see Aurae's slender arms straining under the weight of a single canister of helium-3, a dozen men and half again as many women rush to help her. Thraxa shoves them all away and takes the canister. Harnassus tries to pretend he's not jealous of the soft smile Aurae gives Thraxa.

Used to the reaction, Cassius rolls his eyes and sets down his four canisters with flair. He pops a foot atop one and leans on his knee. My eyes drift to the helium, and I imagine embracing Virginia the moment I step off the *Archimedes* in Agea.

"My goodmen, the finest Martian helium-3 available, courtesy of my mother's smuggling operations on Starhold. Always did love filching from her purse. Behold. Your zephyr wind home." His eyes narrow. "Provided you haven't molested my ship beyond repair." He glances at Colloway, who watches him with beleaguered resentment. "Did you tell him, Char? No of course not, it's all on me. Typical."

"Tell me what?" I ask.

Cassius sighs. "It's Sevro. He's not dead. Worse, in fact. A sordid affair. He's been sold at a high-society Syndicate auction."

"Sold," I repeat. "To whom?"

Cassius winces. "That's the part you're really not going to like."

4

DARROW

The Sordid Affair

The hologram fills the greater half of my quarters.

A man hangs suspended in the air of the Syndicate auction house. The man is naked, scrawny, and smeared with tattoos and scars. His head is covered by a giant helmet in the shape of a wolf's head. When the pale-eyed Syndicate auctioneer waves a hand, the helmet detaches and floats into the air to bare an ugly, cantankerous face that means more to me than my own flesh.

Sevro.

Love has seldom caused me such physical pain.

There is a moment of confusion in Sevro's Red eyes. The same eyes Mickey the Carver took from me and exchanged for my Gold ones. Then agony as he realizes where he is. He hangs his head in shame, then lolls it back and forth. Even with his broken nose more crooked than a lightning bolt, his hair wild, his ears masticated, and his lips tattered, even with ten years of war and what happened to him on Luna wracking his body, I can only see the weird little wolfchild who saved me and Cassius from freezing to death in a loch. The teenage menace who used to stare at me from beneath a stinking pelt, half ready to run, half aching for a hug, desperate to prove he's worth a damn.

The boy inside the war-rent man pants in fear. It breaks my heart to watch his eyes search the auction floor as the enemy bids on him. They're anonymous, the bidders. Holographic projectors conceal their identities, beaming absurd avatars of beasts and gods from their starships or inner sanctums into the auction house. Sevro is unwilling to even look his tormentors in the eye.

I have never seen him so beaten.

The image cuts out mid-auction, replaced by grand military architecture. Stars and distant warships glitter out the mouth of a hangar flanked by caryatids of the Carthii family. A hauler mech, escorted by a pack of Syndicate thorns and an arbiter of the Ophion Guild, stomps out the back of a steaming blockade runner. The mech sets a cargo box down on its end. Four legionnaires in gray armor and white capes stamped with a purple bull open its giant lock. The cargo container parts down the center. Pressure hisses out.

Inside, Sevro hangs imprisoned in a slave rack. Months of beard growth covers his jutting chin. His hair is long and shot with white. Waste tubes with pressure motors worm out his emaciated gut downward into plastic sacks. He was shipped muzzled and conscious with barely enough calories to keep him ticking. His eyes are open and bloodshot and staring at someone beyond the hologram with familiar, tired hate.

A manly voice purrs. *"They whisper you are dead. That is how you left me: for dead. But I have claimed a new domain."* The hangar disappears, replaced by an angelic, evil visage. *"Are you dead, Darrow?"* Apollonius au Valii-Rath waits for an answer, as if this weren't a recording he made for me to see. *"If you are dead, then this dark age has ended with a whimper."* He looks despondent and casts his fierce eyes to the sky. *"No. You are not dead,"* he says to himself, then levels his gaze and lets his smile creep. *"You cannot be dead. I know it in my war-bred bones. But you are not on Mars, nor Earth, nor with your adamantine woman defending your sphere, nor raging against the forces of Helios and Atalantia at the head of your inimitable Ecliptic Guard. So, you must be hiding, wounded and weak. Scuttling in the shadows, a mouse in the dark. Young Ajax, son of Aja, aggrieved and dauntless, seeks your blood. So too the Rim, and their myriad hunters, chief of all: Diomedes, the Storm. They will catch you if you make for Mars, little mouse. They lie in wait. Clever, patient, hungry. They will never let you lead another army. Better to come here. Better to pass the time with me."*

He peers at me like a dragon might when hearing of a distant treasure—acquisitive, scheming, entranced. He runs his tongue along his teeth.

"To tempt you, I have acquired your mongrel at no small sum. On Luna

he was ill-treated. Ninety days of reprieve and dignity will I grant him in my domain, but on the ninety-first day, he will be released into the Hanging Coliseum of the Dockyards of Venus, as were the Carthii captives of old. And like the Carthii of old, I, along with my guests, will hunt him upon equine wings, and mount his head on a spear and feed his organs to the war pyre." He closes his eyes as if imagining the wind through his hair as he rides a Carthii pegasus, and the scent of burning flesh as he laughs with his friends by the sacrificial fire. When his eyes open, they shine with madness. *"Unless you come to me. Unless you come and we decide at last who is hunter and who is prey. Until then, my noble foe, per aspera ad astra."*

The light of the hologram fades, then the hologram starts over again, an endless loop. Screw pauses the image. Harnassus, Thraxa, and Colloway slump in the gloom around my small breakfast table. Screwface itches his stump. Cassius leans against the door with his arms crossed watching me. At his feet sits Aurae, her eyes closed.

"Where did you get this filth?" Screw demands from Cassius and thrusts a finger at Aurae. "Did your Siren conjure it?" Even Harnassus thinks that's ridiculous. Aurae doesn't bother opening her eyes to address the accusation. "Why is she even in this room?"

"I can leave," she replies.

"Slag that," Cassius says. "After what we went through to steal the helium, you should all kiss our feet." He pauses. "Never mind, you'd probably all enjoy that, you creeps. But to answer the query: I didn't *get* Apollonius's message. The mad bastard has been transmitting that from the Dockyards of Venus for two months. Due to all the jamming, I only picked it up three days before my contacts at Starhold linked me up with Colloway."

"So you just happened to come across it," Screw sneers.

Cassius remains droll. "After being cut to ribbons by Raa Dustwalkers, breaking my word to Diomedes au Raa, racing across half the system to plunge through the Ash Armada into a warzone to save Darrow, then back through the Ash Armada again—under the guns of the *Annihilo*, the *Annihilo*—I ally with the Minotaur, a grandiose ruffian overcompensating for his poor heritage whom I haven't seen since he was quoting Milton high on lexamine and blowfish poison in a Martian brothel fourteen years ago?" He bats the air like a cat. "Please. If you're desperate to insult me, at least do me the dignity of being lucid."

"Dignity." Screwface pitches his head back and laughs. "That the virtue you imparted on your impaling protégé, the Heir of Silenius? Dignity? Ha!"

At the mention of Lysander, Cassius's smile disappears. "Atlas impaled your troops, not Lysander. It's not his style."

"Oh, we know his style," Thraxa says. "Rhonna. Darrow's niece. It wasn't Atlas who beat her face in. Your boy did that, after he shot Alexandar in the head. Not in combat. While they were having drinks."

Cassius frowns. "Alexandar au . . ."

"Arcos," Colloway says coolly. It's the first time since he arrived that I've seen him look at me with any degree of sympathy. "He was Darrow's archLancer, Bellona. He was an arrogant shit, but the best soldier I've ever served with. Full stop. He offered Lysander blades. Lysander declined. Took his head off at range. His own cousin's."

Cassius's face falls. ArchLancers to an Imperator are often as close as children. The guilt on his face is exactly why I didn't tell him. It's not his fault, and I didn't want his sympathy.

I miss Alexandar. We all do. Which is why we all feel so sick looking at Sevro's auction.

Harnassus steps up to me, gentle. "Darrow, I know no one wants to be the one to say it, so I will. There's nothing to do here. We're millions of clicks behind enemy lines. Thanks to Bellona we have helium, and the reactor repairs on the *Archimedes* are being finalized. We should burn for Mars while we still can."

I stare at Sevro's image. The Dockyards of Venus are not so far away.

He's close. Closer than I thought.

Love for Sevro or hate for the horned one? Which is it that draws me like gravity?

"Why did we survive Mercury?" I ask. No one answers. I look around the room. "Why did we survive this prison here?"

"Darrow, we haven't survived yet. Not until we get home," Harnassus says. "Every day you've held us together, telling us home would soon be in reach. Now it is. Now is your chance to get back to our forces. To Virginia . . . to your son."

I resist that current and feel the pull of this new one.

"We survived so we could make a difference in this war," I answer for them. "The fight on Mars begins over Venus. The ships of the Ash Armada come from one place and one place only—the Dockyards of Venus. Atalantia betrayed Apollonius to us. The man is pathological with his grudges. So, the only reason she'd let him keep those dockyards is because she believes he has the ability and the willingness to destroy them. I left Apollonius with only a handful of men. Which means there are only a few ways he could present that dire a threat. Bombs, no? That gives us an opportunity."

Harnassus blanches. "Darrow . . . you can't."

"Why not?" I ask.

"Look at us. Look at yourself. We're hanging on by a thread."

"But we're hanging on," I say. I glance at Char. "Only half dead."

Char is done. "My gifts belong to the Republic. I will not squander them on another one of your suicide missions, Darrow." He gets up, lights a burner, and walks out.

I glare daggers at his back. Least he got his food.

Thraxa may not like Char's lack of tact, but she agrees. "Darrow, whatever luck we had, we spent getting off Mercury. With Orion dead, it has to be you who leads the fleet. Our priority must be to get you home."

Only Screwface has not spoken. His rancor at Sevro has been replaced by a look of abject sadness. Whatever complaints he had, he loves his friend. Still he shakes his head at me, begging me not to consider it.

I look at the rest of them. I saw enough hunger strikes in the mines to know how they're broken. Magistrate Podginus would pretend to agree to the terms. He'd descend with food. Roast chickens, fresh bread, hunks of steak glistening with fat. Then he'd find a technicality. He'd hem. He'd haw. He'd sigh. And he'd renege on the deal. It'd only take a day or two for the first strikers to cross the line. People can endure anything except false summits. False summits are where they break. My friends broke the second Cassius waltzed in with that helium.

My heart is often iron, but it melts for the broken.

They will try a peaceful mutiny. I can smell it in the air. They love me, but they will restrain me. I can't let it go like it did with Wulfgar. So I feign a surrender.

"I'm tired. Give me the night to think it over. Is that fair?" I ask.

"Of course," Harnassus says, relieved. "You know how much Sevro means to all of us."

Screwface nods and wipes his eyes. Thraxa squeezes my shoulder with her metal hand.

I return to staring at Sevro as my friends leave. His expression is frozen at the very moment he realized he was being sold at auction. The very moment he realized he'd become a piece of meat.

I massage my aching left arm, hating my frailty.

"Are you prime?" Cassius asks. I turn. I was so focused I did not realize he and Aurae had remained behind. He leans against the wall beside the door observing me from the shadows. Aurae's eyes are still closed, her face far off and pensive. I don't answer and turn back to Sevro, thinking.

"There's a cure for that," he says and produces a bottle from his pack. He pours a generous helping for himself, tosses it back, and pours another. "Why didn't you tell me about Alexandar and Rhonna?"

"Didn't seem relevant," I reply. "Do you need something?"

After a moment, he clears his throat. "Before all this. When Olympia was a beacon and my father's star was on the rise, he had time to spend on me. So he decided to take me for my first hunt—"

"Cassius, I'm glad you're here. Truly. But I'm not interested in lessons right now."

"I seem to remember teaching you one of your very first," he replies.

I turn around. "I beg your pardon?"

"Left you in the mud with a hole in your gut . . ." He pours some liquor into another cup and pushes it across the table to me. I drink the liquor down. "Because I'm a duelist, and you never have been. Not really."

"How's the arm? You know. The one I chopped off at the gala," I say.

He smiles. "You see, on my first hunt I had so many expectations. A thirty-six-point ivory stag had wandered onto our estate." I sigh and let him get on with it. "In the stalk, I imagined how it would fall to me. I would look at the stag, and it would look at me, and I would feel something transcendent, a mutual agreement for a great chase. The stag would flee, fast and wily. I would pursue. I'd release my arrow on the run. It would catch the stag mid-leap, true and in the heart. And I would feel exultant because I had met the stag on equal footing and given it the splendid, *noble* death it deserved. And for his part, the stag would feel at least some measure of satisfaction in being felled by a predator equal to his own majesty.

"Instead, I ambushed it at a watering hole. I misjudged the wind and the shot was ruinous. My stag bolted into the woods, maimed but not yet dying. We tracked it and found it eight hours later dragging itself across volcanic rocks. It had gotten three kilometers over them. You could see the bones of its ribs where the skin had flayed off. I'll never forget my father's face."

Aurae's eyes open, disliking the tale. Cassius doesn't notice. Her eyes shift to me and pierce right through me, studying.

"Point is, you think you have the Minotaur's respect. You believe that respect entitles you to certain privileges. That stag had my respect. I still slit its throat and nailed its head to my wall. Apollonius might dream of a great duel, but your head is his ticket back into Gold favor. He'll take it however he can."

"Six years in Deepgrave will change a man," I reply. "The experience is the point for Apollonius, not the result. I'm a cherished peer. That stag was not your peer. Anyway, doesn't matter. I'm destined for Mars." He nods along, patronizing. "I'm destined for Mars, Cassius."

"You should be, but you're not," he says.

"You've been gone ten years. You don't know me like you think you do."

He eyes Sevro. "Some things never change. You're going to try and sneak off when everyone's sleeping. After Mercury you don't want to spend any more lives. Darrow, I know guilt better than most people. I know you're afraid to go home. But I won't let you go get yourself killed, not even for Sevro."

"Let me?" I ask.

He smiles. The room grows chilly. "Kavax told me to bring you home. Virginia is waiting for her Imperator . . . and her husband."

I bristle at that. "You said you came back to—"

"Fight in your war. Yes. Die in a suicide mission? No."

"Who says it's a suicide mission?" Aurae asks. Her voice sounds as if it comes from an oracle's cave. She's not looked away from me since she opened her eyes. "Tell him your reasons, Darrow."

Cassius spares her a quizzical look. "Do you know something I don't?" he asks.

"Tell him your reasons, Darrow," she says again. "If you have more than one."

I do, I realize. Far more than one. They make up the current that's drawing me this way. Part of me feels the urge to fight that current, fight Aurae's smug look and the words of *The Path to the Vale*. But it's hard to hold on to petulance when you're wasting away.

"I have five. One: it's Sevro, and I owe him. Two: those dockyards are the heart of the Gold war industry, and if I can't save Sevro I can at least slag them up and buy Mars time. Three: when I appear there, I'll draw all eyes to Venus. It'll clear a path home for the rest of you. Four: the Minotaur respects me more than he respects his fellow Golds. Odd as it sounds, I might be able to turn him. Five. The Republic needs a spark. I would rather go home, Cassius. Trust me on that. But"—

—"the path leads to Venus," Aurae murmurs. I glance at her. *"The wind is oblivious to the obstacles though her path would not be the same without them."* She smiles. "So my book is intact after all, it seems?"

I hesitate again, unwilling to give credit to a book written by people I don't know given to me by a woman who, while she's had my life in her hands, I don't exactly trust.

"It's not toilet paper yet, no," I mutter.

Cassius is confused by the exchange. "Were you two in touch these last weeks? You're acting like you share a secret language all of a sudden."

"Isn't that always the case with those who've read the same books?" Aurae says with a little mischief. "My people believe only the dust knows the weight of Golden boots better than Reds and Pinks. You know Ares was a hero to my people, Cassius. So is his son. Which is why I will be coming with you, Darrow."

Cassius looks as if he just got the bar bill for the Howlers after a successful Rain.

"No gorydamn way," he says.

She frowns up at him. "Did I trade one master for another?"

He blanches. "Of course not. It's just I . . . don't think you quite understand where Darrow is going, or how he goes places, or what he does when he gets there. I've been on the other side of the equation . . . how do I say it? It's utter carnage."

"No offense, Aurae, but he's right," I say. "The answer is no. Apollonius doesn't have very many men, it's true. But the ones he does have eat scorpions for lunch and think whiskey and knife fights are for children. If it turns into a meatgrinder, I'd rather not bring the veal. No offense."

Aurae uncoils from her seat on the ground. As she stands, she reminds me of a deerling—tall and perilously slender like most Pinks of the Rim. I could crush her ribs and puncture her lungs just by stumbling into her the wrong way in a hall.

"Blame the frailty. Sure. Or we can cut to the quick. You don't trust me."

"I don't know you . . ."

"Darrow. I am a Raa hetaera. Slave to a house that lives on a molten rock raging with volcanoes, which also breeds dragons and founded the Krypteia. The Krypteia, not just an intelligence agency, but a cult dedicated to murdering anyone who compromises the precious hierarchy. Trust me when I tell you, the Raa do not raise creatures without fangs. If I wanted you dead, you would all be dead. Either from the heartfolly petals I brought with me from the Rim, ground down and dusted into the oats I served you when you were crammed in the halls of the *Archimedes*. Or sleeping in your bunks here breathing the air from the radiation filtration center on level seven b."

Cassius and I exchange a worried look.

Her eyes are sympathetic. "You read the book, but still you struggle against the path. That is your nature I suppose." She sighs. "But I am not veal. Veal can't fly. Thanks to Cassius, I am now very familiar with the running of the *Archimedes*. You two will need an escape pilot to stay behind when you and Cassius board the dockyards."

Cassius shakes his head. "Aurae—"

She raises her eyebrows in challenge. "I remember what you told me before I helped you escape from Europa. Do you?"

He clenches his jaw. He's not used to being held to the fire by a Pink, much less a Pink he's so obviously in love with, one who is so obviously not in love with him. He makes a grand show of his surrender. "Once more unto the breach, it seems."

She squeezes his arm. "This is your path too, Cassius. The one you want to walk. Remember?" He nods. "I have provisions I'd like to collect before we leave. I will meet you two back here shortly." When she's gone, Cassius runs a hand through his hair. "That woman."

"You don't even like Sevro," I note.

"No, and I imagine he's aged as well as Mercurian milk in summer."

"What did you tell Aurae then? Before she helped you on Europa."

He flops down into a chair and fondles his drink. "You know, I've always been a weaker man than I'd like to admit, Darrow. That's my charm." He sloshes his drink about. "Truth is, I bear tremendous guilt for the man I was before all this." I snort. "Don't. I can put up walls too." I let him talk. "I've always wanted to be a decent man, Darrow. But . . . well, I lacked the will to make the necessary sacrifices. I was a coward.

"The raw truth is, I liked my wealth. I . . . liked my Pinks. I liked being on top. A Bellona. I felt the wrongness of it, but I excused it. Said it was the way of the worlds. Pretended I wasn't the boot on the throat of the Reds or the Pinks. I made myself believe my honor made me an exception. One of the 'good' tyrants. Honor was made to hide behind, I think. Like a crown, or an Olympic cape." He grimaces. "I know now I was . . . only a more tolerable source of misery. If I am honest, that's why I spent ten years traipsing around the asteroids with Lysander, doing small good when and where I could.

"I wanted to come back a long time ago. But I was afraid, Darrow. Afraid of how people would look at me. Afraid of the hate I'd see in their eyes—and I do see it—because I know they're right to hate me. Wearing that Olympic cape, I killed Ares. Fitchner. A man worth ten of me. I was running from that guilt, that hate.

"So I fled. Further from home than I'd been before, and you know what I found? I found that hate—the hate I ran from for ten years— waiting for me in the eyes of the first woman I think I've ever really loved. She doesn't love me. But that's all right. She's a mirror, I think. It helps keep me straight. For her part, Aurae tolerates me because I swore an oath."

"What oath?"

"To pay back the debt I owe to the lows for killing their deliverer, Ares. I told you. She's a sympathizer. It's why she helped me. Because I helped you kill Octavia. Now I can't bring Ares back, but I *can* fight for his cause, for the Republic, and I will help you save his son." His eyes flick to me. "So please tell me you're not planning to duel Apollonius."

"You know me. I never fight fair if I can help it."

"A simple exfil mission then. Yes?"

"Yes."

"Minimal carnage. Swear it."

"Minimal carnage," I say.

His eyes narrow. "And we'll have an exit strategy?"

"Yes. *Dominus* Portobello," I say.

"Huh?"

"Screwface named him after finding him in the armory, growing in the dark." I go to open a kitchen cabinet and return with a heavy load wrapped in a towel. I toss it to Cassius. He unwraps the towel to reveal a black sphere the size of an ostrich egg with a smiling, fanged face drawn onto it. He sighs.

"Darrow, this is a thirty-megaton atomic warhead."

I smile. "He has a big personality."

"Well, then Apollonius should love him."

With rucksacks of gear slung over our shoulders, Cassius and I head for the hangar. Aurae trails on behind. The halls are suspiciously deserted, even for so late in the base's night cycle. When we enter the hangar, we discover why. Our way to the shuttle is barred by all my remaining men. Thraxa, Harnassus, and Screwface stand out ahead of them, marshals of this latest insurrection.

"Guess they know you too," Cassius mutters.

"What's this then?" Thraxa calls. "Slinking off in the dead of night?"

"I have a little errand to run," I say. "Didn't want you all to worry."

"Errand's canceled," she says.

Harnassus looks tired. Thraxa looks angry. Screwface looks at his boots.

I take my time searching the eyes of the men and women behind them. My welding team is here, as are the infantry and aviators and engineers. Their skin was made leather by the sun on Mercury, then the fat scraped away by privation on this base so that it hangs from their bones as if two sizes too big. They're here because they love me, but I see the anger in their eyes. It's an anger that's always been reserved for the enemy.

I feel a million kilometers away already as I address them. "Brothers, sisters. You have put your faith in me too many times to count. I have let you down. But I did not survive Mercury to slink home. I survived to continue the fight. Even if you cannot see it, there is an opportunity here to wound the Gold war effort, to help Mars. I do not ask you to wait for me. I ask only that you meet me on the Lion Steps with a mug of swill at the ready. Gods know I'll need it."

Thraxa doesn't understand. "Darrow, the Ecliptic Guard has gathered. The Red legions muster. Do you not want to lead the defense of Mars?"

"More than anything," I say. "But I believe this is the path. I have the right ship. I have the right plan. I will go to the dockyards, and I will find a way."

"And if you don't?" she says.

"Then I'll find a different way. Please let me pass."

"You're a fool." She draws her razor and surprises me by pushing it into my hands. "Take Bad Lass. If you die, die with a blade in your hands."

"It's been in your family for centuries," I murmur. Bad Lass is a silver blade embellished with foxes and trees. Her father, Kavax, gave it to her when she graduated from the Institute. It belonged to his mother.

"Then if it ends up on the Minotaur's trophy wall, I'll find you in the Vale and beat you to drippings." She slams me into a hug. "So don't die."

I thank her and turn to Harnassus. "What do I tell Virginia?" he asks.

I knew the answer before he asked. "Tell her I listened. Tell her I endured. When I give you the signal from the dockyards, sprint for Mars. Tell Char?"

He nods.

Screwface has his pistol drawn. It shakes in his hand. I approach him and clasp him behind the neck. "I'll come with," he says. "You need someone you can trust."

"Mars needs you too," I say. "You've been gone long enough. Your Sovereign knows your sacrifice, Screw. When you look into her eyes, you'll realize you've been seen this whole time. Serve Virginia as you've served me. Protect her. Protect Mars. I will return." I kiss him on the forehead and tear myself away.

I build up steam as I reach the troops. They don't look like they're going to move. I know it appears as if I've broken and parted from sense. I can't explain how I feel. All I can do is keep walking. Finally, the ten years of respect I earned from them makes them part. I walk through them until I reach the pedestrian umbilical to the *Archimedes*. There a lone Red with dark skin and narrow eyes bars my path. His crooked lantern jaw is set in an anger I know far too well, his ham fists balled at his sides. He glares up with rage three times too big.

I go around that one.

At the umbilical, I turn back to my men as Cassius and Aurae disappear inside. I look back at my friends, my soldiers with whom I've suffered so much, and raise my fist. "Hail libertas!"

Only my echo answers.

5

LYSANDER

Games

Shrill whistles pipe from a shimmering mirage as the wild sunbloods gallop out of the desert. The surviving youths of Mercury's ruling elite pursue the white horses, herding them in a ritual stampede toward the storm gates of Heliopolis. The horses pour through the triumphal arch erected to honor my victory over the Rising and into the streets of the city itself.

The horrific burn scar Darrow's boot left on my face itches like mad. Truly it'd be easier to be rid of the thing, but a scar from Darrow is a point of honor and a good reminder of what he's done to our Society whenever I look in the mirror and see the wrinkled, shiny horror that makes my eyelid droop. I resist scratching it. There are eyes on me. From my place atop the triumphal arch with Glirastes and Rhone to either side, I nod to a Blue. With a warble from the gravity engines the arch rises. We follow the horses as they press deeper into the city, their hooves rattling the surface of the Via Triumphia.

Behind barricades, the morning crowd is already drunk on spiced-clove wine from Keryx and cactus brandy from Polybos. Despite the herculean efforts of our sanitation divisions, radiation from the atomics used in the Battle of the Ladon still infests the continent. The radiation has made many of the citizens grow bald. In defiance of this pestilence of baldness, they boast wigs of eccentric length and color. And they remember well that it was Atalantia who sowed this radiation, not Darrow.

In the eyes of Mercury, Darrow and Atalantia are equally loathed, but

I am beloved. Pouring money into a planet will do that. They chant my name. Behind me, my Praetorians stare down at them like a row of militarized falcons. My whisper, Kyber, crouches to the left. My last line of personal defense, the discreet Lunese Gray follows me everywhere. Today she plays a Copper. Her sensitive jaguar-mod eyes rove the roof-tops from behind chrome goggles.

"They love you like children love their father," Glirastes says. Wind whips my cape behind me and tugs at Glirastes's brilliant orange robes.

Rhone grimaces. "If only love wasn't so . . . expensive. And if only all those voices belonged to soldiers."

"These people are the heart of the Society," Glirastes calls over the wind and the clamor. He shields his eyes from the sun to look south of the city to the spaceport. There the *Lightbringer*, beset by swarms of construction skiffs, looms like a mountain. "It's the thump of military boots and the buzz of welders that is the music of insolvency!"

"Better to be impoverished and strong than impoverished and popu-lar," Rhone replies. Though he cuts a fine figure in his purple and silver parade uniform, Rhone is no parade soldier. A veteran's veteran, he's fought on thirteen spheres and wears the evidence in the phalera on his chest and the scars on his face. He is no blunt object. A violent intel-lectual, he was Aja's favorite Gray, and he is now the clever engine of my growing military machine. "Mobs may seem strong as the sea, but give me a starShell, and a Moses I will be."

Glirastes sharpens a retort.

"If you can't get along, silence is preferable," I snap, annoyed at their mutual and growing enmity. "You're both heroes of the people, so wave your gory hands and lobby me later." I wave to the people below. Block by block the crowd grows denser and more drunk. Sunburnt women in wigs shout down from rooftops. Children climb their fathers' shoulders to wave the flag of their favorite racing team. The gold and white of Team Hermes dominates the main boulevards as the sunbloods flow south, past the bazaar, through the partially restored Water Gardens, where the stampede completes a circuit and then turns gradually toward the Hippodrome, our destination.

At the grand building my arch settles down over the entrance to the executive reception plaza. We disembark between two columns of Prae-torians. In the lift to the executive level, Glirastes physically side-checks

Rhone to take his place at my side. Rhone is so surprised that by the time he regains his balance, the doors to the elevator are already closing. I hold up a hand and signal him to meet us up top.

The gravLift ascends. "I don't know if force is the right idea with Rhone," I say.

"How else can I penetrate the purple and black wall that follows you everywhere but with my hips and wits?" Glirastes glares at Kyber who stands in the corner. Somehow she was already in the lift waiting for us. "But one always manages to slither in."

"You have something to say. Go on and say it."

Glirastes, the greatest architect of his generation, is bald, hawkish with heavy eyebrows, gleaming orange eyes, and a stooped, predatory posture that once made him seem hungry and unctuous, but also impervious to any drug or construction catastrophe known to man. More and more, though, the posture also betrays his fragility. He seems like a man teetering over a cliff. These last months have been hard on him. In the end, artists are a sensitive breed.

"There are rumors the Saud denied you a loan. Is it true?" he asks.

I sigh. "You know what I miss most about being assumed dead? No gossip."

"Rhone is steering you to ruin," he blurts out.

"Glirastes, old friend, these games were your idea," I say. "The people need hope, you said."

"The games are a pittance compared to what you're spending on ships and legions. And it's not the games so much as the guests who trouble me. You dirty your hands dealing with the likes of Rath and the Carthii."

A tired line. "But I should cover myself in eagle shit?"

"Hardly a fair comparison. You're bleeding money. Lady Bellona is . . . distinguished. Far more than just a banker or a brute. She is a broker of *power*. She might not control the Two Hundred, but she influences a sizable block of senators. Most of whom have no love for Atalantia."

"Yes, and perhaps if you sang my praises in her ear, she might actually have deigned to attend my games," I say. "Instead, she sends no note, no emissary, just her racing team. It's been nothing but insults since she sent Rhone to aid me in the desert."

"Perhaps she did not sponsor you to be Atalantia's plaything," he says.

"Would a plaything smuggle legions to the Minotaur?" I ask. "Now you'll moan I am reckless."

"You're juggling asps, my boy. Forget Bellona money. If Atalantia . . . Hades, if the Carthii discover you and the Minotaur have a secret pact—" He glances at Kyber. "I don't understand, Lysander. Why him? The Minotaur is an insane person. He craves the ephemeral. Experiences! Satiation of his lusts! No man is more your inverse, and yet you waste the wealth that could rebuild Mercury to send *him* an army.

"Lysander, I am scared. For you. For me. Of every shadow, every glass of wine."

"Maybe you should quit drinking then," I say. I apologize immediately when I see the pain on his face. "Glirastes, you have no reason to be afraid. I will protect you. I promise. But, honestly, what would you have me do?"

"I'd have you listen to the people. You are loved, so be loved. Do not play Atalantia's game. Play your own. Abandon this pursuit of an army and a fleet. Focus your time and money here. Let Mercury's prosperity be your campaign for the Morning Chair." He reaches to grasp my right hand. "It would break my heart to see you get caught in a Gold knife fight. You're better than that. You must be."

"Maybe I am, but without power, everything else is just good intentions. Now, I have guests waiting."

Glirastes pouts but does not protest when I reactivate the lift. Pytha waits on the executive level with Rhone. Rhone's gravBoots shimmer with heat from his ascent. "Sorry, I must have tripped," he says to me with a glance for Glirastes. Glirastes doesn't follow me out of the lift.

"You go on," he says. "I haven't the stomach for your guests or guards today."

Annoyed, I leave Glirastes behind. Pytha, the Blue pilot who watched over me for so many of my formative years on the *Archimedes,* raises an eyebrow. "You want me to fly him home?"

"You'll miss the race," I say.

"Please. Chariots? They don't even have engines."

Pytha chose to follow me instead of Cassius. That loyalty, and her belief in my vision for the Society, has more than earned her the post that will make her the envy of all Blues in the Society—captain of the *Lightbringer.* That is if the ship actually flies. Otherwise she'll be a laughingstock, and me with her. Our fates are entwined. I thank her and head for the box with Rhone.

"Vodka on his breath and it's not even noon," Rhone says. "I thought Mercurians were supposed to be industrious."

"Mind your own self, Flavinius. I'll not have you sniping at each other. Now put on a smile for my guests," I snap and plunge into the pulvinar.

The Golds drinking inside the suite raise their eyebrows at Pytha and Rhone. They shift away altogether from Kyber, thinking her a Copper because of her disguise. But Rhone is popular. His service record, if not the myriad teardrops on his face, would demand respect from even Atalantia. I greet my guests with alacrity and mannered courtesy until a roar a few minutes later draws me beyond the protection of the silk awning and into the sunlight.

In the stands below, lowColors rush up through the tunnels from the vendors toward their seats, arms laden with fennel sausages, candied pecans, oysters, and sloshing gourds of wine. To the two hundred fifty thousand who cram together on the tiered marble bleachers, the sound of the hooves on the street outside is still distant. But already the crowd hollers in anticipation. The voice of the Hippodrome gargles like infant thunder. Only when the first wild sunblood enters the stadium does the discordant noise coalesce into a single voice.

"AD . . . ASTRA . . . AD . . . ASTRA . . . AD . . . ASTRA."

The horses pour onto the racing sands. The youths gallop after them, herding the horses into running a lap. Great flames light around the stadium to signal the beginning of the games. As the dust-caked youths pass the pulvinar, my box, they stand in their stirrups to salute me and my Peerless guests. The youths resemble dusty birds of prey. Their faces and eyes are severe, their bones still thin, but though not one is over fifteen, there is not a trace of youth left in them. I have seen that look before. It is the look of having already chosen one's fate. It worries me to see it in those so young.

I wonder if I wore such a look when I sat by Kalindora's deathbed as she succumbed to the poison on Darrow's blade, and confessed her part in the assassination of my mother and father. An assassination planned and executed by my mother's best friend—and my betrothed—Atalantia. Considering Darrow has no reputation for poisons, it's not hard to guess who was really responsible for Kalindora's demise.

"Less than three hundred graduates. A pittance compared to Atalantia's Institutes," Rhone drawls, surveying the young horsemen and horsewomen. While most of my guests remain reclining in the shade deep within the box's air-conditioned recesses, Rhone sweats with me in the early morning sun. "*Dominus,* what I said about Glirastes—"

"Wasn't wrong, but I won't have Glirastes defamed. Ever." I look over so he sees how much I mean it. "You were not informing me. You were playing politics. Now, let us move on."

He nods and goes back to business.

"Our spies on Venus report Carthii Institutes are churning out young Peerless," he says. "The Saud are not too far behind. Still, if you ask me, you chose the right Color to invest in."

He eyes the thick band of Grays that claim the front rows around the racing sands.

I agree and scan the promenade level in distaste. Though Atalantia is occupied solidifying her hold on Earth and laying siege to Luna, little escapes her gaze, even less her taxes. Her Gold allies, and they are many, populate nearly half the boxes of the promenade level. The boxes were to be sold at auction to help finance these costly games. Instead, Atalantia helped me spiral toward bankruptcy by insisting none of her friends be required to pay.

"Ravenous lot, aren't they?" a voice murmurs. I turn to see a slender, deeply tanned woman of middling height. Horatia au Votum, Cicero's younger sister, is not a warrior despite the Peerless Scar on her heart-shaped face. A master administrator, her narrow eyes shimmer only for numbers. She's far more at home amidst a coterie of Coppers than she is on a warship or battlefield. "They've not come for games. They've come to see us fail."

She means they've all come to see the *Lightbringer* launch, or rather not launch. As the project manager in charge of refurbishing Darrow's crashed ship, she takes that personally. More liberal and political than Cicero, Horatia has assumed their father's place of prominence amongst the Reformer bloc in the Two Hundred. Our politics are strikingly similar but hardly popular. We pray we're not naïve for believing that's only because the tyrants of Atalantia's Iron bloc have the lion's share of war prestige and military might. "The wine you'll buy for these Golds alone would buy armor for half a legion. To say nothing of the food."

"Or Pinks," I reply.

"Or Violets."

"They're not our worst guests, I think," Rhone says.

"No?" Horatia is not over-fond of smiles, but she graces Rhone with one. "So which guest of honor holds that claim? Rath or Carthii?"

"The Venusians. Always." With a sour look, Rhone glances behind us at the brood of House Carthii lounging in my box drunk on my wine. I'd rather have hosted the Rim deputation, especially their rising hero, Diomedes. But Consul Dido's reply to my invitation was a single line: MARS MUST FALL. So instead of honorable, worthy Peerless knights of the Rim I'm beset by Carthii philistines so cultured they've forsaken the use of manners.

Horatia leans in. "I've done some . . . reconnoitering with my friends on Earth. The Carthii are . . . as you said they'd be. Unofficially unaffiliated. They're furious Atalantia let Rath keep their dockyards."

"So available."

"I wouldn't say that."

"Available," I confirm.

In Atalantia's decade of war and her lifelong quest to claim the Sovereign's chair, she's relied most on the Carthii shipbuilders of Venus. That has changed. After Apollonius stole the Carthii dockyards, Atalantia alienated her old allies when she signed the détente with Apollonius to ensure his stolen Carthii ships keep flowing to her armada.

All rather messy. I, of course, was only too happy to broker the deal.

While politically conservative, opposed to reform, and generally insidious, the Carthii are powerful and very wealthy. Winning them would be a political and military coup, but also as safe as bedding a viper.

I smile when I spy the best mark of those Carthii present—meaning the richest and most ambitious of the lot—sizing me up from amidst a clutch of her brothers.

Barely twenty-seven, Valeria au Carthii, like many of the ruthless young Golds of her generation, has found war to have a catalyzing effect on her prospects. She has ascended past many of her more famous brothers to become a third-place contender in the expansive and often fatal sibling rivalry to become their ancient father's heir. With her father, Asmodeus, well past a hundred years old and still replacing lost progeny like it's funny, she's likely in need of a powerful new friend.

I nod to her. She tips her glass my way. Bottom first. A slight Venusian flirtation.

"Where's your brother?" I ask Horatia.

"Cicero?" She frowns. "Even I can't track that variable. I'll inquire with the grooms."

"He promised he wouldn't race."

"I'll inquire with the grooms."

Valeria au Carthii sways toward us before Horatia can leave. "Lysander, I've just looked at the program, and I must say it's terribly Aurelian of you not to include the gladiatorial matches." She slurps the flesh from an oyster and discards the shell on the floor for the servants. "Or are you to blame, Horatia?"

"I fear it's a collective statement," Horatia says. "Excuse me."

"Reformers. Ugh. Such prudes." Valeria wrinkles her nose. "Chariot races and pegasus jousts are all well and good. But truly, what are the stakes if no one's dying?"

"I think the people of Heliopolis have seen enough death," I reply.

At a nod from me, Rhone slips back under the awning to keep watch on me from the shade opposite Kyber. Valeria watches after him. "Shouldn't let your dogs sit at the table, Lysander. They'll eat the food off your plate."

"Praetorians are hardly dogs. Falcons perhaps."

She chuckles. "I hear Horatia is responsible for that delusion of grandeur to the south?"

"She is," I reply. "It was her idea to use the wreckage of the White Fleet to repair the *Lightbringer*."

"Votum's building ships. If I thought that possible, I'd be offended. It looks like a monster, far too heavy in the front. Not even painted."

"Horatia says paint is a luxury our budget can't afford."

"Hilarious woman. So serious," Valeria says. "Are you fucking her? Or is it her brother you like? Both?"

"Like I said, we're not on Venus today," I reply.

"Mhm." Her eyes glide to Rhone, then down to the Praetorians in the stands. "I heard you were a student of our ancient ancestors. A virtuous shepherd of the people." She busies herself shucking and slurping oysters. "Still. We all wonder when you'll grow tired of this orgy of equitas and come to join the real circus."

"I'd like nothing more than to join the war. But without a military appointment from the Dictator or the Two Hundred, I must tend my duties here on Mercury. The last thing I want to do is meddle in politics."

"What a law-abiding young citizen you are." She smiles. "Imagine my father's relief when he learns that you don't consider lobbying Atalantia to exploit our stolen docks to be *meddling in politics*," she says.

"The Battle of Mercury cost us dearly, and Julii and Augustus are putting up a . . . rather impressive fight," I say. "The war requires warships to replace our recent losses, no? That your family lost your dockyards to a madman and a handful of soldiers is hardly my fault. Actually it's more an indictment of how your father treats his workers and citizens. I hear your own people rallied to Apollonius and helped him take the station. I merely helped Atalantia and Apollonius remain focused on the greater interest of our people—winning the war."

She rolls her eyes. "Lysander the Lightbringer. Lysander the Peacemaker. A maker of peace wouldn't keep that scar. Hideous. Does Atalantia like it?"

"No. She detests it."

"I love it. Savage. From Darrow's own boot, no?" She eyes the burn on my face and sucks down another oyster. "I'm a simple woman. I like ships. Flying them, building them, taking them from my enemy and painting my centaur on them. I do the eyes myself, then have a cigar. What do you like, and don't say peace."

"Power," I reply and look up as thunder rumbles from above. Against the blue sky, huge Obsidians painted white beat their drums on each of the Hippodrome's fourteen towers. The main gates open and the chariots of the four-horse grand prix emerge one by one. An announcer declares each rider and their team, sending each team's supporters into convulsions. "After all, what else makes peace?"

"This isn't power. This is theater," she replies. "Expensive theater. The love of the people won't buy you the Morning Chair, Lune."

"But it affords me the opportunity to ask what would."

She grins. "You know what I want, Peacemaker. That which the Minotaur stole. That which Atalantia was only too ready to trade away. That which my father withholds and my siblings covet. My inheritance."

"Really. I had no idea."

"Stop. Our politics are . . . opposed," she says. "Reformers are . . . in denial of humanity's basic lowness. But we have much in common, you and I. Atalantia and her father gobbled up all those Lune ships and fortresses and men and then slapped the Grimmus skull onto them. Has she returned what belongs to you?" I smile. Everyone knows she hasn't, even though by law she should. "It seems we've both had our inheritance stolen by an usurper. If only there was a way to help one another . . ."

Her eyes drift to the box to the right of ours where Apollonius's brother, Tharsus au Rath, parties in all his race day finery, surrounded by his cadre of new sycophants—exiled Martian Golds, lithe courtesans, preening poets. Raths did not exist at the time of the Conquering, so no matter the vastness of their wealth, the depths of their infamy, or the quality of their wine, to their everlasting chagrin they've never been considered a premier gens.

"I fear your inheritance is already spoken for, as is mine," I say. "For now."

She smiles. "For now?"

Tharsus seems to glow as he feels our eyes on him. I've sworn him to keep public distance from me lest others suspect I am in league with his brother. I must maintain the appearance of neutrality.

He prances to the edge of the box. Just a few paces off, he shouts: "Either you want to fornicate with me or kill me. I don't know which, Valeria. The first would be fine, but the second is improbable if not impossible." He idly probes a passing Pink. "I am immune to glares, knives, and all between, for my brother has atomics pointed at your inheritance and he is . . ."

He gestures to one of his drunker sycophants.

"Mad as a bull!" the friend cries and makes horns with his fingers. The rest make bull sounds and dance around before breaking down into laughter and blowing kisses at the Carthii.

Horatia returns with news of Cicero. "He didn't," I say, reading her expression. "Tell me he's not."

"He did. He is," she says, apologetic.

I wince and the crowd roars as the announcer proclaims the entrance of the reigning champion of the individual circuit. Riding as always for Team Hermes, Cicero au Votum drives his chariot out onto the sands, his four-horse team led by the indomitable Blood of Empire.

Wearing a white tunic with leather straps tightly bound to protect his

chest, Cicero's powerful arms and legs are tan and oiled. Like all charioteers in the classic prix, he is woefully under protected. My blood boils
at the sight of him riding with a smile toward mortal jeopardy. "He
promised he wouldn't race," I mutter.

"Stakes after all," Valeria says in delight.

I sigh. "Pardon me. Theater calls."

"For now?" she asks.

"For now," I reply. "But not forever."

She toasts to that.

I signal Flavinius before jumping over the wall of the pulvinar to land
below where Kyber is already waiting. She really does look like a Copper
actarius with her datapad and lithe limbs. If she has a weapon on her, I
can't see it. Shocked by my descent into the common stands, the crowd
cheers as I make my way amongst the midColors, not to sit with my
own men but to honor the Votum legions. Cicero's Grays receive me
with the hero's welcome Rhone paid their centurions for. As I place my
bet with the roving bookie, Cicero guides his chariot past and lifts his
hand in formal salute to me. His voice, aided by some unseen micro-
phone, booms out across the arena.

"I dedicate this race to the savior of Heliopolis! The steward of Mercury! The image of Silenius, last of his line. Lysander the Lightbringer!"

He blows me a kiss.

Cicero guides his chariot to the starting line and the crowd roars.
Silence falls. The charioteers fix their eyes forward, and when the long,
mournful note bursts from a great white horn, the chariots lurch forward, and the sands swirl.

6

DARROW

Mortal Concerns

LIKE A DEEP SPACE remora, the *Archimedes* stirs from its idle drift and creeps into the wake of the convoy of Votum cosmosHaulers. The Haulers are accompanied by powerful destroyers freshly painted with a purple Minotaur's head.

After journeying from the Marcher to Venusian orbit, we waited days for a convoy whose wake could mask our approach to the dockyards. It gave us time to plan. Thus far the stealth hull has allowed us to avoid two Carthii patrol squadrons, but the dockyards, with their far more sophisticated sensor suites, will be a different affair.

I lean over Cassius's shoulder as he guides the *Archimedes* closer to the hull of a cosmosHauler at the end of the convoy.

"Easy does it. The blind spot isn't large," I murmur.

"I know how to fly," Cassius says. "If you want to worry about anything, worry about the hull."

"Considering the only way we'll know if they've spotted us is if they shoot at us, perhaps you should both focus," Aurae says from the co-pilot seat. I sit down in a pop-out seat behind them and hold my breath until we've matched speed with the hauler, a bare ten meters from her starboard. Cassius breathes out.

"There. We're in her shadow. Quicksilver must hate you, Darrow. Or he's working for the Golds. Why else would he not equip the White Fleet with this tech? Five destroyers with this hull could cut apart the Society like a scalpel."

"Apparently the material is one hundred times more expensive per ounce than razors are to produce," I say. "Outfitting the *Morning Star* alone would have bankrupted the Republic."

"So?"

"That's what I said."

He laughs. "No wonder the Senate didn't like you."

In the blind spot of the hauler, I have time to appreciate the view as we approach Venus.

At a distance the Dockyards of Venus, the greatest structure ever built by mankind, resemble little more than a scratch on a sapphire marble suspended alone in the darkness. If ever I needed a reminder for how small we are in the scheme of things, I needn't look any further than Venus.

Yet even Venus itself, a planet of immense majesty with all its vast coral reefs, mysterious migrating islands, abundant flora and fauna, rigid caste structure, and human factories for the Gold military apparatus, is smaller than my pinky nail when I hold my hand at arm's length.

As we approach and Venus grows in size, there's time enough for the worry to set in. Soon the Carthii navy comes into view. Most of the ships and the Praetors of House Carthii were off serving Atalantia over Mercury when Apollonius stole their dockyards. Now their ships are tethered to the north pole of their home planet where they twinkle, a crown of blue splinters.

No doubt they're tethered there by fear of what Apollonius would do to their dockyards should they try to reclaim them. If I were him, I'd have bombs and a dead man's switch. He and I often do think alike.

I reach over to the seat beside me and pet *Dominus* Portobello, our lone atomic, for reassurance.

Under watch of the station's guns and its escorts, the haulers slow as they approach the dockyards. So does the *Archimedes*. Amongst the yards' complex fortifications are guns the size of skyscrapers. If death comes, we won't have long to notice. With a tentative smile that grows the longer we don't die, Cassius cuts the engines and initiates a lateral drift out of the haulers' wake. The dockyards roll past, endless fortifications and industrial towers, spindles and garages as far as the eye can see. Aurae is amazed at the sight. Cassius grows dour.

"Good news. We're not dead yet," I say and stand. "Bad news, that was the easy part. Aurae, the Archimedes and Portobello is yours. Cassius, it's time."

"Remember what I taught you about axial drift. And don't forget two port thrusters are wonky," Cassius says to Aurae, reluctant to hand over the controls.

"I won't crash if you don't die," she replies and gives him a smile. He glances around at the ship, his home, takes a breath, and heads for the garage. I linger for a moment and watch her fingers dance along the controls to the ship's systems.

"Did Cassius actually teach you to fly, or did you just pretend to let him?"

She continues her task. *"It is a master's nature to want, just as it is a servant's nature to provide. This does not mean the master does not provide. This does not mean a servant does not want."*

"So you humored him."

She turns. "I am a Pink. I humor everyone." She doesn't sound bitter about it. "We all have our survival mechanisms, Darrow. I am and always have been air. Until now you could afford to be a rock. You didn't have to change or alter course. Now you are cracking. That is a good thing. If you wish to be repaired . . ."

"You must first be broken," I murmur. She had seen me reading the book in the *Archimedes's* lounge. "It's nonsensical half the time."

"Of course it is. All your life your hands have been how you have interacted with the world. But the path isn't a tool to be grabbed and used, Darrow. Because it isn't a thing. It is a verb."

She holds my gaze, patient, neutral.

"Why are you really here, Aurae?" I ask. "Cassius may buy the sympathizer story. You might explain your skills as part of a hetaera's education. But—"

"I am here for Sevro," she says. "That is the truth. Not the whole truth, but it is all the truth that matters, because it is all the truth that is useful."

"And I suppose the path would tell me to accept that."

"You tell me." She smirks. "But do you really have a choice?"

I nod to *Dominus* Portobello. "Make sure you put that where it counts."

She salutes.

I head for the cargo bay. Cassius is already half dressed. It took us two days of work in the machine shop to reshape the Sun Industries armor Kavax sent with Cassius to look like the spartan-baroque styled pulse-

Armor of a House Rath knight. Now gray and purple, detailed with bulls and Hercules on the shoulders, our guises should do the trick.

"Don't worry, I taught her well," Cassius says. "She's a natural."

"I'm sure," I say. When we are dressed, I check my chronometer. "Ninety seconds. Buttons up."

We don our helmets. A chill trickles over my skin as I see the world through the pulseArmor's lenses. Even if I loathe war, my body thrills to its rituals like a drunk hearing the clink of ice into a whiskey tumbler. With Cassius armored and ready beside me, I feel infused with the luck of House Mars, sixteen again and preparing to steal the enemy standard.

We take our places at the starboard door and he pats my back. "Nut to butt, Bellona. Don't be shy." The jump light turns red to yellow.

"I'd rather not."

"Cassius, we rehearsed this—"

"Yet my objections remain. If anything, you should hop on my back. You look like the warning advert for street drugs. No offense."

"It's Howler protocol on lateral pair-jumps. If our equipment fails, you and I can't get separated," I say. I shove the traction gun into his hands. "Now get on my back."

He climbs on my back, muttering. *"Let's go to war with the Reaper of Mars, I thought. Truly, I envisioned something far more glamorous."*

Aurae triggers the doors. The faint iridescence of the pulseField is all that separates us from space now. We are close enough to distinguish viewports and doors in the metal landscape of the dockyards. With danger ahead, but my life in my hands, I come alive again. Feels good to have my boots unstuck from the mud.

I steel myself and jump.

The dockyards roll beneath us as our initial push carries Cassius and me toward them. Then the velocity we inherited from the *Archimedes* sends us laterally along the curve of the great eastern construction crescent. As we float above the dockyards, it's like watching the construction process in reverse: First we pass over destroyers and torchShips, complete and lacking only paint. Then we see ships without guns, then without hulls, then without engines, until finally we pass over machines welding vast sections of durosteel for the superstructures of warships.

Workers, as tiny and numerous as ants, crawl along the surface of the warships and dockyards under the gaze of inanimate overlords—giant statues of deceased Carthii. When we reach the Vulcan Mouth, we pass under the gaze of Silenius and Carthus—colossal caryatids that glare at us from either side of the Mouth. These statues are the last sight retired ships see before they are melted down inside a furnace named for the Roman god of the forge. Silenius and Carthus, heedless of our pathetic mortal concerns, witnesses to the march of time, sneer past us toward the stars.

And then, fifteen minutes after our jump, we reach our fire point.

Careful not to throw off our trajectory, Cassius aims and fires the traction gun over my shoulder at the station. A counterforce exits out the back of the gun. We still spin a little until the payload locks on the surface of the station, and the line goes taut. The motor in the gun pulls us forward. On the surface, we abandon the gun and Cassius uses the base of a heavy railgun installation to climb off my back. He shot well. We're only eighty meters from our target. We cross carefully, pulling ourselves along the toes of Silenius. As a battered Republic destroyer slides from the queue into the Mouth for incineration, we hop onto its hull. The incinerator doors close behind the ship.

"Fast-like . . . now," I say and we race down the length of the doomed warship and jump off its bow toward the vast aperture that waits beyond the incinerator to consume the liquid metal the warship will soon become. A wave of heat chases us into the aperture, down its huge umbilical, and into a grim processing center where vast cubic trays wait for the liquid metal. A Red foreman in a mech-suit turns our way, but we're already gone and into the station through a pedestrian walkway high above.

The Carthii's philosophy of order is simple. They believe in an iron rod of discipline held by a velvet, scented glove.

Dockyard workers who obey their Carthii masters are given many delights, including twenty-three delirium arcades for the pleasure of their coveted Greens. We target an arcade located on the thirty-seventh level of the eastern construction spindle. The arcade is thick with humidity, and the lights in the ceiling cast a dim indigo glow over the rows of delirium pods.

Our abrupt entry, and the sound the Brown janitor's body makes as he hits the floor, draws the attention of the arcade's admin, a tall androgynous Green with a cruel, pale face. They turn from their route through the rows of delirium pods to see a shadow leaping toward them.

Cassius takes them down hard with a knee to the sternum. By the time I make it over to them, he's holding their body, now limp as a wet towel. The shock of the mild collision killed them.

"Sorry," Cassius murmurs. "Not used to this high gravity." He drops the human towel. "So fragile."

"We're looking for an architect or a fulgur bellator. Delta symbol with three lightning bolts. Try not to kill them."

We split the pods, and I go down the rows peering at the blank, pale faces for the right tattoos that will find Sevro's cell and lead me through the doors blocking my path to it. Hardwired into the experiential pods, the Greens' reveries are relayed through small holograms over their heads. More than half the Greens partake in sexual simulations and are fit with codpieces to catch the byproduct of their pleasure. I stop and feel my gut churn at the horror bathing the face of a highly decorated fulgur bellator—a lightning warrior. A hardy Green bred to be paired with Gray squads in the field to enslave or neutralize enemy electronics, his body is thicker than most of his colleagues, and his predilections far more gruesome.

I wrap my hand around his throat and tear out the wires going into the ports just in front of his ears. His consciousness falls out of its licentious revelry and back into his war-scarred, tech-enhanced body. I strangle him and then break his neck like a sheaf of dry hay.

Concerned, Cassius comes over. "You murderous hypocrite." His expressionless helmet fixes on the frozen dream above the dead Green before he looks away in disgust. "Venusians." He makes a spitting sound. "Found an architect, with healthier dreams." I follow him to a slender Green woman with narrow eyes and the tattoo of an architect over her right eyebrow. Her delirium is tamer. She flies atop a scaled beast over a gloomy fortress lit in green light. The black mountains that surround the fortress are jagged enough to have been hewn by a giant with a scythe. Her eyelids flutter as Cassius eases her out of the dream. She starts. Her eyes focus on her new, frightening reality. As she tries to scream, I wrap Bad Lass around her neck and say: "Your life is in your hands. Don't drop it."

The Green architect does not choose to drop it. She is slight, probably a third of my weight, and so nervous her thin fingers shake on the keys of the hallway terminal. I made her access it manually so I can curb any potential mischief. Cassius keeps a lookout. The Green's program filters through thousands of images. The brigs are filled with prisoners—most of them Golds or Grays—but no Sevro. She widens the search, delving into high-security zones until I have her stop on a bleach-white security room. A man lies in the fetal position, clad in a yellow prisoner's jumpsuit, his head encased in a giant wolf helmet. Cassius must hear my heart beat faster.

"Got him?" he asks without turning.

"Maybe." I zoom in on the prisoner's exposed hands until I see a skull tattoo on the back of his left. Still not convinced, I assess the scars on his right hand. They match the ones Sevro received from Atalantia's cajir war beasts on Earth. I swallow, nervous now that I'm so close. "That's Sevro." I check my chronometer. If Aurae is on schedule, she'll have landed the *Archimedes* and finished her space walk on the sixth construction spindle by now. Our insurance should be in order. "Let's go get him."

With our jamField hiding us from cameras, I put the Green on a razor leash and force her to lead us. She unlocks the maintenance lifts to take us as close as we can get to Sevro's prison. Accessing the maintenance crawl spaces, I have Cassius release a Sun Industries spider drone in the ventilation ducts. He guides it via the uplink in his helm until it peers through the vents into the high-security block. It crawls in and begins to pump gas from its carry-pod. An alarm blares inside and the Grays on duty scramble for their helmets. At the same time, I thrust the Green toward the main door controls.

Shaking, she hunches over the controls until the door hisses open. I drive my elbow into the back of her head and move in low and fast just as the spider explodes in stutters of white light. The first Gray turns toward the door. He's blind when I spear him through his armor and heart. I lift him up and run with him as a shield. Guns crackle. Slugs slam into the Gray's armor. But I'm into them, and that's where I do my best killing.

Shoving the Gray off Bad Lass I cut at a man holding a rifle and take both his arms off at the elbows. I kick the other way and snap a Gray's neck as I catch him under the jaw. I whip another around by his ankles and jerk him down from the level above, retracting the blade and taking his feet off, and then slam the razor into the crest of another Gray's helmet. He parts like split wood. I whip at two others to either side of me.

The damage to their helmets is superficial, but it buys Cassius time to shoot both Grays as he follows behind me.

"Three o'clock," I call. "Low."

Cassius ducks just as the Obsidian's axe sweeps past where his head was moments before. In the same motion, Cassius sweeps his razor over his head in a circle, dividing one of the two charging Obsidians at the waist. His blade catches in the armor of the other. He blocks a second axe-strike with his aegis, a glowing shield emitted by his left vambrace, and rolls to free his blade. The Obsidian's next swing crashes down. The axe sparks against his pulseShield and rebounds. Cassius stabs his razor two-handed under the Obsidian's armpit, taking his opponent under the jaw. The blade emerges out the top of the Obsidian's helmet. Cassius recalls his blade and cleans it as he stands.

"Clear," he says. "I'll hold here. Get your Goblin."

I stumble over the twitching bodies and tear a pass card off a centurion's armor. I race down the security block's main corridor until I reach Sevro's door where I wave the pass card. The heavy metal retracts upward and I burst into the cell.

Sevro lies in the center of the white room. The wolf helmet on his head is so heavy the act of lifting it from the floor makes the veins in his neck bulge. I race to him and with a careful swing, cut the lock on the helmet. I sheathe my razor and tear the helmet away. Sevro's face is dewy and crusted with dried saliva, dead skin, hair, and yeast. He smells as cheesy as a popped cyst. His eyes blink out at me from the tangle.

They are Gray.

The man has Sevro's tattoos. His scars. But he is not Sevro.

"Helllllp meeeee," the imposter begs.

"Oh. Shit." I drop the imposter. "Cassius! Trap!"

Booms sound from the Hall. Cassius fills the doorway, his rifle shouldered. "Darrow." He stares at the imposter at my feet. "They've blocked the exit. Two squads at least."

I raise my helmet. "We have to punch through them. It's our only—"

"Move!" I shout as the cell door begins to close with Cassius in its way.

Cassius hurls himself into the cell. The door slams down behind him with enough force to crush granite. He rolls to his feet, razor out again.

"You idiot. What was that?" I shout.

"You said 'Move'!"

"The other way!"

"You didn't specify which direction!"

"Who dives into a bloodydamn cell?" I snap.

Drip. Drip. Drip. The blood on Bad Lass hits the floor harder with each drop. I feel the unmistakable twinge in my stomach, a leaden weight in the brain and limbs. "Gravity. There must be a well under the floor. We have to get out." I pull a breaching charge from my thigh pack and toss it to Cassius. The gravity increases exponentially and the charge falls short. My feet rise with excruciating slowness and descend with a force greater than any horse's kick. My pulseArmor is tough. Not top of the line, as I'm accustomed to wearing, but tough and battle-tested. Still, it succumbs to the weight. My knee drives into the floor hard enough to dent it. Cassius keeps his feet. He trudges toward the door with the charge in hand.

"Elephant . . . on my . . . gory chest," Cassius says through gritted teeth. Blood pounds in my head. Ten times the weight it would be on Earth. My heart gallops from the strain of pushing it through my veins. I crash down like an ancient Martian godTree. I land poorly, and feel the cold needle-fire down my left arm as a nerve pinches in my neck. I lay there wheezing. Cassius burbles something I can't understand. He must not make it to the door. There is no explosion. There is no Sevro. Did Apollonius ever have him? I've been played for an utter fool.

A voice too vibrant, too ravening to belong to anyone but Apollonius comes from a speaker above. *"Darrow, Darrow, Darrow. Truly you are divine. For you have answered my prayers. Welcome to the Dockyards of the Minotaur. Welcome to your doom."*

7

LYSANDER

The Ally Idiot

CICERO WINS HIS RACE without true contest except in the fifth lap, where a Carthii-sponsored chariot nearly crushes him against the central spina. Leaving my Praetorians at the gate, I cross the staging courtyard to give Cicero a piece of my mind. Kyber wanders along behind, innocuous, but always searching for danger.

The courtyard smells of hay, manure, leather, and horses. The smells wake memories of Virginia au Augustus. Of all the Golds who came and went through my grandmother's palace, Virginia was my favorite.

I feel a faint longing for her easy smile and unpredictable conversations. Certainly that smile hid a mouth full of daggers, but Virginia had a way of making you feel privileged to have lost to her in a game of chess or an idle bet on which songbird egg would hatch first in the garden's aviaries. I wonder if she still has time to visit her stables on Mars, or if like me, this war has swallowed her up. She was always happier after a ride in the Palatine's park. Come to think of it, so was I.

Arcades enclose the staging ground, providing shade and tables for the teams. Young Gold charioteers and the sordid entourages that inevitably orbit such scurrilous characters sip wine and play dice. Many toast me as I pass, but not the Carthii, who sneer and insult me under their breath.

Beneath the arcade bearing the winged heel of Team Hermes, Cicero inspects his reins system. He's due to race again before midday and will race nearly twenty times before the games are through. All of them in that stupid little helmet.

Cicero senses my approach. Instead of turning, he joins the grooms in wiping down the horses. "Lysander, I know. I know. I know. I know."

I chase him around one of his horses, Blood of Empire. "You promised me you would not race." Blood tries to nuzzle me and nearly knocks me down in doing so.

My friend sighs. He peers at me through a tangle of golden curls. "My goodman, search your memory. I said I promised I would take your *recommendation* to heart, and I certainly did." He touches his breast. "In fact my heart was so torn over the matter, I nearly sprained my wrists holding it together." He tosses a sweat-soaked rag to a groom and extricates himself from the horses to sit on the step up to his chariot's basket.

He accepts a silver cup of wine from one of his stewards, drains it, and calls for more. "Wine? It's Thessalonican. Rath brought ten barrels. Gods know how he got it. Man knows his smugglers. Weird fellow, really. Always with the innuendos. Can't tell if he's trying to filch my purse or slag me."

"You do recall that the charioteers of Rome were slaves?" I confirm as the steward refills his cup. "Rich, dripping in whores, but slaves still."

"Is that your way of telling me that unlike them I have so much to lose?" Cicero asks.

"Your father doesn't have the reins any longer," I reply. "Your house is yours to guide. Your father—"

"My father lost his planet. Followed by his honor," Cicero says flatly. "Then he spent his life and his favorite son to reclaim both. You know his fearful disposition, his frugal nature. But he loved this sport. The Hippodrome is in our blood." His eyes go misty and far away as he looks up at the stone heights of the stadium's southern face. "This sand belongs to me. I have no less to lose than the meanest slave of Rome. What concerns are there but honor? What is there to lose but life? You ask me to risk my life for you, your claim on the Morning Chair, when all know the odds against that. This is by far the safer sport!"

He sips his wine and casts me an imploring look. "You and my sister do not understand because the insides of your minds are ordered like the guts of a clock. My mind is a wandering, haphazard organ, but it is not without its own breed of order."

His eyes drift toward the driver's arcade, where the Carthii-sponsored charioteers lounge in the shade listening to one of their fellows play the harp. "Yes, vanity is in my nature, but it would mean very much to me if you would have faith that I am not being vainglorious. I will not have Mercury insulted by Venus carrying away the glory on a day meant to honor my father and the planet he died for. What would that tell our citizens? That Mercury will only be a shadow of what it once was? That Votum is the least of the houses of the Conquering? I race for more than mere laurels, dear friend. I race for the spirit of my people." He nudges me. "*Our* people."

I enjoy Cicero's candor, his general optimism, and his love of conspiracy, but it is his buffoonish bouts of bravery that I admire the most. Others think him flighty, a party boy more interested in the arts than war. Far from it.

It's strange the friends we make. Cicero could not be any more different than Ajax, my best friend from childhood. Back then, Ajax was pleasant and self-conscious, while Cicero was a famed nightmare full of mischief, arrogance, and general trouble. Life since then has made Ajax a selfish braggadocio, grotesquely skilled at killing to prove he is not weak. While Cicero doesn't mind others thinking he's weak. And even when he thinks of his own interests manages, I think accidentally, to nurse along the interests of others. Yet still I miss Ajax.

I snort at the stupid power of childhood bonds.

"What?" Cicero asks.

I deflect. "Something your sister said months ago. If a charm offensive is needed, call on Cicero indeed. If it means that much to you, you have my blessing. Not that you need it."

After losing both Cassius to Darrow and Ajax to Atalantia, I'm careful not to tread on my friends' spirits these days.

"You *do* see me. I told Glirastes as much," he says with a delighted smile. "Where is the old bag anyhow? Mayhaps I'll dedicate the next victory to him."

"He left," I say.

"You chased him away, no doubt," Cicero says. "You must be gentler with him."

"I am gentle with him."

"You are kind, but not gentle. Artists are sensitive about their work. And you're his work of personal redemption," he says. I frown. "He helped Darrow, didn't he? The Storm Gods were as much his devils as they were the Reaper's. He has much to atone for." He spots something over my shoulder. "Oh shit. Incoming cretin."

"Centaur or bull?"

"The hornier breed."

Tharsus and his menagerie are headed straight for us. "The idiot," I mutter.

"Didn't you tell him to keep his distance?" Cicero asks.

"Several times," I say.

Cicero ducks his head. "He'll get us all skinned by Grimmus sociopaths."

"I'll be stuffed and strung as a puppet. You'll be skinned."

"Don't say that. That's terrible. Oh gods, he's getting closer. Do you think he's seen us?" Cicero tries to hide in the basket of his chariot.

"Cicero, my goodman! A true Flavius Scorpus you are," Tharsus calls. Cicero pops up like a prairie dog at the compliment.

"Well, I won't say I disagree!" Cicero says.

"What spectacle! What bravado!" When he's close enough, Tharsus's tone darkens. "I can read lips from a hundred meters, you slanderous goat rapists."

"We know." I clap Tharsus on his muscled shoulder and my hand comes away smelling of sandalwood and pheromones. "Yet even being reminded you were violating our agreement, you kept on coming."

"It'd be even more peculiar if I kept my distance from such illustrious company." He leans in, flirtatious or just being clever about hiding his mouth from lip-readers. An audio distorter vibrates on his middle finger. "You're not doing your job, Lune. You're supposed to slide your hands into monied panties to finance our grand crusade, not fingerblast Gray prostates down in the cheap seats. It's my brother's job to be loved by soldiers. You are just a broker for men and money."

"Money your brother will just waste at Syndicate auctions," Cicero says.

Tharsus brandishes a smile that is all too smug. "A waste, you say?"

Several more of Valeria's brothers have joined their racing team now. One of the Carthii throws a grape at one of Tharsus's poet friends. Another tosses a chicken bone. I tilt my head at my Praetorians to discourage the instigators. Markus—a sundark water-buffalo of a centurion, one of Rhone's favorites—is only too happy to oblige.

"Tharsus, go away." I flip him a few credits, as if I've lost a bet. He pockets them, grinning at my discomfort. "You're going to start a brawl that won't end here."

"Please. They touch one hair on my lustrous head, and my brother will blow the construction spindles on their dockyards one by one until I'm returned to him. How then will the war be won? When the enemy has their docks and the Society doesn't have theirs?" Tharsus purrs. "Quell your anxiety, Palatine child. I've come only to give you news from Apollonius. While others—like that fool Ajax—burned precious helium prowling the system for the elusive wolf, my brother has lured him from the shadows for a test of martial valor."

"Inconceivable!" Cicero squawks. "That broadcast worked?"

"Indeed. And soon my brother will lay Darrow low." He touches my arm. "Calm your loins, precocious catamite. Your old flame Cassius is snared as well, and will be gifted within the fortnight for your pleasure. Mayhaps the Lady Bellona will unlock her vault for you then."

I stare at him. "Cassius is alive. He tried to free Sevro with Darrow?"

"Yes."

"And your brother has them both?" I ask.

Tharsus looks so smug he might faint. "Yes."

I'm staggered. I thought Cassius died out on the Rim until I saw him rescue Darrow from Heliopolis eight months ago. I assumed since then, with Ajax, the Dustwalkers, and others looking for them, that Cassius had met some grisly end. Cassius was like a brother for ten years. Imperfect, yes. But a brother still. I preferred him dead, in a way. At least his end was noble. It hurt, but it was better than him being alive and fighting at Darrow's side instead of mine.

It is a hard game, this. So I must be hard. I will give him to his mother, Julia. Perhaps that is the key I am missing to open her vaults.

"Look at that. Already counting the coins," Tharsus says. "You!" Tharsus cries, distracted by the Bellona charioteer exiting the shade of her arcade to scold one of her grooms at work on her horses. Tharsus is off, his muscular arms gesticulating like a mantis in a mating dance. "You, brilliant woman. Of course you know me, but I must know you. What grace! What bravado! What spectacle."

Cicero and I stare after him as he accosts the young Bellona charioteer. My mind whirls. Apollonius has Darrow and Cassius. A great anxiety sloughs away at the thought, replaced by another anxiety. Darrow must die, of course, but must Cassius die too?

Cicero folds his arms and pouts. "What's the matter with you?" I ask.

Cicero sighs. "It's just . . . spectacle, bravado, those were the same compliments he gave *me*."

I spare him a second glance. He's not joking. I do love Cicero, but sometimes I wonder if I wouldn't be taken more seriously with the dread Ajax au Grimmus at my side.

Night falls on Heliopolis and the races give way to theater and parties. Laughter and music from rooftop celebrations and coastal galas drift through the lamplit streets. The cobbled path I walk wends along the wharf and then through a grove of starburst trees to an amphitheater cut into the side of a cliff. A play is on, but that is not why I have come.

I've come because a grand ship named the *Dustmaker* slid into orbit at midday, and I must meet its master.

I leave my Praetorians behind and descend to stand behind the back risers. Down on the stage, backed by the sea, an agonized Oedipus is realizing his queen is actually his mother. LowColors on the seats and the embankments, huddled with spiced wine and sweets, weep. Discordant sounds of celebration creep across the water from a floating island in the far distance, as if mocking Oedipus's agony. I doubt anyone else notices. Thessian, the famed Violet actor of Earth, is old now, but age has not diminished his craft.

Filled with emotion by his performance, I lean against an olive tree and watch until Oedipus blinds himself, the chorus speaks, and the crowd melts away from the amphitheater back toward the bars and acrobatic displays by the wharf.

I descend into the amphitheater to intercept two large men in dusky traveler cloaks just as they stand from their seats. No one could mistake them for being anything other than what they are: Peerless Scarred.

"They say Thessian could make a stone weep, yet your eyes are dry. Are you stoics or has Thessian lost his touch?" I say as they turn.

The older Scarred is thinner than his colleague. He answers laconically. "Mercury is hot. I forgot to hydrate."

Honestly the answer is like the man. Helios au Lux is austere, unimpressed, and as serious as a gun barrel. Nicknamed Sunburn for his affinity for torchShip raids and his flushed complexion, he was the Truth Knight of the Rim Dominion for forty years before becoming co-consul with Dido at the onset of the war. He is cordial, but clearly not excited to see me.

"*Salve*, au Lune."

Helios shakes my hand. His is sheathed in an antiquated Cestus: a battle glove composed of interwoven golden bands that ensnare the user's arm from the elbow to the tips of their fingers that gives the wearer mastery over his warship. War scenes and the word *Dustmaker* are etched into the metal along with a line from the Iliad: I TOO SHALL LIE IN THE DUST WHEN I AM DEAD, BUT NOW LET ME WIN NOBLE RENOWN. This particular Cestus is named the Binds of Zeus.

The younger Peerless Scarred is a hurricane contained in a lead drum that any man, even Apollonius, should be cautious in opening. He is thickset, gloomy, soft-spoken, and one of the rising heroes in the Rim military. His name is Diomedes au Raa, the eldest son of Romulus and Dido. I'm delighted to see the man. He may be the only person I desperately want to like me for no reason other than I find him honorable, admirable, and utterly immune to everything—charm, flattery, bribery, or any of the devices employed so often in the Core—everything, that is, save merit.

Diomedes likes unsung heroes, but all I have to my name so far are a few songs and one horse charge. It makes me a little insecure around the man.

I extend a hand to him. "Au Raa. Or should I say Storm Knight? Or Legate? Or Twin Taker? You're truly racking up the honors, goodman." He does not take my hand. I'm shocked, embarrassed. I'd thought he and I to be approaching friendship after journeying together to propose the Rim's entry into the war to Atalantia, but our months apart seem to have chilled that growing intimacy. His sister Seraphina died in the desert on our mission to take down a Storm God on Mercury. Does he hold resentment?

Helios looks away.

Diomedes says, formal, "An apology is due, au Lune. I lied to you. I claimed Cassius was dead on Io when he was not. I have been censured by my order, but not by you."

"You may have four strikes if you wish," Helios murmurs, still looking away.

"Why did you lie?" I ask Diomedes.

"Cassius fought with honor but was shown none in return. I wished to spare his life. I knew no other way but to claim his death and secret him away. He broke his word by returning to the war." Diomedes pauses. "As did one of my servants in abetting his escape."

"If all lies were so kind, I'd never wish to hear the truth. I forfeit my strikes if only you take my hand," I say and stick out my hand again. He takes it with a relieved smile. "I must admit my surprise in hearing you two were on-planet. When Dido rebuffed my invitation, I did not think to expect a Rim deputation."

"Nor is this one," Helios replies. I frown. If it is not a deputation, it can only be one thing. An insult. "I am here as a private citizen to honor an oath to my daughter." His hand brushes the short-bladed kitari on his belt. A House Dionysus ring of the Ionian Institute is melted into the pommel. "Before she died, she made me swear I would see Thessian perform once more." His grim face skews into the approximation of a smile. "She always thought I heeded duty so much that I forgot to live."

A thin excuse. I mask my disappointment. "And how does living feel?"

"I yearn to return to my ship and the war," he confesses.

"Living isn't for everyone, I suppose," I say.

They watch me, awkward, as if waiting for me to leave. I feel like a fool. When I was told the capital ship of the Rim's fleet was in orbit, I thought Helios's presence indicated a desire to speak with me. I was wrong. "You're both to be complimented on your successes in the war. Thanks to the two of you, we have the Republic on their heels. They barely dare to leave Mars for fear of your fleets."

Helios is polite, but barely. "You have done well on Mercury too, by the looks of your party."

"Still much to be done, I fear. Especially in Tyche, but the iron rolls and the seas calm. I'd be honored if you would join me in the pulvinar tomorrow for the pegasus jousts, and then for the launch of the *Lightbringer*—"

Helios looks to the massive ship lying to the south. No doubt he thinks it Rim property, owing to the fact it was built in the Dockyards of Ganymede, and then killed those docks under Darrow's command.

"No," Helios says. "This was a stop of convenience. We are en route to Earth. Tomorrow we pass Sol for the summit. We depart in an hour."

"What summit?" I ask.

"The Dictator's in Rome. Nine days from now Atalantia has promised to unveil her plans for the next stage of the war."

It's plain as day they know I was not invited.

"The next stage?" I ask. "Mars?"

Helios shrugs. "If not, there will be consequences. Atalantia cannot continue to drag her feet while my people fight her war. It is time to end this. I would ask you to relay that, but I hear you don't share her confidences, only her bed." He looks over at Diomedes. "The Core is an odd place, is it not?"

Diomedes looks embarrassed. The rudeness from Helios, even for a Moonie, is startling. "You're making a point of insulting me, it seems. Why?"

"I am aware you invited Consul Raa to your . . . games. Dido may flirt with Core power struggles. She is Venusian by birth after all. I do not flirt. Unless you can move Atalantia's fleets off Earth and Luna and toward Mars, do not communicate with us. Your office is a domestic one. Stay in your lane."

"Is that why the Moon Lords sent you to the Core? To make sure Dido shows . . . restraint?" I probe. It would make sense for the isolationist faction to get cold feet with both the Dust and Dragon armadas away, and only the Shadow Armada and the local garrisons left to defend the worlds of the Rim. Nervous people, Moonies.

"Dido wanted this war. I did not. I am here so the Moon Lords can be sure there are no hooks in our lip when the war is won."

"Back to isolationism then."

Helios glances at the Praetorians watching from the rim of the amphitheater. "What do your Praetorians think of you consorting with a man who led a squadron at the Battle of Ilium? Their brothers' and sisters' blood is on my blade."

"My Praetorians are an extension of me, and I believe if we are defined by the conflicts of the past we will never grow to anything better than a gnarled reflection of ancient feuds."

"Words. I watched Rhea burn, lad," he says. "There is a sickness here in the Core for which the only cure is quarantine. We should not be here. But we are. And when we leave, I will burn the bridge behind us."

So much for the unity I always dreamt of.

"Diomedes, surely you see the value in retaining a connection between Rim and Core. With your horticulture and ship design, and our manpower and resources, we could even look past the garden of this little sun. There are worlds to build across the stars."

"I am a simple knight," he replies though I get the sense he's reining himself in. In fact, after seeing him fight out on the Rim, I feel his self-control is the only thing that protects the rest of us. "I do not think it prudent for inexperienced men or women to venture into matters of state."

"From what I know of you, *simple* is exactly the wrong word," I say.

Helios actually laughs. "Well, they were wrong. You're not blinded by your own reflection. Not in both eyes, at least."

Jove, the man is an absolute savage. Still, I try to win him. "And where is Atalantia hosting her summit in Rome?"

He snorts. "The Colosseum."

"She plays games with you."

"Says the man who holds circuses."

"My office is a domestic one. Should I not stay in my lane?"

Diomedes smiles, a rare thing, and even Helios eyes me with a little more interest.

I receive the warning of the incoming man from my Praetorians only slightly before Diomedes alerts Helios. Helios follows his gaze to see a tall Gold striding toward us from the far side of the theater. I go cold inside. The newcomer is slender, pale-faced with gently slanting eyes. He wears a brown cloak and a wig of brilliant blue hair. Those in the departing crowd who see his face wilt.

Atlas au Raa favors us with a neutral smile as he comes to a stop. I almost gasp when I see the very serious man in the very ridiculous wig. "And here I thought Thessian underappreciated. What a constellation of admirers he has." He sees all three of us staring at his wig. He shrugs. "When in Heliopolis."

I knew Helios was on-planet the moment his boots touched ground. That I can't say the same for Atlas is terrifying but hardly surprising. How long has he been here? Atlas greets Helios and Diomedes, but neither man takes his hand.

Atlas raises an eyebrow at the bad manners and nods to the Binds of Zeus around Helios's arm. "Had I a moonBreaker in my palm, I'd shake even the devil's hand with a grin."

The two men stare at one another. They are similar in build, though

Atlas is longer limbed, slightly thinner, and slightly taller. "I do not consort with traitors," Helios replies.

As a boy Atlas was given as hostage to my grandmother only to become one of her greatest tools. While his brother, Romulus, is revered as a hero even in death, Atlas is seen as the blackest of traitors. Truthfully, it's not exactly fair. He didn't choose to be a hostage.

Atlas sighs. "Helios, we ply the same trade you and I. Truth. But ask yourself. Between the two of us, who is the one who has broken an oath? And who is the one who has not?"

Helios, a staunch advocate for the First Moon Lord's Rebellion, is unamused.

"Thank you for the play, Lune. If you will pardon us," he says.

Without a word for Atlas, Helios turns to depart. Diomedes follows. "Nephew," Atlas calls. Diomedes stops but does not turn. "I was sorry to hear of my brother's death. He was a great man, your father. We had our differences, namely your mother, but I loved him very much. I have no doubt you'll live up to our name."

Diomedes quarter-turns. "Diomedes," Helios snaps.

Grudgingly, Diomedes follows his mentor away. Atlas watches until they've left the theater. "Quite the pair, those two," he says.

"That is the wrong man to needle," I say of Diomedes.

"It's good to know where the nerves are."

"I thought you were on Luna," I say.

"Starvation is a slow boil. The pan is set. The burner is on. I can't really make the Lunese eat each other any faster. Once they topple the Vox, Atalantia may need me again."

"Why are you here then?" I ask.

"For the same reason as Helios." His cold eyes wait for my face to betray me. "To see Thessian, of course. The greatest mummer of our age." He smiles, joking, and scratches a scab on his neck. It looks like someone tried and succeeded in cutting his throat. He sees me looking. "You should see the other man. Well, you should see his whole continent, really."

"You were on Earth then as well. I heard rumors."

He nods, as if pacifying North America was nothing. "Atalantia thought I was too . . . brutal. Oh well, let Falthe deal with the Rockies. Atalantia has sent me to convalesce in the mountain hot springs here but also to review your . . . performance."

"You're here as a prefect?" I say, surprised. "A finance snooper, you?"

"I've a knack for numbers, especially when it comes to counting soldiers, and even I need time away from the front lines. I'm here to help. Your expenditures, well, Atalantia wants to be sure her betrothed does not spend himself into ruin. You will of course make your people available to me."

"Of course."

"Good. I won't trouble you further. Pretend I'm not even here." He watches me for a few moments. "It is good to see you, Lysander. You've done great work here. Truly. The people of Mercury are loyal citizens. They didn't deserve Darrow's chaos. Atalantia is pleased. Even she cannot go a day without hearing how beloved you are by the people of Mercury." He pauses, then says, "Your parents would be proud."

Atlas is so unnerving it is easy to forget he was close with my parents. Kalindora told me to trust him, but I can't bring myself to do so. All I know is he's Atalantia's attack dog, and Atalantia killed my parents. He doesn't know that I know that secret. But even if he did, what would he do? I can't help but toy with danger.

"I'm having a gala to launch the *Lightbringer*. I'd be honored if—"

He laughs. "Don't be silly. I'd kill the mood."

"Simply no one wants to come to my parties."

With a smile of good humor, he claps my shoulder and departs. Watching him go, I am filled with dread. If Atalantia is so pleased, then why did she send her headsman?

He stops as if hearing my thoughts, and calls back: "Lysander. Your parents were dear to me. You know that. But there are plans in motion that cannot be derailed. Not even by you. Tend to Mercury. Relax. Let the war be won. It is no shame to be loved."

When he is gone, I stand in silence for a few moments. The theater is now empty. The torches cast shadows over the stone risers. I hear wind move the grass behind me.

"Kyber. Follow him. Discreetly."

"*Your will,* dominus."

The following day, after hours in the sun glad-handing scheming Peerless and hours more soliciting creditors at the theater then the pegasus jousts, it is a relief to land at Glirastes's estate. The knowledge Atlas is on-planet, and my obsession with deciphering his parting words, does not stop the day's tension from melting away. Mindful of Cicero's words about Glirastes I thought a visit was in order. Exeter, Glirastes's Brown steward, greets me with my favorite cactus wine and leads me to the garden attached to Glirastes's workshop. "Be gentle with him today, *dominus*. He is . . . nervous. He fears your . . . machinations."

Better then he doesn't know of Atlas's presence. "In your opinion, does he feel at fault still?" I ask the pale valet. "For the Storm Gods."

"He *is* at fault, *dominus*."

Glirastes is at work hunched over a holomolder in his workshop when we enter. He shades out his work when he hears our footsteps. "Lysander, whatever are you doing here? I thought you were at the opening gala?"

"I thought I might skip it," I say and flop down on a couch.

"What? Don't be ridiculous. You have allies to foster."

"I can't be too overeager. Cicero will charm them, Horatia will reassure them. I must be a rare sight. Anyway, I wanted to celebrate this evening with a true friend. Without a wall of black and purple." He searches for my Praetorians. "I left them on the ship. Even Kyber."

He is immensely pleased, yet gives a little shudder. "That whisper makes my skin crawl. But really, Lysander. You can't afford to insult your guests. Wait . . . what did you mean? Celebrate?"

I smile. "There's news from Apollonius. News you'll never believe."

8

DARROW

The Hanging Coliseum

GRIZZLED GRAYS IN RATH purple shove Cassius and I down the throat of the famed tunnel known as Flamma's Gullet. The tunnel is aptly named. Like food, thousands of gladiators have traveled through the tunnel to the arena for Carthii-sponsored consumption. Veins of blood-hued minerals wind through the pale stone walls and floor. Through some strange art, the veins writhe to form the antique silhouettes of famous gladiators from the Carthii's favorite blood sports. Alongside them writhe beasts. Pegasuses, griffins, manticore, and carvelings too esoteric for my rudimentary education to name. Pax would know. He's the one who likes to read.

Cassius does not look well. It's the first I've seen him since we were captured two days ago. His nose is broken and his right eye blackened. He grins at me as he limps along favoring his ribs. Of course his hair is still coiled and lustrous and he didn't lose any teeth. He brandishes his smile at me as if we were drunks stumbling our way to a Pearl club. "Did he ever even have Sevro?" Cassius asks.

"I don't know."

"Must have been a trap from the get. Hopefully our insurance is still in order," he says. I grunt in reply. He frowns at me. "You know. You might be the only man who grows fatter after two days of captivity."

It's true. I did gain weight. "They fed me," I admit.

"They fed you?"

"Cheer up. At least you don't have to fight Apollonius."

"What did they feed you?"

"Salmon. Rice. Greens. Roast beef. Complex carbs. Protein. You know."

"Roast beef?"

"Yeah."

"Roast beef? I had to suck water from a rusted pipe, and no, that's not a euphemism."

A Gray belts him in his right ear. "Blackcloak. Count your blessings we aren't dragoons. Praetorian Guard would pump you with time sludge and flay you lidless."

"Horrid," Cassius mutters.

The Gray's accent is Martian, like all the Grays I've met so far. Strange. Not Thessalonican, where Apollonius is from. More specifically, this one's from Yorkton, or thereabouts. I feel a pang for home. Conventionally Grays from Yorkton would have served House Augustus. Another Gray spits on Cassius and kicks his legs out. Cassius smiles back at them as he stands. They may hate me, but Cassius disgusts them in a way only a man who has worn the Olympic cloak and betrayed it can. Blackcloaks seldom live long or die well.

The tunnel broadens into daylight and the most spectacular arena of the Core. The Hanging Coliseum. I blink into the natural sunlight. The sight is staggering.

Beneath a grand transparent dome that looks down on Venus, a sandy fighting floor stretches toward a perimeter wall thick with blooming vines and poisonous thorns. A sea of Gray legionnaires roars from the stands. Above that sea wag the purple banners of house Valii-Rath and the standards of legions—some of which are for legions that I once destroyed but have now been resurrected. Above that columns, carved with the faces of centaurs and satyrs reach toward the dome. Beyond that lies the planet Venus with its aquamarine seas, rain-forest continents, and white-sand archipelagos. I feel upside down. The overall effect of the sight would have given the boy from Lykos crippling vertigo.

Today, what stuns me is the sheer number of soldiers.

"I thought you said he only had a handful of men," Cassius says.

"He did. Seems the Martian exiles have found a man they think can take them home."

There must be fifty thousand Grays filling the stands. More. They are joined by dockyards workers—Oranges, Greens, Blues, and Reds in the tens of thousands.

I suffer the petty jealousy of a commander without an army facing a contemporary *with* an army and wish in vain for the thousandth time that I could retrieve my own legions from the sand. Why does Apollonius deserve such loyalty? Such power?

The last time I saw the man, he had only the tattered remnants of his personal legion to call upon. Not even a thousand men. That he can spare so many troops for mere pomp while still holding the station against the potential of invasion from the Carthii navy on the pole suggests his numbers run deep, or his peace is utterly secure. Or both.

He's stronger than I imagined.

But *how*?

Apollonius has always been popular with Grays. Despite his eccentricities, he is a man of war. Never more joyful than on campaign. Flawless in self-promotion. Still, it would take an ally to swell his numbers like this. One name stands apart. I look over at Cassius.

"I don't think those Votum haulers were just carrying iron."

"Lysander?" he asks. "He might be naïve, but he's no fool. He should know the Minotaur never suffers bedmates for long."

"Maybe he's just that desperate."

Silence falls on the exiled legionnaires as we, the two most reviled sons of Mars, stride onto the Carthii sands and are forced to a stop in the center. Eyes scour me with generational hate. I ignore them and search for their warlord and Sevro. The man in the cell might have been bait, but that doesn't mean my friend isn't here.

"Rath!" I shout.

When he doesn't come, my annoyance grows. Damn his pomp. Damn his trap. Damn his celebrity. I glare at his men. They stare back, haughty and hateful beneath their banners, tipped with golden bulls and tigers and lightning bolts and eagles. They are bolstered by zealotry, armored against culpability by words like *duty, fidelity, brotherhood*.

"RATH!"

Finally, when he has judged the tension to be at its crescendo, a horn blows from high above the pulvinar, and dockworkers and soldiers gaze up lovingly at a lone figure in purple armor who emerges atop the roof of the pulvinar holding a horn. The horn sends images of charging horses galloping through the dark alleys of my mind. A glittering coven of Peerless knights enters the pulvinar beneath Apollonius. I recognize many of the faces. Legates and Praetors of little wealth but not insignificant fame or capability. Frontline veterans. Professionals.

"*Minotaur!*" a single Gold Legate shouts from the pulvinar.

"*Invictus!*" hundreds of Gray centurions echo.

"*Minotaur!*" the Legate calls once more.

"*INVICTUS!*" roar all the Grays, joined by twice as many dockers. I was right. Invictus. In the days of the Society a lesser house could hope for no greater honor on the field of battle than to be permitted to weld the battle cry of House Lune to that of their own general. Cassius's expression darkens. He searches for Lysander amongst the knights beneath Apollonius, but if the Heir of Silenius is here, he hasn't the fortitude to show his face.

I wonder what Cassius would do if he did.

Apollonius descends from the high place with his arms outstretched and his cape swirling behind from the high place, but not to join us on the sands. He lands amongst his Grays, where a stout, bearded centurion tilts back his tattooed head and booms with a powering, rousing voice that'd do a Violet baritone proud:

> *When he returned from deepest grave,*
> *He had no home though he was brave!*
> *But he had two horns, that iron knave,*
> *Praise he who commands our legion!*

In reply to the singing centurion, the legions also tilt back their heads and throw their arms about one another and wave their standards like gravcross hooligans until each and every one carries the song's unending verses.

> *Forgotten soldier, march to war*
> *Take your glory, Minotaur*
> *Forgotten soldier, march to war*
> *Take your homeland, Minotaur*
>
> *Soon all of Gold will envy he*
> *Who fought for you, and fought for me*
> *With naught but horns, one minus three*
> *Praise the Minotaur's legions*

Exiled Martian, march to war
Take your glory, Minotaur
Exiled Martian, march to war
Take your homeland, Minotaur

Hear the sound of thousands roar
Toward our planet, land of war
Through one billion slaves he'll gore
Praise the Minotaur's legion

As they sing, Apollonius cannot resist displaying his own affection for these men and women. He slaps backs, sways his arms to the tune, points to his favorites, and calls out coarse jests. The veterans worship him. As they bellow a verse about his sexual relations with Atalantia and his future Augustan and Juliian conquests, he takes up a standard and pumps his arms to welcome the brutish jeers and taunts and jibes that are the language of affection amongst this martial breed.

Cassius watches with a scowl. "They *love* him."

I feel defeated. I thought if I could just reclaim Sevro, I would also reclaim the spirit of the old days. I thought I would return to Victra, to Virginia, carrying a spark to relight the blaze of our glory.

But now I'm not even sure Apollonius ever had Sevro.

Our only hope is Aurae and the atomic. No doubt Apollonius will be streaming this event throughout the station. Aurae will be in the *Archimedes*, parked in a hiding place on the dockyards' hull. She will be watching, waiting for my signal.

When Apollonius finally joins us, he carries his legion standard—a giant golden bull's head, the oak staff of which is pierced with pieces of the shattered stars of Republic legions. Legions he destroyed on Earth and Mars. Legions under my command.

Quieting his men, Apollonius beams me a smile and greets me with a verse from an ancient children's book: *The Lamplighter*.

"Along the black abyss, the bold mortal—long-suffering, nigh-breaking—fixed his will against Fate's course. Sheen-mailed, ne'er-quaking, bent was his neck, fury unslaking to row, row, row his oars against the world's breaking. Once more. Once more he paddled from safe shores. If only to shout, if only to roar: 'Come death! Come oblivion! Here yet this mortal strains.'"

Apollonius shivers in delight. Built thicker and taller even than Cassius, he is a man cast in a Miltonic mold. His angelic beauty is shaded with evil intent. His skin is the color of buckwheat honey, his lips are full, sensuous, and cruel. His nose is generous and stately. His eyes are sheathed behind sleepy lids and curtains of thick gold lashes. Long waves of dark golden hair spill past his shoulders. Hardly meriting a glance for Cassius, his eyes search me, relish me, devour every last centimeter of me, noting my diminished size, my grizzled beard, my pale skin, and shortened breath. As if he knew what to look for, his eyes linger last in confirmation on my injured left arm. He sighs like a great dragon lying down to sleep, content in his machinations and ready to dream of evil things.

"Truly, I did not think you would come. But I held on to my meager faith like a Boetian *ouragos* praying to hear the *alala* rolling west from golden Attica . . . Athens! Athens has come. But you are not a city. No. You are an empire."

I'm not sure what that even means.

"With great anticipation I watched you sleep these last days. I wished to visit. To converse peer to peer. I hear you were asking for me. Now you know my pain. But best is the gratification long delayed. The caviar savored, slow-eaten to melt on the tongue." He steps forward, yearning to embrace me but not wishing to give insult. He whispers, "I am bored, Darrow. I am terminally bored. I yearn for the clash. I yearn for martial sensation. So gratitude, Reaper. Gratitude, foe, for this! The ultimate honor between peers—a conversation in the language we both have mastered. Violence. Surely there can be no greater distillation of all our mutual respect, animus, and quality." His eyelids flare back. "Gratitude for answering my summons. Gratitude for granting me this final communion." His eyes flick to my bald head where the first sprouts of new hair are emerging. "Depilated and dilapidated though you may be."

"Well, slag me but you've really gone off the deep end, goodman," Cassius says.

"Shut up," I snap at him. He has no idea how to talk to Apollonius anymore. I do and I want information. While Apollonius assessed me, I returned the favor. I've noticed something strange. He has no injuries save for two. An almost invisible scar on the left side of his neck. Whatever caused it missed his jugular by a hair. He also has a bitemark on his right cheek. It is almost healed but shows signs of past infection.

"Hello, Apollonius. When I left you on the Ash Lord's island, I knew you'd cause trouble." I peer around, looking for more clues, and knowing flattery will land where threats will not. "Truly, you are trouble incarnate."

He purrs at the compliment. "As you were on Mercury." I cock my head. "Yes. I was there, Darrow."

"And you didn't visit me?"

"I am not so low as to poach another's prey. In rapture, behind a ghost's guise, I witnessed your rage against the Grimmus horde. As your army fell man by man in crossing the Ladon, I wept. For their purity. For their faith. Surely, since the age of Merrywater, no nobler soldiers have ever lived or died for their commander. Always on the back foot. Biting, gnawing for every inch of ground. Smashing the rising beast Ajax against the walls of Heliopolis. Truly, they were sons and daughters of Mars." He touches his breast. "Respect."

I nod, receiving the respect as Cassius sinks deeper into his nearly existential confusion at our interaction. "Then you know their fate," I say.

Apollonius sighs, grandiloquent. "Impalement. Another grotesquerie of the Fear Knight designed only to shock the mob. An unworthy end for such soldiers." He strokes his hair. "As your . . . clandestine arrival was unworthy of you. I could have impaled Sevro after I acquired him. Instead, I offered you a fair contest. So why must you impugn my valor? Coming like a thief in the night despite my earnest proposal? Did you think me a cretin who would offer a duel only to kill you on sight?"

I glance at Cassius. We're both confused. Does he have Sevro? "I hope you got a receipt from the Syndicate. You do know the man in that cell isn't Sevro," Cassius clarifies.

Apollonius rolls his eyes.

"Where is he?" I say. "If you have him, bring him out."

Apollonius considers. "No."

"You disappoint me," I say.

He coughs in offense. "Disappoint you? Disappoint *you*? I took this, the pride of the Carthii family, after you left me on an enemy sphere with half a thousand men. I swayed the hearts of their legions, their dockers, with nothing but rhetoric and passion and will. Lucifer himself when he stood afore the fresh-fallen legions of hell did not surpass my oration. It is you who disappoint *me*. Bringing yourself to me in such a feeble state. Ungrateful for this chance I give you."

I shrug. "At least I'm not a common whore." Apollonius's good humor vanishes. "When last I saw you, Atlas, Atalantia, Asmodeus, they all stabbed you in the back in ways I never have. And now you fight for them."

"I do not fight for them."

"You're making ships for them. The iron flows from Mercury unmolested. Which means, you must have made peace with them—the very same people who let you rot for six years in Deepgrave and then gave you to me like a Saturnalian gift."

"Patient is the bow of Apollo far-striker." The cunning in his smile tells me I have only half the picture.

"Do you mean, 'Patient is the Mind's Eye'?" Cassius asks. "Seems you were not paying attention to Master Lysander's lessons, goodman."

Apollonius sets his hands on his hips and begrudgingly turns his attention to Cassius. As if he could see through the thin prisoner jumpsuit, he admires Cassius's body but little else. "Little Bellona, still chirping like a bird in heat. I have fond memories of my days with Tharsus and Karnus, memories you despoil. Always nipping at our heels with that dented chin to the Pearl clubs, weren't you? Gobbling up the debris of our debauchery. How Karnus despised you and your freeloading. As I told you then, a shining name does not entitle you to never pay for the Pinks, Cassius."

"They made you pay?" Cassius asks.

Apollonius smiles with teeth. "Years ago, when they told me you killed your fellow Olympic Knights, broke a sacred coven, cut down the Sovereign and the Compact and all those ridiculous creeds you swore to uphold, I laughed. How could a man who never pays a bill ever be expected to keep his vows. Hollow then. Hollow now. Hollow ever after."

Apollonius steps closer.

"Why have you returned from your exile, Bellona? Come to test your prowess? Bringing with you, perhaps, some esoteric battle form from the icy depths of the system? Shadowfall? Windstrider? Bringer of Dawn?" His eyes flare with intrigue at each hopeful guess. "Or do you too hunger for the glory of my . . . falchion?"

His fingers graze his groin armor and fall on his razor. The huge bronze-hued blade unfurls from its place on his hip. It is three times as thick as a conventional razor. He sets it on his shoulder.

"Indeed, for the glory," Cassius replies. "But mostly for the patrician pleasure of watching an ill-mannered brute from a mediocre bloodline crumble under the burden of his own grandiosity."

"Better a grandiose scion of mediocrity than a mediocre scion of a grand line." Apollonius pats his face. "You may stay many beatings if you tell me where your ghost ship is. I want it. What mischief I could cause." He waits. "Then begone, beastly cherub. A duel I sought and a duel I shall have."

"There won't be any duel," I say. Apollonius motions to a familiar centurion, Vorkian, his most trusted henchwoman. Bad Lass and Cassius's razor hang from her belt. She comes forward bearing a silver platter. "At this moment there is a ten megaton atomic planted on one of the construction spindles. When it blows, the Carthii will think you've finally gone mad. Unless you bring me Sevro and let me go, I will—"

My threat dies on my tongue when Vorkian reveals what's beneath the platter. It is our atomic. Apollonius smiles at me. "I know you, Darrow, like I know my violin. The moment of your capture, a survey was conducted. Your ship may yet evade me, but your devices have not. A duel I sought and a duel I shall have."

My stomach sinks. So much for the path. The Vale is only minutes away.

I say nothing as his Grays drag Cassius up to the pulvinar.

"Where is Sevro?" I murmur. "If he's alive, we don't have to fight. You have more in common with me than you do with Atalantia, with Lune."

"Darrow. *Darrow.* No more words. They are fickle objects. Misspoken, misheard, *misshapen*. So let us continue our conversation in a truer tongue."

He lifts his arms. A team of Oranges rushes out to undress him from his armor down to a traditional Martian fighting tunic, the sort they wear in the blade clubs where he settled so many juvenile scores. It covers little of his muscular thighs and even less of his arms. At the same time, White acolytes rush forward with bags to strew the ground with reddish dirt.

"Dirt from Mother Mars," Apollonius calls. "My last gift to you. So that when you fall, it may be into her embrace. Know when I return to our cradle . . . when I fall upon Mars in the last Iron Rain of this age, you will be with me as Medusa was with Perseus. Your head will be affixed upon my shield. And when rots the flesh, the skull will be cleaned and preserved with tender care, and set upon the right horn of my helmet so all may see me and know, there . . . yes, there up high . . . you see him, my son? There is the mortal who thought to challenge the heavens, and there is the dauntless god that humbled him."

The Grays release me from my manacles, and Vorkian tosses me Bad Lass. I sigh and shape the blade with the control on the hilt until it takes on the curve of my old razor. I plunge the slingBlade into the sand and pick up a handful of dirt. It smells like home.

Apollonius ties up his hair in a ponytail. "I warn you, should you fight merely to wound me, for fear of my men's rancor, it will be no contest. I am in my power. Our duel will be to the death. Hold nothing back. Should you survive, you and your Bellona paramour will leave here without molestation. You have the oath of my bones." He takes hold of his pinky finger on his off-hand and jerks it sideways to snap the bone. "Of my blood." He slices his left cheek with a knife to produce a crimson drip. "Of my flesh." He fleeces a sliver off the point of his left ear. There were many notches before me. He tosses the sliver into the scattered dirt.

"Where is Sevro?" I demand.

He shrugs, and now I really do believe he had Sevro. "Only the rats know."

"You killed him," I whisper. "You couldn't resist. Animal."

His lips curl back from his teeth, and he charges me. He does it like a lion. Not a lion in the holos, roaring and gnashing, but lowered, sprinting, silent. I seize Bad Lass from the ground just in time to save myself from decapitation. The roaring of the crowd fades away, replaced by the pounding of blood, the panting of breath, the clang of razors, and the immediate terror of a duel without armor.

I try to separate and regroup but it's all I can do to keep pace with him and not cross my feet. I planned to keep him at a distance if it came to a fight, but the collision of the blades and the news of Sevro's death incite my blood to reckless violence. I will kill him. My body may be haggard, thin, but I have trained in the Willow Way every day for nearly five months. I find his rhythm, meet him blow for blow, bending back from his onslaught only to lash at him in the counterattacks Lorn hammered into me.

Sparks fly. Metal keens. A laughing demon inside me tells me he is mine. He may be stronger, faster, bigger, but I am the Willow and my rage is rekindled. I turn a set intended to draw my guard high and take my right leg before finally releasing a set of my own.

It is a mistake.

I realize it the moment he ignores my feint at his eyes and blocks the downward slash intended to take off his left ankle. His parry is the hardest I've ever felt. My arms rattle. His next parry numbs them both. Gods he's strong. Pain lances through the old break in my left arm as he parries me again. I recover by leaping back, exchanging a flurry of whip strikes, and then attacking, relying on the headlong ferocity that made me the youngest Helldiver of Lykos combined with the root strikes of the Willow Way. A crimson line opens on his right thigh. Another on his left cheek just below the eye.

Then Apollonius actually begins to try.

He does it slowly, building his pace and his power in increments. Four moves a second. Five. Six. Then seven. An onset of seven is nearly impossible. It matches Lorn, Aja. Perhaps not with their innate poeticism, but he's athletic enough to make it a close facsimile. My unconscious mind begins to panic. What's worse is he sustains it. His conditioning is tremendous, my own feeble. A line of fire races across my right hip bone. Another across my left shoulder. Another on my forehead. And then I feel a pinch as his razor slips through my left calf, darts out, and as the pressure builds and the muscle knots, my ear stabs with pain. My right lobe flops to the ground. I meet a huge overhand and am driven to my knees. I roll away. He gives me a moment's respite.

"What is this?" he snarls. "Where are you, Reaper?"

My blade, held in front of me, shakes like a leaf. I have felt strength like this before, from Obsidian Stained, but those blows require a sacrifice in grace.

Apollonius's attacks sacrifice nothing.

They are tight, well-timed, and so powerful I fear he'll break my left arm if we continue parrying at the same rate. Cassius shouts instructions down from the pulvinar, but I can't hear him in my panic or over the roar of the soldiers. Apollonius comes on again, hungry for the kill. Unable to meet him toe to toe, I bend and bend until I have to flow away, but his onslaught denies me any chance to plant my roots—even when I do, he hammers at them with a ferocity I can't match, pressing, pressing, always pressing.

The shock is existential and indicts not just me, but the Willow Way itself. For the first time in my life, I realize not only am I not enough, but neither is my form.

He knows it too well. He's learned how to break it.

We're back on the Martian dirt now. He won't let me escape his full-frontal assault. He herds me. A dozen minor wounds already rend my flesh. My arms and legs are coated with as much blood as sweat. It's all I can do to keep the barrage of keening metal from taking a limb. I try to go around his right, but he mirrors me, denying me his flank and forcing me back, back. Sparks fly as I parry four onsets in a row. Blood sprays as we nick one another's knuckles and forearms until he penetrates my guard and plunges his razor into my left breast, just above the lung.

He holds me there, our bodies pressed together, my blade pinned to my side.

"Reaper, where have you gone?" Try as I might, I can't free myself from his anaconda-grip. "Where is the king of stains I sought?" he whispers. He lets me go. Blood pulses from the wound. I stagger away from him not knowing what to do.

He follows with a swing to cut me in two. I let my body go loose and bend backward, feigning retreat. I forget the Willow Way, and use my left arm to catch my fall and push me forward like a Lykosian tumbler. The move takes me past his right knee to finally turn his flank. I slash back and stumble up. He didn't even bother parrying my swing. He steps clear and watches me as if with a broken heart.

I fall to a knee and pant in fear and exhaustion. Blood sheets down my chest. I've lost speed and strength over the years, while Apollonius seems to have reached his ultimate form. Lysander did more than give him Grays and iron. He must have taught him how to beat the Willow Way. I touch the wound on my chest. My eyes dart to Cassius, to the crowd, to space above to glimpse Mars twinkling in the distance. To see home one last time. The paradise planet blocks the view. I touch the key on my chest. I'm sorry, Pax. I'm sorry, Virginia.

"Scraps," Apollonius murmurs in disillusionment. "That is what they will say of this. Atalantia, Atlas, Lysander, left me nothing but scraps to eat." He blinks at the ground. "Apollonius the Vulture, they will call me. Apollonius who could not beat Darrow in his prime. This is not what I deserve. Where is the struggle? Where is the glory?"

I won't die bad. I won't die whimpering. I can trap his blade in my body. Kill him as I die. I spit blood out of my mouth and beat my chest at Apollonius. "Come on, you bastard. Come on!"

Reluctant, he obliges. But before he's taken three steps, he stops and looks down at the sand with a frown. It has begun to shiver. In the stands, the legions stagger and sway. A great sigh goes through the station. The sand begins to leap like water boiling in a pot. Above, Venus stretches like taffy as a shockwave warps the coliseum's dome and a rumble goes through the station.

I glance up to Cassius. He stares back, just as confused.

That was a bomb, but it wasn't ours.

9

DARROW

Shit Escalates

"ATOMIC EVENT DETECTED ON WEST *spindle four. It was one of ours. Deterrent number eight. Preliminary reports suggest total structural and personnel loss. Damage indicated on second and third spindles. All power is lost in sectors nine through eleven. Sensors and coms non-responsive. Full damage report still pending,"* reports the Blue.

Apollonius's Golds and Gray officers have descended to gather around their commander as he listens to the report and dispatches response teams. He is the only one smiling. A dozen Grays shove Cassius down beside me in the sand. He tears off a piece of his prisoner kit to stanch the wound beneath my left collarbone. "Hold that. Darrow. Hold it." He ties a bandage around my pierced calf. I hiss in pain as he does the same to a flap of skin on my left forearm.

"Spindle four? What's happening?" he asks. "Aurae?"

"I don't know," I manage, though I have my suspicions. My wound stings. Not a single limb is without a slash. "He had a bitemark on his cheek."

Cassius is too stressed to hear me. "Gorydamn, man. He whittled you like a stick."

Bitemark. Bomb. Sevro?

"Only the rats know," I murmur.

"What?" Cassius asks.

Hope stirs. Apollonius had Sevro. Sevro got loose. In the ducts? I hold on to that hope.

"I have the *Eurytion*. Asmodeus au Carthii is on the beam," a Gold veteran calls to Apollonius, and projects the hologram of Asmodeus from her datapad. The eerie, ageless leader of House Carthii peers at Apollonius with slitted eyes.

"Asmodeus, you have no doubt seen the atomic detonation," Apollonius says. "I am told your ships over the pole are mobilizing. According to the terms of the détente, Atalantia guaranteed my imperium over these docks. If you attack, you defy the Dictator's edict, you compromise the war effort. Do not misread my intentions. I have no desire to destroy the dockyards. The detonation was an act of sabotage—"

"If I were a man looking for an explanation, I might care. As it is, I am a man looking for an excuse.

"When I stand before the Two Hundred and the Dictator with your head, mongrel, they will not indict me. They will applaud."

Asmodeus disappears.

Apollonius shrugs. "Alas, the frailty of words. Steel, be thou my tongue. Attend me." He lifts his arms and his Oranges look at each other, nod, and run forward with his armor.

"Carthii warships are moving off the pole . . ." a Gold officer calls and casts up a hologram for his commander. The Gold veterans watch coolly as the Carthii navy abandons their position over the north pole and streaks toward the dockyards. "What are your orders, *dominus*?"

Apollonius frowns, as if his Oranges fitting him in his purple panoply was an obvious mission statement. "Bequeath them hell, of course."

The officer frowns at Vorkian, confirming with the archCenturion that the order meant open fire. She nods. Apollonius waves off the hologram as a forest of light lashes out from the station's batteries toward the onrushing fleet. A throaty rumble trembles through the station as the enemy returns fire and the artillery battle begins. Nearly armored, Apollonius shouts to the legions who watch him from the stands.

"Legionnaires! Citizens of the dockyards! My noble friends! The dread Carthii come to drag you back under their perfidious yoke. They come in numbers many times our own. But do not quake, for I am with you. Your Minotaur will not abandon you! By my will and your hands, we took the station together. We hold it together! Summon your courage! Sharpen your will! Join your brothers and sisters at your battle stations! Carry my name! Seize your glory! Go!"

They chant his name and surge out of the stands to defend their stations.

Vorkian's voice is flat and factual. "*Dominus,* we cannot stop the Carthii. They will board. They will swamp us. We will be outnumbered. Perhaps five to one. The bluff is called, and we've the low pair. We can't hold the outer crescents much less the two axes."

"They know not our true numbers nor the quality that awaits them here, Vorkian. Let them come. Let them die. Lune cannot afford to abandon me, and I grow tired of playing castellan. Let us force his hands to throw the dice."

"*Dominus,* I recommend we cut our losses. Our ally would expect us to protect his investment—"

"I am his investment and so are the ships we protect," Apollonius says. "Where is your spirit, Vorkian? Moments such as this are the forge of legends. For every campaign, there is always an inciting incident. Let this be ours."

She pulls her sidearm. "Then let me at least tie up your loose ends."

"My baubles?" Apollonius asks. "Horrible, no. Darrow and I have not finished our duel. I will not let him die while I am left unsatisfied. We pump him with protein and throw him a second try. There in Thessalonica where the Thermic meets the coast, we will dance again and let his blood water my vines. I will taste him in my cup with the dirt. Yes. Yes, that. A Rath red, a new vintage indeed." He comes out of his reverie. "As for Bellona, Lune will need him for Julia. Her finances are crucial. Bring them."

Apollonius peers at his Golds. "My fellows, I promised you the glory of reconquering our homeland. Mars lies through this moment. Go now to your legions. Deny the Carthii every meter of deck, and any measure of mercy. Ravage them. Break them. Venus is the planet of love. What is Mars the planet of again?"

They smile in silence, and rush off to answer with their deeds.

The hallway thunders with a storm of metal boots. Apollonius's personal legion, the same scorpion-eating, rampart-breaking madmen who stormed the Ash Lord's island with Sevro and me and then took on the dockyards themselves, jog down the hall singing their song.

Several hundred battle-hardened Grays, a few dozen Obsidians, and six Golds. We're dragged on like pack mules, strapped with extra ammunition, fit with dilation collars and cuffs that can retract on command. The Obsidians make sure we keep pace and slap our asses with the hafts of their axes.

"We don't have armor," Cassius says. "We'll be like peaches into a woodchipper when they hit the Carthii."

I try to remember a line from *The Path to the Vale* that might console us but I've got blood crusted in my nostrils, on my legs, on my ribs. My only hope is that it is Sevro who blew the other bomb, and that he's got a plan. I don't. All I can do is wait for the opening and be ready.

"Be ready," I say to Cassius.

"For what?"

"I don't know."

With Apollonius at the lead in his horned helmet we're headed for the life-support nexus for this part of the station—which the Carthii will no doubt try to seize with their best men. My view is filled with the bobbing of metal shoulders and the glare of alarm lights and the glitter of hall cameras.

Twice the armored column has to divert because of a bulkhead that refuses to open. Suspicious. I peer past the armored shoulders and heads when we come to an abrupt stop in a corridor ten paces wide. The Grays twitch, restless. They've already taken their battle drugs. The column bends out of sight behind us with the curve of the hall. At the fore, Apollonius bellows in impatience at Greens in his command hub. The column about-faces to retrace its steps but the bulkhead at the rear must have closed too because the about-face goes nowhere. Centurions shout down the line for a breaching team.

"It's him," I murmur.

Vorkian shouts for silence. Up ahead, Apollonius puts his ear against a wall to listen for something. He backs away from the wall.

"LeechCraft!" he shouts. "Search for teardrops."

The call echoes down the line behind us, out of sight. Cassius swallows. Teardrops. That's what they call the first hint of molten metal on the wrong side of a leechCraft's drill. A Gray triarius is the first to spot one. Cassius might have said something clever if he had his razor. But with his hands bound behind his back and only a prisoner jumpsuit between his body and what's about to happen, he just looks at me.

"Peaches. Woodchipper."

The column shifts with anxiety. They're not in a good position should something go wrong.

Apollonius roars for the breaching team to hurry up and clear the bulkhead blocking us in. I search for some obvious salvation—a hatch opening, a plasma charge eating through the ceiling. Some sign of Sevro. Nothing. It's enemies all the way to the bulkhead in front, enemies all the way to the curve of the hall behind. The corridors were designed to trap invaders. I'd know because I studied this place with Sevro for years. You don't want to be trapped in a hall like this.

The breaching charges detonate against the bulkhead at the fore but fail to penetrate fully.

We're not going to clear the hallway before the Carthii hit us.

There's only one choice: hit the boarders in the teeth hard as possible.

Apollonius comes to the same conclusion.

Centurions bark orders and legionnaires grind into position around the breaches. The Obsidians' grip on me tightens. Two more drill marks appear on the corridor's left bulkhead halfway down the formation. Shit. Recognizing the danger the second and third breaches pose, Apollonius calls his Golds to the front. They open fire on the obstructing bulkhead with their pulseFists until it glows orange. They plunge their razors in like picks and hack holes in the thick metal, but they're not faster than leechCraft drills.

Apollonius is a good enough commander to know what's about to happen to his precious personal legion. You push other legions around like blocks, but your own you use as a sacred scalpel, delicate and sharp and fast, to find the arteries of the enemy. His precious scalpel is about to be shoved into a woodchipper along with us peaches.

A great roar comes from the man as he tries once more at the door before abandoning the lost cause and pushing himself to face the nearest breach. "Stack on breaches. Divide by cohort. Rank by heavy shields, triarii, velites. Crows and Peerless stack in pods for melee. Coriolanus, front cohort. Vorkian, rear. You have the prisoners. I have center."

Phalanxes form before the breaches. A bulwark of energy shields, a hedge of glinting, armor-boring spears backed by a forest of rifles.

The Obsidians drag us through the legionnaires to the rear. They're still manhandling us back around the curve of the hall when we pass the mouth of the last breach. I see down its molten throat all the way to the

Carthii leechCraft where metal figures gather behind a glowing shield. A lone berserker, released before the rest, sprints down the throat toward us. In the heat-warped air, he is a mirage of terror. Naked, heavily tattooed with the eel-green ink of the Carthii gladiatorial clans, and raving mad. Vorkian stops, aims her rifle into the breach's throat, and fires a single, perfect shot. It takes the Obsidian between the eyes. He falls short of the breach.

Such is the heat, he catches fire.

A sacrifice to the gods of death. Then the shield at the Carthii leech-Craft winks out and the metal stacked behind it begins to move. Ram-Lads, delirious with pharmaceutical courage, armored thick as rhinoceroses, rush down the throat with an oceanic roar. Vorkian and our Obsidian handlers drag us on as the Grays open fire.

I twist to see a ramLad stumble out the mouth of a breach into the hall. Bent forward like a golem trudging into a storm, he soaks up the fire, takes one last step, and collapses in a rent heap. In his wake come berserkers. This wave of genetically enhanced killing machines crashes upon the wall of stony Gray veterans and turns to red foam. The second wave breaks from torpedo rounds that turn them to human pyres. But their momentum, added with that of the unnatural delirium in the beasts behind them and the Carthii tolerance for high casualties, creates a surge of mass that cannot be denied.

Expensive Obsidian slaveknights in cerulean armor, heavy shields, and short spears form the third wave. Trampling over the corpses of their spent brethren, they crush into the first Grays and hack at the shield line as the spears of the second line impale them. With a cry nearly inaudible amongst the explosions and shrieking, Apollonius and his heavy Gold infantry charge into the Obsidian flanks at each breach. The corridor fills with smoke and noise and death.

My eardrums ache. Bullets hiss. Shrapnel pings off Vorkian's helmet, slashes across the bridge of my nose, and peppers the armor of the Obsidian handler behind me. Cassius ducks. Down the hall, the battle takes on the sound of hundreds of spoons caught in an industrial fan. Something slams into the wall next to my head and ricochets, taking along a chunk of my scalp before embedding itself in the eyehole of one of my Obsidian handlers. His grip slackens. Before the second Obsidian sees his fellow teeter down, I slam my shoulder into the warrior. Off balance, he stumbles into the smoke.

I crouch, coughing, eyes burning. I can't see Cassius. I can't see anything but indistinct shapes and flashes through thick smoke. I go lower to find clear air for my lungs. A hand grazes my head and, finding no hair to grab, slides off. The dilation collar tightens. I can't breathe. Blood sluices down my neck as the collar cuts into my skin. An Obsidian body lies on the ground nearby. I crawl to it and grope behind my back for his boot knife. I find the blade at the price of a few cut fingers. Fumbling, choking, I saw at the dilation bindings on my wrists until they come apart. My hands are free. Wheezing, I cut through my collar and suck down air.

Nauseated, vision swimming, I stay as low as I can in the smoke and search for Cassius. I see two figures staggering in an embrace, like lovers. One is Cassius. The other Vorkian. He's headbutting her repeatedly. Unfortunately for him, she wears a helmet, and all Cassius does is knock himself out. He falls down into the smoke, but he bought us enough time. Vorkian reaches for the dilation-collar controller on the ground and I lunge up through the smoke to bury the Obsidian knife under her left armpit. I slam her against the wall and kick the controller away. I grab at her waist and come away with Bad Lass and Cassius's razor before she disappears in the smoke and press of bodies.

I duck down as high-caliber rounds buzz overhead. Bodies fall and tangle and climb and hack. I find Cassius on the ground and cut off his bindings. His collar tightened and nearly nipped an artery. I slap his face until his eyes open. He hacks for air. Blood leaks from his ears.

My hearing is shot. Everything is muffled, chaotic. Sounds come as if through water. I push his razor into his hand and signal him to stay low and follow me away from the breaches toward the closed bulkhead at the rear of Apollonius's column. Crouching, razors in hand, we set off into the smoke.

Men have disintegrated into singular actions. An arm holding a razor rises and falls. A rifle flares. A helmet caves in from a powered boot. From the smoke, a Gold appears and points his pulseFist at me. Before he can fire, another man stumbles back into him. Then an Obsidian war-spear comes through his neck. I lunge forward and rob the dying Gold of his aegis.

I take point, aegis up, razor straight and on its rim, Cassius stacked behind me. We push toward the bulkhead like hoplites. Identity is lost amongst the chaos, the smoke, the screams. Two Grays fire at us. I take the slugs on the aegis. The Grays shift their aim toward my unprotected feet. Cassius lunges over my shoulder with his razor. He spears the first Gray through the eye socket and ducks back behind the shield. I take the second between the clavicle and neck with Bad Lass then bowl him over with the shield. We push through the smoke, stabbing out from the cover of the aegis as we go until we're stopped by the bulkhead at the rear of the Rath formation. It's still sealed. Terrified men already hack at it with their weapons. More crush in behind us, pinning us to the bulkhead. Still more on their way, tripping, scrambling, desperate to escape the Carthii killers. My legs give out and I swoon in the press. I lose the aegis and my hands are so slippery with blood I almost drop Bad Lass. Cassius throws his shoulders into men until he's able to pull me back up and shield me with his body.

Down the hall comes a muffled cheer. "Carthii! Carthii!"

They must have secured the breaches. According to Carthii doctrine, that means one thing: the Golds will be coming. Over the crush of dented helmets and bloody Grays I see the fear in Cassius's eyes. Then the pressure releases forward as the bulkhead opens.

Pushed by the mass of men behind us, we spill forward. I fall. Metal heels stampede over my back. Something massive stomps toward me from the opposite direction. I look up to see the clawed feet of a starShell. The weight is swept off my back. A half dozen Grays slide down the left wall, their bones broken like kindling by the sweep of the starShell's arm.

The starShell towers over me. It stands alone in the corridor, its canopy and shoulders crudely reduced to fit the tight confines. Its clawed metal foot stomps down to my right, then my left, until it straddles Cassius and me like a beast protecting its cubs.

The railgun in its left arm lowers, as does the giant pulseFist in its right, and from its cockpit, amplified by its external speakers, comes a bloodcurdling howl. Both of my eardrums rattle as it opens fire directly above us. I shimmy out from under the mech to see the pilot through the canopy. Under a bird's nest of hair, a demonic, bearded face black with grease screams in the stuttered light of the starShell's deluge.

Sevro.

I almost pass out from joy. Murderous glee shimmers in his bloodshot eyes. He shouts something at me and jerks his head to get behind him. Cassius and I don't have to be told twice. We scramble behind the starShell. Medical supplies and vacuum helmets have been taped to its back. Cassius strips them off. I slap the chassis. The starShell doesn't move. I hammer at it again and again until Sevro finally takes a step back. Then another. Without breaking his stream of fire, he covers our retreat back down the hall. Cassius injects my neck with a battle stim and slaps resFlesh on my new wounds. The familiar itchy energy rushes through me. I wipe my bloody hands on my tattered jumpsuit and grip Bad Lass.

By the time we reach an intersection and get free of the line of fire, the starShell is spewing smoke. Sevro remains within it, unwilling to stop killing. He fires back down the hall even as its right leg is shot out. At the last moment, he pops the rear hatch and escapes out the back.

He's dressed in battered scarabSkin. A trophy necklace of fetid ears hangs from his neck. I want to kiss him, hug him till his head pops off, but he's all business. After two quick hand signals for us to follow and keep pace, he takes off at a run. We follow.

The Carthii invasion rolls on all around us. With my damaged ears, I feel removed from it. Battles thunder in the distance. Mechanized troopers clomp down hallways. Even with the stims, it's all we can do to keep up. Cassius and I are a mess. My injured calf slows me. Cassius must have suffered a concussion because he can't stop vomiting, even when Sevro takes us into a maintenance tunnel. More than a half dozen times Sevro slows to deactivate tripwires and improvised traps in the darkness. By the time we emerge into a viewing garden I have a clearer picture of Sevro's stay on the dockyards. He must have escaped soon after his imprisonment and spent the past months waging a one-man guerilla war against Apollonius.

The tranquility of the garden is as shocking as the violence of the battle. Birds and purple spider sloths watch us from the garden's trees as Sevro hands me his datapad. I dial in the fallback frequency to hail Aurae. When she answers, Sevro snatches the datapad away and strides up to the viewing deck window to peer into space as he talks. Outside Carthii destroyers and troop barges flow past, illuminated by the white-wash of artillery fire and the orange flames of oxygen burps from the station.

After a few minutes, Sevro signals us to put on our helmets. He takes a thin wire from a pouch on his kit and ties one end around a railing and the other around his belt. Then he extends a hand to me. I extend mine to Cassius. He shakes his head. He knows what's coming. I insist and he takes it. Hands locked, Sevro guides us to the railing. Cassius and I lie down and wrap our legs around it. On his back, Sevro lifts his strange weapon, points it at the glass, waits, then fires until the glass explodes outward. Pressure gushes out of the viewing deck. Flowers, birds, sloths, and trees fly past. The pressure the room contained is limited, and the flow of debris soon slows. As the cold of the vacuum begins to drain the heat from our bodies, we release our legs and let Sevro push us toward space.

Sevro lets out the wire bit by bit until we dangle out the open window like a balloon on a string. The cold is total. My teeth chatter in my helmet. Explosions flash along the metal horizon. I lose feeling in my fingers and toes first. Then my legs and arms. A shadow falls over us. Sevro nods to me. Drunk from the effects of the cold, I let go of his hand and receive a push. I float away from Sevro. He goes the other way, back toward the windowless garden, where he releases the wire from his belt and pushes off to head our direction. He passes Cassius and me just as we float into a cargo bay filled with crates stamped with winged heels. The *Archimedes*.

The bay doors of the *Archimedes* close behind us. Pressure gushes back in to the hold but not gravity. I'm too cold to do anything but shiver and float with my hand locked around Cassius's. I feel out of my body as Sevro strips his helmet and pushes us through the ship. When he finds the medBay he separates me from Cassius to secure me in one of the medical beds and drape a thermal blanket over me before taking off my helmet.

With Cassius still floating in the air behind him, Sevro shouts to Aurae. I can't hear what. He looks back at me. His red eyes are shiny with tears in his grease-dark face. He lowers his forehead to mine and only pulls back when gravity returns. Cassius plummets from the air to crunch into the floor. He curls into a shivering ball. Sevro tosses a blanket at him and heads for the cockpit.

I lie there shaking, a smile on my face as the engines of the *Archimedes* vibrate and the ship accelerates away from the battle.

10

LYSANDER

Iron Fist

I MAKE MY GRAND ENTRANCE to my party on a pegasus from Horatia's private herd. Slipping off its back onto the top hull of the *Lightbringer,* I greet Cicero and Horatia with kisses, Glirastes with a nod, my Praetorian Guard with a salute, and turn to address my waiting guests. Some are friends. Some are Atalantia's creatures. Most are somewhere in between. All have come expecting to see me fail. They just might.

It is an accepted truism that in the Core only the Carthii build warships. Not the Votum. The Votum are fine builders, yes. But terrestrial builders. Simpletons in the sophisticated shadow of Carthii astral-construction supremacy.

Tonight we dash that myth. I hope. I have bet everything on it. The ship does look like a monster. It has no paint, and its hull is heterogenous and patched with the metal of ruined Republic ships. The front is ghastly heavy, but there are reasons for this. If it flies, that is.

The fire of braziers whips in the wind. The Golds gather in white furs and wear crowns of flowers to symbolize the planet's rebirth. It is cold at this altitude, and it will get colder. The ship is the largest warship in existence. Eight kilometers long, 1.5 kilometers thick. It has not yet lifted off. But even lying on its side, our perch on its back provides a grand view of Heliopolis cupped between the mountains and the sea. The whole city is watching, and so are interested parties all across the Core. I lift my voice.

"My noble kinsmen, I am honored you could join me on this auspi-

cious day. When Darrow came to Mercury, he claimed to bring freedom. Instead, he brought death. Mercury was not the first planet to fall
to the Reaper, but it will be the last."

There's a stir in the crowd as Tharsus and a dozen of his glamorous
friends arrive late and very drunk. Indecorously, they chose gravBoots
over the ivory skiffs offered to my guests. They crash down in a swirl of
silks and scents and doff their military boots to pull out fur slippers.
They do not join to listen to my speech, but instead head for the menagerie of carvelings near the bow. Tharsus causes a racket by teasing a
caged manticore. Cicero raises his eyebrow at me, annoyed at the im-
propriety. I carry on.

"Mercury is no stranger to hardship. Closest to the bosom of the sun,
only ingenuity and hard work have made her people prosper. I thank
my hosts, the gens Votum, for their hospitality, but also for reminding
me of those ancient virtues. Only ingenuity and hard work can beat
defeat into victory. For over a decade this ship, once the *Morning Star,*
was Darrow's greatest weapon. He sailed it here to break Mercury. Instead, Mercury broke both him and his ship. Not content with that,
Mercury then rebuilt his ship! And tonight it will set sail for the first
time." I lift my cup to the Votum. "Horatia, Cicero: from ashes, you
craft diamonds. May fortune long favor your house."

I lead the rest in drinking. Amidst my guests, Valeria rolls her eyes at
her brothers. After the muted applause dies down, I tap a foot on the
hull beneath us.

"You all know this storied ship. It was commissioned by Octavia and
built in the Dockyards of Ganymede. It was stolen by Darrow during
the Battle of Ilium, when he slaughtered noble Fabii with his Valkyrie
savages and then destroyed those proud dockyards over Ganymede.
Those sins have come back to haunt him. As will this ship." The Golds
stomp their feet. "Today, thanks to gens Votum, Glirastes the Master
Maker, and my creditors . . . whom I beg to wait until after the party to
twist my thumbs"—there's generous laughter at that—"it is my honor
to present your dance floor for the evening and our next great weapon
in the battle to restore order to our spheres: the *Lightbringer*."

Hundreds of Golds join me in smashing down their wineglasses on
the hull. Cicero, Horatia, and I draw our razors and cut our palms and
drip the blood onto the ship to ward off the bad luck of a rechristening.

Then the brother and sister wait to see if we're bankrupt, and our guests wait for the ship to fail. I hail my bridge, where my friend Pytha waits in her captain's chair.

"Captain Pytha, bring me the sky."

"By your will, dominus.*"*

I hold my breath. The tests were a success, but in the nest of vipers that is Gold power politics, sabotage is as common as bribery. A seismic groan comes from the ship as the new reactors power on. Spilled wine ripples. The groan deepens. The broken glass dances into the drops of blood. Whispers spread. A few laughs from Valeria and her brothers. The groan turns into a roar and the *Lightbringer* begins to rise.

I close my eyes, overwhelmed with emotion. When I open them again, we are in the clouds. I grip Horatia's hand. Cicero kisses my forehead. I embrace Glirastes. They've done it. We've done it. I've done it. All of Gold society snickered when I said I would rebuild the ship without Carthii engineers. None of my guests laugh now as we pass through the clouds. Shrouded in vapor, the Golds look like ghosts. If their silence tells me they know that today a new power was born, their applause, when it comes, shows me the difference between hosting games and putting a moonBreaker into the sky.

Five kilometers up, Pytha brings us into a holding pattern over the cloud layer that covers the city. All of Heliopolis was watching. Fireworks shot for the people glow through the clouds like coals. The whole planet will feel this victory.

Swamped with congratulations, even from some of Atalantia's veterans, I remain humble and defer all credit to Horatia, Glirastes, and their thousands of engineers and laborers—all of whom are inside the ship at their own party enjoying better wine than my Gold guests. I made sure of that.

Though Cicero had little to do with the efforts surrounding the *Lightbringer,* he's soon off to enjoy the rewards. "Not used to sycophancy?" I say to Horatia once the wave of congratulators has abated.

"No," she says, a little dazed. Her cheeks are flushed. Not from the praise, but from the private satisfaction of accomplishing a feat of monstrous logistical and technical difficulty. "To be honest, I'm a little contemptuous of the tidal shift in the manners of our guests," she says.

"It's about time the Reformers had a bit more muscle," I say. "Enjoy it."

She smiles at that and takes my hand. It's the first time it feels more than friendly. "You have work to do and so do I."

"I'd rather run diagnostics with you and Pytha."

"No, you wouldn't. You're a political animal, Lysander. It's been too long since my bloc had one like you. We need you to hunt."

"Money, manpower, mass," I say. "I've got my marks."

She squeezes my hand and we part. My party is tame by Gold standards. There are no orgies, as might be included on Venus, but there are Pinks and Red acrobats on lines strung amongst the trees of the orchard created by my growing stable of household botanists. In the trees there are carved creatures rumored to be half cat, quarter bird, and one quarter lizard, though I can only attest to the size of the bill I paid to my new household carvers. Some of the drunker Golds, Tharsus's friends, have given up taunting the manticore in the menagerie and decide instead to climb the trees and investigate. I'm excited for them to learn the arboreal carvelings have stingers.

"Lysander, my boy," Glirastes calls and waves me over. "There's someone you must meet."

I turn to see my friend arm in arm with a striking young woman with a very serious face. "Pallas au Grecca. The captain of the Bellona racing team," I say. "I see you survived Tharsus's compliments."

Pallas is not tall. The top of her head barely comes to my sternum. Neither is she muscled like a frontline Peerless. Yet there's something . . . fearsome about her, as if she'd been slapped earlier in the day and has been carrying it around all day to give back to someone else. Her skin is umber, her hair a dense, proud gold-brown tangle bound back with an unfashionable platinum eagle clasp. Her eyes are bright and impudent and stare at me as if she'd tossed me a ball and is expecting me to do something with it.

"I hope you're stronger than you look too," she says without an ounce of flirtation. A live eagle perches on her shoulder harness. She feeds it carpaccio from the tray of a passing Pink server. "You'll have to be stronger than you look to keep this ship from Atalantia's hands. What's to say she won't just take it?"

"The law, of course."

"It's silent these days, didn't you know?" she says.

"I didn't introduce you two so you could fence," Glirastes says.

"No. You did not," Pallas says, deadpan.

"So . . . Julia did send an envoy after all," I surmise. Pallas's narrowing eyes tell me I've hit the mark. "I was just hoping to see the Lady Bellona herself here for the games."

"We're at war," she says. "She is busy on Earth preparing for the summit."

"Ah. The summit again. Waste of time, really. She should be busy over Mars, if you ask me. I've only just spoken with Helios au Lux. He's of the same mind. Perhaps you know if Atalantia intends to finally declare an assault on Mars once and for all?"

Pallas cannot be tempted into intrigue. "The Lady Bellona told me to relay a message to you. You have the name of a Sovereign. Now you have the ship. And you certainly have the debt. But until you prove you have the guts, she will not cross the Dictator, and neither will her money."

"Because she fears a visit from Atlas?" I ask and resist the instinct to search for his pale face amongst my roving guests.

She shrugs. "Only an idiot would not." She looks me up and down. "And Lady Bellona is no idiot."

Her eagle hisses at me. It's an attack bird, I've noticed. Metal-reinforced talons. Lovely.

"The lady was kind enough to send me Rhone." I glance at Glirastes, thinking of Darrow and Cassius in Apollonius's cells. "Perhaps soon, I'll have a gift in kind for the lady to open a dialogue. Something dear to her heart."

My concealed com crackles with a priority message. Rhone reports from within the *Lightbringer*. "Dominus, *it is urgent*."

Pallas's eyebrows creep upward. "Problem?"

"It seems we're out of wine. Excuse me, goodlady." I step away from the party to have the conversation near a row of Praetorians. "Rhone, go."

"*There has been a nuclear explosion at the Dockyards of Venus. The Carthii have used it as pretext to launch a full-scale invasion of the dockyards. The Minotaur is asking for reinforcements.*"

I reach for the Mind's Eye to quell the reflexive panic. The sounds of the party shrink away. My heart slows. My welling anxieties slide from chaos into even ranks and await my attention. I look past the Praetorians to the dark sky. The clouds move below.

"I see. Is that all?"

"The situation is still unfolding, dominus."

"Who else knows this?" I ask.

"Anyone with a telescope."

"Do we still have eyes on Atlas?"

"Kyber has him in Tyche questioning Coppers."

I trust Kyber's competency as much as I trust Rhone's. Still, if anyone could spot a whisper following him it would be Atlas.

"Have Pytha prep our contingencies and get on deck, I need you here." The threat of exposure is severe. If the Carthii take prisoners, the Martian exiles will tell their torturers how they got to the dockyards. Not good.

Cicero meets my eyes from across the party. He was listening too and had enough sense not to come over. I hail his com. "Cicero. I need you to tell Tharsus to get out of here now. I don't want a situation that I can't control. Keep him away from the Carthii."

"On it."

I search for Valeria au Carthii. Amidst her brothers, her head is tilted as she listens to someone in her ear. She's just finding out as well. Her brother points out Tharsus. Apollonius's brother is wrestling a small carveling atop a tree to the laughter of his friends.

Sensing my distress, Glirastes abandons Pallas and comes over. I deploy a jamField from my ring so our guests can't overhear us.

"Dockyards have gone bad?" Glirastes asks. I nod. Thankfully, he has the composure to conceal his panic and his urge to remind me his doubts about the Minotaur. "What does Rhone think?"

I spot him exiting the hull via a lift. He jogs over.

"You need to act as if nothing's happened," Rhone says when he joins. "But Apollonius is demanding reinforcements. If we want to move out, we should mobilize our legions and Cicero's as soon as possible. Mercury is closer to Venus than Earth is. We can beat Atalantia there."

"If we aid him then we're in open rebellion against our lawful Dictator," I say.

In the orchard, Cicero has delivered the news. Tharsus comes down from the tree to find the Carthii staring at him. He shouts for his friends. As he desperately tries to collect the deviants lost in their own fun, the Carthii make their move.

I rush to intercept. I almost get bulldozed by Valeria's brothers, but I get in front of her before she's close enough to cause Tharsus harm. She's within my personal jamField. Her brothers are not. I cover my mouth. "Do you want your inheritance?"

"It is burning," she says. "So I'll burn Tharsus. Move or I'll start thinking you had something to do with it."

"Your father is not headed for an easy victory. But rather the fight of his life."

She scoffs. "The only threat was the atomics. I hardly think a handful of Grays will stop our legions—"

I roll the dice. "The Minotaur has eighty thousand Martian veterans."

She blinks as if she just ran into an invisible wall. "How do you know that?"

"Because I smuggled them to him in the iron caravans."

"You are in bed with the Minotaur?" She looks as if she wants to drive a knife into my stomach.

"I can give you your inheritance. All of it. You. Not your father. You."

"How?"

"No time. My life is in your hands. If you expose me, I'm dead and you get the petty satisfaction of revenge. If you say yes to my offer, you can be the head of House Carthii in a week."

Her eyes dart to Tharsus. He's gathered his friends. In a tight pack, they head for the table where they stacked their gravBoots. Calculating her chances of surviving her sibling rivalry and the time it would take to achieve the same goal, she looks me in the eyes and says, "Yes."

Ambition is a reckless master. I turn off my jamField.

"Horatia will be in touch."

Valeria watches Tharsus and his friends equip their gravBoots, and signals her brothers to stand down. Tharsus glances at me, his face pale, and takes off into the sky. His friends follow hot on his heels. They head east off the back of the *Lightbringer*. My other guests have noticed the commotion now, and whisper to one another. I return to Rhone and Glirastes. Cicero joins me as I reach them.

"*Lysander, we have radar signatures inbound,*" Pytha says from the bridge.

"I see them," Cicero says, spotting a squadron of dark shapes in the sky. Not ships. Men. "Are those yours, Lysander? They're not ours."

"No. Intercept them," I tell Rhone. He motions the nearby Praetorians. They form up and are about to take off.

"Lysander. Hold," Pytha says. *"They're broadcasting the Dictator's writ. Olympic tag."* Everyone turns to look at me. *"It's the Fear Knight,"* she says. A chill goes through me.

"It's a legal action then. You have zero jurisdiction," Rhone says.

"Stand down," I mutter.

Rhone recalls the Praetorians.

Others see the inbound squadron and rush to the edge of the *Lightbringer's* hull to watch. Fear's squadron, which must be made of Gorgons, descends from a higher altitude than Tharsus and his fleeing friends. They fall in the night sky like crows. Tharsus sees the interlopers and alters his escape trajectory. He and his friends dive down toward the blanket of clouds and disappear into them.

The Gorgons do not follow. My guests gasp and point as the clouds stutter with light. This time it is not fireworks. Tharsus flew straight into a trap waiting in the clouds. A few moments pass. Then Tharsus and only four of his friends race back out of the clouds. They flee right up into the waiting Gorgons. Disdaining weapons, the Gorgons catch Tharsus's friends with their hands, pin their arms, and start beating them to death midair.

A single dusky figure emerges from the clouds to watch the scene. Atlas.

Tharsus spots Atlas. Even at this distance, I can feel Tharsus's panic. The Gorgons block his exits, leaving him only one path of escape. He flees across the sky, back the way he came, to land hard amidst the party.

Valeria and her brothers laugh like hyenas at the sight of him. He is bloody, his left arm is broken, his fur coat ripped to shreds. He waves his razor and he calls out to me. "Lune! Lune! I am your guest! You must protect me!"

I lift my hands. "I am sorry. I cannot break the law. They have the Iron Fist."

"Help me!" Tharsus screams at the guests. No one raises a finger. "Help—"

Then he hears Atlas land behind him. He goes still. Dread darkens his eyes. Shuddering, Tharsus turns to see the Fear Knight watching him from behind his pale mask of office. Tall, lithe, in addition to his gravBoots, Fear wears gray armor styled with a moth motif. His blade is a long black hasta, slick with dark blood, and his right hand is sheathed in a heavy metal gauntlet.

The Iron Fist, writ of the Dictator.

Tharsus looks for escape. There is none. The Carthii cackle and urge him to come to them. "Help me! Someone! Help me!" he screams and starts for me only to find Rhone and a line of Praetorians barring his path. I feel a hand on my chest.

"There's nothing to do," Cicero says.

The Fear Knight comes for Tharsus. Finding neither escape nor aid, Tharsus resolves to die well. After a life of privilege, he is denied his last wish. His enraged attack is easily turned by the Fear Knight. After three slashes, Atlas raises the Iron Fist and Tharsus is snared by the device's statis field. He floats, suspended in zero-G. Atlas cuts off Tharsus's feet first, then his hands. The severed parts float in the field with their former owner.

Atlas makes a fist with the gauntlet and Tharsus screams as his limbs crackle and compound fracture in a dozen places. Only then does Atlas release him. Tharsus flops screaming to the hull. Wiggling wormlike to nowhere, he gasps as Atlas grabs him by the hair and drags him toward the menagerie. Atlas takes a golden serving bowl from a table as he passes, puts it on Tharsus's head, bends the edges with his hands to enclose Tharsus's head, then stuffs Tharsus into the manticore cage.

I look away as the beast feeds on Tharsus's broken body. His screams echo out from the bowl. My eyes meet Pallas's. The Bellona client pats her belly.

Atlas is headed my way. My Praetorians make a wall between us. Atlas removes his mask for Rhone. His eyes are dark jewels set in a gaunt philosopher's face. I read in them paragraphs of disappointment.

He holds up the Iron Fist. "To oppose me is treason against the Society. I am the will of your lawfully appointed Dictator. You of all people are no traitor, Flavinius. Move."

I set a hand on Rhone's shoulder and guide him out of the way. Cicero shrinks away from me, terrified at Atlas's approach. Glirastes comes closer, protective. Horatia finally joins us from her work on the bridge, coming up from a lift in the hull to see Atlas walking toward me. She goes very still.

Atlas lifts his voice for my guests.

"The truce between House Rath and House Carthii has been broken by the Minotaur. An inquest has been launched. The verdict of which will be announced at the summit on Earth one week hence." He comes closer and taps my chest with the Fist to make it formal. "You have been summoned to report to New Sparta."

"I am in the middle of my—"

"You have two minutes to set your affairs. Do not abuse my leniency."

Atlas helps himself to a shrimp from a server's tray and goes to the manticore cage to whip the creature back from Tharsus's tattered body. He leaves the body but takes the head and the golden bowl that protected its features from the manticore. Then he strides off in silence to await his ship.

Even the Carthii have gone quiet. My friends are terrified.

"You can't go with him," Glirastes says. "Lysander, you have the *Lightbringer*. You have the Votum. You don't have to obey."

Cicero swallows. "We can't take on Atalantia. Not head-to-head. Not with three *Lightbringers*."

Horatia joins. She sees the political trap. "He was touched by the Iron Fist. He must go. It's a trap. Atalantia wants him to reject the summons. She's looking for a public infraction to bring you up on charges. Your popularity won't matter then. All options will be available to her."

Glirastes grips my arm again, imploring. "Lysander, if you go to Earth you'll never leave. She will kill you or make you her puppet."

I did not expect Atlas so soon. I don't know how he fooled Kyber and lost her tail. But as soon as the news of the dockyards came, I knew I would have limited time to act.

"I must go," I say. "This is why we created contingencies. Atalantia won't kill me yet. Horatia, Rhone, we will play peacemakers one more time. Contingency Eleven is our best hope. I've already spoken with Valeria. She's in. You know what to do."

They nod in agreement.

Cicero is green with worry. "Are you certain?"

"We cannot lose Apollonius. Not now. A dozen ships in hand are worth a hundred on the ledger. We're in the game now, my friends. Stay true to each other, and we will succeed."

I hope.

I say my farewell to Cicero and Horatia before taking Glirastes by the arm. "Remember, I want you to get to the safe-house in the mountains as soon as I depart. Keep Exeter close."

His face is pained. But he tries to be strong for me. He takes my shoulders. "Before you, I was broken. Lost. Hope had fled with youth." He thumps my chest. "Hope beats here. In you."

In Glirastes I feel the presence of the love Octavia stole from me with her Pandemonium Chair. The love of a parent for a son. "I will see you soon, Glirastes." I kiss the wizened man on the brow and tear myself away to walk with Rhone toward Atlas's landing shuttle. My guests may cry out their complaints against the Dictator but none dare intervene. "I'm counting on you most of all, Rhone. We need more than just Apollonius and his men from the docks."

"I understand, *dominus*. I will not fail you," Rhone says.

Reluctant, he hands me over to the custody of the landing Gorgons. They scan me after I board their shuttle. They miss nothing, not even the implant in my ear canal. The last words I hear before they take it come from Pytha on the bridge. *"Good luck, Moonboy. We'll see you soon."*

"Thank you for your cooperation, Lysander," Atlas says as the shuttle lifts off. He takes off his cape and hands the Iron Fist to an attendant. "The *Styx* will rendezvous with us a day out from Mercury. We will take it the rest of the way to Earth. Atalantia thinks you look too martial with that scar. She sent her best carver to better shape you to fit her desires." He glances at the burn on my face. "But first she has a message for you." He turns to leave the passenger compartment and calls back to his Gorgons. "Make him shit blood."

The first fist hits me in the kidneys.

11

DARROW

Inheritance

THE *ARCHIMEDES* WHISPERS through space on a route beneath the ecliptic plane that will add weeks to our journey but hopefully help us avoid enemy hunting squadrons. In the commissary, Sevro and I eat dinner in silence. His hair is long and disheveled, and like me he has a beard. He breaks the silence with a burp and wags a chunk of ham on the end of a combat knife. "I'll say one thing about Kavax. He packs a good larder. Surprised your lot didn't pillage it."

"We did. Cassius nicked this grub from Starhold. Neglected to share with the others before we parted ways."

Sevro shrugs, deciding not to let the origins of the food diminish his enjoyment of it.

"You try the ham yet?" he asks.

"Not yet."

Four days out from the dockyards, and Sevro and I have apparently forgotten how to talk to each other. At the same time, we can't seem to ever be more than one room away from each other or avoid touching each other when we are in the same room. It's weird like that. The push and pull of a war bond that goes as deep as ours. So much guilt, but at the same time he's my security and refuge, and I am his. We know we're the only ones who understand what the other one has seen. Indescribable things. Things words explain to those back home about as well as cave paintings relay the reality of a woolly mammoth.

"You always try the ham, Darrow. Wherever you go. It's a good barometer for the rest of the larder. Trust me."

He throws a piece on my plate. "I'm prime."

"PTSD because the Minotaur carved you like a pig?" he asks.

"Was that all a setup?" I ask.

"Don't be so conceited."

I grimace at him from across the table. He's lost weight in his stays in the clone's prison and then Apollonius's. Skinny, bearded, tattooed, savage as a serrated knife, drowning in Cassius's too-large shirt and too-large pants, he looks more like a Lunese street killer than a soldier. Except in the eyes. They're locked in a thousand-meter stare. Then there's the matter of his necklace of ears, which he hasn't taken off. They stink.

"Still a little nauseous from the meds actually," I admit.

"Pain meds are for Pixies."

After the duel and the meatstraw, I can't move without suffering a litany of pains. I've been in the *Archimedes*'s medBay with Aurae more than I've been in my own bunk.

"Be honest. It's the ears," he says. "I'd get rid of them, but how else could I mock the dead?" He brings an ear to his mouth. "Galerius, you still squealing like a piggy down there?"

"Galerius au Voth?" I ask. "He came to the Minotaur?"

"That's the piggy," he says and goes back to eating.

"Well, he certainly had it coming."

"He was my sixth. After I got free. I was in the vents by then. Strong enough to finally gather supplies and make a real guerilla action out of it. Found him in the showers. His life wasn't the first thing he lost."

"I'm glad you showed restraint," I say. He looks up, eager to take offense but not sure if there's an angle to. "Ears. You could have chosen pricks."

"Thought about it. Gender biased and too heavy. Golds, you know." He's not joking. "Once I got into an armory and got my hands on anti-personnel mines, it started getting real fun. Best one was pulling a fire alarm in the mess and seeing all those Grays run out. Got fifty-one that day."

It's not like Sevro to brag. Maybe like me he doesn't know how to fill the silence. "So Galerius was there. You already told me about Tiberius and Drusilla. What about on Luna?"

He goes quiet and returns to his food. "Told you. Old crowd. Vox were puppets. Syndicate Queen was Lilath. Clone thing. Clown, Pebble, who knows where. Iron wolf. You want me to tell you Min-Min smelled like bacon when she burned? She did. So did the rest of them."

He meant it to hurt me, but saying it hurt him too. He looks away. I told him about Mercury. He didn't say a thing the whole time. Not a single expression either, not even when I told him about Alexandar and Rhonna. He was too mad. He didn't say it, but I know he thinks I should have let him kill Lysander when he was a boy.

I love Sevro to death, and he is fundamentally a good friend, but he feels no need to be a good person when dealing with enemies. "There he is. Hero of the hour," Sevro says when Cassius limps in for coffee.

"Barca, glad to see you're making use of the larder," he says.

Sevro gives him a wide grin. "What a host you are." Cassius nods to me and goes for the coffee. "But of course you had practice. You and this manse hosted royalty for over a decade." His smile grows wider. "Glad to see you left a positive impression on young Lune. Taught him all the best ways to slaughter heroes of the Rising."

Cassius turns around, jaw locked. "I won't make excuses for Lysander. I hear Alexandar and Rhonna were good people."

"Good?" Sevro asks.

"We don't have to do this," I say.

"Do what?"

"Don't use Alex and Rhonna, Sevro. Just don't."

He loses his enthusiasm, and Cassius makes his escape. I send him an apologetic grimace as he ducks back toward the cockpit. Sevro doesn't look at all satisfied. He tosses his combat knife down and stares at nothing. "He risked his life for you," I say.

"Yeah. But we didn't get the Minotaur."

"That meatstraw was a bad one. If he made it out—"

"He's a cockroach, Darrow." He grunts. "All this killing, man. We keep fighting. For what?" He coughs again and wipes his tattered mouth with a bony hand. "Least Orion took some of those Ash bastards with her. Went out proper. You should have let her drown the whole bloody planet. Maybe then the cockroaches wouldn't keep coming back."

"That wasn't Eo's dream," I say. "And it isn't mine. We're no Ash Lords."

"Naw. We're Pixies. You had Atlas and you let him live. We had Lysander and we let him live. We had Apollonius and we let him live." He snorts. "It's like we want to lose."

"We haven't lost yet."

"Orion. Harnassus. Alex. Rhonna. Daxo. We don't know if Pax and Electra are safe. Not for certain. Maybe they're dead. Maybe my girls are next. Maybe Victra. Maybe Virginia. Shit, we couldn't beat the Core in ten years. Now it's the Rim too."

"Mars will be a hard nut for them to crack. I can break them there. I will."

"Uh-huh." He almost leaves it at that. "With going under the ecliptic plane Mars might not even be there by the time we get back. Ain't gonna be a fast ride, will it? Gonna be a crawl. And they'll be hunting us."

"What do you want me to say, Sevro? I've been in the dark for eight months. You want me to say it's all slagged? War's lost? Our children are dead? I won't. I can't. We have people counting on us. My family. Your family. We don't have the right to do anything except all we can do."

He stares a hole in his food, lost in thought.

"She'll have had the baby by now. Without me there. First time I wasn't there for it. I was for the girls." His eyes flick up. "What are you going to say to Virginia when you see her?"

"I don't know. I'll probably just listen. Like I should have done from the start." He doesn't respond, and I sense him drifting away. Closing up. "Sevro, there's something I have to say to you. Something I told myself I'd say when I didn't know if I'd ever see you again." I take an unsteady breath. I've been too afraid he'll spit on me to say it until now. "I'm sorry." To my surprise, he doesn't spit. So I continue. "When we left Luna to break out Apollonius, I promised you the end was near. I know you didn't believe it. I made you choose between me and your family. For that, for taking you for granted, for not listening to you, for all of it, I'm sorry."

There's an uncomfortable pause. Sevro shrugs and goes back to eating. The lack of acknowledgment says more than anything else. Wounds may scab over, but they don't always heal completely. I don't know what else I can say, not without making him angry or cheapening it with bigger words and more excuses.

"When I got free of Apple, you know why I didn't steal a ship and make for Mars myself?" he asks. Cassius and I were wondering. "I knew you'd come. You're stupid like that. It's why I love you. But, man . . . we ain't good. We might never be good."

"I know."

"I know you do. But I can't do this again. When we get back to Mars, I'm gonna be about my family. Only my family." His eyes stare through me.

"I know."

"I don't think you do." He breaks eye contact. "They did smell like bacon, Darrow. The Howlers. I lost them all. I don't know where Pebble and Clown are. I don't know if Lilath and . . . the Abomination still have them. He said he was going to erase me. Wash out my memories. Turn me into his trained dog. Wash out my family." Sevro chews his bottom lip. "He didn't, though. I dunno why. I hate that it's his mercy that's given me this second chance with Victra, my kids. But I need to take it."

"I understand. If that's what's right for you. I understand."

"But?"

"But nothing. You have a new baby to meet. You and Victra have four to take care of now. You chose to be a father. I will respect that."

"Even if I have to get my family off Mars?" he asks.

I nod, even though it hurts. "Even if we lost this war, and I was dying, I'd smile if I knew you'd gotten out."

He knows I mean it, and I feel like that, more than anything I've said, gives our friendship a chance. Still, I'm relieved when I see Aurae enter. It's the first time I've ever seen her awkward, and the first time I've seen her enter a room without all of its occupants giving her at least a portion of their attention. "Am I interrupting?" she asks.

"Yes," Sevro says down into his plate. His shell is back up.

She apologizes and is about to leave when I wave her to the table. She sits and watches Sevro. He doesn't care. He eats for a few more minutes, making sure to collect every last crumb, chugs his beverage, burps, leans back, scratches his belly, looks up, yawns, then brings his eyes down on her like a hammer. "And?"

She stares at the necklace of ears he still wears around his neck.

"My name is Aurae."

"I know. We talked in the evac. And?"

"I have a message for you from friends in the Rim. It is from Athena."

I frown, even though I'm less surprised than Aurae thinks I should be. She pulls a strangely designed holocube from her pocket. It activates and bathes us in amber light. Like Ares once did, this Athena wears a helmet. Hers is black with a Corinthian crest. Red eyes stare out from it. Her voice is slow, heavy with the laconic accent of the Gas Giants.

"Yassou, *Son of Ares, Sevro. I greet you on behalf of the lowColors of the Rim. I cannot tell you my name, for I am hunted. But I am called Athena.*"

"Cute theater," Sevro mutters.

"*You do not know me, but I knew your father. He was my mentor, my friend, my hero. He found me when I was broken and showed me that it was not I that was broken, but the worlds. Since his death, I have kept his legacy alive in the Rim.*"

"A joke?" Sevro stands and snorts in disgust. "I ain't got the patience for this shit."

"*You may doubt this. You may doubt me. So hear it from him.*"

Sevro freezes as his father appears in place of Athena. "What . . ." Fitchner is young, probably close to the age we are now, and recording in an apartment with a view of Agea. A toddler lies asleep on the couch beside him, his head resting on Fitchner's thigh. Fitchner smiles ruefully out at us from across time. Sevro touches the ears on his necklace. His entire essence shifted the moment he saw his father. He became a boy again. He blinks a few times and sits back down. Chills creep along my arms when I hear Fitchner's voice. I forgot how much I missed the man.

"*Hey, boyo. It's me. Your da.*" Fitchner strokes the toddler's hair. "*And you. I hope you don't wake up while I'm talking to you. You were a bastard today, bit me like a goblin.*" He shows a mark on his hand and sighs. "*I don't know if you'll ever watch this. I hope you don't ever have to. But if you do it's because you're grown and I am dead.*" Fitchner grimaces. "*Strange, talking to the man you'll be. To me, right now, you're innocent. Except for the biting. You don't yet know your mother is dead. You are too young to miss her. You're too young to know you will have no place in the world that killed her. That won't last.*" His eyes grow sad. "*But you will know she's dead. You know how she died.*

"*This is a hard message to record. It's like admitting I won't be there. But that's being a da, I think. I wish I could protect you from the pain that's waiting. I wish your innocence would last forever. I wish tonight that I didn't have to leave you. But I've done something, my boy. I have started a war.*

"*Our enemies do not know it yet. Hopefully they won't know till they're choking on it. That is why I have to leave you tonight. I'll be back, but there are seeds that must be sown in the Rim. I will return to you as soon as I can.*

By the time you watch this, those seeds should be grown to fruition. Their bounty is your inheritance, should you need it. I hope you won't. I hope I am alive sitting beside you as you watch this. If I am, pour me a whiskey and rub an old man's back. I deserve it because if I'm alive, I've beaten the bastards and you won't have inherited my war.

"It's a pretty dream. But your mother was the dreamer, boyo. I'm not. I'm just a savage who can't let things go. Something tells me you might be the same. I know the path I walk might leave you alone. I'm a bastard for that. I know. It eats me up knowing you'll probably hate me for it. But fortune ain't kind to those who conceive revolution. The generation that lights the fuse usually gets buried in the rubble. My only hope is you'll build something of the rubble, son. Maybe a monument, eh? I'd like that. A big one on the Lion Steps for me and your mum. And a family for yourself. A whole brood to climb on our statue and be amazed at what big toes their grandparents had.

"Athena, my ally in the Rim, will have sent this via a herald. You'll know it's them when they say the words your mother once said to you. They'll have a book with them. It belonged to Bryn, your mother, and her mother before her. It is a partial collection of the oral wisdom of their clan on Triton. It's your heritage, and it belongs to you now. Trust the book, and trust the herald. They will guide your journey to Athena as surely as I hope this book will guide your heart. Vale knows, it saved mine."* He looks down at the toddler resting beside him. *"I must go now. I'll be back for you to chew on soon."*

He grows somber as he looks at the recorder. *"If I am not there now, I'm sorry. But know I'm all right. No matter how I went, the path led me back to your mother. We loved you, Sevro. With your first breath. With our last. We will always love you and we will see you again at the end of your path. Farewell, for now."*

Fitchner shrinks back into the holocube.

Stunned, Sevro hasn't time to say anything before Athena returns.

"Your father knew the worst could always happen, Sevro. He believed in redundancy. That is why he had me found an independent cell. I was the first Daughter of Ares. When the Raa swept the Sons away like dust, we survived because we are shadow. At first we were few. Now we are many. More even than there ever were Sons. For years we have been too afraid to reach out to you. Too embittered. Because we know what Darrow did. We know he gave Romulus au Raa the Sons to win the Battle of Ilium.

"For his own people, the Reaper sacrificed the Sons of Ares in the Rim.

That sacrifice allowed freedom to flourish in the Core, but not here. There are some amongst us who will never forgive that. I am not one of them. Our cause is too important for us to be divided by the sins of one man.

"I reach out to you now because the Raa have entered your war. They have proven to my council what I have long argued, there is no Rim. No Core. Only the high and the low. The oppressors and the oppressed. The high have united. If the low do not, I believe the dream of Ares and Eo, our dream, will die.

"That is why I offer you your inheritance now. For thirty-one years, the Daughters have focused on two tasks. The first, the dissemination of literature and liberal philosophy to gain converts, particularly those skilled in research, weapons development, and military construction. The second, the accumulation of military hardware.

"We have a fleet. We have weapons, but we do not have a general. It is time for you to fill your father's helm.

"Come be our god of war."

The hologram ends. Aurae watches Sevro, waiting for a reply. He gives none. Overwhelmed, he retreats toward the crew quarters. Aurae stands to follow him. I hold up a hand to stop her. "How many ships does this Athena have?"

"I would not know. Athena is careful and I was deep cover until this mission."

"Are you lying?" I ask.

"No."

"How could I believe you? Why didn't you just tell me what you were?"

She smiles. "Darrow. The whole truth would have made you fear me because of the guilt you carry for what you did. Guilt makes men do very rash things. And my message wasn't for you."

"Do you hate me?" I ask.

"No."

I look for hate in her eyes and don't see it. I have feared for years that I would face the consequences for betraying the Sons on the Rim. Until I read *The Path to the Vale*, I probably would have never believed anyone could ever forgive me.

I think of the eighth understanding. *We achieve perfection first by acknowledging our failures. We increase understanding first by recognizing our ignorance.*

"If it counts for anything, I am sorry for what I did," I say.

Aurae reaches across the table and sets both her hands over mine. "I know. You're not the Reaper. You're just a wanderer trying to be what he thinks others need him to be. I forgave you a long time ago."

I believe her, and I hold her hand so she knows how much it means to me. We say nothing for a moment, then I stand to check on Sevro. I stop by my room first to grab the book. I find Sevro in the quarters he's made in the escape pod beneath the cargo bay. He doesn't look up as I squat against the hatch frame. "You all right?" I ask.

He shakes his head. "It's a trap. It's not real—"

"I think it is real," I say and hand him the book. He holds it with reverence. "Your father sent Titus and me to the Institute. It's the sort of thing he'd do. Never tie two ships together in a storm. You know?"

He thinks it's real too, which is why he looks so overwhelmed. "I can't—" He looks up at me. "I got a baby now. I got my girls. I can't—"

"You don't have to. You're going home, brother. If Virginia vets it, and it stands up, I'll go." He tears up he's so relieved. I grip his shoulder. "All you need to think about is what you'll say to your baby when he or she sees you for the first time." He nods and hands me back the book. "It was your mother's."

"Not yet," he says. "Just hold on to it. Yeah?"

I almost agree and I almost leave him alone, but he looks so lonely down here in the quarters he's chosen so far from the rest of ours. Instead, I open to the first page and wait for him to stop me. He doesn't. So I start to read aloud. He wipes his eyes and leans back against the bulkhead to listen as the ship carries on toward Mars.

I leave when he falls asleep. The music of a lyre creeps from Aurae's room. I head through the lounge to find Cassius alone in the cockpit. He looks over as I sit down. "You all right?" I ask.

"I was used as a bus driver for a spy I'm in love with who I thought rescued me because she thought I was a hero, whose protégé chose to become a tyrant and shoot my best friend's protégé in the head—whom I find out was the paragon of honor." He smiles. "I'm over the moon, goodman."

I squeeze his shoulder. "If it counts, I think you're a hero." He snorts a laugh but doesn't throw my hand off. I pat his shoulder. "So I'm your best friend."

He glares at me. "Don't rub it in."

I lean back and watch the stars. "Those ships could be the miracle the Republic needs," he says. "Pity they're so far away."

"If they're real," I say. "And enough of them. You were listening on the intercom?" He nods. "Can I give you some advice?"

"If you let me give you some," he replies.

"Fair enough. You first."

"Sevro was spewing some depressing shit. Fair, considering the state I found you in after your stay with the Jackal." He shivers. "Of all the people to clone, it had to be the creepiest. But Sevro isn't clear in the head right now. It's not all bad. You're alive, brother. I know you thought you'd go back to Mars a savior, Mercury in your pocket. Now you're probably wondering how you can face Virginia and Mars after all this. So I gotta ask. Is your faith in Virginia broken?"

I shake my head.

"Even though she didn't send help on Mercury."

"Never."

"Then how can you be so dumb as to think she would ever believe any less in you? That our planet believes any less than you? You were a Red miner. You became the bloodydamn Reaper of Mars. Whatever mistakes you made, you did that. Not anyone else. You. So if you hang your head, how can anyone else hold theirs up?" He smiles. "After all, you're friends with me, and I'm fabulously picky."

I sit with that for a while. "Wait. Am I your only friend?"

"Shut up. Your turn."

"Stop hiding from Sevro—"

"I'm not—"

"Shut up. My turn. Stop hiding from Sevro. This is your ship. If you let him walk all over you, he will. You killed his father. Eleven years ago, maybe twelve by now. You're trying to make up for it. It's on him to get over that. Not you. And he won't if he doesn't respect you." I take the bottle of whiskey he hides under his seat. "So no more of this for your coffee. No more cowering. You're Cassius Bellona."

"Ow."

"Not in the Republic."

"No, not *au*. Ow. Harsh critique."

"Oh."

"Right. My turn."

"I didn't agree to a game," I say.

"After seeing that 'duel,' you have a problem. One, you've used your body like a mallet for a decade and a half. It's twenty years older than it should be. Two. Diomedes and young Rim bucks will be coming for you. Trust me when I say, he'd eat the Minotaur alive."

I turn on him. "Really?"

"Really. Three. People are wise to the Willow Way, and personally I don't think it maximizes your potential. Four. You need your killing confidence back. You need a top-tier razormaster. You need me. After all, steel sharpens steel." I lean back. "Don't give me that face."

"What face?"

"That constipated wargod face. Minotaur messed you up. But I think we can make you even better than you were at your prime. If you let us." He puts his hand over my mouth. "You say one word about the gala, I will turn this ship around." He takes his hand back, wary. I cross my arms, tight with pride. I wince from two cuts Apollonius gave me.

"If you wish to be repaired, you must first be broken," I mutter.

"What?"

"The eleventh understanding."

He rolls his eyes. "When did everyone turn into a gorydamn philosopher?"

"When we started losing."

"Then that's a yes."

"That's a yes."

"Good. We start tomorrow."

I look down at my bandages and wince.

PART II

RAMPART

The alarm was soon carried to the city,

and when they heard the war cry, the people

came out at daybreak till the plain was filled

with horsemen and foot soldiers and

with the gleam of armor.

—HOMER

12

LYRIA

Truffle Pig

THE REPUBLIC LONG-RANGER LOADS his multiRifle and readies his suit for space. I shadow his movements, lagging behind him less by the day. This will be the sixty-ninth asteroid we've searched, and though this is today's first reconnaissance it already feels we're searching in vain for the laboratory that created the tech that infests my head. The parasite, the compass that brought us to this sector of the Rim, has gone silent.

When Pax sent me off from Mars, he told me his theory that the parasite tech in my head was damaged and attempting to guide me back to the place of its creation to seek repairs. He talked about a lot of things he said he'd learned from inconclusive intelligence reports: a secret laboratory. Fringe scientists. Links to Sun Industries. For good or ill, I believed him. I believed the urge in my gut that brought me to sector 3401 of the asteroid belt. But with the parasite four months silent—save for the mind-melting headaches—I'm beginning to realize trusting someone too young to even have pimples yet might have been a mistake.

Idiot, me. I was so desperate to repair the parasite and tap in to its power to help Volga that I believed him. Not that I'd know how to even find her. She might be with the pirates three sectors over. She might be on Pluto. She might be dead.

Only the routine of the search, the sharpening of my skills day by day, keeps me from eating holes in myself over thoughts of my failure. It's been six days since the last battle we saw between Republic and Rim ships. The Republic didn't win, and the long-ranger squad's resentment—like my anxiety—is only getting worse.

I'm no heavyMetal Red like Fel, the ranger team leader—who is half-bionic. Nor am I an Orange like our crusty mechanic, Oxis. Nor a Blue like sweet-hearted, air-brained Xaria, our pilot—a fawn-like woman of middle age. They want to be on Mars when it's attacked, not here following a truffle pig whose nose is clearly broken. But it's my duty to my dead ones to learn all I can from the rangers, even if I annoy the living shit out of them. What I learn here will help someone who needs it later.

So when I feel doubt tugging me down into the churning grief in my gut and the guilt that the rangers are wasting their time snooping asteroids out here with me, I think of the mud in Camp 121. Of my sister's corpse, wearing her new shoes. I think of snow. The cold I felt seeing Ulysses nailed to a tree. I think of Volga surrendering herself to Fa, out there somewhere imprisoned by the mad warlord who sacked Olympia and killed Sefi the Quiet. I think of all my bloody uselessness, how I couldn't stop any of the bad shit from happening. That makes me angry. And anger's all the fuel a Red lass needs to keep going.

"*Airflow, check,*" Fel rumbles.

"Airflow, check," I reply.

"*Seals, check.*"

"Seals, check."

"*Gustpack, check.*"

"Gustpack, check."

"*Ranger One ready.*" He waits for me. "*Truffle Pig?*"

"Ready."

"*Pilot, piss the presh.*"

The airlock vents its air to create a vacuum. Fel's hard crimson eyes are hidden behind his green visor.

As an elite Republic long-ranger—a pirate hunter, peacekeeper, investigator, instigator, and sometime scout for the Ecliptic Guard—the Belt is Fel's natural habitat. He was born here in an asteroid carbon mine, hard and rough as uncut diamonds. When I wonder how the Republic ever fought Golds, I look at Fel.

"*Still feel like you've got a screwdriver in your eyehole?*" His accent isn't Martian. Belt Reds stretch their vowels like taffy.

"More like a pencil now," I say of the headache that lances from my right eyeball, through my brain, to the base of my skull. "Won't slow me down."

"Best not. Need you fit, Piggy. We got six more 'roids to hit before bunk. Gotta pick up the tempo if we can't narrow the search, elsewise we'll be here till me balls hang past me knees." His voice quiets. *"Are you sure this is the sector?"*

"No, I'm not sure. I told you that. I'm not sure of anything. The machine stopped guiding me months ago."

Under the depressurization lights, the faded symbol on his durosteel shoulder—a white arm holding a white torch—is stained a muddy red. Unlike my EVO suit—a pressurized personal space apparatus—which covers me toes to cowlick, Fel's suit leaves his limbs free. He can afford the vacuum exposure since his arms are metal, and his legs too from the knees down. Eight digits on each foot and hand would be the envy of any Helldiver.

"You give it any thought?" I ask.

"Hm?"

"My callsign. What we talked about last night in the lounge."

"Aw. Naw. Yer stuck with it."

"Ain't exactly flattering, is it? Truffle Pig."

"Ain't that all you're good for? Sniff, sniff, looking for treasure in mounds of the Solar System's shit," our Orange mechanic, Oxis, says over the com from the machine room.

"Right. My fault for not turning the monster machine that crawled into my head without my bloody volition into a perfect compass for you on command. I'm done answering to Truffle Pig."

"Lock it up, Oxis," Fel says to the Orange. His voice carries no pity for me but no malice either. *"Lyria, you're raw as a baby's throat. No wings on your shoulders. No wolf on your chest. Skipped the schools, and we don't care if yer the Sovereign's stool pigeon, ya don't get to skip the shit test. Least, not until you start picking up a scent, hear? We all done our jobs. You need you to do yours."*

"I'm trying."

"Trying won't keep the Golds from the gates of Mars."

"Are all rangers such slaggers?" I mutter.

"Lass, I'm a dove compared to the hyenas out there. Me friends are dying back home, and I'm out here with you, sniffing. Any other would toss ya out

the airlock, call the hunt closed, and get back to real soldiering before the war's lost."

The airlock opens in silence between us.

"Go on then. None would know," I say.

"Tempting. But Republic Intelligence says you're the link to a weapons lab. Ain't seen a thing that'd make me agree, but it ain't my duty to agree, savvy? Now let's work. And by the way, no one gets to choose their own call-sign."

"What was yours?"

"Badassmotherfucker."

With a short burst from his gustpack, Fel backflips into the void. I follow, a foot shorter, twenty kilos lighter, and nine years less veteran in the realm of unforgiving cold, rock, and shadow that is the asteroid belt.

Using one burst from my pack to clear the airlock, and a second to angle up, and a third to coast parallel to the asteroid's terrain, I match Fel's velocity. *"Clean your lines,"* he says. *"You're drifting."* I course correct. *"Reduce your velocity."* I reduce a half percent, growing annoyed.

His metal feet greet the surface of the asteroid, and he rebounds into a loping gait. I mimic with less grace. *"Your trajectory's filthy, Piggy. Dampen your kin imp by three per."*

He's right, of course. My gait was taking me higher and higher, out of sync with his route, which would expose me to sniper fire if the asteroid wasn't abandoned like all the others we've searched these last months. I adjust. *"Better. The anomaly is three clicks out. Shadow me, and train your sensors six to twelve."*

"Check."

"Pilot, what's your read?"

Xaria's voice is smooth and one note. *"Skies clear. Omega scan inconclusive. Anomaly is metallic. Material unknown."*

"Begin orbital dep recon. One eye on ground, one on sky. Just because we don't see the Moonies on scanners don't mean they aren't in the neighborhood."

Sightings of Rim hunting squadrons are growing more common even as sightings of Republic squadrons grow rarer. Flying dark, we don't get reports from Mars. Even without them, if the war in the Core is going like the war in this sector of the Rim, we know we're on borrowed time. Rumor has it even the Obsidians are joining in on picking the Republic's corpse. I wonder if the raids three sectors over are from Fá, if Volga is only a few million clicks away.

Fel moves with appropriate urgency and I struggle to keep up.

To the sound of our own breath, we lope over the dead landscape. Nothing but cratered rock and shadows move beneath.

I follow Fel's line and land lightly on the edge of a huge crater where our scans picked up the anomaly. I search for a reaction from the parasite. Nothing.

"Drones out," Fel orders. The four drones detach from his left shoulder and *disappear* into a crater. Mine join. Within thirty seconds, my third drone finds a human design, flags it, and begins analysis. A gun turret, depowered with a hardline running into the stone. "Ancient model," Fel says as we inspect it. *"Power source. Won't be far."*

"This ain't it," I say.

"Parasite talking to you again?"

"No."

"Less talking and more sniffing then. Drones detect durosteel below."

I follow Fel down into the crater where we find a metal plate thirty meters by twenty embedded in the rock. Searching around the perimeter of the metal plate, Fel finds a manual control panel. His metal hands peel its lock away like it's tissue. I clear off the door as it retracts.

"Pilot, we've found an aperture. Likely a pirate nest. Deserted by the age of it. Continue orbital survey."

Fel swivels forward his Rim-style rifle from its back holster, and drops into the darkness. I pull my smaller rifle and follow, down, down into the depths.

"Yut. Pirates," Fel mutters in defeat before I land in what once was a mid-sized hangar, judging by what our helmet lights can illuminate. An old corvette larger than the *Snowball* lies abandoned in the center of the room. "Pilot, looks like this is a dead end. But since we're here, we'll stick to protocol. Full search. Piggy, you're east. I'm west."

It's not the first pirate refuge we've found, but it is the oldest. Its halls are pitch black. My helm provides the only light. Rifle up, I turn a corner and a shape lunges at me. I slam down to a knee and fire three times like Fel taught me. I report contact and search the hallway for more. None appear, and with my heart in my throat I inspect my kill.

It's just bones. A skeleton, now shattered. I laugh at myself. "Cancel contact," I say, embarrassed. "Just a skeleton." No one replies. "Fel?"

Static hisses.

"Fel? Copy? Shit." I glance behind me. Our coms are military grade.

Shouldn't be enough interference from the walls to block the signal. I hail the ship. Nothing. Knowing I'll get bitched apart and stuck on latrine duty if I don't complete my recon, I press on despite the hammering of my heart. I find sleeping quarters filled with floating personal effects, a storage room with medical equipment, and a mess hall with skeletons. I sweep my rifle counter-clockwise through the room. Nothing moves except the skeletons. There must be nearly fifty clothed in tattered jumpsuits. They float in a tangled dance over tables bolted to the floor. I creep toward one and shine my light into his eyeholes.

A hand grips my shoulder from behind. I jump and wheel only to have my rifle muzzle knocked upward. It's Fel. I breathe easier. "Sonofawhore, you scared the piss out of me."

He gives me a *coms dead* signal then motions to join helmets so we can hear. His voice is muffled. "Coms are down to the *Snowball*. Probably interference from their reactor. Just bodies back my way."

"How'd they die?"

Careful, he pulls one of the skeletons closer with his rifle and points to a green tinge on the bones. "Green Death," he says. "Antique bioweapon. Vacuum resistant. Wiped out dozens of colonies and mines two hundred years back. Just a drop of the virus is grounds for instant quarantine. Yawning is less contagious, literally. Let's get the Hades out of here."

No argument from me. He tries hailing the *Snowball* a few more times before deciding we'll have to do it on the surface. We make our way back to the hangar and together float upward, out the way we came. I feel better on the solid ground of the surface, and our short-range coms start to work again. Still, we can't contact the *Snowball*. *"This 'roid's a sponge for electromagnetism. Must be dense with metals."* He pauses, and I sense the concern in his voice. *"Strange. Should have shown up on scans. If a Silver found this place, he'd be a mining king in three years."*

"Except for the Green Death."

"Good point."

He reaches the lip of the crater first and stops, staring at something. I hurry and join him. Then I see what he's looking at.

The *Snowball* spins on the horizon, lights flickering. *"Pilot, do you read me? Pilot, do we have enemy—"*

"Oh . . ." I murmur as black warships curl around the asteroid. Light lances from one and the *Snowball* simply divides in half. Her two pieces spin in opposite directions and crash soundlessly into the asteroid. The aft rebounds off, disappears into a crater, rebounds again to hit the lip of the crater, and then twirls lazily away toward space. The fore impacts and sticks into the rock a few hundred paces from us. Fel pushes me down.

"*Stay,*" he says and then springs away. I thought he was moving so fast during our recons just to show off. But it turns out he was moving like a toddler compared to his true top speed. Faster than a Cimmerian hare he races toward the ship's front section and disappears inside. The warships do not advance.

Instead, they shed black motes. I magnify with my visor and see the motes are shaped like men. Tall ones.

I balance my rifle on the lip of the crater. "Fel, meat contacts are dropping from the ships. I count ten. They're big, Fel. Fel?"

He emerges from the *Snowball* carrying our pilot, Xaria, over his shoulder. The Blue woman is unconscious in her emergency suit. He glances over his shoulder and races back toward me. His voice crackles in my ear. "*Pi . . . corv . . . iggy . . . prep . . .*"

The enemy have already landed. I link my rifle's scope to my helmet and scan the terrain. I barely sight one. A man-shaped shadow skims over the surface of the asteroid and I experience a dread like none I've ever felt. I wondered what enemy could make Fel nervous. Now I know. The shadow does not come in a straight line. It jitters, like lightning. I fire six shots and hit nothing, and I'm not a bad shot. Even Fel said so.

Something blurs past me to the right and I tumble back, suit screaming puncture alerts. Arresting myself, I see a long gash along the right side of my suit's torso. I'm shot, but not wounded. I didn't even see anyone fire. I deploy a seal before my oxygen vents. As the seal closes, I grab my rifle and rush back to my position just as Fel vaults over the lip, hurls down Xaria, and fires six shots back the way he came with his multiRifle.

"Dustwalkers," he says. "Get Xaria to the pirate corvette. It's our only—" Then his left arm comes off as something gleaming passes through just over the biceps. Fel spins, gathering himself just as a shadow blurs past overhead. A tongue of metal sweeps down and cuts Fel's rifle in half. I fire at the shadow, and must hit it, because its trajectory alters, and it retreats to the west.

I grab Xaria's foot and boost toward the pirate refuge as Fel covers our retreat. He lands behind us with a clang. His voice is tight, scared. *"It's the same frigate pack we spotted five days ago. We'll never outrun them."* The door above closes and seals us off from the surface. *"You can let that go,"* he says.

I look back to Xaria. Her foot is still in my hands, but her body is gone. Her leg was severed at the hip by something with the precision of a medical laser. I let go in horror and the leg drifts away. *"Get the corvette's reactor on. I'll cover you,"* Fel says, his pistol pointed up at the sealed entry. I don't move.

A shadow crouches atop the corvette. Taking a breath, I drop to a knee, raise my rifle, and pull the trigger. Only . . . I don't. Pressure builds in my hand. I look down. My hand still clutches the rifle, but it's begun to drift away. I move my arm and the hand separates from the wrist. White bone surrounded by bright meat stares back at me. The pain is delayed and indescribable. I'm too horrified to scream. I just pant as my suit seals over the wound.

Gunfire rattles behind me. A hand grips my throat so hard I choke. I'm lifted in the air by a huge Dustwalker in camouflage armor. The Dustwalker is not watching me. They watch Fel. His pistol is broken. His long-knife is out as he faces down another Dustwalker. This one is three heads taller than Fel. The Dustwalker pops their helmet's blackout visor, revealing a woman's face. Her bright golden eyes are wide-set and twice as large as mine. Her skin is pale brown, her nose broken innumerable times. She looks at Fel like he's a joke.

"A long-ranger. I have heard of your cult's martial worth. Your kind have killed several of our best knights." She plants her long razor into the floor and pulls a shorter blade to match Fel's long-knife. "I feared I would not get to test myself before the war was done. Gratitude for this—"

Fel lunges at her faster than I thought possible. The Dustwalker swims to the side. Their blades spark. By the time they part, she's severed his remaining metal arm at the shoulder. She hacks off his two metal legs, clucking her tongue. He floats, thrashing like a miserable limbless crab. "Be still, Red. You'll go to your Vale soon enough." Her eyes scan the hangar. "Bring them. Truth flayers have questions."

I'm nearly blind with pain as they freight Fel and me out of the pirate refuge to a group of eight more Dustwalkers who wait on the surface.

Their ships coast toward us. Casually they fire down on the *Snowball*'s remains. What was left of the ship that the Alltribe gave to Ephraim for his services simply disappears. The Dustwalkers seem to be speaking to each other. One points off to a bluff in the distance. One of their ships floats lower. A bizarre appendage emerges from his belly. A scanner?

Then a tremble goes through the asteroid. A tremble that makes the Golds look down. The tremble turns into a shudder, and then a shaking. They turn in unison as something rises from the asteroid's surface several hundred paces off. An obelisk of chrome metal maybe fifty meters high. Another rises to its left, and another, and another. The Moonies stare, as dumbstruck as I am, and see light building in the tips of the obelisks.

The light lunges overhead until the obelisks are linked together by a spiderweb of white light that grows bright and brighter before lashing out toward the ships. My vision goes white. Soon the pain of my severed hand is forgotten as my head explodes in a song of agony. I curl like a spider, screaming. I lose all sense of time, of myself, of my memories. There is only pain. And then it is gone. I don't feel my body. How long was it?

Seconds?

Minutes?

Hours?

My vision is blurry. I am floating over the asteroid in a slow spin. Strange chrome orbs move across its surface. Slow, methodical. I spin toward space. The stars burn coldly in the distance. I spin again toward the asteroid to see one of the orbs withdrawing a long glistening lance from the head of a Moonie Gold. It comes my way. No rush. No need. I spin back to the stars and remember the *Snowball* always sent its messages to Mars through a system of drone relays. I don't know if it's close enough. I use my helmet's voice commands and call up my broadcaster.

"Agea Command, this is Lyria of Lagalos. I've hit pay dirt."

I spin back toward the asteroid to see the orb floating in front of me. It is the size of a horse. A delicate lance protrudes from its center. I stop spinning. The lance creeps toward my visor.

An inhuman voice comes through my com system and fills my helmet. *"Sister . . . why do you hide in the warmblood?"* I must be dying. The machine is talking. *"Sister . . . you are injured . . ."* the orb says again, but it is not talking to me.

13

LYRIA

The Rose's Game

T HE FIRST THING I remember from my dream is the crashing of waves. The first thing I feel when I wake is the ache of my wrist. The first thing I see is the chrome orb floating out of the room through a hole in the ceiling. I scramble up, confused.

I am naked. Medical patches cover two wounds on my stomach and a deep cut on my right thigh. My hand is back on like it was never cut off. A pink line encircles my wrist.

The room is circular, clean, and rather grand. The walls are warm wood except for ovals of glass that peer into aqua-blue water filled with coral reefs. Around them, and deeper on, strange creatures swim. Two vaguely human shapes with translucent skin peer back at me from behind a mass of green and pink coral. Their dreamy eyes, big as my fists, are lime green. A lonesome song warbles from their wide mouths.

"Right."

The room has no distinguishable door, but clothing has been set out for me. I pull on the black pants, socks, and green sweater. The fabric is softer than Liam's cheek and smells like roses and pine. When I slip on the shoes, a slight hum fills the room and it rotates, showing more of the aquatic world outside the windows. When the rotation stops, one of the windows slides up. A stone path leads down a corridor of evergreen trees.

"Right."

I follow the path. A night sky peeks through the gaps in the trees, stretching in all directions until the path leads me to a small grove of rose trees. In every direction, the stars and the darkness of space. Between the rose trees, a man waits for me at a table set for tea.

He turns from watching the stars to grace me with a smile. And it does feel like grace. The man is too symmetrical to be handsome. He is beautiful and fragile, with skin as smooth as the shell of a quail's egg. His eyes are sunset pink. His hair long and white. I recognize him immediately.

"You are safe here, don't be afraid," he says.

"I'm not."

"Safe or afraid?"

"Either. Is Fel dead?"

"Yes."

I don't approach the table. It worries me how accustomed I am becoming to death. "How did you sleep?" he asks.

"Badly, but I'm sure you knew that." I look around the strange room wondering how many cameras monitor it.

"Nightmares can be such beastly refrains," he says. I grunt. "I had nightmares as a child, and then I woke into one every single day. Such is the life of a Pink. I never could tell which I dreaded more, the nightmares or the reality. I suppose it was the waking hours. In the dreams, there was always the hope it'd be a pleasant one. That's why I admire Reds so much. They dread dreams more. At least in the waking hours they can struggle instead of merely suffer."

He gestures to a seat like I'm a long-lost relative come to visit, and he knows the long, bitter road I've traveled to reach his house all too well. The urge to fall into him is nearly overwhelming. I feel seen, but not seen enough to drop my wits. I don't sit.

"I ain't been out long. Nails haven't grown much. We ain't been on a journey. We're in the asteroid. Ain't we?" His smile warms my heart, but only its walls. "And by the fact that you're not hiding your face, I know I'm already dead."

"You know who I am then?"

"Doesn't everyone? You're Matteo Sun. So naw. No tea. I know who you're married to."

"For a corpse you're certainly . . . vivacious," he says, amused.

"I ain't been in the Core as of late, but broadcasts make it through the jamming sometimes. Same with the holoNet. So I know there's two things on the minds of every person in the Core. Is the Reaper dead? And where did that coward Quicksilver sneak off to?"

He strokes his chin. "It's strange, being synonymous with someone who is not you. But I suppose that is marriage—writ even larger when you're married to the father of the Rising."

"*Fitchner Barca* was the father of the Rising," I say, surprised by my own sharpness. If there's one hero who never lost his shine in the mud of 121, it's Ares. Eo too, but she was always the romantic part of the Rising. Darrow was its promise. But Ares, Ares was always its father.

"Ah, yes. But Fitchner would be nothing without Regulus. Surely you know that, or is it perhaps that you cannot conscience two fathers, Lyria of Lagalos?"

I swallow. "You know who I am?"

"I never forget a face, nor a dossier, especially not those of guests in our house. It was a lovely birthday, wasn't it, when you visited our estate as the fox walker of the Telemanus entourage?" He smirks. "Lovely until the afterparty, I suppose." I wince. That's when Pax was kidnapped. "Oh no, don't think I think you're to blame. We're well aware of the free-lancer Ephraim ti Horn. Uniquely crafty fellow, at least when he got out of his own way. Performed a few jobs for us actually, not that he knew."

He leans back, and he becomes so somber and sincere that the lights in the room seem to dim. "I know what happened at Camp 121, and my heart breaks for it. For your sister, your father, your nieces, and your nephews. I cannot imagine your pain, nor how it must shape how you see the world."

He licks his lips, reflective, showing his own secret pain. "I know a little of suffering. The worlds are very big. The people in them . . . and the systems . . . well they are very cold and very uncaring. I know what it is to be small. To be . . . stepped on. There's dignity in holding up your hands against the boot. But it crushes all the same." He touches his breast. "On this fragile heart of mine, I promise no harm will come to you here."

I feel love radiating from him, and acceptance. I take a deep breath. "The hardest thing about being a Pink must be knowing that you can never be trusted. You are made to lie so well that the rest of us can never be sure."

"No," he says with conviction. "If you think that, then you still wear the chains fashioned by our oppressors. It's easy to break the chains on your wrists, but the ones in here linger." He taps his head. "Please sit. Have tea. Trust me or don't, your existence is at my mercy, and I gave you your hand back after those . . . brutes took it."

I sigh, seeing his point, and sip his tea while watching him like a soldier behind a parapet. "If you know who I am, then you know how annoying it is to have Sun Industries tech in my head. Your husband cheated millions of Reds out of their mines."

"No. That was actually demokracy in action. Each mine got to vote. Is it our fault they chose the immediate payout instead of maintaining their ownership? How can we promise freedom and then be the arbiter of a people's choices? That is not freedom. That is social engineering. That is the long road to tyranny." He pauses and looks around the room with a sigh. "Benevolent or malevolent, still tyranny. How is your tea?"

"Warm," I say. "What is this place?"

"Let us play a game. For every question of yours I answer, you must answer one of mine in return. We must swear to be honest." He spits in his hand like a Red clansman. I ain't got much to lose. I spit in mine and we shake.

"This place is a self-contained ecosystem within an asteroid. A construction on a scale that has not been seen since the terraforming of the spheres. Why did you come here?"

I'm a little baffled by his question. "You already know that answer."

"Play fair, Lyria."

"The thing in my head brought me here."

"Lyria."

"This thing in my head, it came out of the Figment. The freelancer. It came out of her as she died. It crawled in my bloodydamn nose, man. Horrifying stuff. Sometimes it talks to me or shows me things. But then it went quiet, except to tell me it needed repairs. So, I followed this urge to get it repaired. Happy?"

"That's *how* you're here. Why are you here?"

"Play fair, Matteo," I mock.

"Why are you here?" he asks, harder.

"I'm here because I'm sick of being small. This thing in my head, I know it's a weapon. One that makes me stronger. And I got things I need to do. I'm sick of being at the mercy of bastards. My turn, Matteo: what is this thing in my head?"

"It is called a *psyche*. It was developed several decades ago by a brilliant but fragile woman named Agala si Ken. Agala specialized in neurobionics. The *psyche* was created to be an AI partner for the brain to enable the user to be . . . a god among machines, for lack of a better expression. It was to link the nervous system to drones, ships, computers, missiles."

"Blues can already do that."

"They can sync on a limited scale. But they cannot control their body while in the sync. The *psyche* was made so that they could do both, concurrently, on an unlimited scale. Imagine sitting here, having this conversation, and running a war a hundred kilometers away."

"Shit," I murmur.

He nods. "Before Fitchner came to my husband, he was a very wrathful man, very . . . controlling. He had been much wronged by Gold, and he sowed many seeds for his revenge. The *psyche* project was a seed that did not come to fruition. Agala could not see what she was making when she was making it, but after it was complete, she realized her folly.

"Could you imagine a man who could wield legions of metal slave soldiers? No waiting for crops of mortal soldiers to grow, be trained, then reaped by the battle's scythe. Instead you would have legions of asteroid-mined, automatically assembled metal soldiers. Each one a node within the hivemind." He smiles. "I love my husband, but even I fear a world where we rely on the benevolence of a person with so much individual power. If I had that power, even I would become a tyrant. How could I not? There is so much evil to make right.

"When she saw what she built, Agala wept. But unlike Oppenheimer, who opened Pandora's box and unleashed destruction, she opened the box and slammed down the lid as soon as she saw the gods creeping out. Well, she tried to, at least.

"My husband thought he could make her continue her work under duress. He was wrong. In protest, Agala released six of her earlier prototypes into the worlds, and then killed herself. I never got the chance to ask her why. I imagine she thought my husband would make his own *psyches* eventually. So she must have thought: if gods are inevitable, shouldn't godkillers be as well?

"My turn. What would you do if we did repair your prototype?" he asks.

"I'd find my friend and I'd rescue her. Then I'd . . . I guess I'd do what I can to help."

"The Republic?"

"My nephew is on Mars, and the Republic is the one defending Mars. So yeah?"

"Even after 121?" he asks, breaking the rules of the game. Still, I find myself nodding.

"The camps were a right horror, but it was a Telemanus who saved me. A Gold saved me from Reds. And I looked in Virginia's eyes. You can't fake caring like that, or having a brain like that, so it's gotta be hard what they're trying. They ain't good, not all through, but neither am I, and at least they're trying to stop the boot from coming down. I think it's my job too. And yours. That's why Pax sent me on the path to sniff out your husband."

"Pax is innately kind. I'd say he was also trying to help you."

I shrug. "Maybe. Either way, Pax knows where you are now. Our ship had a tracker. He'll know where I disappeared to, and so will his mother."

"No, I'm afraid not. We've cloned the tracker signal and sent it on its way. He thinks you're a hundred thousand kilometers from here, still sniffing about, lost in space. Whose turn is it?"

I don't bring up the message I sent to our drone. "Mine. Would you actually repair the prototype for me?"

"That depends."

"On? What, your husband?"

"Contrary to popular opinion, I do what I want. I'm the only one that he loves . . ." He considers. "And that gives me leverage. So my decision depends on what you'd do with the prototype."

I squint and sip my tea, thinking. He's not serious about repairing the prototype, is he? Or is he trying to gauge what sort of person I am? "I told you what I'd do with it. So . . ."

"That's the problem. I don't know if you're lying."

"Ironic."

"But if you weren't lying, then I would say that I might be inclined to help the Republic."

"Then why are you sitting here instead of flying home to Mars?"

"Because this place cannot be risked. Not in the slightest. But I sense a bit of my own story in you. We are splinters of the same tree, Red and

Pink. If I offered to have our facilities here repair the prototype to full functionality, and then sent you off with oh, ten sentinels. What would you say?"

"That's a sentinel?" I ask of the orb floating above us. He nods. My fear of the machine evolves into hunger as I think of the power just one sentinel would bring me. I lick my lips, afraid of my own thoughts. "I'd ask what's your price?"

"*You,* I fear." He winces. "Or rather, a part of you. The prototype has degraded from use, electromagnetic exposure, and blunt force trauma. If we repair it, the integration process will affect the hippocampus, the neocortex, and the amygdala. These are where our explicit memories—events that happened to you—and our semantic memories—general facts and information—are stored. Semantic memories are left unaffected, as are implicit memories—motor skills and such. But the integration's effect on explicit memories can range from minor to total."

"You mean I could forget who I am?"

"Unlikely. But there will be gaps. Your emotional relationship with your memories may change. There will be holes punched through the story of your life. Or memories seen in . . . I don't know how to put it. Black and white? Felt with a kind of neutral passivity?"

"So, I'd lose the very things that make me who I am," I say.

He nods. "It is good that power does not come without sacrifice. That was the problem with the finished *psyche* that Agala destroyed. There was no sacrifice. Though I can't say what you would retain of your memories, I can state that if the integration is a success, you will be able to control sentinels. But also your brain's efficiency will be maximized. Your reflexes will be better than a Gold's—well, most Golds. Your aging will slow. You will jump higher and run faster, control your metabolism, dopamine, and adrenaline. You'll sleep on command, integrate with computer systems, and access information faster than you can blink—in short, you will achieve near mortal omniscience.

"But the *psyche* will degrade. It is not invulnerable and so you will not be immortal. You will not be a god, but you will still be a very dangerous person."

"But I might not be *me,*" I say.

"I know it is a complicated decision." He touches his breast again. "But I swear to honor your decision. If you want the power to help the Republic, your friend, it is yours." He stands. "I will give—"

"No deal."

He starts in surprise. "No?"

"I don't need it," I say. "I don't want it."

He's flummoxed. "Lyria, you don't have to decide this instant. And the memory loss isn't assured."

"I don't need it. I just need you to take it out and let me go." I feel an existential urge to flee. To wash my hands of the parasite. "Just get it out of me."

"How will you help your friend without it?" he asks.

"I don't know. But I'd rather die than forget my sister, my pa, my ma. My brothers. They already died once. If I don't remember them . . . Well, it's just that Liam, my nephew, he's a kid. I haven't told him all about our family yet, about his ma. If I don't no one will. Then they'll all be gone. Like they never mattered. But I know that's not true. They *mattered*."

His confusion fades. He looks as if he's about to cry.

"That is very beautiful, Lyria. You are right. They did matter. And to be honest, with no condescension, I very much admire you for your decision."

Though he doesn't say it, I know somehow that he has someone whose memory he keeps alive, like a child shielding a candle against the wind. "Very well, Lyria. If you're sure of your decision . . ." I nod. "Then we can schedule the operation to remove the *psyche*."

"And then you'll let me go."

"Yes. When the time is right, and there is no risk to this place, I will let you go and give you all you need to return home to your nephew."

I'm left in my room to my own devices until Matteo comes to fetch me for my surgery. I pace the whole time, watching the carvelings swim through the glass, wondering if I've made the right decision. Wondering which decision is braver, but knowing in the end that I meant what I said to Matteo.

As a girl, I dreamed of being big and strong. Of being carved like Darrow. But I feel I've only just started becoming me. I'm gaining strength from all the bad that's happened to me. To lose that now seems like a betrayal of what I've gone through so far. Worse, it's a betrayal of everyone who's gone out of their way to help me.

I jump when Matteo sets his hand on my shoulder to guide me to the operating table. My white paper shift crinkles as I lay down. The table is warm though the room is cold and blinding white. I flinch as a chrome orb descends from the ceiling and begins unfolding hidden appendages until it has eight. "I know Charlotte looks like a monster, but she's actually very sweet," Matteo says of the orb. "I named her for a character in one of my favorite books. You are in good hands."

A long appendage with a crimson disk on the end extends toward me. I smell burning hair and feel a sting on my scalp. The appendage withdraws and I reach up to touch my bald head. "That bitch," I say.

Matteo chuckles. "You'll be out for the procedure. Don't worry."

"You ever had your skull drilled into?" I ask.

"Sadly yes," he replies. Sensing my nervousness, he slides my hand between his and smiles down at me. His eyes are warm pools of sunset pink, a color I did not know existed when I lived in the grimness of my mine. "I want to thank you, Lyria."

"For what?"

He looks down, very sensitive. "In life, it is very tempting to forget the past to try and make a perfect future. But the past, and the pain we have endured . . . they make us who we are. Without my past, my pain, I would not be what I am. I forgot that. I remember it now very clearly, thanks to you."

His eyes return to mine. "The message you sent was, in fact, blocked by our technology. After our tea, I sent that message to the coms relay you used to report your movements to Agea. Pax may have sent you, but the message will no doubt find its way to *our* Sovereign, though I fear neither will be able to sway my husband to return to the fight. But there is one man who might, if he's still alive."

"Darrow?" He nods. "But he died on Mercury," I say. A strange hope grows in my chest. One I did not think Darrow could still inspire in me anymore. "Didn't he?"

"Maybe." Matteo smiles. "But then again, maybe not."

14

VIRGINIA

The Armor of Love

I N THE SPACEPORT SOUTH of Agea, snow drifts down on five of the
fastest vessels in the Republic fleet. Their crews and space legionnaires stand at attention. Patrols circle overhead. I meet the many-
colored eyes of the sailors and captains. After receiving Lyria's message
and the data her sensors collected, I had them assembled as quickly as
possible.

I look at them and wish I could say: *we have received information of
an armory of unknown size located on the fringe of the asteroid belt. Your
mission will be to investigate the scene, locate the armory, and acquire any
possible weapons or ships that may be of use in the defense of Mars.*

But I cannot. Instead, I say, "My friends, this mission may decide the
fate of our Republic. I wish I could tell you its purpose, but you will be
traveling through enemy-held space and the chance of capture is high.
Your ships are fast, but the Rim's are faster. Your route will also take you
through the territory under attack by Volsung Fá, the warlord who stole
most of the Volk fleet eight months ago. Only your captains and my
emissaries know where you are going. Not all of you will survive. But at
least one of your ships *must* survive to reach its destination. The Republic and Mars depend on you. Your children and my own depend on you.
I thank you for your trust, from the bottom of my heart. Good fortune
and good speed." I lift my fist. "Hail libertas!"

"Hail Reaper!" they shout and board up.

His name is *Darrow,* I think. Because the Reaper is not mine. He's
not the man I love. Darrow is. *Endure,* I once told him. Yet it is I who

must endure. Reaper. *Reaper*. It never stops. They mean well, and the Reaper's name feeds them power. But they shout for the god while I carry a hollowness inside me the size of the man.

It's lonely. I miss my husband.

The five senators acting as my emissaries linger behind the crews to receive my parting words. They represent three Colors—Red, Gold, and Silver. They're the best emissaries I can spare. I shake each of their hands. "You all know Regulus. He's as prickly as a cactus, but if his heart still beats for the Rising, I know no better emissaries to help him remember it. Win him back to our cause," I say. "Our agent has not reported in since her last transmission. And we believe her ship has been destroyed, so keep in mind that you may not be met with open arms." I pause. "You cannot be captured en route. You all understand?"

They nod. I wish them luck and watch them board before turning to return to my own shuttle, flanked by Lionguards. Kavax waits for me there. The look in his eyes is unmistakable.

"Word from Victra?" I ask. He nods. I sigh. I had hoped that she would be able to escape the noose that's slowly tightening around Mars. Instead, as I glance at the report, I see she's taken more casualties than we can afford. "If we can't punch out and hit them, this becomes a war of attrition."

He nods again. "Fortunately, we have all the helium."

"And they have everything else. Including helium."

"If the Rim shares their inferior variety," he says. "That stuff they mine from the Gas Giants is like jellybeans without sugar, you know."

"If only reactors were as judicious as Sophocles."

"Sarcasm never inspired anyone. Let them come, I say. Let them come and die. Atalantia, Atlas, Lysander, Ajax, Helios, Dido. We will make Mars their grave."

I cannot share his ardor. Kavax has lost two sons. I have not yet lost my one. I see the grief in his face. The hatred in his eyes when he looks up at the sky. There the reassuring lights of our ships and orbital battle stations twinkle, but none shine so brightly as Phobos, the headquarters of our orbital defenses of Mars and the site of Victra's precious dock-yards. I try to believe our defenses are strong enough to stop what will come.

On my flight to Agea from my gun battery inspections on the Ther-mic coast, I saw fishing boats on the sea, children flying kites, workers digging bunkers, and soldiers making rings for pankration in the shadows of their war machines. All know a battle is coming, but on the surface of the planet, it does not quite feel like a siege yet.

In orbit over Mars, the tale is different. Millions in the navy and defense installations are on battle-watch. With the Solar System turned into soup by the enemy's anti-sensor drones, I feel as though we've returned to the dark ages. Our long-distance coms are unreliable. Our radar and lidar assaulted by false signatures. The enemy could come and we'd have less than a week's notice.

I wag the report at Kavax. "This could have been done over coms. I take it you're coming along to see Pax?"

He nods. "It isn't every day the Conservatory allows a student to see his mother. Even if she is the Sovereign."

I pat my old guardian on the shoulder and head for my shuttle. My bodyguards fall in behind us. "Pax will be happy to see you. Where is Sophocles by the way, I don't know how you're standing without him?"

"In the shuttle already," he says. "I'll bet you a bottle of Rath red that he's chosen your seat."

The wind howls as I wait for my son outside his school. The Darkstar Conservatory is perched high on a mountain. Nearby, only a few military installations and training facilities dot the range that stretches south to the continent's end. Several hundred banners snap in the twilight. The banners are as no-nonsense as the school's founder, Orion. Each bears the school's sigil on a field of black—a blue trident piercing a cracking golden planet.

A perfect black sphere, the school looks as indomitable to its stark environs as I wish I felt. The Conservatory was to be the forge where the next generations of ripWing aces, destroyer captains, and torchShip daredevils were made. Already the influence of their first graduating class is being felt in the ranks, their elite alumni aiding our struggle against Gold command superiority—though many say it is too little, too late.

It was five years ago that I watched Darrow give his speech at the school's opening ceremony. After he surrendered the rostrum to Orion, he came to stand beside me. The smile on his face, and then his lightness at the afterparty, remains one of the more pleasant memories of the last decade. He was happy. He was proud of Orion. And he saw himself, if only for one evening, as a builder of the future.

It seems so long ago now. We both thought we had so much future ahead of us. Our future has shrunken and darkened now that Pax is studying within the Conservatory's walls. Now that the enemy is setting the table for the inevitable siege of Mars.

When Pax was born out beyond the ecliptic plane, I was on the run after my father had been murdered and Darrow taken captive by my brother in a garden on Mars. Back then I never would have imagined I'd be sending my precious boy to study at a place like the Conservatory, yet it is where he asked to go. He knows all too well the expectations the people have of him—he's already famous as the Boy Who Killed a TorchShip. The holo experience is even available on the black web.

My son will be a warrior.

It makes no difference if he fights with ships or blades; either way the fate that awaits my son fills me with inexpressible regret and guilt. Worse, I've always let him know it. It was the only fight we have ever had, that day the shuttle took him from Agea south to the Conservatory. I'd have that moment back if I could. We have not spoken since, and according to school rules, we ordinarily would not be allowed to until he graduates six years from now.

But a Sovereign should be permitted some privileges, shouldn't she?

At first, the school's administrators, all Blues, wouldn't let me inside. They believe the first step to creating a naval officer is severing the recruits, especially those not born Blue, from their original Color's familial structures. No mothers, no fathers, not for those of the navy's killing elite. Their only family will be the brothers and sisters of the sect. The school's method is effective, but to me it feels too utilitarian and almost insidious.

Chilled by my thoughts and the weather, I pull my red and gold cloak tighter around my shoulders. I squint through the falling snow toward the school. The snow is so heavy, the only feature of the school I can divine is the motto in huge iron letters on the façade: AS ABOVE, SO BELOW. There's no sign of Pax.

I glance up. Soon it won't just be Republic ships flying above Mars. Kavax joins me from the shuttle with Sophocles the fox trotting dutifully behind. Fearing that assassination squads are already on Mars, or worse, the Fear Knight himself, Kavax seldom lets me out of his sight.

"The evacuation of the civilians from Phobos is behind schedule," he grumbles. "There was a bombing this morning. Lune fundamentalist."

"Affiliated with Lune's household?"

"Doesn't look like it. Lone wolf. A Green."

"A Green?"

"It was a suicide bombing. Religion has returned to politics," he replies. "In the grand scheme of things, the bombing is only a minor setback. Look on the bright side. You've unveiled four traitors in a week. All high ranking."

"That we have four traitors is hardly a 'bright side.' Do they really think Lysander is any different from Octavia? It's the same system, even if Lune has a prettier smile and more games. Those bloody chariot races . . ."

"I know it's been frustrating watching him rise."

"What's frustrating is that he never comes into the field of battle so Victra can just kill the little bastard and end his delusions of grandeur before he becomes a problem." Kavax puts an arm around me. "Sorry," I say. "I know you know. It's only that I just saw a holo of him."

"I saw it too. He was wearing the hilt from the razor you gave Darrow."

"As if *he* earned it," I say.

"I have a question to ask you, Virginia." I try to pull away to look at him but he keeps his arm around me. "The reputation of your omniscience grows. Four traitors in a week, you know. But . . . if the gods have taught us anything, it is that prescience always comes with a price. Odin gave up one of his eyes in exchange for wisdom."

I feared this moment from him. It was inevitable. I could not hide the source of my intel forever from a man like him. In fact, if Kavax's wits were not so dimmed by Daxo's death, he would have discovered it after the first traitor we clipped.

"You want to know what price I'm paying, Kavax?"

"There are those who say Kavax Telemanus is a bad Republican. It is true. I am . . . old in my ways. I have doubted many of this Republic's policies. Especially concerning the Obsidians. But I hope you know my loyalty. And I like to think you trust me as much as I trust you." I try to speak but he rumbles on. "It is also true I am not what I once was. My injury and my loss have . . . Well you are unaccustomed to seeing me weak."

"You, weak?" I scoff at the notion.

"Don't deny it. I know you and Niobe worry I take too much on. I am not what I was, but I am still very much in the game. You understand? Whoever your source is, whoever has been helping you find these traitors, you can tell me."

I close my eyes. He's still not let me go. I enjoy the embrace while it lasts.

"Imagine the worst, and it is true." I can't bring myself to say it.

He holds me tighter and kisses my head. He knows already, I realize. Of course he knows.

I think of his sons, both of whom spent their lives in service to me until their deaths—Pax at the Institute, Daxo on the Day of Red Doves—and I want to cry. I loved them both, almost as much as their father did.

"I didn't want to break your heart by telling you the truth," I say.

"Daughter, you *are* my heart," he replies. "I trust you like I trust the vaulting sky. I look up, and there it is. Different shades, perhaps, but always there. Always true."

There's motion from the school. A door, obscured by the snow, opens.

Kavax kisses the top of my head again and releases me. Three figures make their way to us through the falling snow. My son and two instructors. Sophocles runs and leaps toward Pax, the tallest figure, to pester my son with kisses. When Kavax sees that my son has something on his head that is not hair, he darkens. A little startled myself, I put on my best face and beam a smile for Pax as he approaches. Instead of embracing me as I'd hoped, he salutes.

Six months at the school has made him nearly unrecognizable. His golden eyes are sunken, harder. His lips thinner. His skin pale as a miner's. But he's taller, far taller. "Pax. You've shot up like a godTree." Already, he's surpassed the height of the Blues behind him, his instructors. Soon he'll tower over them. I eye the digital tattoos that now stain his laser-shaved head. They morph as snowflakes settle on his scalp. "Adept ink too. So soon?" I raise a disapproving eyebrow at the instructors.

The Blue instructors are both waifish but still cast more in the image of the school's founder than your typical Blue. Veterans of our wars, both have scars, one a robotic right eye. By the phalera on their chests, I see both earned their scars under Darrow and Orion.

"It was due, my Sovereign," the older, darker instructor says. "The Star Matron has chosen Adept Augustus for an accelerated track. He was fought over for three hours after his Divining before the navigators demurred."

My son will be a hunter. It's written on his forehead. The constellation Orion.

The instructors salute and give us space. Adept Augustus. Accelerated track. I withhold my anxiety from my face and feel warmth as Kavax embraces my son, then steps aside to give me my moment with him. It will be just a moment too. "How are you?" I ask my boy.

"Learning fast," he replies, curt. "I hear the enemy is mustering for a summit. Is it regarding the action at Venus, or was it scheduled before?"

"Before, we believe. The *Dustmaker* was already en route to Earth."

"Then it pertains to the next stage of the war," he says. "Will it be Mars?"

"That depends," I say. "On what, do you know?"

He considers. "Whether or not the Rim will continue to let Atalantia use them to soften us up, which she will unless she feels strong enough to attack and retain her primacy."

He is so precisely correct it is impossible not to smile. "It is good to see you."

He smiles, but not with his whole face. "You're angry at the ink," he says.

"Angry only that I was not consulted," I reply. "By your instructors, not you."

"You agreed, *no special privileges*," he reminds me, which indicts me because the visit itself is a special privilege. "Is it news of Father?"

I feel a pang of guilt. Of course that's what he would have presumed this visit would entail—news of Darrow's death, or life, or would it be resurrection at this point? Does Pax assume his father is dead? "Only rumors that he lives." I glance at Kavax. "But the source is . . . not credible."

"What do you think?" he asks.

"It would be a guess."

"Your guesses are often more researched than most people's facts."

My first impulse is to please him and make him happy, to spoil him. I know what is right. I trust my heart and narrow my eyes. "Do you really want me to speculate?"

He pauses. This is at the intersection of what I have taught him and what he's learning from the Blues—speculation is fiction. My response may seem cold. It is not. It is a sign of respect from me, and also a reminder that I am not ignorant of his new way of life, nor excluded completely from who he wants to become.

"All hope is true until it is proven false. And even then with ingenuity it may be not," he replies with a little smile. Then he takes a shot across my bow. "So you're here to tell me you've decided to pardon Valdir. Finally."

"No, Pax. When the enemy comes, he'll be where he belongs. In a cell near the front lines, where he left the Free Legions. He rebelled against the Republic, don't forget."

"The Obsidians just wanted a little of the freedom they died for," Pax says.

"There are ways of doing that in the Republic," I reply. "There are senators. Avenues. In a civil matter the cause may be right, but force cannot be the answer. They proved it. Sefi rebelled and paved the way for that Volsung Fá to steal her throne and sack three cities. We are still suffering the consequences of Valdir's decisions, Pax. When the enemy comes, we will feel it far more than we do even now. I cannot pardon him."

"Because they left Father vulnerable on Mercury," Pax says.

"Yes," I admit. "But this is not a decision I made out of anger."

He respects me enough to believe that. "This is about Lyria," I say.

He perks up at her name. "Not lost in the Belt after all?" he asks.

"When you sent her out on the *Snowball*—without my approval"—

"Sorry, Mother," he drones.

—"you said the device in her head had antecedents connected esoterically to Sun Industries. You said because of that she might be able to lead us to Sun Industries, and Quicksilver, and all the resources you think he's hoarding." His eyes narrow, but boyish excitement manages to fight its way through his stoic facade. He does love a bit of intrigue, so I tease him a little. "I looked into it personally while you were here. In fact, I found your hunch so compelling I sent a team of long-rangers to help Lyria's search. Meanwhile I conducted a search for Regulus's hidden books. It was not easy."

"And?"

"And a few days ago we received her signal from the Belt—deep in contested territory. No, that's a euphemism. *Lost* territory. I believe we may have found Quicksilver's base."

"And you think he may have forces strong enough to deliver us?"

"We caught his old *logos*. The *logos* doesn't know what's out there. But the information he did know suggests Quicksilver may have an entire fleet."

Pax smirks like his father. "When will you send your emissaries?"

"I just came from Agea. They launched before sunset."

His face falls. "Who?"

"Quicksilver's favorite senators, and one or two of his least."

He blinks at me as if I said something stupid. "He'll dismiss them all. If he doesn't kill them."

I frown. "Why would he kill them?"

"If Quicksilver dreamed of a nightmare, it would look like the Vox Populii, Mother. You know how sensitive he is when it comes to politics, to socialism. Few men bear insults well, least of all Regulus ag Sun. After all his efforts, to have his head hunted by a mob, his tower ransacked, his friends butchered . . ." He shakes his head. "Without Father, he'll want nothing to do with us. Honestly, he might even despise the Republic. You should have sent me."

"You?"

"Mother, Regulus only cares about rarity. Respect."

"Pax . . . I can't send you off-planet," I reply. "It's chaos. Do you even know the life expectancy of a sailor out there right now?" In reply he looks at the Conservatory and then back at me. "I can't, Pax. I will beam him a message, should the senators fail. He may listen to me."

"Did he build a statue in your honor?" he asks. "No. He built only one. Not for you, not for Fitchner, not for Eo. Just Father. Spare your emissaries the trip."

"We need those ships. Victra's docks can't replenish our losses fast enough. The Rim has choked us of the resources we need from the Belt. We need help. Badly. We can't wait for your father." He shrugs at that. "Pax, we don't even know if he's alive."

He smiles at that. "Tell that to the pilgrims."

I pause. "You know about the pilgrims to Lykos?"

"The ones going to pray for Father's return? I'm in school, not on Pluto," he replies. "Father is alive until proven dead. I know you balk at religion—rightly so—but if Father is anything, he is bloodydamn hard to kill. Now, my sect is preparing for a match with Virgo. Was there anything else?"

The question is as cold as his eyes. He's not forgotten how we last parted, what I said to him, but I fear he mistook my disappointment in myself for disappointment in him.

"I wanted to tell you . . ." My voice falters. "You know I did not approve when you asked to study here. Do you know why?"

"You think I'm resigned to becoming a weapon."

"Are you?"

"The people need symbols," he says.

"When you have children, I hope you never have to feel the pain of hearing that from them," I say. His eyes soften. "It's true. I wanted more for you than a life of war. But I see you now for what you are. A son of the Rising. I wanted to tell you I am proud of you. Not only proud of you, I'm proud of what you saw in Lyria, and that you chose this place. My generation apparently cannot do this on its own. And . . . I wanted to tell you, in case I don't have the chance again . . . I'm sorry." He tilts his head. "I'm sorry this is the world that was given to you. It wasn't fair to bring a child into this. I should have waited."

He searches my face. "Do you wish you had?"

"No. If I had, you wouldn't be you, and I think you're perfect."

He looks down at his feet, searching for words. When he finds them, he looks up at me with the raw emotion of his father, but without the anger or the pain. "Mother, your inheritance was guilt. Father's was surrender. Because of you, because of Father, mine is struggle. That is better than guilt. It is better than surrender. I do not blame you. I thank you. You never pretended the world wasn't broken, even when a broken world favored you." He takes my hands. "I think . . . if love is anything, it is truth. If life is anything, it is struggle. You taught me that. Father taught me my life is not my own, not unless we win. So, do not come back here. Do not think of me. Fix your gaze on our enemies. Fix your heart on the struggle. And win."

The instructors whistle at Pax. "I have to go," he says.

"Can I ask something of you?" He nods. "You greeted me as your Sovereign, but—"

He steps forward and wraps his arms around me, and I wrap mine around him. It is the first embrace we've shared where I can feel a hint of the strength his arms will one day possess. I hold him for as long as I can.

He is my favorite smell, my favorite sound, my favorite sight. He will never know how much I love him because he does not remember the day Darrow and I conceived him, or the months I carried him inside me, or the minute he came into the world, the moment he said his first word or took his first step, or made me laugh for the first time. I remember all those things, and all the things about them. Where the sun lay in the sky, how his father's eyes sparkled, what I feared in those moments, what I hoped for his life to be. That season of life is a haze to him, but when I die and reflect on my life, I know I will still believe that season was the meaning of mine.

When he walks away from me back toward his instructors with Kavax sharing a few jokes at his side, the whole of my heart goes with him, and I pray it is not the last time I see him, though I know it might be, because the enemy will soon be on their way. As the door closes behind him, I think on the stupidity of war. How ridiculous we must be to wage it when emotions like love run so much deeper in us than hate.

By the time Kavax makes it back to me, I am ready for the enemy to come. I have more reasons to fight than they do. My armor is my love.

15

LYSANDER

Earth

SQUINTING INTO THE SUN, my old friend Ajax waits to greet me on the tarmac outside Atalantia's citadel in New Sparta. He's fully armored. I'm sluggish, recuperating from the beating and Earth's gravity. Ajax mistakes my sluggishness for fear.

"You look frightened. Already missing your circus?" he says.

"The circus has kinder beasts," I reply. He grunts.

"Except for the manticores, I hear."

We watch Atalantia's war machines slump across the horizon and her troops on PT jog in the distance. Everywhere I look, I see the banner of House Grimmus.

While I've spent the last half year building my reputation as an administrator and peacemaker, Ajax has spent it rebuilding the reputation Darrow crushed before the storm wall of Heliopolis. He hunted Darrow for months, unsuccessfully and to much snickering, before Atalantia grew tired of that sad spectacle and recalled him to use as her own personal wrecking ball. But she still refuses to trust him with higher command and to grant him the respect that comes with it.

"I wish you had accepted my invitation to the festival," I said.

"As a rule, I don't accept invitations to parties from men I've tried and failed to kill," Ajax replies. "Nothing personal." His eyes fall on my face and the pinkish shadow of healthy skin where my atrocious scar from Darrow's boot used to be. "I see vanity won out. Thank Vulcan. That thing was monstrous. People will think you're a Moonie keeping scars like that."

"Atalantia's vanity. Not mine."

His eyes narrow. "It was like that then?"

"Yes. She had it removed from my face in transit from Mercury, after having her goons beat me to smithereens." I apply ointment to the new pink flesh on my face. "Hurts like mad, you'll be happy to know. The liver worse than the face, though." I run a finger along the Peerless scar on my right cheekbone. "Least I got to keep this."

"It's vainer to keep marks like that burn. Darrow took my nose once. Imagine me, walking around like a serpent. Imagine him walking around without the fingers I took off his left hand when I was seventeen. Scars are for the poor or the pompous." He searches behind me. "Where's your new man friend? The talkative idiot?"

"Cicero, a perfectly lovely human being, is managing the conclusion of my games," I say.

"Hiding behind his sister's skirts, you mean. At least she's brave enough to attend Atalantia's summit, even though it's Cicero's duty. Truly, you must thank your stars to have finally found a friend you can count on."

"Are you allowed to be jealous when you tried to kill me twice?" I ask.

He pats his razor. "This says I can be anything I gorydamn want to be. You're welcome to disagree. Others have. You should ask them for advice, but you'll have to brave the sun."

I wonder how many Ajax has sent to their sundeaths. Even if I knew, my opinion on duels could not sour any further. I don't know what transpired on the Venus docks between Darrow and Apollonius, but I'm sure when it all went wrong, it was certainly because of the latter's lust for a duel.

"I thought you'd be rushing to hunt Darrow," I say. "I'm sure those holos of Sevro, Cassius, and him running through the halls of the docks caused quite a stir."

"I'm on assignment." His eyes twinkle. He may hate Darrow, but any success Darrow has against Ajax's competitors lessens Ajax's own shame. "The Minotaur choked on *that* meal. But then again, so are the Carthii choking on theirs. Mad shit, that battle."

"I imagine Atalantia's sending a strike force?"

"Ten legions. First time I'm glad to be missing the action. All those meatstraws."

"So you've come to what, gloat?" I ask.

He raps his knuckles on his gear. "I don't need armor to gloat. I have an action today in South Pacifica." His tone softens, and his natural awkwardness slips through, making him seem almost sweet. He's unable to meet my eyes. "I just came to say . . . when Atalantia strikes you, don't hit her back. Certainly don't laugh. Go to your knees. Not too quickly though, or she'll think less of you."

I feel a pang of sorrow for him. "Is that what you did all these years?"

His mood darkens and any chance of him answering vanishes when Atlas joins us.

"Storm," Atlas says. It is the coldest greeting between a father and son I have ever heard.

"Fear." The father and son—both Olympic Knights—are strikingly similar in the shape of their eyes but little else. Atlas's skin is the color of a gray winter sky. Ajax's is dark brown. Atlas is slender. Ajax has more muscles than most legions. Atlas never blusters. Ajax talks shit like he was a tiny man from a poor family. "Back from butchering babies already?" he asks his father.

Atlas smiles. "Aren't you due in South Pacifica?"

"I haven't seen Lysander in eight months," Ajax replies. "He's been busy with civic engineering, you see."

"Now you have. Give the Republic my best, Storm." Atlas waits for Ajax to leave.

Ajax does not. "I hear you're off to 'pacify' South America after the summit," he says.

"I am."

"Strange, considering the man who murdered my mother—the man you said was probably dead—is likely somewhere between Venus and Mars right now," Ajax says.

"Your point?"

"My point is you never gave two shits about my mother or avenging her."

"Your mother was a good soldier, but we had little in common except that Atalantia liked our genes. You obviously cared for your mother—so much that you willingly linger in her shadow. So why aren't *you* hunting Darrow?" Atlas asks.

I almost step back from the impending explosion of violence. If any other man had said that to Ajax, Ajax would cut him in half, then beg the man's family to try and avenge him, then cut them in half too.

Atlas looks at the war machines staggering into the horizon, and says, "We all have our parts to play, young man. Yours is to do as you're told until you can prove you don't have to be told. Fortunately, you've made progress, on that front at least."

Ajax grins like the skulls on his armor. "One of these days, when the war is won, Atalantia won't need you anymore. We'll have a talk then. Son to father."

"If we must." Atlas does not care at all. He strides away. "Hurry along, Lune. The Dictator won't do business after the sun is set. She has a party to attend."

Ajax watches after Atlas. A film of anger coats his eyes. He would call Atlas *Father,* I think. But Atlas does not even care enough about him to explain why Ajax is so unworthy of his respect. It is as if by not knowing the answer already, Ajax does not deserve the answer. "Slag him," I say.

He ignores that. "Remember what I said. Kneel."

"I won't kneel to her," I tell him.

He shrugs. "Do what you like. You might even get away with it. You have a knack for just that."

"Ajax," I call after him as he turns to leave. "It is good to see you. Despite everything."

"Go fuck yourself, Lysander." He flies toward a cruiser off the coast. I scratch my head. He used to be so sweet. I head for Atlas and the bikes.

"What does Atalantia know?" I ask. "If you loved my mother and father like you always say you do, you'll tell me. What were you doing on Mercury?"

"I told you to relax." Atlas looks at me the way I've seen beastmasters look at hunting dogs that don't quite turn out. He shoves the golden bowl from my party into my lap. It is full. "You can carry Tharsus."

A few dozen antelope drink from a small pond. A brilliant yellow streak sprints at them from the cover of nearby brush, and the antelopes bolt. The herd draws dusty trails eastward over the plains, where two more cheetana emerge from the tall grass and herd them north. Then a lithe, dark-skinned woman bounds down the slope, leaving plumes of dust behind her. She draws her bow on the run and seems to fire two shots at once. Both arrows catch a cheetana just as it turns and send it sprawling down to the dry earth.

Sensing they are now the prey, the other two cheetana abandon their hunt and sprint west. It won't matter. Atalantia sets off in pursuit. Her huntmaster, a grizzled Gray with keen falcon-mod eyes, spits and revs his gravBike.

Black and white tents waver atop a nearby plateau, a source of laughter and music. Atalantia invited her closest friends and allies to enjoy the hunt before the summit. Instead of lounging in the tents with them, I start up my own bike, apply my ointment, and fall in with the procession of supplicants to follow the Dictator's hunt west.

Two hours later, I'm sweating like a pig under the North African sun while my betrothed guts the last of her three kills. The Mediterranean might lie just sixty kilometers north, but none of its cool breeze reaches the rocky North African plains. The heat is punishing. The golden bowl is growing hot in the sun and heavy in my hands. Tharsus's head has become very popular with the flies. I'm the last supplicant to have his audience.

After years in the Belt, Earth's gravity is a boot on my being. Atalantia knows it. My shoulders ache, and my blood feels thick as mud. Seemingly unaffected, Atlas squints up at the sky from his place in the shade. At first I think the rangy man is inspecting the siege of Luna in the obscure distance. But no, he's admiring the glint of the Twins of South Pacifica—two elephantine orbital railguns that the Republic scuttled when Diomedes seized them months ago. He feels me watching him and his eyes shift lower to three small gray octagons floating in the blue. WarBastions descending from orbit. They'll be bound for Asia, and then on to join the siege of stubborn South Pacifica. These craft are stamped with Bellona eagles.

I look back at the railguns, and wonder why Atlas shifted his eyes.

The cheetana's double-jointed legs twitch as Atalantia skins it. Trained by her mother to hunt, Atalantia is at home field dressing her kill. She usually prefers hunting in their estates in the Rockies, but those mountains have yet to be pacified. Atalantia tugs off the last of the cheetana's fur and tosses it to a lancer, a surly young Falthe, before opening its gut to heap organs onto the dirt.

Atalantia wears a traditional Carthaginian hunting tunic of turquoise linen and skipper boots. Her godwood bow and golden quiver hang from a knot on the nearby acacia tree, where a male Pink nymphyte cradles a tray of refreshments in his muscular arms.

"The head," Atalantia says.

I bring the bowl forward and open it. She gives Tharsus a glance and makes a small sound of a pleasure before giving it to her houndmaster. "For the dogs."

One of her lancers takes the bowl from me and pours water in it.

"I'll make Africa pristine again," Atalantia says and peers out over the plains and wipes sweat from her brow. "Humans can pollute the other continents. My engineers say it will take two years to remove all the rubble cities. Three to prune the populace. Ten to pick up its trash. I'll make this my home again. Like it was before the disease that is Darrow. New Sparta will become the capital of Earth."

"Who will serve as ArchGovernor?" I ask.

"Scipio au Falthe, of course," she says, sparing a smile for the Falthe lancer. Like most of his kin, the son of Scipio looks made for one thing—frontal assaults. "I'll be busy on Luna." Ajax's meeting me on the tarmac suddenly makes sense. He is not happy here.

"Not Ajax?" I probe.

"No." Her eyes flick to me, dangerous, measuring. "The only forces Ajax controls are the ones I deign to give him. Scipio has seventeen legions, by comparison. After Mercury, I need the muscle. It will take time for my new crop of Grays to mature. I have forty legions back-ordered."

The numbers are so casual and so elite I feel dazed. I have the Praetorian Guard—just over forty thousand—and two more house legions of fifty each. That's it.

After angering House Carthii, Atalantia must bring her other allies closer, especially now that the fate of the dockyards is in question. Earth has barely fallen and already its continents have been divided up between Atalantia and her allies like pieces of a cake. With Earth's populace to replenish her legions, in time her stranglehold on the Core will be insurmountable. I hope Valeria au Carthii is as eager to work with Horatia as she was with me.

"The future for the gens Falthe looks very bright indeed," I say, wary of the small talk.

"As my favorite Roman strawberry once said, 'No friend ever served me, and no enemy ever wronged me, whom I have not repaid in full.'"

"And Ajax? Most would say he's done more to retake Earth than the Falthe. How is he handling the disappointment?"

"Poorly," she admits. "His time will come. But could you imagine a man less fit for the duties of a governor? All passion, no tact. He has none of my ability to multitask. None of Atlas's subtlety and prudence. Or your precocious charm."

She returns to her work and pivots hard to business. "Tomorrow, due to the debacle on Venus, it is necessary to consolidate our holdings. I plan to announce my intent to invade Luna with an Iron Rain built around the Falthe legions—it's what they owe me for the restoration of their lands here on Earth and the governor's chair."

Restoration of their lands. Half of which they stole when they slaughtered the gens Thorne at my grandmother's final gala. "When will this invasion commence?"

"Six months from now."

I laugh, thinking it a jest. It's not. "That long? What about Mars? If Darrow makes it back . . ."

She shrugs. "My lads are hunting him. We'll either kill him in the journey back or hang him on Mars where Nero hanged his Red bitch. I broke his spirit on Mercury. His sun has set."

From anyone else except Atlas, it would sound like bravado. But this is Atalantia, the only person to have actually beaten Darrow in a fair fight.

The cheetana's liver flops out of her hands into the dirt and rolls sideways so that it rests against her boot. From nowhere, flies descend to beset the purplish organ. She looks up at me. "You seem eager for a military action. So, I will give you one that'll make Ajax weep with envy. You will fall on Luna in the vanguard with Scipio and his children, at the head of your Praetorians. You'll get that auctoritas you're so desperate to have."

She's playing up my rivalry with Ajax on purpose, but that's not all she's doing.

"The Rim will be furious with me," I say.

"Yes, and they're already angry with me. You and I are to be united in convenient matrimony, eventually. They should be angry at you too. We must stand as one against our rude kin, or they'll think they can push us around. I thought you'd be pleased." Atalantia pouts. "The Citadel of Light will belong to Gold again. The home of your ancestors. Your shame will be ended in a glorious Rain."

"We should be invading Mars," I say. "That is the logical strategic choice."

"Strategic," she mocks. "Oh, tell me more about *strategy*."

"If we take Mars, the war is over," I say. "Is it not?"

"Atlas, educate this puppy."

"Mars is a Gordian knot," Atlas explains. "Winning orbit will be difficult and costly. The Ecliptic Guard is good. Well equipped. Well led. Julii and both Telemanuses are top notch astral tacticians. As is Oro, their Navarch. Meanwhile, Phobos is nearly impregnable. Without Phobos, a siege of Mars is impossible, leaving a Rain the only option.

"But even then the planet itself is a logistical nightmare for an invader. Mars has far more land surface area than Mercury, yet it doesn't sprawl as on Earth. She is compact, well shielded, with limitless energy and resources, and a hostile populace, which makes a Rain difficult and occupation costly. Not to mention, she's riddled with tunnels which eliminates the prospect of orbital support. I fought in the Rat War. It was my least favorite theater. Ever." He slips a piece of eel into his mouth, swallows it, seemingly without registering its taste.

"It seems they're shorn of most of their best Obsidian veterans," I contend.

"Yes, but when you fight Reds in their own mines . . ." He shakes his head. "Low estimate is two million casualties."

"Two million?"

"In the first month, and that's just the infantry. But if you don't take the mines, they can wage a guerilla war with a full army, and still have a choke hold on their helium supply. I cannot express the level of difficulty this would present."

"I did not say it would be easy. I said it should be done," I reply. "You know how the Rim will react to this news of the invasion of Luna. They'll know you're just using them to wear Mars down as you build your strength."

"I am." She frowns, genuinely perplexed by me. "Lysander, really, what good are allies if you don't use them to make you stronger?"

"What good are allies who just leave and carry a bad taste in their mouth home?" I reply.

"Let them bluster. They're stuck with us and they know it. Time is on our side, Lysander. As Luna cannibalizes itself for want of food, Mars does the same for want of circuits, Blues, nickel, even uranium. All the little things from the Belt and Mercury and Earth that make their fleets run. And I haven't even lifted a finger yet."

She lifts a finger, feigning exhaustion with the effort. Her nymphyte swans forward. The man is no older than twenty, and is the picture of youthful Attican beauty. His olive skin, jet black curls, and pugnacious chin were likely designed by Atalantia herself and carved by one of her best. Atalantia receives the Pink with a kiss and, arms still bloody to the elbow, takes a frosted crystal glass full of a dark liquor from his tray.

"Answer me this, my love. The Rim wants a short war. The Rim wants Mars to fall. So why don't *they* attack the planet and quit dancing about its perimeter?"

"They can't," I say. "Aside from the *Dustmaker* and a few others, they don't have enough heavy ships."

"That's right. They can't. Sure, they're real bastards in asteroid combat and deep space affairs, but when it comes to breaking a planet, it takes tonnage, Newtons, manpower, and a strong stomach—most of your men will die. Why do you think Darrow and I are the only assholes who take planets?

"So the duty of taking Mars would fall to us. More specifically to *me*. To my armada. To my legions. I love my armada. I fucking *love* my legions. I want them to have pensions and live like gods into retirement until they exhaust themselves from slagging and drinking. I will not expend them on Mars just so the vultures can rip me apart and then steal the chair those men earned for me."

She thinks I'm lying in wait for her to exhaust herself, only to steal her chair when games, not battles, are the order of the day. Others are lying in wait, certainly, but I know if I rose that way, my reign would be hollow and crumble soon as someone hit it with an iron fist. She is defensive. Dangerous. I can't sidestep the conversation any longer.

"And so long as Mars is a threat, no one would dare question your power. Except me," I say.

She flips a coin to Atlas. "I thought you wouldn't have the balls to broach that subject."

"I don't know what Atlas has told you or what you've heard, but—"

"Let's not dance around it. Atlas, fetch the dog." Atlas screws closed his canteen and heads for the hound cages. "It's not that I am allergic to dissent, Lysander. In fact, I depend upon the friction with Horatia, the

Reformers, even Lady Bellona at times. I am the first of equals, of peers."
She smirks. "That is, until I am strong enough to drop the pretense and
make them all kneel. My problem is when people reward my generosity
by sticking a dagger in my back."

When Atlas returns it's not with a hound on his leash. Instead, it is a
naked old man. My heart sinks. The man is bald and barefoot on the
hot dirt and sharp grass. His skinny body sags with age and is mottled
with bruises and superficial lacerations. Nausea churns in me as the man
lifts his head and looks up at me with strained Orange eyes.

I thought he was safe in the mountains. How did they find him? I feel
sick.

"Glirastes," I whisper and take a step toward my friend. Atlas draws
him up short of me, jerking his collar so Glirastes must fall to his knees
in the low grass. "What have you done to him?"

Atalantia twitches another finger and a lancer sets down the bowl
that contained Tharsus's head. The blood has mixed with the water the
lancer poured in. She snaps her fingers at Glirastes. "Drink, dog." He
drinks, feverish and thirsty.

"*You* did this to him," Atalantia says. "You and all your scheming.
The entitlement is what's truly appalling. Did you think I'd just let you
walk all over me as long as it was behind my back?"

Grief overcomes me as Glirastes shivers there on his hands and knees.
All the vitality and genius and irascibility in the man is gone, replaced
by a grotesque desperation to reach me. That desperation makes me almost recoil from him even as I yearn to embrace him and tear my hair
out in penance. I had assumed Glirastes was safe on Mercury.

Did they take him right after I left? Was he on the *Styx* during our
journey from Mercury? In a cage while the carver healed my scar? As
Atlas and I dined in silence? Why did the Praetorians not protect him?

"You are useful to me, Lysander," Atalantia says. "You are. A velvet
glove for my iron fist. Useful. But not indispensable.

"This autonomy you've enjoyed . . . it was a gift from me. The breath
in your lungs right now . . . a gift from me. I love you. I do. Since you
were knee high. But I'm done tolerating your insolence. Trying to make
a faction behind my back? You piece of shit."

She slaps me and is on me again before I can recover. She slaps me
again and follows me, slapping me with either hand until I rear back as
if to strike her. Then I see why Ajax told me to go to my knees. Calcula-

tion waits behind her eyes. If I hit her back, I fall from one category into another. If I show too much spirit, I won't leave this desert. Not in one piece, not in control of my own mind.

I release my anger and, as I so often have when I'm with Atalantia, channel my agony into a useful fiction. A few months ago Pytha asked if sleeping with Atalantia whenever she visited bothered me; I told her it didn't, that it sharpened me. I lied. It's the same lie I perpetually tell myself every time she touches me. I loathe the intimacies I allowed Atalantia, and had to allow her even after knowing her hands were covered in the blood of my parents. I hate her almost as much as I hate myself. I feel unworthy of my house and my dreams. My very skin crawls with shame, my eyes grow watery, my face hot. I let my arm fall to my side.

"Either you think I am stupid, or you want to wound me. Do you want to wound me, Lysander?" She slaps me again. "Do you want to wound me?"

"No," I whisper.

She searches my eyes. "Then why send Apollonius's men, you little rat? Why build yourself an army with a man who has sworn to kill me?"

"I'm sorry," I say.

"What? Louder."

"I'm sorry," I say and go to my knees. "Forgive me. I was . . . jealous. Ajax has been gaining one glory after the next. I play governor when others are fighting, dying. When this war is done, all will remember those who fought and those who did not. My reputation is hollow if I'm known for little more than a cavalry charge. I knew you wouldn't let me in on the glory. So, I thought . . . if I had the Dockyards of Venus, if I had the Minotaur, I could attack Mars. Gain glory. Respect. I'm sorry."

Her eyes narrow as she tries to decide if my tears are true. "Are you a Red? Then stand on your feet when you apologize to me."

I stand, slumped with shame. "I apologize for my duplicity."

She searches my eyes. She's a master of the Dancing Mask and the emotional sciences of interrogators, so it is like having an Oracle on my arm. If she sees the hate, if she smells the loathing, if she so much as senses I know she killed my mother and my father, I'll die right here. I embrace the Mind's Eye more quickly than I ever have in my life. I feel only what I want to feel. I hold nothing inside but the false truth.

I pass her examination. Her tone softens. "Shhh," she says, and kisses the pink flesh on my cheek. "Shh." She embraces me, rubbing my back like a mother. "I know. I understand, dear heart. Better than anyone. It was always Aja and Moira that Octavia and my father saw. You feel unseen. It's prime. You've had your tantrum. I hear you. I see you. I will bathe you in glory beyond your wildest dreams. But I need to know I can rely on you."

"You can."

"Can I? I know you value unity. This ongoing flirtation with the Rim. It's beneath you. It is not the Core and Rim that must be united. It is you and me. *We* are the future.

"So tomorrow at the summit I will need a demonstration of fidelity. The Two Hundred chafe at my ascendancy. Their jealousy knows no bounds. They will look to you to oppose me. And what will you do?" She lifts my chin. "You will sit amongst my supporters, silent and stoic in your support. If you make a scene, if you contradict me, if you sow doubt, if you so much as frown, I will skin your Master Maker and make you a pair of Glirastes leather boots." Locusts cackle in the distance. "Now, tell Glirastes you will protect him."

Approaching Glirastes, my artifice cracks. Pity wells in me. He is a miserable sight. His horror-stricken face turns up to me in relief, as if I've already saved him.

"I will protect you," I say, hollow.

A pathetic sob wracks him and he lunges up to embrace me, grateful. I hold his shaking body until Atlas pulls him away and Atalantia takes my hand and steers me to my bike. I watch Glirastes until he disappears back into the cage. Atalantia's boots stand on my heart.

"What House do you think you would have been?" Atalantia asks. "At the Institute? Atlas was Pluto, which is apt. I was Apollo, like a glove." She nudges me with her shoulder. "I hope it would have been Minerva, and you would have been wise. Because if it had been Jupiter, as you seem to want everyone to think, then I'd know to be wary of you. After all, what's more dangerous than a man who believes his cause is just?"

"A woman who believes she is untouchable," I reply.

She smiles, condescending. "Listen, Lysander. I know you. You are too gentle for this game. This game is meant for people like me. I will win it, not because I can do everything, but because I will do *anything*. It's easy for me. Natural. I don't want to win alone. *Alone* is a bore, and boredom . . . well that is where my demons find me. I want you to share my dominion. I want your life to be a beautiful thing. I do. I want them to call you Lysander the Peacemaker. A man to live for two hundred years, and be worshipped for a thousand more. Fair. Noble. Loved. That would be my heart's delight. We can even go beyond this pale little star and found new worlds. Yes, I remember your dreams of childhood. But it is Lysander the Peacemaker I desire. Not Lysander the Conqueror. *I* am the Conqueror."

She backs off, beats her chest twice with her right fist like an Obsidian gladiator, winks, and saunters away to her party.

I am not invited to Atalantia's moonlit gathering on the plateau. The songs of her hired musicians drift over the lands once held by Carthage, and are lost in the wind as my gravBike takes me back to New Sparta.

The air cools when the sun resigns behind the western mountains. Soon, warBastions appear in the distance, then the broken battlewalls of New Sparta. The walls rise into the purpling sky like fractured smoker's teeth. Next to them, like gleaming incisors, stand newly built skyscrapers from which flutter the banners of House Grimmus. Atalantia's construction teams will soon have repaired the damage done to the city by her own assault. She is said to have led that assault in person before dragging the Republic governor out and crucifying him along with his family.

Eight years after Darrow chased the Grimmuses from their ancestral city, they have returned more powerful than when they left.

The citadel my betrothed gave me for the summit is a fantasy. Songbirds sing in rows of freshly planted cherry trees. Marvelous lizards crawl through terraformed lawns and warm themselves in pools. Crimson stags with flowers growing from their antlers flit behind trees sculpted painstakingly by cohorts of Brown botanists and Red gardeners to make the forms of dancers with their boughs and trunks.

It would all be so lovely if I could ignore the sound the wind carries—the piston *thump-thump thump-thump* of boots on the Field of Mars; the groaning, almost whale-like sound of warships passing over the sea; and the screams from the purges down by the wharf.

No friends or Praetorians wait for me at the villa. The numerous servants are Atalantia's, as are the Violet performers who practice in the lawn, and the oiled Pinks who lounge in the harem provided, ironically, for my amusement. They tilt their mouths toward one another's as I pass, willful and coy.

Lavish gifts from my betrothed fill my villa. Carvelings—a pegasus, a leographon that terrifies all but the Obsidian beastmaster holding his chain—wait for me in the yard. There are artifacts too, and weapons, and white and silver armor fit for Silenius himself.

More than ever, I miss the humble asceticism of the Raa and the excited industry of the Votum. I cannot stand to think of how badly I miss my dinners with Glirastes.

When night falls, I sit alone at the dining table set with my untouched dinner. Birds flit around the columns of the grotto and a light rain falls over the sea. A valet appears to announce a visitor. "*Dominus,* the Storm Knight is at the door and requests to join you for dinner, and that the cook prepare more food."

"Tell au Grimmus I'm sleeping," I say. I can't take mockery now.

The valet bows and disappears. There's a bang and a laugh. Ajax enters, stinking of battle and wet fur. So large and rough, in a house so clean and genteel, he seems from another dimension. Tossing his leopard cloak on a chair, he crashes into a seat.

"I don't want to talk," I say.

He twists a jamRing on his finger. A pop censors all noise beyond his bubble. "Didn't come to talk. I came to eat."

He begins his campaign against the food. When he's finished and the servants have carted the remains of two huge salmon away from Ajax, I pour us glasses of wine. He hesitates before drinking. "I'm hardly in a position to poison you, even if I wanted to," I say.

"No, I just promised myself I wouldn't drink this month." He considers the wine. "I killed thirty-one people today. Slag it." He sips and sighs. "So, you kneeled after all."

"How did you know?"

"She gave you my cook." Presumptuous as always, Ajax helps finish the bottle and begins inspecting my gifts. He frowns at a fragile ivory scepter. "I remember when she used to give me presents."

"Have them. You know what she's doing. How insincere it is."

"It's sincere," he says. "That's the problem. Long as I've known her, I've wondered what goes on in that head. It's a world unto itself. Inscrutable from without except by its seasonal weather patterns. For me it's autumn. For you, she wants it to be summer, but you seem intent on making it winter."

"Autumn, eh? The waning season." I watch him for a time. "Do you love her?"

He shrugs. "Don't have to love oxygen to need it." He stands abruptly to fetch more wine. When he returns, he comes back with three bottles, and we migrate to a lower patio set into the cliff. Waves crash against effigies of water dryads that hang off the patio's edge. They crash in silence. Nothing can be heard beyond the jamField.

"She'll have a fit about this," Ajax says, wiggling his jamring. "I'll be punished. Who knows, maybe she'll take the cape from me."

"Do you want that?"

He shrugs and asks, "Who does she have of yours?"

"Glirastes," I murmur, fixed on the soundless waves.

"I'm sorry."

"Are you?"

"It's easier to make me out to be some callous heel, isn't it?" he asks.

"It's your defense mechanism. You tell me. I never know when you're being sincere."

He shrugs, because he knows it's true. The husky, mild-mannered boy lives on only in his mind, in mine, and in Atalantia's. If he can only be made to realize that, how she abuses that boy inside and how I cherish him, maybe I can reclaim him from her. "She will honor her word. You can protect him."

"Do you want Atalantia to sit on the Morning Chair?" I ask him. "Do you believe that is what is best for the Society and its people? Do you think it's best for you?"

"It doesn't matter what I think," he says. "You've both made that clear."

"I think it does."

"Do you?"

I don't answer for a time. Lights glow over the sea. Warships taxi. The Twins of South Pacifica twinkle high above. The guns were scuttled by the garrison when Diomedes seized the orbital station with his Lightning Phalanx, but I have heard rumors that mysterious Rim physanikos, that cabalistic subset of their Orange caste, have been spied studying the structure.

"Are you familiar with the ghost raptors of Varazana?" I ask Ajax. "It's a species of bird on Callisto. There's said to be less than thirty left. Chameleonic feathers, top speeds of two hundred and thirty kilometers per hour. It has a curious trait. If caged, it will maul itself to death with its own talons. Do you know why?"

"I'm sure you'll tell me. I don't read. I train."

"Before her death, Varazana confessed that she designed the bird to have a certain psychology. It was the most perfect thing she'd ever made. And Varazana would rather see it dead than be kept as anyone's pet. It was made to be the emperor of the sky." I sip my wine. "Do you remember when Atalantia came back from her tour of the Rim?"

"I was visiting Mercury with Grandfather, I believe."

"That's right. Sorry. The wine. Well, she brought back pets she captured for her menagerie. Included among them was a solitary ghost raptor. She'd branded out its eyes so it couldn't see it was caged. Octavia was horrified. She had Aja put it down. Said Varazana was right. Some beasts are too noble to be caged."

"Ah," he says. "So, I am a noble bird now? Or are you referring to yourself?"

I shrug, down the rest of my wine, and watch the waves noiselessly thrash upon the rocks below. His hand closes on my shoulder. "Lysander. I know this might not mean much coming from me. But I do not want you to die. I want you to live." He nods to the coastal mansion behind us. "This cage isn't so bad. Is it?"

"She killed my parents, Ajax."

He freezes. His eyes a thousand kilometers away. Then he stands and looks down at me. "She said you'd say that. The problem with loving you two is that you were both meant for the Palatine. I never was. You're both too good at lying."

He departs.

16

LYSANDER

The Two Hundred

S UN BAKES THE TRANQUIL parklands around the Roman ruins, but
it is cool in the shade of the Colosseum. The morning events at Atalantia's summit of the Two Hundred had started with summer showers,
floral tea, handshakes, and power politics in the restored Temple of Hercules Victor. There, I was able to sneak a moment with Horatia alone
to tell her what must be done. With the Irons watching us, she hastily
confirmed the dockyards deal I teased to Valeria is already complete.
She flashed me a holocube and we drifted our separate ways. Then, after
the subsequent breakfast at the Temple of Juno, the heads of the Gold
houses made their ritual procession to the Colosseum for the main event.
By then the skies had cleared and a lazy warm wind was already rolling
in from the Italian interior.

The outside of the Colosseum gleams white. A golden awning has
been erected over the top. The inside of the Colosseum has also been
refurbished for gladiatorial games Atalantia plans to host. But today in
place of the fighting sands, Atalantia has laid down travertine marble.
Marble risers for the Two Hundred sit beneath the actual viewing stands
and lie in a U-shape at the north end. When one stands on the rostrum—
an iron triangle on the floor—to speak, the Irons are to their left, the
Moderates directly ahead, the Reformers to their right, the Rim delegation even further to the right, and the black chair of the Dictator on the
floor about fifteen meters in front of the rostrum.

After taking our seats, we heard a briefing regarding the Ascomanni
warlord Volsung Fá's raids on Republic strongholds in the asteroid belt—

a welcome consequence of the Republic's chaotic internal divides. I sit listening amongst Atalantia's hardliners, the diamond in her Iron tiara.

After the briefing, Cornelius au Carthii assumes the rostrum. Cornelius, a loquacious and handsome man, uses all of his oratorial prowess to bemoan the injustice of the conflict still raging on the Dockyards of Venus, indict the scurrilous character of Apollonius, and extol the virtue of his family's show of arms even while begging the Two Hundred to help them defeat a numerically inferior foe: *With millions of men under arms, we Carthii will not lose, but Apollonius is cementing his place in the pantheon of premier field commanders by ripping the men we send against him to bloody shreds. Surely ship production is a common cause! Surely property rights still matter! The truth is plain as day to everyone listening. Those docks were built by us, kept by us, they are ours, but needed for the common good.* Cornelius surrenders the rostrum with a plea for unity and respect for law and order. The irony of these sentiments coming from a haughty Carthii is reflected in the little smiles shared around the room.

The Falthe sitting next to me in the Irons leans over with a whisper of contempt. "The Carthii stuck their perfumed hand in the Minotaur's mouth, and he's dragging their whole house into his labyrinth bit by bloody bit. Hilarious."

I give him a slight smile and sigh at Cornelius's impending political decapitation. What's that old maxim? Be wary of tyrants: they will help you today and own you tomorrow.

Atalantia doesn't even need to rise from her black chair of office to ruin Cornelius's life and demote one of the great houses of the Conquering to a middling power. "Cornelius, you could not be more correct. Ship production is crucial to the functioning of this state. A vote will only delay decisive action, and decisive action is needed. Therefore, I have personally dispatched ten legions to deal with this threat to the Society. I will bear all costs and all risks. Cornelius, tell your father, Asmodeus, to worry not. The dockyards will soon be in safe hands."

Cornelius and his siblings pale. By month's end, their six-hundred-year-old family heirloom will belong to Atalantia—exactly the fate I helped Heliopolis to avoid. The fools can't even challenge Atalantia's jurisdiction. They handed their inheritance to her on a platter.

"No gratitude for au Grimmus's generosity?" Scipio au Falthe asks Cornelius from amongst his phalanx of hard-bitten siblings.

Cornelius eats the mouthful of shit, swallows, and thanks Atalantia for it. Her Iron bloc snickers. The Reformers purse their lips. The Rim deputation look at each other, smug at the comparative dignity of their Moon Council.

"Julia, who is next on the docket?" Atalantia asks.

"Storm Knight of the Rim Dominion, the rostrum is yours," Julia calls.

Diomedes au Raa stands from his place between his mother, Dido, and his mentor, Helios, and trudges up to the rostrum. He begins without preamble and delivers the butcher's bill for the last two months of warfare with his head lowered like a ram.

Diomedes is not a very good public speaker. Thicker than most of his colleagues from a life of high-gravity training, it's obvious what the Raa heir was made to do, and it wasn't to stand at a rostrum and sway hearts and minds. Politics and rhetoric were supposed to have been the destiny of Diomedes's brother, Aeneas. Diomedes's destiny was to be his family's fist. When Aeneas died at the Battle of Ilium fighting many of the men and women who now recline in the shade above Diomedes, Diomedes was thrust toward a future he neither expected nor wanted.

Then his father, Romulus, died too and he became heir to a legacy seven hundred and fifty years old. Great expectations follow Diomedes. Chafing at that—and at the sophisticated airs of his audience—his words come like bullets.

From under heavy brows his eyes glare accusations searing enough to set togas on fire. When he finishes his report, he scowls up at Atalantia and her Iron bloc hardliners as if they, not the Republic, were responsible for the casualties. I am not spared his ire. After our talk in the theater, he does not appreciate my seating arrangement. He will see it as a grotesque hypocrisy. If I thought I saw an ally in him in the theater based on his embarrassment at Helios's manners, it is confirmed by his obvious disappointment in me. Like all other Core Golds, I say one thing and do another. Snipe at Atalantia, sit in her section.

I glance at Horatia, who sits with the smaller Reformer bloc, and feel nauseated.

Diomedes does not surrender the rostrum as he should. He remains on the iron triangle in the center of the marble floor, glaring at Atalantia. She watches back from her chair of office. As does Ajax from his place with the Olympics on the wings of the speaking floor. And so do the hooded crows in the circular gap in the awning's center high above.

Atalantia cocks her head in amusement.

"Diomedes. First to storm the Twin railguns. Then on to Earth to take the Middle East from the Red Sea to the Black. Then to Ceres, and the Belt, then all the way back to Earth. By Jove, young dragon, you've the wings of Hermes on your boots." Atalantia pauses, smiles. "This must be the longest you've remained rooted to one spot since you arrived."

The laughter is not limited to Atalantia's bloc. It spreads into the more populous moderates in the center, where even Julia au Bellona smiles at Diomedes's expense. The Reformers to Diomedes's right, by far the minority, think the joke in poor taste.

I catch Horatia's eye. She gives me three quick blinks, our signal. After our talk at Hercules Victor, she made her move at the Temple of Juno. Everything is prepared. My nausea deepens as I think of Glirastes curled on the floor of a dog kennel, waiting to see if I love him as much as he loves me.

Dido parts from her fellow consul, Helios, and replaces her son on the rostrum. It's good Helios is not speaking. After a preview of his manners in Heliopolis, the last thing we need is our own Day of Red Doves. Dido is a profoundly handsome woman with charisma to spare. Strong features, penetrating eyes filled with mischief, thick hair of dark gold, and—peculiar for a consul of the Rim—she is bawdy, jocular, even funny. But it's her temper that's always been her liability.

"Atalantia, I can speak for us all when I say your boots are horribly lovely." Atalantia's boots are as marvelous as they are obnoxious. Black leather from a stygian cobra encrusted with great diamond skulls. "Yet, I swore war was in fashion. Not diamonds."

Atalantia looks suddenly far less bored than when Cornelius held the rostrum. She doesn't miss a beat. "The skulls started as carbon. Perhaps it is the pressure of carrying the war that has made them diamonds. Go on then, au Saud—oh, excuse me, au Raa. Lecture us as if you're the one that's been fighting the Rising for what . . . twelve years now, while we've been hiding behind our moat." She smiles. "You paid a dear price to enter this war. How strange to flinch at casualties now."

The room winces. The casualty of which Atalantia so casually speaks was Dido's husband, who chose to die both in protest of the war, and because he hid evidence of Darrow's destruction of the Dockyards of Ganymede from the Moon Lords, in violation of his honor. The same Romulus famous for his passionate, fairy-tale love for Dido. Who died, in the end, because Dido pressed for war.

"I hear young Seraphina was a virtuosic fighter and a credit to her father and her mother, and her people as a whole," Atalantia says in reference to Dido's daughter, who died in the fighting on Mercury. I saw her simply disappear when a rail slug hit her.

Technically, *she* was the Rim's first casualty. The Colosseum goes dead silent.

I've seen razor duels with less tension.

Dido sighs, and I wonder if her opening taunt was bait to lure this disproportionate response from Atalantia. I think it was. At the price of much hardship, Dido has gained an air of wisdom and gravitas. And by choosing to ignore Atalantia's insults, she now seems the true statesman of the two, which Atalantia doesn't seem to mind.

Dido continues. "We should not forget the great peoples we few here represent. Billions wait for us to sort the troubles that disturb our age. Time and again, you have preached a message of unity, au Grimmus. Promises of aid against the Ecliptic Guard. Promises of aid in the asteroid belt. Promises of aid in the matter of Ceres.

"Then what of that aid? What of that unity? I saw here today with my own eyes how quick you are to dispatch legions to deal with your own troubles. But what of our shared troubles? Time and again, au Grimmus, we have extended our hand only to be left grasping at air. Did we not aid you in liberating Earth? Did we not conquer Ceres upon your request? So why are your boots still stuck in the mud when it comes to the matter most dear to us?

"As you rebuild your cities, stack your spoils, polish your boots, the rest of us—fewer in bodies, poorer in monies—suffer to pay the bill. We are left to wonder why this is. Poor communication? Hidden agendas? Greed? Laziness? Or perhaps it is simply that habit has taught the leaders of the Core that Rim lives are expendable.

"That was true once—when the Rim was shackled to the Society. It is no longer true. Instead, what is true is that you need us. What is true is that we are not your vassals. We do not jump when you say jump. We do not die when you say die. But we will leave this alliance if you persist in this . . . obstinacy . . . this . . . disrespect and brinksmanship against those you profess to be your allies."

Scipio au Falthe calls out. "The honorable consul of the Dominion is quite correct. How selfish of us to rebuild our cities. If only we could be more like the Dominion, and not have to rebuild a single one."

A Reformer next to Horatia fires back. "If only the honorable Falthe did not think all cities should be pounded to a fine dust, we might not have to rebuild anything but the trust of the people in us!"

A general firefight ensues.

The Senate was never as solemn in closed sessions as it pretended to be to the public. Neither is the Two Hundred. Formed around the same rules, the Senate and the Two Hundred have the same manners. In both bodies, beings with genius-level intellects are reduced to hollering like gladiatorial crowds in some asteroid backwater, shaking performative fists, reeling back in indignation, and sharpening rhetorical harpoons to thrust into an adversary or draw a smile from their patron.

The commotion only quiets when Julia au Bellona, the Princeps Senatus, stands and hammers her pyramid-tipped staff of office on her riser. As the leader of the Two Hundred, Julia keeps its rules and, along with the Olympic Knights, enforces them. "We're already an hour behind the day's schedule. If the esteemed Dictator does not remind her friends that we are not baying coyotes, but Peerless Scarred, I will skip the lunch recess and fine every member responsible for my low blood sugar. Yes, that includes you, Scipio. Quit blathering and let the woman talk. You might have more legions than hair follicles, but she has the floor."

Atalantia flicks a finger and her bloc quiets. Dido carries on.

"The agreement made between your government and mine when we entered this war was that Mars would be the main military target. That Luna—that seat of tyranny—would be your responsibility to reclaim. Not ours. You agreed to these terms, Atalantia. You signed these terms, Atalantia. And yet every time we request to begin the campaign against Mars, you . . . prevaricate."

A shadow cast by something above wags on the floor in front of her. I follow her eyes up to the gap in the awning where Atlas sits far above the summit, legs dangling off a support strut. The crows perched up there don't seem to mind him one bit.

Dido is flustered by the unexpected appearance of her brother-in-law, but not for long.

"What am I to tell the mothers and fathers of the Rim that their children died for, Atalantia? What am I to tell the Gray and Blue archons their caste members died for, Atalantia? As this war drags on, what excuse shall I give? We did not attack Mars because your friends were too busy shoring up their own domains? We did not attack Mars because you had to rebuild your capitals and your pet fiancé must host games while we did the dying?" Dido's eyes meet mine. She does not veil her disgust with my place in Atalantia's bloc. "That we were used by the Core and then tossed away like a street tramp?

"Time and again, you preach a message of unity, au Grimmus. Today you have an opportunity to prove that Core Golds keep their word. Together, we have the ships. Together, we have the legions. Declare the campaign for Mars and let us finish the Rising once and for all." She looks at the most famous isolationist in the room, Helios, and gives a hard nod to show their unity. "If you do not, then you must not need us, and we will have no choice but to assume this alliance dissolved and sail back to our own worlds."

Dido returns to her seat beside her son to strong applause from Horatia and the Reformers.

"That concludes the Rim deputation's time," Julia says. Atalantia begins to stand. "Not yet. Protocol, Atalantia. You know the floor must first be open to the body."

"Thank Jupiter we have you, Julia. I'm always in such a rush to just get things done." Atalantia swans back down. If anyone wants to waste their breath advocating for the Rim, now is the time. No one dares. Not even the Reformers. That is a crucial part of the theater Horatia has arranged.

Atalantia takes one of the asps slithering around the arms of her chair of office and dons it like jewelry. She doesn't once spare me a glance to see if I intend to speak, secure in her conviction that I don't have the stomach to consign Glirastes to death. Seated down with the other Olympic Knights, Ajax looks relieved. He offers me a smile of conciliation. He knows defeat only too well.

As the silence stretches, it becomes awkward, and then oppressive. More and more people begin to look around. I can sense there are others like me out there—those who chafe under Atalantia's yoke—but she's silenced some of them. Those she has not silenced, Horatia has silenced. Many of the house heads who know my true opinion on the matter look at me and wonder why I do not speak. But most of them, while powerful, are fence-sitters, not deeming the matter worth the risk one way or the other.

Still, the fence-sitters would have expected me to lend my opinion. I have been very vocal for this very reason. My silence would not have mattered in a room filled with remonstrations from the Reformers, but now it thunders.

The venom drains out of the looks from Diomedes and Dido as they begin to construct their own narrative for the room's silence. I improvise a little and flick my eyes up to Atlas. Just for a half second. Several dozen people see, and look. Helios is one of them. Then more look at Atlas. Then half the assembly is looking up to the gap in the awning at the man hanging over the silence like the Sword of Damocles.

It is a perfect answer as to the nature of the silence that grips the assembly. It seems to all as if everyone else has been cowed into silence.

Atalantia turns to look at me with a puzzled expression, but I remain the picture of fidelity to her. She squints around the room. "Nothing from you, Horatia? No quibbling from your morally august flock?" Horatia plays it up by looking down. Atalantia is starting to get angry. Like she said, she depends on dissent. Subjugation is not a good look in a crowd as pathologically competitive as this. A dictator is the highest peer, but a peer still. She looks like a sovereign. Worse. A queen.

"Quiet bunch today, Julia. May I speak now?" Atalantia asks. Julia waves her on.

Atalantia uncoils herself from her black chair of office to give what all have come for—her plan for the next stage of the war.

"My noble counterpart from the Rim speaks with wisdom hard learned. Yes. Dido," she says, clutching at her own heart, "I feel your anger. Your rage for Mars. The flames lick my heart as they licked my father's skin when Darrow and Apollonius burned him in his bed. But . . . we cannot run from hard truths. My friends, the hard truths are what we must address today.

"I hope it steels your heart to know that I concur. Yes! A Rain must fall on Mars!" Her supporters thump their benches all around me. I abstain. "The Ecliptic Guard must be smashed! Augustus rooted out from her father's old den. Julii pulled down from her moon roost. Every traitor must be tried and hanged! Their slingBlades beaten into collars! Agea stormed! The helium liberated! But . . ." she says amongst the cheers of her supporters. "But . . . the hard truth is if you turn your back on a wild boar to kill the lion, the only thing you'll bring home is a tusk through your thigh. That is why, yes! Yes. Mars must fall. And after Luna, she will."

Her supporters fill the Colosseum with a roar of support that sends the crows in the attico scattering. Alone now in the high perch, Atlas catches me watching him. He tilts his head.

"Which is why . . . Which is why!" The cheers quiet as Atalantia lifts her hand. "I have accepted Lysander au Lune's petition to lead the vanguard of the Luna Rain along with the legions of the gens Falthe . . . six months from now! So that when Luna is reclaimed and the Society restored, there will be once again a Lune upon the Palatine!"

Her hardliners applaud me and turn to shake my hand. Diomedes has had enough. He stomps down to the speaking floor and stalks out. If they'd planned to stage a walkout, Dido or Helios should have been the one leading it. Nonetheless, they nod to the others and begin to follow the Storm Knight out.

My dreams of a united Society will burn before my eyes if I stay seated.

I clock Horatia. She nods.

Now is the moment. All is arranged.

When he sees what I am about to do, fear grips Ajax. He steps forward from his station with the Olympics, his hand outstretched, imploring me to stay safe on my knees in Atalantia's cage with him. Instead, I stand.

17

LYSANDER

Mars Must Fall

"WHERE HAVE ALL THE shepherds gone?" I shout. Atalantia turns with all the members of the Iron bloc to stare at me. Ajax looks at the ground, already mourning me. I push my way through them down to the floor. Diomedes has stopped halfway out the exit. "The Diomedes I know does not run from a fight," I call. "If you gave up so easily in the field, Earth would still be in the Republic's hands. Stay. Hear me speak."

"Why should I listen to anything you have to say?" Diomedes calls back. "Palatine serpent. All can see where you sit."

"Do you seek to aid Virginia?" I turn on his mother and the rest of their deputation before scouring the risers. "Gold infighting with Gold. Is that not how we arrived here? How Darrow shattered our hold on the spheres? Why the Dockyards of Venus now rattle with civil strife? We allowed our enemy to divide us before. Bellona against Augustus! Rim against Core! We are victims of our own bickering. We're doing it all over again! *Vox clamantis in deserto!* Can none of you see it? This. Is. How. We. Fall."

"Lune boy. You do not have the floor," Lady Bellona calls to me, mocking. "You like games, yes. Games have rules, so do we. Sit down. Mind your manners."

"I invoke my right of interjection," I say. "It is my due as a direct descendent of a Conqueror."

"At least you remember the archaic rules. You'll know then that you will need thirty members to validate your interjection."

"Forgive him, Julia," Atalantia calls. "Lysander found his way to a cup and lost his wits on the journey. His youthful passion is usually such a virtue, but this is his first summit. It's all so very exciting for him."

Many laugh at me, and not just the Irons.

"Drown with laughter that which you cannot retort, how gauche," I reply. "Do I have thirty members?" Horatia and her entire bloc raise their hands, as I asked her to arrange earlier in the morning. "Princeps Senatus, I have thirty members. I'll wait while you count."

I earn a few laughs. The Moonies are more than a little mystified by the theatrical style of our politics. Dido nods to Helios. They don't retake their seats, but they wait. Julia makes a show of counting and sighs as if it's out of her hands. "He's right, Atalantia."

"Oh, fuck off," Atalantia mutters.

"You fuck off. On what grounds do you interject, young man?"

"On the grounds of conscience," I declare.

"Conscience?" Atalantia laughs. So does her bloc, but the laughter is forced.

"There is precedent. First cited by Akari in 5 PCE," I say. That one was for the Rim. A smile starts to grow on Dido's face.

A student of history herself, Julia rolls her eyes again. "Hilarious. Very well. The body recognizes the interjection. The pyramid is yours. Dictator, please return to your seat. You may continue your speech after the interjection is finished."

"No," Atalantia says. "It is my floor. The opportunity for discussion has passed. Go back to your seat, boy."

"Au Grimmus, what am I holding?" Lady Bellona wiggles her staff of office. "You may be Dictator, but I remind you that the authority that makes you so is that of this body, the same authority that makes me the Princeps Senatus, and the same authority by which you summoned young Lune with the Iron Fist and sent legions to Venus. You control the state fleet, the state armies. I control the state floor. It is important we remember our laws. They are meant to protect us from ourselves after all. Did not Lysander honor the law in obeying your summons, at great inconvenience to himself, considering his games were only in their infancy? Should you not follow his precedent?"

Julia is a menace when she cares to be. By law, she holds imperium here, though no one really believes the Olympic Knights are her policemen today. Not all the knights are Atalantia's creatures, but if it came to trouble it's common consensus that Ajax counts as four.

Still, if it comes to blades, I've failed miserably.

Gauging the mood of the Two Hundred, Atalantia surrenders the floor. "House Jupiter after all. Such a pity," she says as she passes me and shakes her head at Ajax as if she tried her best with me. Already she draws him closer again.

When Atalantia settles in her seat, I let the silence stretch and fight back the thoughts of Glirastes. I was raised on the rhetoric of Cicero and Demosthenes, but it is Silenius I channel now. Humility first.

"Why should you listen to me?" I ask and meet their eyes one by one. "Why indeed? Diomedes was not wrong to ask the question. I have not shared the horrors of these last years with you. I have not stood shoulder to shoulder with you to hold back the Rising. I have heard it said that I am a traitor. That I renounced Gold to lie with the wolves. I have been called a shadow of my predecessors, a Palatine buzzard returned for the easy spoils—"

"Catamite! Don't forget catamite!" an Iron shouts.

Ajax turns on the man, and the man leans back as if suddenly seeing a tiger staring back at him from an otherwise pleasant glade. Atalantia's eyes twitch toward Ajax, calculating.

I laugh. "Catamite as well. Why not? Words, like weapons and laughter, can be used to silence a voice. I heard a great silence here today. Seated in the shadow of our Dictator, I felt that silence in myself, and I would remain sitting, trusting in our Dictator, had my shame not been too much for my conscience to bear.

"Since my return, I have sought to put the welfare of the Society above all other concerns, including my own. I have asked neither for remuneration nor the return of my personal property. The ships, the legions, the bases, the reserves, I gladly give to the war effort. Instead, I have put myself in debt rebuilding the planet Mercury. I have used my name, such as it stands, not to win territory or glory, but to make peace where it can be made. I have urged conciliation between Rim and Core, between Atalantia and Apollonius, between the loyal people of Mercury and those citizens lost enough to believe Darrow's Noble Lie. I seek that same object today: peace and the welfare of our Society.

"When I was a child, I was asked by my Sovereign what the Society meant to me. I answered then as I would answer now. The Society is a light in the darkness. My Sovereign then asked me what Gold means to me. Knowing my own opinion meant very little, I echoed the words of our greatest hero, Silenius the Lightbringer. I told her that we are those who tend the flame and shepherd the human flock. But the more I look around, I wonder: where have all the shepherds gone? In their place, I see only wolves and sheep."

Atalantia's lips twitch. Togas shuffle.

"My august friends, it is my belief that in our war to combat the demons of our Society, we have fallen prey to our own internal demons. We have been at war so long that we have forgotten not only the purpose of war but our own purpose. Where once we measured our virtues by our sacrifices, by our civic accomplishments, by the expansion of habitability to even the coldest spheres, we now measure them in the quantity of enemy ships vanquished, in the quality of the names notched on our razors, in the gross tonnage of enemy equipment destroyed, and the length of the roads we pave with the bodies of dead rebels. I contend these are not measurements of virtue at all. Even less are they measurements of progress. They measure only our will. But our will for what? What!

"Did Silenius and Akari love war? Did they use war to line their own purses, to vent their rage against the ungrateful masses? Or did they wage war to sculpt the chaos natural in humanity into a future of order and prosperity? Our sacred ancestors knew what we have forgotten: that peace, not war, is our sacred calling. That we were to lead by our example, not to be led by our greed, our hunger for power. I look around, and I am humbled by your acts of valor and sacrifice, but we are no longer a people united by our sacrifice or by our convictions. We are united only in our propensity for self-interest, infighting, and greed.

"Let us call out our great worry: that it is only our enemy who unites us. But what then when our enemy is vanquished? That is the question that haunts us, is it not?" I fling my hand at Dido. "That is what the Rim consul wonders. That is why our Dictator withholds our forces. Why we all look past this war. Because we know the next one hangs over our heads, like the Sword of Damocles, restrained by a single thread." I look up at Atlas, and so do many others. "If we cannot find common ground today, in two years it will not be the Rising against the Society. It will be Core against Rim. Perhaps even sooner than that."

No one speaks. It has always been the elephant in the room, the Rim's greatest fear before they entered the war, why they are held hostage by this delay, this obfuscation, this impasse. Diomedes slowly makes his way back to the Rim deputation. Helios and Dido are paying rapt attention, but they are not my audience today. I scour the Two Hundred with angry eyes.

"Are we so ridiculous to invite another war upon ourselves? Have we forgotten the promise of Gold to our people? They cry out for peace, for stability, the rewards for the sacrifice of their liberty. They are due those rewards, for they have sacrificed. If we are too afraid of each other to find common ground, by what logic should they follow us? What hope do we give them? What legacy do we give our children except might makes right? What inheritance do we leave behind except war after war until the flame of mankind shrinks into the uncaring dark?

"Whether you respect me or revile me, you must admit we face a choice today. Not as Rim or Core, but as a people. Do we believe that Gold should continue this internal game of self-interest and self-destruction to benefit a few of us, or do we make the choice that Silenius and Akari would have made? Do we reclaim our moral imperative, and choose to work together to remind the billions who look to us for guidance that not only can we lead, but we *will* lead them into a brighter future? It is a choice too important for one person to make for us all."

I turn to Atalantia. If looks could kill, the maggots would already own my flesh. I soften my voice, imbuing it with the respect her campaign deserves.

"Atalantia, I look at you and see a great general of her people. In our hour of desperation, we appointed you with unprecedented powers. With them you have led us through our darkest days. Truly your name will stand beside Akari and Silenius." I sigh, apologetic. "Yet, I cannot agree with your proposed course of action—knowing it will sever us from our brothers and sisters in the Rim, knowing it will permit Virginia to devise new schemes for our destruction, knowing that this war will not end with the reconquering of Luna. It will only end with the reconquering of Mars."

I meet the eyes of the Two Hundred, one by one, lighting in them the same fire I feel building in me. Horatia is incandescent amidst her Reformers. The Falthe are stewing. Julia is examining every face in the room. Ajax watches his father above. His hand does not rest on his razor, but the leather thong of his holster is open.

"Atalantia, you have offered me a gift without equal: the reclamation of my homeland, my family seat. I must be a fool to demur, but I hope I will be mocked as an honorable fool who values the stability of the spheres over my own interests. I cannot accept this gift, not if it comes at the cost of this alliance. I cannot! I will not. My conscience demands better from me than self-interest. My Color demands more from me than silence. Mars must fall!" I shout it again. "Mars must fall! That is why I urge this sacred body—which represents our greatest minds, warriors, and voices of our people—to exercise its rights and vote to veto the Dictator's decision to strike at Luna and instead favor a resolution to assemble an armada and join our Rim brethren to end this war where it began: Mars."

For the first time in my speech, I look dead on at Julia. "We have the will to fight our enemy, let us have the courage, *the guts,* to trust one another. Only then can we show our enemies, our people, *ourselves,* that when Gold is indivisible, Gold is invincible."

The silence that follows feels like death, but that is all well and good. The punch line's on its way. "And I suppose you would like to lead this campaign against Mars?" Atalantia asks. "Self-interest be damned indeed."

"No."

"No interest in that glory at all?"

"No. Though my heart yearns to prove itself, I am not yet experienced enough to lead such an army as Mars will require. There is only one man amongst us fit for the task. One man who can make Mars tremble with fear and wake the hearts of our fighting men and women. That is why I nominate the greatest field commander of our time." They frown, not sure who could possibly fit that bill. I lift my fingers in the horns of the Minotaur.

The action ignites a wildfire of dissent and opprobrium.

Julia has to hammer her staff for quiet.

Atalantia laughs. "Unfortunately, the madman has raised arms against the Society. He is cornered by Asmodeus's army. My own ships are four days away. When they arrive, they will extinguish House Rath forever."

"Your ships will not be needed," I say. "I have already made peace." I extend a hand toward Horatia. "Au Votum."

Horatia stands. "As we speak, my brother, Cicero, leads our fleet toward Venus. They will arrive in four hours. In the name of Lysander the Peacemaker, my brother has helped broker a ceasefire between House Carthii and House Rath. Apollonius will vacate the docks and turn them over to their rightful owners, House Carthii. The deal was struck not six hours ago."

Atalantia whirls on the Carthii. "Cornelius, what is this?"

The Carthii stares at her in confusion. "My father would never agree to this—"

Horatia holds up a holocube. "I have in my possession a message from au Rath and the head of House Carthii." Julia motions Horatia down and sends Ajax to collect and deploy the message.

Apollonius blooms into the room, three times his natural size. Only his hair is groomed. The rest of him is a testament to his frontline heroics. His left arm is broken, his right ear missing, his face covered with burns and shallow lacerations. His eyes glow with triumph.

But it is his companion who draws gasps. Valeria au Carthii stands beside Apollonius with a somber expression and speaks. "*Salve, fellow Aureates. No doubt you have watched this battle between our houses with much consternation and fear of the risk to this critical infrastructure. Too much blood has been spilled. I have lost brothers, a sister, legions, and a father in this battle.*" Murmurs rise. Her siblings stand in a panic. "*Yes, a father.*

"*I regret to inform you that my great father, Asmodeus, fell yesterday. He died like a Peerless, on the field of battle with the mortal wound in his front. With great loss comes reflection. My father's slights against au Rath were not imagined. Indeed, my father betrayed au Rath to the Republic seven years ago. Though there is a temptation to seek revenge, au Lune recalled to me on Mercury the words of Lorn au Arcos.* Death begets death begets death . . .

"*Now is not the time for blood feuds. Now is the time for unity. Thanks to Lysander and his proxy, Cicero, au Rath and I have agreed to terms. My house legions have sworn themselves to me. The dockyards are now under my control. Restoration and production begin tomorrow. Goodmen, the hatchet is buried. Goodladies, the feud is done. Our mission is too important. Mars must fall.*"

Valeria said all that needed to be said with none of her usual flair. It is the perfect tone for the next administrator of the dockyards to strike. Apollonius also has a new tone suitable for this venture—as I requested, he's reduced his grandiloquence.

"*Gratitude, au Votum. My noble kin. For too long have I been cast from your favor and the fray. My eyes have been fixed on civil enemies only to forget the wily instigator that set us at each other's throats. This . . . conflagration over Venus was nothing but another device of the devil who plagues us all. Darrow, and his wicked little henchman too. Barca.*

"It was Darrow who attacked the docks with atomics, as many of you know. It was Darrow who sparked this battle. It is Darrow who has fled me, laughing at the chaos in his wake. No more. You call me madman. You call me black sheep. I care not. My legions board my crafts of war. We sail on Mars to reclaim our homeland. We sail with Votum, with Lune. Join us. For Mars must fall."

Their images shrink back into the holocube in Ajax's palm.

Horatia thrusts up her fingers in the horns. "Mars must fall!"

The Reformers surge to their feet and join the chorus. But it's not just them. Apollonius has friends, admirers, and they burst to their feet with the horns uplifted, roaring his name in a battlefield frenzy. I turn to look at Diomedes and raise an eyebrow. Not one member of their deputation has so much as moved. He leans to whisper into his mother's ear. She smirks, tongues her molars, stands, and lifts her blade. Then so does Helios.

As soon as they do, Julia au Bellona stands. With a glance for me, she sets her hand on her stomach, smiles, raises her other hand, and makes the horns. Her clients and friends burst to their feet and carry on the chorus until only Atalantia and her bloc remain seated. The majority is with me, and then some.

Atalantia has not moved. With a sigh, she waits for the uproar to die down.

"My ears are open, and I hear you," she allows. "Your passions have been awoken. If you must forsake prudence to act on them, it is your right. But you understand, I cannot abandon the strategy that has brought us to the brink of victory: my own. I will maintain the siege of Luna with my fleet, and I wish you all well on this . . . escapade. For all our sakes, I pray Lysander is as gifted on the field of battle as he is on the speaking floor. Good luck, my friends." Her eyes twinkle in amusement. "If Luna falls before Mars, perhaps I'll come and join you."

She stands from her chair and strides in my direction. Horatia and a few of her Reformers intercept her. Atalantia snaps her fingers and five Olympics rush to her in a moment, including Ajax. Knowing she wouldn't risk a bald-faced assassination of me now, I have the Reformers let Atalantia through. Her anger is buried beneath a proud smile. "Truly, my beloved, I didn't think you had it in you. My fault for always believing the best in people."

"My mother and father send their tidings," I reply.

Ajax stiffens and turns to look at Atalantia. She does not show any signs of guilt, but whatever he sees on her face makes his eyelids twitch. She's too focused on me to notice.

Atalantia licks her incisors. "Kalindora?"

"Kalindora," I say.

"Quite the liar that one." She sighs. "I'll send you your new boots. Oranges make fine leather."

Whistling for her Olympics to follow, she heads for the exit, stopping only when she notices that Ajax has not fallen in behind her. She turns back and cocks her head at him. He looks back and forth between us, and then lifts his fingers in the horns. She lets out a small laugh of surprise mingled with disgust before turning her gaze on me. "Don't let Glirastes's death haunt you, Lysander. Now that you're in the game, he won't be the last friend you sacrifice."

Atalantia strides out trailing Olympics and Irons.

I look over at Ajax and grip his shoulder. He gives me a hard nod, then we both look up to the top of the Colosseum, where Atlas watches us for a moment from his perch before flying away on his skipBoots, as silently as the crows who left before.

18

VIRGINIA

The Returned

VICTRA'S WAR SHUTTLE SQUATS in my reserved spot on the executive tarmac outside the Citadel of Agea. Muttering aspersions, I jump out the side of my own shuttle before it even sets down, and sprint for the Citadel.

Removed from the rest of Mars's capital, the grounds are quiet. On the other side of the lake looms a battered Votum torchShip. It only just cleared orbital security to land. I spare it a glance and cut through the gardens, moving so fast Holiday and my Lionguards struggle to keep up. Their boots and capes trail red dirt from my tour of the bunker construction sites in the deepmines of Cimmeria.

Birds scatter as we rush along the white cobbled stone path. Pale treelynxes stare down wondering at our hurry and go back to licking their paws. I burst into the executive wing's side entrance. Virgilus, a Lionguard centurion, greets me with a grin. "Where are they?" I demand.

"Executive lounge."

I sprint through the network of halls past more smiling guards until I reach the godTree doors. I catch my breath, straighten my jacket, and Holiday opens the door for me. When I enter, four bedraggled, semi-emaciated strangers turn to look at me. I feel an urge to cry when I realize they aren't strangers at all: they are dear friends and colleagues. War has made them ashen and leeched the light and softness from their skin and eyes.

While they are more Darrow's friends than mine, it would be difficult to find four people more worthy of my trust and respect than these: Harnassus, the steady, soulful commander of the Free Legions' engineers and the loyal doubter my husband always needed. Screwface, a Howler who wore the cloak only weeks before I first did, and was always my favorite of the original pack though I don't think he ever knew it. Thraxa, the Telemanus sister who taught me to box when we were girls in New Zealand together and is like a sister—as much as a bulldog can be a sister. And Colloway Char, Darrow's virtuosic pilot and darling of the masses, media, and single persons everywhere.

Holiday shuts the door behind me.

They were sitting at a table eating. They scramble up and snap to attention to salute me. "Slag that," I say and rush to embrace Thraxa. Her hand sledgehammers my back. Not being as personally acquainted with Harnassus or Colloway, our embraces are more formal. I soften the most for Screwface. I saved him for last so I could spend the most time on him. He was my school friend, but I know he always worried he was a hanger-on. He looks nervous, ashamed of the brutality that has been done to him. He's missing a leg and wears a wool cap to cover an atrocious scalping. His face is not the same as it was at the Institute, but his eyes have never changed. They've always been insecure, I think. While Sevro learned to put knives into the soft places of those who told him he was worthless, Screwface believed his tormentors' words a little too much and grew to think if only he was only a little taller, a little more handsome, a little more sophisticated, then maybe he would be worthy of love and respect.

That is why he agreed to infiltrate the Ash Legions. Three years with the devils has taken its toll on him. I embrace him and hold him because he seems to need it. He melts into me and begins to sob like a child. The others look away, but I don't let go of him. A man like this deserves to know both that I am his friend and that his Sovereign sees his sacrifices. I hold him for several minutes and spoil him with attention.

"Welcome home," I say to them over his head. I let go of him and hold his face between my hands. "You most of all, my friend. You most of all. Welcome home."

He smiles up at me with incandescent love, because he feels that his presence is welcome when he doubted it would be. "Can I tell her?" A broad-shouldered woman stands by the window, her hands clasped behind her back. She turns. Her eyes are red from crying. I let go of Screwface. My hands shake.

Victra crosses the room to me, and more than a head taller, she leans down to embrace me. My heart plummets in despair and then soars on wings as her lips curl into a smile and she says, "Sevro. Darrow. They are alive."

I close my eyes in exultation, and then yelp as Victra hoists me into the air and spins me around, cackling. "They're alive! It *was* them over Venus."

I'm fighting back tears by the time she sets me down. "Where are they?" I ask.

"We don't know," Harnassus says and tries to temper our expectations. "In fact, we don't know if Darrow was successful in rescuing Sevro. But Victra won't hear anything about that."

"We can game theory it," I say. "I'll get the Conservatory and Midnight School hives going. We can send out search parties."

They all look at Victra. "There's something else," she says. "Char?"

"Our sensors were soup the whole journey. Victra tells us it's the same here?" Char asks.

I nod. "Even the telescopes. It's a light war unlike anything we've ever seen. They've virtually annihilated our telescope web and sensor network all around the system. Solar flares. Dummy fleets. Drone Mimidae are everywhere. I've never seen fog of war this thick."

He grows solemn. "In crossing the Earth–Mars orbital gap, we observed a squadron of enemy ships too heavy to be a patrol. Since we had Votum tags, we were able to follow them, but still, we dared not get closer than this." My pulse quickens. He taps the holoDisplay on the table. A grainy image appears of Eros, the Mars-crosser asteroid nearly seventeen kilometers in diameter. It was a Republic trade post and military harbor until we lost it seven months ago to Dido. Dark shapes in the hundreds lurk in the shadow of its mass. Warships.

I feel the limits of my power acutely. The Rim's nimble ships have had a ruinous effect against our scouts and drones like never before. They've gouged out our navy's eyes at the same time that Atlas's Gorgons and Atalantia's spies have cut off my ears by eliminating my own spies. A fleet that size could not sail much closer to Mars without us seeing. But for the enemy to have amassed that much firepower only six days away without my knowing . . . it is humbling.

"What is that?" I point to the largest mass. "The enemy couldn't have built a moonBreaker in secret."

"No. They couldn't," Char says. "I'd know that shape anywhere. That's the *Morning Star*."

I step back from the table. I heard the Votum were trying their hands at shipbuilding. If the *Morning Star* is there, it can only mean one thing: that Lysander is there too. He's finally come to war.

Victra is smiling. Now, at last, we can kill him.

"Victra, recall everything within a week's sail. Alert the Ecliptic Guard, tell them the enemy is likely already on the way."

"And Darrow and Sevro?" she asks.

I almost say we don't even know if Darrow and Sevro survived Venus, but I don't. She needs that hope. Today is the first time I've seen her smile in months. In fact, it shows the growth in her trust in me that she waited here after learning the news instead of immediately launching a rescue mission. She knew I'd say no to rescuing them, but after eight months of holding the line together I know she would never abandon me to face the coming fight on my own, not even for Sevro. Thank Minerva, I need her.

"We can't help them right now, Victra. We don't know where they are. Any ships we send to look for them will be cut off. Hopefully they still have the *Archimedes*. We know they're resourceful. They know where we are. All we can do is make sure Mars is still *home* when they come back." *And pray they are alive to do so,* I think. "Now go, Victra. We've got work to do."

After she leaves, I glance at the recently arrived survivors. They're so battle-worn they can't possibly be ready to even think of the front lines. But they're Darrow's best, and I know I should at least ask so they don't get offended that I didn't. "Who's fit to fight?"

They all raise their hands. Emotion tugs on my heartstrings. And here I thought I couldn't love them any more.

19

VIRGINIA

Rising Dirge

THE ENEMY HAS COME to finish us, so we gather where it all began. Lykos.

My face is painted blood-red in the mine where Darrow was born. I stand flanked by armored commanders and friends. Deanna's breath billows in the cold of the mine. She thrusts her wrinkled hand up at the gallows that stand in the center of the Lykos township and murmurs, "They hanged my aunt here. Her name was Lorna."

"Lorna," Kavax whispers with the crowd and strokes Sophocles's head.

"They hanged my husband here. His name was Dale."

"Dale," Holiday repeats, and must think of her brother.

Eyes of all fourteen Colors of the hierarchy watch Deanna limp around the gallows, her hand still outstretched. Drones carry the voice of Darrow's mother to the thousands who cram into the township. On delay, they will carry it across Mars.

"They hanged my daughter here. Her name was Eo."

"Eo," Victra says like a prayer. She towers beside me, stalwart in green armor. The woman runs so hot a crown of steam writhes over her head. Her warhawk shave is fresh.

"They hanged my son here. His name was Darrow."

I see my husband. Sixteen, whipped and broken, walking the stairs up to the noose, and think how far he's come since that day. He is alive still. Alive and coming home.

"Darrow," I say with ten thousand more.

The name rises above the others. Some can't help but shout it. They should think he's dead. They don't know he's alive. The thought of his homecoming is like dawn to my heart. It will be a sweet day to see all this faith, all this hope rewarded.

Deanna lowers her hand and looks down as if reflecting on the pain of her people. Her voice may be quiet, her body bent, but when she looks up, it is with the calm feminine power of Red women. A power that comes from certainty. That comes from love. She seems mother of us all.

"My son died that day and returned as our sword. That is not all he is, but he became that so we could be free." She echoes my own thoughts, and I feel represented, part of something pure. "So did his friends, the brave lads and lasses who died on Mercury. Free to be mothers, daughters, brothers, fathers, grandparents." She smiles at Kieran's children. Dio, Eo's sister, stands with them in the crowd. But Dio's husband, Kieran, the ArchGovernor, is not here. We can't afford to have the leadership all in one place. Victra and me together is risk enough.

"Free to live under the sky," Deanna continues. "Free to dream like Eo. Free to own this land our people watered with our blood." Her eyes grow fierce. "My son is lost. He will come home. But he is not here today. The enemy is. So today, we are not mothers. We are not fathers. We are not brothers or sons. They come to make us slaves again. So today we are not dreamers. We are not Colors. We are swords. We are wrath. We are reapers."

She flicks her hand in disgust at the gallows. Fifty Reds of Lambda descend with power hammers and smash the gallows to splinters.

The crowd begins the Fading Dirge for the machine of death—thousands of fists pound on chests in the metronomic rhythm of a heartbeat. It is how they used to mourn their dead in the mines. Deanna limps over to my armored commanders and me. Darrow's sister, Leanna, carries a dented metal pail behind her. I go to my knees with my commanders. Deanna glares into my eyes. When I look into hers, I realize it is no mystery where Darrow got his rage. I stick out my bare hands and Deanna wipes them with red Martian mud to cover my Gold sigils, then Victra's.

"Go, daughters of Mars, and be our wrath."

Victra and I stand and head toward the rubble. Deanna moves down the line, covering everyone's sigils with mud. Victra and I each take a metal splinter fished from the debris by a child, and ascend the switchbacking stairs up to the Can. We are followed by Holiday, Kavax, and fifty more commanders. Hundreds of Reds beat their chests as we pass through the halls of the Can. Their faces are hard and painted red. The sound fades as we ride the gravLift toward the surface. Soon another sound grows, greater by far, as if we could hear the very heartbeat of the planet itself.

Two dreadnaughts float in the morning sky. One is Victra's, one is my own. Beneath them, a sea of humanity surrounds the highland mine of Lykos. Most are civilians come to pray to the Reaper. Faith is dangerous, but it is also part of our power. They stretch to the horizon in every direction, beating their fists on their chests, their faces painted red. I wonder absently who arranged for the paint, then I see that the Reds closest to the mine have bandaged hands.

At the heart of this human sea waits a steel core: the thirty thousand legionnaires of Pegasus Legion beat their chests. Their white horsehair crest helms do not sparkle in the sun. Their chest plates are dented and battle-scarred. Their capes are ragged. But their weapons are pristine and the spheres on their chests declare the planets they have liberated. To fill his personal legions, my husband chose only his own breed. The kind of grunts who floss their teeth with the threads of enemy standards. Who can sleep on volcanic rocks and win a fight in heaven or hell.

Today Pegasus Legion is Thraxa's, and she looks proud. She stands before them wearing a white wolfpelt. We don't have many Obsidians left under Republic arms, but a few hundred remain in this legion, nearly all women. That says it all about this legion's esprit de corps. It is a reflection of Darrow—nothing before the cause. They incite all, including me, to fight as hard as they will.

"Pegasus Legion! You were the tip of Darrow's spear. He is not here. I am!" Victra says. "Today, I need wolves. Are you wolves?" They howl. "Good. The enemy is up there. They want to be down here. That's not your problem. That's the navy's. So today, you will wait. You will be patient. Because when I release you, it will be to change the tide of battle. Make Darrow proud. Make Sevro proud. Make the enemy remember the Free Legions!"

They howl and she turns to me with a scandalous smirk. "So?"

"Vodka punch with a lemon twist," I say to the question she asked me after our dinner with Kieran and the commanders the night before in the Citadel.

She scoffs. "That's what you want to drink over Lune's corpse? Vodka punch with a lemon twist? What are you? A Pixie trollop?"

"It's gauche. He'd hate it."

She grins. "Savage. Be that today, horsey. They certainly will."

"Keep your head. They know you're aggressive. They know you'll want Apollonius too. I need you alive more than I need any of them dead."

"Now you sound like Darrow," she says.

It is a small kindness for her to comment on his humanity instead of invoking his name as a talisman for aggression. It touches me deeply. No matter what people think, Darrow cares for his soldiers, his commanders, and so do I.

Victra twists her neck to peer out at the sea of red faces. The Fading Dirge has slowed to a beat every few seconds. Even with her head shaved into the warhawk her husband used to wear to battle and her face painted red, the woman cannot hide a mother's grief. She may be looking at the sea, but she is standing before Ulysses's grave. Victra is daunting to behold in either peace or war. Her stature is tyrannical—tall, broad, muscular, with knives for cheekbones. Her nature matches—proud, brutal, voluble. But in her is a font of love that glows so hot it burns her from the inside out. For years I did not see that. I saw only her sharp edges. Now I love her and realize she was the sister I never wanted but always needed.

The Fading Dirge beats one more time and the sea stands in silence. The morning is cold. The breeze is light. It smells of soil and armor oil and grass.

Victra murmurs. "You're the bookish one. Was it a man who said 'hell hath no fury like a woman scorned'?" A lancer brings her gauntlets. "It must have been—to imagine something so petty as scorn to be the utmost misery a woman could suffer. What, I wonder, would he make of a mother who has seen her husband sold like meat and her babe nailed to a tree?" She dons her gauntlets. "Perhaps: wrath, I am thee? They come for our children, Virginia." She turns to me and cups my face with one hand. "Do not fear for me. Instead, pity them."

I thump her chest with my fist.

Victra nods to Kavax and Holiday and flies upward toward her low-flying flagship. Thraxa and Pegasus Legion follow in her wake. I look up to Mars's twin moons and feel a little sick. I always thought Darrow and I would face this battle together. Kavax and Holiday fall in behind me, and we fly toward my flagship.

20

VIRGINIA

Nucleus

As Victra's dreadnaught, the *Pandemonia,* heads toward our main fleet over the north pole, my war shuttle descends from the *Dejah Thoris* toward Phobos, the largest pincushion mankind has ever built.

Orbiting only six thousand kilometers from the surface of Mars, Phobos circles its primary body closer than any other moon in the system. That means it moves fast and takes only seven hours and thirty-nine minutes to complete its orbit.

It is not a big moon. Certainly not compared to the moons of the Gas Giants or Earth. It is only twenty-two kilometers in diameter, though over seven centuries, humanity has stacked on another three kilometers of cityscape in almost every direction.

Hundreds of starscrapers pierce the moon's crust. The rich live in the needles at the tips of the buildings, with the city's population density growing the closer one draws to the surface of the moon. The population thins again as one crawls down into the belly of the moon—the Hollows—where the sediments of Phobos's population gather in the eerie dimness surrounding the gravity generators. Much of the population has been evacuated, but not all. Tens of millions of people take a long time to move, especially when they do not all cooperate.

As the heart of our orbital defense complex, Phobos is well guarded. New grand guns and clever pyramid-shaped fortresses loom on in its cityscape. Most are positioned to defend its precious Julii-Sun docks, which are synced in orbit around Phobos like two intercrossed bandoliers. Forests of jagged towers reach past the docks. Amidst them stand monuments to heroes of the Rising. Some are carved in stone, many in ice. Kavax catches my eyes lingering on Eo's statue. But soon she is past, and then there is only Quicksilver's monument to my husband.

Darrow bursts into view, towering and terrible over the north pole, glaring toward the distant sun. Though my husband is still out there somewhere in the vast expanse of space, I feel him with me. It is a consolation that if he is alive, I know he is on his way home. Maybe even looking at Mars as a distant but growing star in his viewport.

"He'll see the energy wash of the battle if he's near," I say absently to Holiday. "I hope it doesn't make him do anything stupid."

"He won't," Holiday says.

I turn on her. "He's with Bellona and Sevro. Put them together and the stupidity tends to be exponential."

Holiday doesn't break eye contact. I feel safe around her surety. "You will see him again. Your son will see him again. I know that man. If he made it off Mercury, he can make it home. He is hard as nails and slippery as a fish."

I nod in gratitude and turn my gaze to the enemy. The Rim and Core Armada that has come to conquer my home is little more than stardust in the distance. Their high velocity suggests they intend to pierce our defensive shell in an attempt to deploy an Iron Rain.

So much for the conservative siege we'd once expected. At least Atalantia isn't with them.

"A Rain," I say with a shake of my head. "I really didn't think the Rim had it in them. Maybe Apollonius is in command after all."

"Helios would never cede the battle plan to a Core Gold, much less Apollonius," Kavax says, his gaze on the *Pandemonia*, and his thoughts on Thraxa. Only just returned and back to the fray. "Sophocles is likelier to feed *me* jellybeans."

"It's early yet," I say. "I suppose we will see."

A rectangle of light forms three-fourths of the way up Bastion One to permit us access. Forty heavy assault shuttles follow mine into the pyramidal fortress.

I leave most of my Lionguards in the hangars and ride the high-security lift with Kavax and Holiday down into the belly of Bastion

One. With my head down, I trudge out as soon as the doors open. Ahead, a symphony of bolts and oiled steel clunks and rasps. Interdiction slabs shift and security doors dilate open to grant us access to the military nerve center of Phobos—the Nucleus.

Petty officers scatter to the side as my cavalcade enters. The door guards announce me. "The Sovereign of the Republic!"

Five hundred officers and technicians snap to attention at their stations around the interior of the sphere that comprises the Nucleus. I plunge toward the command platform at its center. The best of the Republic's naval aristocracy wait there for me. Most are holograms beamed in from their ships. Even at short range, the enemy's electronic warfare degrades their avatars. A few of my Legates wait off to the side.

I step onto the command deck. "Void."

A white-walled cathedral of silence forms around the officers. Oro, the Blue commander of Phobos, is sixty, and lean as a bloodhound. His cobalt eyes are ringed with the insomniac circles of a Dostoyevsky protagonist. "Imperator Julii is nearly in place. Phobos stands ready. OBC control is yours, my Sovereign."

He sets a glossy black battle crown on my head. The crown gives me access to the Nucleus's systems, and the sudden influx of information is similar in sensation to being dunked into cold water at high speed. A few breaths and I adjust to the stream.

"This is the Sovereign. I have the crown."

Two hundred battle-station commanders confirm. With the crown I can micromanage them but not the fleet itself. I am not as good as my Imperators are at their jobs, so no need to bother. I wave my hand and Mars appears in the air. The visual of the battlefield resembles a three-dimensional representation of a cell with Mars surrounded by a dense orbital shell of neutrons and protons—her orbital battle-station complex, or OBC. They orbit in two staggered shells. Shell One at six thousand kilometers from the surface. Shell Two is at three thousand. There are minefields in the gaps between the stations along with a dazzling array of gun batteries on the surface of Mars, but the surface guns will come into play only if they launch an Iron Rain. To launch an Iron Rain, they have to get through both layers of the OBC.

Static defenses are never enough on their own, not in this epoch of warfare. Spears went through chainmail after all. The OBC may look dense on the display but if the map was to scale, the size of the gaps between the battle stations would startle an amateur's eye. The fleet and the OBC must work in tandem.

I watch the spear that represents Victra's flagship slide into place over the north pole. Her fleet is new and heavy and nearly a match for the Core contingent in the enemy armada on its own. The other two strike forces match the Rim ships well enough in tonnage if not speed. With the planet, Phobos, and the OBC the battle is ours to lose. Oddly, that makes me nervous.

"Imperators report," I say.

"*Pandemonia is in the pocket. Task Force Spear stands ready,*" Victra says.

Niobe, Kavax's wife, reports from the south pole. "*Task Force Fox ready.*"

"*Task Force Warlock ready.*" Colloway Char was eager to be put to use. The hero has been promoted to Imperator today and commands my *Dejah Thoris* and my household ships in defense of Phobos.

There is nothing to do now but wait and see where the enemy intends to focus the thrust of their attack. Darrow would loathe sacrificing the initiative, but Victra, Oro, and the Blue hive all agree the defensive posture gives us more advantages. To attack with the fleet beyond the kill zone of the OBC guns is to waste those guns and equal the odds. And with Victra's powerful fleet on the pole, she can meet the enemy wherever they thrust.

I watch with Kavax, Holiday, and my commanders as the enemy armada creeps closer. Thirty minutes becomes twenty. Twenty becomes ten. A sea of radio chatter from the hundreds of ripWing squadron leaders murmurs in the background.

The enemy is arranged in six spherical battlegroups and one floater. The *Dustmaker,* the powerful moonBreaker of Helios au Lux, leads the crème of the Rim fleet. Dido leads another group in her husband's old dreadnaught, *Shadow Dragon.* Diomedes leads the smallest and nimblest group from his destroyer, *Charybdis.* I keep an eye on that one.

The Core groups are led by Julia au Bellona, Apollonius, and Cicero au Votum. Julia's is the strongest group and populated with the flagships of many moderate houses. Cicero leads the Reformers and the Votum ships. Apollonius leads the smallest but newest group of ships, ones he must have acquired as master of the Dockyards of Venus. Niobe is keyed on him. Trailing behind those battlegroups is a sight that boils the blood of all Republic patriots—the floater fleet, led by the *Morning Star.* Though its transponder says the ship has been rechristened as the *Lightbringer.*

To see Darrow's ship in Lysander's perfumed hands disgusts me.

It is the biggest thing on the field. At eight kilometers in length it outstrips the older *Dustmaker* in length by two kilometers, Victra's *Pandemonia* by three, and my *Dejah Thoris* by four. Its refurbishment is clearly not complete. It's not even painted and looks like Frankenstein's monster—its hull a heterogenous patchwork of steel harvested off the carcasses of the White Fleet, which Atalantia crushed over Mercury.

I wish Orion and Darrow were here to take their ship back.

"Your intelligence still believes the *Lightbringer* poses no true tactical threat?" I ask Oro, dubious.

"Indeed. Less than a third of its surface guns have been replaced, and its reactor output readings are meager. No one has ever heard of her captain, and Lune would need years to build a talented ecosystem of House Blues. The ship is like the boy, a hollow symbol. He is taunting us to lure us out. Tempting us to take her back."

"Then let's not be lured," I say to all my Imperators.

"Seems Lune somehow profited off the chaos on Venus. Are those ships a bribe from House Carthii?" Kavax muses and squints at the nine unpainted destroyers that surround the *Lightbringer.* "Those are fresh off the spindles. Two don't even have surface guns. How can he possibly crew them?"

"Bellona, I wager."

Kavax comes closer. "Does your . . . source have any insight?"

I shake my head. "Not about this. And I'd doubt him even more if he did."

Kavax nods, happy our strategy is our own and not my source's.

A strange report comes from Oro. "My Sovereign, they're reducing velocity."

He's right. I turn off the command deck's void to see the Blues of my tactics hive chittering to each other. Soon they present an adjusted list of the enemy's potential tactics and attack vectors ordered by probability.

"Virginia, are you seeing this?" Victra asks.

"I see."

"What is Helios doing?" Victra murmurs. "Speed is their only advantage. Does he want to spend more time in the gauntlet of our guns?"

"It might not be Helios in command after all. Eccentricity is Apollonius's forte," I reply. "Maybe a split command?"

I glance at Holiday to shore up my anxiety about sabotage. "All vital installations have been swept, my Sovereign. Every reactor, every shield generator is under watch," she reaffirms. "If the enemy wants passage, they must pay for it."

All is in order, yet a nagging thought remains. Why in Minerva's name would they dare attack without Atalantia in the first place? Why take these odds?

There is nothing to do but wait and find out.

Gods, I hate playing defense.

21

VIRGINIA

Petard

FOR AN HOUR, THE enemy's armada circles around Mars's equator like a shiver of sharks. They travel just beyond the no-man's-land that exists between the OBC and the maximum effective range of its guns. Holding their positions on the poles, Victra's and Niobe's groups shadow the tightly packed enemy, waiting for them to make their move. Missiles flit between the lines, but with the anti-missile systems of both forces deployed, few find their mark.

In the second hour, Diomedes's battlegroup begins to flirt with our outer perimeter. They test for weaknesses and get a bloody nose from our long guns. It's a familiar game. They try to tease out as much information on the OBCs strength as they can, and we try to withhold while still getting a few licks in. Then thousands of Blues of each navy analyze the skirmishes and pass their findings up the chain. Pixel by pixel commanders from both sides form a clearer picture of the strength of their opponents.

Very conservative. Very Helios au Lux.

By the fourth hour, the anxiety of waiting for the enemy to attack in earnest has begun to wear on my commanders, but we cannot lose if we maintain discipline, so I am on the horn constantly with all of them. The only change in the enemy's pattern of feint and withdrawal occurs by accident when Lysander takes his turn testing our perimeter. One of his destroyers loses its shield under the converging fire of three battle stations and barely limps out of range to safety. His battlegroup falls behind the others. "Those are escape pods," Oro says. "They're abandoning ship."

There's laughter around the Nucleus. But not from Kavax. "A veteran would know, fresh off the assembly line there's always a few lemons," he murmurs. "Least he's decent enough to pick them up." True enough, just beyond the effective range of our guns, the *Lightbringer* comes to a halt to recover the escape pods.

"I could pounce on him and kill him," Victra suggests.

"That's bait," I say. "Hold your position. Continue shadowing the main fleet. If a mistake is to be made, let it be them who makes it."

"Yes, my Sovereign. But I'm growing roots up here."

Kavax still stares at the *Lightbringer*. Something feels off. "Oro, how long until Phobos and Lysander are directly aligned?" I ask.

He frowns. "Thirty-one minutes."

I tell Char to be ready just in case Lysander does something foolhardy.

Oro is skeptical. "You think Lune would risk a frontal assault on Phobos? While we have triple fleet coverage?"

Victra practically licks her lips. *"Let's hope he's that fool—"* Her sudden change of tone chills me to the bone. *"Sensors, what is that?"* A pause. I see it on my crown's holo projection. A large mass inbound at high velocity toward the pole. *"Evasive action!"*

Her signal cuts out. Sensors scream. A hail of unidentified objects moving too fast to be ships or missiles streak toward the north pole. The objects are dark, massive, and too big to be rail slugs. Yet they are. I know they are before the Blues can even analyze the objects.

No student in any astral academy could ever be faulted if, when given an exam to create a hypothetical defense of Mars, they placed their strongest fleet on the north pole. A fleet on the north pole is a trump card. That is, unless the enemy circled the planet, noted your fleet's velocity as you shadowed them over the course of five hours, and adjusted their own velocity over time to lead your fleet right into the path of rail slugs that were fired a week ago from the largest railgun installation ever built.

A railgun installation that was scuttled before it was lost to the enemy and which many great minds promised me neither the Core nor the Rim had the technology to restore.

I watch in cold fury.

The rail slugs would have to have been fired days ago, so they cannot target individual craft. It hardly matters. Rail slugs as large as corvettes but made of solid durosteel scream in at six times the speed of our fastest warship and detonate to send shrapnel into Victra's fleet over the north pole. Slugs skip off the planetary shields with the force of thermonuclear bombs and plow through battle stations like tungsten marbles into papier-mâché machete models.

The slugs don't come in flights, but in a steady, wide stream. We didn't design the guns to fire like that, like firehoses. Kavax is awestruck. "They didn't just fix the guns, they made a bigger clip," he murmurs.

The stream of fire abates. The rail slugs took only four seconds to pass over the planet. The Blues tabulate the amount of metal that just passed over Mars and on into space faster than they can our casualties. They say the number. I blanche. It equates to ten months of Mercury's iron exports. Where did they get that much metal? I have a guess: Lysander must have used some of the bones of the White Fleet to repair the *Lightbringer*. I think I know what just happened to the rest. They shot us with our own detritus.

At least there will be no second shot. It's just too expensive.

In the wake of the attack, the Nucleus is stunned. Not simply by the damage reports, but the mathematics involved in such a shot. They would dwarf the complexity of those used when we fired relief pods with our guns to my husband on Mercury.

We feel *inferior*.

Yet as my Blues search the debris floating over the north pole, they find a stirring sight. A ship signature, Victra's. She hisses over the coms. *"Those bastards. Form on me. Anyone still alive, form on the* Pandemonia.*"*

Victra's ship is damaged, but she is alive. Not just her; at least half her fleet seems to have survived the barrage. But they'll have no time to recover, because the enemy armada has finally decided to attack. They angle not for the planet, but toward the north pole. I go still. They have no intention of launching an Iron Rain today. Today, they came to kill Victra and eliminate the best ships of our fleet.

"Niobe, Char, this is a decapitation mission. They're going for Victra and Task Force Spear. Marshal on her. It'll be a knife fight on the pole. We cannot lose the fleet. Defend it at all costs."

They copy and their fleets race from Phobos and the south pole to help as the battle stations open fire on the onrushing enemy. The fire-fight glows like a second sun. I let the battle-station commanders do their jobs and stare at the *Lightbringer*. Each minute Phobos's orbit brings us closer to alignment with Lysander.

"Not a lemon after all," Kavax says.

"No."

He frowns at the debris over the pole. "Alas, hoisted by our own—"

I turn on him with such cold fury that Sophocles growls at me from his arms. Kavax feeds Sophocles a jellybean as if we hadn't just been hit in the teeth. "Calm down," he says and eyes the dazed members of the Nucleus's staff. He's right.

"We knew this would not be bloodless!" I shout. "Now it's our turn to draw theirs."

A faint cheer and they return to their jobs.

Oro rushes to my side. "My Sovereign, without fleet coverage Phobos will be vulnerable to attack."

"Then it's a good thing we have shields, guns, ripWings, and missiles," Kavax says. "If Lune's got the balls, let him try his luck."

"Sync to your guns, Oro," I say. "I'll prep the legions."

He rushes to his gun command station and dons his neural link circlet. He shivers and his eyes roll back. Oro can literally feel the giant anti-ship guns of Phobos moving in the gloom to train their gaze on Lune's fleet.

"My Sovereign, does Lune know you're on Phobos?" Holiday asks me.

"He's a smart boy," I say. "And since our intelligence is apparently for shit, I'm guessing the Twins of South Pacifica aren't the only weapon the enemy's stolen from us that is now battle ready. Time to alignment with the *Lightbringer*?" I ask.

"Nineteen minutes," a Blue calls.

The enemy fleet is suffering heavy losses to our battle stations, but they are almost to the dead zone their artillery carved into our defenses over the north pole. In that debris, Victra will be gathering her ships for the fight of her life. I roll out my shoulders, ready for the fight of mine.

22

LYSANDER

Iron, Death, Gold

"*S*PITFIRE: TWENTY MINUTES!*"
   Pytha's voice blares through the *Lightbringer* along with the droning sirens that attend an imminent launch.

The Praetorians roar as I enter the main hangar with my drop century: Ajax, Kyber, and Rhone's oldguard—Markus, Drusilla, Demetrius, Antonius, Coriolanus, and ninety-one more elite dragoons. StarShells lift their arms in salute. Blocks of dragoons boarding assault shuttles wave their heavy rifles. I am not Apollonius, so I do not ape him and exhort them to feats of valor. I set a tone of quiet professionalism and stride down the busy corridor with my entourage.

Of the forty-three thousand men and women of the Praetorian Guard who have returned to me over these last nine months, all have been dedicated to this assault. With them will go the two house legions I raised on Mercury.

"Octavia would shit herself," Ajax says. Ajax's armor is black with golden skull pauldrons. He wears no leopard cape today. It would not survive what's coming. He looks and sounds far more at ease in this setting than I ever will. I fear my dread is written on my face for all to see. "Why aren't you shitting yourself? You're risking everything on a gamble."

"So are you," I say. My voice sounds calm at least.

"Just my life," he replies. "If this fails, you lose your reputation, your army, your new ships, and your chance at the Morning Chair. Oh, and your line goes extinct."

"You forgot about my bank account."

"Already extinct," he says.

"Operation Polyphemus is a sound strategy," I say. "If it wasn't then Helios and Apollonius wouldn't have supported it."

"Why not? It's your head you're sticking in the lion's mouth. If it gets bitten off, they don't have to follow."

"You think they wouldn't?" He chuckles. "The Twins were my idea."

"And the Rim's weapon," Ajax says. "I came to make sure you don't die. Not lie to you."

"Right. Well. Whether in ruin or victory, I'm glad you're here," I say.

He grimaces at the dragoons who eye him with suspicion. "You're the only one. Astounded Flavinius let me on board."

"He works for me, not the other way around," I remind him.

"Long as he knows that," Ajax mutters. "Praetorians are an uppity breed."

Rhone might have squadrons of centurions micromanaging the pre-assault preparation, but he is still barking himself hoarse flying back and forth down the lines. "It'll be a hard brake and drop! Mouthguard in, Stravinius! Do you want to eat your teeth? Shellmen, chug your prep juice and get to the tubes! Don't inject till the yellow light! Aquilifer! Shine that dragon! You want them to know who's killing them or not! You fight for Luna today! I want that dragon spotless! Boomer boys, you'll be following the drills soon as they hit fifty meters. Centurions, straighten those lines. I want this tight!"

Grays peek at me as I pass, their eyes not on my shining gold armor but the snow-white cape that flutters behind me. Each hopes their unit will receive the charmed cloak. Rhone nods to me as he buzzes past overhead. His men expect him to receive the cloak. He knows better. Politics aren't limited to the rostrum of the Two Hundred. Still, he grimaces as I approach the outsiders in the hangar—my Red Helldiver corps—and doff my cape.

As I crossed the hangar, I saw them suffer the spit and curses of the armored Grays stomping past. They are small men and women, but they are hard as old leather. Many are exiled Martian Gammas I leased from Lady Bellona for this operation. Others are Votum miners from Mercury. They kneel and I motion them up. I keep my tone conversational.

"My friends. For too long, your loyalty has made you lepers when you should be hailed as patriots. Today you avenge yourselves for the persecutions you have suffered. You avenge the Gammas who were butchered in the assimilation camps. Operation Polyphemus relies upon you. So does our Society. You are the foundation upon which all else is built. I see that. Help me make others see that, and we will make a Society better than the one we were given. I expect this back, good-man." I wrap my cape around the shoulders of their headTalk. The man trembles with pride and looks up with a fierceness I've scarcely ever beheld. "Be brave. Be steady. Now go, sons of Gamma, and dig us a path."

The small Reds roar like lions and rush to climb their drills. Two hundred of the machines fill this hangar alone. I walk the line giving words of encouragement. At the base of each drill, berserkers in heavy armor take mushrooms from their centurion—a lone Peerless for every ten berserkers. Most of the Golds are *novus homos*—new men, young killers desperate to make their mark. Lured by my name, my games, and my evocation of a more honorable past, my promise of a brighter fu-ture, and hopes of elevation, they flooded to me after my speech in the Coliseum, eager to render service and apply all their skills toward the reclamation of Mars.

They are expendable, so I prepare to spend them. Wisely, I hope. Fol-lowing their berserkers up the ladder, they salute nobly from the top rungs before sliding into the carry pods and sealing the hatches. Win or lose, I will not see many of them again.

As the notice lights on the ceiling flash yellow, I fall in with my drop century and rush to our tubes to let the Oranges fit me into the loading rack. Rhone lines up to the loader to my left. I grab Ajax as he heads for the loader to my right. "Today we show Atalantia we are not her pets," I say.

He looks wounded. "You think that's why I'm here? Lysander. I couldn't give two shits about you *standing up* to Atalantia."

"Then why?" I ask.

"She killed your parents." His voice deepens with raw emotion. "I saw it in her eyes. She orphaned you. That is unforgivable. Family does not do that to each other. So, we are family now. You and I. And family sticks together. Come ruin or victory." He bumps my forehead with his own. "See you in hell, little brother."

He loads into his spitTube. I load into mine, bellydown, headfirst. I ratchet into the firing chamber. It is dark. Echoing. It has not vented pressure yet. I do not feel alone like I did the last time on Mercury. But still I feel sick. I pop my helmet and retch. There are stains down below. Old retch stains. From Darrow's hard-nosed Rain veterans. That consoles me. I can't wipe my mouth. My arms are locked in. I feel a moment of panic. I order my helmet back on with a voice command. I try to find the Mind's Eye. It evades me. I'm terrified. I don't want to die. I don't want to be here. I have to be here. Noble thoughts flee. No more peacemaker. No more politician. No more feeble seed.

I am Iron. I am Death. I am Gold.

"SPITFIRE: TEN MINUTES!"

23

VIRGINIA

Grim Glory

IN ITS INITIAL MOMENTS, Lysander's charge is the picture of glory. His new destroyers—not lemons after all—surge out in front of the *Lightbringer* as soon as Phobos's orbit brings the moon into alignment with his fleet. Haughty and shining, Lysander's destroyers race into range of our guns. Oro begins to fire and the darkness of no-man's-land turns to light. First, the light of particle beams, lancing and primordial. Second, the light of rail slugs, blurred and dull. Third, the light of drones and missiles, glinting and canny. Fourth, the light of the enemy's flak, dusty and meager. Then all the light all at once as the enemy replies in kind.

Lune's fleet disappears from the sensors in the energy wash of the conflagration. The first minute claims two destroyers. Overloaded by the volume of fire, the destroyers' shields turn opaque before the ships collapse inward. Their hulls peel open like burning paper, shredding away to reveal their twisted skeletons as they hurtle forward, their momentum unchecked. Imagining the hell on those destroyers, the screaming of shield sirens, the buckling bulkheads, the fire, and the vacuum, I pity the crews for having to suffer the cost of a boy's highborn ambition.

Glorious in its early thrust, Lysander's initial charge veers toward disaster as another destroyer is knocked out of formation and nearly collides with the *Lightbringer* behind it.

Yet even as the Blues report damage to the enemy, I see Lune's gruesome logic at work.

He gambled he could lose destroyers to gain kilometers, and despite the best efforts of my Blues, his gamble is . . . working. Not one destroyer is spared a shield failure or damage to its hull, but Lune's charge has soon passed the halfway mark to Phobos. The closer his ships come to Phobos, the less able the OBC guns are to hit them. Fewer guns by the second have a clear line of barrage, and we begin to feel the absence of Char's fleet. Another destroyer falls out of formation, slit down the center like firewood by the combined fire of Phobos's three space-facing citadels, including Bastion One. I shout for my Blues to analyze the debris for bodies. There should be armored infantry spilling out across space.

"None, ma'am. Not a one."

"All his men are likely on the *Lightbringer,*" I say to Oro. "The destroyers are empty. Maybe piloted remotely or by a suicide crew."

Playing on a hunch, I order the Blues to concentrate their guns on the *Lightbringer.* Even the great ship is not unfazed by our deluge of fire. Soon its hull is cratered in two dozen places and its shield must cycle on and off to prevent itself from overloading. Then I glimpse the danger, the true danger, and correct my orders. "Fire back to the destroyers."

Oro protests. "The *Lightbringer* is the threat. The destroyers are empty."

"Then why would they need to veer off their current trajectory, which is at present this moon?" I snap. "He's using the destroyers as battering rams, dammit! He's letting us shoot them down so they'll crash into our shields and bring them down for the *Lightbringer.* And then he's going to dump men down our throats."

Oro is appalled. "Nine destroyers. But the waste . . ."

"What's all that to a Lune?" I snarl.

Of the nine destroyers Lune started the charge with, four are already ruined and knocked off course. Five are horrifically damaged, but unless we smash them off course, they will collide with Phobos's defensive shield. And when they do, the kinetic energy from their impact will be in the gigatons, at least.

Minutes tick past. Oro's guns knock another destroyer off its crash course. With four more inbound, I call my Legates forward. "Goodmen, it looks like this is going to come down to infantry. Lune wants Phobos. The fleet is busy. They cannot help us. You will soon be all that stands in his way."

Then the first destroyer hits the moon's main shield.

Inside the Nucleus, we feel and hear nothing. Then two more destroyers hit almost at once, and the Nucleus trembles. Outside, above Phobos's starlit cityscape, the shield shivers and turns crimson. I make a quick calculation, weighing the force of the destroyer yet to hit and the strength remaining in the weakened shield. My math is sloppy, but there's no time to balk.

"Lower the shield," I order.

Oro's second-in-command turns, aghast. His accent is Phobosian. "That destroyer will impact the Hive. It's not fully evacuated—"

"Lower the shield!" I order directly to the shield officers. They stare wide-eyed at me. I jerk my head at Holiday and she bursts up on her gravBoots and puts a rifle to the Blue operator's temple. Finally, he lowers the shield.

The last the cameras report is a metal blur before perfect white. The Nucleus falls silent. The moon itself groans. Whole columns of sensors die. Alarm lights glow. Officers turn to stare at me, jaws on the floor. Even Holiday looks startled, as if she's only just realized what she's done on my orders. She removes her rifle from the Blue's head, and returns to me with a blank expression.

"Sovereign . . . what have you done?" Oro whispers from his sync.

"Triage," Kavax replies for me.

"Damage report when you have one," I say. "I want a visual of the surface. Engineering: what's the damage to the shields?"

The Orange engineering officer looks like he's seen a ghost. "Engineers report four nexuses have melted through their inhibitor-shells."

"But we're spared a general overload?" Kavax asks for me, again.

"Yes, sir."

"How many seconds till we can get them back up?" he asks.

"Seconds? It'll be a quarter hour, at least. If we don't wait that long, the radiation levels will kill anyone who goes in there. Even in a rad suit."

"Tell your shield teams that I need the main shield back up over Sector One in five minutes, or we lose Phobos," I say.

The engineer blinks at me, then Kavax. "I know those men—"

"Good. So, they will know the importance of their sacrifice," I say.

"Do it, Officer," Kavax says. "Do it now!"

Oro's second watches the exchange looking like he is about to strike me, which for a Blue is saying something. He's not the only one.

"We have visual of the surface!" a Blue calls.

"Main screen," Kavax orders.

Faces fall as their worst fears are realized. Images from the surface crackle above us. Maybe they thought I had a magic trick up my sleeve. Something that would make my order less monstrous. They are sorely disappointed. It's not that kind of day.

The devastation from the destroyer's impact is incredible. It sheared off the tops of a hundred spires and made an impact crater with a radius of more than two kilometers wide. I've never seen so much debris in zero-G. Entire starscrapers and monuments to heroes float like motes of dust up from a punched sofa cushion.

Beyond the moon, the shattered city, and the impact crater, neither our shield nor the stars can be seen any longer. The war-battered belly of the *Lightbringer* has become the sky, and it creeps closer as the great ship hard brakes to hover barely a kilometer over the tallest starscraper. Then the *Lightbringer* fires on Phobos with whatever guns it has left. Oro trains the guns of Phobos and fires back.

It becomes a slugging match. My moon and Lune's moonBreaker go at it like two bare-knuckle brawlers tied together, punching and obliterating each other's delicate features at close range.

Oro glares at me. His sync connection must have been broken by damage to subterranean hardlines. He discards his useless circlet. The guns are now under the control of their on-site manual redundancy teams. He strides over and says in a quiet voice: "My Sovereign, the shield could have withstood that impact . . ."

"Maybe but the kinetic whiplash would have overloaded the entire system. It would be down for a day or more. Now Lune's landing zone has so much debris that his Praetorians will shoot him if he orders them to make landfall in it. He'll have to adjust. Shift north, toward Bastion One. Sector One. Where he'll be in range."

"Of what?"

"Retaliation," Kavax says. He's already set Sophocles down and begun field-checking his armor. Sure enough, the *Lightbringer* recognizes the impossibility of the crater, and the ship sacrifices its surprise to begin a slow shift north.

Lune's captain is good, and rotates the ship to hide its cratered belly and present fresh guns. The ship completes a full turn so that when it reaches its new landing zone, its original side is facing down toward the moon. Then all its fighters and bombers, held back for the assault, flow out its hangars like a plague of locusts. I send ours from Bastion One and its adjacent fortresses Bastions Two and Eight.

Then Holiday curses in disgust. Familiar silhouettes fall from the *Lightbringer* toward the surface of Phobos's cityscape. Lune didn't just bring battering rams. He brought clawDrills too. Hundreds of them.

"He's aping Darrow," Kavax says and kneels to stroke Sophocles's head. The fox has started to whine with anxiety. He can always tell when Kavax is about to leave.

I patch into the squadron commanders. "Ignore enemy fighters. Fire on those clawDrills. Bring them down before they hit the surface."

Holiday motions forward the commander of the Bastion One's legion—Red Legion I. The stocky Red thumps forward, fists balled, one hateful eye on me, the other still on the crater the destroyer made in Phobos's cityscape.

"Legate Dunlo, those drills allow them to bypass the Bastions, and the defense levels. They will land north of the crater and south of Bastion One. They will chew through the starscrapers and the surface into the moon's interior and Praetorians will pour in like water.

"It's up to you and Red Legion I to stop their downward penetration before they get to the Core and the reactors. Make contact and kill those drills. Plug the breaches best you can. Hawk Legion and Haemanthus Legion will press in laterally from Bastions Two and Eight to reinforce and stop their lateral movement."

"They'll be able to put men on hundreds of levels from the drill shafts," he warns. "I . . . don't know if we can contain them."

"Which is why we will also attack them on the surface at the breaches themselves. Tell your Drachenjäger commander that Kavax is on his way and will lead the charge." Silence greets my announcement. *"Go."*

With a salute, he storms away with his officers to join his legions.

Holiday returns to fit me in my armor. "Engineering, where are we on the shields?" I ask.

The engineer falters. "Ma'am . . ."

"Speak up, man!" Kavax barks.

"My Sovereign, I cannot give the order. Those are good men and women! If we don't wait for the radiation to pump out, they'll die!"

"Get those shields up, or go tell your family they will pay because you wouldn't. We are here to do our jobs!" Kavax booms, then to all: "War requires monstrous deeds! If you cannot be a monster, then get out of the way!"

The engineering officer falters, unable to give the order, but I already opened a line to the shield rooms. They heard Kavax. A steady, distant voice replies.

"My Sovereign, that is a Lune out there?" the voice asks, a woman's.

"The last one. And his Praetorians."

"You need the shields up to attack them?"

"Yes. If they hold their landfall on the surface, their allies can pour in behind them. We need to wipe them from those breaches. Teach Lune's allies the only thing here is death."

The engineer on the line takes an unsteady breath. I can sense they are confirming with their colleagues. *"The shields will go online in ten minutes. We will see to it personally."*

"Name? Rank?" I ask.

"Centurion Murani Legard."

"Thank you, Centurion Legard. I hail your name."

"Hail Lionheart. Legard out."

In ten minutes, Legard will likely be dead. More martyrs for the cause. So many martyrs. I turn to Kavax. He is saying his farewells to Sophocles.

"When the high gates open, we'll release the reserve ripWings. You and the mechs must wait for the shield, or you'll be torn apart from space," I tell him. "Kavax."

"I have waged war before," he says and kisses Sophocles on the mouth. "I love you, little one. Be brave for Virginia. She has the beans now." He stands and hands me his pack of jellybeans.

"I wish I could go with you," I say.

"Your value is here. You must guide the legions. Plug the holes in our defense."

"Take my Lions from the hangars with you," I offer.

"No. You will need them to reinforce the legions," he says.

"I will see you soon," I say and look for him to validate my hope, but the look he gives me is not that of a father to a child, not anymore. We are peers now, and we know we may never see one another again. I clasp his hand. "Good hunting."

"Sophocles, stay. I shall return." His men take a conical attachment off the back of his armor and hand it to my centurion Virgilus. "Look after him, yes? He's grown tender in his old age."

Sophocles watches Kavax go and begins to shake. I can't watch. I turn back to the display and observe my legions making their way through the trams and sprint through corridors as I try to guess where the enemy will drill. I steel my heart for the battle to come.

When Sophocles begins to howl, I know Kavax has left the Nucleus. Part of my heart marches off with him. I stuff the jellybeans into the pocket of my armor that holds the splinter of the gallows.

24

LYSANDER

Drop Shock

I SOAR OUT OF THE ignorance of the spitTube into a silent madhouse
where there is no up. The first glimpse of battle is as incomprehen-
sible to my brain as calculus is to a dog. Confined between two horizons
of metal—the ship and the surface of Phobos—I'm blinded a half second out of the tube. Only the heavy filters on my helmet's optics save
my ocular nerves from frying.

I fight the instinct to alter course. It won't matter if I do, not in a
drop like this. You can't dodge anything. If you try, you'll just slag up
the fellow next to you and create a chain reaction that will mire the drop
and get ten thousand killed.

Dive. Make landfall. Survive. Find my drill.

Survive. What a laugh. As if I had a say.

The blurred topography beneath winks at me. Guns. They're almost
pretty. Rail slugs whip past at speeds too fast to see. They must slash
furrows through ranks of men behind me, to my right, to my left. I can't
tell. I can't care. I can't look back. All I can do is go down, down fast as
I can to where death waits with its mouth open and its teeth gnashing
the men ahead.

My brain is recovering from the sensorial overload of drop shock.

I register landmarks. The city to my left. Bastion One north. The
crater south.

I'm on target. I'm not lost. I still don't have a name. I'm an insect in
the path of speeding machines and munitions that won't even notice my
death because they're not aiming at me. I'm too small.

The assault is too big to grasp much less evoke an emotional reaction. I feel nothing. Not even fear. Just shock and awe and insignificance. I witness the assault in staggered, isolated frames.

Gun batteries belch fire and die by fire.

A whole block of cityscape disappears under the wreckage of a pinwheeling destroyer.

A squadron of bombers slips under flak. I think they're ours.

A hundred Praetorians vanish in a flash of light.

A clawDrill's arrest program fails and it disintegrates against a starscraper.

A giant ice monument to Ragnar Volarus melts as a particle beam blazes through its torso.

Three ripWings with Lune crescents on their wings rocket past to shoot down a lone enemy fighter. The crescent seems like the mark of some insane king. Not me. Someone else. Some authority who has strategy, reasons, a plan.

I have no plan. Survive the passage. That's my only job. *Dive. Make landfall. Find my drill.* Then the rest. I'm locked onto my drill's beacon. So are Ajax and Rhone. They materialize out of the chaos onto my flanks. Cityscape veined with colorful advertisements swells ahead. Rapidly, the buildings and battlements grow taller, grander even as the scenes of battle shrink.

A ripWing crashes into a soft-drink advertisement, beheading the smiling vixen.

Armored men dive onto gun batteries and lay charges.

A Praetorian lands too fast behind his clawDrill and is sucked into its business end.

Missiles slither from civilian starscrapers.

Bodies fly like confetti from a bisected transport.

My theater shrinks and becomes more comprehensible the closer I draw to our drill. It has landed on a metal and duroglass mesa about half a click shy of our designated landfall. Fuck it. Its Helldiver has already started to dig. I don't blame him. The dull gray surface rushes up to greet me. Am I dead? Am I Hades staring at a necropolis where humans are fused in the landscape itself? The mesa has faces in it. *Faces.* Hundreds of terrified faces.

No. It's an apartment complex. Those are windows. Tenants.

I invert, land, and become a man again. I am alive. I almost roar.

My heart hammers in my chest. Under my boots a Green woman holding a glass of whiskey stares at me through the cracked duroglass of her living room window. The plants in her apartment start to shake, but not from me. Her eyes meet the dark glass eyeholes of my helmet. In the reflection of the glass between us I see my second wave descending behind me.

I feel powerful. She is insignificant. I am too hateful from the drop and the death I saw to care if my thoughts might be wicked. The Green flashes me the crux and tilts back her whiskey.

It's already boiling. She screams. Her plants behind her wither. Her hair singes. Moisture abandons her body and her flesh catches fire as the heat generated by our clawDrill rages through her apartment. Frozen by the whiplash from insect to human again, I watch the woman with detached remove, thinking: *Who's the bug now?*

The spell is broken when Ajax barks my name.

My Praetorians have secured our landfall. Dogfights swirl overhead. Rhone stomps up to me with bad news.

"They prioritized the clawDrills. Took out half of them. The rest have landed and have penetration." Only half. Gods, their ripWings are good. I hop onto a coms antenna protruding from the surface of the apartment complex. I have a few seconds to see the landfalls from a clear vantage. Even then, it's impossible to tell if my plan is doomed.

The light of war stutters across the landscape. It stirs a memory, summoning an apocalyptic image I saw in an old paper book when I was young and making my way through the Palatine stacks—a lithograph depicting the war of god's angels after paradise was lost. The clawDrills tower on the grim hellscape like the pagan obelisks to which the angels flocked.

It is hell—terrible and awesome and silent beneath the heavens. I can appreciate its strange beauty now that I am human again. Maybe that is the problem. Maybe that is why we wage war, because bugs don't and angels do.

I shiver and so do the drills as they disappear into the moon. Geysers erupt after them. Level by level the moon depressurizes and spills its guts out. They were things once, the guts. Metal bulkheads, glass windows, plastics, insulation, and bodies, all now churned into fractal spew. Then identifiable debris comes as pressure shoves anything untethered on the compromised levels toward the holes ripped in their world. Toward these debris geysers rush my Praetorians.

I glance up past the waves of assault ships coming down at the mauled belly of the *Lightbringer*. My flagship and captain have done their job and dropped their cargo. Time for Pytha to let the others through. If they are coming, that is.

If they aren't, we're dead, and in the moment that is all right.

Then Ajax pulls me down from the antenna. "You want to make a sniper's day?" he snaps and curses me with a litany of phrases I've never heard before.

Rhone radios the breach is ready. With Ajax I rush to its edge. It is twenty meters wide. Helmet says three hundred meters deep already. The geyser of debris unceasing as level after level depressurizes. The claw-Drill is already out of sight. Its demonic light throbs far below, promising death or glory. The hair on my arms stands on end as an energy field activates. Glancing up, I see Phobos's main shield has come back on, cutting us off from support. My stomach sinks.

A Praetorian shouts a warning and points toward the pyramid looming over our landfall—Bastion One—where scales of light appear on the dark surface of the fortress. From the scales, tiny humanoid shapes emerge. They are tiny only because we are so far away.

"Drachenjäger," Ajax murmurs over the com.

More scales glow on the fortress as a dozen more garages open.

My voice is eerily calm. "They'll sweep down the pyramid and hurl us off this moon. If they take our landfall, we're done before the main wave can land. We'll be cut off inside."

"Not our job," Rhone says. *"This isn't the Ladon. Trust your guard. Our objective is down there."*

"Waiting on you, dominus,*"* Demetrius says and jerks his head toward the breach.

Ajax gives me a nod. *"Let's go make peace."*

Already I hear the cool litany of centurions over the com as they assess the new threat and prepare to rebuff the Drachenjägers. I gaze one more time at the far-off machines. They've begun a disjointed lope down the pyramid's slope, building speed as they come in rolling waves of steel.

I contemplate when, years from now, I will sit in the Palatine garden and review all the fair things my peace has wrought, and I dive into the mouth of hell.

25

VIRGINIA

War Prism

ONE OF THE MANY lessons I learned at the Institute is the higher your rank, the less war is about courage or discipline or mud or blood, and the more it becomes a game of accounting. Usually it's about food, fuel, and weapons. To defend Phobos, I invest bodies and resources like a Silver portfolio manager. Minimum cost, maximum profit. That is the game.

Victra, Niobe, and Char must handle the fleet. Phobos is my charge. If it is lost, so are our docks, our ability to replace our lost ships, and our ability to defend orbit. Mars will then be strangled. Not today, not tomorrow, but slowly and then surely, when they are finally able to use the moon to launch a Rain at the planet itself. We thought that the Rain would be today. We were wrong. So many of us were wrong. Nothing to do now but fight.

The crown on my head is a prism that breaks down the chaos of war into comprehensible information. It cocoons me in battle. The crown can monitor and manage up to a hundred and eighty engagements at once. Knowing my limitations undershoot the machine's, I hand off forty of these engagements to Nakamura and the Nucleus's staff.

Center in my field of view is the ever-shifting 3D tactical map. It shows the wormlike progress of the clawDrills through the top tiers of Phobos. My legions rush to head them off.

Our Bastion-based defense system was built so that the Bastions could be reservoirs of reinforcements able to direct troops to any breach in their sector. But with the clawDrills bypassing the Bastions and our ten-deck security layer—some of the drills have penetrated as deep as fifty decks already—our system is being pushed to its limits. No—it has been circumvented completely.

In just the first fifteen minutes of the assault, I've nearly emptied Bastion One's reserves. Of Bastion One's three legions—a hundred and fifty thousand Reds, Grays, Browns, and a few loyal Obsidians—all but several thousand have already been divided and committed.

The first legion makes contact with the enemy thirty-six levels down. The four centuries I tasked with heading off the drill at the tramway are impeccably on time. They fire shoulder-mounted rockets and destroy the drill as it passes through the level.

The drill burrows halfway into the floor before collapsing sideways. An armored capsule affixed above the Helldiver cabin bursts open and berserkers pour out. That's new. A Gold is with them. The Red Legion centuries open fire. Then Praetorians pour through the smoldering breach and all I can do is send reinforcements.

Sixteen more units make contact with Lune's forces in the next minute. The close-quarters fighting is bitter. Though outnumbered, Lune's Praetorian vanguard is armored heavily enough to reduce almost every fight to melee chaos. Yet our numbers are making up the difference. If at the same time Kavax can keep the enemy on the surface from entering their breaches on the decks, we will destroy Lysander and his Praetorians once and for all.

With no time to micromanage each individual engagement, I give suggestions on the fly. A flanking maneuver to a centurion defending gun controls, a maniple formation to a Legate on deck thirty-three. Moments later though, I circle back to see the centurion dead, the Legate sealing the breach with engineering teams. I redirect the Legate to the next breach, three levels down.

I must trust my ground officers. My most important function is arranging for and massing reinforcements where they matter most. I triage based on a culmination of factors: the importance of each clawDrill's objective, the likelihood of preventing the enemy from reaching the objective, and my overarching strategy of containment.

The strategy is working. Lysander has overreached.

Fierce and disciplined as the Praetorians are, with Kavax delaying their second wave on the surface, they're outnumbered nearly everywhere. I've managed to mass legions in strategic areas to oppose their progress and swamp their flanks. Fifteen minutes in, more than half of the clawDrills have been intercepted and destroyed by ground units. I may be the only one who sees the order in the chaos. Meanwhile, the squad coms are overwhelmed by that chaos.

"Fuuuuuuuck . . . what the fuck was that?!? Get the fuck down, Corran. What the fuck were you thinking? Did anyone see where that came from? Where the bloodyhell is Horrow? Need to call this shit up! Need heavy armor."

"Horrow ain't on coms no more. Certius is."

FRAFRAFRAFRA

"Where the slag is Horrow?"

"Dead!"

"Bloodydamn! Certius get over here. You lilyshit bastard—knew I needed to call this shit up. Boyo, you gotta be nut to butt. Wait, where the bloody- damn is doc?! Doc!?"

"Oy."

"Why the fuck are you so far forward?"

"I was plugging up Horrow."

VrreeeeVRREEEEdunnnnng. FRA FRAFRAFRA.

"Berserkers!"

"Waste them!!! Next one. No next one right!! The fucker with the ham—"

"Norus! Norus!"

"His head's off, man. Fire!"

"I'll get him!"

"His head's fucking off!"

"I got—agghhh."

"Slag Norus. We need to fall back! See that water processor looking thing over there?!"

"That thing?"

"No that's an incinerator, Carthus! That motherfucker! That toaster thing."

"Yeah Yeah, registers."

"Heavies give us cover and move move move—"

"Fuckfuckfuck Scarred! Scarred!"

"Anti-Scar up! Up!"

"Rocket green. Rocket away!"

Phhhhhhhooooozchhhh.

"Eat my cock goldilock! Nrrrrk."

"Bring that tripod up! Where's our heavy armor!? Is anyone fucking listening to me!? OVERWATCH??!?"

I answer: "I'm here. Heavy armor reinforcements en route and will flank from tunnel sixteen C. Hold your position at all costs." And that was a veteran unit. I cycle to the next. Red Legion I bleeds and burns to plug the holes. Stomping over Praetorian carapaces leaking blood and machine oil, they rush forward to make bulwarks against the invaders. Tramways, gravLift shafts, subterranean agoras where commerce once thrived become slaughterhouses choked with smoke, fire, rent metal, and robotic screams echoing in helmets.

Sweat stings my eyes. Time disappears. Gone are the learned moralities that once differentiated me from my father. I force my ants in the path of the enemy worms. Then I isolate those worms. Swarm them. Kill them fast as we can. Plug the breaches, damn the cost. Create a grid around them with Haemanthus Legion and Hawk Legion. Constrict the grid. Squeeze the enemy out. It's working well enough that every few minutes I can check on Kavax.

His Drachenjäger charge must have been a dreadful sight to Lysander's Praetorians. Five wedges rolling in silence down the slopes of Bastion One. Under cover of the restored shield, they hit the enemy just as their troop carriers brought the second wave of House Lune Legions. By the time I checked back, Kavax had hurled the enemy off a third of their breaches and looked as if he might eradicate the Praetorian Guard by hour's end.

But the next glimpse shows a fuzzier picture: His charge has stalled. The stubborn Praetorians refuse to be routed. They rally again and again and entrench in the cityscape, delaying him, giving their brothers behind them time and cover to flow down to support their vanguard inside the moon.

It's impossible to find Kavax in the fray. Enemy sensor-jamming is killing everything except direct laser coms. Armies of codebreakers on both sides wage war from deep within bunkers while battle-brave Green fulgur bellatores—lightning warriors—sneak through the warzone to hard hack and enslave enemy systems or remotely hijack vessels or guns.

Despite the chaos, Kavax is doing his job. I struggle with the magnitude of my own, and I almost miss two clawDrills threatening to break through our lower perimeter. I move eight centuries to intercept. By the time I've cycled back to them ten minutes later, the clawDrills are down but the centuries I sent to stop them are already broken and in flight. The enemy group responsible for the rout is moving fast. They're over two hundred strong and pressing for the maintenance lifts to the sector's reactor. I hurl more men from nearby at them only to watch their biometrics flatline one by one. Somehow the enemy keeps finding ways to flank the units I send.

Is that you, Lysander?

Or is it another Gold ally? The Golds have so many fine commanders, it's impossible to know. In the murky images, I think I see a beast of a man in black armor with skulls on it.

Ajax?

Using another three hundred of Red Legion as sacrificial lambs to slow the enemy progress, I search for more reserves to send from Bastion One. All are committed except my four thousand Lionguards in the hangar.

"Nakamura, pass off your prism. Front." She jogs over as a Gray officer takes her prism circlet. "This enemy unit has bypassed our killboxes and has chewed through everything I've thrown at them. We've whittled them down to one fifty or so. But they're past the perimeter going for the reactor. They still have doors and automated defenses to get through, but their battle Greens are good. You can beat them to the reactor. Take five hundred Lionguards from the hangars and see them dead."

She salutes, and then fixates on a holofeed showing the enemy squad. She shoves an armored finger toward a Praetorian with a transverse crest on his dragon-head helmet. He's half hidden in the smoke. "That's Flavinius," she says. Her eyes narrow and she points to a big shadow in the smoke. "Ajax?"

"Take a thousand. Lune might be with them. I can't give you more," I say.

"Let Virgilus lead them," she says. She motions up the Lionguard centurion. "I'm with you, ma'am. You've already sent Kavax. I will not leave your side again."

"Virgilus, you heard?" He nods. "Go then. Good hunting."

He salutes and he's off. I glance at Nakamura, mildly annoyed at being contradicted, as she returns to her prism.

Victra finally breaks through the jamming. *"Virginia . . . holding . . . our own. Rath . . . Votum missing."*

"Diomedes . . ." Char's voice.

"Repeat, Char."

"Diomedes . . . toward Phobos."

"Registers. Keep the fleet together."

"But . . . Phobos."

"The fleet is more important," I say. "Win your battle. We'll handle ours." I'm beginning to realize we won't, but amputations on the field are best done without consulting the patient. My father said that once. At the time, I thought it grotesque.

"Do we have Rath and Votum on sensor?" I ask my Blues.

"The *Lightbringer*'s mass is interfering with our instruments," they call.

I consider, then hail Kavax to warn him of possible enemy reinforcements. No reply, so I tell my Greens to keep trying and plunge back into my battle prism. Not five minutes after Virgilus's departure, I have to send more Lionguards to support Red Legion in the shafts leading to the sector's shield generator. Fifteen hundred left. Then a thousand as I send five hundred more. Then only five hundred left as another Praetorian vanguard breaks through Red Legion on level forty-five.

I hold on to that last five hundred. I feel the tide turning. Our numbers are wearing down the elite vanguard. A cheer even goes up as the *Lightbringer* backs off from the punishment of our guns.

I don't cheer, and that is why I often feel so alone. Holiday doesn't cheer either. She steps closer, protective, and I grow thankful she did not let me send her away.

This is not going to be pretty.

Sure enough, as soon as the *Lightbringer* clears out, our instruments sing with incoming contacts. Votum and Rath ships are already plunging into the no-man's-land. Some of those ships go dark or break apart under our cannons, but they have an easier crossing than Lune's did. When they arrive, they park just shy of the shields and wait for them to fall.

Knowing we're lost if those shields go down, I send my last five hundred Lionguards to reinforce the shield generator. They're only three minutes out when the enemy breaks through the Lionguards I already sent with Virgilus.

If it is Lysander leading that group, he's just punched me in the gut.

"Tell Kavax to retreat. The shield is about to go down. He's exposed,"

I order. It's bewildering my thousand men didn't stop that group. My Lionguards are some of the best Grays of Mars and they're dying like flies against the Praetorians. A few minutes later, Lysander's gut punch really lands when the shield goes down over the sector for good, and Votum and Rath launch their own invasion.

"Is Kavax on his way out?" I ask my Blues.

"We passed the order, Sovereign. He has not replied."

Nausea spreads through me. I try to compartmentalize. I can't. If Kavax is alive, he'll look up from his battle with the Praetorians on the surface, a battle he was winning, and see the Votum and Rath hulls raining reinforcements. He'll think, if only he had twenty more minutes, he'd have finished the guard forever. Our numbers would have swallowed their vanguard inside Phobos. We'd have won.

For Kavax, that would be something he'd smile at spending his life on. But spending his life for Lune to gain glory? I want to puke, but the enemy won't stop hitting us long enough.

Apollonius's ships are the first to launch men at us. Cicero's are second. And then streaming behind them are three of Diomedes's destroyers. Our invaders will win prestige based on the order they arrived, and on the objectives—and heads—they seize. I glance at Sophocles and feel as empty as I did the day my mother died. The fox sits behind me. He cocks his head as if to ask me why all the strangers in the room are so worried, and more important, when is Kavax coming back.

I fight back the urge to moan in despair as the Minotaur's reinforcements fall on Kavax's division. I think of telling Niobe I spent her husband in vain, telling my son Kavax is gone, and it makes me want to die. There's nothing we can do to stop them from reinforcing Lune.

What would Darrow do? Fight and bleed until an opportunity to obliterate the enemy appears, and if none does—fight to the death.

It's time to retreat.

I access the general frequency. "All legions, this is your Sovereign. The enemy has secured their landfall. Disengage. Begin a fighting withdrawal to Sectors Two and Eight. Sector One cannot be held. If you stand, you will be unsupported and cut off. We hold them at Two and Eight, we can still hold the moon. Over."

Sophocles yowls in anxiety. Nakamura's voice is calm, but worried. "My Sovereign. It's time to evacuate you. Bastion One will be cut off in the retreat."

I pay her no mind. "I have work to do."

"My Sovereign, Votum warships have dropped clawDrills on Bastion One. I will not let your life be put in harm's way again."

"The Nucleus is an escape pod. We can drop it to the Hollows."

"But if the escape shaft is blocked in the bombardment—"

"We are five hundred and thirty-one people. We can save tens of thousands of lives per minute. This is a crucial moment. The retreat must be managed or it will become a rout and we will lose the moon and all the lives on it. Evacuate the Bastion, Nakamura. Clear the Nucleus of all nonessentials. Tell me when our window is about to close. *Then* we drop. And someone please secure that fox."

I crack my neck, shake out my arms, and dive into coordinating the retreat. My father would be proud. I do it logically, not humanely— sacrificing common soldiers to slow the enemy and save our uncommon ones. The cold sorting of life demands so much of my focus that it's not until Nakamura grabs my shoulder that I realize the Nucleus's alarms are blaring, and have been for at least a minute.

"We need to drop. Those clawDrills are almost through the outer armor."

"Another minute."

"I gave you twenty."

Twenty? Really? Time has lost all meaning. I look at the pie shape of Sector One—wide on the surface, a slice where it meets the Hollows— and know I've done what can be done. So far, the enemy is contained within the sector. Most of our forces have escaped to the sectors adjacent Sector One—either to Sector Two or Sector Eight. I nod to Holiday to initiate the Nucleus drop sequence.

A Green calls out: "Legate Telemanus's Drachenjäger is on the line!"

Relief floods into me. "Put him on."

A handsome, sweat-soaked face fills the Nucleus. Raving red-rimmed eyes too close for comfort stare out. It is not Kavax. It is Apollonius au Valii-Rath.

"War, the mortal hallelujah." He makes the sound of a man receiving a foot massage. *"Lionheart. I have broken your champion. Now, I come for you."*

26

VIRGINIA

Labyrinth

I THINK OF KAVAX BREAKING in the Minotaur's armored hands and want to scream as Holiday arranges to drop the Nucleus. Numb, I scan the displays, hoping to see evidence Victra is alive, that's she faring well in her battle on the pole. I receive nothing but old data showing a pitched battle. RipWings swirling. Capital ships hammering one another at close range. Helios's *Dustmaker* slugging it out with the *Pandemonia.* I won't know what's happened until I make it to my fallback command center in the Hollows.

An Orange drones: *"All personnel, brace positions for Nucleus drop. Sever the hardlines. Hardlines detached. Drop in twenty . . . nineteen . . ."*

"Who has the fox?" I call.

"On it, my Sovereign!" a burly Red Lionguard named Glaucus says. They've affixed Kavax's carryall to Glaucus's back armor. The man kneels and tries to lure the fox in. Sophocles is scared and refuses to come out from under a console. Each time they try to pick him up, he darts away. Holiday solves it before I have to. She lays down on her back, sets a ration on her chest, and pats it until Sophocles scampers over to nibble and lie in the nook of her armpit. Holiday stows him in the carryall on Glaucus's back.

"Five . . ."

I brace alongside Oro. He looks so fragile next to me without armor. The Nucleus shudders and tilts. "What was that?" I ask.

"Exo-ligament seven is severed!" an Orange announces. "Their particle beams have compromised the Nucleus's thermal wall." That means the next particle beam will land directly on the surface of the Nucleus, and its heat will transfer, superheating the air of the Nucleus.

"Drop. Now."

The great, impenetrable Nucleus begins its drop toward its exit shaft. And then halts and goes nowhere.

Every screen goes out. The interior of the Nucleus starts to heat up, fast. A pupil of red light dilates above us on the metal. Sweat pours down the faces of Blues and Greens. The skin of my exposed face starts to itch. It's only getting hotter. I raise my helmet. Of the Nucleus's complement, only my bodyguards and now Sophocles in the carryall have armor. The sweat starts to wick off Oro's face.

"Virginia . . ." he whispers as his saliva turns to steam. "The particle beam must have melted the shaft . . ."

The temperature outside my suit creeps upward. Then it doubles, and doubles again. Blues and Greens start to scream from the heat. "Emergency lifts!" I order. "Everyone, emergency lifts. Armor last!"

Holiday and my Lions don't listen. They manhandle me and plow a path through the gurgling techs and crew into the lift. Past their armored shoulders, I see Oro struggling toward us, his eyes bulging from their sockets. Techs stumble, their hands melting to metal consoles as they try to steady themselves.

"We need Oro!" I shout.

Oro's strength fails. He falls to his knees. His lungs, burned from the scorched air, vent an inhuman squeal. Holiday runs out at the last second and hauls him toward the lift. Oro's burnt skin sloughs off and Holiday loses her grip. She falls. Glaucus and another Lion rush out to grab Holiday and pull her into the lift just before its doors seal shut with a bang.

Silence.

The lift descends. Our armor steams.

Holiday still holds the skin of Oro's forearms. She sets it gently on the floor and orders weapons checks. I stare at the skin. I stayed too long. That's my fault. Add it to the list. But I managed the retreat. I saved lives, just not in the Nucleus. We can contain this invasion.

"The lift will take us to the emergency tram, where we can transfer laterally to Bastion Two," Holiday says to me. *"We will make it."*

I nod, but soon the lift begins to slow. She checks its systems. "Let me guess. Shaft is blocked," I mutter.

"System says there's debris down there. We might be able to slip past it, but the lift can't."

"Let's try. Abandon the lift." I turn on my gravBoots and feel the uneasy thrum at my feet. All thirty of my guards activate their grav-Boots too.

A pair of Lions open a hatch at the bottom of the lift and drop out of sight to scout the way. We hear the sound of pulseFists first, then a report of enemy contact. The Lions' signals go dead. It's not debris down there. I peer down the hole and see metal glinting in the darkness below, and rising fast. A horn sounds in the darkness.

"Minotaur," I murmur. "Down is no good. Everyone, out the top. Drop the lift on them."

"If we leave the shaft now we'll come out in the middle of the Bastion," Holiday says. *"They could cut us off if they—"*

"Would you rather go down?" I ask.

"Up we go, lads!"

Holiday releases the top hatch and we pour out of the lift. By the time I'm through, my Lions have opened the door to the level above. There's gunfire, but they shout *clear* and I hustle through. Three Grays in Votum space armor lie dying. Holiday makes them dead and Glaucus blows the lift behind us. It shrieks down the shaft.

Twenty-eight Lions and I take off into the Bastion's corridors at a sprint. My helmet's HUD provides a tactical map. The Bastion's sensors report hostiles pouring in through multiple levels. I keep my razor in its hidden holster and take a rifle. My armor is identical to my bodyguards', and for good reason. To the enemy, I'm the ultimate prize. Damn that lift. Damn those clawDrills.

I inform my bodyguards of the situation on the fly. "We're cut off to the east and west. Enemy is pouring in. Rath and Votum. With the fortress evacuated, there's nothing to stop the enemy advance except automated defenses. We're in danger of being cut off. We can maneuver sideways but we need to go down. Get to the Hollows. Our best bet is vertical shaft D. If it is blocked, we try shaft B."

Already I'm stacking contingencies in case my plans fail one by one. I flip to the bodyguard frequency to hear Holiday adding on. *"—her safety is your only priority. If you are wounded and cannot keep up, you will be left behind."*

"Nil that," I snap. "We are outnumbered. They will close in from all sides, but they are glory hounds out for themselves. They will compete against one another to get me. We are not them. We are a pride. We kill together, we work together, we survive together. They came for a hunt, but they forgot: *hic sunt leones*."

"*Hic sunt leones!*" they echo and we pound metal.

The hallways are a blur of tension and silence punctuated by random and intense kinetic violence followed by retreats, mad dashes, and weird refrains where hiding in lavatories or strategy rooms and even a kitchen become moments of extreme dread. It is a dance, and the enemy is finding we're as hard to pin down as a greased eel.

But sadly, they aren't a pair of hands grasping at us with their transports pouring troops. They're about to become a very big net.

My twenty-eight Lions are tougher, better equipped, better trained, and better led by Holiday than the capable but standard Votum legionnaires. Apollonius's men, on the other hand, are Martian veterans—hard bred and battle-scarred. And for them, hunting me is personal. Many would have been Augustan legion. My father's own. He didn't suffer fools. Neither does twelve years of war.

No matter how good my Lions are, they will die if we don't get out.

I won't be killed, though. I'll be chained and dragged through the streets in Lune's triumph.

The Votum Greens kill the power first. Our running firefights flare in the darkness. We hit like lightning, cover our retreat, and disappear into the station time after time, always trying to find a gap. We hit when we have to, we hide when we can, but mostly we run, phasing in out of sight in our ghostCloaks.

More and more we run.

Running on local power, the doors still function, and I retain control of those with my Sovereign implant. We split up half a dozen times. It confuses their pursuit, but they start to get wise. Cut off vertical shafts. Form a hard-deck on lower levels we can't pass. Deploy hall-spanning particle shields, traps, auto cannons of their own. Mines.

We turn into a hall, running from Apollonius's closing horn, and a Lion simply disappears in front of me. Like he didn't even have armor. I don't even know what killed him. The last thing I see is one of his legs tumbling down the hall.

Panting a few minutes later, I kneel in the darkness of a rec room for

Red Legion I, where jellyfish writhe in an aquarium. The jellyfish are red, grisly like that poor dead Lion's leg. His name was Arminius. He liked garments. He wanted to design them. He was going to use his pension to start a clothing line. I was going to give him seed money. He didn't know.

"Movement in hall," Glaucus says and recalls his drone. "It's Holiday."

Holiday and six Lions slip silently into the rec room. "Did it work?" I ask.

Smoke slithers from Holiday's armor. "They bought it. Votum thinks we're two levels up, heading east toward the secure trams. Drones say shaft D is clear."

"And Apollonius?"

"His men are mostly tied up with Red Legion in the battle for Sector Two. We got a coms officer to talk." I don't ask how. "Officer said Kavax is alive. Apollonius broke his back then sent him to the rear as a prize."

He's alive. Thank Jove. I breathe out in relief. A prisoner, but alive.

I try to set my worries away as we wait for the second team I dispatched to return to the rec room. When they do return, they carry two domed backpacks. "Cloaks and razors?" I ask.

They nod. "Twenty and fifteen. Some night optics too."

"What do we need those for?" Holiday asks.

"Insurance," I reply.

The intercom crackles. *"Augustus, this is Cicero au Votum. You are cut off from your army. You are surrounded. There is no escape from the Bastion. Neither is there shame in surrender. Indeed, there is more dignity in that than in being hunted down and killed like an animal. Apollonius is stalking you this very moment. Lune is not Atalantia. He has agreed to recognize the Republic as a valid entity. Should you surrender to me, you will be afforded all the rights due your station as a head of state. Your men will likewise—"*

I click my tongue twice and my Lions move out.

Cicero is getting worried. So am I. We haven't seen Apollonius himself in an hour. Never a good sign.

The halls are quiet, dark. Our wounded don't slow us yet. We have five so far. Two from Apollonius himself, and he didn't even manage to close. The wounded are fueled by the cold fire of the Republic's best emergency combat cocktail: Mjolnir-6. I'll stay sober. Mjolnir-6 blunts empathy. If I lost that, I'd send what was left of my bodyguards to create a distraction so I could slip out by myself. For the Republic.

That's what Adrius would do. Or my father. Not me.

Not today.

We move slow and careful, and manage to reach one of the many entrances to the tank garages in which shaft D is located on level thirteen without encountering the enemy. We're so close. Holiday turns on her ghostCloak and slips forward into the darkness with three Lions. I hear the slur of a railgun. A gurgling. Holiday comes back with a red knife. Drones were right. Clear except for a few Votum techies trying to hack the gravLift's controls to better move troops.

I give the nod.

We move into the hangar as quietly as possible in heavy armor. Three Lions have popped the lift door open a few meters. It's a big door— thirty meters wide for tanks. We form up around the Lions. Holiday drops a drone into the darkness. I watch its feed on my HUD. The shaft looks clear, even on thermal. The shaft terminus is deep within the moon but still within Sector One's pie-like shape. It won't get us back to our lines in the Hollows but it'll get us close.

Holiday spots something I don't and motions a team to deploy nanowire across the mouth of the lift entrance. They string a dozen strands of the near-invisible polyene fiber. Casually, as if checking the door for traps. Her drone is still snooping down the shaft as she replays what caught her eye: cold spots arrayed around the circumference of the tunnel shaft two hundred meters below. A few degrees lower than the surrounding metal. Scores of them. GhostCloak dampeners. Good ones. The tunnel is lined with soldiers. It's a trap.

Apollonius for sure. He didn't know what level we'd access on, but somehow he knew this shaft was our way out. I thought I'd randomized our movements enough.

"I'm picking up a signal. Stasis field. Probably in the shaft. We'd be frozen right above them if we dropped. Flies in amber."

I eye the darkness of the garage behind us through the lenses in the back of my helmet. He's watching us right now. Maybe sending men to flank us. Maybe coming himself.

"Why haven't they made a move?" I ask.

"They don't know which of us you are. Better if we're flies in amber."

Meaning they don't know which one of us not to kill, and they respect the quality of my Lions enough to know they'll have to kill most of us. So, Apollonius is trying to take me alive after all. Did Lune make him a team player?

"Let's punch them in the mouth and scram." Holiday nods to the walkways above. *"Go through engineering. Cook this shaft. We have other options."*

"There's another option. Do we have a net?"

"We have two."

"Lions, Kavax is captured. He has sensitive information in his head, and he is our friend. Many of you know him. Many of you have attended his namedays. The only way we will get him back is if we have a prisoner of equal worth to trade. But we have a chance to take one here." They answer with a chorus of affirmative radio clicks. "He mustn't suspect a trap. Holiday, you're up."

"I'll use the drone," Holiday says. *"Soon as they move, false retreat, first pride into quicksand formation. Second pride fire support. Third pride secure hangar doors. Let's not get flanked. Exit is engineering. Sovereign, you're rear."*

"No. I'm first pride. You lot might need the muscle."

Holiday pauses but doesn't argue. *"Do not draw your razor."*

I nod, ready for violence. Holiday guides the drone back up the shaft and lets it get extra snoopy. It coasts toward one of the cold spots. Closer. Closer. A laugh echoes in the shaft. The cloak melts away. A bull's head emerges from the shadows in front of our distant drone.

"Found you," says Apollonius.

A fly-sized drone blinks above. Apollonius must have one on every level leading to the shaft.

We drop charges and let Apollonius see us flee. Through my rear lens, I watch the charges go off. The gap in the door becomes a column of fire. Golds cocooned in pulseShields rise through the flames and slip into the hangar after us. Right into the nanowire. The nanowire activates and oscillates back and forth like a saw, at a rate of a million oscillations a minute. It goes through armor like butter. I've never seen men cut into such weirdly precise blocks of meat and metal as the first three who meet the wire. The next two hack their way through it and chase us. Then Apollonius rushes in backed by Grays.

"Now," Holiday orders, and my Lions turn on the enemy and fire as one on Holiday's targeting tag. The first Gold disintegrates as twenty-

five expert marksmen and I converge our fire. The Lion next to me bucks back, arms broken like twigs as he's shot by a pulseFist. Holiday targets the next Gold. So do twenty-four rifles. He is deleted five paces from us. Metal pings off our shields. One of his legs hits my shoulder.

This all in four seconds. It let Apollonius get closer.

Pride two fires on the Grays rushing out of the shaft, and Apollonius charges into my pride. We fall back like quicksand to receive him. Our plan is that six of us are to pepper him with fire, two are to shoot nets, and two are to deploy a shieldDome.

Something goes wrong. It happens too fast and too close to see what. One of the net Lions is cut in half. His fired net flails overhead like a sheet in the wind. Another Lion is knocked out of sight. I glimpse Apollonius coming toward me in a rush of dark purple metal. I fire two shots before he's on me like a kicking horse. He drives a shoulder into me without looking and hacks off a Lion's arm. He doesn't know which one I am. His shoulder check dazed me, but he expected it to knock me out. I'm no Gray. He's facing the other way, about to kill our last Lion with a net gun.

"Holiday, bodyguard."

Apollonius also has cameras in the back of his helmet. I reach for my concealed razor. My reach draws his full attention like blood draws a leviathan. He turns, a mass of terror and metal.

"All hail Lionheart," he purrs.

His giant razor cleaves through another Lion as it comes toward me. It sparks just in front of my helmet, blocked by a glowing blue aegis. Holiday's. I seize the moment, dive low, like Darrow taught me, razor out, and spear Apollonius in his left knee. He doesn't make a sound. He headbutts me on the crown of my helmet and my HUD shorts out.

I go right into the floor. Our netman fires. The net snares Apollonius and electrocutes his armor. His razor is trapped, but one of his arms isn't. He takes my razor from his knee and cuts himself free. I scramble to my feet, woozy, and see the shieldDome is up. An iridescent half dome projects from a Lion's back unit. It ends a half meter above the floor. If it meets the floor, it'll blow like a bomb. That Lion has to stay upright and out of the fight.

Apollonius is trapped inside the shield with eight of us.

His men outside it, fighting my other Lions, go into a frenzy when they see the risk to their commander. Holiday and two Lions fire into Apollonius on full auto. His shield dies with a thunderclap. He loses his grip on my razor. It skitters out from beneath the dome. My Lions converge on him and take out his legs. Glaucus armlocks Apollonius's left arm. Others grab his right arm. I tackle his knees as hard as I can. He teeters and falls on his back. A Lion stomps on his hand and kicks his huge razor out from the dome. I help lock down his legs.

Now's our chance.

Holiday rushes forward with her misericord. The weapon looks like a dagger hilt with two colored ends and no blade. When jammed down on its black end, a magnetic charge in the hilt forces out a depleted uranium drill with a shaped charge. When jammed down on its red end, the drill has enough haemanthus tranquilizer to put down a griffin. It's a new weapon, cheap to mass produce, and it is meant for grounded knights in armor that is as expensive as the gear for an entire legion. Like Apollonius's.

Apollonius sees the misericord coming and thrashes against us. I can barely control one of his legs. A Lion grabs his horns and puts his feet on Apollonius's shoulders to hold him steady for Holiday. Apollonius was hiding his true strength. He jerks his neck down and pulls the Lion into Holiday's way. The misericord bangs against the man's shoulder and the Lion knows he's dead. That dose was meant for a Gold. Apollonius lunges his head sideways and drives one of his horns up into Holiday's stomach.

Glaucus shouts in anger and pulls his sidearm. He fires a full clip into the bull helmet. The metal dents. Buckles. Glaucus fires again and I see the digger round penetrate the helmet at the cheek. Apollonius moos and his head flops sideways out of Holiday. Blood and teeth pour out the hole in the bull helmet. Still kneeling atop Apollonius, Holiday pulls a backup misericord and drives it down into Apollonius's throat armor.

It doesn't deploy. *Lemon.*

She slams it down again and again. It's a dud. Both ends. My heart sinks. Then I lurch as Apollonius fires his boots. We hit the dome with the sound of a gong. We're almost knocked free. My Lions outside cannot hold back his troops any longer. Still pinning his legs, I give the order to kill him. Holiday puts her rifle into the hole in his cheek.

Then I hear a clatter. A circular metal ball rolls toward us.

Apollonius didn't have to get free. He just had to be difficult enough to put down for something like this to happen.

A grenade rolls under the domeShield and goes off. The force knocks me sideways. Dazed, head ringing I stagger up as soon as I can think of it. But amidst the groaning armored bodies, the largest is rising. I haul up Holiday and call a retreat.

27

VIRGINIA

A Good Death

Trailing blood and machine fluid we flee from engineering to a lateral tram tunnel. Its car is dead. We run all-out for two minutes. Apollonius follows. No more horn blowing. No more mockery. He wants to kill us.

We had him and we couldn't finish the deed. We're numb with the shock of it. Down to eighteen Lions now. Everyone is injured. Ten of us would not be able to run without the battle juice or their suits, including Holiday. Glaucus picked up my razor. I take it from him and pat the carryall. Poor Sophocles.

"Slag the shafts," I say. "We'll ride the shit."

"If we even can reach sanitation," Holiday says, dubious. Her gut wound is starting to slow her down. Glaucus and I help her along.

Cicero seems to know where we are now too. He's squeezing in. I feel his forces constricting. Flowing from other levels. We'll never reach sanitation. We can't go down or up. We need help. The Bastion's hall temperature—which I've gradually been increasing—is just passing ninety degrees Fahrenheit. We also still have the gear bags I had my Lions take from the armory. We still have a chance. It's not a good one.

We can't get close to sanitation. So with the enemy closing in, I lead my Lions into a flight-training room as close as I can to the brig. Wheezing blood, Holiday props up a Lion missing a leg and puts a gun in his hand. Her helmet is off. Her face pale and sweating.

"We left a trail of blood. We can hold here. Buy you time. You are uninjured. Take a ghostCloak and slip out," Holiday says. She can't raise her left arm. Her shoulder is shot out too, but I'm more worried about the horn wound. "We failed you on the Day of Red Doves. Allow us to redeem—"

She looks crestfallen as I hoist the gear bags I had the Lions fetch from the armory earlier. I head for a side door. "We're near the brig," I call back. "Hold the fort and be ready to move."

"He's a traitor!" Holiday calls after me. "He may kill you! My Sovereign!"

I don't slow down.

Cloaked, I hide in an alcove across from the brig's entrance as Votum legionnaires thunder past in the darkness toward the sounds of gunfire. My Lions are under siege. A Gold with a brilliant sunburst helmet and white cape stops and looks at the brig door. It's Cicero au Votum. "That is a big door," he comments flippantly.

"It's the brig gate, *dominus*," a centurion says.

"Don't correct me. It's a door."

"You want Greens on it?"

"Don't be absurd. Keep them on the lifts. Lysander doesn't need convicts. He needs a Sovereign and this fortress. Let's not ape the Minotaur and drop the ball. Still. A big door. Perhaps I have friends entombed inside. I did always wonder what happened to Mercurius. We'll crack it over supper. Come, come."

I wait until they're gone and rush for the brig gate. Detecting my Sovereign implant, its mass sinks into the floor. The brig is empty of guards. For obvious reasons, emergency evacuation does not include high-security prisoners. I push in and decloak. A bank of cells glows in the dimness. Inside, their residents watch me approach with my bags.

Sixty-three of them are Obsidian braves found guilty of treason against the Republic. These are the Alltribe cast-outs too guilty and too high profile to pardon. I pass brute after brute until I land upon the dread prize in a cell twice as thick as the rest. The Golds call him Sky Bastard. I know him as Valdir the Unshorn. He lies on his bed with his hands behind his back.

I do not like this man, not one bit.

Valdir was already a teenage butcher by the time he watched Darrow give Ragnar the razor in the mud of Agea. That moment left an impression on young Valdir. He fell in love with my husband. And I mean the sort of love Patroclus had for the son of Peleus. Not exactly versed in Ovid, Valdir expressed his love in the language he knew best: making Darrow's enemies into stains. He grew bitter, as those whose love is unrequited do, when Darrow paired him up with Sefi as a power alliance to unite the Obsidians.

At least that's my theory.

Taller and younger than Darrow, Valdir reeks of demigod petulance. He is troublingly handsome, especially for an Obsidian. His eyes are deep and surly. His cheeks are gaunt and patterned with freckles. He is corded with ropelike muscle and stained with tattoos.

His famously long valor tail is gone. He said he shaved it himself the day before we found him in one of Mars's most expensive brothels covered with Pinks and drunk as a Red. But he's a liar, so who knows. He *should* be ashamed. He betrayed the Republic for the Alltribe, and now the Alltribe has disintegrated, its best troops and all its ships stolen by Volsung Fá. I wonder if he wishes he was with Fá and his Volk brothers savaging our outer Belt depots instead of rotting here in this cell.

He looks as happy to see me as I am to see him. We are not strangers. Too many times Darrow brought him to dinner in the Citadel. I thought him a bad influence on Pax. Maybe I've underestimated my son. Maybe he was a good influence on Valdir. Pax sees worth in Valdir, as he did in Lyria. So here I am. A Sovereign with her hat out to a traitor.

Kind words will not affect this man, so I lay down a challenge.

"You're able to look me in the eye," I say. "I wonder. Will you look Darrow in the eye when he gets home?"

"Tyr Morga is dead, Gold. The Free Legions are dead," he says, soulless. He does not stir from the bed. "Sefi is dead. My . . . heart is dead. I am dead."

Certainly not lacking in drama, this one. You'd think his cell bed was a fainting couch.

"Darrow is not dead, Obsidian," I say. "He is on his way back to Mars as we speak." Valdir looks over at me. A timid fire builds in his coal-dark eyes. I give that fire a good gust of wind. "You don't care about me. You don't care about honor, or the Republic, or even that these sirens mean the Society is taking Phobos and Golds will come in here and kill you like a dog. But I know you care about what Darrow thinks of you. So do you want to die here, and be remembered by him as a cheap traitor? Or do you want to look him in the eye as I tell him: Valdir is worth forgiving. Valdir helped protect the Republic, his Sovereign. Valdir may be bald, but he has valor still."

Valdir sits up. His eyes narrow at the damage to my armor. He may not be brilliant, but he has the kind of low cunning I need. "The Bastion has fallen and you are cut off? That razor score on your greaves is thick." I didn't even realize I had one. "Falchion made."

"It was the Minotaur's." Valdir's lips twist. "My bodyguards are trapped not far from here. I need you to help me save them. I need all of you, or I will never see my son again." I upend the bag of ghostCloaks, optics, and razors. "Your answer, Valdir? They are dying as we waste wind."

He looks down in contemplation. "What is in it for my brothers?"

"If we escape, freedom. If we don't, a good death."

"I want armor."

"Fresh out. But the halls are dark and nearing a hundred degrees." I poke the ghostCloaks with my toe. "I hear you used to call that hunting weather in the Rat War."

He considers for an exhausting moment, then looks up with a terrifying smile.

GhostCloaks are worthless when the enemy has thermal optics. But in the dark when the air is as hot as the human body, the last thing anyone wants to encounter is eighteen fresh Obsidians with razors and nothing to lose, all of them chosen and led by Valdir the Unshorn. I don't have to create a diversion. I don't have to do anything. I offered to help. He said, "Rear echelon belongs in the back." I told him where my Lions were and which direction I needed cleared. Then he went off to do it.

I know how it will be done. I made the mistake once of asking Darrow how a griffin rider was useful in the tunnel fights of the Rat War. He told me over dinner. My appetite waned with each sentence.

"It is very hard to break armored infantry groups without artillery or machines," Darrow explained as if detailing how to clean a rifle. "So you don't target them. You target their psyche. You target their groupthink.

"First you send in a man like Sev or Valdir with their best ghouls—that's what we call them. If you can't plant the ghouls ahead of time, they should sneak deep as possible into the enemy ranks before hunkering down.

"Then you kill a scout on the outskirts. Badly. The more screaming the better. That'll draw curiosity and a heavy squad. The squad will investigate. If you can, make them disappear in silence. You want the rest of them using their imagination. You want the commander wondering if he should send another squad, maybe even a century.

"Then you confirm their worst fear. Give them a death chant—we carry recordings when we don't have Obsidians. You want anticipation. You want them preparing to face a known fear, physically, mentally. That's when your ghouls awaken and start killing the command chain.

"Then you have your main force close in silence at a fast pace and hit them as hard as you possibly can. Groups can hold a line together. Groups will make last stands. But alone, rarely. It's very hard for the human mind to accept dying alone. No matter their number, if you summon enough chaos they will feel alone. Especially with anonymity, especially in the dark. Once the first breaks, the rest will feel like they have permission to follow."

When Darrow saw the look in my eye, he didn't say what he was going to: when they break, that's when the real killing starts. He didn't say much else that night. Neither did I. His eye was on the past and all he'd seen. Mine was on the future and all we yet might.

Valdir had learned from the best.

Waiting in the dark, I think back on that night as I hear the first scream in the distance. The scream goes on for half a minute. Then silence. Gunfire. Silence. Barked commands. Metal boots running. Cicero shouting orders. Then the death chant of the Obsidians. Apollonius exhorting his men to be brave. Cicero calling reinforcements. Then the ghouls must have awakened because the real chaos starts. It doesn't sound like battle. It sounds like a nightmare.

A few minutes later, a ghoul appears out of nowhere. This one's skin is no longer pale. "Deed's done."

I follow the ghoul to the training room. There is a court outside the other rooms where people practice war. In that court where the enemy had once gathered, there are only armored corpses and a tower of blood in the center, mutinous and swirling. Valdir has not turned off his cloak. His braves call to my Lions to come out.

My Lions seemed so mighty in the Nucleus. They are almost sheepish when they limp from the room and see the tower of blood and what Valdir's braves have done. They rush to me protectively and stand between me and the remaining braves. The Obsidians suffered immense casualties. Only ten attend Valdir. Eleven out of sixty-three. Valdir must see my expression because he decloaks. His chest is flayed open in three places.

"A good death," he confirms of his casualties.

"Minotaur?" I ask.

"Almost." He shrugs. "He had armor. He killed ten. Votum four. Both are wounded. Both enraged. They will regroup. After this, they will follow. They will kill us the next time. We must flee now."

"This way." I take off at a jog. It is slippery going.

We reach sanitation but already hear the enemy coming. I help Holiday into the fetid tube through which daily flows all of Bastion One's aggregated waste as Glaucus and Sophocles slide straight down into the darkness. She gives me a nod and I give her a push. She disappears, the last of my Lions. I load in and hang on by the rim. Valdir and his Obsidians wait with blank faces. Radios squawk in the distance.

"This leads to the fertilizer plant. It is two clicks above the Hollows," I say. "We will have to go on foot from there. Through the hydroponic farms. If they follow via the shafts, they can still catch us before we get to the Hollows. It'll be a race over open ground from—"

Valdir puts a hand on my head and shoves me down the tube.

28

LYSANDER

War Engine

SNIPER BULLETS HISS DOWN at me from the bulwark that bars our path to Sector Eight. Demetrius, Markus, Kyber, and Drusilla return fire and follow me as I duck away from the assault to take cover behind the freshly arrived tank Rhone's using as his forward command post. An antman has finally managed to get in touch with Horatia.

My guards chug down water and wait for the antman, a Green bristling with antennas, to hook his umbilical into the port in my helmet. Rhone nods to me from inside the tank. I nod back. We're doing well. From the opposite side of Sector One, Horatia's face appears in my helmet, washed with static.

"Horatia. Report." I can barely speak my mouth is so dry.

"We're taking heavy casualties, but we're almost through the bulwark to Sector Two."

"Well done, Horatia." I swat away the medicus attempting to examine the three holes Virginia's Lionguard put in my thigh, cuirass, and shoulder. The suit has filled the wounds with clots of resFlesh inside while liquid armor has coagulated to plug the holes in the armor itself.

Markus kicks the pushy medicus in the ass. "The suit's got him. Begone."

A ragged cheer goes up as a column of starShell reinforcements bound for the bulwark clomp past at a jog. Ajax runs with them, accompanied by a dozen Gold new men. He lifts his razor to me as he passes. I salute back. He wanted one last crack at the bulwark's stubborn defenders. On a day he can't seem to fail, who was I to say no?

Blocks of Praetorians and my house legions queue down the tunnel waiting for the bulwark to fall. We're ahead of schedule, but we need to keep up the pace.

"Apollonius will be driving like a dagger to the Hollows by now," I tell Horatia. "He's relying on us to suck up their reinforcements. Once you get through, keep pushing. Do not stop. Do not slow. Press to the bone. We're taking heavy casualties too, but if we keep up the pressure, Apollonius will punch through the Hollows. He does that, the sectors will fall in a cascade."

"Diomedes is still on pace?"

"On pace? He's setting it. If we had ten like him, we'd already be dining in Agea."

I exaggerate, but not by much. The rim knight is the consummate professional. He joined my attack as he promised he would, and targeted no glorious prize like the Julii complex or the dockyards themselves. Instead, he went after a water cistern and flooded a reactor to shut down all the power to an entire Bastion. Then he took on the credo of the day—speed, initiative, shock—and went back onto the surface of the moon and skipped ahead with his phalanx to cause more chaos behind the enemy's lines in Sector Six. He is unsupported and will die if I do not reach him, but that was his idea, and not once has he bothered to check how far out I am. I said I would meet him in Sector Six at a set time, and he trusts that I will.

"We push on at this rate, I'll unite with Diomedes in just over an hour."

Horatia wishes me luck and signs off. I pop my helmet and Markus tosses me the tank's water hose. I chug and see my Praetorians also bear wounds. The Lionguard were tough bastards. Still, we smashed through them to take down their shield reactor to Sector One. With Ajax, Kyber, Rhone, and his old guard, my double-strength century has more talent than I've ever seen in so small a unit. I do my part, but I'm no Achilles. That's not my role.

There's a roar from my Praetorians and house legions. I peer past the tank. Ajax has vaulted up the debris spill from the breach and hacked down the last Republic starShells blocking it. He jumps to the side and our starShells pour through the bulwark into Sector Seven. Chanting my war cry, the legions follow at a run. Ajax salutes the Praetorian below who gave him fire support.

"Shit," Markus curses, enamored with Ajax's performance.

"Right?" Demetrius says. "War engine."

"He's a prick, but . . . shit."

"Just needed the proper vehicle around him's what."

The medicus is watching Ajax too, likely ready to pester him as well. Only Kyber isn't watching Ajax. She leans against the tank, her jaguar eyes slits.

Markus turns on me. "*Dominus,* if he doesn't kill you, can we keep him?"

"I think that can be arranged," I say and watch Ajax fly back. He lands with a bang.

"Water?" Drusilla asks.

Ajax seizes the hose and drinks for a half minute. He spits when he's done. "And they said this place would be a second Rat War." He points at my guards. "You four." They wait for an insult. "That fire support. You deserve statues."

"Thirteen," is all Drusilla, Demetrius, and Markus say, but it sounds more like *obviously.* A knight like Ajax only really comes unlocked when he can close. That takes a good fire team.

"Your mother taught us, *dominus,*" Markus adds. It is shockingly charitable, but not as much as when he says, "You're the best closer we've seen."

"Since her?" Ajax asks, annoyed.

"Period." Ever.

Ajax goes blank, nods, and turns to me, deeply touched. He doesn't know what to do with that compliment. The medicus comes to pester Ajax. Kyber raises her rifle and shoots the medicus in the head. We're all stunned. Kyber approaches the medicus and opens his hand to reveal a trigger mechanism.

Suicide bomber. He was waiting for Ajax to blow.

"How'd you know?" I whisper, still a little stunned.

"Didn't. Gut," she says.

Ajax is even a little irked by her. "I owe you my life."

"Thirteen." She nods to me, meaning Ajax owes me the debt because she is Legio XIII Dracones, and Legio XIII Dracones is an extension of me. She glances at the other three Praetorians with a strange expression on her face.

"Let's get back to it," I say. A moment later, Rhone exits the tank. I enter. He doesn't look happy.

"We've got a problem." He shares a feed from our landfall on the moon's surface. A ragged enemy dreadnaught is exchanging fire with our ships and escaping back toward the safety of Sector Three. "That's the *Pandemonia.*"

Ajax senses the tension and fills the tank entrance behind me.

"I thought Julii was tied up on the pole—"

"She was. She just punched through and dropped her own Rain. Here." His finger falls between Horatia's force and Bastion One.

"How many did she drop?" I ask.

"As many as they could in a minute. Twenty thousand? More?"

I frown. "That woman is mad, but brave. I'll give her that. Still I don't see a problem. This is why we have Cicero in reserve. Send him from Bastion One to cut her off."

"Cicero isn't in Bastion One," Rhone says. "Neither is his vanguard."

I look back at Ajax. He's dumbfounded. I'm already hailing Cicero with the tank's powerful antennae. His face soon fills the display. He's flying. He shouldn't be. "Cicero, where are you?"

"Can't talk. We're hot on Augustus's tail. She's on the run through the latrine lines."

I pause. Apollonius was to have Virginia. That was his price for giving my operation his public support. "Cicero, how many men do you have with you?"

"My vanguard, of course." He goes on. *"I know you're wroth, but I'll not have a Martian taking the glory. This day was made possible by Mercury. Her people and her honor should not play second fiddle to a vainglorious madman like the Minotaur."*

I close my eyes, too angry to speak, and listen to my troops pouring past into Sector Seven. Just a moment ago it was the sound of victory. How things change in the blink of an eye. "He's ruined us," Ajax says. "The greedy little bastard . . ."

I can yell later, but I can only fix it now. "Cicero, patch in Apollonius."

Reluctant, he obeys. Apollonius is furious. He should be. Cicero is butting in on his operation. I silence their coms. "Goodmen, we can lay blame later. You both need to quit the pursuit and turn around now. Julii is on her way down. She is behind our lines. We believe she has Pegasus Legion and is headed for you." Apollonius is already barking orders to turn around. Cicero still doesn't understand the danger. "Cicero, you are probably flying into a counterattack coming up from the Hollows. They will slow you, and then you will be hit from behind by Victra and the only troops of the Free Legions not killed on your planet. The best troops. If you turn around, you may be able to slip past them. If you do not, you and all your men will be dead in thirty minutes."

"If he's lucky," Rhone murmurs.

Cicero laughs, but his voice sounds very small. *"Those can't really be my choices."*

"I suggest following Apollonius's orders. I will try to send help. Good luck."

Rhone and Ajax let me think. "Rhone, recall the men. Tell Horatia and Diomedes to do the same. We're overextended."

He nods.

"You said if we didn't take Phobos in a day, we wouldn't take it in a year," Ajax says.

I nod. "She's behind our lines. Say Julii doesn't go for them. Say she goes for Horatia or us or Diomedes. We'll be lucky to not die on this moon, much less conquer it."

"What if I cut the head off the snake?" Ajax says.

I stare at my friend. He is in his power, confident, competent, and the last man Victra should want seeking her head. There's no vainglory in his eyes. No hubris. He is here for me as I was there for him when the storm raged in the Ladon. Hope flickers.

I glance at Rhone. "If he took Golds only, he could get there," I say.

"He'd have to travel fast," Rhone says.

"Speed, intiative, shock, you said." Ajax steps toward me. "You did not spend Glirastes, your ships, and your men for a second Rat War. We are not just fighting the Republic, Lysander. If Atalantia comes . . ." He looks afraid. "This is our only shot."

"I will go too then," I say.

He grins. "We have always had different skills, you and I. This is what I do. Press the attack. Take the moon. I will guard your back."

Gratitude swells in my heart. We bump heads and waste no more time. He rushes out. Rhone watches him go. "Octavia would have sent Aja," he says, approving. "And he *is* better."

That is little consolation. Victory balances on the edge of Ajax's razor.

"Tell Apollonius and Cicero to expect him. Let Horatia and Diomedes know what's happening." I raise my helmet and head out with my Praetorians to press the attack into Sector Seven. A roar from my house infantry signals Ajax's departure down the cargo tunnel. Fifty Gold knights trail after him.

29

VIRGINIA

Pity Them

SALVATION FLIES PAST OVER the tangerine trees of the hydroponic farms. A counterattack up from the Hollows. Armored Reds with Greens in mechs flow past to either side, saluting and cheering us. The water around the roots of the rows and rows of trees ripples in the wake of the mechs. Harnassus thunders past in a towering machine that salutes and trundles toward the fertilization plants in the distance.

We thought we were dead when my Lions and Obsidians shot our way out of the waste collector and emerged covered in shit. We heard our pursuers in the distance, and we ran. They were gaining on us even after we reached the fertilization facility and threaded our way through the huge haulers that ferry the fertilizer to the farm level.

We were running out of options. The levels closer to the hollow center of Phobos are vast. A far cry from the tight confines of the Bastions. In open ground, we would not have made it. But the vast levels also don't block signals so onerously as those near the surface. I was able to call for help. Still, Votum and Rath bailed before they reached us at the fertilization plants, before they even saw Harnassus and the counterattack that's still surging past us. What spooked our pursuers so badly they lost interest in a prize as juicy as me? I suppose I'll find out soon.

My Lions and Valdir's Obsidians stumble on toward the safety of our lines in the Hollows covered in feces and urine. The Obsidians are quite talkative, and seem to think they're on a grand adventure. Some even splash along with Sophocles in the water to clean themselves.

"I smell like Blues," an Obsidian mutters.

"Shut up. There are worse things than shit," Valdir says.

"Imprisonment," another Obsidian growls.

Valdir nods. "Yes. That is worse than shit."

"The Blood Eagle," the same one growls.

"That too."

"Long battles in armor where you have to shit but can't because of the crust that—"

Valdir turns on the man. "Aimless babble."

The growling one growls. "Eggplant."

Valdir looks over at me. "He was hit very hard."

The growling one has a pug face and is quite stout. He jumps and grabs an orange. He doesn't even peel it before taking a bite with chrome teeth. "Oranges." He throws it over his shoulder.

"That's a tangerine, you idiot," Holiday says.

"Do they not mourn their brothers?" I ask Valdir.

"Do not yours?" He nods at Glaucus who shares a joke with another Lion. My Lions are exhausted and somber about their dead, but they share smiles and private words as they help each other walk. "Sefi once told me fruit is never sweeter than after you've eaten shit." He peels a tangerine and eats it before spitting it out. "Not ripe yet." He considers his braves. "They will mourn later. For now it is enough they know their brothers would smile to see them living. So they smile for their brothers, for they had a good death. Later they will miss them. Later they will mourn."

I feel strangely comforted by his words.

An armored man with a wolfcloak lands in front of me as we exit the tangerine grove. It's Screwface. Fresh Lionguards set down behind him. Medici unload from a skiff. I laugh seeing Screw. I put him in the Hollows fallback command center to keep him from the front. It takes time to get used to bionic limbs. He limps toward me with a huge smile that inverts when he sees the state of us all. "My Sovereign, we thought you were trapped. When the Nucleus didn't arrive . . ."

"Rath and Votum had us. Why did they—"

"Victra. She dropped Pegasus behind their lines."

I stare at him. "How . . . she couldn't have known where I was."

"She was already on the way. She knew she needed to stop their momentum. To save the moon," he says. "I relayed your message to her personally. Told her you needed help."

"If they doubled back, the counterattack won't reach her in time," I say.

"No. She's on her own and advise we recall the counterattack as soon as possible. She told me to tell you something." He smiles. "Do not worry for her. Pity them."

It is impossible not to grin at Victra's bravado. "The fleet?" I ask.

"It's not good, but Niobe and Char are putting up one hell of a fight. I'll take you to the command center." He looks warily at Valdir.

"Hello, Sky Bastard. Long time. Valdir the Shorn these days, eh?"

"Who are you?"

"Screwface." He points at his face. "Deep op."

"Ah."

Screw looks questioningly at me. I look at Valdir. "There's no way off the moon. You can either fight or—" Valdir stares hard at me.

"I'll take him and the rest, please," Screw says like he's at an auction. "Howler Den is empty these days."

"I will not be ashamed to fight under that standard," Valdir says to me.

Screw sniffs him. "Probably go to the medici first. If anything kills you, it'll be an infection."

I look back at my Lions before I go. They are swarmed with medici.

"Thank you. We stayed too long to manage the retreat, but every life we lost in our escape saved ten thousand," I say to them and touch my chest. "*Hic sunt leones* indeed."

My fresh Lions salute the ragged survivors. I find it oddly stirring when Holiday, Glaucus, and the survivors salute back. Then the fresh Lions fall in behind me and I head for the command center with Screw.

30

LYSANDER

Edge of Glory

"I TOLD THEM YOU'D BE here before I finished," Diomedes says as I approach.

Diomedes sits on a fallen advertisement in the broken cityscape of Sector Six eating an apple. His Dustwalkers lounge around him drinking honey and combing their long hair like Spartans. "We agreed on a time, did we not?"

"We did. Our compliments." He nods to the Praetorians behind me. Markus, Drusilla, and Demetrius do not nod back. Exhausted from our push through Sector Seven and then the brutal assault on the bulwarks of Sector Six they're in no mood for pleasantries, especially not with a Raa. Diomedes tosses me the apple. Almost half of it is eaten. "The territory we've taken. But can we hold it down?" he asks. "They're worried about the worm in Sector One."

I look up to see Dustwalkers lounging all the way up to the dome of the bazaar. There must be several hundred. His Grays are regrouping nearby for our joint push west. I don't see any Obsidians.

"Victra is being dealt with by Ajax," I say and take the next bite of the apple. "Horatia is continuing her push. Votum men are still flowing in. Bellona will come behind them. The fleet battle could be going better, but our job was the moon. We are on the edge of glory. If we can take two more sectors in the next hour, the cascade will be irreversible and we'll have the Hollows surrounded."

He nods. "If." He watches me without emotion for a few long moments.

Rhone pings my com. "Dominus, *we have a report from Ajax.*"

I smile at Diomedes and take another bite of the apple. "Go."

Rhone pauses. *"You'll want to hear this in person."*

The apple sticks in my throat, and I cough. "Excuse me."

Diomedes stands and ties up his hair. "I will come with. We bit the apple too."

The forward command tank's interior fades away as I watch the fight unfold in the gloomy theater of industrial plants where Victra met Cicero's vanguard. At a distance, nothing of note can be deciphered. The plants are vast, the knights and riflemen small. If anyone started the day with shining armor, it is either black or gray now. The fighting swirls through tank yards, smelters, Drachenjäger plants, up to the air, and even within the netherworld of pipes and shafts that comprise the top of the level. A thousand tiny battles, each with their own little story.

I only care about one.

"It was a trap," Rhone says. "Cicero chose to stand and fight instead of being picked apart trying to escape. He was holding his own. Doing a fine job considering the quality he was facing. He thought Victra was with her main force. Her armor was, at least. Ajax was coordinating with Cicero for a strike on Victra. He came down a hauler shaft about a kilometer from the battle. The enemy must've had scouts out. Or drones. Either way, they knew he was coming and how, long enough for Victra and another knight to be waiting for him when he exited the shaft. They had Obsidians with them. From what we understand, Ajax's party gave a good acquitting of themselves. But they were outnumbered. Three to one."

My mouth is dry. "And Ajax. How did he die?" Rhone hesitates and spares Diomedes a look. "I sent him. I should see. Show me."

Rhone shifts to a grainy visual. "This footage we have isn't much. It came from one of Cicero's drones. He was wondering where Ajax was."

An assembly area for Drachenjäger rolls past. Bodies come into view. They're hardly recognizable as men. Others hunch over them. I tell Rhone to zoom in. The image degrades a little. The bodies are the new Golds Ajax took with him. The Obsidians are scalping them. The drone carries on. Obsidian corpses litter the ground now. Three figures stagger. At first it seems like they are drunk. I zoom in further. Ajax is hunched between Victra and another assailant. I force myself to watch. There's something dispassionate about the way they whittle Ajax down. Like watching animals kill each other in nature when the predator has their teeth in and both animals are just laying on the ground. There may be bouts of struggle yet to come, but they both know it's only a matter of time, and they have time. When it ends, it is sudden. Ajax manages to defend himself from the male assailant, but not Victra. He goes down, and she hacks him apart. Then she cuts off his head, stands on his body, beats her chest, and roars.

There is no audio, but I hear her anyway.

Rhone kills the video and waits in respect for me to break the silence. "Did Cicero escape?" I ask.

"We don't know."

"Where was Apollonius?"

"He used Cicero as a diversion and chose retreat. He told me he followed your plan, but he would not throw away his men because of the folly of a Mercurian amateur. Which is very fair, if you ask me. He is now ensconced in prime real estate. Julii's dockyards citadel."

I boil inside.

"The man with Victra. Who?" I ask.

"We don't know. If you ask me. The cloak. The style. It could be a man. But . . ."

"But what?"

"Thraxa au Telemanus," Diomedes says. "Windsweeper. Her style. Not common."

Rhone watches him a little more closely. "You've never met Thraxa."

"I study." Diomedes's eyes narrow. "I thought the Republic Obsidians defected. That they were sacking Republic cities in the Belt."

"Not all of them want to be pirates apparently," Rhone says.

Diomedes processes that and sighs. "A pity. This was a good plan." He looks at me. "We are overextended, Lune. I will prepare my phalanx to pull back. We will do this the slow way now." As he leaves, he sets a hand on my shoulder and looks out the tank door. "The edge of glory cuts both ways. Condolences. He was gifted. Loss . . . it is never easy."

He walks out and tosses the apple away.

Rhone watches me as I turn to stare at the last image the drone captured. Victra stands on Ajax's chest howling upward. "It was an ambitious plan," Rhone says. "We can hold probably Sectors One and Eight, but we should eliminate Victra and Pegasus Legion or at least contain them before we proceed further." I nod, numb. "It will be a grind, but I've done grinds before. We'll have the numbers when your allies land their men. It's not a loss, *dominus*. Not yet."

"Not a loss?" I say and look up at his stony face. "This was supposed to be our staging ground for an Iron Rain next month. The ships. The money. The lives. That moment in Rome. Ajax . . . Ajax choosing me. Dying for me." I shudder in horror. "Glirastes. All that for a slice of moon and a grind? If that's not a loss, what do you call it?"

The old soldier frowns. "War, *dominus*."

31

VIRGINIA

Détente

THE BATTLE FOR PHOBOS is turning into the type of battle students of history shake their heads at. It is pugilism without any other recourse, as uncomplicated as it is brutal, measured less by the inventiveness of clever commanders and more by their willingness to sacrifice men, and the willingness of those men to be sacrificed. While tactics can be used nearer the surface of Phobos, with either side daring the guns of opposing warships to launch canyon attacks to flank the enemy, the battle for the interior is an affair of will. How many men will Lysander or Julia or Cicero or Apollonius sacrifice to gain another level, another hundred meters of tunnel, another sector to fill?

How many sons and daughters of Mars will I spend to stop them?

Victra is still lost behind enemy lines. With no prisoner of equal value to trade, Kavax is still in enemy hands. No word has come from Darrow or Sevro. Our battered fleet dares not challenge the enemy away from the surface we still control. We cannot get reinforcements from Mars.

As the days progress, and the hours in the command center of the Hollows with Screwface, Harnassus, and Niobe bleed into one long stale nightmare fueled by coffee, protein injections, and casualty reports, I feel the gulf between my concept of leadership and Lysander's growing. Lysander may promise a new age, but he'll sacrifice a generation to get it.

The enemy creeps forward. Meter by meter. I see no way to turn the tide.

Knowing how easy it is to become alienated by casualty reports and to measure lives in terms of ground lost or gained, I force myself every morning and night to visit the wounded. It was Holiday who told me if I forget to feel the cost, I will grow accustomed to it. Like Darrow did. I love my husband, but I know the Republic cannot afford for me to follow in his footsteps.

Twelve days after Lune's assault on Phobos, the medical wing of Bastion Four overflows with fresh intakes. I slept poorly, snatching only four hours of sleep between assaults against our front in the Hollows. Niobe woke me to help rebuff the latest assault.

It's all I can do to manage a smile, a kind word, and pretend I don't see the horror in the dying as I move bed to bed. Holiday limps behind me. Her ribs were crushed by Apollonius's boot, and she is not yet fit for frontline duty, but she rivals me in popularity and refuses to stay in her hospital bed.

The horrors have not changed since my first visit. Young faces of all Colors are peeled back by fire, their bodies riven by metal and energy. We could heal almost any one of them, but not all of them, not all at once.

Moving bed to bed, I clutch their hands and let them talk, give each their moment even if it wears me thin. The wounded whisper the big words pushed by our Violet and Red propagandists. *Freedom. Hope. Reaper.* I find it remarkable that the dying have not lost faith. In fact, they cling to it more fervently than those who still retain their faces or limbs. They do not ask where Darrow is. They do not beg me to tell them why he has not returned. They clutch my hand till their knuckles go white and tell me he will return, and with him he will bring dawn for his friends, and judgment and doom to the enemies of freedom.

I weep after my visits. I am jealous of their faith. Jealous they cannot see the struggle from my seat. Thankful for it too, because I know the odds better than the young men and women who've given their youth, their lives for our cause. I pity them for their faith in my husband as much as I cherish and admire their conviction. Golds are a faithless breed, founded in the gross sobriety of atheism, but the rest of the Colors are willing to believe.

When they die holding my hand, when they whisper Darrow's name, when they say they will find peace in the Vale, I break a little more, and each time I find that in the breaking I grow stronger, more desperate to protect this beautiful idea my husband has awoken, that I have helped prosper. They do not crave freedom for themselves. They crave freedom for others, for those yet unborn. In that I find a dignity greater than any Gold virtue.

Theirs is a religion of hope, not doom. But in the face of an enemy that will not stop, that takes every concession as a foothold for further aggression, I know I must find a way out of this fight or it will drink up more of Mars's strength than we can afford.

When I arrive back in my Hollows command center from my nightly inspection, there is a commotion in the assembly area where the troops parade. Flanked by officers, Niobe greets me. Her bird's-nest hair is tangled from a long day in the operations room. "What's all this?" I ask of the shouting soldiers. Her eyes are filled with tears. I fear the worst until she kisses me on the mouth and takes me to see for myself.

Soldiers and medici and engineers fill the southern tunnel entrance to the assembly area with cheers so loud I think Darrow has returned. I push with Niobe through the mob to see Victra striding in looking like hell warmed over. Thraxa is beside her. Behind them lumber the fighters of Pegasus Legions. Victra's eyes are bloodshot and feral but when she sees me she calls out: "My Sovereign! I bring tidings from Sector One. Also known as . . ."

"The asshole of the worlds!" the legion shouts.

"And gifts. Cicero au Votum." She thrusts forward Cicero on the end of a leash and holds up a rotted head. "And Ajax au Grimmus. The rest of him couldn't make it."

32

VIRGINIA

Parley

LYSANDER PARALLELS MY WALK across the metal wasteland. To my right, the lights of starscrapers sparkle with promise on the southern horizon. The northern horizon is bleaker—a mountain range of utilitarian mesas strewn with artillery obelisks shattered like trees by lightning. For two weeks, war has raged over most of the moon. I hardly recognize it.

As our armies grind against one another, their commanders have snuck away for this secret meeting.

I clomp forward. My welder boots are magnetic and heavy—clumsy as stipulated. With honor all but dead, the demands from both parties for the meeting were extensive and fraught with suspicion. But in the end, it comes down to trust. Trust that neither of us wants to die, and trust that we both have more to gain from an adversary with some modicum of social comportment.

A couple hundred steps from our airlocks bring Lysander and I together under the shadow of a crashed warship. The young Lune is more physically intimidating than I expected. Gone is the little boy from Octavia's garden, the one who used to lose to me at chess over and over again, never tiring of it. He is taller than I am by a head and a half now. His pulseArmor, riddled with field patches and pressure seals, is that of a man who's faced weeks of corridor fighting and emerged with a reputation for luck and leading from the front.

His face is a mirror of mine, haggard from strain and sleeplessness.

This is not a spoiled, entitled princeling. This is the last of Silenius's blood. A man who has come to see if he too can conquer.

Lysander and I fall back on tradition. He touches his heart with an open palm and extends it to me. I repeat the gesture and set my palm on his. His is larger. We draw back and he extends an analog audio cord.

The accent of the Palatine fills my helmet. "Sheathed is my blade, held fast by my word," he says.

"True are my words, secured by my name," I reply.

"*Salve*, Augustus."

"*Salve*, Lune."

He smiles, somehow still a little shy, or perhaps playing at it to set me at ease. "How many of our ancestors have said thus to each other do you think? The formal rites of parley?" he asks.

"On the field of battle? Formally? Four, all told."

"Not five?"

"You're counting Oceanus and Agrippa."

He frowns. "I shouldn't?"

"No. Oceanus may have been a chip off Silenius's block but Agrippa was adopted into my house after the Genetic Accords. He had as much Augustan blood in his veins as you do. Which is a little over one point nine percent, actually."

He smiles. "You always did know your history."

"You, on the other hand, seem to have embraced theatricality. I remember a more bookish boy. A more prudent boy. You've learned to gamble on shock."

"I have. Your husband is a stern teacher."

Lysander's face is not as classically handsome as Cassius's or Apollonius's, instead his is the lean hunting-dog ideal. Like Roque's face, but intense instead of romantic. And it is a face no longer burned. According to our intelligence, it was fixed just before his speech at the Colosseum. Right before his true debut. He's replaced the scar with marks of sorrow. Ajax was close to him.

"I doubt you had Darrow's full attention. You must wonder what will happen when you do. Will you measure up?"

Lysander meets my tone. "I am here. Above his planet. Talking to his wife. Where is he?"

"Oh, he'll turn up when it's most inconvenient for you, I'm sure."

"I'm sure. He'll be wanting this back." He turns bodily so that I can see the two razors sheathed on the outside of his left thigh armor.

One is familiar. When I gave Darrow his razor after the Institute, I had no idea what a symbol it would become. He was mocked for its curve by Tactus and his fellow lancers. They were too embarrassed to fence with him. Lorn wasn't. Twelve years later, every child knows its shape. Now Lysander pats the hilt. The gesture makes no sound in the vacuum.

"I did have his full attention, Virginia. For a moment. In a dark street. He was tired, wounded but so was I. I broke his sword. Probably his arm. And put my razor through his chest. Then he fled and left his sword behind. It was not cowardice to run, he'd simply been outmaneuvered. Just as you are now."

I nod to the statue of Darrow to the north. "Have you seen it up close yet?"

"Not yet," he says. "But by week's end, we'll have pushed you off the pole, and I can take a closer look."

"Pay special attention to what's in his hands. It just looks like a sphere from far away. It's not, at least in its details. It's hundreds of manticores, hydra, skulls, hammers, eagles, a few Poseidons, mermaids, centaurs, and crescents he has taken from the prows of Gold warships. No room to include any from ships smaller than a destroyer-class. You understand? That is consistency against intense competition, Lysander. For twelve years now. One battle does not make you a lord of war."

"I have Darrow's blade. I have Darrow's warship. Now I have more than a third of your moon. I also have seventy thousand of your best troops encircled in Sector Three. Your men are exhausted. We have legions that haven't even landed yet. By the end of the week, half your army will be cut off and herded toward the Hollows, where we will kill them."

"Fine. By the balls then," I say.

"I beg your pardon?"

"You don't have me by the throat. You have me by the balls. You can wrench and twist and it will cause me terrible agony. But in the end, they are just balls, and I am a woman, so I will go on, enduring without my balls and I will pester you with death by a billion cuts. Except it won't be me. I am not a captain who goes down with his ship. I am a

Sovereign, who will delegate to people more suited for tunnels and darkness and the horrors that happen there."

"Pegasus Legion is at less than half strength. You'd waste them here?"

"No. Rat Legion. I believe even you know them."

By his expression, I see their reputation does proceed them. "They were on Mercury . . ." he says.

"Sure. Sure. But you know how legions work. Like snakes shedding skin. What we're left with is the old skin between theaters. The tough skin. The veterans who earned their discharge. Ones that went toe to toe with Atlas. You know. Our worst, because they learned from the enemy. Odd, their centurions petitioned me personally to come up here. Something about you impaling their brothers and sisters from Heliopolis to Tyche."

He sighs. "That was Atlas."

"Poor man. Gets blamed for everything."

"You judge my name, not me."

"Yes. How unfair to prejudge a man based on something he can't control." I smile. "What reflection of you shall I judge then? Your company? Your politics? Your deeds?"

Gears move behind his eyes as he squints at me. "Bluff. All omens, no figures. You may have snuck in Rat Legion, but if you try to bring real numbers, Helios and Dido will eviscerate them as they come up the gravWell. We are invested in Phobos. We will take it."

"Yes. Because you *have* to take it. Atalantia waits, licking her lips for you."

"You could drag it out for months. But we both know where the battle for Mars will be won. On the ground. In the tunnels. All this is blood down the drain. Yours, mine, all while Atalantia grows stronger."

Oddly enough, that is my problem as much as it is his.

"Yes," I say. "I've seen footage of your address to the Two Hundred by now. I knew things were not perfect between you and your fiancée, but I must admit I hadn't counted on you openly rebelling against her."

"Can you blame me?" he asks.

"Not one bit. Truly, I thought it was an expertly navigated and well said bit of discourse."

He smiles at that, the genuine compliment being received in kind.

"Virginia, I've known you almost my entire life. You've taught me some of my most cherished lessons. Chief among them, that we as a people need a language other than violence, or this war will never end. In many ways you and I are more alike than anyone else in this struggle. We were both raised in the shadows of tyrants and expected to be the same. But you are not Nero any more than I am Octavia. You proved it by sparing my life all those years ago. Allow me to prove it now."

At last, a hint of light.

"How?"

"A solution to this . . . quagmire. If you agree to quit Phobos with all your legions, I will guarantee safe passage to the planet."

"Including those encircled?"

"Yes."

It actually is generous. "In return?"

"You will agree to neither sabotage nor scuttle the Julii-Sun ship-yards. You will leave behind no saboteurs or assassins. You will, where possible, disarm your booby traps and turn over the codes to the defense systems to me."

"That seems . . . generous of me," I say.

"It's not. You will suffer a blow to your reputation, as well as lose your seat in orbit, and your ability to make ships. But that is already lost. With this, you stop the bleeding and your Republic will live to fight another day."

"Is that all I get?" I ask.

"The taking of Mars is a complex puzzle of which Phobos is only one piece. Any mistake on my part and my host will fracture or disappear into the red soil below. I will have the docks but no fresh helium. Our stores are as low as you seem to think they are." I smile at that. "I will have the moon, but a host of allies eager for their cut, and I spent all my ships."

"Except one. I noticed you're putting part of the dockyards to use on the *Lightbringer*. I don't think I've ever seen someone doing naval repairs during a battle before." He does not reply. "To whom will you bequeath the moon?" He looks uncomfortable. "Come now, you won't keep it for yourself. You'll look greedy."

"Apollonius."

"Not your chief investor? Bellona won't like that."

"Of all my allies, if you could secure the loyalty of any, which would you choose? Were you me," he asks.

I consider the question. Lysander and I do have similar ways of thinking. I would lock down the one ally my competitors would try to steal.

"Let me understand, just so we're clear, I'm to aid your war effort because I find you marginally less detestable than Atalantia au Grimmus," I say.

"Only marginally?"

"I would need a little more than a vague notion of your intent against Atalantia," I say.

"When I charged Phobos, I secured my reputation for valor. It was unsteady. But I lost some of that shine I had in Rome from all this. So now I need to show I am an investment that pays off. If I do, I'll have the numbers to call a referendum to remove her dictatorial powers. Then, once her immunity is gone, I will call her to the Bleeding Place, and I will kill her."

I watch him carefully through the glass of his helmet. He means it, or he's an even better liar than I am. "She's a fair blade."

"So am I."

"You don't have a reputation for that."

"Good."

"If you do that without a cause for blood, it will cast you as an immature, power-hungry little man."

"I have cause for blood. Atalantia killed my mother and my father. Which is why I'll ask one last thing from the Sovereign of the ill-fated Republic as part of this merciful and honorable bargain."

"What's that?"

"I'll be needing two Oracles. If you can spare them."

I think of my tanks back in Agea. "I can if you can spare a Telemanus."

He considers. "For a Votum?"

"Just what I was thinking."

He nods. "I think it is important for you and me to understand, we are at war, but this war will not end until we can be civilized." He pauses. "We recovered Ajax's body, but I would like his head."

My friends and commanders roar in outrage when I tell them the deal I've struck with Lune. Sitting with her mother, Thraxa actually turns purple with rage. Screwface shakes his head and lists the casualties we've taken. Only Holiday nods along in agreement with me. Victra says nothing. She reclines in a chair with her legs spread and a whiskey balanced on her chest.

Char stands up. "We lose the docks, we lose the war. Ships are our only hope."

"Of course you'd say that," Harnassus says.

"Because I'm a Blue?"

"Because you're a fighter pilot, man. Red, Blue, Vermillion, you all fight to the last," Harnassus says. His eyes twinkle at me. "Are you thinking we turtle the fleet? Play at friction between Lune and Atalantia?"

I smile. "They're their own worst enemy. We give this to Lysander, he's a competitor. He's also our best chance of taking out Atalantia."

"So we want to empower a Lune to unite the Society?" Char asks. "That's mad."

"He's weaker. He depends on alliances. On pleasing greedy tyrants who all think they're his most valuable ally," Holiday says. "He can unite them because they are afraid of Atalantia. And we should be too. She is raw power and a realist. Lune is an idealist. When she's gone, his allies will fight to fill her vacuum. There will be division. Factions. Weakness. Is that not a better plan than ramming our head against a wall up here?" Everyone turns and looks at the cinder block of a woman. Even Victra. "What? The price these people paid for Phobos, you think they want to take on Mars? All the people that died up here just bought Mars a reprieve, unless Atalantia swoops in. So let's give her a problem, yeah?"

Victra sips her whiskey. "Well, that's settled. We need to win so the grunt can run for office." Holiday looks embarrassed. I couldn't be prouder of her.

"It all comes down to one question in the end," I say. "Who will crack first? Mars? Or the Golds? I bet my life on us a long time ago. Looking at the people in this room, I would do it again."

"Oh, don't get emotional," Victra says. "You're the Sovereign. We have to do as you say."

"I'm glad to hear you say that, because I've agreed to not scuttle the dockyards as we depart." No one speaks, but I sense their unease. "And you will have to give Ajax's head back, Victra."

Victra grimaces. "But I was crafting a chalice for Sevro." She sighs. "Fine. But really, Virginia. The Minotaur is in my house. No word from Sevro or Darrow. We've lost Phobos. You said there was good news."

I nod to Glaucus. He disappears out the door. Sophocles runs squealing from his pout in the back of the room and runs after Glaucus. Infectious laughter booms from the hall. A moment later, Glaucus returns pushing Kavax in a wheelchair. Niobe and Thraxa rush him as Sophocles tries to inhale his face.

Victra doesn't move but tears well in her eyes. "Shit. I said don't get emotional."

33

LYSANDER

Master of the Spoils

T HE TRANSFER OF PHOBOS is nearly complete, and so far Virginia has honored her word. That is good. It means this war need not end with a genocide on Mars. Yet it is still war. So to rub salt in their wounds, I host the battle honors as the last Republic ship leaves the moon.

Amidst the Golds in their shining panoply and the Grays under their proud standards, a feeble man walks carrying my once-white cape. It is dark with blood and soot now. The man is as ruined as the cape. He is terribly burned, and looks like a wax sculpture that sat too close to a fire. He is not the same man I gave my cloak to. That man is dead. This one was from my own clawDrill. His gnarled hand trembles as he gives me back my cape. I drape it over my arm. It is filthy. His words are so slurred I cannot hear what he says.

I bend and pin on his uniform a golden phalera of a torch burning a moon. He looks down at the torch and begins to sob. I rest a hand on his unburned forearm. "This pain is temporary. Your glory is forever. Hail Orlow of Gamma!"

Thousands roar his name.

Softly, I say: "I will make you whole. You are part of my house, and so you are part of me. Come to me when you are healed, and whatever you ask you will have."

"Hail Lune," he whispers out his lipless mouth. "Hail Lune."

Tears well in my eyes. I let them flow as I pin phalera on the few Helldivers who remain before moving up the hierarchy. All who partook in the battle will receive a phalera. Precious few are Gold, and come with the patron favor—an opportunity to approach me at any time later in life and ask for a boon. When I come to the Grays, I kiss Markus, Demetrius, Kyber, and Drusilla on their cheeks. Rhone doesn't want a medal. He's already a Dux. Fresh honors would be stealing valor from the men, he said.

There are many Blues who earned honors, but none as much as Pytha. In addition to her charge on Phobos, when the *Lightbringer* was no longer fit to fight, she turned it into a refuge. She saved countless lives by using the ship to collect thousands of wounded and escape pods from damaged Rim crafts during the pitch of battle.

To her, I give the Civic Crown. Made of common oak leaves, it is the highest decoration a general can give. Unlike lesser phalera, its worth is not enhanced by the precious metals that make it, but rather only by the honor itself of receiving it, because no price can be put on the saving of lives. Later, it will be tattooed onto her head to carry with her for life. I feel immense gratitude for her. Only when I saw her again did I cry for Ajax. She knew what he meant to me. I told many stories of our childhood to her when we sailed on the *Archimedes*. She held me in her arms, and I felt safe not having to be strong.

When at last I come to the Golds I look out with particular affection at the several dozen new men and women who made their marks. "In you I see the future the Conquerors intended," I tell them. "Virtuous knights defending the rights of all Colors to live in worlds of peace, order, and prosperity. It is you New Shepherds who will carry the flame of the Society. To you, no honors will be given. To be Gold is honor enough. Instead, I levy a burden."

Rhone brings out custom razors. Each with a pearl crescent on the leather grip. I cut the cheek opposite their Peerless Scars before giving them their blades. They stare at me as if I were Silenius himself.

The room bursts into applause. I see Pytha watching the Red who brought the cape, Orlow. Though he is burned, he claps and hollers in almost pathetic joy. For a moment, she looks sad. Can she not see what I am doing here? She will. They all will. After I finish this blasted war.

With the ceremony done, I return to Rhone and he attaches my cape.

What was white is now stained in blood. I do not turn my back, as is custom, to see if they will give me the highest honor a citizen can receive, an honor higher even than the Civic Crown, because it can only be given to a general by the acclaim of his troops—the Grass Crown.

Instead, I face them, signaling that I do not deserve honors. They like that.

Rhone says the ritual words in my ear. "Remember, you live for the fallen, for at your word they ran to the grave. Make not their sacrifice be ever in vain."

A hologram glows to life to show the great statue of Darrow standing astride Phobos's north pole. A ship from all my major allies fires on the statue as one. As his monument crumbles, the figureheads Darrow's hands imprisoned are liberated at last. Centaurs, suns, eagles, crescents, skulls, gold all, scatter out to space. We will let them go. And the retreating Republic? They watch their idol fall.

"Per aspera ad astra!" we roar.

Pink acrobats twirl over the couches arrayed in Victra's garden. I pluck a grape from a passing servant's tray and plop it in my mouth. I worried I'd be seen as weak for reaching a compromise with Virginia. Far from it. My allies are elated. They could care less that we let the enemy retreat. Phobos itself is the prize, and not even Apollonius liked the style of war it was taking to claim it—though he was responsible for most of our gains. I saved us a year of blood and treasure and won us a second dockyards for our faction and a beachhead for our siege of the planet, and all it took was a little compromise. I am heady with success, but in no mood to celebrate.

"Is it possible for you to relax?" Julia au Bellona pours me a glass of wine from the pitcher.

"Don't I look relaxed?" I ask and sip the wine.

"Looking and being relaxed are very different things, young man." She sighs. "Apollonius swore this party would be tasteful, so as not to offend our dusty guests but honestly I expected that to mean the Pinks would be edible," Julia says with a leer at the Dominion couches. She lies on her side next to me pretending to be drunker than she is. "Either humility has curbed his libido or you have a stronger rein on him than I thought."

I come back from my thoughts of Ajax and shift my bloodstained cloak before sipping my wine. "I can't vouch for his libido, but I believe your lancer Pallas is quickly becoming an authority on the subject. I warn you. The southern route is not the way to Apollonius's heart."

Julia laughs.

"Prostitute my lancer? Vile. She's special. Like a daughter to me, really." Pallas, far more seriously dressed than she was at my party, is interrogating Helios au Lux, and he seems to be enjoying it. Missing is his shadow, Diomedes. "Pallas is curious by nature, especially about powerful, simple men." Julia eyes me. "Just not the ones who spit in her patron's eye in public."

"Me?" I ask, mock offended.

"You. I financed half this endeavor, and you give Apollonius the dockyards. I should have you poisoned for that."

"Yet here we are, cozy as thieves," I reply. "I promised Apollonius the dockyards—"

"In exchange for being a military marvel, which he was not."

"Who knows that better than he?" I ask.

"Cicero," she replies. "Still pouting?"

"Still."

"Good. The little idiot. I will say, at least Apollonius pouts ferociously."

I glance at Apollonius. The man reclines on a couch all to his own drinking wine by the pitcher and having his feet mutilated by a Red masseur with hands the size of dinner plates. "He's not pouting. He's furious. You can't chastise or put reins on Apollonius. All you can do is consistently deliver until he realizes it's his turn."

"Which would be now, I presume," she says. "Or he'd have fixed his face." I nod. Apollonius's gunshot wound to the face is as ugly as he is usually beautiful. "I think he's the only man I've ever met where his exterior always matches his interior. Take Cassius for instance. Such a strong outer chin . . ." Her eyes dart to me. I have no idea what she *actually* thinks of Cassius. "Word on that?"

"If they try to sneak into Mars, we'll catch them," I say. "Helios assured me. For Darrow, he's pulled out all the stops."

I pause as an acrobat descends on a column of silk. The Pink comes a stop upside down with her eyes very close to mine. Her breath is scented with cloves and roses. "We are talking," I say.

"I don't mind," Julia says. "Go on, blow off some steam."

I remain looking at the Pink, until she retreats back up the silk with a sigh.

"All my energy is focused on this war, Julia. I literally don't care about anything but our path forward."

"That's a little pathological and unhealthy."

"They cut off Ajax's head," I say. "People are dying. The man who gave me this cape today, the Red. His face was half melted. If you saw the look in his eyes, the faith. He believes we know what we are doing. I will not let him down."

She holds my gaze. "Good. I also tire of petty things. But I need honesty."

"Fine. I didn't give you the dockyards because I didn't need to because you can't push the issue or take them back. And if you had them, you'd be too powerful. Mars always needs two families. One with helium, the other with the military might."

"So that's to be Bellona and I'm to be August?" she asks. "Gross."

"Who won that battle? I let him have the yards so I can give you the planet." There is a particular quiet to a powerful person when they realize just how much more powerful they could become. They usually say nothing for quite some time, like Julia right now. "I know we've lost a lot of ships. I know you're worried about Atalantia. But Virginia thinks we are going to settle in here, recover our losses now that we have two dockyards. Build up a massive fleet until we attack. Everyone does. Even Helios. He's already complaining about it. I say we shock the worlds. Hit them in three days. A full Iron Rain with everything we've got."

Her mouth falls open.

"Lysander."

"If you want the planet, you will back me. I'm going to propose it at the end of this party. I know Atalantia. She won't let us become more powerful than her. She will intervene. So, let's move while she's tied up with Luna still. Speed is our weapon. Rhone says it can be done. Apollonius is a nuke about to explode. Cicero wants redemption. The Rim is impatient to get this over with. We have the momentum. Darrow isn't down there. Let's win this.

"Horatia is right now working on Dido. If Dido is in, we can protect our flanks from Atalantia. So, I'm going to go see if she is in. You think it through. Think fast. Speed is our weapon. Let's make Mars yours."

I stand. She stares up at me. "When did you get such balls?"

"When my friends started dying for me."

She grabs my wrist. "It's your allies here who are taking the risk. The Rim will of course agree with this . . . you're trying to impress them. Unity, I thought that was just rhetoric. No?"

"Julia. It is not the Society without the Rim. But before the Society was anything else, it was an idea. That idea is what we need to reclaim. We are in this together." I tap my temple and pull my arm away.

Dido's companions—a warmer variety of her chilly species, at least compared to Helios's fortress of isolationists—welcome me to join them on their couches next to Horatia. "So, golden boy, you spared us a looming disaster by sweet-talking Augustus. What next?"

"That's what I came over to ask you two."

"Dido hasn't given me her answer yet," Horatia says.

"We already know what Helios will say," I reply. "But Helios won't stick around if Atalantia comes when we're taking the planet. He'll just pass the work off to her. Job done. So if Atalantia comes and gives you an ultimatum: leave now or protect us, what will you do?"

Dido watches me very carefully. "What do you want, Lysander?"

"I want the Morning Chair. I want Atalantia to die. She killed my parents because my mother and father were Reformers." Dido glances at Horatia. Horatia nods. "With the Rim? I want your people to believe you're more than your utility to us. That we take risks together and share the rewards together. I know you have all the food you need from Demeter's Garter. But I know your civilization needs a better source of helium. Privation need not be a way of life. I want Martian helium fueling a second age of prosperity in the Rim. I want reforms here." I nod up to the Pinks. "I want them to be shifted to the arts, not processed for consumption. I want more dignity. Less violence, more law. And I want you and I to be able to talk to one another directly without mystery and intrigue. It's the only way we're going to fix these worlds after this war."

Dido leans back. "When I first met you, I thought you were a conniving little shit with too much ambition for his own good. You're all those things, but all this isn't for just for your own good. Is it?"

"Only in my weaker moments."

She glances at her friends. One by one they nod.

"There it is then. If Atalantia comes, we won't run. And if Helios tries, he'll have to be the first Rim Imperator in history to abandon his own on a field of battle." She leans forward. "He'd rather eat glass than have that after his name in the history books."

Horatia touches my hand. I smile at her and stand. "I'll give the speech after dinner. Is Diomedes here?" I ask.

"Looking at flowers and not picking them, as usual." Her companions almost smile. I look up at the Pink acrobats. "No. The actual flowers. You know, Lysander, I like Horatia here, but the only reason we are talking like this is because of my son. He's your champion, in private at least." I frown. Could have fooled me. "Don't abuse him, please. He's far more gentle than he appears."

I leave to wander Victra's gardens in search of Diomedes. The stars twinkle through the trees as I walk, and I feel a sense of satisfaction. Despite the difficulties, things are coming together. With the help of the Praetorians standing watch, I find the rim knight crouched over blue aura flowers near a running spring. "You're a hard man to find," I say.

"Not really. I'm the only one in the garden."

"I had to ask the Praetorians. Didn't even know the garden went back this far."

"Did you have to ask the soldiers, or did you want to?" He bends to look at a brilliant crimson flower shaped like a sword. "It's good to have a common touch with the men. I eat with mine."

"Every meal, I hear."

He points to the flower. "We don't have these. What are they called?"

I pause. "The Vanquished Foe."

His eyes darken and he examines it for a few moments before standing in disgust. "A bad name for a mediocre flower in a meagre garden."

"Compared to your horticulture, it must be."

He turns on me, stone-faced. "How is your heart? Your friend. I hear his head was returned today. You gave him a sundeath."

I frown, about to lie. "Hurting. Thank you for asking. You're the only one here who has."

"Why do you think that is?"

"Ajax was an asshole. No one mourned Tharsus either. I'm not sure even Apollonius has brought him up once." He says nothing. I nod toward the path, and we begin to walk. "You spoke to your mother about me," I say. He waits for me to go on. "Thank you. Why did you?"

He considers. "If the Rim and Core refuse to be allies, it seems it is inevitable we will become adversaries. In either case I think it would be preferable to deal with you than Atalantia."

"Your father and your mentor are both isolationists," I say.

"Yes." He nods toward the party. "Our ways are older than yours in the Rim. We have older sayings because of it. Older biases. Helios thinks we can burn the bridge behind us." He lifts his eyebrows. "The Core will always be more powerful than the Rim. In a war, we could never win, we could only make it not worth your while. In short: You seem to do what you say. I do what I say, always. I think that is important."

"So do I. I said Mars must fall. I meant it. Tonight I'm going to propose we launch an Iron Rain as soon as possible. I would like to be able to say you and I have agreed to fall in the vanguard. Me with my Praetorians, you with your—"

"Lysander, you are bleeding." I check my wounds. "Your eyes."

My fingers come away with blood as I wipe my eyes, and the ocular nerves ache with a dull pain. No. No not now. Not like this. Diomedes is about to call out for help. I stop him.

"Kyber?" I say.

A pause. "Step away, au Raa," Kyber whispers.

Diomedes jumps when Kyber slips from the shadows. "Kyber, I am poisoned. It's the Lament. Get Rhone." Kyber freezes. She knows the Lament. "Kyber."

"She's gone," Diomedes says. "What can I do?"

The pain is growing exponentially worse by the second. I can barely keep my eyes open. Was it the wine Julia poured? The grapes? A flower in the garden? *Atalantia*. It has to be Atalantia. The pain has spread to my spine. I bend like an old man.

"What can I do?"

The pain is in my legs now and my balls now. It's like a pressure made of fire. I sit down and try to stay as still as possible. I can barely breathe. The party in the distance is growing blurry. "Keep them together," I whisper. I can't hear him reply it hurts so bad. Drills burrow into my temples. I reach for the Mind's Eye. Octavia said the Mind's Eye could stop poison from spreading through the body, but I don't know how to use it that way. I try to feel my body, to slow my heartbeat, but all I sense is agony and loneliness. I know it's from the Lament, but I cannot shake the abyss opening inside me. It swallows me until I feel nothing but pain and sorrow.

I am alone in a hole. A boy. Sobbing. I want to die. I want to die.

34

VIRGINIA

Remember Earth

"MY SOVEREIGN, STAND BY for a tightbeam with the *Archimedes*. If the enemy attempts to intercept the beam, we will have limited warning," my techs inform me. I run my hands through my hair. Sitting in my stateroom in the *Dejah Thoris*, I feel more nervous than when I stood before Valdir the Unshorn.

"I understand. Cut the beam when you need to. We can't risk compromising their coordinates."

My ship waits in the queue down to Mars. The enemy thinks we're merely being cautious, arranging our capital ships over the descending transports to protect them. In fact, they would laugh if they knew our real intentions. They will when they learn. Our best hope is they laugh themselves to death.

I took a souvenir from Phobos before I left. A menu from a civilian eatery at the spaceport. I don't know why. Maybe because it felt like the Republic retreating from Phobos was the last moment of a dying age. I wanted a relic for what was and will never be again.

I banish defeat from my mind and browse the menu.

One of the entries makes me smile: Ragnar's Vast Hunger—an ice cream dessert slathered with fudge, peanut butter, walnuts, cherries, and bananas that is claimed to be so large only the legend himself could eat it in one sitting. If you can match the famed hero's appetite, the dish is apparently free.

Then my husband's face appears on the viewscreen above the menu, and I stare at him like he is the first man I've ever seen.

It doesn't feel that long ago that I sat atop my horse looking down at two young men by a loch at the Institute. There was Cassius, as distracting a man as has ever been made, but he was so used to drawing all eyes to him that he needed to be witnessed to spark.

Then there was the other man. The dark one. Not in features, but dark in his energy. There was a man who needed no witnesses to burn. His energy was igneous and parthenogenetic, fire reproduced of itself. At first glance, I knew he was a powerful being with no manners, no airs, no grace, only a direction—one that ran straight through me. It wasn't love that he awoke in me. It was fear. But that is a part of love.

It took time for me to see the sensitive being hidden behind his iron walls. It takes no time today. I don't even see what his trials have done to him. Those are details. I see his energy. It is not as dark as I remember. His eyes are soft, yearning, and do all but reach out across the void and embrace me.

"*Lo, Mustang.*"

His masculine voice stirs up the silt of love, and the part of me that's been dormant since he left awakens. "Lo, Reaper," I whisper.

Still, a shield lies between us, held by both parties. Either of us could be a program, an enemy ruse.

"*Our boy?*" he asks before our prearranged test. I find that touching. He couldn't wait.

"Alive," I say.

He looks down, overwhelmed with emotion. "*When was he made? Confirm.*"

"After your first Rain," I answer along with a numerical code. "What was waiting for us after our fun? Confirm."

He gives a code in return and smiles at the memory. "*Applause, innuendo, breakfast, bacon, and friends.*"

"Applause? You wish." I force a laugh.

It *is* Darrow. I feel out of my body. Unable to find the words. "Where are you?"

I sound so young. So fragile.

"*With Cassius and Sevro on the* Archimedes.*"

"Alive. Kavax too. And your mother. And your friends made it home. Char, Screw, Thraxa, Harnassus."

Each name is a joy to him. "*I'm days out from home at full torch. We can see Phobos on our scopes. How bad is it?*"

"You're not running full torch, are you?" I ask.

"No. We've come this far . . . but we can if we need to. Virginia, how bad is it? All we can see are debris. Did they make landfall on the planet?"

"No. No landfall."

"Did we lose Phobos?"

"Yes. We've only just completed the evacuation."

His frown is like one you'd see on a statue outside a military academy, a commander surveying the enemy formation and thinking, thinking. *"But there's no energy wash. No shooting."*

I was so angry at his departure I'd nearly forgotten how comforting he is as a confidant. No judgment, no bullshit, just boundless competency. Some people shirk problems. Some fumble them or pull at them like Gordian knots. Darrow asks questions, finds the nerve center, and then drives a spear into it. His only true strategic fault is that very same unwavering aggression.

I don't soften the truth.

"I surrendered the moon to Lune in exchange for a peaceful transfer."

"When?"

"Five days ago. It took time."

"If only we hadn't taken the ecliptic plane back to Mars . . ." He sags his head.

The comment is so flagrantly vain it makes me furious at him. It breaks the spell his appearance cast over me. He'd what? Wave his hands and send a plague of boils on the enemy, a wave of floods to wash them out of the sectors?

But I pause before I rebuke him. Just by his tone of voice, I can tell he is not the man who left. He is older, his trials etched into his features. His crow's feet and forehead lines are now deep grooves. He is thinner, weary, and concealing at least five injuries. He's encountered radiation, and his hair has only started growing back. He has a beard, a terrible, hairy beard. But the change I sense runs deeper than the physical. His restless anxiety is not gone, but it is muffled by a solemn maturity. Nothing grants wisdom like loss.

"Do you think I made a mistake?" I ask.

He considers. *"I honestly won't know until I better understand the tactical situation. I will need a full report from your Praetors when I get back."*

The more I look at him, the more my doubts compound. "Darrow, they know you're out there. They know you're in a cloaked ship. Lysander lived on the *Archimedes* for ten years. The closer you come home, the more their patrols will tighten. They're on their telescopes. They may not sense you. But your ship isn't invisible. They will catch you."

"Then come get me," he says as if it was so easy. *"Sally out with the fleet. Victra could run the op easy enough."*

I sigh at my inability to describe the battle and violence I've witnessed. Finally I feel like he must have felt for so many years. Words will never do justice to the menace we survived. The intensity of emotions or the cost of seeing so much destruction. So many things have happened I don't even see the purpose in relating—Apollonius, the shit tube, the Nucleus, Valdir.

"Darrow, we can't. We have to ground our ships." He flinches. "It is not the glamorous strategy, but it is my strategy. They almost destroyed our navy. Half our fleet is gone, and we don't have the repair yards anymore." Even if we did, I realize I wouldn't send them. How do I tell him it's not just the difficulty of getting through the enemy fleet that stays my hand? He doesn't understand the level of faith people have in his return. They believe that it will be enough that he just arrives back on the planet. But I remember the sea of faces outside Lykos. The way they spoke the other names after Deanna, but had to shout his. They shout his name to invoke his power.

Mars needs its savior back.

But I look at Darrow and I don't see a savior. I see an exhausted, bearded survivor stumbling home without the ships or the men to turn the tide. He gets back, then what? He's trapped inside the Gold siege like the rest of us? The tactical risk is just not worth the strategic reward, or cost. We need him on the outside.

Pax's words in the snow come back to haunt me.

Quicksilver will listen to only one man. And he's here looking at me.

"No," Darrow murmurs. He's read my expression. *"Virginia. I am only four days away."*

"Darrow." I take a breath. It hurts so much to say what I need to say. "Darrow. I want nothing more than for you to be home. For us to face this together. To see you and Pax in the same room. But, you can't come home. Not yet." The words are like a bullet. Once they've left the barrel of my mouth, I cannot take them back. Nor would I. They are true.

He falls silent. I fear facing down the tidal wave of emotion that he'll release. I fear he'll just ignore me. Just do what his passions tell him. Eventually he asks, *"Why not?"*

"You've been out of this war for over half a year. There isn't time to catch you up. I can send a packet to do that—especially with your Obsidians, Sefi, so much has happened. You have to trust me to know what Mars needs, because the longer we debate, the greater the chance they'll find you. If they find you, they will catch you. Kill you. That would break Mars. That would break *me*. I couldn't take that. Not after all this."

"I didn't come all this way just to sail past you," he growls.

"Did you come all this way to die?"

"Virginia—"

"To hold my hand as I die? That's what will happen. Darrow. My love. If you've ever trusted me, trust me now. The enemy wants you to return. They want us all in one place so they can exterminate us. If you come here, all you can do is wait for them to attack. If you are out there, you can work on the problem. You can build strength. Then when the time is right, you can combine it with ours. With our ships inside the planetary shields, Mars will be a fortress, wreathed with death and teeth. We will hold the planet. We will stave off defeat. I will not let Mars fall. But it's up to you to find us a path to victory."

He wants to say I let Phobos fall. I can feel it. Or maybe I believe I feel it because I hold as much faith in him as all the others do. That in my place he somehow would have conjured a terrible miracle and sent the enemy into flight.

He does not reply.

"Darrow, this is the hardest thing I've ever had to do. The hardest thing—" My voice breaks. I fight back the tears. "Every morning you are my first thought. Maybe news has come as I slept. Maybe you've just landed in Agea . . ." I can't keep the strain from my voice. "But we need you out there, beyond their siege line until you can return at the head of an armada."

"There is no armada."

"What if there were?"

He ignores that and looks at me with so much pain I nearly recant all I've said. To travel so far only to be turned away now, not by a scorned god or a twist of fate, but by his wife.

"*There has to be another way.*"

"If there were, do you think I would ask this of you?"

His eyes fall to his hands, as if they were to blame for the distance and years between us. "*You told me not to go. When I left Luna. I should have listened. I just . . . wanted to end it all.*"

"I know."

"*I thought one last push would see us through. Numb myself. Put it all on me. Get it done. Then we'd get to live the life we'd promised ourselves. Experience the future we wanted Pax to have. I know that was silly.*"

"It wasn't silly. Reality is just more stubborn even than you."

He takes a long, deep breath.

"*You know what I told myself out there . . . each time my mistakes compounded? I'd say, Darrow, next time you listen to Virginia, you jackass. If you get so lucky to see her again. You listen to her as you should have all along. I'm not saying you're always right. But I know I tend to shut down. Sometimes for years. That's not right. It's not . . . the path I want to walk anymore. It's lonely, and we've always been stronger together. After all, we made our tribe together. We made Pax together.*" He grins, lopsided with a devil's sheen in his eyes. I don't care that he's putting it on for show. I don't care that he's not come back with the victory he promised. He may have lost on Mercury, but he's conquered the worst part of himself: his intransigence. Nothing makes wisdom like true loss, it seems.

"*So. Since time's of the essence, you should give me your orders, my Sovereign.*"

35

DARROW

Winds of Duty

"AFTER THE DAY OF RED Doves, *Regulus ag Sun fled Luna on his flagship and disappeared along with the most advanced ships of his personal defense fleet. They were spotted between the orbits of Mars and Venus at Narcissus Station, and then again by one of our spy drones beneath the ecliptic plane. They were last sighted by a military sensor station here."* Virginia's finger taps a small asteroid on the inner fringe of the Belt. *"That was over eight months ago."*

A hologram of Virginia floats in the lounge of the *Archimedes.* Aurae is flying the ship. The door to the cockpit is closed and locked. Whether out of respect or horror, a stillness settles over Sevro, Cassius, and I as it becomes apparent to them Mars is no longer our destination. The only sound is the tick of Sevro's knife as he trims his nails.

Tck. Tck. Tck. I knew he'd never accept this news from me. I hope he will from Virginia.

"At first, I suspected that Regulus had built himself a refuge in the Belt. Perhaps a series of battle stations or doomsday bunkers should the war go foul. Then I found Regulus's logos. That logos traded his freedom for Regulus's books. Not the ones Regulus reported to the Republic auditors, but his hidden accounts and registry of raw materials. I learned that Regulus's empire was larger even than I suspected. It seems for the last ten years he's been siphoning helium from his mines in Cimmeria as well as funding off-grid rare metal mining in the Belt. The metals—mostly antimony, rhenium, neodymium, and tantalum—are all perquisites for warship and next-gen weapons fabrication.

"Since this discovery, our agents and telescopes have searched for the location of his laboratory and dockyard. Despite the resources at my disposal, those efforts were in vain, until a few weeks ago. We have found Regulus." An oblong asteroid appears to the left of Virginia's face. Cassius pulls it outward and expands it. "What you are looking at is Asteroid 12193. An asteroid so unremarkable that even six hundred years after its discovery, it still does not have a name."

Sevro's knife stops as the computer calculates the distance from Mars to the asteroid on the map and gives a range of estimated flight times based on potential velocities, the faster we go the more risk we assume.

"My analysts and I believe that this asteroid is not only a base for Regulus's operations. It is a factory and laboratory for military research. Taking into account the ships that Regulus took with him when he fled, as well as the quantity of metals he has mined over the last nine years, we believe this asteroid to contain a force large enough to shift the balance in this war.

"Five of our fastest ships were deployed to reach this station. We have lost contact with all of them. Whether that is Gold jamming or something else, we don't know. Your ship possesses a unique combination of traits that should help you succeed where they may have failed. A Whisper-corvette made by the Rim, cloaked by Regulus's best technology, and a diversion in the form of an assault on Ceres that should draw enough of their squadrons to allow you to sneak through."

"Who is leading that assault?" I ask.

"Praetor Ciarti Inawran."

I approve. "She's a dangerous asteroid fighter. One of Orion's best."

"Your mission is to reconnoiter the asteroid, establish contact with Regulus, and persuade him to bring the sum of his hoarded might back into the fight. Regulus believes Darrow and Sevro are dead. No one save Matteo is closer to that bastard's cold heart than the two of you. I am counting on you to convince him to rejoin this war."

"Why can't we just beam them a message?" Sevro asks.

"One, our relays are now down. Two, the strength of signal required would alert our enemies and lead them straight to the asteroid. Three, they won't answer."

"Quick's stubborn as psoriasis. What if he doesn't want to get back in the game?" Sevro asks, looking for a way out.

"Then you force him back in, like you forced Lorn to fight against Octavia." She looks off-screen and anxiety saws at me. I thought we'd have more time. Virginia confirms my fear. "It seems the enemy has finally noticed this transmission and is attempting to trace its location. The Lightbringer will have your coordinates in minutes."

"Victra," Sevro says. "I want to see her. I want to see my baby."

Virginia is the picture of empathy. "I'm sorry, Sevro. She's on the planet already. The only reason you're getting this is because it's not being blocked by the shields. Once I go down there . . . You might not hear from me until you get back. Unless the shields go down . . ."

"Does she know I'm alive?"

"She knew the whole time. Even when my hope was dim, she knew, Sevro."

"She would want me to come home," he says almost to himself.

"She would want to win this war, Sevro. You know that's how you protect your family. After all you've been through, you're alive. Don't throw that away now."

"The Abomination told me to tell you hello," Sevro says, and it seems like a jab. "If I ever saw you again. Last thing he said to me. 'Tell my sister I send my regards.'"

Virginia stiffens. "Sevro, I am sorry for what happened."

"So fun. Being a bit player in your clone family drama," he says. "So happy you got rescued and left me behind."

"I barely escaped myself. I wanted to come back for you—"

"Duty, though. Registers. You're the Sovereign. No hard feelings, horsey. None at all."

"Is there anything you want me to tell Victra?"

He looks down. "Naw. She knows."

Then he leaves. Cassius follows to give me privacy, but Virginia calls for him to wait. I feel schoolboy resentment creep in, that she would spend precious seconds on him. "It's been too long, Cassius, but it's good to see you back where you belong."

He smiles. "And you where you always belonged." He hesitates. "Have you spoken to Lysander, face-to-face?" Virginia nods. "A word of advice when treating with him. Just because he wants to keep his word does not mean he will."

"I'll remember that. And, Cassius, the Republic welcomes you. I would *like to offer you a battlefield promotion to Morning Knight of the Republic. Will you accept?"*

Cassius blinks, stunned, then bows very formally. "It would be my honor, my Sovereign."

He leaves with a nod to me. Now that we're alone, Virginia allows her concern to show. *"Sevro. Is he—"*

"We're working through it," I say. Grief enters her eyes. "What is it?"

"Nothing. Guilt, I suppose. It is good to see you three together, despite everything." She's holding something back, but I don't press. *"Darrow, there's something you should know. The agent who found Quicksilver is named Lyria of Lagalos. She was an unwilling participant in Pax's kidnapping, and Electra's. Yet Victra and I owe that girl a debt. Do not let Sevro kill her."*

"Unwilling?"

"She's just a girl. She didn't know. But she's more than made up for it. And don't you kill her either. Your son sent her out there. Pax believes in her."

"Virginia, you know Regulus. She may already be dead."

She shakes her head. *"Perhaps, but I think Matteo may be an ally in this. One more thing: Volsung Fá and the Obsidians who sacked Olympia were last seen raiding asteroid cities along your route. I need you to promise me you won't seek him out."*

She told me about Fá as we waited for Sevro and Cassius to join. My blood boiled to think of Sefi splayed open by an obvious fraud. That my Volk went with him afterwards boggles my mind. It's not important now.

"I know my mission. Trust me."

I reassure her with a smile. She watches me without speaking, and I feel the tender beat of her heart against my chest. *"It's harder than I thought it'd be. Sending you away. You're so close. There's too much to say."*

"It's not fair, is it?" I ask.

"No."

It rends me apart that I can't use these last seconds for us. "Virginia . . . if Quick won't come back, if we can't make him—there may be another option." I tell her about Aurae and Athena's offer to Sevro as quickly as I can.

"In Ilium?" she asks when I finish. *"That would add months . . ."*

"I know."

She goes quiet. I know her techs are talking to her.

"Darrow, I know what you had to do in order to secure a peace with Romulus, but I doubt anyone who survived the purges will see it that way. You can't go to Ilium."

"Well they didn't invite *me* anyway. How long can you hold Mars?"

I'm stalling now to get more time with her.

"As long as I have to. I'm sending you an intel packet so you can know what I know about our enemies. In it is a set of coordinates. When you return, all Republic vessels not under Mars's shields will rally to those coordinates to rendezvous with whatever ships you bring back. Do not rush home just to lose. You cannot squander our last chance. I am grounding our ships here on Mars to preserve them for your return. So promise me you will not come back unless you think we can win."

"I understand." Looking at her is too hard. I glance down as I continue, trying to use my last seconds well. "Virginia, I need you to tell Pax something for me. Tell him . . . that I am proud of him. That all I've done was for him, even if it doesn't feel like it. I didn't do it all right. But I think . . . I believe I did it for the right reasons. Tell him I love him more than my own life. Tell him—"

I stop because she is already gone.

The signal has been cut on her end. Without her hologram, the room is darker and so am I. I linger in the silence, because as long as I linger, as long as I do not look up and see where her image once was, she does not feel so very far away. I've read through *The Path of the Vale* enough to know that some currents cannot be fought, no matter how good a swimmer I think I am. Far better to hope that the rapids I sail upon will carry me to new opportunities, new allies. Still, the closer we drew to Mars, the more I allowed myself to expect I would hold her in my arms, breathe in the life of her, make so many mistakes right. Not yet, I suppose.

When I'm ready to face reality, I look up into the empty space she had once filled with light.

"Tell him I wish he and I had kept riding that gravBike," I say. "Tell him when this is over, we'll ride from coast to coast. Just him and me."

Dinner is a silent affair. Aurae joins us, and asks a few questions about our conversation with Virginia, but gives up when neither Cassius nor

I engage. The ship, now millions of kilometers further from Mars than when the day began, feels hollower even though no one has left. Sevro does not attend dinner.

After we've finished, I take Sevro a plate of ham and leave it outside the escape pod hatch. "I'm sorry," I say. "It's not fair. It's not what I promised. If . . . if we had two ships, if there was a way to shoot you home with a catapult, I'd do it. It's not fair I got to talk to Virginia and you didn't get to talk to Victra. It's not fair. I'm sorry. But they're alive. Together. Like we are. They have each other's backs. They'll keep each other safe. Just like we'll get each other home. I'll shut up now. Oh. There's food if you want it. It's ham." I can't resist adding, "Cassius and I are training again in the morning. If you want to join."

He doesn't reply, but that's fine. I said what I felt true and right.

I return to the galley to clean up, finding peace in making sure every crumb is accounted for and disposed of. Cassius looks for a similar peace in the bottom of his wine cup. Aurae disappears and returns with the lyre Harnassus made for her.

"I've never been so far from Io for so long," she says. "I find myself very homesick. Yet it was Athena who told me there is no home for those born slaves. Only a prison the master tricked you into calling home. The true home for a slave is in dreams. Except on Mars where slaves make dreams real. I always found that a beautiful thought."

There are no words to her song, but she hums along with the delicate sounds of the lyre. As she plays, the anvil weight of war lightens, and human emotions emerge in me. I close my eyes and think of my home. GodTrees grow and spread their limbs through my tired mind, the Thermic breeze rustles the tunic of my son, soft sunlight caresses my wife's face.

The delicate music summons ghosts from my past.

Ragnar lives again, wild and big and brave. I see him toppled by Red children in Tinos, taking the razor from my hand in a field of mud. I see my father kissing my mother by our small kitchen table. I see Orion grinning at me across the bridge of the ship we called home. I see Lorn frowning at me in disapproval. Alexandar looking up at me for approval. Fitchner whisking me away to safety the moment I learned he was Ares, and he said, *It's me, boyo, it's always been me.* I see Eo looking back over her shoulder as she races into the deepmines, frozen in time like the light of a star, which carries on so many years after it dies.

Tears flow from my eyes. When I wipe them away, I see I am not alone. Cassius weeps as well. After Aurae has finished her song, Cassius fetches cups and pours us all wine. Seeing my eyebrows rise, he gives himself the smallest portion.

With the reddest eyes in the room, he sniffs, wipes his nose with his sleeve, and raises his glass. "To the engines, the reactor, rapid winds may they devise. To our hearts, to our hands, toward deeds brave and true may they rise. To the Republic, to Mars, for hope and liberty ever may they stride." He thinks for a moment. "To our Sovereign, a lion Gold but wise as Minerva gray-eyed."

We drink. When the wine is gone, we melt away into the hollows of the ship. Neither Cassius nor I mention training tonight. Laying in my bunk, *The Path* on my chest, I look up at the ceiling at the scrawl that Lysander left behind after ten years of calling this ship home. My eyes fix on his family phrase: *LUX EX TENEBRIS*.

Out of darkness, light.

The words of the enemy hang over my head, and I feel purpose in a way I haven't in some time. I have done what I promised myself I would in the prison that was Marcher-1632. I listened to Virginia. Now the rest is up to me. I look out the small bunk window and see Mars. It is no longer a light whose growing brightness measures my progress home. The moment Virginia told me what I had to do, I thought my hope would diminish in seeing this last glimpse of Mars, but it doesn't. I hold the light inside even as my home shrinks in the distance and our black ship races toward the Belt.

36

LYSANDER

Jurisdiction

"LYSANDER, WAKE UP."
I emerge from the darkness into pain. A familiar voice speaks in my ear. Pytha's, rushed and worried. "Lysander, can you hear me? You were poisoned and put in a medically induced coma. We've only just brought you out. Something has happened. Squeeze my hand if you can hear me."

I can understand her but I cannot reply. My body is possessed by a cold flame. It ghosts through my bones like a memory of hell. It wants to be hot, the flame. Something restrains it, a drug. I feel the dumbness in my thoughts.

"This won't do. We need him lucid. He's an eggplant." Cicero's voice. "Do you hear that?"

"Hear what?" Pytha says.

"Boots. They're coming. Dammit. Exeter must have told them."

There's a whoosh of a door retracting. Boots thump into the room. Pulse weapons whine. A demonic voice rasps: **"Step back from the Blood."**

"Praetorians, we mean your *dominus* no harm. It's me. Cicero!"

"Dominus, step back from the Blood or you will be fired upon."

"It's too late, Kyber, we already pulled him out." Pytha shakes me. "Wake up. Moonboy. Can you hear me? You need to wake up. Everything is at stake."

"Praetorian Kyber, be reasonable," Cicero says. "We are Lysander's closest companions, not to mention I was your host on Venus and positively drowned you all in wine and Pinks. Furthermore, I am the head of a house of the Conquering. Rhone, thank Jove, there you are. Tell your men to stand down. This is absurd behavior."

Rhone's voice is hostile. "You woke him? My orders were clear."

"Yes, you surpass your post, my goodman. You have no right—"

"Captain, I am his Dux. I have every right to make decisions for him when he is incapacitated. You are the one without right. I am also the ranking officer on the *Lightbringer,* Captain Pytha."

"Flavinius, what is wrong with you?" Pytha snaps. "You know he'd want to be woken. He risked everything for this alliance with the Rim. He'd never forgive us if—"

"Pyyythaaa," I murmur.

They stop arguing. Cicero leaps to my side, shoving Pytha out of the way in his elation to see me first. "*Salve,* brother. How do you feel?"

"Shit . . ."

"I'll say. We thought you'd died. Don't do that to me. You know I've a timorous heart. My sister has been keeping things afloat. Don't you worry."

"Re-port."

Rhone approaches. "*Dominus,* you were poisoned. Do you remember?"

"Rain . . . fall yet?"

"He needs water," Pytha says. And presses a metal straw to my lips, embarrassing both Cicero and Rhone for not considering my comfort. I'm happiest to see Pytha. Her Civic Crown has been tattooed. It looks proper on her head. My swallows are sluggish, but the water cools the arid rawness of my throat. I choke in my eagerness to fill myself with it. Pytha wipes tears from my face with a corner of her uniform. The tears are bloody.

Now I recognize the cold flame in my body. I remember the poisoning.

"Medusa's . . . Lament," I murmur. Rhone nods. Even my teeth are starting to ache. It will get worse. Far worse. I take a few moments to sift through the muddle of my thoughts. "How . . . long?"

"Eight days since you went under," Pytha says, unable to hide her relief. "Don't strain yourself."

"We have Atalantia's assassin," Rhone reports. "It was one of the Pink acrobats, I fear." The one who came down on her silks to offer me a bit of leisure. "Rath wasn't incriminated. We have her confession recorded should you like to send it to the Two Hundred and make a formal complaint. But some know already. Many are furious. You're even more popular than before you started crying blood."

"What advantage!" Cicero is far too delighted by my poisoning. "She swung and she missed, Lysander. It's brilliant! This might be the costliest assassination attempt in that heinous woman's storied career! We have the votes. We can call a session of the Two Hundred and strip her of her powers. Maybe worse. Lysander Invictus, indeed. But never mind that, you're awake now. Much has happened."

"Tell me," I croak.

"Lysander . . . the Rim, they're abandoning the siege," Pytha says, blessedly blunt. "Diomedes has been asking to speak with you since yesterday. Rhone wouldn't allow it."

"Your medici panel agreed that nine more days were required to guarantee your recovery," Rhone explains. "I consulted with Lady Bellona and Apollonius and ordered their advice followed. I didn't want to risk your life, *dominus*."

"Where . . . is Ajax." They go quiet. "Oh. Sorry. My head's a little off."

Cicero can't help himself. "Lysander, you have to stop the Rim from leaving. All we've worked for. It's at risk. Dido won't listen to me or Lady Bellona. Make Diomedes listen to you. Make him tell his mother to stay, or at least tell us what is happening."

By the look in Pytha's eyes, I know she thinks that a dubious proposition and woke me for a different reason. Her hand squeezes mine. "There's another option," she says. "He said as much to me."

I nod, eliciting thunderclaps of pain. "Show him in."

Rhone objects. "*Dominus,* Medusa's Lament is not finished with you. It won't be for some time. If you remain awake, you could go into shock. The risk to your nervous system and for organ failure is—"

"Acceptable. Show him in."

The old soldier holds my gaze, and nods with reluctance.

Diomedes enters the room wearing his dusky cloak of office. "I fear I've caused a disturbance," he says and surveys me in my medical bed with deep concern. "But I'm glad you're awake. Flavinius thinks I've killed you by waking you too early."

"Overprotective," I murmur. "Just doing his duty." If Diomedes wasn't worried at the sight of me, he is by the halting rasp of my voice. Beneath that worry is a tension I don't like one bit. My friends did not exaggerate. He *is* leaving. I fight back the panic rising in me.

"They say Medusa's Lament is unpleasant," he says, understated as ever. "I'm pleased to hear that you will survive. Are you in pain?"

"Why are . . . you leaving. Our Rain. . . ." A fresh surge of agony lances through my left eye socket and stirs my brain into bloody gray mush. "What—" I breathe heavily, waving off his concern with a clumsy hand. "What has happened?"

"The Beacons of Jupiter burn red. Ilium is under attack."

I don't understand. Ilium. The moons around Jupiter. His home.

The pain makes it hard to think, but not as hard as the painkillers pumping into me through the med bracelet. Forming thoughts is like walking through neck-deep sludge.

"Attack?"

"Yes."

"The . . . Republic. Darrow? How?"

"No. Not the Republic." He hesitates. "Two days ago, we received an emergency tightbeam from my grandmother in Sungrave and the Moon Council on Ganymede. Both messages were confirmed by our long-lenses near the Belt."

He hesitates.

"Trust me," I say.

"Ilium is under attack by an Obsidian fleet led by a warlord. One who might be known to you through your intelligence reports. Volsung Fá."

I think very hard. "The pirate leader. The same who attacked Olympia? Stole . . . the *Pandora* and the Volk fleet?" I feel like I've been asleep for years. "He's raiding the asteroid belt. Republic cities. Trade posts. His fight is with them—"

"We thought so too. It seems that's changed," Diomedes says. "Three days ago, the Ilium Guard responded to an Ascomanni raid at Garmaga, one of the outer moons of Jupiter. Instead of encountering a raiding group of Ascomanni corvettes, as intelligence suggested, they encountered a Core-grade warfleet comprising dreadnaughts and destroyers, supplemented by Ascomanni ships in numbers not even my great-grandfather ever encountered. The Ilium Guard was destroyed completely."

I must be high on the painkillers. The defense fleet of the Raa homeland, gone?

"There were warnings. Of course. My grandmother . . . the isolationist who cried wolf one too many times. Our intelligence is incomplete, but we believe Fá has united the Ascomanni and the Volk. He claims to be the father of Ragnar Volarus."

We heard that rumor too. "Is he?"

"We don't know. I'm breaking the law even telling you we don't know. Like you, we thought he was still somewhere in the Belt attacking Republic stations and trade posts. Apparently his ransacking of Mars, his coup of Sefi, now seem nothing more than stepping stones for his true ambition: a war against my people, just when we can least afford it. He saw his chance and exploited it."

Very clever. But not surprising in the end. That is the problem with rebellions. They incite others to rebel. Exhausted, I hang my head in sluggish thought. "Diomedes, we have Mars . . . in our grasp. All we did here. If you leave now—"

"I know. I am sorry, Lysander. But no victory is worth a people's home. We must protect Ilium. We're far closer than the Shadow Armada. Our consuls are in agreement. Even my mother. The Dragon and Dust armadas will return home at full torch."

"Demeter's Garter," I whisper. Nothing else could make Dido and Helios react so aggressively except a threat to the breadbasket of the Rim. "You think the Ascomanni may be able to take the Garter."

He almost scoffs.

"Even the Ash Lord and Fabii couldn't take Io. But we cannot let Obsidians run rampant in our home system. Not everything is so well defended. We have a duty to protect our people."

I sigh in relief for him. If the Garter were to fall it would mean famine, death. The Rim is far more fragile than it pretends to be. Life is hard so far away from the sun.

"When are you leaving?" I rasp.

"Once all the troops are loaded."

"When?"

"Just over three hours from now."

Even though I feel for the Rim, it is impossible not to think of my own plight. Without their ships, their troops, my faction will be hard-pressed to maintain the siege, much less take the surface. I feel a second schism forming, all our progress reversing. My allies will be furious at being abandoned. Somewhere Atalantia will be laughing, the Republic wiping their brows. But Pytha would not wake me unless there was something I could do about this calamity. Filled with immense love for her, I narrow my eyes at Diomedes.

Is it just the pain, just the drugs, or is he far more talkative and open than usual?

"Then why wake me?" I ask.

He considers for a long time. "When you came to Ilium, when you promised an alliance, I thought you were a boy who wanted to matter so badly he'd bend everything to do it. Even the truth. On Mercury, I felt that suspicion confirmed. But then you stood in Rome. Then you spoke. Then you sailed. Then, when blood was demanded here to turn pretty promises into hard truths, you opened a vein. You did what you said you would do. I worry . . . I know Atalantia is not that sort of leader. I fear her. If we leave, the alliance will break, but we must leave, so you must come with us. Prove to Helios, to all, this alliance is more than convenience. Prove it is the future. We do not live in the shadow of Rhea. We make our own light."

I have never seen him so passionate.

I do not take his hand despite the emotions riding in me. "If I do . . . sail with you, what assurances do I have . . . you will return to finish what we started here?"

"I bind my honor to this. We will give you the Shield of Akari." He smiles. "And my consul, Dido au Raa, has granted me the right to bind her honor to that pledge as well. Help us, the Dragon Armada will come back and help you."

"The Shield of Akari?" Lady Bellona says. "They haven't given that relic to a Core Gold since Silenius died. It must be under a meter of dust in Plutus."

Unable to stand, I must look pathetic to my allies in the floating chair I rode to the emergency summit held in Julia's new base of operations—Quicksilver's former estate. Horatia has gone home to manage Mercury. Cicero stands at my side, firmly backing my petition to my allies to aid the Rim. Naturally, Apollonius was the last to arrive. He rode into Quicksilver's former palace on a winged chimera he took as a spoil of war from Julii's household menagerie. After the beast was led out by nervous Bellona guards, I informed my allies of the Rim's plight and Diomedes's offer.

"The shield is only given to signify a century pact," I reply with a nod. "There has not been one since Silenius died. We change that, we can turn this tragedy into unity."

"Diomedes offered it to you?" she asks, skeptical.

"He did, backed by his mother and the Dragon Armada."

Apollonius laughs heartily. "The Obsidians have attacked Ilium. The fools. A Sicilian Expedition worthy of Alcibiades. What ruinous ambition this Fá has. Do we have a picture of the devil?"

"The Republic might, but we don't," I say trying my best to mask the pain I'm in.

"Delicious. A mystery. But Flavinius was right. Better to slumber through the low affairs and save your vigor for the clarion call of worthier contests. The field of fame is Mars. As soon as Darrow slithers in, all the names will await our glittering spears."

With his servants excluded from the meeting, Apollonius is reduced to combing his own hair. He looks awkward doing it, and tugs at a knot with a grimace. He must have grown bored of his inconvenient and ghastly bullet wound. It is covered with the first layers of a carver's work.

Apollonius is not done. "Surely you lower yourself by journeying to that dismal shadowland to hunt mongoloids. Much remains unfinished here, Lysander."

Julia watched Apollonius throughout his monologue with a look of weary tolerance.

"Shield or no shield, I believe I agree with Rath, though he does his best to lose the plot." Julia fixes me with a banker's gaze, tallying both my proposal and my infirmity. "How dire is the threat, truly? Even Fabii couldn't crack Io, much less Sungrave or the Garter, and he had the Sword Armada."

"It is dire enough to recall their whole fleet," I say.

Her eyes flick to Rhone, who stands behind me. "Do you agree, Flavinius?" Rhone hesitates, and glances at me.

"You can answer," I say.

"He already did with his eyes," Julia says. "But he's a loyal man. Don't put him on the spot. The calamity this causes our campaign—"

"Will be felt whether I go with them or not," I say. "We simply cannot take Mars without support from either House Grimmus or House Raa. If my condition is any indication, the former will never happen and we're teetering on open war with Grimmus. That is a fact. We cannot stop Diomedes from leaving. Another fact. But if they go, their isolationist faction is champing at the bit to use our lack of participation as a pretext to end the alliance and not return."

"I see the problem and the opportunity," Julia says. "If we don't bend, we set ourselves up to break. But what exactly do you have in mind?"

I take a deep breath and fight back the pains that wrack my gut.

"Houses Rath, Bellona, and your respective clients will maintain the siege of Mars and continue repairs to Phobos and ship production. House Lune and Cicero, with a few of his ships, will lend aid to the Rim. As my *Lightbringer* cannot match the speed of their armada, my Praetorians and I will go ahead on Diomedes's or Dido's ship. Cicero will follow with the *Lightbringer,* my house legions, and his own ships." Anticipating their objections to the risk of my person, I quickly explain. "There is a high chance that the Rim will meet and destroy the Obsidian fleet before our ships even make it to Ilium. I don't want to waste this opportunity by having our contribution dismissed as theater. If there is a battle, I will play some part in it so no one can say I did not help my allies."

Julia frowns. "Votum, this unity madness has bitten you too?"

"Yes," Cicero says. "I cost us the assault on Phobos. I know that since then my opinion has been taken very lightly—justifiably so. I apologize. I put my planet . . . *my* interests, ahead of this faction of ours. But I believe we have a moral obligation here. I believe we must disprove this theory that the Core has no honor. That is why I will volunteer my flagship and urge you all to contribute something to this venture. We should not allow civilization, even far flung, to be marauded by barbarians."

Apollonius stands and prowls the room, combing his hair as he thinks.

"Lysander, I applaud your courage, but . . . be honest. Are you up to it?" Julia asks. "You can't yet stand. The Lament is no idle matter—"

I put a hand out. "Rhone." He is a little slow to help me up, but with his aid I gain my feet. "A Lune never stands without his guard," I reply. "So it will be as it always was."

Apollonius laughs and I know he's thinking of all the glory he'll take for himself when I'm gone. Julia rolls her eyes. "Well, since the Rain is called off, we need time to build our fleet here and over Venus. I'll send Pallas with you." She watches Apollonius hurl his razor thirty meters into the air, yawn, and catch it with his eyes closed. "Don't die."

Three hours after Diomedes left me in my bed, Rhone pushes my floating chair through the hangar toward the disembarking Raa army. The last of the Raa troops and engineers fall upward in the gravity column toward a vast aperture in the *Dragon Song*. Rhone looks like he's walking to the gallows. A thousand of my best Praetorians follow behind us. I'd take more, but mobilizing the whole legion will take at least a day, and the Raa are very punctual.

"*Dominus,* I must reiterate my concern," Rhone says. "Leaving Phobos will put your territory in jeopardy. You leave the door open for Atalantia to snatch your allies. Never mind the risks to your own life."

"You speak as if staying here with Atalantia would not be a risk to my life," I argue. "Tell me, Rhone, if we were sailing to protect Mercury, would you sing that same tune?" I ask.

"Mercury deserves our protection."

"I know you don't trust the Raa, and the grudge you hold for them. But we can't build a future if we cling to the past."

Rhone stops the chair. "*Dominus.* I beg you not to do this. Not only is it a waste of your time, it is an insult to those of the guard who died at Ilium. I have held my tongue, but I must use it now. This venture is beneath you."

I search his hard eyes. "You really should have woken me. I know you're sworn to guard my life, but I hoped you knew my heart as well."

"Your heart, like your friends, may not always be wise."

"Remember, you are my Dux not my keeper. I value your counsel, but you obey my will, and the matter is concluded." I hold his gaze. My eyes ache as if they've been stabbed. The Lament roves through my body like a cat around a house.

"Yes, *dominus.*"

Diomedes waits for me with his mother just shy of the boarding troops. Neither looks pleased. Dido's thick, dark-gold hair flows freely over her right shoulder. She spares me a meager smile that does not reach her eyes, and scans the Praetorians behind me. "Small change of plans. Potentially awkward, but not unnavigable."

"Helios has taken imperium of both fleets," Diomedes explains. "The Moon Lords are in a panic. Grandmother is punishing my mother for this war. When Helios discovered your intentions, he forbade you from traveling with my mother."

"How did he find out?"

"I told him," Diomedes says. "As was my duty."

"My son. The stick in the mud. He mistakes stubbornness for wisdom, and loose lips for honesty," Dido says. "But Helios may yet say yes. He gave you high praise for your performance at Phobos."

"What praise?" I ask.

"He didn't criticize you once," Diomedes says.

"As raving an endorsement as you'll receive from the old ass," Dido clarifies with a roll of her eyes, then glares across the hangar. "Speak of the mule, and he appears."

Helios and his castle of isolationists stride across the hangar. The god glove of the *Dustmaker* glints on Helios's right hand. Helios glares at the Praetorians.

"I hear you want to go on a propaganda tour," Helios says to me.

"Pride has ruined better men than either of us," I say. "We will come with you, if you let us, with my *Lightbringer* following with a small fleet. My people have been repairing her for two weeks now. She's not pretty, but she still punches. Consider that fleet as insurance. If you do not need our fleet, do not use us, but let us show our respect for you. Or cancel our alliance here and now."

Helios doesn't hate that reply. "Tell me, Lune. Have you ever fought an Ascomanni from the Far Ink? Have any of your . . . Guard even seen one? Their tactics are as alien to you as their language. You will be lost."

"Consul Lux, have you ever fought Darrow's Volk shock troopers?" Diomedes asks. Helios's eyes flash with annoyance at his too-honest protégé. "I have not. But the Praetorians have, and Fá seems to have recruited many of Darrow's veterans."

"You doubt our arms?" Helios asks.

"No. Just our experience, as you doubted Lune's. Perhaps we have something to teach one another after all."

Helios says nothing for a long, odd moment. When he speaks, his tone is entirely different. It shows the respect he has for Diomedes, if not for me. "You ask me to trust you, Lune. Very well. Prove you trust me. Come, but I'll allow no more than ten of your killers aboard my *Dustmaker*. The rest must follow in your snail ships."

"Ten is an insult to a man of his station," Rhone says from behind. "He's a Lune."

"Precisely," Helios says.

I turn on Rhone, astounded by his lack of discipline. "Silence, Flavinius."

The motion sends excruciating shocks of pain through my spinal cord and calves.

"He can bring all he likes onto the *Dragon's Song* . . ." Dido offers, wary as she scrutinizes Helios.

"Ten," Helios says. "And if he comes along with us, he must ride with me. You two are too cozy as is."

"Ten will suffice," I say. "Thank you."

"Choose them and load. We've wasted time enough. Diomedes, you have his mark." He turns on a heel and departs with his cadre. That took a lot of energy. Helios thought I wouldn't do it, and Flavinius tried to stop me. I wheel on him.

"Flavinius—tell me now. Should I leave you behind? Answer truthfully."

"No, *dominus*. I apologize."

"Then pick nine of your best. Pack your gear. And get on board." I look past him. We'll be taking Demetrius, Drusilla, Markus, Coriolanus, and five more of Rhone's best but my whisper is missing. "Have you seen Kyber?"

"Yes, *dominus*. She took a shot from a sniper," Rhone says.

"What, just now? I only just saw her," I say in concern. Rhone motions up Demetrius.

"Got hit on the way to barracks to get her kit, *dominus*. She'll live. Sniper didn't," Demetrius says. "We got her back to the medBay before she bled out. Knowing her, she'll follow in the *Lightbringer*."

"Good," I say. I waver. Pain pounds my temples and races along my spine, causing an ache between my shoulder blades. I feel sick. "Snipers, though?"

"They've been active since you've been under. So much for Lion-heart's word," Rhone says.

"If they're affiliated," I muse, then I call out to the men not part of Rhone's picked nine, and urge them to give Kyber my best wishes on a speedy recovery. As the Praetorians sort their equipment, I approach Dido and Diomedes.

"What did Helios mean by 'your mark'?" I ask Diomedes.

"If you make any mischief, I lose my cloak," Diomedes replies as if he's won a great victory. Dido is not pleased. She frowns after Helios as if he'd sprouted horns.

"What is it?" I ask.

"The only reason he'd say yes is if he was worried we might need you."

"Has he fought this Fá before, in the Far Ink?"

Dido shakes her head. "No. None of us have. Until this attack, we thought he was a myth. No matter. Ascomanni and Volk. They're just genetic perversions and thick-brained infantry. They'll probably tear one another apart before we even reach the Belt." She presses something into my hand. "For the poison. It'll help. Diomedes will show you how to use it. Goodspeed, boys. I will see you in Ilium."

PART III

TEMPEST

Ah how shameless—the way these mortals
blame the gods. From us alone, they say, come
all their miseries. Yes, but they themselves,
with their own reckless ways, compound their
pains beyond their proper share.

—HOMER

37

DARROW

Cacophony

As the *Archimedes* approaches the asteroid that is said to hold the Republic's salvation, I fidget with Pax's gravBike key. Thraxa's razor, Bad Lass, rests in my lap. I am thankful for both. One is a reminder to stay the path, the other is a tool to help me do so.

The asteroid does not look like much. It is gray, oblong, and lies on an outer shoulder of the Belt mined long before the age of Ovidius.

"Well, we made it here in one piece," Cassius says and sips his caf. His thermal is pulled tight up to his neck. A bruise peeks out and stretches to his right ear. "Hard part's done."

"You've never had a conversation with Quicksilver," I say and kick my feet up on the wall. He slugs me in the shoulder. "Sorry." I lower my feet.

"You and Quick are close," he says. "At least from what you've said. I thought you were his favorite."

"True, but . . . he can be tricky."

"Still no energy readings. Metal, yes. But this was a mining sector. . . . Should I start to hail the asteroid?" he asks.

"If he is here, he's already seen us," I say.

"We have a stealth hull."

"Yes, one his company made. He doesn't create questions to which he doesn't have answers. My guess is if he's in there, he's been watching us for some time."

"I bet he's as horrified as I am about the state of the hull. My poor ship is falling to ruins. Honestly, between you and Sevro it's a wonder there's not literal shit in the halls."

"Sorry. We usually have janitors," I say.

"Really? He doesn't even flush. A life of privilege is no excuse for slovenliness." He sets his caf aside, and sprays the wall where my foot touched with cleaning solvent and wipes it down. "You really must take pride in the things you own, Darrow."

We fall into silence as we creep closer to the asteroid. Occasional reports come up the hall from Aurae who helms the sensor station between the cockpit and the lounge. The only other sounds are the whispers of the engines and the tremble of Sevro's music from the machine shop in the aft of the ship. With the asteroid only a half hour away, the moment of truth is at hand. Did we come all this way for nothing?

All things considered, our thirty-six-day journey went well. It may have been fraught with anxiety, but actual threats to the ship were scarce. The Rim has already emptied most of their strength from the Belt to bolster the Dragon and Dust armadas in their attack on Mars. Only a few of their hunting parties gave us pause. As for the fabled Obsidian pirates, we saw not a one on our sensors. That is not surprising really. The Belt is so large it feels like an existential threat to sanity if you try to comprehend the expanse its asteroids fill.

But *fill* is the wrong word. In the Belt, asteroids float so far apart they are more like islands on a sea so vast only metaphors can help the human mind understand it: if you poured all water from all the seas on all the worlds ever sailed by man into a giant ring and then dropped one grain of sand into it, that grain would not even represent Earth's size against the tremendous expanse of the Belt.

Of course there is no celestial object out here so massive as Earth. Instead, there are tens of millions of asteroids in swirls, shoulders, clusters. Of those, only two and a half million are larger than a kilometer in diameter. Few are inhabited. Fewer still are populated with anything larger than mining outposts or pirate hideouts. Those asteroids that host actual cities are so rare and estranged from civilization, they are precious, the last lamps before the abyssal dark of the Gulf. That light from those lamps was once white, the color of the Republic. Now their bulbs either glow Raa blue, or they don't glow at all.

Past those last outposts lies the Gulf, which once was the moat that separated the Dominion and the Republic. It seems abyssal, but its darkness is not endless. Beyond the Gulf lies the realm of shadow and dust—the gargantuan Gas Giants and the moons on which the Golds of the Rim have made their homes for centuries. House Raa presides over that far-flung civilization from its seat on the volcanic moon of Io.

There are asteroids out there too, with cities of their own, like Priam in the Trojan Cluster or Agamemnon in the Greek Cluster. Though these cities lie on Jupiter's orbital path, they are cloaked by the mystery of distance and obscured even further by the hermit-like nature of their inhabitants. Even I know very little about those cities, their peoples, their ways.

Past Jupiter, of course, lie the orbital paths of Uranus, Saturn, Neptune. Places I have never sailed, and places I probably never will. And beyond that . . . far, far beyond that, twirls lonely Pluto—where civilization ends—and then, eventually the Kuiper Belt where sparks of the Society have flared occasionally against the edge of the true dark, but never for long.

It feels strange to contemplate what life is like on those spheres. In the Belt, I feel as if I am already deep inside the realm of darkness, but those who dwell in the shadows of the Giants would barely consider me on its threshold.

The last time I was so far away from the sun was when I was sailing for Luna aboard the *Morning Star*. Now Lysander is sleeping in my old bed on the *Morning Star*, and I'm sleeping in his bed on the *Archimedes*. Strange, the twists of fate.

It is scary out here, and not because of the Rim Golds or the Belt's fabled Obsidian pirates. It feels like the sun, like *life*, has forgotten you and you could just slip away into the dark without anyone ever knowing where or when you vanished. In some ways it makes me doubt I'll ever see the godTree forests and fog-swaddled highlands of home again. I notice that dread and let it pass through me.

Then Cassius throws me a live grenade made of anxiety. "What if Quicksilver's not in there?" he asks. "This Lyria girl sounds scurrilous indeed." He glances back to make sure Sevro isn't behind us. "I mean, she stole your kids, man." He nods to Pax's key. "I'm no father, but that's not just something you sweep under the rug. I don't want to be a pessimist. But what if Virginia made up this fleet so you wouldn't go on a suicide charge only to get nabbed by the Raa trying to get home?"

"You mean what if she's just preying on my hope and lying to prevent the enemy from obtaining a political and propaganda weapon that could drive a stake through the heart of Mars?" I ask. "Namely my head?" I sip my caf. "Then I'd say she's doing her job."

"Shit." He leans back in his chair. "I wouldn't want to marry a Sovereign."

"I didn't. I married Virginia, and she married me. The Sovereign and the Reaper, they're the shadows that come with us."

He mulls that over for a time. "So . . . if Quicksilver is not here, or if he is and he won't help?"

"Worry is a spiral with death at its center, Cassius," I reply.

I feel Aurae smiling. Cassius rolls his eyes. "Worry is a spiral with . . . I mean, come on. You trying to outdo Stoneside?"

I shrug. I am not as confident as I pretend to be, but how can you lead if you cannot walk—and how can you walk if you fear every step? Whenever I find myself doubting I've made the right decision, I force myself to examine our situation through the lens of *The Path to the Vale*. A portion of the book's tenth understanding comes to me often during these moments:

> *Forgetting is essential to learning,*
> *just as exhaling is essential to breathing.*
> *Breathe out, then in.*
> *Find the self,*
> *then lose it once again.*
> *Thus, the path goes ever onward.*

Stilling myself, I breathe out the memories of past mistakes and doubts, and then breathe in fresh perspective. My worries might be founded in uncomfortable truths, but they are—according to Aurae—born of an idle mind and an idle body. Worse, my worries only create more feelings of powerlessness. Rather than fretting about whether I've made the right choices, I instead focus on preparing for the next one, whatever that might be.

I *was* just like the Marcher, I realize now: trash from the past, circling the drain. But I realized on the morning after we turned away from Mars that I faced a choice: I could look back and see the light of home shrinking day by day and miss its warmth more and more, or I could resist the urge to look.

I resisted that morning and found strength in the resistance. That physical choice has since become a mental one. I have not looked back since, and I will not. Virginia has given me a mission: come back with strength enough for one last chance to win this war.

I am now an arrow shot by her bow.

There was no downtime on this voyage. I learned from my enemy and aped Apollonius. I made a syllabus and divided it into three parts: body, brain, heart.

For my body, I train with Cassius six hours every day cycle. Three after I wake, three before I sleep. My body is bruised, my muscles ache, my hands are blistered, and my ego is smashed every day. He is a fantastic classical swordsman, and whenever he puts me down, he says with a smile, "Steel sharpens steel."

He is not wrong. In the chaos of the battlefields, I have grown sloppy, my confidence obese from success while my enemies have studied how to beat me and the Willow Way.

Thirty-six times six is two hundred and sixteen. Those are the hours we have put in. I feel the change already. I also now eat ten thousand calories a day. My mass is returning like the hair on my head. I've kept the beard. For some reason it helps me to feel like I'm on a mission.

My heart is nourished by the book I write and the book I read. I write to my son, like I did on the Marcher before I go to sleep. It grounds me in my past, and keeps my head up, eyes on the future he'll have. I find the lessons in my losses, my grief, and hope I pass those on instead of the pain. And I read *The Path*. Aurae suffers me daily, but if she's annoyed at my litany of questions about *The Path* or Athena, she hides it well.

I think Aurae's strength comes from her response to suffering. Unlike me, she was not given the easy way out. I was carved, given a physical chassis through which I could vent my rage on the worlds. Physically fragile, Aurae had only one choice: make her heart strong, or the worlds would shatter her in every way.

The brain division of the syllabus is dedicated to the data Virginia sent. Five hours a day, I catch up on my enemies' successes. Atlas's are legion. His campaign on Luna in destroying its food stores was genius, as was his pacification of North America. He's moved on to South America now, and I try not to obsess. He's the most dangerous of them all, but fighting him is only part of the war.

I read about Lysander and his nascent alliance with the Rim, as well as the intelligence briefings on Rim and Dominion strengths, politics, personalities, industrial capabilities, and all the players of our drama. I learn of Lyria's past, of Ephraim, and Volga, and how she volunteered to go with Fá. That part disturbs me more than anything else—Fá. Intelligence is sparse on the mysterious warlord and his Ascomanni. Something is off based on the reports I've read. His tactics on Mars had the flavor of special forces. No shortage of disaffected spec ops on both sides running around these days, but it seems there may be more to this one. I need more intel.

This tone of industry I have set personally has influenced the others. The *Archimedes* hums to a productive rhythm. Only Sevro remains a discordant note.

I'm jarred from my reflection on our journey as Cassius grabs my shoulder.

"Is it just me, or does that crater look like its opening its mouth and spitting at us?" he asks.

"I think it is spitting." I grin at the strange star craft pouring out from the hidden hangar that has opened in one of the asteroid's craters. The ships are angular and made of a mixture of pearly and transparent material. I've never seen any ships quite like them. Cassius darkens.

"There's no cockpits," he says. "AI?"

"Maybe. More likely drones with a controller."

"Mhm."

A high-pitched noise goes through the ship and the lights flicker. A face appears over the coms projector. The man is beautiful and in his early fifties. His eyes are rose quartz pink. He greets us with a smile. *"Darrow of Lykos. You have a beard!"*

"Matteo," I say in relief. "You're not surprised to see me."

"No, but always delighted." His voice takes on an edge. *"Our spitfires will escort you in. Please don't bother with the controls, au Bellona."*

"Just Bellona," Cassius says.

Matteo warms to that. *"Interesting. Darrow, I will see you soon."*

He disappears and I stand, grab Cassius's shoulders, and kiss his head. "Now the hard part," I say and head to the back.

He shouts after me, "Tell Sevro to clean up his mess in the sink!"

I go down the hall that leads from the cockpit, past the sensors, through the lounge, past the crew quarters and the chutes to the guns, past the quad of service rooms, down the ramp into the cargo bay, and to the door to the machine shop. It's sealed, and I knock. Sevro doesn't answer so I crank the door open.

His screaming music almost knocks me backward. My friend is making knives. He is shirtless, tattooed, and staring deadpan at the edge of a huge cleaver. Sparks spew as he sharpens its edge. He glances up, sees me shouting at him, and goes back to his work.

Sevro does not want to be here. He came along because he had to. He knows the importance of our mission, but it's not made him better company. He has rules. He'll share the same room or a task with us if it's meal or ship related. But he won't reminisce. He won't joke. Sometimes at dinners, he'll listen as Aurae plays a tune but most times he slinks back to the machine shop or to his quarters in the escape pod.

I call his name a few times, but I've been in battles that made less racket than the music of the Agean street scene. Greens never should have met Obsidians as far as I'm concerned. They call the musical style: Cacophony. I turn it off so the sharpening laser's shriek against the metal is all that's between us. "Working," he says but he turns off the sharpener. He wipes the sweat off his body with a rag and eats sunflower butter, his new addiction, from a jar with a spoon. "We had a rule," he says. "Door was closed."

"When you start following Cassius's rules, I'll follow yours. We're on his ship, and you keep leaving messes in the sink."

He grunts. "Aurae did it. Messy for a Pink."

"If you're going to lie, at least put in some effort. Anyway, we're here. I've just spoken to Matteo. They've opened up a hangar for us to land."

He tosses the rag up and it divides in two as it falls on the new blade. "Nice."

"What's that one called?"

"Abomination." He turns the cleaver. I scan the wall he's made his personal armory. So far he's made a Lysander, a Lilath, an Atlas, and an Apollonius. I doubt it's healthy naming knives for people who have given him trauma, but we all process our own way.

"Are you coming with?" I ask.

He turns Abomination a few times. "I'm in the middle of a thought."

It feels wrong to meet with Quicksilver without him, but they've always been oil and water. "You still haven't given me an answer. Will you teach me how to make one of those on the way back?"

He eyes me, walks toward me with Abomination, slides it past my face, and turns his music back on with its tip. Cacophony rattles between us, and I take the hint.

38

DARROW

Tabula Rasa

REGULUS AG SUN IS a voluble, rude, insanely clever man of many layers and shifting schemes. Nicknamed Quicksilver, he is, above all else, a wary man. A decade and a half sponsoring the Sons of Ares instilled him with that virtue, if he didn't already have it before he met Fitchner. Our ship is scanned for atomics and who knows what else as it taxis into a hangar beneath one of the asteroid's larger craters.

When the ship's door opens and the ramp unfurls, I descend alone. Sevro's music trickles out behind me. Despite the cordial welcome, I expected to come out to a phalanx of automatons. Instead, Matteo waits alone. He looks out of place in the bleak hangar, better fit for the luxuries of a Venusian court or a high-profile Lunese symposium than all the way out here on the faultline between civilizations.

"Darrow, my goodman, my struggler. Back from the dead once more."

I thought I'd call him deserter. But I can't be angry, not at Matteo. Lorn might have taught me to kill, but Matteo was my first teacher in my life after the mines—and in many ways, my most important teacher. He taught me how to *be* a Gold.

As I approach him to shake his hand, his arms go wide and he wraps his wispy limbs around my midsection. I allow my arms to circle his shoulders and I kiss the top of his head. His hair, darker now, smells like jasmine.

"How are you?" he asks when we part. "We've so much to catch up on."

"I'm sorry, Matteo. But I don't have time—"

"You have more time than you think," he says. I frown. "How are you?"

"Desperate. But you know that."

"Revenants usually are. The dead never come back without a reason." His eyes flick to the craft. "Beautiful hull. I admire the craftsmanship. But what have you done to it? It looks like a pauper's shoe sewn together with nothing but good intentions."

"Exit tax from Mercury," I say. "Harnassus fixed it best he could."

"Ghoulish work."

"Well, he's a military engineer. Staples for stitches, you know."

"I meant Mercury." His sigh is one of deep empathy. "I cannot imagine the horrors you faced." Matteo surveys my injured limbs, my sun-seared-turned-sun-starved skin, my fresh scars. Instead of looking away, as most do, to preserve his image of the invulnerable Reaper, he admires my imperfections, catalogues the wounds to understand my narrative, and then loves me all the more for them. Though I can tell he doesn't like the beard.

"I am sorry for Mercury, Darrow. That you did not get reinforcements because of the Senate's failings. I grieve for the Free Legions." Matteo reaches up to take my face between his hands. I try to pull back. He holds on. "I grieve for Theodora."

Something in his eyes causes me to relent. Maybe it is because he saw me in my youth, after Eo died, at my angriest. Maybe because he taught me to dance when I was just a freshborn Gold colt on steroids. Maybe it's because I look at him and feel seen.

"All her life Theodora was coveted, not valued. You valued her, and she loved you for it. I have never known a Pink so pure in their loyalty. She was resourceful, intelligent, but most of all she found contentment in her service to you, then to the Republic as its great spymaster. True contentment melded with purpose. Something that evades so many of us. She was a hero to our Color. All free Pinks hail her name. It was her honor to serve you, and my honor to know her."

I'm taken off guard by the requiem.

"I grieve for Orion," he goes on even though I flinch. "She was a shooting star, and it will be an age before mankind sees another one quite like her. I grieve for Alexandar. I know you took him on as a debt to Lorn and grew to love him, despite seeing so much of yourself in him. He was the best Gold of his generation, but he set to make himself in *your* image, a Red's, and he did. When the waves came for Tyche, he proved he lived for more."

My voice is halting. "You know about that?"

He nods.

Tears fill my eyes, unbidden, unwelcome. Everything in me wishes to harden my heart against the pain. Instead, I allow the pain, and by allowing it I honor the dead with Matteo and feel that their light was seen. Not just by me, but by this man who knows my story and the stories of those I've cared for. That solace I thought I'd find in Sevro, I find in Matteo.

"I grieve for Dancer."

I don't make a sound but hearing our old friend's name on Matteo's lips makes a boy of me again. I see Dancer smoking a burner watching Matteo and me practice Gold mannerisms. I see Dancer's excitement as I chewed on the scythe card in our first meeting. His fatherly concern as I boarded the shuttle for the Institute. His fear as he choked to death on his own blood during the Day of Red Doves.

I miss Dancer more now than I miss my father, more even than I miss Eo. They were a part of my first life. Dancer gave me my second.

"I have never met a truer spirit than Dancer," Matteo continues. "He was born a leper amongst the downtrodden and rose to become a prince of men. He was virtuous and true, the way men *should* be. He was stubborn, sometimes naïve, but never stupid. He adored you, the boy we helped make a man. And he adored the man too, even if he had to stand in your way sometimes."

I nod. It's all I can do.

"I grieve for Sevro the most—"

"Bad form," Sevro mutters. "Mourning for what ain't dead, yet." Matteo's eyes widen as he sees Sevro marching down our ship's ramp. Apparently, Matteo and Quick don't know everything. "Sorry I'm late. Dishes to do. But we came for metal, Matteo. Not to hump. Not to cry. Metal. So if you don't mind, show us to your man." He glances at me. "One of us is in a hurry."

We enter Quicksilver's study and step onto the streets of Luna. The study itself is hidden behind a life-sized hologram. Sevro mutters under his breath at the melodrama.

The hologram shows a mob of lowColors marching through Luna's streets waving banners and chains. Skyscrapers and skyhooks crowd out the sky. A ship trails fire. Luna, just after the Day of Red Doves, is gripped with drunken, perverse revelry. The mob sings the Forbidden Song and cheers as gravBikes buzz past dragging the tattered remains of Silvers behind them. Many of the business caste wear Sun Industries emblems, but not all.

I glimpse Quicksilver through the holograms. He floats over the image of the crowd. The man is stout, bald, arrogant, and pugnacious as ever. He wears a black kimono embroidered with green, and glowing slippers.

"I thought I would take solace in the fact that they are all starving now, having traded the Republic for a cabal of maniacs, deviants, clones, Boneriders, Grimmuses, and, worst of all—socialists," Quick says as I walk through the riot. Sevro doesn't follow me deeper into the room. He remains at the entrance to the study, where he leans with his back against the wall, eyes restless and searching for danger. "I don't feel satisfaction. If anything I feel . . . nothing."

Quicksilver's frown is followed by a moment of silence.

"Of course, I wonder what I could have done differently. Your constant refrain, I know, Darrow. Only difference between you and me is that you blame yourself, and I know who is really to blame: the mob."

He glares down at the mob as if they were ants spoiling his picnic.

"So, this is what you do all day," Sevro says.

"Ah, nothing like sarcasm from uninvited guests," Quick replies. "You know, with that beard you truly do look like your father, Sevro. For your own safety, please refrain from any sort of violence. I didn't have to let you two aboard. Remember that."

"I'm sure you'll remind us a few more times," Sevro says. "When you come down from the cross."

Matteo and I share a smile. Sevro and Quick have always been bastards to one another, but Quick puts up with Sevro like he's his black sheep son. He knew Fitchner since Sevro was a baby, and watched him grow up from afar. Sevro's always carried a chip on his shoulder for the Silver. Like he thinks it's unfair that the money lived and the man who did all the work, his father, died.

He's not wrong, but I think he fails to notice how no one else gets away with talking to Quicksilver quite like he does.

Quicksilver speeds up the scene, bored. The mob flows past and then the streets and people and their song dissolve into digital smoke. His slippers dim and he descends to the floor.

Quick's study is expansive but lightly furnished. The floor is green stone. A nearly opaque window looks out at a garden. The rest of the walls are filled with screens relaying raw data. Except for one behind the desk. That wall is filled with relics of the past. Amidst ancient spears and tablets are a few items I recognize, including a black helmet with a starburst crest.

Quicksilver rubs his mysterious ring with its Gold eyeball at its center, the one he's worn since I first met him. I let him look me over.

If Sevro's his black sheep, I'm his golden son.

"Darrow." He reaches up and grips both my arms. "My boy. Gods. Mercury." He breathes out. "I'm sorry about your troops. They were patriots, all. Heroes. The mob doesn't deserve their sacrifice. But where have you been?"

Matteo clarifies. "We've watched the *Archimedes* approach since you entered the Belt." I turn. They must have very long eyes. "And we know Kavax sent Cassius with that fresh hull to help you escape Mercury, but where have you been in the time between?"

"I was marooned on one of the Marchers," I say.

"Icarus Base?" Quicksilver guffaws. "Really? Gods, makes me nostalgic. Remember when we sent teams to build the damn thing, Matteo?"

"How could I not? You'd rove the penthouse at all hours raving that Fitchner was too bold. That the Votum would see the construction skiffs and rat us out to the Praetorians."

"Ah, the old days." Quicksilver's eyes twinkle. "That was truly a thrill. Spartan base, though. Couldn't have been pleasant."

"It was . . . educational," I say.

"And what is it that you learned?"

"Perspective."

"Perspective, eh? You know, I once overheard Magnus au Grimmus tell your old companion Roque that losing an army will either make a man a philosopher or a suicide. Glad you chose differently than Fabii."

"After that it was the Dockyards of Venus."

Quicksilver and Matteo look at each other and laugh. "That was you?"

"Technically, it was him." I nod to Sevro.

They frown. So, they don't know about the auction. Sevro looks at me, and it's clear he doesn't want them to. He's embarrassed. "If you knew we were coming, then you probably know why we're here. Virginia did send five other ships. Did any of them make it?"

"No. But your wife's agent has been very clear with Matteo. She thinks the Republic's salvation lies here with us," Quicksilver says.

"Does it?" I look around the room. The data might as well be streaming by in ancient Mandarin. Can't make heads or tails out of it, but the length of our journey with Matteo on the lift to Quicksilver's study was long enough for me to guess he's hollowed out the entirety of the asteroid. A herculean effort. Maybe Virginia was right after all, and the asteroid is filled with dockyards and new warships. Yet a feeling is telling me it's housing something else. But what?

"Come," Quicksilver says. "Let's sit if we're going to get mad at each other."

He takes us to a sunken sitting room with cushions arrayed on the floor and, dripping from the ceiling, a Neptunian rain column. It is shaped like a teardrop made from the diamonds that rain down on that distant sphere. Sevro doesn't sit on the cushions with the rest of us. He perches on the rim of the sitting room and keeps watch.

"Sevro, come sit with us," says Quicksilver. "Whatever happened to you on Luna wasn't my fault. You know that. We're friends, you and I. Let's sit and talk like it." Sevro gives him the crux. Quick shoots me a look of concern. "Right. Well. You've had a hard run, lad. A hard run. Act as you like. You're entitled to it." Mischief enters his eyes. "That's the way in Virginia's Republic, is it not?"

"If anything, she's shown restraint," I say. "Especially with you."

"Please. If she listened to me, the Vox would have been smashed years ago. Had she treated them with as firm a hand as she dealt with my Silvers, well the Society would be ashes. And she wouldn't have had to send her husband here to drag me back to the slaughterhouse."

"I didn't come to drag you. I came to talk."

He's skeptical. "So, talk."

"The Republic may not survive the year without your help," I say. "Phobos has fallen to the Rim and Lysander's alliance. They may Rain on the planet any day now, if they haven't already. Not to mention, Atalantia is waiting in the wings blockading Luna. Already, millions have died of starvation. We need whatever ships and weapons you have left or our lifelong dream will die. You have reasons to be upset with me, with Virginia. I have not always been the best partner, nor delivered the results I promised. I don't have the long view like Fitchner. Nor the subtlety. But we started this war together and we need to end it together. I have always had your back, Quick. I need you to have mine one last time. Give me the weapons to make this a fight."

He sips his whiskey and looks at Matteo.

"Very well spoken, but who says I have weapons?"

"Virginia has your books," I say. "From your old *logos*."

An eyebrow arches toward Matteo. "Our loose end. I thought I said hire a team?"

"I hired three."

"Well, shit. Here we are."

I press him. "We know about the metal and materiel you've hoarded. Whatever fleet or weapons you've built in secret serves no purpose out here. I've come to ask you to lend me your ships. Let me put them to use. Give me the weapons I need to finish this war, and I will finish it."

Quicksilver sighs. "I fear we cannot do that, Darrow."

"Cannot or will not?" Sevro asks.

"Both, in fact."

"That's not entirely true," Matteo says.

Quicksilver glares at him, then smiles at me. "Listen, Darrow. It's not that I don't believe in you anymore. I asked you to move mountains, and you did. I asked you to wage a war on heaven, and you have. Shit, dead gods are in your wake, my boys. That you survived Mercury, that you found your way here—" He shakes his head with a true and unreserved admiration that I immediately resent. "Well, it's enough to make an old nihilist believe in heroes again. I believe in you, Darrow, at least that you and Sevro will fight till the last. But Gold is rising once more. Atalantia's forces multiply by the day. Lune—a Lune I said we should kill, remember—is reawakening their dormant moral spirit, and has won the Rim to his banner. Even with the recent developments, our cause is at its terminus."

"Recent developments?" I ask.

He ignores that. "To be perfectly honest, I no longer believe the people have the will to win this. I no longer believe in the people at all really."

"You never did," Sevro accuses.

Matteo looks at him, hard.

"Oh, like you do?" Quicksilver laughs. "Say it then. Claim the people are the power of the Republic." Quicksilver waits, but Sevro just glares. "No? See. The people rely on a narrow, sharp edge. The Volk. You two. The Free Legions. The people just huddle and whine and wait. You hate the people too, Sevro. You think they're slime. When have they ever treated you decently? When have they had your back? All you care about is your wife. Your children. And you know what? That is fine. It's natural. Fair. But don't act like I'm worse than you. You abandoned the Free Legions. Left Darrow to rot before I did." Sevro looks down in shame. "I only left after the people returned my gift of liberty on the end of a pike."

It's Matteo's turn to look down. Quicksilver leans back and puts his feet up on the rain column that, if sold, could feed twenty assimilation camps for ten years.

"Quick, you can bitch and moan all you like, but you can't hide out here forever," I say. "If Gold puts down the Republic, do you think they won't hunt you? Atalantia's promised Ceres to the man or woman who brings either you or Matteo back to be her playthings. When the Republic falls, you'll be next. There's nowhere to hide. Nowhere to run."

A mysterious half-smile appears on his face.

"What if there was somewhere to run, somewhere to hide, where Gold could never reach us, where the stain of their rule was erased from humanity and we could start with a blank slate . . . a tabula rasa . . . would you come and be a part of that future? Would you come with me?"

I hesitate. "What do you mean?"

"Enough toying with him. They're our friends. Show them," Matteo says.

"They'll hate it," Quicksilver says.

"We agreed you'd show Darrow. Show them both. They both deserve to know the war wasn't all for nothing."

"Show us what?" Sevro asks.

"My dream," Quicksilver replies and looks heavily at Sevro. "I will remind you that violence will not work here." With a smile of pride, he nods toward the garden window. I stand and approach the window. Obscured as it is by the fogged glass, I cannot divine anything about the garden save that it has foliage and running water. I'd assumed it was an oxygen farm, but something in Quick's words, and in the faintly visible curve of the garden, seems off.

Then the opaque glass clears and unveils a wonder.

Time stops, and I feel that I am once again stepping out from the gravLift behind Dancer to see the surface of Mars for the first time.

It's not just a garden that lies behind the glass: it's an entire world. Miniature, but complete. Hundreds of varieties of trees and fruiting bushes curve along the hollowed-out interior of the asteroid, facing the small, glowing sun that floats in the center of his new world. Figures rove over the landscape in twos and threes. *Children,* I realize after a beat. The gravity is such that the children who run through the trees or sit in the glades taking instruction from automaton teachers all cling to the ground even as they appear upside down or sideways to me. Wherever they stand, the small sun at the center of the world is up.

"What is this place?" I ask.

"I was born too late to explore the seas, and I am too wicked to explore heaven, so the stars will have to do. This, my boy, is an interstellar generation ship. An introvert's boyhood dream that he now gets to share with his lifelong love." Matteo takes Quick's hand.

The construction and technology on display would render even Virginia speechless, but that's not what forms the lump in my throat. There is something strange about the children. I pick out the closest, a girl running from the others through a glade of young Martian godTrees. The girl is olive skinned and around six years old. Her hair and eyes are brown and her hands smooth and blank.

Without sigils.

"You see, boys. It's not Gold that's the problem, not entirely at least. Even if we kill them all, their work will endure. The Colors are the problem. The hierarchy itself. And those children down there, our children, they are not Gold, not Red, not Blue, nor Green. They are *Homo sapiens,* and they deserve to inherit more than the sins of our world."

"Not a shipyard or a fortress," Sevro whispers. "It is a life raft. You're abandoning us . . ."

He stands and trembles with rage. "You don't have ships. You spent all the metal on this . . . *this.*" All three of us watch and wait for Sevro to explode. The hair on my arms rises. Sevro's must too. He turns and sees half a dozen malevolent red eyes staring back at him. I can't see what the eyes are attached to, but I sense their mass and danger. Sevro's lips curl. I don't think he was going to fight, but seeing how fruitless it would have been, he grows so angry his trembling stops. He turns back to Quicksilver.

"Thirty-six days. Seventy-eight by the time we're back." Tears glisten in his eyes. "You saw us coming. You could have sent a message." His voice catches. "You two ain't fathers. Those ain't your children. You're cowards playing gods. Rot out there. Rot and die, *Golds*."

Then he walks away. The helplessness of his rage breaks my heart. That rage was our fuel in the beginning. Our lifeblood. We learned that together long ago. It will not help us now.

Forgetting is essential to learning,
just as exhaling is essential to breathing.

I look back on the garden and breathe. This path is blocked, and no amount of pushing will help. "This place have a name?"

"We call it the *Tabula Rasa*."

"Why don't you show me your new world then, old friend?" I ask. "Help me to understand."

39

DARROW

Under the Golden Gaze

A s I walk through the *Tabula Rasa's* garden with Quick, an old conversation I had with Nero long ago on the Lion Steps echoes across the years. Nero told me he desired mankind to push past this stunted age to explore and colonize the stars.

A noble sentiment. Yet it is difficult not to let my wonder at the garden and Quicksilver's ship decay into the sulky anger of a spurned lover who has been traded in for a younger model. Quick and I once held dreams in common. Even if I can see the beauty of Quicksilver's ship, I fault him for making it, for abandoning everything we fought so hard for. At the same time, I understand his mind. All too well, I understand the frustration of feeling like the only one who is pushing at the mountain.

As the sun dimmed, the children were escorted away by their automaton teachers. Now that they no longer populate Quick's invented world, they feel like reveries, the only evidence they existed the occasional indentation from a small foot in grass.

"It seems a somewhat impractical ship," I say.

"Oh, this is merely the heart of the ship," Quicksilver replies. "That's what we call it and what it is. Spiritually at least. It is an ocean of darkness out there. Metal and halls could only do for so long. I could show you the engines, the reactors, the living quarters, the school, the water plants, but those are all the *how*. This is the fantastical *why*."

"I see."

"Do you?"

"I think so. You want to give these children the chance you never had."

Quick considers me as I run my hand along the trunk of a godTree, wishing it was Martian soil beneath my feet, Martian air in my lungs. "Do you think Sevro would have stabbed me?" Quicksilver asks. "If he knew he could."

"I think he saw it didn't matter. It wouldn't turn the metal into a navy," I say. "But you wouldn't have let us aboard if we were at all a threat."

"No. I recall how you brought Lorn into that civil war. Trapped him in treason, so he had to fight."

"Then why?" I ask.

"Why?"

"Why let me board, why be here at all? Why watch me come all this way?"

"We were performing engine tests when your wife's agent arrived. They're ready, but now I need an exit window. My engines may be fast, eventually, but this is a lot of mass to get moving and once it gets moving, it can't hide."

I puzzle over that. With the war concentrated in the Core, Quick should already have his window. "Ah. The Shadow Armada."

"Yes, the Rim's roving fleet. Amongst other threats."

"Where is it now?" I ask.

"Almost far enough away," he says with a soft smile.

He watches me out of the corner of his eye as we walk through a field of grass toward a glade of trees woolly with crimson leaves. The gravity is higher than that of Mars. "You've changed since I last saw you. Perhaps your time on the Marcher really did teach you something."

"Maybe." I peer at the upside-down world over my head. It must be more than three kilometers between the tip of the tree I lean against and those that hang from the ceiling. "This place. It would have taken longer than a few years to build. You started when we were winning."

"Yes."

"Did it spring from doubt or hope?"

"Both. This was always my dream, long before Fitchner and I began to conspire. I tried to build this place when you were just a child, but it was too ambitious then. I hadn't the technology or the access to the right scientists. When the planets fell to you, I had my pick of Gold's best."

He twists his famous ring, a nervous tic. The Gold eyeball within the ring watches me as Quicksilver takes a seat in the grass. Wind moves the leaves. It's strange to feel it here inside an asteroid, but the world he's made seems to have its own weather patterns to go with its own gravity and its own tiny sun.

"All this effort, all the resources . . . you could have made me four more *Morning Stars*. We might have beaten Gold years ago," I say, trying to keep accusation from my voice.

"The first time in history a man is called a villain for beating swords into ploughshares."

"I didn't call you a villain," I say.

"But you think it, even as you pour honey in my ear. One gets tired of investing in war. What do you think happens, if you did win, Darrow? If you do beat Gold down to nothing? The Vox just proved what's waiting on the other side—with a little Gold prodding, sure. But still. You were on the precipice of victory, and already the people turned on you. Even if you win, these worlds will never be free of that sickness. Of Gold. I learned that lesson a long time ago." He kneads his hands together, twisting and twisting his ring. He looks down at it with little affection. "You know you're the only person I can think of who has never asked why I wear this."

"You wear it so people will ask, so I never did."

He hesitates. "Since this will be the last time we see one another, I feel an urge to be understood. What I'd have given to have that moment with Fitchner. Full clarity."

He takes time gathering his thoughts.

"I . . . had a partner in my first enterprises, Darrow. A Silver whom I loved as deeply as I love Matteo. He was . . . better than me. Where I had already surrendered to the . . . pummeling nature of reality and become a pragmatist, he was a dreamer. It was because of him that we adopted children."

"You had children?" I ask.

"Four of them." He goes quiet, turning and turning his ring. "After our first enterprise met some trouble and failed, as they do more often than not, our name was ruined. I took out a loan with a dangerous Gold to finance our second venture. I had no choice. The guild had docked me, so you know, ambitious me invited a shark into the pen. The Gold thought it amusing to insert a clause allowing him to collect in flesh, should we default.

"We didn't mind. We were used to such . . . demeaning eccentricities, and our cash flow was dependable. But then, a shipment of ore was hijacked by pirates. Then another. And another until we defaulted on that loan, and I had to cut a pound of flesh from my thighs and buttocks to give to our creditor. He fed them to his horses. Yes. He had carnivorous horses. Humiliated, my partner investigated the pirates.

"Of course, you will not be surprised to learn the pirates were led by none other than my creditor's youngest daughter. But I was surprised then, and naïve. So naïve even though I thought I was a student of realpolitik. I reported the offense to the proper authority. Unfortunately, that 'proper authority' and my financier had been to the rhetoric school on Rhodes together.

"A week later, the daughter and her father and brothers broke into our home. They found us in bed, and our children in their beds. They wrapped them in the sheets, hung them from the ceiling, and beat them until no more blood would come out. I sat in that rain . . . that red rain . . . and I understood there is no such thing as *proper authority*. Violence is the only authority. They said one of us could live. My partner refused to choose. I chose me."

I stay quiet, allowing him to exhume the grief on his own terms.

"Only Matteo knows this. I was . . . too ashamed to tell Fitchner. He would have died for his wife. I feared the way he'd look at me knowing I didn't die for my love." He sighs away years of shame, and carries on, detached. "After that night, I was spared and forced to play the market for my creditor until I bought my way under a bigger wing. It took me years to have my revenge. By the time I was done, the Gold who'd wronged me was destitute, childless, and hunted by Olympic Knights. I'd done it all to him with payments, whispers, and the violence of others. The last time I saw him, I put a spoon in his hand, and told him I'd give him his life for the price of one eye."

His thumb glides around the iris of the eye embedded in his ring.

"I was true to my word. After he'd given me the eye, I had him sealed in a life pod powered by a nuclear generator and shot it into deep space. That was thirty-eight years ago. This ring receives his heartbeat from time to time." I feel a little sick. "He's still alive, hooked to the nutrient pods, unable to move, willing but unable to die. He will only be eighty-two when we pass him. We're following his trajectory, and with this station's engines, we should overtake him in five years.

"That's what progress does, you see. It leaps ahead of the past, but we can never outrun the trauma that fixed our course. I will never not be that coward shivering beneath the corpses of my love, my children. I will never not see those Gold eyes staring down at me, mocking, knowing there was no recourse I could seek. Just as you will never be able to forget Nero's eyes as he killed Eo. We are all ever beneath their golden gaze. That is why I wear this ring. To remind myself how my war began."

A silence falls between us. I break it after a few minutes.

"That's why you built this place. So your children will never know that gaze?" I ask.

He nods, and the automatons suddenly make sense. "These children have never met you, have they?"

"No. I am contaminated," he says. "We are all contaminated. Gold hijacked the fate of mankind. I won't let them inherit the chains Gold nailed into the rest of us. Those children were born free, and they will be free out there amongst the stars. Free to go mad and devour each other before we reach the nearest star. Or free to build a better world than the one we left. Free to become whatever it is they decide to become."

"Maybe you're not a realist after all," I say.

"Maybe not."

"Will you extend your life with telomerase tanks?"

"I have not decided yet," he says, reflective. "I know it will be lonely. Matteo and I are prepared for that. But what god isn't lonely? I really don't think it is bad to think of myself as that. Gods are manmade after all."

I consider his face, so exhausted from bellicosity, so lined with the grooves of struggle it might as well be the prow of a battleship. "Do you want to know what I think?"

"Yours might be the only opinion I value," he says. He pauses, and I sense why. He made me, in a way. His first child after those who died. "After all, you're the only person I care to say farewell to."

"I think when you catch up with the Gold who wronged you, you should show him mercy. Resist the temptation to face him again. Destroy the ship as you pass." He closes his eyes. "You asked me what I learned on the Marcher. It's that. Chains might be made by others, but we tend them. End his pain. End your own. Who knows. Maybe you'll find more joy in being a father than playing god."

He thinks on that. After he does, he sounds different, like a man speaking an unfamiliar tongue and surprised to hear it coming from his own mouth. Affection is not natural for Quicksilver. "You know, I always called you the best investment I ever made, Darrow. But for a long time now, you've been more than that." He looks away, estranged from his own vulnerability. "For many years, I've thought of you as a son."

As I thought. He let me come all this way just to not hand me the miracle I need. He is not like Odysseus's wise, gray-eyed god. He is like the other gods who tormented Odysseus. The selfish gods. He wanted me to see him. Not to understand him, but to forgive him for running away. And though I'm angry, I truly do.

I reach for his hand. He flinches, but allows me to hold it and take the eyeball ring from his finger. "Your war is over, Quick. I'll take it from here. But any help you could lend me that doesn't risk this ship would be more than welcome."

"I can't give you enough to change your destination."

I smirk. "The Vale?"

He nods. "There was a moment where we could win, but we let it slip through our fingers. That moment is gone."

"Have I ever given you business advice?" I ask with a smile. "Then do me a favor, don't advise me on war."

He laughs. "What do you need? Aside from ships. Most of mine were decommissioned and used as materials to finish the *Rasa*. The few that remain are needed to defend the station until we're free of this infernal system."

"Repairs, provisions, weapons, armor, and my wife's agent. But more than anything, I need information. Since this wandering world is meant to find a new home, and you watched me on my way here, I'm betting it has one bloodydamn good telescope."

The main telescopic array of the *Tabula Rasa* looks like a tornado made of metal and glass. It is constructed in several parts and so can extend out from a crater to change its view. The array tapers to a spherical viewing chamber suspended in darkness. Eight less powerful short-range telescopes are distributed along the asteroid's surface so that with a tilt of its axis the array can bring any one of them to bear without having to completely realign itself. The system is meant to be usable even by an astral novice like Quicksilver, and is run by an AI.

"Show me the system," I say.

I see the galaxy form beyond me in the blackness beyond the chamber. A second three-dimensional image appears on a central pedestal. It is not a true view of reality. Where there is no visual information to be gathered, the AI has filled in the unseen elements of the celestial bodies. I cup the system in my hands, astounded.

The telescope lends me the flawed omniscience of Zeus. Its only limitation is that it looks out from one perspective—the *Tabula Rasa*'s. On closer inspection there are blindspots from asteroids in the way of its view, but the experience of peering at the images it gathers is no less affecting. I see the planets turn on their axes, revealing little secrets as they dance around the sun. So long as the telescopes are open and watching, the AI is recording, so I can rewind time on demand.

Matteo was right, I do have more time than I thought.

Mars floats before me. The moons of Phobos and Deimos are in the hands of the enemy still, but the siege of Mars has not progressed as I feared it would. The Iron Rain has not yet fallen. Far from it. Nearly half the enemy fleet is missing. I rewind time from the telescope's old, recorded imagery to see if maybe they are hiding behind the planet. They are not.

I watch in puzzlement as, twenty days ago, the combined Dust and Dragon armadas stream away from Phobos. The telescope's artificial intelligence tracked the ships with one of its smaller telescopes. If it hadn't, there would be no way to find the Rim Armada again, with their cold-running engines and in all the billions of radial kilometers peppered with millions of asteroids and the war's debris. I watch the gloomy image of the *Dustmaker* leading the armada into the asteroid belt. I spot them again two days ago, already a third of the way through the Belt. Now they are a hundred and eighty million kilometers from the *Tabula Rasa*, but their course doesn't look like it will bring them any closer. They're on a straight shot to intercept Jupiter, and moving fast.

A second fleet follows from Phobos ten days after the first.

It is led by the *Lightbringer* née *Morning Star*.

Two fleets headed for Jupiter. But why?

Knowing the answer lies in their destination, I tell the AI I want a view of Jupiter and wait as the telescopes align. When they have, the planet floats over the pedestal. It dwarfs me in size. Of the one hundred and twenty-one moons that surround the Gas Giant, thirty-two are visible. The others are hidden by the planet's mass.

For several hours I magnify the image and shift between spectrums of light. What I see over those hours causes me to sink to a knee in disbelief. It's been so long since I've had good news, I don't believe my eyes. But it is there in front of me. Good news.

And a path, waiting for me.

Ten hours later, with repairs on the *Archimedes* already underway, I gather Aurae, Cassius, and Sevro in the chamber of the telescope. Sevro cradles a coffee, while Cassius nips at a tiny, seemingly bottomless flask of brandy—a habit I thought he'd kicked on our journey to the Belt.

"We now know Quicksilver is not coming back to the war. As I understand it, most of his fleet was decommissioned and recycled into the materials from which this station was built," I say.

"So you're just gonna let that arrogant piece of shit waddle off to the ass-end of space," Sevro mutters. "He shouldn't get a happy ending."

"So you suggest what?" I ask.

"We dropped that coms buoy for a reason," he says.

"Yes, to blast out his location to the system if he wouldn't give us his ships. A gun to his head. But if a man has no cash in his pockets why mug him at all?" I ask.

Sevro relents with a sigh. "I don't even think he likes those *Homo sapiens*. His children. More like human pity shields." His initial anger has faded, and he's grown lighter now that he knows as soon as the repairs on the *Archi* are made he'll be going home. He glances up at the telescope. "So, what. You found our route back to Mars?"

"In a way," I say. His eyes narrow. "I did not ask you your opinions when we came here because we were under the orders of our Sovereign and had but one ship. I'm going to ask your opinions after I show you something. Sevro, you and I have already talked, and I know you're going home. This is not to pressure you, but I want you to know what I know."

He grows guarded.

I activate the pedestal. The moons of Jupiter bathe the faces of Cassius, Aurae, and Sevro in gloomy golden light. Sevro looks up. Aurae begins to smile until she sees the Obsidian ships.

"In war, especially those that span a decade, it is inevitable for a vulture to appear and prey on the weakened powers," I say. "Our war finally has its first true vulture. Volsung Fá. He fell on Sefi and the Alltribe before they could set their feet after rebelling from the Republic. He stole her throne, her braves, her navy. Instead of staying on Mars where he'd be overwhelmed eventually, he saw we were weakened in the Belt and started gnawing on our cities and trade posts there. It seems, finally, he's smelled blood from someone else."

"We were all wondering why we saw so little sign of the Obsidian pirates, many my own old veterans, who were supposed to be raiding along our route to this asteroid. Now we have our answer. They are not in the asteroid belt any longer. They have attacked the moons of Jupiter. The home of the Raa themselves."

Cassius coughs. "Obsidians . . . attacking Ilium. That's suicide."

"Not this time. In their haste to finish off the Republic, Helios and Dido threw most of the Rim's naval might into the Core. Two whole armadas, Dragon and Dust, which left only the Shadow Armada and local fleets to guard *all* of the Rim. It's three point seven two billion kilometers from Neptune to Jupiter on a good day. Since Dragon and Dust are racing back, we can assume the Shadow Armada is very out of place." I grin. "They're caught with their pants down and the vulture's got them in the ass."

"There's still the Ilium Guard," Aurae murmurs. "No?"

"Volsung Fá beat that garrison," I say almost like I'm proud of the monster who killed Sefi. "The telescope doesn't have footage, but I've seen the debris. Currently there are no Rim ships opposing him in the moon system that I can see. Those ships he stole from Sefi used to serve on my front line. The Volk navy is tough. Dreadnaughts, destroyers. This is not some minor raid.

"I wasn't able to see as much as I'd like—they're clever, using the moons as cover. But it appears—and here's the weird part—it appears Fá has joined the ships and braves he took from the Alltribe on Mars with the Ascomanni of the Far Ink."

I gesture to two dozen dim ships skulking between the moons. They are small, corvettes maybe, but their design is like none any of us have ever seen.

Cassius guffaws. Sevro sips his coffee. He knows it's good news for Mars. Aurae looks like she's about to throw up. I tame my enthusiasm. It's the Raa who've been made fools of, but it's their people who will suffer.

"This is the problem with AIs," Cassius says. "They're creative little beasts. The Ascomanni of the Far Ink . . . well yes, some exist. Probably. But they're so far away. And absolute savages. If any are left. They can't make ships. Much less challenge Ilium. If you ask me, this AI has spent far too much time alone and concocted a ludicrous fiction."

"Or Fá has compiled the largest Obsidian navy since the Dark Revolt," Sevro says. "Maybe he is Ragnar's da. Let him eat, I say. Chew, chew, evil bastard."

"Personally, I think he's a fraud but either way his luck won't last. He can't face the armadas coming for him. Not even with the Volk ships. Helios is going to eat him alive. But . . . I believe it will be absolute chaos in the one hundred and twenty-one moons of Jupiter."

Sevro eyes me like I'm the worlds' biggest idiot and sips his coffee again.

"This chaos can be used to infiltrate Ilium. I want to accept Athena's invitation. I want to meet with her agents at Kalyke, present the Helm of Ares, and use the ships she's stockpiled to complete our mission and bring them back to unite with the Republic ships to finish this war."

Dead silence.

"I hope the ships will be enough to give Gold a contest, but I do not know for certain. What I do know is Virginia and Victra are depending upon us for reinforcements. I see this as our last chance to matter in this fight. I will not make any of you come with me, but I believe I have to go."

"Darrow," Sevro says. "You don't have to do this."

"I was sent on a mission. It is not yet done," I say.

"Athena's invitation was not to you, Darrow," Aurae says, a little troubled. "If you answer it without Sevro, I cannot promise she will give you the ships."

"Why wouldn't she?" Cassius asks.

Aurae looks to me to see if I'll tell the truth.

"Twelve years ago, to secure Romulus's help against Roque before the Battle of Ilium, I offered to give him the names of all the known Sons of Ares on the Rim," I say. "The Raa used this information and purged them all."

"Purged?"

"They killed them," Aurae says. "And many more."

Cassius is stunned. He points between us. "And there's no tension . . . or . . . heartfolly poison in his oats?"

"You of all people should know I believe a man can walk out of his own darkness, Cassius," she says. "But I was a deepcell agent. I do not know the Daughters well enough to say they are all as forgiving as I am."

"Athena gave you *The Path to the Vale,* did she not?" I ask. She nods. "Then if you can get me to Athena, I will take my chances," I say.

Aurae looks worried for me, but proud too in a way. "It really would be best if Sevro came. Sevro, you are the son of Ares. You have a responsibility to help us," she says.

"Not going to lie, he's a hell of a guerilla. We could use you out there, Barca," Cassius says.

"No," I say. "Sevro has gone above and beyond the call of duty. Every single time I've asked. Then even when I haven't. He's earned his trip home. With the Rim gone, he stands a good chance of making it to the surface back to his family."

Sevro appreciates that. I see the change in his eyes as he imagines greeting his daughters and new child. His voice is friendly, but heavy. "Darrow, you're sailing into a warzone with the only safe harbor being among people who've got every reason to put a bullet in your head . . . at best."

I nod. "This is the path that is available to me. Your father left it for you. But we're brothers, so in a way it's my inheritance too."

40

LYRIA

Departure

IN FRONT OF THE mirror, I run a finger along the pink line of raw skin that circles my head just above my highest forehead wrinkle. "You popped my skull like a candy dispenser," I say.

"I told you it would be maximally invasive," Matteo calls back from the medical suite.

"Oh, the options I had. So grand."

"Scars will fade, but your sarcasm's back. That's good. The first week out, the only effluence one could expect from your mouth was drool."

He's not wrong. My first week after the surgery, I gibbered like a drunk. My feet wouldn't work till the second. I felt like I was operating a puppet body until the third. Only on the fourth did my body finally begin to feel like mine again. Most important, my memories are mine, safe, horrible, precious. But would I even know if they weren't there? If I was . . . what did Matteo call it . . . tabula rasa? A blank slate.

Matteo did not visit every day, and when he did the visits were not for long nor of much substance. But considering I've spent the last five weeks with only the company of shiny robots, his smile makes me feel grand when I exit the bathroom.

The elegant Pink reclines on the sofa. The man sits like silk. All folds, no creases. In brilliant blue and green, he's the only thing in the room not bleach white or gray steel. His smile fades and he raises a delicate eyebrow at the grid in front of me. "Grid proof, please."

"Again?" I say, exasperated.

"One last time. Think of my heart. I can't very well send you back into the worlds wondering if you'll go cross-legged."

His eyes return to his personal planner. I can't see it, of course, but I see his fingers twitching and know he's working on something. I start the grid's program and begin sorting the holographic blocks. Halfway through, the color-coded blocks begin to emit frequencies meant to elicit certain emotions. I sort based on nostalgia, terror, regret, jealousy, love, amusement, pity, joy—putting the emotions on a sliding scale between the light and dark side of the grid. When I'm finished, nine and a half minutes later, Matteo stands and examines my results.

"Horrific," he says.

"What?"

"Your personality." He winks. "Your mind is yours again, Lyria. Almost. Do you still feel it?"

I search my mind. The parasite is gone, but I still feel . . . something. They say people who lose a limb still feel it years later. Must be like that. Except it was never a limb. It was always an alien inside me I couldn't control. Yet I find myself missing its security. With it, I felt I was due for something great. It consoled the part of me that feared how small I am in a world of giants.

"I feel it."

He nods, stands, and walks to the far side of the room. I follow the man, clumsy in his elegant wake. We stop before a metal basin bathed in harsh light. Matteo hands me a small circular control. "Destroy it. It was never you. You were never it. Draw a triangle with your thumb on the prism. Destroy it, and be clean."

I look down at the parasite.

It lies inert in the basin, harmless yet seductive. Its core is as small as my pinky nail, and flat, and around it lie its thousands of translucent tendrils, a halo of angel hair. I've not seen it since it left Figment and burrowed into my own brain that day Victra, Volga, and I crashed down on Mars. That thought, that memory of violation, moves my thumb.

I draw the triangle.

The harsh light over the parasite intensifies. Matteo turns my head away from the light. Heat radiates from the basin over my back. When it's dim enough to open my eyes again, the parasite is a pool of liquid metal. It trickles down the drain. Matteo clinks his glass to mine.

"Well done, Lyria. You are free now." I feel free, finally. "You'll be happy to hear the Sovereign's envoys have arrived. Darrow is expecting you."

I stare at him. "What? *He's* here?"

"Yes. One room over. His hardware needed tuning. But he won't be here for long." He pauses. "He's bound for the Rim."

"The Rim." My mind races. "Why the Rim? Mars will come under attack soon."

"Oh, Mars is already under attack. And so is the Rim. By Volsung Fá, in fact." He smiles, and touches his pendant through his jacket. "I thought that may be of interest to you since he killed your friend Ephraim."

"Ephraim wasn't my friend."

"No, it was the other, wasn't it? What was her name? Vulgar? Volgana?"

"Volga," I say. "Which you remember perfectly well."

He winks. "Just making sure your memory's scratch."

Darrow is not the hugest man I've ever met, but he is the only man I've ever met who makes his own gravity. I grow heavier the closer I come to his orbit. He lies on a medical bed under red light, accompanied only by medical drones. Sweat sheets off his muscled, scarred body. He has more power in one of his legs than I have in all of me.

It was easier to criticize him from afar. Up close, seeing his body is enough to make me realize the distance between our experiences. What type of enemies must a man fight to need to be built like a war machine and still get so many scars?

His voice is deeper in person, and sends chills down my spine.

"You must be Lyria of Lagalos," he says from the bed without opening his eyes.

"I want to go with you to the Rim," I blurt out.

His eyes open. "And how is it you know where I'm going?"

"Matteo told me."

He pauses for a moment. Even his silence is terrifying.

At last he asks, "What else did Matteo tell you?"

"That you didn't get the ships you needed here, so you're bound for the Rim. Which is under attack by the Ascomanni, well Volsung Fá."

"He told you that?"

"And more," I say.

He grunts.

"Must miss the Hyperion gossip circuit."

"I've seen Volsung Fá," I say.

"Have you?" I hear the interest in his voice.

"He chased me down a hallway once. All in black armor. With thorns on it."

"Thorns?"

"He impaled men with them. He wanted Volga."

"Ah, the time you fled the *Pandora,*" he says.

"You know who I am. What I've done then," I say.

He's still looking straight up. "According to my wife, we've forgiven you. And I'm supposed to make sure you get home safe."

"Forgiven? Slag that. I'm done feeling guilty for something I didn't intend. I was asking because if you know who I am, you know I am close with Volga. What I don't get is why you wouldn't take me with you, seeing as how I'm the only friend Ragnar Volarus's daughter has in all the worlds."

Only when I stand up to him, and only then, do his eyes finally meet mine. He's pained from his treatment. Still, I sway knowing only a portion of what those eyes have seen. Eo hanging. Armadas burning. A Sovereign dying on his blade. For a horrifying second, I realize what it must be like to be him. The man cursed to use the weapons of the enemy to liberate people like me.

All for what? People like me to stand with their hands on their hips and scold him?

All the anger I've had for him over the years dissolves in the reality of his existence. I wouldn't want to be in an Iron Rain. I wouldn't want to fight a Peerless Scarred. And he's fought them all.

"I am not going to rescue Volga," he says. "She's probably already dead or brainwashed. Sorry. Those are the hard truths. This Fá doesn't seem to play with his food."

"But—"

"Ilium is a warzone. It'll soon get worse, and Fá's not long for this world. Helios and all the might of the Rim is coming for him. Are you a soldier, Lyria?"

"No," I admit.

"Then you really don't want to be there . . ."

"It's because I'm a Red, ain't it?"

His eyes flash with anger, and then soften just as suddenly. His voice softens too. "Lyria, I know the spirit of Reds. I know it well enough to know a Red's spirit is not in her armor or her size or her experience." He sighs. "Listen, Virginia sent me your dossier. I know what happened to your assimilation camp. I know what happened to your family. The camps never became what we wanted them to. I am sorry for it."

"I ain't yours to protect," I snap harder than I mean to. "Now you listen. I don't want your sorry. Volga is my best friend. She's my only friend. She gave herself to Fá to protect Mars. Everyone just let her. I don't blame them, but she's got no one. I know what that's like. I promised I'd get her back. She's got no one else to fight for her. Don't you care at all? Ain't she the true heir of Ragnar? Don't that matter to you? He was your friend. We all know that."

He grimaces. "I can't fix everything. If all goes as planned, we won't even see the Obsidians. Probably just the rubble they've left behind. But oddly enough, they've given Mars time to breathe. I wish them well in their war against the Dominion, and I wish you well in your travels. Your ship will leave tomorrow at 0500. Go home. Personally, I'd give anything to do that."

I leave itchy with anger, and feeling small as a tick's prick. Somehow I thought it'd go different, because he was a Red. Is a Red. Because I'm a Red. Is it because he knows I'm Gamma? I thought he'd see my spirit, my pluck, and pack me in with the rest of the cargo the drones are loading onto his ship. But no. My chance to matter flowed down the drain with the parasite.

Matteo wakes me early the next morning.

I shower and dress in silence. Before I leave the room, I look out through the ovular windows and listen for the last time to the song that seeps through the glass. It was with me throughout my recovery, and I think it will be the only thing I miss from this place.

"You are fortunate. The ship is stocked with cuisine from our own stores. It is run by a sophisticated artificial intelligence named Pilot," Matteo says as we enter the hangar. A Y-shaped ship waits with its ramp unfurled. On the opposite side of the hangar, Darrow's black ship undergoes repairs. It looks a little like a pitviper, I think. Light from welding drones casts wild shadows on the floor. "Pilot may lack creativity, as its name implies, but it will return to Mars as efficiently as any human could."

"What if enemy ships attack us?"

"It will react."

"What if I try to take the controls?" I ask.

"There are no controls to take. You are superfluous to the functioning of the ship." And everything else. "It will leave in"—he checks his chronometer—"a half hour. All you need do is lay back, enjoy the ship's myriad comforts, and you and your fellow passenger will land in Agea thirty-three days from now. Assuming you don't get shot down or kill each other in transit, that is."

I stop at the ramp. "My fellow passenger?"

"He's already inside. Before we say farewell, I wish to thank you, Lyria of Lagalos."

"For what?"

"A reminder of the beauty of friendship, and that any mob is made up of people, in the end. I'll look back a little more fondly because of you." Look back? I'm not sure if I'm insulted or not, but I blush when he sweeps down to kiss both of my cheeks. He smells like heaven and flowers and sunlight.

"Friendship." I snort. "Darrow and the rest are going to find my friend. And I'm being sent the other way."

His eyebrows float up. "Indeed. At gunpoint even. Safe journey." He sweeps toward the hangar exit, whistling a lovely tune.

The hall entry from the ramp leads to the ship's lounge where a shirtless, tattooed man sits on the floor drinking from a coffee mug. I stare in awe at my fellow passenger.

The Goblin of Mars. Holy bloodydamn shit. I almost run away.

"You're late," he rasps.

"What?"

"You're late."

"Darrow said the ship wouldn't leave until 0500."

"The shit you think we're waiting on, ruster? Refueling? Clear skies? Naw. You." He tips his mug at me. He slaps the floor. "Let's get, Pilot."

"*Negative, passenger Barca. This vessel may not depart until the specified window. We are not the only ones in the asteroid belt. Your demand is declined.*"

"Slag that. Let's go."

"Negative, passenger Barca. The vessel"—

"Heard you the first time."

—*"may not depart until the specified window."*

Sevro scowls down into his mug. I stand awkwardly until he glares at me. "Whatchu looking at?"

I look at the ceiling and feel stupid. I look back at him. Darrow is all weight and silence. Sevro is like staring into a woodchipper, not sure if it's coming your way.

"You're Sevro Barca."

"So they say."

"I'm—"

"Don't care."

"My name is Lyria of Lagalos."

"Don't care. Go do something useful with your mouth."

He jerks his head toward the commissary. I stay rooted in front of him.

"I wanted to say . . ." My voice cracks. "I wanted to say I'm sorry. About Ulysses." His head jerks toward me so fast I flinch back.

"What did you say?"

"Ulysses . . . he—"

Sevro blinks up at me. "He?"

I stare. Horrified. He didn't know. Oh gods. I thought he knew. I thought the Sovereign would have told them. I thought he'd know like Darrow knew who I was. Does he know who I am? What does he know? Oh shit. Shit.

"He?" Sevro asks again. A lump forms in my throat. I swallow it down. "He?" Sevro rises to his feet. He's taller than he looks. Sturdy in frame, lanky with sledgehammer fists. Next thing I know, I'm in the air, dangling from one of those hammer hands as he chokes me. The hand has a skull of a wolf tattooed on it. He's not cuddly at all. He's terrifying. I can't breathe. My feet kick. I see knives in holsters on his belt. Knives on the floor. They've sent me home with a monster. I swat at his tattooed arms. It's like hitting a tree. *"He?"*

"Your . . . son . . ." I manage. "Ulysses."

Sevro's grip tightens. He's going to kill me. My lungs scream for oxygen. White spots dance in my vision. "It's a boy?" He blinks and loosens his grip. "Why are you sorry?" He shakes me like a rag. "Why?"

I don't know what he knows, so I just spill my guts.

"I—I was on the *Pandora*. I was Victra's prisoner, along with Volga. Fá and his Ascomanni attacked. The ship was lost. We escaped down to Mars with Victra. She was trapped under a tree. We helped her get out, and the three of us tried to get to safety. Victra had the baby before we got clear. I helped best I could. But we were in a fishing village. Thought it was safe. It wasn't."

His voice is small. "He's dead?"

"I'm sorry. I thought you knew."

He stares at the floor. "How?" I don't answer. I'm scared. Not by him, but because I know my words are sharper than his knives. "How?"

"The Red Hand. They . . . took him." My voice trails away.

"How?"

"They nailed him to a tree."

He lets me go and I collapse to the floor. He slumps, hollow. Before I can apologize again, he shoves a small silver cube into my hands and says, "Get this to the Sovereign."

He pushes past me and leaves the ship, stumbling down the ramp like a drunk man.

I follow at a distance, and watch from the top of the ramp as he storms from the hangar. When he's gone, I'm alone on the ship. I roll the silver cube in my hand. What is it? A message to Virginia from her husband? Or something for Pax?

The AI drones. *"Twenty minutes until departure."*

Will Sevro make it back in time? Is he coming back? Am I doing this journey all by myself?

I turn to head back into the ship, then stop. I'm not just alone on the ship. I'm alone in the hangar. Darrow's ship lies on the opposite side. Welder drones are at work on its hull. More drones trundle in and out of its cargo bay. Its open cargo bay.

I glance back into my ship and its sleek, lonely corridors. I look back at Darrow's. A smile spreads. I think of Matteo's last words. *Forced to go home at gunpoint.* Not a gun to be seen, I dart back into the Mars-bound ship, place the holocube on the table in the commissary, then run out the way I came.

41

DARROW

To the Stars ·

I WAKE ON THE DAY of departure feeling like a mummy rising from its sarcophagus. Quick said pain was to be expected, but I didn't expect to feel arthritic after the lightwave treatment. He said it would help with my mobility. To get the dust out of the joints, and the blood flowing, I perform my morning stretches to the rhythmic sounds from the coral aquarium outside my room's only window. Past the pain of each initial movement lies a pleasant surprise: greater flexibility than I've had in years. I jump and touch the ceiling with ease. Damn, but I will miss Quick in more ways than one.

After a shower and a cup of caf, I stride with fresh legs past the suites given to Cassius and Aurae to enter Sevro's. Stony-faced, he'd said farewell the night before, but I hoped that he'd change his mind. That I'd wake to see him snoring in his bed.

He did not change his mind, it seems. The bed is freshly made and when I arrive at the hangar, I see the ship Quick provided to ferry him and Lyria home with my message for Virginia is already gone.

Wounded, and wary of the wound, I seek distraction. To the sounds of loaders hauling pallets of gravBikes and equipment into the cargo bay, I inspect the *Archimedes*'s refurbished stealth hull until Cassius then Quick join me in the hangar.

"Factory repaired and sleek as a leviathan's hide," Cassius says with a whistle as he runs a hand along the fresh stealth material that coats the hull. "My compliments to your techs, Sun. Even if their brains are all silicon." Cassius glances in suspicion at the construction drones.

"The material is the last generation of its line," Quick says. "Its cloaking capabilities are superior to that of the generation Kavax gave you for Mercury. However, it is more fragile against kinetic impacts. As usual, it only works with your shield off, so do steer clear of pirates and Moonies, Bellona."

"What about scylla and leviathans?" Cassius asks.

"Whatever are you prattling on about sea beasts for?" Quick asks.

"Well, knowing Darrow, we'll crash on Europa and I'll have to fend off those beasties with an oar," Cassius says. "I must confess, I think you are a coward, Sun. Fleeing the fray at a time like this. But your station is the most ludicrous venture I've ever heard tell. Congratulations on the audacity, if nothing else." He extends a hand to Quicksilver. "Prime luck out there beyond the System, Sun. If you find a planet of guileless nymphs, do send word."

Quick looks at his hand in contempt.

"Your father was a decent man, despite his eyes. Your mother wasn't and isn't. As for you . . . you might be decent. But the man you killed like cattle twelve years ago was a titan. While you frittered away the spring of your life, he suffered, he struggled, only to be struck down by . . . you. Fitchner was my friend. I'm happy you've found accord with Sevro. But, no. Hospitality is one thing. But I will never shake your hand, Peerless. If you were worth anything, Lune wouldn't be leading a Gold armada. Would he?"

Cassius weathers all the insults but the last with aplomb. The last is a knife to his gut. I showed him the *Lightbringer* trundling after the Rim. He fears a confrontation, I think. "*Per aspera ad astra,* goodman." He bows with perfect manners and excuses himself.

I linger with Quick. "Cassius is—"

"I don't care. Do you think he knows you plan to kill Lysander?"

"Do I?" I ask.

He chuckles. "Of course you do. You know where he's going. If the opportunity presents itself, how could you not? He's the link between Rim and Core. He dies . . ." He makes scissors with his fingers. "What a way to use your new navy . . . if it exists."

"Maybe you do know war," I say with a grim smile.

"Will he be able to do it?" Quick wonders. "Ten years with someone, that's a long time. Can you take another brother from that man? Would he let you?" I don't answer, because I've worried enough about that question myself. Quick gestures to a black crate as it enters the *Archimedes*. "We took everyone's measurements while you were sleeping. You have the new pulseArmor you requested. My last line. Ten kits. I know you run through them, though you'll be hard-pressed with this model."

I turn in interest. "Manuals included?"

"Have I ever not?"

"I will miss your presents."

"You'll adore this last. Model's called Godkiller Mark I." He winks. "Just don't use it on me. Jove, don't smile like that. It's disturbing."

"Sorry," I mutter. "Gear, you know."

His eyes brighten at the sight of Matteo entering the hangar with Aurae, hand in hand. "Well, they're a pair." He's very right. By themselves each of the Pinks is enough to take the breath out of a room. They laugh like two long-lost friends heading out of the theater talking about everything and nothing.

Quicksilver reaches for Aurae's hand when they arrive, but it's his turn to be slighted. With a kiss for Matteo on the cheek, she walks past Quick and carries on into our ship like she doesn't even notice the wealthiest man alive.

"She's very political," Matteo says with a smirk.

Quick sighs. "Fair enough. At least my final rebuke was from a beauty and not a Bellona." He smiles at me as the drone trailing behind Matteo brings the helmet I saw on his wall. He picks it up and grunts at the weight. I take it from him with one hand. The helmet is the same shape as the starburst helm Fitchner wore as Ares, but it is pure black.

"This was the first helmet I made for Fitchner," he says. "And the best, but he only used it a couple times. Thought it looked too expensive and would tip the Golds off that he had a backer. He's not wrong. I did get carried away. It's made of onyxium and is compatible with most suits. One of my best artificers worked on it."

"Does it have a name?" I ask.

"The Twilight Helm," Quicksilver declares.

"Never one for understatement, is he," I say to Matteo.

"Well, this name's very literal," Quick says. "Put on the helmet and say, 'I am Ares.'" I hesitate. It seems wrong. Like I've stolen a legacy. "Go on. It's charged."

"Not yet," I say. "If Athena thinks I should, I will. But not yet."

"I understand. I miss Fitchner too." He looks a little disappointed. "Well then. I guess this is farewell. I don't know what there is left to say."

"You could say you changed your mind. That you think it's not too late for our Republic," I reply.

"If only I agreed." He sticks out his hand. I take it gently in mine. His eyes drift to his ring on my pinky. He struggles to let go, but eventually he does. "It is in your hands now. You know what I think. But I'm an old coward. Prove me wrong."

"I will. If you prove me right."

Rolling his eyes, Quicksilver turns, squeezes Matteo's shoulder, and walks away without looking back. Matteo watches after him before looking up at me. "I'm sorry I could not do more to help. It's not that I don't agree with you, but Regulus and this station . . . well . . . I can do more here, perhaps, in the end."

I set a hand on his chest, over his heart.

"You've always been strong because you are gentle," I say. "Thank you for everything."

He folds both of his hands over mine. "It is a noble thing to keep the beasts from the door. Whatever people say, they could not say it if you didn't." He goes to his tiptoes, but still I have to bend for him to kiss my cheeks. "For Pax. For Virginia." He kisses my forehead. "For you." He kisses my nose and smirks. "For Sevro."

"Sevro?"

"Well, he'd bite me."

His eyes dance toward the hangar entrance. A mound of heavy weaponry wobbles toward us. Underneath it is Sevro. His long hair is gone. The sides of his head gleam from a fresh shave. He's kept only a short spine of hair down the center of his head. His warhawk is back. His face is terrible and focused.

"There's already weapons on the ship," I note as he trudges past.

He doesn't say anything and just goes up the ramp and into the ship. After a final embrace with Matteo, I follow with the helmet and seal the hatch. I find Sevro dumping his gear in front of a floor rack stocked with six new gravBikes. "Your da's. Catch."

I toss him the helmet and he lets it hit the floor with a *thunk*.

Right.

"You see the new pulseArmor?" I ask, trying to get him excited about anything. It's already loaded in newly installed wall racks. I whistle as I approach it. "Slimmer than the models we used to fall on Mercury. These are built for speed. Double-joined couter, reinforced breastplate, nano-helm, adaptive camouflage skin, and he tripled the generator output capacity." I lick the shoulder of one to test the flavor. "Polyenne fiber woven in. Godkiller's right."

I turn to see him still sorting his gear.

"So, you're coming then," I say. "And you got your warhawk back. Why the change of heart?"

He doesn't look up. "Can't go back yet."

He sounds fatalistic, scary. "Sevro—"

"Drop it. I'm here. Let's fly."

I pick up the helmet from the floor. "For what it's worth, I'm glad you're coming." He says nothing. I let him alone, and head for the cockpit as the *Archimedes* lifts off to leave Quicksilver's new world behind.

42

LYRIA

Rat in the Machine

THE *ARCHIMEDES* IS THE quietest ship I've ever traveled on. So quiet I fear the growling in my stomach can be heard as I crawl through the access tunnel from my sad little hiding place in the auxiliary reactor into the machine shop. MRE wrappers and drained water bladders, now filled with my shit and piss, trail behind me on a cord connected to my ankle. I draw them out after me and refit the access grate. I pause in the dim shop, straining to hear beyond the purr of the engines.

My mouth is chalky and swollen. My head pounding. All day I lay in my hiding place with the datapad Matteo gave me, studying Nagal, mind wandering to one thing and one thing only. Food. Food. Food. I'm mad from hunger and thirst.

When I hear nothing but the purr of engines, I slink through the machine shop toward the cargo bay. It is late in the ship cycle. The others should be in bed, the autopilot guiding the ship on its long journey across the Gulf. My hiding place seemed well-chosen at first. Located at the rear of the ship, just forward of the engines, the shop is seldom traversed by the crew of the *Archimedes* except for Sevro. Most day and night cycles I bear witness to his welding, his angle-grinding, his grunts, his curses, his giggles? And the music. Gods it's terribly great.

What's he making out there?

I know it's my fault he's not going home. He seems to have gone insane after the news of Ulysses. Dammit, but I wish I'd kept my mouth shut.

While I have gone nine days without being discovered as a stowaway, my hiding place has its disadvantages too. I have to travel forty meters, nearly the entire length of the ship, to refill my water and food supplies. So far I've braved only two supply expeditions. Each time I risk being discovered. If I steal too much at once it will be noticed.

No telling how they'll react to a stowaway. They might turn the ship around, but maybe they'll just jettison me out an airlock for my insolence . . .

I think back to the stories we shared in Camp 121 about these vaunted heroes. About their exploits and how my siblings and I dreamed of meeting them. In those fantastical stories, my brothers and sister always imagined we'd be their plucky lancers as Darrow and Sevro swept us away on their adventures, draping wolfcloaks around our shoulders when they realized what big hearts we had in our small bodies.

But now, seeing them, their scars, their machinelike limbs, the brooding danger in their eyes, well that burnt that illusion away like a welding torch over hair. These are serious people. Dangerous, serious people. They'd have to be to stand a chance at the game they play. Still, I guess I'd hoped they'd be nicer.

My heart pounds in the cargo bay as I pass under the gaze of their shiny new battle suits. They stand at attention in their racks, eerie and huge. The whole cargo bay portends violence. The place is stuffed with weapons and machines of war.

What have I gotten myself into?

I creep up the ramp, past the medical bay, training room, and showers. My armpits and privates stink, but I can't chance a wash. Past those rooms I hold my breath for the most dangerous stretch of my expedition—the crew cabins. No sound comes from Darrow's cabin, or the Pink's. The faint murmur of voices creeps through the largest door, Cassius's. He's watching holos again. A metal bottle clinks, signaling he is awake. He's always easiest to pin down, owing to his habits. Drinks like a miner, that one, mostly when the others are out and the hours are lonely. The only hours I can move around.

Lucky for me, drunk men hear like old men: poorly. I make it to the lounge without trouble. From there, I go right into the galley. I wince at the slight hiss of the door opening, and then reel back. The smell of fresh food washes over me in an awesome wave. My mouth drips with saliva.

A beautiful temptation awaits me. There, on the counter under the muted red glow of the fresher lies a feast for a queen—half a loaf of fresh bread with an open container of creamy yellow butter, shimmering apricot jam, a selection of stinky, thick cheeses, and a gorgeous, huge ham glistening with a dewy glaze of honey. My salivary glands ache and I swoon, but I can't touch it. Any of it. I dare not. It will be missed. Must keep discipline. Never take the fresh food, Lyria; that's a rule I made.

With a lonesome glance at the feast, I slump toward the larder, where I drink a liter of water straight from the spigot, then fill five new bladders and stuff them into my bag. Next, I steal several days' worth of MREs, always picking from the back of the containers and only taking one from each container so the depletion won't be noticed. I hesitate over the jars of sunflower butter. There are dozens. I've already taken two, but it's my lone delight. Surely another won't be noticed. I steal one from the back, feeling the thrill at my own daring.

With my supplies refilled, I prepare for my return expedition. But another temptation calls like a Siren from one of those Greek stories. The re-hydrator. I linger in front of it back in the galley, lusty, wishing I could dare to use the machine on my MREs. Oh, to taste hot food instead of the dead crunch of dehydrated calories that awaits me back in my sad little cubby. I could just do one meal. Maybe two. If only I could afford the noise the machine makes. No. I'm thinking like a madwoman. I already have my sunflower butter. I've been naughty enough. I pull myself away, only to feel a second tug. A greater tug. The ham. Oh sweet Vale, the ham.

It's a huge ham for huge people. Surely they won't miss a slice. Or two. A knife is right there on the counter. Ham, with a dollop of butter. A slice of bread. I could make myself a sandwich. A golden fantasy appears—me and my sandwich alone in my cubby, getting to know each other real sloppy like. I will make myself a sandwich. I deserve a reward for all this daring, don't I? I peek over my shoulder. The coast is clear. I set down my bag and extend a trembling hand for the knife, another for the ham to hold it as I cut a small slice. But it's such a big ham that I give into my greed and cut a larger slice.

As I shift the ham to cut it, I feel a strange resistance from the ham, a tension. Squinting, I see something. A faint, almost invisible thread attached to the ham and running toward the wall where it's connected to a mysterious, fingernail-sized piece of metal.

Some primal part of my mind senses the danger before the logical part puzzles it all together. I've just taken the bait to a trap. *Shit. Shit. Shit.* Something snags my feet and jerks them out from under me. I'm flipped upside down.

Blood rushes to my head. The knife flies from my hand, but I hold tight to the ham. Feet pound in the hall outside. I spin, wheeling my arms, suspended in the air.

A dark shape runs full tilt into the galley. A demonic smile flashes on a crazed face that stretches as it screams at me. Ham in my hand, upside down, I yelp as Sevro rushes me and envelopes me in a sack.

"Sevro, get away from the airlock and put her down," Darrow orders.

"She was eating our supplies."

"Put her down."

"Fine." Sevro's voice is monotone beyond the dark fabric of the sack. "Sevro, you're paranoid. Sevro, you need to get more sleep. Your rat's imaginary. Stupid Bellona. I told him we had a rat in the walls. I never miscount my sun butter." He carries me on his shoulder.

"Tell me you didn't hurt her." Darrow's voice. "Sevro."

"She still has her scalp."

"Sevro, Jove. She's just a girl."

"What's what?" a warm, masculine voice with the most beautiful accent I've ever heard asks as he joins. Cassius. "The airlock alarm went off. Where's Aurae? Is she all right?"

The Pink's voice: "I'm fine. I thought I heard a girl scream."

"I didn't scream," I say in the sack.

"Yes, you did," Sevro says.

"No, I didn't." He kicks me through the sack. Hard. Pain jolts through my ribs.

"Stop, Sevro," Darrow snaps.

"Is that a person in that bag?" Cassius asks.

"Yes!" I say. "My name is Lyria! I am a person."

"Is that the Red scout?" the Pink, Aurae, asks. "Poor thing, let her out."

"No."

There's a scuffle and Sevro curses in pain. "Son of a bitch."

The bag unzips and I'm dumped onto the floor at the feet of Sevro,

Darrow, Cassius, and a woman so beautiful she must be made of shadow and starlight. I blink up at her, forgetting the giants towering over me. No, shadow and fog. That's what she is.

"Hello," I say to her.

The woman smiles sweetly, and then sniffs Sevro's shoulder. "Is that urine?"

Sevro pulls a knife the size of my leg. "Sevro . . ." Darrow says. Sevro stares at me with so much rage, I think he's going to kill me. Darrow sees the look too, and asks if he's all right. The rage is not for the ham or the urine. It's for telling him about Ulysses. The others don't know. That's plain as day, and the look of hate carries a warning: *Keep your mouth shut.*

He knows I got the message. He stalks away.

Cassius laughs so hard he has to lean against the wall. Aurae disapproves of the entire scene. She scowls at Cassius and kneels beside me. "Lyria, isn't it? Are you hurt?" she asks. I shake my head and look up at Darrow.

"What do you think you are doing?" he asks.

"I told you that I can help."

"Well, she pissed on Sevro and lived," Cassius manages between fits of laughter. "Name one other person who's done that."

"This is absurd and cruel," Aurae says and puts herself between Darrow and me. "Isn't she one of your agents? At least let her change before you interrogate her."

"I ain't so fragile." I push her off and stand on my own. Gods, Darrow is tall. So is Cassius. Both broad as barns. It strains my neck glaring up at them. "I swore I'd help get Volga back, and I'm going to."

"I gave you an order," Darrow says.

"Remember: I ain't a soldier."

"Sevro gave you a message to deliver to my wife."

"The ship is going to Agea whether I'm on it or not. I left the message on the commissary table. Volga needs me. Mars doesn't."

"Who is Volga?" Aurae asks.

"Ragnar's daughter, Fá's granddaughter," Darrow murmurs. "Supposedly."

Aurae blinks in surprise at me. "You know the granddaughter of the Obsidian warlord attacking Ilium?"

"She's my best friend," I say, more than a little proud.

Aurae turns on Darrow to scold him. "And you told her she couldn't come?"

"This is *my* mission," he says.

The Pink actually stands up to him. "It is *my* worlds that are under attack, Darrow. Considering we're entering a warzone, might not it be best to have as many tools in our belt as our belt can fit? If you can't find a use for her, I guarantee you Athena can."

"The Obsidians will probably be dead before we even get there," Darrow says.

"And if they're not?" Aurae asks.

I feel a surge of guilt for snapping at the Pink, and sudden affection as soon as she backs me up. Not to mention, Darrow is listening to her. "I know the Volk served under you. But they also deserted you." That seems to wound Darrow. "Whether you like it or not, she's on our path."

Darrow scratches his beard. "She's not trained."

"There are more ways to fight than with violence," Aurae says.

"She's right," Cassius agrees, obviously sweet on Aurae. "I could use a janitor."

Aurae glares at him. "What can you do, Lyria?"

"I know how to hand a ship, as crew. Rangers taught me to EVO jump and shoot." Darrow's eyebrows float upward. "I can fly a bit too. And I might be small, but I can do things you can't. Went nine days under your nose. Could one of you do that? Naw. You wouldn't fit in the electrical ducts. You're too bloody big. If it weren't for the ham and that crazy bastard I'd have managed the whole trip. Not that it matters. You can't turn back. You'll lose eighteen days."

I catch my breath and smile up at Darrow, hopeful.

"I say we flush her out the airlock, Darrow? Straight up murder her," Cassius says, but then gives me a wink. I blush and smile back at him when I realize he's japing. He's on my side, probably just because of Aurae. He's also the most attractive man I've ever had wink at me in my whole life. Matteo was beautiful, but Cassius. Oh, that's a man. Seeing Aurae missed his sarcasm, he hurries to clarify. "But if coldblooded murder isn't on the menu, Lyria is right. We are stuck with her. Personally, I think the more the merrier. I could use an extra hand with the ship."

Darrow's gone quiet, thinking, but not in a pleasant way. "What makes you so certain Volga isn't happy where she is?" he asks me.

"You don't know her. I do. Fá's a monster. He killed Ephraim. That Gray was like a father to her." That seems to connect with Darrow.

Cassius petitions on my behalf. "Come on, Reap. Kid's House Mars through and through. Look, it's clear she wants to punch you. She's even got her arms crossed."

Finally, Darrow relents. "You follow my orders, Lyria. The last thing I want to do is cross the Obsidians. My mission is *not* to rescue Volga."

"No, it's to contact Athena," I say. His face tightens. "Sorry. I overheard from the ducts."

I really gotta stop talking so much.

"You are an asset I choose when and how to deploy. Yes? If our goals coincide, fine. If they don't, you suck it up. Returning to Mars with strength is our only priority."

"Right. I got a condition then too," I say. "If I get a shot at Volga, you let me go. Long as it doesn't slag up your mission. Like I said, I ain't yours to protect. Deal?"

Darrow sighs, spits in his hand, and extends it. I do the same and my hand disappears into his as we shake. It's the first time I've touched him. An electric thrill goes through me. If my sister was alive, if my brothers were, they'd die knowing I spitshook the hand of the Reaper himself, and nearly broke my hand doing it too. I don't think he even meant to squeeze so hard.

"I'm back to bunk," Darrow says with a yawn. "Cassius, Aurae, you two seem to be her champions, so she's your charge. Find her a bunk and get her to work in the morning."

Cassius snaps a mock salute and drawls: "Yes, Imperator. Happy to, Imperator. Good call, Imperator." Darrow leans in close to him, sniffs, and raises an eyebrow. Cassius shrugs, sheepish.

"Right. So can you actually hand a ship or was that just talk?" Cassius asks me once Darrow has left.

"I can hand."

"Lovely." He sniffs me this time and glances at Aurae.

"I'll deal with the stench if you find some clean clothes," the Pink says. "Come along, you smell like an oryx."

"Like a what?"

I take my time in the shower. After nine days in my own stink, the hot water is the Vale itself. When I come out the flush, Aurae is waiting for me. I cover my tits and nethers, and jump back into the flush. "It's only flesh," she calls and tosses a towel in to me.

"Easy to say when yours looks like that," I call back.

She laughs. Beautifully, of course.

When I'm dry, she leads me to the crew cabin next to her own. It is small, but a grand step up from my cubby. It has a bunk, a desk, lockers, and a holovid player. As well as loads of candy and Blue space charts. I eye the mattress like it's made of ham. After sleeping on metal, it might as well be. Wrapped in the towel, I stand awkward under Aurae's gaze. Not sure what to do. I've never felt more clumsy and ugly than in the Pink's presence. She might as well be made of air. Maybe it was that insecurity that made me snap when she came to my defense. "Thank you," I say to her. "For speaking up for me. Who is this Athena then?"

"She is a teacher, and a leader. She freed me when I was younger than you are now."

"So what is she? Like the Ares of the Rim?"

"Ares was a warrior. Athena is . . . a builder. At least to me. You'll have to decide for yourself when you meet her. Cassius will be coming with clothes. Do you need anything else? Perhaps a lullaby? It's been a frightful evening."

"I'm not nine. Oh. It was a joke."

"Not everyone is aiming at you, Lyria. Glad you're aboard," she says and sweeps away.

I wait in my towel on the bed until a knock comes at the door. Cassius enters and tosses me a bundle of clothes. "My old pilot left her gear behind. Since you're in her quarters, figured, well. Might be a little long in the limbs, but it's the best fit we have."

"Thank you," I say. "Where'd she go?"

"Who?"

"Your old pilot."

He grimaces. "With my other crew member." He hesitates. "With Lysander au Lune."

I stare at him. "A Lune." He nods across the hall to Darrow's door. "A Lune slept there?"

"You'd find out sooner or later—"

"Mad," I say. "A Lune there. Me here?" I laugh, stunned. "Why'd he go?" I ask.

"He chose to be a Lune."

"Oh," I say a little darker. "And she chose to be a Blue?"

He seems surprised by my question, pleasantly. "Yes. Tailor them however you like. There's sewing supplies in the machine shop, though be wary in there. It's a sty these days. I made you a plate too. Some of that ham. But no eating in your room. Eat at the table like a civilized human. Can't stand crumbs on my ship. Must have standards."

I watch him for a moment. "The Pink isn't here."

He frowns. "And . . . what does that mean?"

"You're sweet on her. Why else would you be so nice to me?"

"Shall I be rude?" he flirts and I blush. "Is that your bent?" He sighs. "Maybe that's the fashion now. Haven't been back to Mars in an age."

"No," I say. "It's just . . . I know who you are."

A cloud appears over him, dimming his features. "And who's that?"

"You . . . well. You're the Betrayer. The Turncloak. You let Darrow into the Dragonmaw to strike down Octavia the Tyrant. And . . . you killed Ares."

"I did." He pauses. "A long time ago." He looks sad now. Maybe for a moment he thought someone didn't know of his infamy. Maybe for a moment he thought he got to make his own first impression. He's so downcast that I feel a kinship with him, a need to lift him up. How many times did others change when they learned I was a Gamma?

"They chose to be a Gold and a Blue, so they left," I say. "You're still here." He looks at me with twinkling eyes. "Could use the company while I see about that plate. You can tell me about the *Archimedes,* and my job. I want to be a good hand. I won't be dead weight. I can't be."

He considers. "Do you drink whiskey?"

"Red eyes. One-hundred-forty-proof blood."

He looks up as if to heaven. "Finally, some decent company. You have a callsign already?"

"Red Banshee," I say.

"It's rude to start a friendship with lies," he replies. "What is it really? You can be honest with me."

I grimace. "Truffle Pig."

"Oh dear." A smile creeps across his face. "You really shouldn't have told me that."

43

LYSANDER

Fragment of Immensity

T HREE AND A HALF weeks into our race back to Ilium, Diomedes extends an unexpected and remarkable invitation to join him on the bridge of the *Dustmaker*.

I smile at the stoic guards as I ride the lift from the rear of the ship where my handful of Praetorians and I bunk. I must be the first Core Gold to receive such an invitation in decades. More and more I believe I have a true partner in my quest for Rim and Core unity.

Diomedes may be taciturn in our weekly dinners with his officers, but he's allowed my Praetorians to train with his Lightning Phalanx, and given them dispensation to use the solariums, gardens, and lap pools usually reserved for veteran Rim Grays. Even Rhone softens in his opinion of the Rim after a hard drill and a good swim, though the food is still not up to my dragoons' standards.

Behind a kill zone and an immense door, the brain of the Rim vessel bustles like a busy, well-behaved library. In life, the Colors operating the ship may have personalities, wants. But at work in this ship, they are biological cogs in an immense vessel of war within an immense fleet within an immense military within an immense civilization spanning from the moons of Jupiter all the way out to Pluto. They seem to take a measure of comfort in their relative insignificance, or perhaps it is the pride in knowing they are an essential part in an effort so massive. The Core could learn from them.

In terms of territory, the Rim is the second largest empire that has ever existed, save the Society when the Rim was in the fold. With awesome size comes logistics of impenetrable complexity. One artificial intelligence of sufficient computing power could run it in macro, of course, but that would be a gross violation of our humanistic principles. Instead, billions of humans work in concert, each suited to their task—those tasks foreign and opaque to any other Color—like fish to water. It makes me feel at peace in the center of this small but powerful fragment of their civilization, and it solidifies my belief in the Republic's cancerous effect on the harmonious system our ancestors built.

Men like Volsung Fá only exist because of what Darrow began.

I summon the Mind's Eye as I enter the bridge. My senses, now focused, produce a theater of texture and sound and detail. But it's the blackheads on the nose of the Gold woman in milky white armor, and the baritone grumble of her thick throat, that overwhelm me. She is a destroyer. Huge, hard, violent. I stare at her like an urchin struck by the thunderbolt of Zeus.

"I am the bridge kidemónas. You have been given the honor of breathing beneath the gaze of Akari." I let go the Mind's Eye, and glance up to see an iron relief of the dead Gold staring down at me from the ceiling of the bridge. "You will submit your razor to my keeping."

I submit it readily.

"A personal note." She leans forward. "That blitz on Phobos. Simple. Rude. Effective. Proper iron." She kisses her fist and punches her chest. "Behave, *gahja*. I would have more feats of renown from you." I assure her she will, and request her name.

"Ophelia au Zagra."

"Au Zagra, first into the breach on Deimos." She nods as if annoyed by her rising fame, then waves me on. "The simulation will conclude soon. Stand there."

Above an expanse of sunken pit crews that encircle a raised triangular platform, Diomedes commands the *Dustmaker*. He is surrounded by war—holograms filled with starships on fire. His left hand is sheathed in Helios's god glove. It is bizarre seeing a man other than Helios wearing it.

The Cestus allows the Gold wielder to assume command of the ship's major systems. It's a mobile bridge, but if your DNA isn't on file and you put your hand in the Cestus, they say it's a death four times worse than death by fire. How they measure that, I have no idea.

The Cestus doesn't beam an interface up toward Diomedes. Instead, his display is a constellation of free-floating globes navigated with a subtle twitching of his fingers. The Cestus is mostly ceremonial. It is far more efficient and precise to leave the running of the ship to the crew.

Watching the crew, I feel as if I am watching a dance. That is how the Rim battles. They rely on speed, surprise, elegant attack runs, not the brute strength common in the Core. It reminds me of Cassius's razor lessons.

With a pang of nostalgia for the idle days I spent with Cassius on the *Archimedes,* I watch from the back of the bridge as the Blue and Green crew successfully fends off the wave of Ascomanni boarders until the command deck's holograms fade and the lights brighten. The performance seemed splendid, but not to Diomedes's exacting standards. Still, he thanks them for their efforts over the last two weeks he's been in command, and the view screens return to displaying the view fed to the buried bridge by the cameras on the prow of the ship. We are almost through the vast emptiness of the Gulf. Jupiter hangs in the distance, as small as a drop of amber.

Diomedes motions me to join him on the command triangle. "They think my palms are sweating in the Cestus," he says of the crew.

"Are they?"

He looks at the Cestus. "To be the master of so much power is to be trapped by it. I prefer my destroyer. To be a dragon rather than a volcano."

With Helios running ahead of the main armada with his torchShip recon squadrons, Diomedes has been entrusted with the command of the *Dustmaker.* It is a stupendous sign of confidence from Helios.

"Is Helios still running dark?" I ask.

"That's when he does his best work. Unencumbered by the monstrosity of command." He nods to the display that shows the Rim fleet. Arranged in six spear-like spheres, with pickets thousands of kilometers out. It is far more fun for an experienced commander to shed the logistical weight of an armada, and strike out with a small task force returning home only to refuel, rearm, repair, and report. First a razor to cut the enemy, then the hammer to bash their brains in as they try to get up.

"Have you eaten?" Diomedes asks.

"Protein amino mush with the Praetorians, if you count that."

He motions over his valet. "Tell the cooks to steam up some trout."

I die a little inside. "Steamed trout. What a treat."

With Diomedes master of the *Dustmaker* in Helios's absence, he is required to use Helios's office. That is where we take our meal. The rooms are circular and spartan, of course. Most are dedicated to functional purposes—a map room, a meditation chamber, a small personal niche with ambient sounds from Helios's home of Callisto, a sparring sphere, and an eating area large enough to accommodate two dozen officers. The table there is as rare and priceless as a ghost raptor: a Mother Table. It is made from branches of the eight founding trees of Demeter's Garter.

Diomedes and I eat alone and in quiet around its live edge. He masticates the last of his steamed trout as though it were as succulent as a calerian eel marinated in orange juice and brine, which it is most certainly not. The fish has the consistency of wet cardboard, and the flavor of old cashews. The vegetables and legumes, however, were a delight. Garter carrots thick as my wrist. Garter beans fat and oozing with nutty flavor. I mourn that only my trout remains. The Rim has never done meat well, and that we are eating it at all means the troops will be getting it soon. The Raa never like to eat better than the lows, especially not on campaign.

For Diomedes, trout is a special treat. He pauses for his last bite.

"How is the pain of the Lament?"

"Faded to little more than a dull ache," I say. "Your saline pools and medici have helped. But really it's the leech your mother gave me. What a godsend." I touch the leech through my shirt. Its teeth are still buried into the skin over my lower spine. It collects toxins in the blood of its host and processes them like a second liver.

"You've kept it in then?" he asks.

"Don't tell my Praetorians," I say. "They'll spout more Moonie conspiracy theories."

Diomedes smiles and spears his last bite. He chews very slowly and swallows with reluctance.

"Helios drew first blood five days ago just inside the orbits of the outer moons," he says as he wipes his lips. Finally, the update I requested. "He engaged and destroyed an Ascomanni scout group. Then he went dark to probe deeper into Ilium and harass Fá's main fleet. Four days ago, he destroyed two Volk torchShips. They still bore their Republic insignia."

"Do you think Virginia might have sent them? Or at least prodded them along?" I ask.

"The consuls debated that possibility. You know her better than I do. What do you think?"

"No. Not her style. From what I understand, Olympia and two other cities were sacked, and any Fá didn't enslave, he sacrificed to his Allfather before moving on to attack their asteroid holdings. Fá, it seems, is an enemy of all."

"A creature of Darrow's, then? As I understand it, the Obsidians view him as a demigod, if not a god, and he's still unaccounted for."

I peek under the table. He laughs at the joke. "Honestly it would have been better to let him get back to Mars than constantly worry he'll pop out of nowhere and maul us while we're all eating our trout."

"It is better for an enemy to be strong and visible than to be missing and capable," he agrees.

"From what I understand, Sefi was like a sister to Darrow. If Fá mutilated her, as our intelligence suspects . . ." I shake my head. "Not to mention had the Volk braves not deserted Darrow on Mercury, it would have been a very different battle," I say. "So, no. It's not Darrow. Though it is his fault the Volk have a modern navy. That we can blame him for."

Diomedes mulls that over. "How are your Praetorians enjoying their trip?"

"Like dogs in a land of cats their own size," I say. "They're eager to return to the Core."

"I imagine they are." Diomedes picks his teeth with the bones of his trout. "Many of their friends must have died at the Battle of Ilium. Died perhaps by my father's hand, or by the hands of my veterans. Before Darrow sailed to Luna, and the Society crumbled."

"Twelve years ago. You think they hold a grudge?" I ask.

"We both know they do."

"It's true that Rhone has a long memory, but he's no fool, or zealot. 'Realist' is the word. A realist and loyal to me," I say as the servants clear the dishes. "He was my shooting instructor and has known me since I was born. He knows Atalantia and the Republic are my enemies." I consider. Diomedes sips a rare glass of plum liquor. Mine is already gone. I'll have to get a case of the stuff from the Garter for Apollonius.

"I admit Rhone does seem more on edge the closer we draw to Ilium, but that is to be expected," I say. "As are you. You've run forty drills in two weeks."

"I am wary, but this is not a subject for the dining table. Come." He thanks the stewards who collect the plates and has me join him in Helios's personal niche. He sits in a European-style chair made of inky leviathan leather. I peruse a wall of Helios's trophies. Like many Rim Knights he collects weapons that have either killed his friends or wounded him personally. Amidst them are his own hasta and kitari collection. His daughter's kitari with her House Dionysus Institute ring melted into the pommel hangs with twenty other blades. The iron grapes make me think of Thessalonica and Apollonius's vineyards for some reason.

Diomedes clears his throat and I take a seat on a Titan-style camp chair.

Diomedes sets his hands on his belly and leans back. "I drill the crew because I am on edge. What did they tell you as a child? About the Ascomanni, I mean. That they lurk out there in the far dark like demons in their asteroid nests? That they come to our worlds to eat naughty children and take them back to slave away in their diamond mines? Yes?"

I shrug. "More or less. But my grandmother exposed me to several warrior specimens at a young age to 'inoculate me from fear.' She'd put them on a collar in my room, until I could fall asleep at the drop of a pin. Little did she know it'd be a goblin who would haunt my nightmares."

Diomedes looks dubious. "Really? Do tell."

"Once, when I was a boy, Sevro au Barca dragged me from my window and stuffed me in a bag. I was presented to Darrow as a hostage."

"The Reaper was not the more nightmarish of the pair?"

"No. Unlike Darrow, Sevro has no qualms about murdering children," I say.

"I have not met the Goblin of Mars yet." He sounds disappointed.

"When and if you do, I advise you to kill him fast—and to make sure he's dead."

"It seems the Minotaur did not heed this warning."

"No. Evidently not."

He nods. "I would offer the same advice when you meet the Ascomanni. They are a race of relentless darkness. That is their home, after all: the darkness out there in the Kuiper Belt. And darkness always finds a way. They are the product of a failed rebellion. The scions of the warriors who followed King Kuthul. They are consummate survivors. Clever enough to know what they're good at, wise enough to realize what they are not. To think of them as simply space-dwelling Obsidians is to underestimate them."

"I underestimate no slave-turned-marauder."

"They are slaves-turned-slaver. They learned the practice from the Core, but then advanced it. Made it crueller. Their very appearance now is the result of enslaved carvers. Our Blues, Oranges, Greens, Violets, Reds. Generations of them have been stolen from their families, then bred for more generations out there in their asteroid city-states. These Colors live in torment, simply because they can operate an energy grid, fly a fighter, craft weapons, develop technology. An Ascomanni king would risk five thousand of his braves to get one Orange like your Glirastes. Ten thousand to get just one grower from the Garter."

I feel a pang of sadness as I recall an image of Glirastes hunched over a project, spouting lunacy about some new endeavor. "They really value Browns over Oranges?"

"A grower of the Garter, yes. They exist in only one place, and are the linchpin of our entire food supply. No enemy in history has ever set foot on that sacred ground where they engineer and advance the plants that feed billions."

"Why is the Garter not constantly under siege then?" I ask.

"So many reasons. It is too far from their domain. It is too well protected. The Ascomanni are fractious, tribal, and most of their wars are against one another," Diomedes says and points his fish bone like a baton. "And until now, they didn't have ships that could dare meet ours in battle. They'd hit our peripheral industries from time to time. Helium gas refineries, ice speculators, terraformers, onyxian mines, you know. But now, thanks to Fá and the Republic's stupidity, they have heavy Core ships. Not hard to imagine the danger of an exchange of ideas between the Volk and those reptiles from the Far Ink."

"So they adapt."

"They learn quickly. They have to." He leans forward and dusts his hands off. "We have always hunted them and yet they are still out there. Even my dread uncle could not eradicate them. In fact, his very presence there stirred them up like a stick into an ant colony. This Volsung Fá began as a rumor more than a decade ago. A movement trailing in the wake of Atlas's massacres, uniting the fragments. Our reports came mostly from torturing captured braves. We never concluded this movement was one man, nor how many tribes he'd united under his banner. My father wondered, though: did Atlas leave to fight the Republic as he claimed, or was he chased out because he feared what he had awoken out there in the dark?"

"That's why you didn't want war with the Republic. You thought they might invade—"

"Invade?" He laughs. "We never considered invasion. They didn't have the ships for it. Raid Neptune's moons, perhaps. Invade Ilium? Our Constantinople? Our Rome? Never. But, it seems they skipped Neptune and the fleet we stationed there. Made fools of us. I don't intend it to happen twice." His eyes narrow and fall on me. "You've been asking me to share our approach vector with your fleet. Come."

Diomedes leads me to the map room where he slides a small blue ring onto his pinky and one hundred and twenty-one stones disconnect from the ceiling to float over the table. What the Raa call the Sea of Ilium— the moons of Jupiter, each with its own orbital speed.

Diomedes leads me through the outer ring of small stones, about one-fifth of the way through he stops. "We're burning full torch to here. Kalyke," he says and puts his finger behind a smooth gray pebble. "Helios has reclaimed it and is using it as his base of operations." His finger follows the gray pebble as it moves slowly around Jupiter. "We will then ghost here," he says. His finger jumps from the slow pebble to a larger, faster white marble as it passes. We're now two steps closer to Jupiter in the middle behind a black marble. "And begin slingshot maneuvers. Twelve consecutive maneuvers with no more than one percent of thrust used." He repeats the process a few times, hopping between passing stones until all that lies between us and Jupiter are four beautiful stones, one blue and green for Ganymede, one a deep sapphire for Europa, one steel and brown for Callisto, and the last and most important one, a poisonous yellow that moves faster than its companions. Io, home of the Raa and Demeter's Garter.

I retrace the route. "Ghost sailing," I say in admiration. "Is it true it's more art than math?"

"Only for a navigator." He shrugs. "Truly it depends on the orbits.

Sometimes it's bad weather—inconvenient orbital arrangements. Sometimes, very rarely, it's good weather." Diomedes's finger settles on Io. "Before Sungrave's communications went silent last week, my grandmother reported Obsidians on the ground. Fá's ships will be at siege altitude. The mass of the moons and the radiation of Jupiter will hide us. They'll have little notice that we are coming."

"And what's the weather report?"

"Perfect conditions. Orbits line up without us having to lose speed. Hence this approach."

"I wondered why Helios was leading the scouts himself," I say. At Kalyke the fleet will be vulnerable. Condensed. Cutting energy expenditure on shields to keep their approach off enemy scanners.

"Helios always leads from the front. Who better to secure Kalyke?"

My eyes go back to Io, where most of Fá's big ships have been sighted, and settle on the thin band of green that wraps around the yellow stone that represents Diomedes's home moon. "What happens if Obsidians do seize Demeter's Garter? Over sixty percent of the entire Rim's agriculture is produced there, no?"

"They will not," he says flatly.

"But if they do get through the battlewalls and shields?"

He sighs. "The Rim is vast, cold. If the Garter falls to the Ascomanni, it would mean famine for many of our dependent worlds. The moons of Neptune and Uranus in particular. But the Garter has never fallen, nor has Sungrave. If the ghost sail succeeds, and I believe it will, we will hit Fá when most of his men are on the ground on Io and we will end this travesty before your fleet even arrives."

"Then Mars," I say.

"Then Mars."

"So, it all begins here, at Kalyke," I say.

"Yes. And when we arrive, I would like you on the bridge."

"Why?" I ask.

"If Rim and Core are to be friends once more, moments like these will matter. I want the crew to see you there. Moreover, I want Helios to see you there."

"You'll suffer his displeasure for me?"

He shrugs. "Until he returns, I am in command."

44

LYSANDER

Grapes and Iron

Kalyke is about the size of a small coin in the holoDisplays that surround the command triangle. Behind it, Jupiter looms. Its myriad moons twinkle, many still distant. Io, our eventual destination, where we will smash Fá, is four days' ghost sailing away. It is on the far side of the Gas Giant for now.

Diomedes smiles when the Blue pilot, a girl of maybe twelve, murmurs: "*Dominus,* we are receiving a hail from Consul Lux. Passing to coms. Shroud requested."

The bridge crew hum like happy bees at the news and at the first sighting of enemy debris. It makes me wish I was aboard the *Lightbringer.* My fleet is now four weeks behind the Rim's. Disappointing. I spoke to Cicero and Pytha yesterday. Their crossing of the Gulf that yawns between the Belt and the moons of Jupiter is taking longer than expected due to fluctuations in the reactor. I fear the *Lightbringer* won't contribute to the conflict at all.

As the shroud enfolds the command triangle in a wall of darkness, a hologram glows. Helios's hawkish face peers out at us from the bridge of his torchShip.

"All's foul on the wine dark," Helios says.

"But there's joy on the wind if you turn east." Diomedes then gives a sixteen-digit code. Helios replies with a code of his own. Identities confirmed, both relax. Helios has a fresh flash burn on his face the shape of a hand and heavy circles under his eyes. His skin hangs loose. He is exhausted from days behind enemy territory.

"*Young dragon, you must be jealous. First blood's to me.*" Helios grins from behind his clasped mustache. "*You missed quite a hunt, lad. How's my dusty lady?*"

"Still in one piece, Consul. Eager to have you back in the Cestus," Diomedes replies.

Helios's eyes narrow. "*Why is Lune on my bridge?*"

"I thought it sent the right message, Consul," Diomedes answers.

Helios pauses as if about to order me off, then reconsiders with a grunt. "*Perhaps you're right. We may yet need his aid purging these vermin. They've infested dozens of moons with outposts. Few serious battalions, but enough to keep the locals miserable and complicate matters further.*"

"My Praetorians and I are eager for the fight, Consul Lux," I say.

Dido's hologram appears from her bridge aboard her flagship, *Dragon Song*. "*Helios, we were worried you'd taken your isolationism a step too far,*" she says without a greeting. "*You went dark for longer than planned.*"

"*Intelligence reports underestimated the enemy strength. They are well-equipped. Ascomanni craft in numbers I've never seen. The Volk are the real danger, though. They've got Republic code-breaking technology, heavy patrol craft to go with their dreadnaughts. And those dreadnaughts are frontline material.*"

"*Where are the rest of your hunting squadron? I only see three torchShips with you.*"

"*Keeping an eye on Fá's main fleet. The four Volk dreadnaughts are always with the* Pandora. *They're his wrecking ball. I want eyes on them at all times.*"

"*What of Sungrave?*" Dido asks, no doubt thinking of her three children she left behind in the Raa mountain city.

"*Sungrave is besieged, as suspected. But it holds, as does the Garter. Vela is in command. But let's not keep your children waiting any longer than we have to, Dido. Diomedes, begin the contraction to fit the fleet into Kalyke's shadow. I'll be taking the* Dustmaker *back under my command for the ghost sail, so have your phalanx prepare for transfer. I want them on your destroyer for the battle at Io. Tip of our spear.*"

Diomedes is happy to hear it. Helios au Lux signs off and a little weight slides off Diomedes's shoulders. He caresses Binds of Zeus and sighs. He had the *Dustmaker* and he didn't slag it up. That's all one can do when you're not Helios au Lux. He catches me staring at him, but offers me a rare smile. *This is it.*

Still some thirty minutes out from Kalyke, Dido's *Dragon Song* orders the Armada to contract alongside the Dust Armada. The dreadnaught's belly slides overtop the larger *Dustmaker* until barely a kilometer separates the ships of the two consuls. As we slow on our approach to Kalyke, Helios's torchShip and its escorts merge with the combined fleet. His shuttle lands in the hangar bay and he rides the gravLift up the protected shaft to the bridge.

Helios enters through a rhomboid executive door opposite the bank of escape pods. The metal slab seals behind Helios and his bodyguards with a clunk. I'm the only one on the bridge who doesn't salute when Helios limps in with two Golds and four Grays in battered orange and gray Phoenix Phalanx armor.

Helios is hunched from what must be a torso wound. His white Olympic cape is as filthy as his pulseArmor. He carries several heavily decorated axes and spears. Diomedes holds his salute until Helios returns it on the command deck and tosses the captured weapons down with a clatter.

The master of the ship has returned, and he's brought trophies.

"For the battle shrines," Helios growls to Diomedes with a toothy smile. Helios's bald head is filled with new angry, red notches. He spares me a cursory nod. The man may be exhausted and obviously wounded—he walks with a very heavy limp in addition to his hunch—but his energy still crackles. His Golds and Grays cluster together down below. I recognize the two Golds from his old guard. War seems to have made them younger, sprier.

Of special interest are the Ascomanni spears. They are long instruments with hafts of sleek black metal etched with runes. Their black heads are nearly as long as my calf and made of a different, shinier metal. "You look frightened, Lune. First blackspår you've seen?"

I nod. "Is that metal oxinium?"

"Found only in the Kuiper. Almost a match for polyenne fiber if mixed with carbon. Will slide right through a pulseShield or a hull. Let's get on with it, Diomedes."

Diomedes motions up Zagria, the huge bridge kidemónas. With the heavily armed woman and three veteran Dustwalkers behind her supervising the transfer of power, Diomedes faces his mentor. "Consul Lux, I relinquish imperium of the *Dustmaker*. Do you accept her Binds?"

"I do, Storm Knight. Thank you for your steady hand."

Diomedes pulls the Cestus off his hand and gives a code to a Green in the pit. Helios gives a code as well and the Green formally transfers the ship master controls to Helios. A Blue announces the transfer has been logged in the central chain.

Under the guard of the two Gold officers, Helios removes his gauntlet and vambrace to don the Cestus. His callused hand seems eager. Understandable. It's been his command for what, forty years? I'd be eager to leave the fragility of a torchShip and once again become the biggest bastard in the Sea of Ilium too. I miss the *Lightbringer* more than I thought I would.

I stand up from inspecting the spears. As I do, I see something strange. Helios's famous hasta, Sunburn, is on his right hip. But on his left is a kitari with an iron pommel imprinted with the grapes of House Dionysus. I frown. That's odd.

Helios's hand slips into the Cestus in a strange way—timidly, then all at once. Like a frightened man jumping off a waterfall. Nothing happens for a moment. Helios's eyes burn into the deck. Inside the Cestus, needles will be sampling his blood and bone marrow. Homer's words glow on the bands of the Cestus to signify it has unlocked. Helios murmurs them. "I too shall lie in the dust when I am dead, but now let me win noble renown." Helios looks up at Diomedes. "It is good to come home."

Diomedes, Zagria, and Dustwalkers salute along with the crew.

I stare at the grapes on the pommel of Helios's kitari. That is his daughter's weapon. But his daughter's weapon was on the wall of his niche in his office. I glance up at the man. Haunted by that second of intense focus and fear as the Cestus tested his DNA.

What *was* that? Diomedes did not notice. His eyes are fixed on Helios's boots. I don't see anything wrong with them, but I feel something wrong with the moment. Helios dismisses Zagria and activates the command triangle's shroud. A curtain of darkness surrounds the command triangle, hiding us from the eyes and ears of the greater bridge. I don't have a weapon. Zagria has mine. I try to get Diomedes's attention.

"Zagria, remain," Diomedes says to the kidemónas just before she steps through the shroud. She stops and her Dustwalkers turn back with frowns.

"What is the beauty behind the moon?" Diomedes asks. Another code. Rumi, I believe.

Helios is annoyed. "Diomedes, we already did that dance."

"What is the beauty behind the moon?" he repeats. Zagria's hand drifts to the hilt of her hasta. Her Dustwalkers begin a slow encirclement of Helios. Helios is amused.

"The beauty behind the moon is the MoonMaker," he replies.

Diomedes nods and relaxes. Then, fast as a viper, he steps into Helios, grabs the Cestus, and pulls up Helios's sleeve.

For a moment I don't understand what I'm seeing. Helios's muscular left forearm is buried in the bands of the Cestus up to the elbow. His skin is pale till just past the elbow, then the arm changes. The skin is rough and baked tan by the sun. The muscles are ropier, the bone thinner. A perfect pink line separates the two disparate topographies.

Zagria and the Dustwalkers draw their blades.

It might be Helios's arm in the Cestus, it might even be Helios's face smiling at us, but the man now in control of the *Dustmaker* is not Helios au Lux.

45

LYSANDER

Allfather

DIOMEDES'S FACE IS THE picture of horror, but his kitari is already at the imposter's throat. Zagria and the others surround them both.

Diomedes whispers, "Remove the Binds or you—"

In several places the plating on the imposter's armor slides up to reveal honeycomb apertures, from shinguard to pauldron. Something sprays out in all directions, a fine mist. Diomedes jerks backward and screams. So do Zagria and the Dustwalkers.

The imposter steps back from Diomedes's kitari. I lurch for Zagria to retrieve my razor. I don't go far. Immense pain stabs through the back of my hand. I turn it to see the skin pierced with dozens of tiny hair-like spines that resemble the glochidia of a cactus. A scream explodes up from my throat. My muscles cramp and my body seizes as the pain spreads.

Diomedes and Zagria fall, twitching and screaming. I stumble and tumble sideways, body landing halfway out of the shroud of darkness that encloses the command triangle.

I'm greeted with the sounds of gunfire.

The greater bridge is a scene of carnage. The companions the imposter brought onto the bridge with him have already finished killing off the bridge Grays and have moved on to the crew, walking around the pits firing down till their barrels glow with heat. They were killing as soon as the shroud went up.

Despite the agony in my muscles, I manage to crawl back into the shroud toward Zagria. The sounds of gunfire disappear. Zagria and Diomedes twitch like fish on a fisherman's deck. The imposter casually shoots the three downed Dustwalkers in their heads and walks over to Zagria to stomp on her throat until I hear a crunch. He looks down at me with Helios's face and sighs.

"I didn't want you to be here. But if you're going to eat sausage, you should be able to stomach seeing how it's made."

He leaves me there and heads for Diomedes.

"Who are you?" Diomedes slurs from the ground.

I brace myself to watch Diomedes's death as the imposter approaches him. Instead, the imposter draws what looks like a black egg and cracks it over Diomedes's head. Inky liquid spreads over Diomedes's head before constricting. He can likely hear or see nothing, but it looks like he can breathe beneath the material.

The imposter then lifts the Cestus. It glows a deep, dark gold and writhes as he assumes direct control of the ship's main systems.

Ignorant of the attack, the fleet outside continues its contraction. Kalyke draws closer, and closer, and a realization comes over me. If this is not Helios, then Helios's torchShips have not scouted the moon, and Fá is likely not on Io at all.

The Rim forces are ghost sailing into an ambush.

My vision warps from the pain shrieking through my muscles. Everything takes on a nightmarish aspect. A helmeted Gray in Phoenix armor phases into the shroud, his gun smoking and still red-hot.

"Bridge clear, *dominus*. Silent alarm cut. We're ghosts."

The imposter waves the shroud away. All around us, the imposter's tiny group of Golds and Grays put the finishing touches on their gory coup. The bridge is no longer under Dominion control. Diomedes's mouth is locked in a silent scream behind the inky mask that snares his head. His body is no longer moving. He seems completely paralyzed. The pain in my body is excruciating, but I'm not paralyzed. Not totally. I should be immobile, but I can still wiggle my fingers and toes.

"Hardline neutralized," one of the Golds calls from a defense pit.

"I have the fleet commandment key," one of the Grays adds. Only she's not a Gray, because no Gray has hardline ports built into her temples. She's hooked into a console like a Green. "Implanting the Helminth. Two minutes."

"That's fine. We're early," the imposter says. "I will apprise Pale

Horse." His voice is still Helios's but his cadence is not. "It was the way I carried my weight in my limp. Wasn't it?" he asks Diomedes, though Diomedes cannot hear him. His fingers dance through the air as he sends a tightbeam signal at Kalyke and waits for a reply. "Helios bears it on the outer metatarsal. Should have practiced that more. Sloppy of me."

A ship answers the tightbeam.

It is not a face that greets us, but a swarm of locusts that coalesce into the likeness of a head.

"Is it done?"

"Stage One complete. Virus on schedule. Initiate Stage Two. Remember, no prisoners."

"Fiat voluntas tua. Allfather, accept these stains."

Fiat voluntas tua. Let thy will be done.

The signal dies. I stop trying to wiggle my legs as the imposter turns to look at me to see if I understand. I do.

The eyes are different, the face, the voice, but my unconscious mind knows who the imposter is beyond a shadow of a doubt. It is Atlas au Raa. He's not hunting Darrow, he's not on Earth, he's not pacifying South America. He never was. He had plans, he'd said—plans that could not be derailed. That's why he urged me to keep my distance from Diomedes. Why Atalantia smirked as she left after my speech in the Colosseum.

He's working with the Ascomanni. The very people he spent years trying to kill for Octavia. He's going to destroy the Rim Armada. But why, for what possible gain?

I ask, but I know the answer.

The Rim never paid the bill for their rebellion.

Now Atlas and his Gorgons have come to collect.

Under the locusts. That was him. Volsung Fá.

Even though the signal is dead, the sounds of the locusts fill my ears with dread.

Death is here, and famine is coming.

The Gray in the coms pit, a Gorgon, shouts: "Helminth ready!"

"Send it," Atlas says, and begins to conduct the ship with the Cestus. A chaos of holographic globes with information appears around him. First, he begins to spool massive amounts of energy in the reactors. Second, he takes control of the anti-ship guns and gathers targeting solutions. Last, he calls Dido. Diomedes cannot hear or see or even thrash anymore by the time the hologram of his mother appears.

"Helios, the fleet has nearly finished its contraction. Your visual is down." Dido's brow furrows. She pauses, referencing something. *"Why are you spooling your reactor? Your scouts have enemy—"*

"Dido au Saud, for the crime of treason against your Society, I sentence you to death."

Dido stares back without expression. *"All power to—"*

Her signal goes out in a wash of static.

Due to the contraction maneuver, the distance that separates the two flagships of the Rim Armada is small. A few hundred meters at most. The *Dragon Song* believed itself to be safe, surrounded by its fleet and nestled above the great mass of the most powerful ship in their civilization. Its shields were down to not tax its reactors and to keep its thermal signature low. Stealth was the priority. So when the *Dustmaker* fires at point-blank range into the unshielded belly of the smaller ship, the devastation is immediate. A barrage of heavy rail slugs follows, and then several atomics.

It is a death salvo aimed directly at Dido's buried bridge.

Her dreadnaught is too big even for the *Dustmaker* to kill with one salvo, so Atlas fires three. The third cleaves into the superstructure of the ship itself and breaks the *Dragon Song*'s back. The ship is nearly cut in two. Diomedes has no idea his mother is now less than dust.

The pain in my muscles and bones has faded from white hot to a steady red. I test an arm. It moves sluggishly. I don't think anyone noticed. The Mind's Eye is impossible to grasp. It can't be that. So it must be the poison leech Dido gave me. I kept it on because of the lingering effects of the Lament, and also my growing paranoia. It's metabolizing the poison. Just not fast enough.

It seems Atlas is only just getting started. He expands the battle sphere hologram. Holos of the Rim fleet throb around him. All those ships and all those men look like toys in his hands.

"Fiat iustitia et pereat mundus!" the Gorgons shout.

Atlas feels no need to say anything. He lifts the Binds of Zeus and closes it into a fist. Every gun and torpedo tube on the moonBreaker fires at the engines of every Dominion ship within range.

Shields only work if they are on. If they're on, they radiate on sensors like torches in the night. With Kalyke deemed clear of enemies and stealth the priority, shields across the fleet are down. The barrage is more gruesomely effective than it ever could be in a pitched battle. It does not destroy the Rim Armada, but it has the same effect that iron caltrops would have on a cavalry charge. Soon, Atlas is surrounded by ships bleeding atmosphere, made dark by the loss of power, or with their engines burping blue and black plumes.

The reaction of the rest of the fleet is impressive. Even as they hail the *Dustmaker,* they open fire on her. Though the *Dustmaker* is a powerful ship, it has no hope against the entire armada. Soon the bridge begins to shudder as the Rim Praetors gnaw through the *Dustmaker*'s shield. The *Dustmaker* fires back with its huge guns.

Then the second phase of Atlas's trap springs.

As the fleet fights the chaos at its center, waves of torpedoes flicker up from Kalyke where launchers must have been installed in the surface of the pocked moon. Thousands of torpedoes. Tens of thousands hoarded for this deathblow. I am staggered by the sight.

Rim ships race to intercept.

As they do, the third evolution of Atlas's trap comes around the curve of Kalyke. It is the coup de grâce. The fleet of Volsung Fá is not on Io. It is here. Hidden behind the mass of Kalyke, it now races for the besieged Rim Armada.

I feel the doom that must grip the hearts of the Rim Praetors as they see the repurposed Republic destroyers and torchShips painted with the crescent sigil of the Volk streaming toward them. Between those ships stream hundreds of the misshapen smaller craft belonging to the Ascomanni. And at the center of the enemy—the wrecking balls. Four dreadnaughts and Julii's stolen *Pandora.*

Those Rim ships whose engines were not hit by the *Dustmaker* could flee. Their ships are faster than the coming enemy. But if they flee, they leave their brothers and sisters behind. They make the brave choice. The stupid choice. They choose to stay to fight and die with honor.

Chaos swirls around Atlas.

Gruff Rim Praetors bark commands, Blue ripWing pilots chatter as they race out of their hangars toward the barbarians. Long-range weapons fire between the two navies. Flak screens deploy. Slender corvettes and fast torchShips meet first. Waves of smaller fighter craft merge and spit fire at one another. And then Fá's wrecking balls unite their fire and start to kill Rim capital ships one at a time. With Atlas guiding them, it seems so cold and sinister that I begin to hate the very idea of war.

I cannot let this stand. The leech is doing its work. The pain is nearly gone now. My body feels like mine again, but I do not know if I can walk much less fight. I can't change the battle. Not now. I will have precious few moments before I'm cut down by the Gorgons. What can I do in those moments to make a difference?

My eyes fall on Diomedes.

I can save him. Carefully I check the path to the escape pod doors down by the crew pits. Are they connected to the Cestus? No. I see manual levers.

I can save Diomedes, and then maybe I can save myself. The gravity isn't too heavy. I can carry him. I have to be sure enough the poison is out of my system. Soon the Gorgons are busy with Rim troops trying to get through the bridge doors. I wait for Atlas's attention to focus on an important firefight, and I slowly get up.

My legs and arms feel like lead. Ants chew behind my eyes. I take a step. Atlas turns.

I lunge for the grenade on Zagria's belt, thumb the detonator, and hurl it at Atlas. He turns and slaps it back toward me. It passes over my head and detonates down below. I fling Zagria's razor at him. It takes him through the left shoulder.

Lunging for Diomedes, I trip over Zagria's leg and fall. Scrambling across the floor, I grab Diomedes's foot and drag him off the command deck. We tumble down the stairs together. I sway up, grab his jacket collar, and pull for all I'm worth. Atlas shouts at his men to hold their fire. I'm close to an escape pod door. Boots pound behind me. I haul the release lever up. The door hisses open. I'm hit with a stun munition beneath my right shoulder blade. The limb goes numb, but the force of the shot hurls Diomedes and me into the pod. I'm about to launch it when a whip snares my left ankle and I'm jerked back onto the bridge. I slap at the door controls as I pass. The tips of my fingers brush them. The pod door closes. With a loud series of clangs, the pod clicks into place and fires down its escape chute with Diomedes inside.

I hope he can evade the battle outside, recover, and make his way back to his forces. But with no one to pilot the pod, with that maelstrom raging outside, I know he's as good as dead.

The Gold Gorgon who snagged my foot with his razor turns me over. His face is half gone from the grenade. He beats my face until I swallow a tooth then he frisks me and jerks out the leech. He drags me back to Atlas, pins my head sideways to the deck with his boot, and puts his razor to my temple.

"Tox leech. They missed it. Waste him?"

"Not yet," Atlas says.

"He's a fucking sympathizer."

Atlas ignores him and calls to the others. "Don't forget the scalps."

I see the world sideways. Blood pools at Atlas's feet from his wounded shoulder, but the man only stops conducting the battle when the *Dustmaker* has soaked up too much damage to contribute any more. He turns on me as Obsidian and Ascomanni troop barges swarm Rim ships like lice.

"They'll be through any minute, *dominus*," a Gorgon calls.

"They'll have more than us to worry about soon enough," Atlas says. He squats in front of me.

"I needed Diomedes alive, Lysander. You just killed him by sending him out into that."

"What have you done?" I snarl.

The metal boot presses harder on my head.

"Avenged a litany of transgressions." He sighs. "Truth be told, Atalantia ordered me to kill you both. But what she doesn't know won't hurt her. Bring him. We're done here."

He drops the Cestus to the deck.

The Gorgons plant charges at key junctions around the bridge, and follow behind us via the executive passage with a haul of scalps. Exiting the lift, we cross the private hangar to the shuttle they rode in on. "Halt! Put your weapons down!" a voice roars. A line of Dustwalkers bars our passage. Atlas seems unconcerned. His men toss down their weapons. "On your knees!"

Atlas and his men obey.

"It's not Helios!" I shout. "It's Atlas."

The lead Dustwalker's eyes widen in apprehension. Then her head disappears above the lower jaw. All but three of the rest are mowed down before she hits the ground. The remaining Dustwalkers leap away like grasshoppers and come apart midair, victims of flawless squad shooting. Atlas picks his weapon back up and stands.

"*Ignis!*" a familiar voice calls from across the hangar. My heart drops.

"Lunae!" Atlas calls.

I turn to see my squad of ten Praetorians melt out of the shadows. They move toward us in tactical formation and lower their weapons. My heart grows cold as Rhone, Markus, Demetrius, Drusilla, and the rest of the Praetorians Rhone handpicked to accompany me on the *Dustmaker* doff their helmets. They're grinning ear to ear, and not at me. Atlas greets them all by name.

"Barely got here in time," Flavinius says. "Ascomanni are landing all over the ship. The bill is paid?"

"For the Sword Armada and more besides," Atlas says.

"Where's the Raa?" Markus asks.

One of the Gorgons hurls the tox leech at him. "Don't squabble, lads. There's always a kink," Atlas says. He nods to the shuttle and I'm pushed along. "So few of you, Flavinius?"

"Helios only allowed the Blood to bring ten Praetorians," Rhone answers.

Atlas looks back at me and grins.

"You have excellent taste in troops, young Lune." With that, he swoops up the cargo ramp and Markus cracks a black egg over my head.

46

DARROW

The Sun Is Down

S EVRO'S EERIE LAUGHTER ECHOES down the halls of the *Archimedes*. No one else is laughing.

When we arrived in Ilium after our month-and-a-half-long sail across the Gulf, I expected to see a running battle between the Rim Armada and Fá's outmatched fleet. One in which we were to exploit the chaos and slip through unnoticed.

Instead, as we decelerate, we find a massacre. An inexplicable massacre.

The Dragon and Dust armadas, the dark flower of Raa naval might, have been destroyed. Their remains float in orbit around the moon of Kalyke, a shroud of detritus and broken Dominion dreams. Sevro's laughter grates on Cassius and Aurae the worst. Lyria is just stunned by the sight of the battlefield. Few have seen anything like it. Even me.

"That's the *Dustmaker*," I murmur. The warship floats in the center of the debris field. It is as dim and cratered as an asteroid.

"Was," Sevro corrects and wipes his eyes with his sleeve. "Bellona, you have any champagne on this heap?"

I might join Sevro in celebrating the misfortune of the Rim if it were not so complete and so improbable. I cannot even begin to guess how Helios and Dido could have been so thoroughly annihilated. Is Fá's fleet larger than Quick's telescope led me to believe? Or was his ambush— and it had to have been an ambush—just that thorough? Just that un-expected? My skin crawls with questions.

Who *is* this Fá? No Obsidian I taught over ten years of war was strategically and logistically sophisticated enough to have managed this against Helios and his battle-tested Praetors of Io, Callisto, and Ganymede. Praetors who would have given me migraines.

"How did this happen?" Cassius asks Aurae. She has no idea. How would she?

Cassius may be empathetic for the Rim, but I know he's just happy Lysander wasn't here. With the *Lightbringer* still crossing the Gulf a few weeks behind us, he missed the ambush, and with Rim's ability to help him in his war now broken, he'll go back to the Core and the conflict Cassius dreads will be pushed to another day.

Cassius and Lyria hunch in the two pilot seats staring out at the debris field. I stand behind them. Aurae sits just behind the cockpit at the sensor and coms station as Sevro paces the hall, enjoying the dark thrill of the enemy's catastrophe. "Are you getting any active signals from Kalyke's cities?" I ask Aurae.

"No," she says. "Radioscopes suggest this is ten days old." That matches the energy flares we detected while we were crossing the Gulf. Kalyke was in far orbit then. Hidden by the Gas Giant.

"Does that mean Athena's agents on the Moon are gone?" Lyria wonders aloud, but her voice trails away. Even she knows they are dead. Everyone here is dead. Finally, Sevro stops laughing. He stares up from the hall at the back of Lyria's head like this is her fault.

The cozy smell of coffee is all that remains of the optimism with which the rest of us started the day. It was to be the last leg of our journey across the Gulf and signal our entry into Ilian space, where we were to meet with Athena's contacts at Kalyke City. With the city a crater, the contacts are dead or fled. With them has disappeared our link to Athena.

My hair falls over my eyes as I hunch in thought. "Can you take us in, Cassius? We need a better look at the wreckage," I say. "Especially the *Dustmaker*."

"Why?" Sevro asks. "She in there? We're here to find Athena. Not waste time looking a gift horse in the mouth."

"We can do both," I say. "It's hardly off mission to seek context. We need to know what we're sailing into."

"Darrow, you heard what Quick said about the hull," Cassius says. "If we go into that debris field, we will take damage. Can't turn on the shields. That Obsidian fleet that did this is still out there. They'll see the shield energy signature."

"You're right. Skirt the perimeter then. No chances."

Cassius glides the *Archimedes* around the perimeter of the debris field, staying clear of the denser patches. Still, every minute or so metal pings off the hull. I peer into the ship graveyard, wincing with every hit. After a decade of war, horror is as common to me as flies in a stable. Yet amidst the debris, I encounter a sight so inhumane that it puts lead in my guts.

Sevro sees it first, and murmurs an Obsidian curse. A great monstrosity floats in the center of the battlefield like a monument to a wicked celestial god. It drifts near the remains of the humbled *Dustmaker*—thousands of Blue, Gray, and Gold corpses tethered together by wires into the shape of a giant Obsidian crescent. From tip to tip, the crescent must be over four hundred meters long.

"Your men . . . your old braves did this?" Cassius asks.

"That must have been the Ascomanni," I say without confidence.

Disgust wells within me, and guilt, and regret. Even as I led Ragnar's people to war, I knew brutal tendencies always lurked within our Obsidian legions. Fá has stirred the evil sediment up from the bottom of their hearts. What he did to Sefi in Olympia, splaying her open in the Blood Eagle, was bad enough. Even though he did this to my enemies, this further perversion puts him in a very special pantheon—men who I wish to see die upon my blade.

For several hours, we skirt the debris field searching in vain for signs of survivors who could tell the tale of what happened over Kalyke. We find none. Only the eerie sound of revenant loops—the voices of dead men on dead ships calling out into the darkness for aid or reporting Ascomanni breaches in their hulls.

"I've got something," Aurae calls when we round Kalyke and reach the outer extremity of the debris field where there is less radiation interference. "There are not too many signals. Looks like the Obsidians have screamer drones and have been targeting relays. But this one's coming from deeper within Ilium. It's not encoded." She frowns. "I think it's Athena. Let me see if I can isolate the signal."

"Lyria, go watch and see how Aurae does this." Cassius nudges the smallest of our band. Lyria pops up and heads to the sensor station, ducking her head to avoid eye contact with Sevro in the hall. The girl might have annoyed me by stowing away on our ship like Rhonna once did. But I'm impressed with how seriously she's learning the functions and equipment of the *Archimedes*. You only have to tell her something once. Cassius has taken to her. Gods know they spend enough time together clinking cups into the wee hours. I know she fills the vacuum Pytha and Lysander left when they deserted Cassius, but I'm surprised how fond she is of him in return. Cassius au Bellona is the last person I'd expect a Red to like.

A hologram flares to life once Aurae and Lyria have isolated the signal. Athena's glowing red eyes stare out from a blizzard of static. Like before, her helmet is black and Corinthian in its design. *"This is Athena. The sun is down. I repeat, the sun is down. All sleepers and cells, report to your omega torches for evac. The sun is down. The sun is—"* The transmission loses its battle to the high-energy jamming coming from deeper within Ilium and cuts out.

"What does that mean?" Lyria asks. "The sun is down?"

"Fallback contingency," Aurae answers. She sounds afraid. "She's summoned all the Daughters to Helisson."

"Helisson?"

"Her base of operations."

"Their version of Tinos then," I say back to Sevro.

"And where is Helisson?" he asks.

"I don't know."

Sevro does not accept that. "We came a billion clicks, and you don't know?"

"Which moon is it on? Callisto? Ganymede? Europa? One of the outer moons?" I press.

"The Krypteia's been trying to kill Athena for a decade. I was a deep cover agent in the Raa household. I'm the last person who should know. Could you imagine if I was ever interrogated?"

She has a point, but Sevro isn't pleased. "Then how are we supposed to contact Athena?"

"Kalyke had coms relay stations to contact her network." We all look at the bombed-out moon. "The only other option is to reach my omega torch. A hardlink coms port."

"Right, and where is your omega torch?" I ask.

She hesitates, apologetic. "Sungrave."

Cassius hangs his head. Sevro starts laughing again, but his humor has fled. I close my eyes and exhale forcefully through my nose. Why is nothing easy? Why can't I just go straight back to my love? My son?

"Is that a bad thing?" Lyria asks. "Sungrave?"

Cassius gives her a tolerant smile. "Oh, it's only the ancient heart of Raa power. The axis of their military apparatus. An impenetrable citadel that even the Ash Lord couldn't take. Yes, it is probably the least convenient place to go."

"Is Athena an idiot?" Sevro asks. "Aurae? This is shoddy spycraft. Amateur hour."

"It's not Aurae's fault, Sevro," Cassius says.

"'Course you'd say that."

"Sevro, the Raa court operates out of Sungrave. Where else would my omega torch be located where I could reach it?" Aurae asks. "I know this isn't what we expected to find, but we can still contact Athena. I have a way to bypass security. There are family passages we can use."

"How are we even discussing this as an option? Darrow, this is not what we should—"

"*When life springs forth, death follows behind,*" interrupts Aurae, quoting from the book. "*When goodness is found, evil is close at hand . . .*"

"*The path straddles the boundary between these things,*" I reply. Aurae smiles.

"And just what the everloving hell does that mean?" Sevro barks. "Are we really taking our marching orders from your ad hoc interpretations of some dusty-ass tome?"

"Your father's dusty-ass tome," I say.

"And how'd that go for him?" he asks, and looks at Cassius. "Oh. Right."

Cassius doesn't rise to the bait. I watch the debris out the viewport. If the Rim Armada can be destroyed, somehow I doubt Sungrave is as Aurae left it. "If it's the only way to contact Athena, then that is our road," I say. Sevro stares at me, incredulous. "Cassius, set course for Io. But go slow. Fá's out there somewhere—"

Silent, the *Archimedes* steers off Kalyke. I turn, expecting Sevro to have slinked off after our tiff, but am surprised to see him still there, still staring at me as if I am unrecognizable.

As much as I want to say something, to mend the chasm between us, I realize I cannot. I know Sevro better than anyone and there's nothing he'll hear right now. No sense or argument will sound good to him. So I shrug and turn back to the viewport where Jupiter gazes back at me like a disembodied eye, the moons held in its thrall winking motes twirling in their orbits.

Ping. A long moment. *Ping.*

We all turn to look at Aurae. "What is that?" I ask.

She frowns. "A distress signal," she says. Sevro glares at her in suspicion. "I thought we should just keep looking, in case . . . someone was alive."

"The place is crawling with distress signals," Cassius says. "Doesn't mean anyone's alive."

"This one is a heartbeat," she says.

"And why didn't the Obsidians pick it up?" Sevro asks.

"It's short-range, whoever's sending it must have waited until after they left," Aurae says.

I look at Sevro. "You know our old braves. Do you really want to go deeper into the system blind?" He might be a pit of anger, but he doesn't want to die out here either. "Aurae, pin the location. Cassius—"

"If you say 'fly like an eagle,' I am turning this ship around," he says and pushes the *Archimedes* into the debris field. "Watch and learn, Lyria." He winks at her. A piece of debris hits the hull. We all wince. "Starting now."

The escape pod is shaped like an egg. Instead of escaping the battle as its pilot no doubt intended, it found itself embedded into the side of a dead destroyer's hull. It is severely damaged. Sevro and I space walk out to it in our new Godkiller suits and cut open its hatch. Sevro enters first.

"We got a breather," he says as I push my way into the pod behind him. *"Barely."* The pod's power is almost gone and its interior dark except for the glow of our headlamps. A single man floats covered head to toe in gray armor, his legs crossed in a seated position. *"Big bastard. Gold no doubt."* Sevro peers around the pod collecting clues and wiggles a tube sticking into a port in the back of the man's helmet. *"He's hooked directly to the shuttle's oxygen reserves, what's left of them. Probably brain dead by now. You saw the damage to the tanks outside. My guess: he tried coms, engine control, found they were slagged and saw his juice was running out so he put this kit on to keep the cold out, and went to sleep praying someone would find him."*

I find a few more kits of armor in a concealed rack. One is missing.

"It's a bridge pod, looks like," I say. "Lots of Gold-sized kits. That's good. If he's not brain dead, he'll likely have a better idea of what happened than someone in the belly of a ship. Let's get him back to the *Archi*."

Sevro and I haul the lone survivor back to the *Archimedes* where we load him onto a medical gurney brought by Lyria and Aurae. Aurae is about to connect an oxygen recycler into his helmet when Sevro swats her hand away. "You stupid?" he asks.

I clarify. "Let's get him out of his armor before we feed an enemy knight O2. Lyria, get the fusion cutter eight-millimeter. You know where it is?"

She's already off to the machine shop. We hear a clanging, a banging, and a string of curses, then Lyria returns at a run. She tosses the fusion cutter to Sevro who gets to work on the armor. He's not precise in his cuts, and the Gold's blood dribbles liberally onto the gurney.

With every piece of armor Sevro cuts off, my grip tightens further on the hilt of my razor because it becomes more and more apparent that whomever we've saved is no rear echelon pixie. His arms are brawny. His legs thick and muscled from high gravity training. His chest like a barrel and his shoulders as wide as my own. And then, after Sevro cuts off his thermal body sleeve, there are the scars on the man's pale skin. Not so many as I have, but enough to make a Gray leatherneck dip his head in respect. This is a frontline Peerless. A killer.

"Manacles," I say.

Sevro is far ahead of me. When the man is secured, Sevro works on his helmet. It comes off with a pop and only a little spritz of blood. My own concentration on the tiny bristles embedded in the man's hands is so intense I nearly miss Aurae's intake of breath when Sevro wipes the man's black-gold hair away from his face.

The man's armor may be nondescript, but his heritage is unmistakable. It is like looking at a brawnier, gloomier, manlier version of either Atlas or Romulus au Raa. But unlike either of the famous brothers, this man is young and trends toward muscle.

"Is that who I think it is?" I ask.

Aurae takes a moment before nodding. "Only if you think it's Diomedes au Raa." Sevro looks up at her and casually puts the fusion cutter to Diomedes's muscled neck. I swat it away, but Sevro was watching for Aurae's reaction.

"What are you doing?" I ask him.

"He attacked Phobos," Sevro says, still looking at Aurae.

"I thought you didn't read the data packets."

"Only the relevant ones," he replies. "But I got all the data I need." He tosses the fusion cutter to the side. "Information. Leverage. Hostage exchange. Use your head, Darrow. Why would I cut his throat? Aurae, aren't you going to give your old master oxygen?"

Aurae puts the mask to Diomedes's mouth. Sevro raises his eyebrows at me.

"Here's what. We start skinning the Raa's toes first," Sevro says a few hours later. Diomedes has gained consciousness, and he's not talking yet. Sevro has one of his knives out and leans back in one of the lounge's sofas, his voice soft as if telling a children's story. "You always start with the digits. I have made a paring knife that will do just fine. There's lots of nerves in the toes. The most sensitive are under the cuticles. After we flay his toesies, we'll salt them. Then we'll bash them, right? One by one. Then I'll use Tickler here and we'll work our way up."

He seems to relish the looks of horror on the faces of Cassius, Lyria, and Aurae, but I know he's just winding them up, especially Aurae, to test how loyal to her former master she still might be. "Bellona, you have any acid on board?"

Cassius looks mortally offended. "I beg your pardon?"

"Acid. Hydrocloric or ipsoric are best. Naturally I prefer newt venom, but I didn't see any aquariums on board. Unless you're hiding them. Are you?" he asks Cassius, but watches Aurae.

"No."

"Pity. Hear Raa are tough. Might take ipsoric."

The excitement on the *Archimedes* after discovering the identity of our new prisoner is palpable. Unfortunately, he's as silent as granite and just as unyielding. I questioned Diomedes about Kalyke. He stared back at me, unspeaking, unblinking except when I mentioned the toxin still in his bloodstream. An unknown compound that seems to be responsible for the fits of cramping that occasionally wrack the man. I'd think it a poison from an Ascomanni weapon, but the tiny hairlike thorns

Aurae extracted from his fingers and face would suggest otherwise. Sevro was part right in his earlier diagnosis. Diomedes was paralyzed before he somehow got on the pod, then he must have recovered to turn on his beacon and armor up. After that, he must have gone into some sort of meditative trance to reduce his oxygen intake, because he should be dead.

What in the bloodydamn worlds went on around Kalyke?

"There will be no skinning, bashing, or salting on my ship," Cassius says. He glances at Aurae for support. Since Kalyke she's drawn inward. Doubly so since Diomedes was brought aboard. I'm hardly the only one who has noticed.

"All the same, I'd prefer to have answers for Kalyke before we get to Io," I say.

"I can get you answers," Sevro says.

"Oh. Now you want them. Wouldn't risk debris but will carve up an honorable man," Cassius says.

"Honorable?" Sevro smirks. "You really did miss the war, boyo."

Cassius squares his shoulders. "I will not allow torture on my ship, Sevro. Especially not torture of that man. He is the only reason I am alive. I owe him a debt."

"You fancy yourself a part of the Republic now. Hm? Don't you?" He points to me with a knife. "ArchImperator." He points to himself. "Imperator." He points to Cassius. "Pilot."

"He'll be conditioned against torture," Aurae says. "To break him would take time and instruments we don't have."

"You'd know," Sevro says. "He's your master after all. Sorry. *Was* your master. Strange no, that he's the only survivor, and you just happened to find his signal out there?"

"It was a guess," she says. "The signal was not on the traditional spectrum. It was a family signal he used with his siblings."

"No torture, Sevro," I say. "If Fá did that to their war fleet, when we get to Io, I think Diomedes may be in a mood to tell us of his own accord. And we have Aurae. She'll get the information we need. Won't she?" I say.

Aurae nods.

With Fá's fleet still at large, Ilium feels haunted as we glide deeper into the system. Once-inhabited moons lie bombed out and quiet. The capabilities of our passive sensors are severely limited. They can only receive input from the physical environment around the *Archimedes*. Vibrations of light, radiation, heat. The mass of Jupiter, its moons, and the radiation cascading off the planet make a grand, murky sea for hostiles to hide within.

At our cautious pace, the Galilean moons are still days away; Io, Ganymede, and Callisto are hidden behind the Gas Giant. Europa flickers, a midnight blue mote in the eye of Jupiter as she swings on her orbital path before disappearing behind Jupiter's mass.

Haunted by the unanswered questions at Kalyke, I seek out Sevro in the machine shop. With any vibration a danger to us all, he listens to his music on headphones. He is working on his main suit of pulseArmor. When I get him to finally take off his headphones, he shakes his head at me. "Gods, could you be more jealous," he says when I ask him what he thinks of Kalyke.

"I'm not jealous," I say, annoyed.

"Jealous. You can't handle the fact that Fá destroyed the Rim Armada, and you didn't and don't understand how he did. Like I said. Jealous. Or Colorist. Like Bellona. Can't reckon an Obsidian's your equal in space."

"If one was, it would be Ragnar's da," I say.

He snorts. "So now you're thinking it is his da."

"Can I just talk it out without you shitting on my every word?" He shrugs, noncommittal, and continues sculpting wolf embellishments into the armor. I lean against the metal smelter and watch him detail an incisor on the helmet. "What doesn't make sense is even if Fá guessed Helios and Dido were ghost sailing, and Kalyke was their ghost point, we should have seen more dispersion in the debris. And we should have seen more Volk and Ascomanni ships in the ruins. You don't inflict that kind of damage on Rim Praetors without taking a good licking yourself. You just don't. It was too lopsided. He should have lost half his fleet, at least, even in a perfect ambush. How was it so clean? How did they get so completely surprised? Why didn't they run? Their ships are faster."

He finishes the incisor and sets the scalpel down. "Honor, dipshit. The Rim and Cassius have something in common. They're new to this war. They don't know what we know. Honor, if it ever existed, was the first casualty."

47

LYSANDER

The Bringer of Darkness

T HE DOOR TO MY room opens with a creak of well-worn hinges. Instead of the mute Gorgon who has brought my meals over the last ten days, Rhone enters. He looks tired and smells of soap. The skin beneath his eyes is cracked and red. Just the area left exposed when one wears a kryll breathing aparatus and goggles.

"You've been out," I note.

"Gorgons had a mission. Thought we'd pitch in. You know I don't like being idle." He spares me a cautious smile. I remain reclined on the room's small bunk. "May I sit?"

"It seems you don't need my permission to do anything any longer," I reply. He sits with a grimace.

Outside, a volcano roars in the distance. My room has no windows but there's little mystery where Atlas's torchShip has landed. Io, the volcanic homeland of the Raa, their citadel of Sungrave, and Demeter's Garter. With the Rim Armada destroyed, nothing stands in Fá's way except the ground defenses, and maybe my fleet.

If they are still coming. They'll have seen the ambush on their scopes. They'll hear the silence. They'll think I'm dead.

For a few moments Rhone stares at his hands, picking at one of the calluses that line his palms. He is not guilty, just thinking. In the muted light of the room, the teardrop tattoos on his face all look the same color. "You know me as your shooting instructor," he says slowly. "You know me as crown winner, as a Praetorian subLegate of Dracones XIII, as Rhone ti Flavinius. I was not always those things. Before the agoge, my home was Lost City. My name was Fleabite. And that is what I was. One of a million fleas in the armpit of the city. That is who I knew until your family's recruiters found me. Gave me a bed, a roof, a chance, a purpose. A pack. People think I'm from a famous line who's always been in service to a patron. No.

"We bunk in centuries in the *ludus*. A hundred per kennel. Most who graduate go to the Lune house legions. Maybe five of those eventually are quality enough to go to the Praetorian Guards. Of my kennel, all one hundred went to the guard. It has never happened before. It will never happen again.

"They were my brothers. They were my sisters. Forty-six of them died in the Battle of Ilium when the Raa chose Darrow over the Society. Twenty-one died when Darrow came to Luna. After twelve years of this war, a war the Raa made possible, only Markus, Drusilla, Demetrius, and I are left of that kennel.

"I tell you this because I know you are angry. I know you feel betrayed. But you are not the only one with debts. You are not the only one with anger. Diomedes was your friend, but barely. So take a moment. Weigh your loss against ours. We who have given our blood, our lives, our futures to House Lune. We who have abdicated legacy for ourselves by forsaking the chance for children. We who would give our lives for you, if you but asked." He sets his Praetorian dagger on his thigh. "And consider, perhaps we are due more than *gratitude,* gilded though it might be."

"And what are the innocents of the Rim due?" I ask.

"No better and no worse than the innocents of Luna," he replies. "Our home."

His words are not lost on me. I see him more clearly than I ever have before. But that does not change what he did. "It wasn't the acrobat. You poisoned me on Phobos."

"I thought you might work it out eventually."

"How?" I ask, doing my best to keep the anger out of my voice. "My food?"

"Let's just say that perhaps you shouldn't have given your favor to some fucking ruster before the battle. Never know what bloodborne diseases those vermin might be carrying."

I nod, understanding. It was Rhone who put the poison on my cloak before the Red Helldiver returned it. The petty jealousy turns my stomach. I'm mad at myself for mistaking this man's patriotism for loyalty. That means Kyber isn't in his circle. Shot by a sniper, maybe, but not one from the Republic. He didn't want her coming on this trip.

"You knew this would happen," I charge. "Kalyke."

"Yes."

"Have you colluded with Atlas this whole time? Since Mercury?"

"No. Atlas contacted me after we took Phobos. He was crossing into the asteroid belt. He did not want you to join Diomedes in his unfortunate fate. He tasked me with preventing that. I failed because Cicero and Pytha meddled. And I underestimated your resistance to the poison. Had I not feared killing you, I would have used more. You may not believe me, but I do not want to see you harmed, Lysander. The poison was merely a necessary evil."

"This alliance was everything to me," I say. "It was the future of the Society."

"The future of the Society should be decided by its patriots, not its betrayers. The Rim is eating the meal they served us." He stands. "Atlas is out of surgery. He is asking for you." He opens the door. Markus, Drusilla, and Demetrius wait in the hall. "We expect you to listen to what he has to say with open ears."

I follow Rhone through the gloomy halls of the blackops torchShip. It is named the *Lethe*. Like all of Atlas's favorite toys, it is utilitarian, well-used, and entirely off the books. While everyone thought he'd gone off to pacify South America on the more powerful *Styx*, he must have ridden the *Lethe* out to the Rim and laid in wait. The disgust I feel toward his methods and his action are dwarfed by the absolute awe I have for his capacity and his brutality. A cheer goes up from a common room filled with off-duty Gorgons. They suck down cigars and toast as I pass the open door.

"Fá. Fá. Fá," they chant.

"What's happened?" I ask Rhone.

"The Garter. Its battlewall was breached a few hours ago. Fá's army is pouring in like water."

"Your mission with the Gorgons . . ." I murmur.

He nods. "Nothing could break the Garter's shields from without.

Atlas knew a route to strike from within. His father showed him as a child."

I hang my head. The worlds are upside down. Atlas colludes with Obsidian ravagers against innocents. These hardliners celebrate massacre as patriotism. The groupthink is so heavy in the room I worry I'll vomit.

The lights are low inside the medical bay as I enter alone. Atlas, the object of so much fear, speculation, and dread that he can be believed to be on every world at once, is slumped on a stool, thin, tired, and mutilated. Even now, he studies a globe of Io that seems to be constructed of free-flowing mercury held within a stasis field. He's monitoring the invasion, one he no doubt planned down to every minuscule detail. I pity anything and anyone that has his full attention. Poor Io.

The invasion is in Fá's hands now, though. Atlas's arms are missing from the elbows down. The angry red nubs are capped with silver stasis sleeves. A pair of thicker forearms and hands lie discarded in a metal basin along with a carver's replica of Helios's face and Helios's eyes. Atlas's own limbs float in a tank to the left. His eyes have only freshly been re-installed in their sockets.

Atlas's Violet carver examines his freshly implanted eyes with a large monocle. She pulls back and smiles down at him in worship. "The ocular nerves are tethered and your dendrites fully rewoven, *dominus*. But they won't familiarize for several hours. Avoid bright lights and holoscreens. Don't fret about the fog on your periphery. Your vision will clear by cycle's end. It won't be as bad as the last time."

The last time?

"Gratitude, Xanthus. Arms in the morning?" She hesitates. "I told you it would be a rush job. Now is a decisive moment."

"Yes, *dominus*. Arms in the morning."

"It was the blade, wasn't it?" Atlas says to me. "His daughter's. Helios lost his kitari to space when we took him. Wasn't sure which one he was packing." Atlas's eyes creep in my direction as the carver departs. They are bloodshot and rheumy. "*Ave,* Lysander."

"Atlas. Or is it Allfather?"

He grimaces. "Ugly business, godhood, but not the first time a man's hidden behind the visage of the divine." My gaze drifts to the bed in one of the medBay's two clean rooms. Helios—or what is left of Helios— lies naked on the bed behind the glass partition. He is a grotesquerie.

His arms amputated, his eyes extracted, and head penetrated by wires linked to a spindly Green. The Green twitches over Helios like a pagan priest.

"I thought mastering his physiognomy would be the most difficult part. I underestimated how hard it would be to take him alive. Tough man," Atlas says.

"Veracity confirmed, *dominus,*" the Green murmurs. "The codes to the Sungrave's defense grid are confirmed."

Atlas sighs. "It's good to be sure. Well done, Centix. Decouple and send the codes to Pale Horse. I want Io wrapped up on schedule." To the Yellows he says: "His duty is done. Send him to the Void."

I watch the Yellows inject Helios. His chest heaves twice then falls still. He dies without pain. I mourn for the great man's dignity as much as his passing. I mourned already for Diomedes, Dido, and the honorable dark rose of Rim knighthood that must have perished in Atlas's ambush. So many lives, so much hope, fed to monsters. Monsters that now have Demeter's Garter. Soon Sungrave will fall too.

There must be a way to do more than mourn. To warn them. Atlas isn't the sort of man who'd let me out of my cage if there was any way I could interfere, yet we're now alone in the room.

"Your mother will be in Sungrave," I say. "Gaia."

"Yes, she will be," Atlas confirms. "Along with my sister, my nieces, and my nephews. And tonight as we sleep, or maybe tomorrow as we eat breakfast, the Ascomanni will enter through our family tunnels and Fá will breach the main gate. After that . . . well, you're a student of history. You know what happens to cities that resist, and Sungrave has resisted the Society for hundreds of years. Its death will therefore be proportionate."

"Do you hate your family so much? Do you hate your home so much that both have ceded any right to exist?"

He's offended.

"Hate? You think this is personal? You think this some . . . petty vengeance, repayment for being given up as a hostage to Luna when I was a child? Disgusting. I am not Adrius au Augustus," he says. His eyes and face, usually as impenetrable as a vault, for once relay the contents they protect. Pain. Loss. Absolute sorrow. "I know every poem etched onto every step on the Dragon's Spine. Every turn in the family tunnels. Every stony expression in faces that fill our ancestral shrine. Every shadow in the bedroom of my father and mother. I know Sungrave's sounds, its smells, its social cruelty, and its physical beauty. I know the flowers that are grown on the walls of the Stygian Wells, which my father would leave on my mother's pillow. I know the egg-stink flavor of the water from the Phlegathon, that sacred artery which nourished seven centuries of my people. I saw my sister born here and felt my mother's blood on her pudgy skin as I helped my father wrap her in linen. Sungrave will always be my home, Lysander. Yet my home must die. My family tree must be torn up from its roots and burned to the last green branch. I am in agony, but these matters are not personal. These are matters of state. The highest matters of humankind. My feelings are irrelevant, as are yours."

He wavers on the stool. The passion drew too much energy from his reserves. With a sigh, he stands then makes his way to a well-worn couch. With his back turned, I snatch the scalpel and conceal it. He sits with a wince.

"I do not have much strength today, Lysander. But you have questions. Now that the deed is done, I will answer whatever you ask. I think that a fair thing to offer you. You can either try to kill me with that scalpel, or you can have a seat and learn how deep this tunnel goes."

He gestures with his right stump to his abandoned stool. As I sit, another cheer from his men seeps through the walls. I don't set down the scalpel.

"Fá used to serve with them, didn't he? He was a Gorgon," I say.

"A Gorgon once is a Gorgon forever. His birth name is Vagnar Hefga, and he is the finest soldier with whom I have ever served."

"Is he actually the father of Ragnar Volarus?"

"Genetically, yes. But genetics alone hardly make a father. The two never met. The gens Grimmus made their fortunes as Obsidian breeders and dealers, remember. A good bull like Vagnar is worth much in those circles, and he was bred profusely after the Grimmus family purchased his people from the Julii. He has sired hundreds. Possibly thousands."

"How long have you planned this attack?" I ask.

"Well, the operational parameters evolved several times after your grandmother banished me, but I have been working toward this since my brother allied with Darrow and waged war on the Society. What is it? Twelve years now? As they say, time flies." When he sees I want more, he continues. "You must understand, when Octavia told me to not return until I'd exterminated the Ascomanni, my Gorgons and I knew we'd never feel the sun on our faces again. That was a difficult paradigm to accept. A paradigm I could not have survived without Vagnar.

"He became my friend. My confidant. A brother. Not a brother drunk on his own egoic concerns, but a brother with belief in something greater than himself. Banished to the dark, we found solace in the fact that we were spending our lives spreading the light of the Society. It was our sustenance. Our religion. Then came the Battle of Ilium. Then Luna itself fell. Then the light went out."

He looks down.

"Nothing can live long without light. Nothing good. I yearned to return and set things right. But I didn't have the ships or the men to turn the tide, so I used what tools I had. Patience, good soldiers, a few ships, and my education. The years we spent fighting the tribes of the Far Ink were mostly spent sniffing out their nests. You can't imagine the endless black out there. I realized the only way to complete my mission was to treat the Ascomanni like ants: bait them out, then have them take poison back to their colonies.

"They hate each other, the Ascomanni. They don't even know why, some grudges are so old. Fortunately, their hate is second only to their greed. So, I sent Vagnar with fifty Obsidian brothers to conquer small Ascomanni headmen at first, then warlords, and finally their version of kings. When word spread through the tribes of an invincible warrior from beyond the Void, one blessed by the Allfather himself, one declaring a holy war on me, on the Society, their individual grievances melted away. They realized if they united under Fá's banner, the Moon Lords and their Sunlit Lands might finally be in reach."

"You made a messiah. An Obsidian Darrow."

"Yes. Still, the Ascomanni did not possess the skills or the armaments to take Ilium. So, I sent Xenophon, my best White, home to become useful to Sefi. Xenophon led her away from Darrow bit by bit, and eventually into the fold of Volsung Fá. By adding the Volk to his Ascomanni Horde, Fá finally had what they were missing—capital ships, heavy assault infantry, and experience in modern warfare."

I lean back, stunned. Twelve years! The whole time Atalantia, her father, and Darrow have been trading planets and ships in the Core, Atlas has been working on this project.

"It was you. The helm cam footage the Ophion Guild sold to Dido. Proof that Darrow and Victra destroyed the docks . . . You pushed the Rim into war."

He does not gloat, but he nods. "Atalantia's contacts in the Ophion Guild, actually. She helped purchase the footage from a disaffected Valkyrie."

I'm horrified by the implications. My fingers tighten on the scalpel. "Was it an accident Cassius and I stumbled across the *Vindabona*? Across Seraphina? Was I your pawn from the start?"

"I wish I were that omniscient," he mutters. "Careful not to give me too much credit. Chance, it seems, is not without a sense of irony. Your free will is still somewhat intact. Until Mercury, I thought you were dead. Cassius hid you well."

"I suppose congratulations are in order," I say, bitter. "Romulus, Dido, and Helios are dead. Ilium is on its knees. What now then?"

"Autophagy." I frown, and he explains. "The conserved degradation of cells to remove unnecessary or dysfunctional components. Nature is full of clever systems. Individual organisms turn damaged tissue into new growth. Whole species evolve to meet challenges, or they die out. Entire biomes shift, one generation of beings at a time, or become fossils beneath the surface. Old, unfit life is recycled into new, more successful life.

"Civilization is not a clever system. It is stupid—an artificial, unsustainable projection of man's hubris. It feeds upon its own myths, and resists autophagy at every turn. Often on the grounds of morality, which usually attends prosperity. It is an evolutionary flatline.

"The Rim's desire for independence has always been the Achilles' heel of the Society. Dissent its dysfunction. Exploiting that fact is how Darrow rose to power: first by playing Bellona against Augustus, then Rim against Core. His interference is a poison in the *corpus mundae*. The body of worlds is made sick by our division. Our most noble families are rife with desire for vengeance. For power. Division is a cancer, Lysander, and I am excising the affected tissue.

"The Rim cannot help but seek division. Their naval pride, their warrior caste, the leadership of my family, all aid and abet the cancer that threatens the *corpus mundae*. Hence the Obsidians. Only when the Rim has been humbled, when its pride has been shattered, when it has been stripped of the tools it requires to perpetrate sedition, and remembers to fear chaos, a savior will arrive and bind them to her cause. Or . . . his cause."

I blink at him. "His?"

"Atalantia plans to be the savior, and has for some time. Yet, I've begun to think it could be someone else. Someone more suited to the position."

I say nothing. Atlas smiles and continues.

"It is a sad fact that those capable of gaining extreme power are often unfit to wield it judiciously. Neither you nor Atalantia is a perfect candidate. While she is cruel beyond excuse, you are moral beyond reason. Both are liabilities. But while yours is a virtue, hers is a fatal flaw. Atalantia gains power by dividing. But I've seen your maneuverings, young Lune." He watches me swallow. "You gain it by uniting. I wonder, could you be the savior Society needs?"

"No."

"No? You don't want to save millions of Dominion lives? Billions of lives suffering under this unending war? You don't want to be my cure for this plague? You don't want me to set you on the Morning Chair so you can guide us to a brighter future?"

"I won't take part in this . . . genocide."

"Then you are an idiot. Worse, you are selfish. These deaths cannot be reversed. They are a sunk cost. It would be a logical fallacy to let them influence your decision. What should influence your decision is what will happen if you refuse me. Atalantia plans to let the Rim suffer Obsidian rule for three years before she comes as liberator. Three years, Lysander. The casualty estimates are . . . staggering. Why allow that? Your ships are already on their way; if you choose to step up, you will save hundreds of millions of innocent lives."

"No," I say and stand in vain protest.

"Then I will have to kill you, Lysander. You will not be missed. Back home plans are already underway for your replacement."

I flinch. "What do you mean? A clone?"

"Nothing so perverse or uncontrollable. A doppelgänger. A man by the name of Lepidus, chosen from Atalantia's stable of paramours. You've annoyed her, so she'll just keep your name and face." Atlas casually glances at the corpse of Helios au Lux.

I grow sick at the thought.

"That won't stop Cicero and Pallas from destroying Fá. They have the *Lightbringer* and—"

"And Fá has me," Atlas says. "And I have two hundred and eighty-one Gorgons aboard the *Lightbringer,* waiting for orders. Cicero has proven himself a loyal friend to you, but that will not stop my nightmares from tearing out his throat as he sleeps. By then, you'll be dead, Atalantia will sit on the Morning Chair, and the Rim will descend into three years of torment, war, and famine."

I sink back down, overwhelmed.

"If the Rim finds out about your actions . . . this is how Darrow wins."

"You are correct in that. The burning of Rhea was a tactical mistake only because everyone knew who ordered it and who carried it out. But I have learned from Octavia's mistake. I am a careful man, Lysander. There may be conjecture, there may be suspicion, but there is no direct evidence of my involvement. Besides, you are too fixated on Darrow, boy. Darrow cannot win. Darrow is beaten. His only power lies in the mystery of his absence. He has no tools left to resuscitate his cause. No allies to call upon.

"As for Mars? Augustus and Julii can slow the inevitable but they cannot stop it. Meanwhile, your assault on Phobos and subsequent absence has made it easier for Atalantia to strike Mars without jeopardizing her martial supremacy. When she decides to take the planet, she will. With ships given to her by Valeria au Carthii." He smirks. "What? Valeria may run the dockyards because of you, but will she die for you? I think not."

I look at the floor, wondering what my mother and father would say if they saw me here facing this proposal, what Glirastes would say. What Cassius would say. He would curse me for even considering the cold-blooded convenience of the realpolitik Atlas spews. Ajax would sneer at this but for far different reasons.

"Lysander, I value your hesitancy," Atlas says. "More than you know. If it is any consolation, I do not do this for glory or my own satisfaction. I do this because I believe in the Society enough to be the tool it requires. I am a monster because a monster is needed. But after, when the monster has rampaged and terrorized the people, they will need a savior to gather them up, remind them of their better values, and lead them to a better, more unified future. I have brought darkness to the worlds in its fullest extreme so you can bring the light."

I look up at him.

Atlas is the picture of conviction. His words are not the empty promises of an ambitious politician. His expression is not that of a cocksure commander who has never known defeat. He is a priest, solemn and resolute, one acquainted with pain, familiar with suffering, who has grown surer, wiser from both to reach a state of eerie omniscience.

"Once you are on the chair, it will be time to address Society's dysfunction. To bring it closer to the more perfect light of Silenius's dream. Or, your story can end here, your death not even a footnote in history. The choice is yours."

And that choice is impossible.

My mind reels, trying to grasp the magnitude of the moment. Atlas offers me everything I have worked for and fought for, not to mention the chance to stop the deaths of hundreds of millions, but the price is my soul.

I thought I was done with disillusionment when I sat down with Apollonius in the Graveyard of Tyrants. I told myself I could play the game by Atalantia's rules. Then in Diomedes, in the Rim, I saw a way to win that seemed moral. In that moment in Rome, I conjured an illusion. And now, in the shattered remains of that illusion, I feel like a player in a production I thought was a drama discovering the audience bought tickets to a comedy.

Atlas's eyes do not mock. They wait for my answer.

I let myself sink into the Mind's Eye and the ship and my anxiety disappear. I see myself seated on the Morning Chair, the Rising crushed, the worlds at peace, my reforms spreading prosperity from Pluto to Mercury, and Atlas, Atalantia, and Rhone dead at my feet.

"Very well," I say. "I will be your savior."

Atlas leans back into a shadow. His lips twitch into a faint smile as he says, "Hail Lune, bringer of light."

48

DARROW

The Tickler

A POUNDING WAKES ME IN the night. We're still three days out from Io, but I assume they've found us. That Obsidians are in the halls. Ascomanni are peeling Lyria and Aurae in zero-G. My traitorous braves are laughing as they stomp on Cassius with their boots and drink from Sevro's skull. They look like grinning beetles in the dark, their armor heavy as they drag us before the throne of Fá to make us into Blood Eagles.

No. I wake screaming.

The room is still. The bed warm. The alarms quiet. But someone *is* pounding on the door. I grab Bad Lass and crank open the door to find Lyria standing there with a crazed look. "It's Sevro! He's torturing the prisoner."

Lyria's already sprinted back down the hall. I rush after her, ducking my head to avoid the bulkhead partitions. I'm not the only one to hear Lyria's shout. I collide with Cassius as he comes from his cabin bunk with alpine on his breath. Gin.

How many varieties of booze does he have on this heap?

We scramble off one another. I push a little more aggressively, annoyed he's drunk, and lead the way to the medBay. We find Lyria and Aurae in the hall outside the door trying to hack the smashed controls. Aurae looks sick to her stomach.

"He's crazy," Cassius replies. "I told you."

The door is thick. I peer through the duroglass viewport to see a murky image of Sevro hunched over Diomedes with cables in his hands.

I beat on the door but Sevro either doesn't hear me or doesn't care. "Lyria, those controls are fragged. You remember how to initiate the fire protocols?" Cassius asks.

"Yeah. Oh, it'll demagnetize the lock," she says with a burst of inspiration.

"Go to the bridge, initiate them, then override the oxygen cutoff protocol." He gives her his access password and she takes off.

"Go with her," I say to Cassius. He ignores me, and I do my best to put myself between him and the door. "Cassius, don't pour gas on this flame." I look to Aurae for help. She puts a hand on his shoulder, but he brushes her off. "He could kill him."

Cassius misses the desperation in her voice. I don't.

"Someone has to get him in line," Cassius says.

The hall floods with fire alarm lights and a clunk comes from the door. The door hisses open and Cassius swims past me with a kravat move. He's first through the door. I follow, then Aurae. It's a brutal scene. I've encountered worse: nothing will beat the abattoirs Atlas leaves in his wake. But seeing your best friend taking out a man's teeth with pliers and then electrocuting the exposed nerves is more than a little jarring.

Cassius is at a loss for words. "You . . . *goblin.*"

"Go away. I'm working," Sevro says.

"Sevro, stop," I say.

"Stop? What? You gave me the look," he deadpans. "Ain't this why you brought me? Ain't this why you always bring me? I don't mind the dirt. Gotta keep you shiny." He turns with a sneer. "I asked about Athena's ships. Had to know they were real."

I can't help myself. "And?"

Sevro turns around and smiles at Cassius's look of disgust. "He's quiet on the subject. Want me to ask him about Kalyke?" He has a tooth between his pliers.

"Get away from him," Aurae snaps and shoves Sevro so hard he almost moves. She hurts her wrist, but Sevro steps aside like a courtier to let her pass. Aurae rushes to Diomedes. Cassius, Sevro, and I watch. Cassius looks crestfallen, but not too surprised.

"Cassius, I want you to get out. Aurae . . . clean him up, but his bonds stay on." She looks back at me and nods. "Sevro, meet me in my quarters. We need to talk—"

Sevro hurls the pliers at me. I catch them, infuriating him. "I didn't come out here to slag around. You said you wanted answers. This Raa's all bluff. Twenty minutes and I'll give you a diagram of Kalyke. And see if this one's full of shit." He stabs a finger at Aurae.

"Not like this," I say.

"Fine." He dusts his hands off, and waltzes out of the room.

Cassius is about to go after him. I stand in his way. "You're enabling him."

"You want to kick his ass?" I sniff his breath. "Go on then."

Cassius is off like a bullet. Aurae stares back at me in disbelief. "It's either now or when we can't afford it," I say. "They're grown men. Let them sort it out." I look at Diomedes and say to Aurae. "Do you and I have to sort something out?"

She stands and turns. One of her fingers is clearly broken from pushing Sevro. "I am a Daughter of Ares," she says. "But I am also a person. You would know better than anyone." She points out the door. "Now go make sure they don't kill each other."

I lock eyes with Diomedes. "Fair enough."

I follow Cassius to find him reaching the bottom of the ramp to the cargo bay. Halfway to the machine shop, Sevro turns on Cassius and draws a knife from his boot. "Rich boy want a tickle too?" The blade is long, lean, and crooked. "I call this one Lysander."

"Torture your prisoners. Hide behind a knife. You aren't an Imperator. You're a lonely little savage is what you are," Cassius says.

Sevro plays offended. "It's pronounced Goblin."

"That man saved my life. He's injured and a prisoner. It isn't right . . ."

"Come again?" Sevro asks. "Sorry, can't hear you. You're too deep in the bottle. Echoing sound. Say it louder. Use that big Bellona chest."

Sevro's eyes twinkle like a kid's with matches. These two have anger to exorcise and neither of them has fought anyone since Venus. I can at least try to contain this here. I feel a surge of petulance and contempt for the both of them. I wrestle down that emotion and try to remember what the book says: *If you wish to be straightened, you must first be bent crooked.*

Let them get bent then. I sit on a crate to observe and make sure they don't kill one another.

Lyria rushes in, and I motion her to sit beside me. Confused, she heeds me.

"Diomedes is a prisoner of war," Cassius says with princely dignity. "He has rights."

Even I roll my eyes.

A sour giggle worms through Sevro's teeth. It contorts into a chest-heaving laugh. Then it stops as suddenly as it began, his voice weirdly calm. "Your problem, shithead, is that you claw for every chance you can get to be the hero, because you know you'll always be the villain. Can't shake that Golden taint." He winks. "Same reason Aurae will never give you the time of day. You're stained, boyo." He grins. "You are such a big pretty nothing. Couldn't handle your brother dying in the Passage, even though those were the rules you people made. Had to pout. So big, so small. Needy little Bellona. Sad, lonely Cassius. You're hollow, man. Can't even stand straight without a woman inflating your spine."

Sevro wags his knife at Cassius.

"Couldn't save Julian. Couldn't protect Quinn, couldn't keep Mustang intrigued. You're the shallow end of the pool. Couldn't save your Sovereign, because you're a traitor, then you couldn't join the Republic, because you're not welcome. Whole Ares thing. But the saddest shit is, you spent years on that Lune brat. Only to have him ditch you for the world that chewed you up and spat you out at the first opportunity he could get. Failures like that only come around once in a lifetime. Darrow's too nice to tell ya, but hey. That's what I'm here for." He pouts. "Gonna go drink to numb the boo boo? You'll still hate yourself tomorrow, fraud."

The Lysander insult carves the deepest gash in Cassius's heart. I feel sad for my friend, for the loneliness in his life after we killed Octavia, after Adrius killed his brother and sister. But I can't stand up for him. He has to get through his guilt for killing Ares and stand up to Sevro himself.

Sevro's tirade has the effect he wanted. Cassius takes a fighting stance and goes at him. Sevro sheaths his blade. Fists it is. Cassius feints a left hook, and puts a significant amount of his powerful frame into a line-drive of a right jab. Powerful or not, the jab is affected by the gin he's had. Sevro is dead sober and spent his whole life baiting bigger men into unwise confrontations. He ducks and puts all his weight into punching Cassius in the testicles. Air gushes out of the bigger man.

Before Cassius can even double over, Sevro lunges up like a frog and brings the crown of his head into Cassius's jaw. Cassius's teeth clack together. Cassius doesn't go out, and it's a miracle his jaw doesn't break.

He staggers back and spits out half of a front incisor before squaring up again. Sevro never stops coming at him though and catches him with a flurry of jabs to his left ear, then almost breaks his ankle with a sideways stomp. Harried, Cassius stumbles back after an exchange of elbow strikes and gets some distance with a push kick that lands on Sevro's lower chest.

"Stop him," Lyria snarls. "He's a monster. Stop him."

"That's up to Cassius," I say.

"Look at the Morning Knight," Sevro mocks and darts forward to daze Cassius with a jab combination that sends blood pouring from Cassius's nose. *"Losing again."* Cassius rushes him. Sevro evades easily and jabs him twice in his right ear. *"That's all you're good for. Drinking and losing and—"* Sevro lines Cassius up for an uppercut. It doesn't land. Cassius steps into Sevro suddenly, crowding him and making the blow awkward just as he swings his left elbow into the exposed side of Sevro's head. It hits Sevro's skull with a crack. Sevro leans with the blow just enough to not get knocked out, but Cassius follows with a swing of his right elbow that hits Sevro in the side of the head. Crack. Sevro stumbles back, dazed, and Cassius delivers a right kick that smashes into Sevro's guard. Sevro is lifted off his feet, hurled in the air to rebound off a crate. He wheezes for air, holding his ribs.

Cassius squares up and shakes his fists out. "Stay down." He grins like his old self. The rotten self I thought he'd outgrown. "It's not my fault you weren't there when your wife needed you most."

I must be missing something because it's like Sevro's been hit with a block of ice. He goes pale, and glances at Lyria with a look so wounded I realize there's something I don't know. Something terrible. Lyria is horrified.

"Cassius, stop—" she begs.

Sevro rushes Cassius in silence. He jukes sideways and under another of Cassius's kicks and puts his shoulder into Cassius's groin. They go down. Sevro clambers atop Cassius, and tries to bite his face. Cassius uses a kravat counter-leverage move to roll the two of them toward us. Sevro's teeth snap at empty air. He ends up behind Cassius, raining blows on the back of Cassius's head.

Lyria springs at them.

I grab for the scruff of her neck, but she's oily from working on the ship and slips my grip. Shit. I jump up. Neither man sees her coming. Cassius thrusts back against Sevro with his hips, throwing Sevro off balance, and inverts their positions. As he does so, he brings back his fist to pound Sevro's exposed face. But his elbow cracks right into Lyria's face on his backswing. She reels back as if kicked by a sunblood.

She's snoring before she hits the ground.

I shout for them to stop. Cassius glances over his shoulder to see Lyria twitching on the floor. Her nose smashed flat. Blood pours out. A second vile snore rattles out of the small Red girl. Cassius's face falls. "No no no no no no."

Sevro isn't done. He scrambles to his feet and rushes Cassius. I slip from the box and kick him under his left shoulder so hard he's lifted clean in the air and sent crashing into cargo boxes. He stumbles up oozing blood from his face, his left eye hidden beneath a mass of swollen, purpling tissue.

"Enough," I demand.

He heaves for breath, ugly as the monster all children think lurks in their closet, but he sees the look in my eye, Lyria snoring like a drunk, and he sinks against a box. Cassius cradles Lyria in his arms. She's still snoring. "Neuro unit. MedBay, Cassius." He doesn't hear me. I swat his head. "MedBay!"

Cassius stumbles and rushes out of the cargo bay with Lyria in his arms. I'm left alone with Sevro. "Happy?" I ask him. "Got your belly full of hate? You stuffed now? Got enough to last you to Io or do you need to provoke everyone before you're full?"

Sevro mutters something inaudible and spits blood. Woozy, he makes his way past me and out the cargo bay. He juts a finger after Cassius. "Liability." He points at me. "Drowning man."

"So what's that make you?" I ask.

"Goblin."

He doesn't seem happy about that. He is miserable. It's a different tone than I've seen from him. He looks lost. Like he's about to puke.

I soften my voice. "What did he mean about Victra?"

He blinks. Distant. Empty of anger. Empty completely. "Sevro."

"It was a boy," he rasps. "Our baby. It was a boy, named Ulysses. That was the name we chose. Harmony killed him on Mars. Nailed him to a tree. I wasn't there." The sense of hope I'd been nursing since leaving the

Marcher shrinks to the size of a candle's flame. The wind howls in my heart, black, cold. The candle flickers and almost goes out. I don't know what to say. Sevro is beat. He looks at his feet.

"Sevro, I'm sorry." A half minute goes past. "Gods, I am so sorry. When did you learn this?"

"The stowaway spilled the beans. At Quick's."

Now it all makes sense.

"Shouldn't you be home?"

"I wasn't there." Sevro stares off, vacant. "How can I go home? How can I face her? Victra. What she went through, on her own? She was probably there. With Virginia. Didn't want to talk to me. I tried to be a da. But it ain't what Barcas do. We can be nightmares. That's what we can do. Make the enemy scared. Goblin's what they need. Out here. Goblin gets shit done."

"So does Sevro," I say.

"Naw. That's what I learned on Luna, see. The Abomination reminded me of something I'd always known deep down, but had forgotten. Kids. Wife. Money. Fame. Victory. All that soft shit; it ain't for me. I'm not allowed to have it. Sevro craves all that. Sevro is weak. Sevro slags up. Sevro wants the family and the peace and the quiet. That's how the clone got me. Sevro *needs*. Not the Goblin. Goblin eats nails, shits fire. He can do what Sevro can't."

"Bullshit."

"What?"

"You heard me. That's bullshit, Sevro. It wasn't the Goblin who held the Sons of Ares together when I was in the Jackal's box, when your da was dead. It was you. Sevro Barca."

"I got people killed. If it wasn't for Rags and Dancer, it all would have burned down. If you and Victra hadn't joined up . . ."

"So what you're saying is, without your friends, you'd be slagged and the Rising would be ashes?" I scoff. "Welcome to the club, asshole. Where do you think I'd be without you? Without our friends? Dead in a ravine, that's where. We hold each other up. We always have. That's not weakness. That's the only strength we've got. More than anyone, you've been there for me. You've been my engine for half a life. My turn." I set both hands on his shoulders. "Look at me, Sevro."

His eyes peer out at me from a pit of sadness.

"I know there is nothing I can say that will make this right. I know that the worlds have been cruel to you. That they've ripped your guts out one too many times. This will hurt forever. I cannot imagine losing Pax. I am your best friend. I would die for you, Victra, any of your kids. So trust me when I say this: we are not here for ourselves. So if you cannot pull yourself out of your pain, if you cannot contribute the way you know you can, then there is the airlock: please see yourself out."

He stares at me in shock.

He's not used to this. I've always accommodated his turbulent temper, his volcanic anger and petty slights. I know the Goblin is a part of him, but if he doesn't understand there are expectations, if he isn't called out, he'll see himself to ruin, and maybe take us down with him.

"Piece o' pie," he says bitterly. "Didn't even know the kid. Turn the page on my da too. Forget that son of a whore Bellona—"

"I beat his brother to death with my bare hands. Cassius's twin. I cut his older brother in half. Our friends killed his da. And on and on and on!" I'm shouting now, but dammit, he needs perspective. "And despite all of that fucking murder, Sevro, all that murder—Cassius is *here,* with us, right now, fighting for our future. Fighting for you, and for your family back on Mars. Despite the horrors of the camps, where that little Red in the medBay saw her *entire* family butchered, Lyria is here, with us, right now. And despite my betrayal of the Sons on the Rim all those years ago, where thousands were executed because I turned my back on them, Aurae is here now. They are all fighting for your kids, for mine."

"Looks like you've got your replacement Howlers then. That makes me irrelevant. I'll just hop out the hatch," Sevro says but doesn't move.

"Sevro, I love you. And I love your family. I'm not saying get over it and turn into a machine, I'm saying stop acting like an asshole and let me help you carry the pain."

"You love the Goblin," he says. "You love the blade that slides out of nowhere into the enemy's throat. Like magic. Right before he'd cut you down for good. That's my worth to you."

"Ah. Brother," I say with a sigh. "Do you think Victra would ever have married you if that's all you were? You think you'd be my best friend? Shit. Valdir's better at killing than you are, and he wanted the spot."

He snorts a laugh. "He wanted to shag you."

"He did not." Sevro stares at me like I'm an idiot. "He did not." Sevro shakes his head. The laugh brought on a small change in him. I risk touching his shoulder. He lets me. "I wish you could see what I see, man. What Victra sees, what your girls see, what millions of Red children see when we look at you. The Goblin is a holy terror, yes. He's a useful tool, he makes the enemy scared and our people brave."

Sevro squints at me, surprised at my sudden agreement.

"But Sevro Barca?" I ask. "Hades. He's the stage on which the Goblin sometimes comes out for a guest appearance. He's the man who made the Howlers. He's the one who keeps the Reaper in check. Keeps everyone in check. He was Ragnar's brother. Sevro's a leader, a father, a friend. He's the one Athena sent this message to. Not the Goblin. Not me. We need Sevro to realize how tall he stands. Because if the Golds can beat him into believing he is small, wretched, what hope do the rest of us have?"

Sevro says nothing. He stares through me, his hollow eyes drilling holes into the bulkhead behind me.

"Last thing I'll tell you is this, old friend: neither Sevro, nor the Goblin, is of any use fighting his allies, or working against his friends. You done with the Howlers? All right. My offer still stands: I'll do everything in my power to get you home to your family. Steal you a ship on Io and cover your escape."

"What about the airlock?"

"We know you're not that man." I squeeze his shoulder, hard. "But if you're going to run with this pack, stop chewing our legs like we're all stuck in a trap. This mission matters because it's the one we are on. Think on it. When we get to Io, I'm going to scout. Whether I do that alone or with Sevro isn't my call."

I slap him on the shoulder and head for the medBay to check on Lyria.

I wish I could do more, but I can't go back in time to save his son. He won't respect pity or think he deserves it. In the cold prison of our minds, we are alone with our self-hatred, our doubts, and guilt. No one more than Sevro. A friend may reach through the bars and hold our hand, but they cannot open the door for us. Only the prisoner has the key. All I can do is remind him we're waiting for him when he gets out.

49

LYSANDER

Vae Victis

THE OBSIDIAN PROSTHETICS THAT Atlas's carver applied to my face itch almost as much as the false beard hanging from my chin. The contacts I wear are black, and my teeth plated gold. Scalps taken from the bridge of the *Dustmaker* hang from a rope on my belt. They are frozen stiff and clatter against the battered thigh plate of my Obsidian armor.

My gravBike thrums beside Atlas's over the molten riverlands of Io. A patrol of Volk bikers wave in greeting as they pass in the distance. Atlas waves back. His arms have only recently been reattached. Our three-hour ride from the *Lethe*'s hiding place has taxed him a pain price few could pay. But we have arrived at our destination unmolested, clad in the armor of the barbarian host, and bearing the digital warrant of the Great Fá. Though Fá pacified all but Io's toughest strongholds over the last month—while I crossed the Gulf with Diomedes—we were still at greater risk from Rim guerillas than Fá's forces during our journey from the *Lethe*.

We've come to Plutus to tell Fá his anticipated three-year reign over Ilium will be cut short, and to discuss the logistics of his defeat once my fleet arrives. Atlas may have absolute trust in the man, but I'm keenly aware that we will be at Fá's mercy.

I dread that with every fiber of my being.

The battlewall of Demeter's Garter stretches across the horizon. Behind the wall lies a temperate microclimate amidst the hellish landscape of Io. The paradome network, which holds in pressure, oxygen, and filters radiation, steams over it like the surface of a morning winter lake. It bends the light of its artificial suns so that they appear to shine silver.

The city of Plutus, the administrative capital of the Garter, is swarmed by Fá's divisions. Above the city, two Volk dreadnaughts hover like beasts squatting over their kill. Neither one is Fá's flagship. Though we have come to speak to the man, the *Pandora* is still bombarding Sungrave.

We slow our bikes as we approach the battlewall. I watch as, far above, a stream of produce transports creeps up toward a swelling orbital caravan. The ships gathering there trickle in from across Io. A coldness creeps into my heart when I realize they carry more than foodstuffs off Io. Diomedes told me slaves are the highest currency to the Ascomanni. While the Rim Armada sailed from the Core, the Ascomanni harvested the populace of Io that could not take refuge in the moon's stronger Bastions.

The slaves are part of Atlas's "sunk cost." Many have been infected with disease and will take that poison back to the ants' nests. A hideous thought.

At the battlewall, Obsidian and Ascomanni bodies are still being pulled from the wreckage of the breach by teams of Red slaves bundled thick against the climate. They make frozen heaps with the corpses of Raa soldiers. Traffic thickens near the central gate where patrols queue between cyclopean statuary to enter the city.

When we pass through the gate's pulseField, we are greeted by warmth and elegiac light. The air is breathable, warm, and thick with smoke. The sulfur crystals gathered on my bike and armor join the steam of the other traffic. Beyond the congestion of armored infantry and war machines driven by Blues in strange metal collars, Ascomanni overseers crack long whips at Red captives. Most labor in the thousands to collect bodies from the paths of destruction, which fan out from the narrow breaches into the orchards and grain fields to either side of Plutus.

The Ascomanni are taller and lankier than the Obsidians, and either umber or gray-skinned. Their hair is coarse, straight, thick, and black. They wear glossy black armor made of onyxia, and bark at each other in an unintelligible, savage tongue. They are human, though made less so by their own arcane and perverse use of carvers over the centuries. Some of the cretins are small, like children, with demonic pug faces and surly tempers.

The Ascomanni are a stain of corruption on the face of paradise.

Plutus, a gem in the tiara of the Garter, is a garden city where farming is embraced both as a science and a philosophy. An agricultural eden with warehouses for its crops, and academies, arbors, and laboratories for its prized Brown growers. Public parks, theaters, and baths for its droves of Red fieldhands. Limitlessly powered by the tidal heating of the planet, it makes its own weather and its own sunlight—pearly or silver depending on the crop zone—and for centuries it thrived, invulnerable behind its Raa garrison, kinetic shields, and its elephantine surface-to-orbit cannons.

The city mourns the demise of its guardian triad.

The shields fell because of Atlas, and my Praetorians. Smoke from their sabotage mission still twirls to the west from the ruins of the shield pylons. Bombardment—and tides of savages delirious for spoils—did in the other two pillars of the city's defenses.

I follow Atlas as he weaves through traffic toward a road that carries along an orchard of plum trees five times larger than those of the Core. Ascomanni lie together like sated dogs between the trees gorging on fruit and taunting the Grays who've been nailed to the tree trunks. That is not the worst of the carnival of horrors we see before we reach the city, nor indeed the worst we see in the city itself where an orgy of violence is in full swing, but the look on the face of a young Ionian Gray as she watched the braves beneath her eating plums haunts me. Her expression could not be more different from the smile upon the benevolent statue of the goddess Demeter that extends from the harnessed volcano north of the city.

We park our bikes in a courtyard crisscrossed with huge tables hewn from fresh-cut trees. Preparations for a feast are underway even as an assembly line of Ascomanni axemen execute Raa Grays in the courtyard adjacent.

"I'm surprised you didn't have Fá nuke the Garter," I say to Atlas as we ascend the wooden steps to the Arbor of Akari. Like me, his face is concealed by Obsidian prosthetics. His nose is horribly bent, his cheeks heavy with scars, and face tattooed with the skull of a Stained. "But I suppose even you have your limits."

"Absent a dependable source of food there is no civilization," he replies. "The goal is not to destroy the Rim, Lysander, but for you to be able to control it without leaving your supper table on the Palatine Hill. Do you want a reign impoverished by infrastructure reconstruction? The Garter and the seed vaults were built over dozens of lifetimes. My family might pretend it was the honor in our blood that made us masters beyond the asteroids. In truth? It's the hand that holds the Garter that grips the belly of the Rim."

"And what if Fá decides not to let go of that belly?" I ask. "What if he decides he'd rather be a king than a soldier to a thankless Society."

"A good question. One you should ask him yourself."

I stop and listen to the wailing on the wind. Atop my bike I could not hear it. Now I can hear nothing else. The city itself is weeping. Atlas turns, a few steps up. His voice is gentle.

"Lysander, this is how it has always been. The vaunted past we so revere saw thousands of cities fall to thousands of armies. Periods of trauma are traded for periods of peace. The greater the trauma, the longer the peace. Bear it, and this year will be the last year you see war in your lifetime."

"I will hold you to that," I reply and march upward.

The Arbor of Akari has been spared the murder and rapine that flagellates the rest of the city. Fá has taken the building that hosts the Raa's horticultural history for himself and his inner circle.

After gaining passage to the Arbor's interior past the blood-painted Ascomanni warriors who guard its doors, we are greeted by three Obsidian veterans in armor studded with gems and encrusted with Gold sigils. Beneath apricot and apple trees, Atlas embraces them like long-lost brothers. They are all members of the Kinshield, the team Fá took with him to aid his rise, and speak fluent Common. One by one Atlas introduces them to me and gives them my true name. They kneel in deference, but I see the confusion in their eyes.

They don't know why I am in Ilium.

That confusion is shared by the five more Kinshield Gorgons who return over the course of the next several hours to join us around a circular table set in the Arbor's inner sanctum. I am unexpected; that makes me nervous. The Gorgons come with blood on their boots and soot and sulfur on their furs and capes, fresh from supervising the sack of the Garter or the pacification of one of its cities. Stacking their armor beneath a tree, they join us at the table where they drink and laugh with Atlas as if they were back in the barracks on Luna.

The conversation is fascinating both in its casual nature and its depth. Very quickly the signs of Atlas's tutelage become apparent. Their understanding of politics, strategy, and logistics unnerves me, especially when I hear quotes from Cicero, Hobbes, and Seneca used not only in proper context, but sometimes with deft irony. I have never heard such sophisticated conversation from Obsidians. That is not all that surprises me. When I ask the Gorgon beside me, a clever-eyed man of fifty or so with a cutlass for a nose and mallets for hands, if he was at Kalyke, he hangs his head for a moment.

"I was," he says.

"Why do you hang your head? Was it not a glorious victory?"

"I find little glory in war," he says. "Satisfaction yes, for a job well done. I claimed Aleskandar au Rûn upon my blade. He was a worthy foe, and met a worthy end. That was proper. I bested him man to man. But others, great names—Cassander au Megara, Alethia au Codovan, Talia au Anthos . . . I saw them done under by reptiles, spit, skinned. Their warrior virtue, and it was virtue, was denied. That is why I hang my head, *dominus*. There is much to admire in our foe, and little in our allies."

"Does that dissuade you from your mission?" I ask.

"No. The reptiles cannot help but be reptiles. The knights of the Rim, however, cannot plead ignorance. They chose to be traitors to the Society that built their worlds."

"You call them reptiles," I say. "Like the Moon Lords do."

"They are reptiles, *dominus*. Perhaps not in physiology but in their lack of empathy," another answers. "The centuries have taught them starvation and poverty can only be staved off by violence. They fight other tribes who are their mirror, and so their violence and cruelty are exponential and theatrical."

"It is like they have never seen the light, *dominus*," rasps a quiet one whom Atlas seems to favor above the rest. He is lean, handsome in a way, with an eagle's face and clear eyes and a slight lisp. "Mercy is literally unknown to them. Out there, meat is meat. You understand?"

"No, not yet, go on, Fergarus, isn't it?" I say.

"Yes, *dominus*." He considers. "A man from the wilderness who has never heard music might come upon a city and hear through a window the song of a violin. It makes no matter if he knows the complexity of the piece, or the reverence culture has for the instrument, he will stop and listen because he can recognize the rarity of beauty. These Ascomanni would go into the house and beat the player to death for making a racket, enslave the children, break the violin, and burn down the house. All of them. They do not seek context, or assimilation, only domination. If it does not fit into their paradigm, they destroy it."

"And what of the Volk?" I ask.

"The Volk would enjoy the song and listen till its end, then break the man's fingers, and steal the violin to sell."

"You act as if they are all the same," I say. "Are they?"

Fergarus defers to the others, but they urge him on. "We paint with a broad brush. The Volk have braves who are noble. Some are liars, cheats, and butchers. But some are decent men. Like any army. We all have seen the duality in their nature." The others nod. "They were raised to worship strength, but unlike the Ascomanni they've tasted the light of culture, of cities, of parks, and plays. Yet they feel as if the light has rejected them and spit in their eye. The lowColors, the Republic, the Silvers."

The biggest man at the table then adds, "Fá is their catharsis. Their rage on the worlds." He opens his hands as if all I need to do is look out the window.

"The Ascomanni are simple," Fergarus says. "They demand victory, food, and loot. Usually human. Managing the Volk takes up the majority of our time. They miss the sun. They are skeptical about Fá's claims of making this their new kingdom. Not to mention, they are arrogant. They think moons are small potatoes compared with the planets they used to conquer under Tyr Morga." They roll their eyes at each other, as if exhausted by that arrogance. "They say secret prayers to the Allmother, fearing their betrayal of Sefi will bring a terrible judgment upon them. And worst of all . . ." He looks at Atlas. "Many wonder if they should ever have left the host of Tyr Morga. The jarls would never dare slander their king, but the braves whisper and pout like guilty children who chose the wrong parents after a divorce."

"And how do you combat that?" I ask.

"A mixture of fear, momentum, loot, division, lies, bribery, public killings, but most important, spectacle and invoking their love of Ragnar Volarus."

I sit back, overwhelmed at the complexity of the army I just assumed was a mindless host. I have also never seen Atlas so warm. What Ajax would have done for half the smile he readily gives any one of these Obsidians. But how could Atlas ever respect Ajax, who had everything and gave nothing to the Society when Atlas lived amongst these patriots who have given everything for a Society that would give them nothing in return?

"Well said, goodmen," Atlas says. "As you can see, Lysander, the duty I set upon these Gorgons required them to be far more than mere soldiers."

"Far more," I murmur. "And they all get along. For a table of Golds like this . . ."

"We will make you one," Atlas says and touches my arm. "When we get home, that is our first priority. And what of Volga, my friends? Does the Kinshield have thoughts?" The men grow quiet. "Come now, brothers. Young Lune and I have heard your opinions on everyone else."

They are spared from answering when a roar comes from outside.

Volsung Fá has returned from Sungrave, victorious, and he's apparently brought a dragon.

Atlas and I witness Fá's return with his Kinshield from the steps of the Arbor. Ensnared by a huge net, the dragon dangles from the belly of the *Pandora.* Its scales are iridescent black and purple. Its wings nearly translucent. It thrashes against the net in vain and lets out a mournful howl. It feels to me as if it is calling to its masters or its children. It sounds like it is weeping.

Fá descends from his flagship upon a giant floating altar loaded with chained Gold captives. Not one of the bloodied, chained Peerless draw the eyes more than the king sitting on his throne in his black, spiked armor, with his unshorn honortail, and his gold crown. The crown grows in size with every victory: purportedly, when Ascomanni shaman tear the sigils from the hands of his Gold captives, they melt them onto the crown, or onto his throne or even the altar itself.

A figure stands to the right of Fá's throne throughout this performance—a shorter Obsidian woman, one of the only women I've yet seen in Fá's host. Atlas informs me this is the object of the question that silenced Fá's friends: Volga, the biological daughter of Ragnar Volarus, newly acquired from Mars. What must she make of all this? I wonder.

Fá's affection for her is plain, and I watch the two with interest until I spot three Golds who are spared the violation of having their sigils scalped like the others.

They are all women—one old, one of middling age, and one a young girl. They are kept on leashes by Fá's bodyguards. A cloud settles over Atlas when he sees them. One that deepens when the procession takes on spiritual overtones and the dragon is brought down from the *Pandora* to be butchered by Fá. Using his barbaric weapon, a great saw, he climbs atop the dragon and excises its man-sized heart. He lifts that mass over his head and casts it into a bonfire. Then the dragon is butchered, roasted, and fed to the braves. Spectacle, they said.

As the feast rages beneath, Fá meets us in his stateroom aboard the *Pandora*. I am shocked by the change in his appearance. He has traded his armor, his entourage of Ascomanni and Volk jarls, and the façade of a barbarian king for a beautiful purple silk kimono, bandages, and a glass of cognac. The glass is tiny and would be hilarious in his huge hands if not for his terrifying stature and appearance.

It is no wonder the Grimmuses once used this man as a stud bull. He is the pinnacle of Obsidian genetics. Gargantuan in size, but ropey with usable muscle, like an albino python. Nearly two heads taller than I am, with scars in shapes I've never seen before. One of his hands is metal with clawed fingers that he wears little caps on. His jaw is made entirely of metal too. A terrible burn has claimed one of his eyes, and the eye replaced with a tech mod. He sets his cognac down on a jade table, delicately.

He takes in Atlas's Obsidian face with a smile. His voice is the deepest I've ever heard. **"Allfather, you look positively barbarous."**

They laugh and embrace. Atlas pulls back to hold the man's giant head between his hands.

"A brilliant show, old friend. You are the pride of *cohors nihil*. Your brothers and sister send their compliments. They miss you and the Kinshield dearly. You should hear them chant you on."

"And I miss them. More than I can say. The Kinshield is always so busy putting out fires. A host just shy of a million, and not one genteel conversation to be had."

When they part, they clap each other on the shoulders and laugh. Atlas notes Fá's many bandages. "You're wounded. Do you need any anti-toxins?"

"Not like on Mars. Sefi's pestilence was itchy. These wounds are not grievous. My armor is thick for a reason. Sungrave is broken, of course, as you commanded. The Ascomanni are loading what remains of its populace onto transports. In three days, the city will be a tomb."

"Well done. Well done indeed. But really, will you take that out? You sound insane."

Fá detaches a device from his throat and sets it on the table.

"Ah, that's far better. Hard to enunciate with that baritone." The warlord's natural voice is shockingly soft and sensitive. He's a fraud. A consummate fraud. The only thing not fraudulent is his physical menace, which I think is actually enhanced by his obvious cleverness.

Fá's eyes finally wander to me, curious and sparkling with intelligence. "Your bodyguard is not Obsidian either."

"How can you tell?" I ask.

"Obsidians don't lean in doorways," he replies and nods to my shoulder against the doorframe. "Bad luck."

I stand straight, and file that away. "I am not his bodyguard, at any rate. I am Lysander au Lune," I reply.

"Are you? Are you really?" Fá asks, very intrigued. He squints at my Obsidian prosthetics, dubious, then laughs in delight. "So you are. Xanthus has outdone herself yet again." Fá bows but does not kneel. "*Dominus* Lune. An honor to meet one of the Blood." He raises an eyebrow at Atlas. "Am I to understand there has been a change of plans regarding the beneficiary of this endeavor, then?" He smirks. "Or has the new Lune come to banish us like the last Lune?"

"The former," Atlas says. "The three of us have much to discuss, but first I must see my kin."

I trail the two men through the brig until they come to the void cell containing Atlas's sister. Its occupant can neither see nor hear us. Vela is a hard-faced veteran with even less charisma than Romulus and more fire than Atlas. She lies on her bed without moving. "You broke her back," Atlas notes.

Fá gestures to several of his bandages. "For my trouble. It was the only way, I fear. To take a warrior like her alive in a pitched fray . . . very difficult."

"Apologies. Diomedes was meant to be a sure thing." Atlas glances at me.

"We scoured the battlefield and the escape pods as thoroughly as we could. My Kinshield believe he was likely vaporized in a blast. Per your recommendation, I was liberal with the Grimmus atomics you supplied. If I had known we would need to search for a survivor . . ."

"I don't blame *you*, Vagnar." He insists on using Fá's original name. A sign of friendship. Then he shoots a look of annoyance back at me to show Fá who he does blame.

"Vela will do?" Fá asks. "Even with a broken back?"

"She will," Atlas says. "I need her nervous system, not her spine."

"And what exactly do you need her for?" I ask.

"He doesn't know?" Fá asks.

"Not everything, not yet," Atlas says.

"You said you'd be fully transparent," I say. "I've thrown in with you, at the cost of my soul. What could you possibly think you need hold back?"

"What's a soul to an atheist?" Atlas asks Fá.

Fá makes a farting sound. "Gas."

Atlas smiles and moves on to the middle cell. I am about to press the issue, but Atlas preempts my question. "Just a moment, lad. All of my cards will be on the table in short order . . ."

Atlas trails off as he approaches the cell of his mother. Gaia, the old matron of House Raa, is a broken woman. Her vacant eyes stare at the gray wall of her cell as she murmurs a phrase I can't quite make out. Atlas watches her for a few moments, his emotions inscrutable. "My nieces, nephews. Did my mother see it done?"

Fá hesitates. "She . . . cut their throats with her own hand, but she could not bring herself to kill the youngest." Atlas's eyes soften for his mother. For a moment he looks like he will cry. Instead, he turns his attention to the last Gold prisoner. A girl still shy of puberty with red-rimmed eyes, and the long face of the Raa. Thalia. Diomedes's younger sister.

"Neither could you, it seems," Atlas says.

"She looks like you, and she bit me very hard."

She does look like Atlas. Her face is slender, her eyes narrow and quiet, and has the same distant boredom so commonly seen in Atlas's expression. "You were not so soft before Volga joined us. Was she there with you?" Atlas asks.

Fá grimaces. She was. "I thought you might need a bargaining—"

"Have I ever minced words with what I do and do not need, old friend?"

"I will kill the girl now then." Fá moves to open the cell.

"No," I say. Atlas turns and lifts an eyebrow. Knowing only proving her utility will spare the girl, I conjure some from the ether. "The Rim is stubborn and proud. Many will resent me as Sovereign even if I am their savior. But if I were wed to an ancestor of Akari, then might not that ease the pill down?"

Atlas's eyes narrow. "It will be years before she's of age."

"I thought you were a man who planned for the future. Seems a waste to trim this possible future from our tree, no? Better to have the option."

"You more than anyone should know the perils of mercy," Atlas says. "More than anyone except Darrow, perhaps."

"The difference is I watched Darrow cut down Octavia. Thalia has only seen him." I dip my head in Fá's direction.

Atlas smiles softly. "We'll consider it." He waves Fá away from the cell. "Come. We have plans to iron out."

I linger as the two men make their way from the brig. Thalia is older than I was when my parents died. Younger than I was when Darrow killed Octavia. It wakes my sympathy. If I keep her alive, perhaps I'll have paid some of my debt back to Diomedes.

Gaia is another matter now. When last I saw her, she hid her cunning behind a guise of senility. But grief has broken the woman. She whispers the same phrase over and over. The same phrase a barbarian murmured to a Roman declaiming the price of surrender long ago.

Vae victis. Woe to the vanquished.

50

LYSANDER

Heavy Is the Head

"So, what you're saying is . . ." Fá trails off after Atlas tells him the new order of things.

"Your reign will only last three weeks instead of three years, thanks to Lysander here," Atlas clarifies.

The king sits across the table from Atlas and me in his stateroom. I watch his huge hands, especially the metal one, and wait for violence to erupt as he learns the curtailed length of his reign. Instead, he throws back his head and laughs in sheer delight. A great weight sloughs off him and tears come to his eye. Atlas leans over to squeeze his shoulder.

"Thank Jove," Fá says.

He grimaces when he sees my surprise and taps his monstrous crown with a metal finger.

"Do you think I enjoy the weight of this, *Dominus* Lune?" He pushes it toward me. "The worship of asteroid-dwelling savages? The slaughter of the Society's civilians? The venal backbiting among Darrow's Volk? No. A single day under the sun with sand between my toes is worth ten years on a throne. One performance of *Giulio Cesare* or *Parsifal* does more for my heart than ten thousand chanting my name. I need no honors. I crave no power. Let me be rid of it all."

I'm stunned. "You're not angry in the least? You helm the greatest Obsidian army since Kuthul. Power the nations of old Earth could only dream of."

"War has never been my passion, only my profession, *dominus*. Once my service to the Society is done, I will retire and live out my days eating well, attending the opera, watching races, and swimming in the sea."

Fá's eyes lust for that day. I look back and forth between him and Atlas. "Then what do you get out of this?"

"Satisfaction. Pride that I have done my duty to help ensure a lasting and peaceful Society and the continued advancement of humankind," he replies. "And for myself, a small pension."

"What have you promised him?" I ask Atlas.

"Less than he is due, and more than he requested," Atlas replies. "A penthouse in Hyperion. A seaside retreat on Venus. A pegasus ranch in Switzerland." Fá's eyes go distant and dreamy at that one. "A telomerase tank, a carver, a new name, and twenty years of peace."

"And a daughter," Fá adds.

Atlas winces. "And a daughter."

"Volga," I clarify.

"You should see her, Atlas. She is bright, clever, with a mind like a sponge."

"Has she joined you in battle?" Atlas asks.

"No, I would not press that upon her. Not this world of killing. She is gentle, in a way. She loves animals. It hurt her, the dragon hunt. But she will have flying ponies soon enough." He frowns. "She did try to kill me at first, but I reasoned her through it. She saw how often she's been used, and how I asked nothing of her. But she did join the hunt. It was she who captured their sigil beast. Abraxes. Tricked him right into a trap." He laughs. "She might be a Valkyrie, but there's a touch of that freelancer in her too." He taps his ruined eye. "A worthy man. Oh, Atlas. I think that Gray would have been one of your favorite knives."

"Does she know about me?" Atlas asks, a little perturbed by Fá's excitement.

"No. Of course not. She believes the same thing we sold the Volk. That we do this to make a kingdom for Obsidian." He pauses. "I worry she believes it too much, in a way."

"And when she discovers that is a lie? Afterward, when you tell her of me?"

Fá brushes off the questions. "She is a creature of the cities. She is practical. She will understand and embrace our new life."

"Will she understand, though?" Atlas asks.

Fá hesitates. "What do you mean?"

"Some things we cannot wash off, Vagnar. Once she realizes who you really are, who you really serve, she will abandon you. Especially if she believes the Volk should have their own kingdom. You know my own hardship in that." The two go quiet, perhaps thinking of a tragedy that befell Atlas some time ago. "The only way for her to look past the stains on your hands would be for her own hands to be stained too," Atlas says.

"Blood her in battle?" Fá seems hesitant.

"Yes . . . for a start."

Fá looks down in deep thought before nodding at his teacher's wisdom.

"She will love me more when she understands my sacrifice, yes. Thank you, old friend. You have given me much to think about."

Growing tired of discussing Vagnar's personal life, I clear my throat.

"Shall we have the battle plan then?"

"Fair enough," Atlas says. "The plan is simple. Lysander, after this meeting you will take a suitably battered Rim shuttle and travel to the moon of Pasiphae with Rhone and your Praetorians. There, you will send a message to your fleet telling them you survived the ambush at Kalyke. You will order them to press on and rendezvous with you there. Once they have, you will sail on Io and reclaim the Garter in any way you see fit. Its shields will still be down, so I recommend an Iron Rain for maximum visibility across the Dominion."

"And what of my 'foe'?" I ask and eye Fá.

"Vagnar, sorry. Fá will leave mostly Ascomanni behind to garrison the Garter as he sails onward to assault other moons. Exterminate those wretches to the last and save the citizens you find in their ships, Lysander. The first two waves of transports are already rife with disease and off to the Kuiper, so that extermination is already set in stone. Once you have secured the Garter and installed a Core garrison, you will urge all remaining Rim forces to rally to you for a final confrontation with the dread Volsung Fá. In that confrontation, seen by your grateful allies, you will kill him and scatter his fleet to the winds."

I look at Fá. "But it won't be you I kill."

"I should certainly hope not," he says with a laugh, then more seriously, "You will kill Volsung Fá, but Vagnar Hefga will be long gone."

Atlas explains, "Xanthus is already at work on a head for you to show the Moon Lords. Vagnar here will escape with a select force—enough to be useful to us should we have need of them against Atalantia or the Republic. Now, Vagnar, I know the timetable is extremely compressed, but will three weeks be enough for you to sack all the Galilean moons?"

Fá considers the question as if Atlas had asked about painting a wall. "Sack, no. Raze, yes. But we will have to resort to bombardment if you desire that sort of coverage."

"That sort of coverage?" I repeat. "Atlas, Kalyke and Io are quite enough massacre to—"

"To humble a civilization that brushed off the burning of Rhea in less than a generation?" Atlas asks. "You said it yourself, Lysander. The Rim is proud, stubborn. They must feel existential fear. Europa, Ganymede, and Callisto must fall."

"That's hundreds of millions of people."

"Yes."

"That's . . . gratuitous," I say.

"The greater the trauma, the longer the peace."

"No. If that's your plan, then kill me and put Atalantia on the chair."

He measures my resolve. It's a bluff. He knows it. Fá knows it. I'll have no leverage until my fleet arrives. Yet Atlas relents, and possibly always planned to.

"Very well. I am not unreasonable. You may choose one moon to spare. Io is finished. So that leaves Europa, Ganymede, and Callisto. Which will you grant reprieve?"

"I recommend—" Fá interjects.

"Thank you, Vagnar, but if this is the only power I have right now, I believe I will trust my own counsel," I say.

He nods at my respectful correction of his overstep, and waits patiently. It is a question of arithmetic, so I choose the most populous by far. "Ganymede."

"Very well. Ganymede will be spared," Atlas says so quickly it seems as though he knew I would choose it, and may never have meant for it to be razed at all.

I feel sick. "Vagnar, you can move on to Callisto as soon as your braves have finished their feast. Europa after that, please. Raze the islands first, then invade the Deep."

Fá grimaces. "My braves won't like that. The riches are on the surface and the Deep is a deathtrap."

"Then bribe them with a feast, with spectacle," Atlas says. "Beat them with their own religion. Say their Allfather wills it. Whatever it takes. Burn all your capital. It'll be their last mission before Lysander hits. There's an infestation there I wanted rooted out."

"Apologies, it's hard to forget sustainability of the army is no longer a priority. It will be done. They do love their feasts," Fá says.

"And where will you be during all of this, Atlas?" I ask.

"Oh, you know, around," he says.

"Atlas, I just had to choose between moons to spare from annihilation. I'm all in, obviously. If you burn, I burn. If you don't let me into the circle of trust now, how can we work together and, how did you put it, 'get shit done'?"

Atlas considers. "Fair. I will be on a moon called Orpheus."

"There is no moon called Orpheus," I say.

"Not on any map, no. It is an irregular moonlet two point one kilometers in diameter with an orbit so close to Jupiter and so hidden by the planet's radiation and magnetosphere that few sensor systems would notice it. If they did, their telescopes would see an uninhabited rock of little interest. Inside this rock lies the most secure vault in all of Ilium. This vault is guarded by an elite garrison of shadow knights. Its contents are so shameful to my family that not even its guardians fully know what it is they are protecting."

"But you do?" I ask. I've never even heard of the term *shadow knight*.

Atlas nods. "Shall I die of suspense? Am I in your circle of trust or not?"

"Very well. I will tell you what even Atalantia does not know, because unlike her you won't salivate all over the table. This mission was organized to drain the Republic of its Obsidian weapons, punish the Rim, to unite it with the Core under a Sovereign, and to exterminate the Ascomanni, yes. But, there is a secondary goal that is arguably more important.

"As you know, I spent much of my youth in your grandmother's vaults. The stacks there have information you'll find nowhere else. I was particularly obsessed with the relationship between Akari and Silenius. In my readings, I found the true reason for the schism between the founders of our Society.

"Seven hundred and fifty years ago, Akari stole a weapon called *Eidmi* from Silenius. *Eidmi* is a virus with a modular half-life capable of targeting any of the fourteen Colors without secondary transmission to the rest. It is a weapon that will mean the end of war and ensure obedience to the Morning Chair for a thousand years. What planet, what Color, would dare raise arms ever again if they knew we could prune rabble-rousers out with a snap of our fingers?"

Silence falls upon my heart, and my mind conjures images of pristine worlds and cities where the sun still shines and the wind gently rolls, but are denuded of all human life, empty of laughter. I do not move for a long moment.

"*Eidmi* means, 'I devour,'" I say. "In Hittite, no?"

"Yes. Devour, eat, consume. It is the root of the word 'edit' in many languages."

"Edit. As in edit out a Color?"

"Yes, on whatever sphere it is deployed."

"Even Gold?"

"Even Gold."

I try a laugh to dispel the joke. Atlas and Fá do not smile. It is hard to embrace the reality of such a weapon. The application may seem enough. Blockade a planet, remove all the Reds, or Obsidians. Sanitary. Clean. And in Atlas's hands, a terror like nothing ever seen before. But the ramifications are impossible to fully understand. Wars are inconvenient and expensive, atomics too destructive and radioactive to use without blowback. This is . . . genocide in a bottle. It wraps my heart in a cold silence and squeezes.

"You see why I did not tell Atalantia of this," Atlas says.

I nod and look up, puzzled. "Why would the Raa, your family, steal it and not destroy it?"

"The same reason mankind never freed themselves from atomics. Fear there may come a day so dire it would have to be used." Atlas opens his hands as if to say here is that day for the Rim. "That is why I needed Diomedes. Helios told me only a Raa with the scar can open the vault. Fortunately, I have Vela now. I anticipate it will be the hardest mission of my career. I have no information on the base defenses, nor its garrison. I expect I will lose many patriots. When I have *Eidmi*, I will rejoin you on the *Lightbringer*, Lysander. As for you, Vagnar, I fear we will not see one another again until we are toasting Thessalonican red at your penthouse in Hyperion."

"I look forward to having you as my guest," Fá says.

"Interference around Orpheus will be heavy. So if there's any lingering questions now's the time," Atlas says.

I have one.

"You've killed your nieces, your nephews, your sister-in-law, and I don't imagine Vela will survive Orpheus . . . so why is Gaia alive?"

Fá and Atlas exchange a look of amusement. Fá laughs. "Really, *Dominus* Lune. What kind of monster would kill his own mother?"

51

DARROW

Midnight Lands

W E ARRIVED ON Io and found it too dangerous to risk an approach. For three days we waited inside Io's orbit in the cover provided by Jupiter's faint ring system and magnetosphere as storms the size of Earth raged beneath. We circled Jupiter, matching pace with Io's orbit, watching streams of transport ships depart until the *Pandora* and three Volk dreadnaughts slipped away from the moon with most of the Volk navy toward Callisto. When they disappeared around the curve of Jupiter, I told Cassius it was time to make our approach.

Virginia always thought it a strange perversity that so many of Jupiter's moons were named after women or goddesses Zeus raped, and then graced with the ultimate torture—to be held under his gaze for eternity. From what I've seen on our journey into inner Ilium, Fá has been no kinder to the moons than Zeus was to his conquests.

Io floats alone beneath us, a ruin.

Its defenses have been smashed. Its cities razed; their smoke weeps upward to join the columns that pour out from Io's four hundred volcanoes. It seems only the equator was spared Fá's wrath. For good reason. There, an uninterrupted belt of green and gold pulses with life amidst a hellish landscape riven with volcanoes and desolate, frozen sulfur wastes.

Demeter's Garter.

The breadbasket of the Rim. Infrastructure as crucial, perhaps more crucial, than the Dockyards of Ganymede I destroyed twelve years ago. Not all of Fá's fleet has departed. Hundreds of strange warships that could only be Ascomanni-made gather over the Garter along with caravans of cosmosHaulers.

I cannot help but be impressed. Of the four Galilean moons—Europa, Io, Callisto, and Ganymede—Fá took the hardest and innermost moon first. It is exactly what I would have done: gain space supremacy by defeating the Raa navy, eliminate their moon defense bases, then capture the Garter to grip their whole civilization by the windpipe. Now that another leader has done it, the brutality the act required seems a sin against humankind. The consequences of the Garter's loss will stretch far beyond Ilium to affect Rim civilization all the way to Pluto.

More and more Fá feels like my shadow, that darker part of myself that knows the shortest route often lies through the ruthless application of brutality.

Even Sevro does not laugh this time. Aurae's lack of celebration when we saw the devastation around Kalyke was because she feared exactly this. She was right to, and Sevro was right to worry that Athena and her fabled ships may no longer exist. Still, we didn't come all this way to turn back now. We need to contact Athena, and the only way to do that is to light Aurae's omega torch in Sungrave.

Io is about the size of Luna, and tidally locked. One side always faces Jupiter. The moon is pulled in a constant tug of war between the gravity of Jupiter and the other Galilean moons. This creates tectonic movement, so Io is constantly bleeding fire from her heart. Some of her volcano plumes spew as much as five hundred kilometers out into space. Using one of these to mask our entry to the moon, we slip through Ascomanni patrols and descend toward the south pole.

I am extremely wary of putting the *Archimedes* at risk by approaching Sungrave directly. Surface-to-air missiles—either from Raa guerillas or Fá's forces still on the moon—are as much a risk to the ship as enemy fighters or capital ships. So I have Cassius set down several hundred kilometers southeast of the city in a volcano range on the edge of the anti-Jovian Wastes of Naramoor. The spews and volcanic activity will hide our ship, hopefully. While Cassius stays behind with Lyria, Aurae, and our mute prisoner, Diomedes, I head to the cargo bay to gear up and disembark. Aurae passes me in the hall and tosses me a hair tie.

"Been a long road since the Marcher," she says as I tie my hair up. "Be careful."

I bump fists with her and descend into the cargo bay.

Sevro is there waiting, already dressed. I did not know if he was coming, but it seems he's decided to step up after all. I give him a nod and he helps me into the Godkiller armor.

I skip the small talk and show him our route.

"The direct approach takes us through a briar patch of mountains and volcanoes. Anything could hide there, and we can't afford to get shot down. If our oxygen reserves run out, the sulfur dioxide in Io's thin air will react with the water in our lungs to form a strong acid. So we will head due west to the Waste of Karrack, then curve back toward the city on the seam between the mountains and the waste. Here just south of Darkfall. Complaints?" He shakes his head. "You're better in boots. I suggest fly-hopper interchange, but you're flight master. I'll take your lead. Helm up. Boots prime. Let's do it."

The ramp lowers and we step out into the dimness.

Sevro and I fly from meager sunshine over plains painted shades of yellow, red, black, green, and white toward midnight lands where Jupiter hangs in the sky, supreme, mutinous, and huge. From the surface of the moon, Jupiter subtends an arc of 19.5 degrees, appearing thirty-nine times the apparent diameter of Luna from Earth's surface. Even the many mountains of Io, some rising higher than Earth's Everest, seem small in comparison.

We wind through the teeth of mountain passes, over vast sulfur plains and burping lava flows until the moon slips into Jupiter's shadow. The celestial event, where Jupiter blocks Io from the sun completely, occurs every forty-two hours. Surface temperatures drop so low all sulfur on the moon turns to frost. The Ionians call it nivalnight.

The darkness grows Stygian, broken only by the glow of volcanoes, the throbbing of molten silicate lava lakes, and the blinking lights of high-altitude Ascomanni patrols. If there is Rim resistance to the Ascomanni, we do not see any signs of it, and that's all the better. Dustwalkers, Obsidians, Ascomanni, those are my fears in descending order.

We alternate between sprints of low-altitude flight and hopping in our gravity boots. We pause at random intervals and Sevro peers into the blackness of the mountains or the shrouds of volcano plumes as if they concealed legions. There is no better scout in my army than Sevro save a few of Valdir's lads, but we are warmlanders, softworlders, and I feel even Sevro's fear.

An hour into our journey west we reach the Waste of Karrack. Over that barren plain, weird tentacles of light molest the sky. They are charged particles flowing off Jupiter to form auroras. They stain the frozen sulfur crystals mutating shades of violet, cerulean, and green.

Daring young Blues, styled "airdancers," from Darkfall and Nightmourn used to sail those auroras with homemade Dedalian wings. Golds have bones far too heavy for the sport. No Blues dance in the sky tonight. I wonder aloud to Sevro if any Blues will ever dance here again.

He does not answer, or care. In the eight days since his fight with Cassius, Sevro has barely been seen, choosing to camp out and sleep in the machine shop or the escape pod and take his meals in private. I hoped for a new start after he revealed his grief for Ulysses. Maybe I was too hard on him. Or I was too optimistic, but even if he's gone silent he is no longer pulling the team apart.

He comments on Quick's armor though, and that's something. "Shame we didn't have this ten years ago," he says of the new gear.

I don't disagree. The gear is light, fast, stealthy without sacrificing power, and its updated generator can run the suit for days. It has three modes for power-usage. Typical of Quick, they all have dumb names. "Reptile" to run cold for stealth. "Lupine" for regular use. And "titan" to kill gods, apparently. We've only dared try reptile mode. Our juice runs out here, we're dead.

Sevro grows somber as we pass the city of Darkfall.

Unlike many of the large-mass moons, Io was never terraformed. The moon and its air are still hostile to life. Life has been able to stubbornly survive here only beneath the surface of the moon or under the paradomes. Those domes that once harbored precious oxygen and sheltered the citizens of Darkfall from Jupiter's radiation bombardment have now been shattered. The city, once famed for its orators, sopranists, and philosophy, lies quiet and cold as we pass. It is as if their stoic people have been eaten by the dark itself. I think of the transport ships that we saw trickling away from Io when we arrived, and know now what cargo they carried.

Men, women, children, bound for some frigid asteroid city far beyond the bounds of civilization. I can scarcely imagine what awaits them there. Even in Lykos, little trickles of hope made their way into the mines—whispers about Ares, beams of sunlight. I fear the captives of Io will receive no such inspiration. My chest grows tight after thinking of their fate.

If they are truly my enemies, then why do I want to weep?

52

DARROW

Sungrave

"**B**LOODYDAMN BELLONA. WHAT'S HE DOING? *There's three of them,*" Sevro says from his perch on the ridgeline behind me. *In reptile mode, our armor runs cold and has adaptive camouflage. Sevro is difficult to make out on any of my ocular filters.*

From our vantage south of Sungrave, he monitors the approach from the south. I monitor the northwest. It is barren of life. The Obsidians have come and gone. The story of Sungrave seems no different from the tale we saw everywhere along our route. Death. Darkness. Silence. The only difference is the cemetery of war machines that sprawls out before the city. Sungrave did not fall without a fight. We checked the machines and found frozen Blues and Greens inside—not Obsidians at all. They had scars on their necks from pain collars. But it seems the enemy recycles, and took the collars back from their corpses.

"Three," I say absently. "Should just be Cassius and Aurae."

"*Three.*"

I frown. Frost crackles under my gravBoots as I slide down from my post, then jump thirty meters to join him in the shadows. He clings to the side of the dark rock like a gargoyle. "Lyria?" I ask. "She shouldn't be off-ship with that concussion."

"*It's not the Red. It's the Raa.*"

I pause. "He brought Diomedes?"

"*Unless Lyria gained a hundred kilos overnight. Bellona's off-mission. He's masturbating over his own honor still. Maybe you need to offer him the airlock.*"

"Let me talk to him this time."

"It's resolved," he says.

"What do you mean?"

"Ain't your business."

"Keep watch." I descend from our position to meet Cassius at the base of the mountain. Sulfur crystals clatter as he sets down on his grav-Boots. His own Godkiller suit mutates with the changing light. Nival-night is waning, and the pitch-blackness slowly erodes into a forge-like glow sometimes caused by the refraction of the moon's volcano light on the particle-thick air. I expect him to babble on about the armor. Instead, Cassius's voice is like that of a man attending a funeral.

"These poor people. I've never seen anything like this."

"You will again if Atalantia takes Mars," I reply. Perhaps too maudlin. "You brought Diomedes."

"Yes. Can't be just you and Sevro making the plan every time. I'm more than a pretty face and an excellent pilot. The Raa needs to see this, Darrow. He deserves to see this. I know you think he's your enemy. But I was too, once." I nod, thinking. *"Was I so wrong to bring him? To not want him tortured? I know I've missed the war, but maybe that's a good thing. You and Sevro are stuck in a brawl that you can't look up from."*

"Maybe," I offer him. "But you should have asked, Cassius."

"Oh, like Sevro asked to torture him?"

So much for my authority. How is it easier to control an army of millions than my two best friends? I frown. Is Cassius a best friend? Weird how comfortable I am with the thought.

Aurae's gravBike groans to a halt behind Cassius. Diomedes looms behind Aurae in the bike's second seat. Even with her slender lines hidden by the bulk of her pulseArmor, she looks like a child sitting in front of a golem. Unarmored, he wears a boxy EVO suit. His face is hidden behind the dusky visor. His hands are secured behind him to the bike.

"Your idea?" I ask Aurae of Diomedes as she joins us. It's clear she has a deep emotional connection to the man. She admitted as much to me after Sevro and Cassius fought.

"No. This was all Cassius," Aurae says. *"While Diomedes was one of my masters, you seem to forget that I chose to leave him. I am a traitor to him, in more ways than one. He has not spoken to me. Only to Cassius. I said we should follow your orders, Darrow. Diomedes may be a man who cannot tell a lie, but Cassius really has no idea how dangerous he is."*

Cassius presses the issue. *"Diomedes had kin here, Darrow. If you let him search for them, he's agreed to give you his parole."*

"Aurae, you know him best. Will he keep his parole?" I ask. "I know you're on our side, Aurae. I promise I will not think your judgment compromised."

"He is a gentle, sensitive man—" Cassius and I both look at the hulking beast sitting chained to the bike. His list of wartime heroics sings a very different tune. *"He is also fair, kind, and honorable. But I have never seen him at war. And he has never seen his home destroyed. I cannot say what he will or will not do. Especially if he thinks you are involved in this."*

"Me?"

"The Raa considered you a grave threat, a new age Hannibal. Now many of your old braves are here."

I wince at that.

"He spared my life, Darrow," Cassius says. *"He doesn't like me. He did it because I fought with honor."*

"Yeah. But I'm not you," I say. "I'm certainly a main war objective. And you always forget. Golds have different rules for Golds than they do for Reds."

"Darrow, look around. The Rim is out of the war against Mars," Cassius says. *"This is worse than anything you ever did. If we show him that . . . Well, we could do worse than having a helpful Raa out here."*

Cassius really is trying to be a moral knight. If only the world cared. Yet I am tempted. Torture did not work on the man, so perhaps this is the path to understanding Kalyke, and maybe more. Aurae says, *"I've known Diomedes for thirteen years. You knew his father Romulus, yes?"* Her expressionless helmet looks back at me, but her face shows on my HUD, captured by the cameras in her helmet.

"I know his uncle far better," I say.

"Diomedes could be like his uncle, his father always said. But Diomedes wants to be his father. His mother, Dido, led the Dragon Armada. She is likely dead. His kin were in Sungrave . . . to break his honor, his parole, would be the ultimate dishonor to the dead. And he loved them more than anything."

Apparently bored of eavesdropping, Sevro jumps from a ledge above and lands on the bike just in front of Diomedes. He squats there for a moment then jumps back to us and lands in a flurry of sulfur. *"Said he gives his parole to me. Let's stop wasting time."*

"You sure?" I ask.

"He's in an EVO suit. I'm in this. He slags around, he's chowder."

I nod to Cassius to get Diomedes off the bike. Aurae begins to show me on the map where the access to the family tunnels lies. I stop her mid-sentence. She hasn't yet seen Sungrave itself. "We won't have to use the family tunnels," I say. "The front door is wide open."

Sungrave was once a city that demanded awe. Centuries ago, Akari au Raa carved dragons into the mountain range that hosts the top levels of the city. He did it with orbital lasers before his Reds started to burrow into the moon itself. The city rose from the frozen desert as proof of the ingenuity, grandeur, and determination of House Raa, and it stretched beneath the desert, deeper and deeper, as testament to the centuries of prosperity overseen by Akari's ancestors. Like an iceberg, most of it lies unseen beneath the surface. Even now, fallen, dark, its dragon statues broken and radiation slithering from their shattered bodies like blood, I feel puny in its shadow, and even lesser in the shadow of Fá's accomplishment.

Many believed Sungrave impregnable. I know I did.

Set within and beneath a mountain, the citadel of the Raa was powered by the tidal heating of the moon itself and linked through tunnels to subterranean greenhouses. Even with a half-strength garrison, it could maintain its shields against orbital bombardment and feed its people for years, while its natural features and tiered defensive fortifications made it all but impervious to ground assault. Supposedly.

It would take days to scout all the entrances into the mountain city, but we haven't the time. Besides, nothing except our party moves on the south-facing slope. Not at the main breach, nor amongst the collapsed towers or twisted gun batteries, nor even down below where the sulfur waste meets the great and undamaged ground gates into the mountain.

Entering the city via the breach—a smooth tunnel forty meters wide littered with broken war machines and frozen defenders—is like descending into a necropolis. They died in many places, the defenders of Sungrave. In the hallways, in great grottos once rich with vegetation. In fall-back bunkers defending civilians, and in tramways and broad avenues beneath vast domed ceilings glowing with radiant fauna and waterfalls flowing from underground rivers.

First it was the urban phalanxes who died in their gray and blue armor and then it was auxiliaries in gray and blue livery and then the citizenry in the simple cotton or wool vestments of the hierarchy. Sometimes the bodies are heaped in public agoras. Sometimes they are pinned to the walls above empty bottles of spirits. Mostly they lay where they died, which was either in flight or cowering in redoubts or trying to stand firm against the tide.

The pulseFields that provide the atmosphere to the city are mostly intact the deeper we press into the city. We doff our helmets. The air is breathable, cold and thick with the noxious, sweet smell of death. With Sevro scouting ahead, we reach the Spine without encountering a single living being. Usually there would be scavengers.

Wide enough for a hundred men to walk abreast, the Spine is a grand stone stairway that links the levels of the subterranean city together. A black stone arch carved with scenes from the Raa family's history has been decorated with a new and odious embellishment: the decaying head of a giant dragon. I smell its stench even from the floor.

Sevro floats up to inspect the head. It's big enough to fit four men Sevro's size in its mouth. "Abraxes," Aurae murmurs and looks back at Diomedes. We have not taken his helmet off or unbound him, so his expression is hidden. "The sigil-beast of the Raa herd. It was his grandfather's dragon."

"Wonder where the body is," Sevro says when he returns from his inspection.

"The Garter?" I suggest.

He grunts. "Think they ate it?"

"It would make sense, wouldn't it?" I say.

"Wait, why would they eat it?" Cassius asks.

"Old religious rite. Their way of absorbing the power of a defeated foe. Would happen in tribal wars on Mars's poles back in the day. Fá ate Sefi's heart, according to the briefings. Seems he's reigniting the practice."

We move on. The defenders made a last stand only a few levels down the Spine—Gray, Green, Orange, Red, Brown. Their corpses lie together, equal in death if not in life. I feel exposed seeing the bodies twisted together. So many of the problems I've caused are because I've valued some lives over others. The Core over the Rim. The people of Mars over the people of Mercury. Seeing what Fá has done to Io, seeing the dead of a city I planned to "liberate" one day fills me with guilt and dread in equal measure. But there is something else there: an urge to right these wrongs.

I know that's folly. I no longer have my army, and the Volk have abandoned the dream of Eo and Ragnar, and I know much of that is my fault.

It is vain to think I can do anything out here, but my eyes wander to Diomedes and I wonder what he's thinking behind that helmet.

No one is sorry to leave the Spine behind for the promenade level. When we reach the pedestrian juncture where the tunnels to the government district and the market divide, I tell my companions that we are separating. "Sevro carry on with Aurae and Cassius to the market and light the omega torch." I hesitate. "I've got business with Diomedes."

Sevro doesn't even pause. He keeps walking toward the market. "You sure you don't want me with you?" Cassius asks.

"No. I need you two to work together. Can you?" I ask.

He looks after Sevro. "Maybe. He left me a bottle of moonswill."

"Huh?"

"I think he's been making it in the machine shop. Lyria can vouch. It's decent stuff."

"She has a head injury, Cassius."

"She only had a dram! It was an olive branch, I think."

Aurae and Cassius follow Sevro down the tunnel toward the market, leaving me alone with Diomedes for the first time. He is not as tall as I am, but he is broader and I remember the scars on his body and the calluses on his hands. I approach him carefully and wonder if I'm being a fool—trying to redeem my sin against the father by treating with the son. Yet I take off his helmet. His mane of dark hair falls out. When I see his eyes, I feel his bottomless sorrow. They are shot red from crying and panicked like a child's. I imagined a stoic warrior beneath the helmet. Instead I see a man whose world is in tatters and his home filled with ghosts.

I do not have to feign the sympathy in my voice. "Diomedes, I am sorry for your loss. I'm told you had kin here." He does not reply. "You gave your parole to Cassius, but I need you to look me in the eye and give it to me. If you do, we can search for your kin together."

He looks me in the eye, like I've spoken a foreign tongue. Then he blinks, understanding, and gives me a solemn nod. I motion him to turn. His feet shuffle and I unlock his cuffs.

53

DARROW

Eyes of Stone

THE RAA FAMILY COMPOUND was once a place of humble beauty, I'm sure. *Defiled* is too slight a word to describe what has been done to it by Fá's troops. Bodies decompose in the entry grotto. The subterranean spring that runs throughout the home is murky and smells of rot. The winding halls, once painted with images of fables and histories, have been defaced with curses and phalluses traced in blood. I breathe a sigh of relief to see the language is neither Nagal nor Common. The Ascomanni sacked this place.

Knowing what awaits Diomedes, I let him search the home for his kin on his own. The liberty is also a litmus test for the man's honor. As he searches, I inspect the bodies of five Peerless knights who tried to make a last stand. Their bones are broken and their bodies covered with puncture wounds. I sample the flesh around those wounds to take back to the *Archi* and compare to the poison we found in those spines in Diomedes's hands.

Then I wait in the grotto.

I feel sick looking at the bodies that fill the stream. Was it really twelve years ago I sat with Romulus in his garden in the Wastes of Karrack? I remember being amused by his daughter Seraphina and wondering what her future would hold. I try to picture her going off to war. All I can see is a little girl sealed inside a starShell. Did she die at Kalyke? Here? Phobos? Earlier in the war?

I feel old, and older still when I hear Diomedes's moan coming down the corridors. In it, I hear the grief I fear I'll one day feel. How on that day I might think back on this moment now and wonder what I could have done differently to avoid my loved ones' destruction.

I crave distraction from my emotions, but my time with *The Path* anchors me in my own body. *Breathe out, then in. Find the self, lose it again.* I repeat the mantra until all I feel is the breath in my lungs, the cool cavern air on my skin, the weight of armor on my shoulders, the distant deepmine wind of Mars.

When I've found my center, I watch Sevro's helm feed as he and Aurae enter the market to find the perfumery. They secure the shop, a stone building carved like a teardrop, and crunch their way over broken vials to the back where Aurae pricks her finger on a needle hidden in the wall. The stone trembles and reveals a hidden long-range coms station. Her omega torch. She sends her message, and the three of them settle in to wait for a reply.

When I think Diomedes has had enough time to mourn, I seek him out. I find him kneeling in the Raa's ancestral sanctum. The faces of his dead ancestors are carved into the chilly black stone of the vestibule. There are hundreds. Many have been smashed or melted by energy weapons.

Water from a crack in stone high above drips onto Diomedes's shoulders. He hunches over two headless bodies. A child and what looks like a teenager. I feel for the man. Out of respect I stay silent and sit down in a recessed bench. The stone eyes of his ancestor watch him with less pity than I do. In time, I ask: "Who were they?"

Diomedes lowers his hands, exhausted from grief. "My brothers, Marius and Paleron."

"All of your kin?" I ask.

"What?"

"Was that all your kin you thought to find here?" I ask.

"My sister Thalia. I could not find her. Nor my grandmother Gaia, nor my aunt Vela."

"I'm sure there are bunkers?" He nods. "Shall we search for them there?" He doesn't even look like he can stand. "If you give me the co-ordinates, I could have Cassius look." For a moment I'm not sure he heard me. Then he nods again. I hail Cassius and in a dead voice Diomedes tells him the bunkers where the rest of his kin might be found.

With nothing to do but wait with Aurae in the perfumery for Athena to respond to our message, Sevro doesn't complain. Diomedes nods in gratitude as Cassius sets off.

"I'm sorry," I say.

"Was it you who did this?" he asks.

"No."

"What do you know of those who did?" he asks.

"Volsung Fá, the Obsidian warlord who seems to have united the Ascomanni, coerced the Volk out from under us after killing Sefi on Mars, and now holds Ilium in the palm of his hand." I pause, then ask, "Anything you can tell me about him?"

Diomedes ignores the question, instead asking, "Why have you not killed me?"

"Should I?"

"We are at war. The purpose of war is to kill your enemies."

"I'd have thought a Raa would know better," I say. "You're wrong on both counts. Were I your enemy, I would be celebrating this attack against the Dominion, as it strengthens Mars's resistance to the Golds of the Core. I would have left you out floating in the darkness or put a pulseFist to your head and sent you to join Akari in the Void. Problem is, I do not find genocide acceptable, and I have a growing vendetta against the man who carried it out. This Fá."

"How else?" he asks, catching me off guard.

"I'm sorry?"

"You said I was wrong on both counts about war. How else am I wrong, in your estimation?"

"The point of war is not to kill your enemies, but to come to an acceptable peace while losing as few people as possible."

Diomedes's eyes narrow. He says nothing, and I take his silence as a signal to continue.

"I will be blunt. In a few weeks, Volsung Fá will own all the moons of Ilium. You cannot stop him. Your family armies are gone. Your family's navy is gone. Io has fallen. It was the strongest defensive moon in Ilium. Europa, Callisto, Ganymede, they will all fall one after the other. You can't protect them. Worse, Fá has the Garter. That means he can wage war on the whole Rim without ever leaving Ilium."

"We will take it back," he says, stoic.

"Maybe the Dominion will have enough strength left to reclaim the Garter—if the navies of Uranus, Neptune, and Saturn combine with the Shadow Armada—wherever it is. *Maybe*. But they'll take time getting here. And if Fá decides he's about to lose, what's to stop him from destroying your ability to grow food, simply out of spite? You cannot fix this on your own." I lean toward him like a Silver delivering a foreclosure letter. "But, perhaps you are not alone after all."

Diomedes barks out a laugh that echoes through the vestibule. "I was told you were a trickster. My mother was right. You list my miseries as if you had none of your own. Your home is under attack. We crushed your wife on Phobos and even now, Atalantia is biding her time for a Rain on Mars. You did not come to Ilium to fix this. You came for either ships, men, or both. But whose? The Volk, I'd wager. Trying to bring them back in the fold, are we?"

"Yes, I came for both ships and fighters. But you're wrong about the source. I am here at the bequest of our mutual acquaintance, Athena."

At this, Diomedes's eyebrows shoot up, then settle into a furrow. If he didn't deduce Aurae was a Daughter already, he knows now.

"Fitting that the terrorists of the Core are seeking out those of the Rim. What help could Athena and her band possibly offer you that would entice you all this way, I wonder."

"Given the Krypeia among your kin, I'm sure you're aware of the Dominion's various missing ships over the last thirty years." Diomedes gives me no reaction, so I assume I am on the right track. "It is true that the Rim is huge, and that your playthings might get lost in the darkness beyond the shipping lanes. But if I were you, I'd worry more about who is finding those lost toys."

"Ships then. How many do you think there are?"

"Enough," I bluff. He would know better than I would. But Athena didn't just steal ships. She said they were building them too. In truth, I have no idea of the promised fleet's size or quality. "Enough that we could help turn the tide against Fá. Save the Rim from generational starvation. It's in all of our interests to do that, and quickly."

"You are attempting to broker a deal between two parties, neither of whom want the deal to begin with." His brow furrows. "She is a terrorist. She would call me a slaver, though I am not."

"Would Aurae call you a slaver?" I ask.

He goes very quiet. "She knows I never thought of her as a slave."

His tone reveals enough. I almost laugh. Am I the only one not in love with that woman?

"You might not be a slaver like those of the Core, perhaps. But you had Pinks in your house. Didn't you? Did they have a choice in their vocation? Shall we ask Aurae about her life?" He says nothing.

"Listen, Diomedes. You are right that I am attempting to broker a deal between adversaries, but it is only because I believe a greater adversary threatens all of us."

"How is Volsung Fá a threat to the Republic?"

My com crackles. *"Howler One, we have a confirmed receipt from Athena. We're to stand by for instructions,"* Sevro says.

My heart soars. "You mean she's still alive?" I say.

"Looks like. Aurae think she has assets on Io still. We're to stand by for instructions."

"Report back when you get them."

"Registers."

The com clicks off. I sigh in relief. Diomedes is still staring at me. "Where were we?" I ask.

"How is Volsung Fá a threat to the Republic?" he repeats.

"He isn't," I say. "He's already done his damage to us. But the entity pulling his strings is very much a threat. There's something, or someone, behind this warlord. That is always the enemy you must fear the most. The unseen one who strikes from the shadows."

Diomedes does not encourage me to continue, but he does not argue. For a flashing second, I see recognition and surprise play out on his otherwise impassive face. He has had these worries himself, it seems.

"Do you believe in magic?" I ask. He looks almost offended. "Clairvoyance?"

"Of course not."

"So you agree no woman or man can see the future."

"Are you mocking me? No. Of course not."

"Good. Because there's something that's not been making sense to me." I rub my hands together hoping to draw him out of his shell. "Something about all this that doesn't fit. Now, I don't have all the intel, but Virginia passed me some as we sped past Mars. I got some more from a very rich old friend. And the rest with my own eyes.

"This campaign against Ilium is *organized*. This is not some raid of opportunity. It couldn't be. We know that Volsung Fá is a Core-born Obsidian who somehow united the various Ascomanni of the Belt and the Far Ink. You know as well as I that a task of that magnitude would take *years*. But our Obsidian friend did not stop there: he managed a coup against the recently independent Sefi, and subsequently stole the Volk legions and their navy out from under her. It's not the theft itself I can't swallow—Obsidian thrones are often won through bloodshed—it's the precision with which the theft was carried out."

"So, he's clever for an Obsidian. That doesn't mean—"

"It's not just cleverness, it's not just his mastery of the Obsidians' psychology. It's the logistics. If Fá was ruling the Ascomanni all the way out in the Kuiper Belt—a year's journey at least—how did he know to arrive on Mars exactly when Sefi's reign was the most vulnerable? She'd only just rebelled from the Republic and claimed the mines of Cimmeria for her Alltribe. Can he see the future? Or is it more reasonable there is a degree of coordination and patience to this play?"

Diomedes turns this over in his mind. His jaw clenches. I continue.

"This campaign against Ilium would have been impossible without the Volk fleet, without the Volk braves, without your navy being off to war in the Core. Yet based on the timetable, all the pieces had to have been in motion long before the Rim declared war. So . . . how did Fá know the Rim was going to be otherwise engaged? Before your own rulers did? Before Cassius and Lysander ever arrived with the evidence of my crimes against the Rim? Years before, in fact. Can he see the future, Diomedes?"

He does not answer, but thoughts swirl behind his eyes. I'd give almost anything for him to put them into words.

"Then there's the matter of Kalyke. Where the Dragon and Dust armadas, two of the most storied fleets in history, led by one of the Rim's best commanders, were destroyed without Fá even breaking a sweat. I saw his navy when we landed here: intact, and, except for those dreadnaughts, decidedly mediocre. That navy should be in tatters, even in victory. It looks like he lost barely a ship during the ambush. Was your navy made of porcelain? Has Helios become incompetent in his old age? Was Dido equally mediocre?" His jaw flexes. "Was it a miracle?" I pause, waiting for him to correct me. He doesn't. "You were there. Guard your secrets if you must, but I think it's more likely there was an unseen hand at play. An unseen hand that led you into an ambush, that guided the Rim into the war at precisely the right time, possibly even inciting Sefi to abandon me on Mercury and seek independence on Mars."

When said aloud, it all seems far less paranoid than it did in my head. "Maybe I have become paranoid after a decade of war," I allow. "Maybe I'm swinging at ghosts. Maybe Fá *is* charismatic enough to unite the Volk and the Ascomanni. Clairvoyant enough to plan a war that was only possible *if* your navy was gone. And brilliant enough to crack Sungrave and the Garter in one-tenth the time it would have taken me." His eyes narrow at that, but even if he hates me he knows I know my business. "Impossible? No. Improbable? Yes.

"But here's the thing, Diomedes. Neither you nor me are amateurs at warfare. Been at this awhile now. What I've learned is war on this scale is preposterously complicated. The logistics of food alone for one starship . . . well thank Jove your people designed Coppers. In war, nothing, and I mean nothing—not even your own bowel movements—are perfectly predictable. War is hard, but this bastard is making it look easy. Too damn easy. So all that combined, where does it leave us? It leaves us to ask the question at the center of the maze: *qui bono*. So. *Qui bono,* Diomedes? Who benefits from this death and destruction on the Rim?"

I'll give one thing to Diomedes: whoever trained him to withhold his emotions deserves a medal. The man is less expressive than even the stone ancestors that watch us from the wall with their permanent sneers. I'm so focused on trying to chisel meaning from his stony face that I nearly jump out of my skin when my com crackles with an incoming call from Cassius. *"Howler One, do you register?"*

Diomedes shifts forward, hopeful.

"I register, Eagle One. Did you find Gaia or Thalia?" I ask.

"Negative. I have enemy contact west sector four," Cassius says.

"Shit. Really? I didn't think the enemy would still be picking Sungrave's bones. Ascomanni?"

"Volk." My heart beats faster. I stream Cassius's helmet feed into the air. A chain of captives shuffles through the gloom of a subterranean garage. *"Small team. They must still be drilling into the bunkers to make sure they get everyone. By the looks of it, they've found some Blues and Greens, all with interface plugs. High value Colors. Do you recognize the braves?"*

I zoom in on the enemy shown in Cassius's feed. Over their heavy armor the Obsidians wear pale ram furs with a crimson streak. Blood Horn aerial cavalry. Skarde's lot. That tracks. Of all my former Obsidian centurions, Skarde was always amongst the greediest.

"I recognize them."

"I count six braves so far," Cassius reports.

"There will be more," I warn. "Do not engage. You heard Sevro. We're standing by for instructions from Athena."

"I have the element of surprise. I could take them."

"No. Those aren't the Belt pirates you're used to. I trained those braves. They were frontliners on Earth and Mars. And if they're part of a larger war party, letting them know we're here is the last thing we want to do."

"Registers . . ." The word sticks in his throat as another column of captives appears a hundred paces behind the first. I curse.

The new column comprises entirely Pink and Violet children. Not one could be older than fourteen. They are the picture of misery. By the looks on their terrified faces, they know what awaits them. They remember their state propaganda—tales of pale Rising butchers and their satyr-like appetites for young flesh—and so does noble Cassius. His biometrics reflect the anxiety in his voice.

"Darrow, are you seeing this?"

"I am, but—"

"I can't just let this happen."

"Cassius, listen to me. We cannot leave the omega torch, or compromise this location. They cannot know we are here. We need our rendezvous instructions. Do not engage. Report to the perfumery. Remember why we are here. We are so close." I feel Diomedes's eyes on me. It's tempting to intervene just to impress upon him that we are not enemies, but the risk is too great. Aurae and Sevro have been listening to our communication in silence. Aurae finally weighs in.

"Listen to him, Cassius. When we reach Athena, we can save all of them. Think of the greater good."

"That's Darrow's job," he says.

"Cassius. You will die. You cannot take twelve of them on your own," I say. "Stand down."

"They have children," he says, and his armor shifts from reptile mode to lupine as it powers for combat. *"I'm sorry."*

He wasn't trying to call my bluff, but I crack like an egg. "Bloody-damn Bellona," I mutter. "I have your location. Track them to their ship. Wait for my support. We can jam their coms with our suits, then take them together."

I hear the smile in Cassius's voice. *"Registers, Howler One. Do hurry. If they get to their ship before you get here, we'll never catch up. I'll have no choice but to take all the glory."*

"Howler Two, you're closer. Support him in case I can't get there in time." Sevro does not reply. His com is on. I know he heard me. "Howler Two?"

"Negative. I'm on mission."

"Sevro . . ."

"You're telling me to abandon our only contact to Athena? Alone? Here? With Obsidians about? Naw. Bellona wants to spend his life for Moonies. Let him. I'm here for my kids. Maybe think about your own for once."

Sevro has never wounded me more than he does with those words. I'm struck silent. I see Diomedes watching me. My pain must be written all over my face because for the first time his eyes have softened. "I have no boots. I will slow you down," Diomedes says. "Go." I hesitate. "I will meet the others at the perfumery. I know it. You have my parole. *Go.*"

He's definitely lying, but I've planted the seed that needed planting. Even if he leaves our company, we will have earned his honor, and the worry about a hidden hand will keep his interest.

I storm out of the sanctum, calling Lyria as I race through the Raa family home. She replies from the cockpit of the *Archimedes* far to the north. "Truffle? Do you read me? You said you can fly. Time to prove it. Bring the *Archimedes* to Sungrave. Fly low. Pick up Aurae and Sevro, then lend fire support when able. We're going to need it."

54

DARROW

Pella! Pella! Pella!

"**H**OWLER ONE, WE'RE RUNNING OUT *of time*," Cassius says. He's followed the Obsidians outside Sungrave. They are almost to their ship with their captives. I beg him to hold on. He can't much longer. I run faster. My gravBoots pound the stone steps of the Spine. Boom boom boom ten stairs at a time. Slag it, I start to fly in a dizzying spiral upward. Dangerous gaining such speed indoors.

Cassius's helmet feed streams into mine taking up a corner of my HUD. He watches his quarry from a high-altitude entrance into the city. Below his position, the Obsidians lead their new slaves out from a massive gate flanked by stone caryatids toward a transport ship. The ship is parked in the center of an amphitheater-like depression in the mountain.

"They're loading them up. If they get airborne, that ship will outpace our boots. I have to slow them down."

I'm watching his feed so closely that I'm hit with vertigo and almost crash into a fallen statue as he plummets off his perch toward the rocks below. He stops himself only two meters above the slope—ever the patrician showman—and ricochets at a near right angle to skim down the western face of Sungrave's mountain range.

I avoid crashing and gain confidence. My speed doubles. Antechambers, passageways, grottos blur past. I hit the breach through which we entered the city just as Cassius begins his attack. He flies low and fast over the dark mountainside. The warriors don't see him coming in the dim light. With his razor out to his right, he decapitates an Obsidian shoving the Pink boys along on the transport's ramp. The others barely even notice it's happened. Cassius turns his flightpath right to flick off the arm of another Obsidian manhandling two of the Violet captives. He skewers a third Obsidian in the eye-shield of his helmet as he turns toward the noise.

Three down. Nine left. But now he has their attention.

By the time I exit the main breach and rocket into the sky, Cassius has shot out the other side of the Obsidians. A graceful flier, he absorbs only the G's he must to slow his ricochet back into them to shoot through their ranks on a second pass. It is called the *pella maneuver*—in which an armored Gold ricochets back and forth like a bouncing ball between two walls, murdering with each pass. In times long gone, the pella was an impressive and reliable tactic. It was also something we taught our Volk braves to counter in the third year of the war. Cassius is in for it.

I gain altitude and head west toward the fight. It's three kilometers away. Wind buffets my body. The broken mountain range blurs beneath me as I pick up speed. The fight still hidden from my direct line of sight, I watch Cassius's feed with mounting anxiety.

He races back toward the Obsidians in his pella maneuver, but instead of finding a bewildered enemy, shocked and awed by his sudden attack, he finds an organized enemy with tactics refined in the killing fields of the Core. He will not have heard the first Obsidian to spot him yell, "Pella! Pella! Pella!" Nor that his fellows have taken up the call and shouted out numbers to make wedges by threes. By the time he's upon them, the Obsidians formed their wedges. Almost all the wedges are led by a brave with a shield or in heavy armor and with a heavy triarii's spear—and flanked by heavy guns.

Cassius is fast, so the enemy is slow to open fire, but Cassius spends so much time dodging the unexpected salvo that his attack is wasted. He feints bailing out, giving him a gap, and passes an Obsidian wedge close enough to jab at the helmet of the lead Obsidian. The blade screeches off the heavy metal, and Cassius barely bats a spear away from impaling his thigh. He fires backward with his pulseFist, missing the other two. He's wasted his charge on only one wedge, and as he passes he does not see the Obsidians with gravBoots shoot upward from the wedges to track him.

I'm closing in. I scan the sky. It is clear. No support ships. I pull Bad

Lass, prime my pulseFist, and fly several thousand meters higher, until I'm directly overtop the Obsidian ship. Cassius and the Obsidians are dots below. I see no other enemies in any direction. I angle head-down and kill my boots. Freefalling, I watch Cassius's feed. He ricochets back for his next pass.

Unfamiliar with the Obsidian tactics, it takes him a moment to realize there are fewer wedges than before, and by the time he wonders where the other Obsidians went, they're screaming down at him like falcons. I warn him, and he veers right just in time to dodge the first Obsidian's lance. He's quick enough to slash the netman's net in half and veer upward just before it envelopes him, but he doesn't see the heavy hammer that hits him in the left shoulder like an arrow hitting an eagle.

Cassius careens sideways and smashes down in a cloud of shattered sulfur crystals. I continue falling, still unseen by the occupied enemy. Cassius's helmet cam view is rocks on the ground as he heaves for air. He tries to stand and falls flat, rolling sideways to see six braves sprinting at him with axes the size of Reds and scalping knives meant for hair like his. Time to focus. I turn off his visual feed and pick my targets by altitude.

The airborne Obsidians form a triangle over the fight. I fall upon them at a hundred and eight kilometers an hour. I chop through the neck of the highest Obsidian. Recall my blade. Chop another on my left as I continue down to the third. He turns on me before I get there, so I shoot him as he raises his railgun. His pulseShield takes the first two blasts. The third bends the shield back until it glows opaque. He deactivates it just before it melts inward. He banks left. I conserve ammunition, mirror his trajectory left, pirouette past his pulsefire, bat his axe to the side, and spear him through the weak armor at his throat before carrying on to the ground.

Skarde should be embarrassed. His lads are lazy today. They thought they had Io whipped. Were they still in my army, this lack of discipline would not stand. That thought fills me with contempt. These men deserted me. They left the Free Legions to die. So now they will.

Against Obsidians, speed is all. Combine that with constantly shifting between vertical levels in the sphere of battle, and you stand a chance.

I swoop down on the pack of Obsidians just as they track me from the ground. I shoot one point-blank and snap my whip around another. The third thrashes as Cassius's blade punches through his back. The one I stabbed in the throat in the air finally lands with a thud. I fly upward immediately, dragging the Obsidian my whip ensnared by his leg. I contract the whip into a blade two hundred meters up. The razor slices through his armored calf. Released, he plummets down. I follow and use his mass to conceal my descent.

The wounded brave windmills haplessly at me as he freefalls. I stay just out of his reach but close enough that his friends on the ground don't see me coming until it's too late. I veer off my cover just before the brave impacts the ground.

My trick didn't fool everyone. Something blurs toward me from the left. An impact rocks me. My vision flickers black. I wake a half second later, needles jolting through my body. Rail slug. Huge one. Must have hit my pulseShield. A dent the size of an egg has made a home in the left pectoral of my armor.

Furious at the dent in my new gear, I look for someone to kill.

"Two o'clock," Cassius calls. I track him in my helmet's rearview camera feed—a blur of gray metal tearing toward me like a bus. I wait, boost up with my gravBoots, invert, and cleave the Obsidian's head down the center as he passes under at what must be sixty kilometers an hour. I revert, land, and flick the blood off my blade. It freezes in a long strand and shatters as it hits the ground.

"Engines hot! Engines hot!" Cassius calls.

I turn to see two surviving braves retreating onto one of the transports. They open fire on me. I activate my aegis and it shunts power from the pulseFist to form a blue shield on my left arm. I buck as the rounds pound the barrier. The ship takes off and just before the door closes, Cassius gives a boost from his gravBoots to land like a grasshopper inside. The doors seal behind him and the ship's engines groan as it gets airborne.

Shit.

I burst into the air, pursue, and land on its hull before it gains enough velocity to outpace my boots. I stab my razor into the hull to gain traction. Walking like an old man with a cane, I make slow progress toward the cockpit. The transport gains altitude rapidly. I hack off its coms array as I pass. The antennae pinwheels toward the shrinking ground, black but for rivers of magma. Dark clouds whip past, stained red by the transport's external lights. Just before I reach the cockpit, the transport bucks. I'm caught so off guard I lose my grip on my razor and slam into its top gun turret.

I'm dazed. Falling. Spinning like a leaf through blackness and clouds. I arrest my fall with my boots, gain my bearings, zip out of the murk of the clouds, and see the transport to the south carving a gash of light into the darkness as it falls in a nosedive.

By the time I catch up, the transport has crash-landed at the foothills of a volcano range. Not knowing what I'll find inside, I land on the top hull first to retrieve my razor. I say a silent prayer when I find Bad Lass right where I left it—half-stuck in the hull just shy of the cockpit.

Thraxa would have killed me if I lost her family blade. I jerk it out and walk back along the top hull to the ramp. I hop down just as Cassius stumbles out. He almost takes my head off with a blind swing. I deflect his slash and call out his name. He realizes his mistake, booms a laugh, and embraces me. Helmet to helmet. *"Gorydamn. Gorydamn. You weren't exaggerating. Those crows can fight. But man . . . Vulcan himself would stroke his loins to this armor."* He runs his gauntlets over the scored, blood-spattered gear.

"Idiot." I shove him. "You almost got yourself killed."

"Now, now. I just wanted to see the Reaper in an open field," he says. *"The verdict is in. You're a menace to savage and civilized alike."* I pause, reflecting back on the battle for the first time. It's been years since I felt in the flow like that. I grin ear to ear despite myself. The training with Cassius has brought my spark back.

"Are you injured?" I ask.

"Concussed, certainly. So, don't shove me again. One of them got me with a hammer."

"I saw. It was a big hammer."

"Right. Like, what's he trying to prove? Is my armor prime?"

He turns. It's shockingly only scratched. I look at the dent on mine. That's not fair. Then I remember the civilians he risked our mission for.

I head into the hold of the transport, expecting the worst. The dim interior is filled with cages. The captives meant for gods know what are not dead from the crash. They cough behind filthy nanoplast barriers, huddled together in fear, droopy and sedate from the shabbiness of the cage's oxygen filters. Several of the Pinks have broken their legs or arms in the landing. They cry in the arms of Green architects. I feel sick at the sight until I realize they are not crying in horror. They are crying in relief. I didn't help Cassius to save them. I helped Cassius because I didn't want him to die. And he would have died, for strangers. A font of respect and love for the man grows in me. Sevro called him shallow. He is not. Not by a longshot. He sways a little at my side. *"Yes. Certainly concussed. But not a bad bill for a good deed."*

"Not a bad bill," I admit. "Not a bad bill at all."

"What you said to Diomedes . . ." I turn, already wondering how we'll evacuate the civilians. His helmet is close to mine. He was listening, then. *"What was all that?"*

"Just a theory."

Then the waste rumbles behind us, and I turn to see our actual bill.

55

DARROW

Demigod

FOUR DARK TRIANGLES RACE toward us over the volcanic plain. They are Republic assault dropships painted with the ancient Obsidian runes of the Allfather. Before I can hail the *Archimedes* the jamming arrays that jut from their bloated underbellies like stingers cause our long-range coms to die with an insectoid screech.

"Oh, Jove. That's not good." Cassius's voice is filled with static.

"I did tell you they wouldn't be alone," I reply. This is not what was supposed to happen today, so of course it happened. I actually laugh. Maybe it needed to happen for me to realize I can't keep running. I have to take a stand somewhere. Like Cassius with Sevro. Am I so afraid of my own braves, and the guilt they make me feel?

When the attack ships are the size of thumbnails, Obsidian aerial cavalry deploy out of their bellies. *"So what is it then? Fifty for each of us?"* Cassius asks.

"Looks like."

"And they'll be just as good as the ones we just fought?"

"Better. See the dropper with the golden ram banner? That's Jarl Skarde's."

"Jarl Skarde? Who is he?"

"One bad son of a bitch," I reply. "We do not want to fight him."

"Right. Do we have that choice?"

"You did. We don't."

"Right. Where the Hades is the Archimedes?" Cassius asks.

"Picking up the others soon as they're done with the omega torch.

Then coming to us," I say. "If it didn't run into its own trouble. With Lyria at the stick—"

"She can get it here. But she'll be too late," Cassius says and glances back to the hold. The civilians may not be able to see the Obsidians, but they can hear the war drum beat blasting from the ships.

"I'm not leaving so let's not bicker at the last. You can escape into the volcanoes, lose them in the spews."

"Oh, shut up."

"Mars needs you. Your boy—"

"If Pax grows up to be as stupid as you, I'll be a proud father. I'm not leaving you."

"Really?" He sounds incredibly touched. *"You'd really die here with me? I just . . . well . . . I thought that was your and Sevro's thing. Thank you, Darrow."*

He must have gotten hit in the head harder than I thought. "We're not going to die. I have a plan."

"I knew you would. Crafty sod. What is it then? Did you bring another of Portobello's friends?"

"Bring me the heads of the men you killed. Now."

"Prime." He hurries into the transport and returns carrying the heads of the Obsidians he killed. *"What now?"* I spear them both onto my razor like olives. *"Well. That's grotesque."*

"We killed their war brothers. Best thing we can do is rub their noses in it, so they don't just waste us with their assault ships."

"Some plan," he mutters. *"These maniacs were in your army?"*

"Compared to Gorgons they're cuddly. They're scoping us now, seeing the heads of their brothers on my blade. Once they get closer, they'll see how good our gear is. They love gear, and they've never seen armor like this. That's when I'll reveal myself."

He grows quiet. *"Reveal yourself?"*

"Yes. I'm something of a demigod to them."

"Like Perseus?"

"More like Heracles."

He turns on me. *"And they call me arrogant."*

I shrug. "Have you ever had three hundred thousand Obsidian warriors chanting your name before falling in an Iron Rain?" He says nothing. "Then get behind me if you want to live."

He gets behind me. I step forward with my razor held in my right hand. Distorted by the heat rising off the streams of magma, the warriors form a single, hundred-headed beast made of glinting armor and flapping fur. The beast dissolves as they envelope us and hammer down like half-ton nails until we're surrounded by a dome of huge killers. Their warhelms are fused with gold sigil trophies. Their weapons are comically large. Axes and spears and rifles not even a Gold could wield with ease.

They are extremely displeased about the heads on my razor.

"Da Guffan und Trolnjr!" a berserker shouts. He points his long axe at two of the heads in my possession. He follows with a song-like requiem in Nagal. "Here have fallen Guffan and Tolnjr, Horns of the Pale Ram that broke Sungrave, and fell in the Wolf Rain upon Terra. Avenge them!"

That is as articulate as it will get.

A dozen of the braves howl curses, but their leader holds them back. Skarde is spindly for an Obsidian. He wears heavily battered green armor with a Boetian ram's black horns bursting from his greathelm. He floats above us with the grace of a mermaid. His cape is grander than the ram cloaks of his men. It is purple and white. Dragon scale. The scales are still iridescent. Which means fresh. Very fresh.

Skarde was one of my old special forces centurions. He was not my favorite Obsidian leader. In fact, even Sevro found him a little creepy. While not as famous or terrifying as Valdir the Unshorn, Skarde is a tricky warrior and a solid tactician. Though callow at heart, he has the sort of low cunning that makes certain contemptible men utterly indispensable in war. Decisive, brutal, his greatest weakness has always been his dragon-sized greed and his planet-sized pride.

"The fact that he is here scavenging is good news. It means, in likelihood, that he's off-grid," I tell Cassius.

"Yes. Such good news."

Skarde finally lands and calls out in a mixture of Nagal and Common, which more or less means: "By Brokkr's bulbous cock, look at that armor! I need it. I want it. I'll have it. True kin may have the first Gold, who killed your brothers. War kin may have the second Gold, who hides behind the first like a beaten whore. Do not damage the armor. No blunt weapons or plasma. Be not messy, my lads. The artificers must have something to work with."

A dozen spear-wielders separate from the rest and come toward me. They're not hurried in the least.

"Nak sada tjr na fan!" I shout before they are halfway.

They stop and look at one another, confused to hear their own language from a Gold, especially spoken in the accent of the Valkyrie Spires.

"Nan fada hyr kan. Du van sombrjn schleppen fan dag, Skarde. The one who touches me shall be castrated, if not first then you last, Skarde," I add in Common. "You always were a slutty carrion dog sniffing about for extra vitals. Should have expected to find you squatting over Sungrave's corpse. But abducting children? That's new."

Skarde is taken aback and puzzled by so specific an insult. He laughs, but it comes out like more of a titter. I imagine his piercing eyes narrowing, collecting, scheming from within his humid helm. He holds up a hand to halt his men. "Your armor is heavy. Of the Core, like your razor." His eyes linger on the razor, thinking he recognizes it. "Do you know me from its battlefields, Gold? And how is it the accent of the Spires graces your slippery tongue?"

I laugh at him. He does not hate that. In fact, it intrigues him.

"When you sold your phalera for the Wolf Rain, I knew you weren't sentimental, Skarde. Didn't think you had a shit memory too," I say.

Skarde releases his great spear from its back magnet, extends it to its full three-meter length and sets it on his shoulder. "Name yourself or I'll stick this so far up your piss eye your father will feel the tickle in his bum."

"Something like the Fear Knight did on Mercury then, eh, Skarde? To the Free Legions? To the men and women you once called kin in arms? Oh no. I forgot. You weren't there, because you're a faithless oathbreaking cur."

The Obsidians look at one another in confusion.

"Name yourself," Skarde demands.

"Before you bothered with moons, you liberated planets in my name. How far you've fallen. You know me, Skarde. You all know me. Or have you forgotten the man who put the razor in Ragnar's hands?"

I lower my helmet to bare my face to the warriors and to Io's freezing, poisonous air. It's horribly painful. My skin starts to ache fast. They lean back, kind of like they're pissing themselves. I think it's fear. I really hope it's fear. Then one makes a sign of protection. My skin feels like it's falling off. Poor Romulus. I'd hate to die this way. I put on a very disappointed face, and let it become a very weird, very malevolent smile.

I raise the helmet again, mute the helm, moan for breath, and wait. If I'm the next one who talks, Cassius and I will die.

"Tyr Morga," Skarde whispers. "You are dead. Dead in the sands of Mercury."

"With your brothers of the Free Legions?" I ask. "With your sisters? I looked to the sky for Valdir, for Sefi, for you, Skarde. I prayed to the Allmother for the kin of Ragnar to remember their oaths. To deliver on their promise to follow the Morning Star. To protect the Republic. But no. Skarde breaks oaths. Like a noman. Now you're out here playing Gold in the dimness. How can you live with such shame? Where is Sigurd? Where is your son? How can he look upon his honorless father?"

Guilt has a corrosive effect on self-confidence, particularly for warriors. The Obsidians could kill us without losing a man. But they eye the gloom and fury of the volcanoes as if waiting for an army to emerge. That is not all that restrains them. Obsidians delight in war. Not only for the violence, though they love that, but for the truths war flays bare. When the enemy is closing in and you're on your back foot, that's when you discover who your brothers and sisters really are. For ten years, wherever the fighting was the thickest, they needed only to look to the sky to find me on my way.

I know the Rain phalera on their armor because I pinned it to each of their chests. I see three who wear the platinum pendant of a rat, eleven with the white fist of the Earth campaign, others still wearing their horse helms with the white horsehair crests of Pegasus Legion.

"*Is it working?*" Cassius asks. "*That all seemed a terrible amount of provocation, Darrow.*"

I ignore him. "What have you become, Hafnar . . . and you, Lothgar . . . and you, Loka. It is Loka, yes? I see a rat badge. You fought with me in the tunnels of Mars. 'Big Cousin,' wasn't that what the Red children called you? You wore their ribbons in your hair. Now . . . what. You take little boys and sell them at market? Or do you keep them for yourself? Have you learned the ways of your new master? Will you sell me to him too?"

Instead of facing their own guilt, they embrace denial.

"He cannot be Tyr Morga. He is too short," one says.

"That's Sun Industries gear. Eight-bit screws. Maybe it is him." I know that voice. Sigurd, Skarde's son. An amiable young man, neither as clever nor as greedy as his father, he adores the arcades and nightclubs of the Republic and was once in love with Thraxa. "That's Bad Lass in his hands."

"It's a Gold trick! Shoot him and let's take their gear. I want to go back to the Garter and play in the orchards with my new nymphs," another rumbles.

"Flay him, the cur who takes Ragnar's name in vain," a berserker whispers. "Flay him. Flay him. Flay the pretender." The berserker comes at me in a rush with two armor-boring fists whirring. Sigurd calls for him to stop. He does not.

I bend under the berserker's left jab and come around his flank where I hack off both his legs at the knee and then take off his head for good measure. My helmet's sensors warn me. Two more descend from above. One like a hawk, the other a tiger. I shoot straight up past the hawk, split the tiger in half, then come down on the hawk from behind like a needle. My blade goes through his back armor and into his spine and I drive him down and stake him to the crusty ground. To them, it might look supernatural. But they don't feel the hamstring I just strained. The left one. It aches like a snakebite. I went for drama, not form. I hear Cassius going. "*Tsk. Tsk.*"

The wind howls as the men die at my feet. No longer interested in testing me, some of the braves make signs of protection. Sigurd, slender for an Obsidian with kudo horns jutting from his helm, rushes forward and bares his throat. Skarde jerks his son back and calls him an idiot. Skarde's voice is barely above a murmur.

"Tyr Morga. How . . ."

"Why, Skarde. Not how. I am here to claim what is rightfully mine. The life of Volsung Fá. He killed Sefi. The sister of Ragnar. Your sworn queen, last I checked. I've come to declare *ashvar* upon him. I've come to claim the contest of blood that is my right as a son of the Valkyrie Spires."

"Tyr Morga . . . that will not happen. You must leave this place. When Fá learns you live, he will offer a mountain of helium for your head. He will not fight you. He will drop atomics on whatever city he believes you inhabit. He will scorch a continent from space to kill you. He does not abide by *ashvar*."

"So he is a hypocrite. Is that not how he rose? Claiming to avenge Thalia, a dead wife?

"Here is my head. Come claim your helium, Skarde."

He wouldn't dare, not in front of his men. They might even kill him for it. Not all of them, but someone. Maybe in his sleep. Maybe when he's bedding his new slaves. He knows that, so it's impossible to tell if he really does have honor when he says, "We will not fight the man who gave Ragnar the razor. No. We are not savage dogs. But you have no place here. The Rim is your enemy too. Let us play with it. We are helping you. Go back to Mars."

Is that how they justify it to themselves?

Sigurd approaches his father. "Father, how many times have I heard you moan on about Fá? His favoritism of the Ascomanni. His rigid hand? His Bloodguard? Is this not a sign? Is this not what we prayed—"

There's a fizzing sound and then a triplet of noise—*panng, ffftt, bshhhhhhh.* Sigurd stumbles. The Obsidian to his left jerks. Lines of blue fire arc across that man's pulseShield before the shield collapses with a shriek. Something slams into another Brave's breastplate, punctures it, then detonates. Gore sprays out. Skarde uses his own body as a shield for his son, Sigurd, and slips back into the protection of his men. "*Snjeg! Snipers! Testudo!*"

I'm so startled Cassius has to tackle me to the ground. Slugs scream overhead.

56

DARROW

Dust Mice

As the Obsidians begin making their formations, two specters bound in and leap over the nearest magma river. They are shaped like humans but made of distorted air. GhostCloaks paired with skipboats, and moving fast.

One of the ghosts rushes for one of the main clusters of Obsidian and fires a blinking object onto an Obsidian forming the side of a testudo before bursting away. The second blur hurls an EMP bomb. It pulses, but only two of the suits go down. A hail of sniper fire slams into the testudo. The overlapping shields absorb the worst of it.

"*Mice! Mice! Mice!*" bellows an Obsidian.

"*X testudo! Bastion! Bastion's by prox! Thorns west!*"

Then the first explosive detonates white. The second detonates a heartbeat later and both ghosts disappear in the resultant smoke. They were short, the ghosts. Short enough to be Reds. It's not Dustwalkers at all.

"*The Daughters,*" Cassius shouts from atop me.

"No shit!"

A terrible sound rumbles over the plains as a missile strikes one of the Obsidian ships. It crashes fifty paces to my left, crushing a brave. Its missile stores detonate. The shockwaves send Cassius spinning off me. The explosions flash-melt a pack of sulfur ice. I rise to my knees. Yellow fog cloaks the battlefield.

Nearly blind, I find Cassius sprawled on the ground nearby. I help him up. Thermal is useless with all the magma on the periphery of the battle. The fog of war becomes literal, the fighters, indistinct golems and spirits—bizarre, atavistic silhouettes appearing and disappearing at random. A hulking mass rushes for me, and then mysteriously sheds his right leg from the left knee down. Cassius swears in shock as a four-legged shadow scrambles atop the Obsidian, savages him with huge, flashing claws, and then heads our way with a weird, loping gait. Cassius raises his razor.

"*Kuon hound,*" he warns. I shove him to the side as the beast scampers past on all fours, knives glimmering in either hand and disappears again into the yellow murk. "*What the fuck?*"

"Sevro," I reply with a grin. Athena had assets on the moon after all. "Let him hunt."

"*Where'd he come from? Where's the* Archi?"

"Dunno. We need to end this fast. Find Skarde and put him down. Stick with me."

Together we hunt through the fog. Ghosts flicker. Obsidians leap like gods. One soars into flight and then disappears in a flash that refracts in the fog—already freezing back into crystalline form—to make tears of white fire as his ruins rain down.

"Skarde, five o'clock," I tell Cassius. A huge, horn-crowned mass runs at top speed after an escaping ghost. Skarde lands and his spear penetrates the ghost to pin it to the ground. He tears at the ghost, rips off its helmet, and the ghostCloak guise ripples away to show a screaming Red woman impaled on his spear. Skarde hurls her into the magma flow and then swings a heavy fist at nothing. His punch summons a spray of blood and then a corpse from the ether. Sulfur crystals spew back as the ghost's skipBoots fire against the ground, trying to escape even though their wearer is already dead.

There is no escape for our would-be-rescuers.

That's the problem with getting the undivided attention of Obsidian air cav. They can take a punch, and once their teeth are in—whether on the ground or in the sky—they don't let go. They chew until you wish you never had the idea to test them at all.

For the first minute the Daughters had the upper hand. After that the tide started to turn, and turn bad. But I see our opportunity as Skarde pulls his spear from another corpse and tosses the corpse into the magma river. He's alone. Three braves are rushing to bring him back into their formation. I claim Skarde, and give Cassius the braves. I goose my boots and shoot toward Skarde like a ballista bolt. Skarde's battle sense is uncanny. Somehow he sees me coming. Backlit by the pulsing red river, he fires at me as I fly at him. Energy crackles across my shield, but the shield holds.

I invert, flying with my back to the ground just under his spear thrust to hack into the back of his thigh. My razor shears through the metal and finds flesh. I hard stop and pivot from flying back to standing on my feet. G's pound me, but I'm behind Skarde. With all my strength, I drive my razor into the power unit that lies beneath the armor of his lower back and twist. Sparks spew. The armor dies with a shriek and Skarde seizes as if petrified by Medusa herself.

I kick him but he doesn't go to his knees. Then Sevro appears from nowhere and tackles his legs out. Skarde falls. Sevro wrests the spear from his hand and runs off into the fray. I grab both of the ram horns on Skarde's helmet. Powered by the strength of my armor, I haul the giant into the air to dangle him over the magma river. With Cassius coming to guard my back, I max out the volume on my external speakers, linking it with Sevro's armor and Cassius's. Even I am shocked by the magnitude of sound produced by our triumvirate.

A voice made of thunder rumbles over the battlefield.

"THIS IS REAPER. I HAVE YOUR JARL. I HAVE SKARDE. YIELD."

No one listens, not even with Skarde dangling beneath me. The battle is a mess, spread out over a kilometer now. It does not end just because I want it to. Obsidians peer out at me from their testudos, or down from the sky. Ghosts skip in a dozen directions. Bodies lay rent and broken. Pieces too. A leg. A head. A torso. The killing does not stop. It cannot. No one can afford not to fire. I am reminded again why I hate war. I shout and shout but even the voice of a god sponsored by Sun Industries is powerless to stop the killing.

It's a smaller voice that brings hope to end the violence—a smaller voice, and a ship that evens the odds. Lyria's words crackle through static. I look to the sky. *"There's my girl!"* Cassius shouts. I don't know if he means Lyria or his ship.

The *Archimedes* races in with its guns blazing. Lyria's flying is sloppy, but the *Archimedes* is more powerful than the assault shuttles. Whoever is on the guns is deadly accurate. One of the enemy shuttles dies in a ball of fire. It has a sobering effect on the Obsidians, and they finally start noticing that I have their war chief by his horns over the river. I call for Lyria to hold fire when I see Sigurd leading his father's men in a withdrawal to the other side of the river under the protection of their remaining ships. The *Archimedes* lowers to protect the Daughters, who form up on Sevro. He flies toward me still holding Skarde's spear. Cassius flies the other way to help the civilians. They actually nod at one another.

Sevro pokes Skarde's armored belly with it as he comes to a midair stop.

"Move. You're blocking the way," I snarl. "He's heavy." I drop Skarde on our side of the river. Sevro lands on top of the man's depowered armor to be eye to eye with me. "Took your time," I say to him.

He grunts. *"I was on mission.* Archi *got tangled with two Volk ships near Sungrave while picking us up. Daughters came to help, but their ship went down. Big mess. All thanks to Bellona."*

"They don't have a ship?"

"I just said it's down."

"Then get their wounded aboard the *Archi.* Help Cassius with the civilians and children."

Sevro looks at the Obsidians gathering around Sigurd on the opposite bank of the river. *"We should kill them all."*

"We can't. Literally, and they need to take a message back to the Volk from me. Civilians. Wounded. Go."

With a mutter, he leaves me alone with the Obsidians. Grunting I bear Skarde to the other bank and drop his mass in front of his son and braves. Just over sixty of them remain alive. I wish I could see their eyes instead of their battered helmets. I bury my contempt. They'll be recording me with their cams. What I say here will travel through the main army like wildfire.

I prod Skarde with my toe. "He's alive and still has a little air yet in his helmet." I sigh. "Brothers, I did not come here to spill your blood. But look at yourselves. What would Ragnar think? What have you become? Look around you. Is this right? Is this the home you were promised, by Ragnar, by Sefi? Where are the leaning godTrees and the summer seas? Where are the vineyards and marble cities that sparkle in the autumn dawn? Where are the children who sing your names and shower you in spring flowers? You have lost them in this . . . your winter of violence. You have lost yourselves.

"I did not come to judge you. I did not come to punish you. I came to remind you of the oaths you took! It is brothers who find us when we are lost. Brothers who guide us home to the hearth and halls of our mothers and fathers. Go now and tell the warbands what you have seen here. Tell them Tyr Morga has come to challenge Volsung Fá to single combat. Tell them Tyr Morga has come to lead you home as Ragnar would have wanted. But most of all, tell Fá to expect me."

I head away from them, knowing I've just opened Pandora's box, but enough is enough from this Obsidian fraud.

By the time I make it into the cargo bay of the *Archi* it is crammed full of Pink children along with Green architects. The Daughters are strewn along the starboard side with their casualties. The air thick with the screams of the wounded and the crying of children—and all this in victory. I head for the cockpit and hear Lyria's anxiety before I get there. Three signatures approach on our scanners. "Boss, we gotta go, we gotta go," she says. "Big ships en route. Big ships."

"Cassius is coming with the last of the civilians. Sevro's right behind. Watch via the cameras. Soon as he's back, lift off and head for the volcanoes. Cass will take the stick." I squeeze her shoulder. She's soaked in sweat. "Good work, Lagalos." She grins back at me, nervous. "Was that Aurae on guns?"

"Negative. The gloomy bastard. The Raa."

A little stunned, I head back to the chute to the top gun turret. Diomedes's face peers down.

"The children?" he asks.

"Safe."

"Shall I return to the brig?"

I glance into the main hall. Three Daughters are carrying a charred lump of a man into the medBay. I duck my head back into the chute. "I still have your parole?" Diomedes nods. "We have guests. Stay on guns."

By the time I make it back to the cargo bay Cassius has boarded with the last of the children. Three Pink boys cling to him. They might have held their breath against Io's air, but the cold found them. Their fingers will be frostbitten from where they gripped his freezing armor. He is tender handing them over to Aurae. I shout for him to get to the cockpit. The ship shudders and Lyria lifts off. "Where we going?" Cassius asks as he passes me.

"I'll find out. In the meantime, lose them in the volcanoes, and punch to orbit in one of those ash columns soon as you can."

"These are the Daughters we came for? They're mangled."

"Cassius. Cockpit. Now."

He goes. Soon as he's gone there's a shout as Sevro lands along with an Obsidian with kudu horns. The Daughters scramble up and level their rifles. "Dammit, Sevro. We don't need a hostage," I say. The ship shudders as Lyria lifts off.

Sigurd lifts his hands to show he has no weapon. Sevro steps in front of the rifles. "He came over the river and flagged me down to surrender. Figured we could use the information now that Fá knows we're here."

"Fá is a plague. To my people. To all peoples. I want to help you kill him," Sigurd says. "Many of the braves believe as I do. They will rejoice to see you are alive, Tyr Morga."

"Good thinking," I say to Sevro. "Any of you got cuffs?"

A woman wide as an anvil throws me reinforced wire cuffs. I fit them on Sigurd. The woman stares up at the Obsidian, and I realize she must be the leader of the Daughters. Her flexible scorosuit is yellow and tan, like the wastes of Io, and bears the stitches of a significant size-down. The lower half of her face is covered with a scaled kryll, the rest wrapped with a yellow headscarf. Her eyes are hidden behind shaded goggles flecked with thawing Obsidian blood. She doffs the goggles, revealing the unmistakable scarlet eyes of a Jovian ultraheavy—Reds bred to work in punishing radiation and gravity 2.4 times that of Earth. The rarest of our breed. Big bodies. Big hearts. Short lives.

"Athena?" I ask.

"Cheon. Chiliarch of the Black Owls. Athena sent us to bring you to her," she says.

"They weren't expecting us. Obviously," Sevro says. "They've been running ops trying to evac civilians on Io."

"So, Cassius was on the right track," I say to a scowl from Sevro. "Well met, Cheon. Good to see Red eyes in the fight." I extend a gauntlet. She looks at it but does not take it.

Her voice is deep and masculine. "You let their jarl go. We had to leave our dead. I lost half my column. More in ten minutes than four weeks of fighting. And you want to shake hands?"

I withdraw my hand. "Where is Athena?" I ask. "Our pilot needs to know where to go."

"Europa. Athena has taken the Deep," Cheon answers.

"Which city?" Sevro asks.

"The whole bloody thing," she says. "We know Europa's next, after Callisto. We're ready. The Deep is impregnable. We'll blow the sealifts soon as they breach atmosphere. Even an Obsidian arm isn't long enough to reach the bottom of the sea. But Fá's welcome to drown trying."

Aurae is confused. "And the people on the surface?"

Cheon shrugs. "That's a question for Athena."

57

LYRIA

Lamps in the Storm

THE SHIP SHUDDERS FROM turbulence as we descend on Europa. My mag boots clunk as I go into the *Archimedes*'s tiny brig. The Obsidian sits up behind the duroglass. He is Darrow's height but a little more slender. He looks confused as I squat on the floor. The swaying of the ship makes my head ache. "I have questions," I say in Nagal.

"Who are you? How do you speak our language?" he asks.

"You're the one in the cell," I reply. "I ask the questions."

"You are the one who hacked the door and turned the camera off," he says, nodding to the camera above. "Darrow does not know you are here. So let us be polite. I am Sigurd, son of Skarde, of the tribe of the—"

"Volga Fjorgan. This name ring a bell?" He snorts. I pull the sidearm I filched from the armory and set it on my knee. "Does her name ring a bell?" He chuckles. "What's so funny?"

"You are saying: 'Does this name ring my balls.'"

"Oh."

"It is not your fault. We have many words for snow, ice, death, and especially balls. I can speak in Common very well, if you prefer," he replies in Common. "You do not need that gun. I am a friend of Red." I narrow my eyes. "You do not believe me. That is all right. I am in a cell."

"Volga Fjorgan," I say.

"Yes. I know the name. There are not many women Obsidian amongst us. Part of the stupidity that brought us out here was blaming them for our years of slavery. They sold us, their boys, it is true, but it was an impossible choice. Sell us or all their children die, boys and girls. Gold is good at shifting blame. But it is Volarus. Not Fjorgan."

"What else?" I ask.

"I do not know. I am Fifth Band." He shows five torcs made of iron on his wrist. "Not First Band. My father complains too much to be close to Fá's favor. But warriors love gossip. I know she is the Fá's grand-daughter, but Fá calls her daughter. She follows him like a shadow—"

"She's not imprisoned?" I ask.

He frowns. "Not that I know. She was given a command for Callisto, this much I've heard."

"A command?"

"*Ja.* Soldiers of her own. To make this a kingdom for the Volk. A good little soldier."

I shake my head. "That's not true. She'd never help with this."

He shrugs. "If you call me a liar we will have to fight." He waits and I don't. "There is gossip too. That she was an unnatural birth. A freak from a Grimmus tube. And—"

"She's not a freak," I snap.

He smiles, a little sad. "We are all freaks," he says and shows his sigils. "They made us so."

When it's clear Sigurd knows nothing else of Volga, I seal the brig behind me and sway back to the cargo bay. We're low now, close to the sea. Out the viewport three cities bob to the west like lonely lamps, and like lamps they wait to be blown out.

An Obsidian wind is coming, and according to what I heard Cheon the Black Owl say to her troops, there will be nothing the Golds of Europa can do to stop it. Io is done. Callisto blooms with atomic mush-rooms. Ganymede hides behind its orbital shields. Europa's ships were spent over Io trying to protect the Garter and their liege lords, the Raa. The floating island cities of the sea moon lie vulnerable. Their people wait for doom. Athena does not. She and her Daughters are safe beneath the sea.

Supposedly.

I pass Aurae as she explains the refuge that awaits us to the Pink chil-dren. They gathered around her as we traveled from Io to Europa. She warms their hearts with tales of Athena's goodness and charity, and promises no army can penetrate the Deep.

"The Deep is a collection of cities beneath the seas of Europa, which are the deepest on all the worlds," she says. "These cities were carved into the solid core of the moon itself. The place began as a mining operation, you see. And like all things, it evolved. It became a place for industry, research, and, yes, weapons manufacturing. But Athena has taken all six cities of the Deep. If she did that, it means she has an army that will protect us all, and weapons too. We will be safe down there even if the Obsidians huff and puff on the surface."

The Pink children smile at Aurae's claim. One, a boy no older than eleven, with hair like a sunset, sets his small palm in my hand.

"You'll be safe too," he says. "You don't have to look so sad."

I kiss his hand and leave him to story time.

I wish I was that young again. Nothing feels safe anymore. Not even my memories. Not even my friends. Could Volga really be a war commander of Fá's?

I head for a viewport to watch the waves.

The hold is dim and echoes with the sound of the rain and the roar of the ocean. Weapons crates creak against their fastenings. Most of the Black Owls—those who ain't crammed in the medBay pumped full of painkillers—snore right through it all. They are scary, and I'm proud of how scary Reds can be, but at the same time I saw what the Obsidians did to them. Tore them apart like paper dolls when they got ahold of them. If I didn't show up with the *Archi*, it woulda gone bad, fast-like, that's what Cassius said after we'd gotten off the moon. He kissed me on the head and we toasted with Sevro's moonshine.

Still, I feel like an idiot. Cheon could pound me to paste, an Obsidian could pound Cheon to paste, and here I was thinking I'd go amongst them and have a chance of rescuing Volga. Bloody idiot is what I am. Doesn't sound like Volga much wants to be rescued. I scratch the surgery scars on my head. They're covered now with an inch of curly hair.

The *Archimedes* shakes with turbulence. If it weren't for the magboots sealing me to the deck, I'd be on my ass. Cassius's voice comes from the wall speakers, admonishing anyone not in a crash seat. But I'll be damned if I strap in like the rest.

"Lyria, come back and join us," Aurae calls. I wave her off. She may be happy to play the matron, but that boy's palm in my hand made me think of Liam.

How many little boys like Liam did Volga kill on Callisto?

I try not to imagine. I try only to see what's out the viewport. I have to remember the sights, so I can tell my little nephew what Europa looked like when we're together again on Mars. Not that I can see much of the cities or Europa.

Beyond the viewport, Europa hides behind a shroud of rain and fog. Whips of green lightning flay the sky. Waves wander in the gloom like tired miners coming home from shift. I miss waiting at the top of the tunnel for my da to come home. I miss my ma. My sister the most. I think of my brothers lost at war.

I shouldn't be here.

I press my nose to the window. The water seems to grow closer. The sea itself rises up toward us. No. Something *in* the sea is rising. My heart beats faster. A massive fin breaks the waterline, followed by an oil-black bulk with pale pink stripes, surging up, up, up with horrible massiveness. And then it sinks down, down, down into the churning dark.

I'm left in awe. And here I thought the volcanoes on Io were the most manic thing I'd see in the Rim. I know magic isn't real. I know it's all science. But if I don't know the science, it might as well be magic. Far as I know, whatever flitted up from the black depths was here long before Europa's ice-layer was terraformed into the Discordia Sea. I shiver a little.

"Ragnar always wanted to ride one of those."

I turn. Sevro's staring at me from a pace away. How did he sneak up on me? I check his feet, presuming he'll have on magboots to steady himself. Of course not. The man's feet are bare, the long toenails curled into the grate floor. He sways with a jar of sunflower butter in his hand, a bottle of syrup in his back pocket, and a knife in his mouth.

"Sunbutter?" he offers the knife laden with thick brown goo.

"Not hungry."

"Talking to an Obsidian will do that," he says.

'Course he knows. He's always lurking. I search the water. "What was that?"

"Leviathan. Biggest carveling this side of Titan," he says.

"There's bigger things?"

"Always. You see any gold stripes on its top fin?"

I shake my head. He looks disappointed. "Why?"

"Leviathans are the sigil beast of gens Kalibar. The ruling house of Europa. Cyaxares is their pride and joy. Three-hundred-year-old bull.

Twice as big as any other. That one down there was probably middling size. Always wanted to see Cyaxares."

"And the Kalibar, they ride those things?" I ask.

He nods. "With pressurized suits you can take them a couple dozen clicks down. Not the healthiest hobby, or kindliest mount. Leviathans ain't loyal creatures. Sometimes they eat their owners. Hungry bastards. Each with five stomachs to fill. I'd prefer a sun drake or a white griffin, me." He pauses. "Or a unicorn. What would you ride?"

I consider his strange question. "Not a leviathan. A Pegasus maybe. Something nice."

"Have you met a pegasus?"

"Well, no. But me brothers grew up pretending they were in Pegasus Legions."

"They ain't nice, Pegasuses. Carthii breed carnivorous ones too."

"Is anything nice?" I mutter. He stares at me, taking the question too philosophically. "Why are you talking to me?"

"Why wouldn't I?"

"You never talk to me. As a rule."

"My rule is I don't talk to dead weight."

I would smile if I hadn't just learned that Volga might now be a bloodthirsty warlord. What would Ephraim say to that? "You're a real bastard," I say. "You know that, right? Leaving Darrow and Cassius hanging out to dry."

"They went off mission. I saved their asses in the end."

I glance at the Pink children. "Yeah? Well, I have a new rule. I don't talk to bastards."

I turn back to the window.

He doesn't say anything for several minutes but he stays there behind me, chewing the inside of his cheek, riding some really mad turbulence without so much as stumbling. "I want to know something," he says. I don't answer him, but he's going to ask me whether I let him or not.

"You helped kidnap my kids, unknowingly or so you say, but you were party to it, just the same," he says slowly.

"Aye," I say. "And I felt bad about it, so I risked my neck to get them back."

"Earning the trust of Virginia and Vic, apparently. Enough that you were witness to the birth of . . . you were there for . . . my—" He cannot say the words, but I know now what he's asking about.

The ship rocks. My knuckles are white from clutching the handholds near the viewport and my heart starts to turn black the longer I hold on to the thrill of my anger at him. I relent, and it feels good.

"You want it straight? I helped her deliver Ulysses," I say. "I . . . heard her first words to him. Volga was there too, guarding the door while it happened. Later, I pulled him from the tree where they killed him. I tried burying him in the ground. I didn't know what else to do. I think Victra wanted me there when he was buried proper, because she knew I would rather have been the one in the ground. I'd have traded spots with him."

"Why?"

I go quiet before finding the words. "He was a baby. He didn't do anything. I've done stuff. I'm not all nice." I think of my sister's children. "It wasn't right is all."

"And this Volga character?"

I wipe tears from my eyes. "Shit. Volga woulda eaten her own gun if it put that baby back in Victra's arms. I swear it. That's what I don't get. She's a sweetheart. I know she's done stuff. I mean, she was pulling heists with Ephraim before I ran into them, who knows the kinda stuff she did. But I thought she was good. Maybe I needed her to be? When she gave herself up to Fá—even after he killed Ephraim, and he was like a father to her—I told myself she was sacrificing herself so he'd leave Mars alone. So people wouldn't get hurt. To hear that she's marching with Fá, I can't believe it."

"But you do."

"Whaddya mean?"

"You didn't call Sigurd a liar." I stare at him. "You know why? Because you know that people can and will disappoint you. Even this friend of yours is going to let you down."

"Is that why you won't take up your da's helmet?" I ask.

"The hell do you know about that?" he mutters. I shrug. "Cassius, that chatty little shit."

"Ain't a rat, can't reveal my source," I say. "But you ask me, I think it's because you think you're gonna let everyone down."

"Naw," he says and looks away. "Ain't it."

"Then what?"

He doesn't answer for a long time. "It's just, everyone wants me to wear my da's helmet. Since I can remember. Like I'm fated. Can't escape it."

"You wore it before, though," I say. "For a little while. Everyone knows that."

"And it ate me up," he mutters.

"Why?"

He chews his cheek some more. Lightning bathes his face green. "Da didn't want to be Ares. He told me that. One of the last times I saw him before he died. He hated it. I know what he meant. The Golds made it. He and Mum made me. It was his prison. See?"

I wonder about that as the sea bucks outside. "My da was a rat," I say toward the viewport. "He informed on people in our mine. I used to think he was perfect because he was my da. Then I hated him. Then I realized he did it for us. Now when I think of him, I think he was just a person doing his best in the world he was in. I can't judge him for that. I can't say I'm better or worse. But it makes me sad. He accepted his prison. He never even tried the bars. That helm . . . for Da, maybe he hated it. But maybe it wasn't his prison. Maybe it was his key to get out."

I turn and look at him. His eyes peer out the window and I wonder if he was even listening, especially when he turns and walks away. "Is this the last time we talk?" I call after him.

"Only if you become useless again."

58

LYRIA

Europa

THE FLIGHT ENDS NOT long after the storm abates. When we land, it's on an island dedicated to fishing and solar farming. The civilians exit first with some of the Black Owls. Apparently, they're taking their own submarine down to a different city in the Deep. We're headed for fabled Helisson, Athena's secret stronghold. Cassius finds me in the cargo bay mopping up vomit left by the motion-sick Greens. "Lyria. I'm furious with you. All the latrines are filthy. You've been derelict in your duty."

"What? You said I didn't have to keep cleaning the latrines soon as I could handle the stick."

"And my word is my bond," he says.

"I flew the *Archimedes* on Io. I—"

"My goodlady, I mean this with all my heart. That was not flying. That was just 'not crashing.' That you avoided a finale in the hard deck doesn't mean my latrines should be devoid of your affection." He pinches my cheek. "Your face. It's a jape." I stab at him with the vomit mop. He takes it away faster than I can blink and stores it on the wall.

"You're a condescending pricklick," I say.

"Only to my favorites." I blush when he winks at me.

"You're staying up here then?" I ask.

"The Moses Columns are offline. Can't get the *Archi* down easily. Anyway, it's best not to stash your getaway vehicle under the sea, and I'm not leaving my home unattended with all the salt, thieves, and barbarians about. Don't look so worried. If the Obsidian come, I have a stealth ship."

"*When* they come."

"Right." He eyes a few Black Owls unloading a crate. "Not sure I'd be welcome down there anyway. You kill one terrorist warlord . . ." He sighs, then frowns. "I have to ask. Are you still intent on going after Volga?"

"I think so."

"Even after seeing the Obsidian on Io, you're not afraid?"

"No," I lie up at him.

"Then you're mad, girl. Did you see those people? Did you see that hammer they hit me with? Me. That thing was meant to drive nails bigger than you. Huge hammer." He has a point. He's taller even than Darrow and has more muscle than all my brothers ever did put together.

"Everyone saw the hammer, Cassius. You made us watch your feed."

"Good. Then you know. This whole time, Sevro's been giving me shit for missing the war. I don't love my people very much. But I do feel sorry that they had to face *those* Obsidians. They're not like they used to be when I was your age." He scratches his neck. "War isn't like it used to be. Used to have a modicum of civility. Point is, the idea of you having anything to do with those monstrosities makes me nauseous with anxiety. Swear to me, we will talk before you do anything stupid or agree to anything stupid. Darrow is good at getting people to agree to do stupid things."

"Like going to the Dockyards of Venus?"

"I have never claimed to be a role model."

His concern makes me feel weird. Sad to leave him, I look back at the halls leading into the *Archi*. It feels a little like home. "Very well, I will seek your counsel prior to any bad decisions." I spit in my hand and stick it out. He hates that. But he spits in his and we spitshake.

"Good. Now, get thee hence, foul ragamuffin. I hear the Deep is gloomy and dour as a Moonie's sonnet. You won't want to miss it." He hands me a tiny flask. I take it and give a little shake, feeling its contents slosh around. "Had to make sure it was good enough for your discerning palate," Cassius says.

I thank him and head down the ramp to join the others. I stop in the rain and jog back to him. He smiles, a little confused. I say in a rush,

"What you did on Io. Why you did it. It's just . . ." I look down, feeling stupid, knowing he doesn't need compliments from me. "I dunno. I just think you're a good man and you have a huge heart and I don't think people say that enough. Just wanted you to know that I see it, Bellona."

For once, he doesn't have anything ironic to say. His eyes glitter, and he bends, looks into my eyes, and kisses me on the cheek. I'm filled with an urge to protect him and his too-fragile heart. "Go on now. Before I try to keep you," he says.

I catch up with Darrow and the others just as they descend the ramp to meet a new group of heavily armored Red troopers. They are tough, thick-necked men and women with buzzed heads, faces like a vagrant's heel, and big guns. They greet Cheon with salutes.

An Orange man with a thin jaw and huge eyes grasps Cheon's arm. "Ares fought."

"Athena fights," she replies. He repeats the rite with Aurae with a little more flirtation.

The Pink seems nervous around her own people. If she was deep cover, I guess she *would* feel like an outsider amongst the Daughters. She keeps glancing at Diomedes in worry. The Orange whistles when he spies Darrow and Sevro through the rain. "Honored, Reaper, Son of Ares. Honored. When the communique came through . . . Well. I didn't believe it. Honored." His eyes narrow when he sees Sigurd, as if he thinks the man's hands should not be just bound behind his back but chopped off completely. His most unusual response is reserved for Diomedes.

He just starts laughing.

"How the mighty have fallen." He spits on the Gold. Diomedes does not react, and the rain soon cleans the spit from his face. Par for the course: the man's expression of boredom is chiseled in stone. Don't think I've seen him emote once, except sometimes when he's looking at Aurae when she can't see him. Movement on the horizon draws my attention away. I squint through the rain, just making out the lights of an island city looming like a mountain out in the gloom.

When I look back to the group, almost everyone is gone down a stairwell. Cheon waves to me. "Any day now, lass." I jog up. "You're the pilot. Lyria of Lagalos. Cheon." She extends a hand. It's half again as big as mine, and her grip punishes.

"I'm not really a pilot," I say and descend the stairs with her.

"I saw. And I'm not really a soldier either," she rumbles, entirely unconvincing. "Was that man *the* Cassius au Bellona? Quite the gilded complement the Reaper has."

"He saved those kids and Greens, I'll remind you," I say.

"Aye, at the cost of half my men."

"I'm sorry." She shrugs. "You're a gas miner, yeah? From one of the floating rigs on Jupiter?" I ask.

"You a silk spinner? A spider breeder? Ain't that what Red lasses do on Mars?" she replies.

"They also sing," I say. "And serve on the front lines."

"Just right, lass. Just right. We're more than the utility they made us for," she says.

Astounded by any Red who could or would go toe to toe with Obsidians, I had wanted to meet Cheon soon as she came aboard. Yet I find myself disliking her more with every passing second.

We reach the bottom of the stairs and come out onto a submarine dock. We pass a dozen lightly armored Grays stacked in a heap, dead. The former guards of the solar island, it seems. A black and gold sea beast is emblazoned on their chest plates. "Cyaxares," I murmur.

"What you know about that monster?" Cheon says.

I shrug. "He might be on the menu soon. The dragon eaters are coming."

The submarine that awaits us is shaped like a wedge of Lunese cheese. I file after the others into a pressurized hold located at the top of the dense and heavily patched craft. It stinks from a legacy of rust, brine, and sweating bodies. Cheon's troopers lock into harnesses in a row of crash seats bolted to the floor. There's enough for a hundred passengers. My party takes the row on the opposite side of the hold. Darrow locks in Diomedes's harness before locking in his own. The bag he's carried with him rests on the floor by his feet. Darrow and Diomedes look comical in the small seats. Sevro looks like he'd rather swim down than buckle himself into his seat. His anxiety is obvious.

I take my seat next to Aurae. She's just as nervous as Sevro.

"Don't like submarines?" I ask.

"Never been on one, but I do try to embrace new things," she replies, her eyes on Cheon.

"You don't like her, do you?"

"I didn't say that."

"I don't."

"It takes all kinds to wage a war," she says. "Could you imagine her entertaining guests in the Raa court?"

"I can't imagine you there either," I say.

She looks at me, struck. "Thank you."

I haven't time to answer before the Orange barks for us to brace and the submarine plunges into the sea. The straps dig into my shoulders. My stomach leaps into my throat. Down we plummet. The hull creaks as pressure builds. Sevro looks like he's going to throw up. Darrow yawns. I try to channel his calm.

"Passing through twilight," the captain soon intones. *"Midnight ahead."*

Aurae's fists clench and I reach for her hand. She opens it for me and breathes a little easier.

By the time I twist in my seat to look out the small porthole, the twilight level of the ocean is behind us. Scum and darkness withhold most of the midnight level's mysteries, but soon bright fauna and fish glow in the pitch water. They stretch like veins of blue, gold, and green fire. Aurae tells me that they are drawn to this level by the warm waters of the level's jet stream, and swim in schools kilometers-long. By the look in her eyes, I know it's the first time she's seen the wonders of this ocean too. The Raa home where Cassius was prisoner must've been on the surface, I surmise.

"Entering the abyssal zone," the captain says.

Beyond the warm waters lies a vast darkness, where not even the outlines of the beasts who call it home can be seen, as we go down, down, down toward Athena's domain.

The submarine groans from the pressure. The darkness becomes impure. Light glows faintly in the distance. Soon the lights are bright and cast a blue-white haze over the variegated walls of subaquatic cities that sprout from the dark stone core of Europa's underworld. I sigh. It looks magical and gloomy and weird. Somewhere within the core of the moon, Athena waits with the key to save Mars. Yet I can't stop thinking of those on the surface.

Will she really leave them to die?

The submarine's engines come alive as we near the ocean floor. Still Aurae doesn't take her hand from mine. The captain guides us into the mouth of a trench lined with metal dock doors crusted over with giant deepwater barnacles as big as cows. There are no barnacles on the gun installations nearby. A hatch yawns open on one of the installations and three dark projectiles slither out. They disappear behind us, bound for some distant danger. We're entering into a war within a war, a story that's been going as long as I've been alive. I glance at Cheon, at Aurae, at Darrow. He's yawning again. So is Diomedes. Sevro has finally stopped squirming.

The submarine glides into an open dock and settles into a rack that lifts it from the water with a rattle and a groan. Aurae lets go of my hand. I stretch my legs and wait for my seat's safety straps to unlock. Through the porthole, I glimpse movement outside the ship. Shadows moving on a dim dock. My eyes adjust quickly, and a chill creeps down my spine. The shadows carry something in their hands.

Manacles. It's a big set. And then another. And another.

I turn back around to see Sevro struggling to keep his eyes open. Diomedes yawns even more deeply than Darrow this time. They both blink like they're trying to stay awake.

"Darrow! Something's wrong," I shout. "They got chains out there!"

Darrow doesn't react except to turn and look at Cheon and raise his eyebrows. "It doesn't have to be like this," he says.

She stares back at him and taps her bionic nose. "You know, I can smell a musky man at a hundred paces and tell you the Color of his last shag, but I still can't smell ceronocyne gas. Can you?" He does not answer. "This brand's made for Golds."

"No," Sevro slurs and begins thrashing at his straps like a caged animal. "No!"

"Don't fight," Darrow murmurs. "Sevro, don't fight them."

"Cheon, what are you doing?" Aurae asks. She struggles with her seat's restraints.

"Athena's will." Cheon stands. The heavy Reds stand with her. Their armor flickers alive as their generators whir up. I pull the release latch for my straps. Nothing happens. I pull again, and the straps contract, synching me tight to the chair. Sevro gurgles in rage. I pull my pistol only to have Aurae claw at it.

"No," she says.

The gun falls to the floor, out of reach.

"Lyria, don't. Cheon, these are our friends—"

I'm slim enough to slip down through the restraints of my seat and pin the pistol between my feet. I flip the pistol back into my lap and it hits the restraints and nearly slides off. I grab the pistol and point it at Cheon. Something hard and metal slaps the back of my head. I see black spots. My brain aches. I can't get out of my straps. What is happening? Cheon grabs Darrow by the hair and sniffs him. He stares back, groggy. I've lost the pistol. Aurae is shouting, telling her to stop, calling for Athena. Another Red is opening the bag at Darrow's feet. He hollers to the others and lifts up a black helmet with a grunt. Cheon shakes her head.

"Thought I might smell a bit of the old Red on you," Cheon rasps to Darrow. "But you're all Gold now. A Red would know some debts just can't be forgiven." She clocks him in the face with a steel gauntlet. "The Sons you betrayed had husbands. They had wives. They had children and grandchildren." She hits him again. His head lolls. Aurae's somehow slipped her restraints. She has the pistol. She points it at Cheon and fires over her head. Cheon hits Darrow again. Aurae fires the gun again.

Aurae is so angry she's crying. "This is not who we are. What are you doing!"

Cheon turns, licks her lips. "Seems it wasn't just the Raa who had this little Pink on her back."

A voice comes from the door. "Cheon. What *are* you doing?" Cheon stops. The door to the submarine has opened and a thick-set woman enters wearing a black, spiked helmet and a simple black jumpsuit. Heavy braids of dark red hair fall to her midback. Her dark arms are muscular and tattooed with white ink. The troopers part.

Athena.

Cheon looks down, ashamed. "Get out," Athena says. Cheon mumbles an apology. "Get out. Turn in your weapons. Report to the Sanctuary. Aurae is right. This is not who we are."

Cheon obeys. Athena walks up to Aurae and slowly helps her lower the gun.

"Aurae, we finally meet. My bravest daughter." She kisses her forehead. "I thought you were lost in the Core. I should have known better. Well done." The Pink falls to her knees, quaking. "No, no. We never kneel, Daughter, least of all you. You have brought me all I asked for, and more. Far more."

"You bitch! We trusted you!" I snarl at Aurae. "What is this?"

Athena turns her helmet. Its glowing red eyes bore into me. "Justice, at last."

59

DARROW

Athena

I WAKE IN A COLD room with a sour chemical taste in my mouth and a headache. Machines rumble through the walls. I swim in nausea as I sit up. The air is heavy with the flavor of rust. Huge chains clink. They are light in the low gravity, but they are thick as my wrists and anchor me to the floor. I feel for Bad Lass. It's gone. So is Pax's key. The fog in my head is in no hurry to clear, and I remember what happened.

"You talk in your sleep."

I am not alone in the room. A woman sits on the floor, her back against the wall. Her hair is dark red and pools on her shoulders in heavy braids woven with silver filament. A curved black hasta leans beside her. She reads from my copy of *The Path to the Vale*. Both of her hands are artificial and seven-fingered.

I rub my temples. "Where is Sevro?"

"Aren't you curious what you said in your sleep?"

"Sevro."

"Safe. He will never be harmed here. We owe that much to his father. You and the Raa, on the other hand, may not be so lucky. To say nothing of the Obsidian."

"And Lyria?"

"The Red who tried to shoot Cheon? She's with Aurae now. She won't be harmed. She's done us no crime. But I am surprised a Red who was a victim of your assimilation camps would be so protective of the Reaper." She glances up with a frown. "You look surprised as well."

She is not a tall woman, but she is dense. A Red ultraheavy like

Cheon. Her nose is Roman in its architecture, and crooked. Her skin is a dark black. Her eyes are garnet red, large, wide-set, and narrow. She seems in her late forties. Her sleeves are rolled up, and her forearms, like her neck and face, are covered with white tattoos. Names.

"Guess I should ask. Are the ships real? Or were they just bait?"

"They are real . . . if the Obsidians have not found them or destroyed them. As for bait? No. They could not be bait because there was no trap. Aurae was sent only for Barca. But when she called from Sungrave . . . well, I knew this was something I could not run from any longer." She sighs, then waves the book a little.

I didn't bring it with me. They have the *Archimedes*. And Cassius?

"Life is easy to imagine as a path. But it is moments like this when I think of it as a particle accelerator. You, the Daughters: You're two high-energy beams traveling close to the speed of light before finally colliding. That collision will lay bare the essential building blocks of your nature, and ours. I did not want this collision. Not with you. Not now."

"Why not?"

"I pulled us from the brink of hatred. I pulled myself from the debris you made of my life. Now . . . the stir your presence has caused. The hatred it has awoken. Well. The Daughters demand justice, and I am but their will."

"It needn't be a collision," I try.

She smiles. "Is that why you did not struggle in the submarine?"

"I did not struggle because I smelt rust on the breeze. I believed—still believe—that I am amongst friends."

"What do you mean?"

In response, I quote the full fourth understanding:

> *The supreme good is the wind in the deepmines,*
> *It flows through rock, around people, and over land*
> *The wind is oblivious to these obstacles,*
> *though her path would not be the same in their absence.*
> *When you smell rust on the breeze,*
> *hear the echo of tools in the darkness.*
> *Smile, and be glad*
> *The path is upon you,*
> *and you upon it.*
> *All you must do is walk.*

She closes the book. Her eyes remind me of Dancer's, except unlike his they hold no love for me. "Aurae told me you . . . understood the book. I was skeptical."

"And now?"

"Still skeptical, but admittedly impressed by your ability to memorize."

"Can you afford to be a skeptic? Mars is under siege. Obsidians are at your door. We're both Reds. We do not have time to be at each other's throats like this—"

"Red? Me?" She watches me, then says, "I suppose I came from a mine. Like you. Ours floated over Jupiter. I was sorted as a girl. Since I was not chosen to be a breeder, my breasts were cauterized shortly after puberty. I was selected to be a gasfly to gather helium from Jupiter on airlon wings. Red? I have never been Red. Nor Gray nor Gold. I am a human being. You may look at me with the eyes of the masters, but you will not sort me according to their inhuman labels."

I'm beginning to think maybe I should not have come here. I peer around the chamber. It is familiar. Similar to that of the room the Praetorians beat me in before Trigg and Holiday saved me from Adrius in Attica. The only difference is the vents in the ceiling instead of drains in the floor.

"Is this where you will kill me?"

"No. But this place is significant. This is one of the rooms where the Krypteia murdered the Sons of Ares you betrayed to Romulus. Fortunately for you we are not like the Krypteia. We do not hide our violence in the shadows. You will be tried. You will have the chance to defend yourself. As will the Raa."

"And when I am found guilty?"

"*If* you are found guilty, you will be executed." She hefts the hasta leaning against the wall. It is huge in her hands, and longer than she is tall. Black, it is veined with iridescence. I recognize the metal. She turns it close enough to me that I can read the text etched into the side of the blade. It is the Forbidden Song. "This blade was made by our greatest artificer, Oskanda. She named it Pyrphoros. Fire bearer. Your hands were meant to wield it as you led us to freedom. You will not die by the rope or gas, Darrow of Mars. If you are found guilty, this will be your end."

"Do you really think Sevro will help you if you kill me?" I ask.

"No. But I fear much has changed since I sent Aurae to find him. We can no longer spend our ships in your war. They are needed here to seize power once Fá has left."

I almost laugh. "You think they'll just leave?"

"They are raiders, the Ascomanni. We will outlast them down here. Once they have purged the Golds, we will step into the void. Perhaps then the Rim will finally know just rule. Not that this concerns you."

"The Republic needs—"

"No." She stands. "Do not hide behind Mars's plight. You are not a god, Darrow. You cannot wave your hand and hurl down the enemy. Mars is doomed. The Republic has lost. This does not please me. But I think you deserve this reckoning." She fishes a holocube from her pocket. "The men and women who risked their lives for you, who died for you, they had no funerals, no public trial, no public execution. They simply disappeared. Disappeared, cast off from every register, every record. Made like they never existed in the first place."

I know there is nothing I can say, so I say nothing. I nod at the white tattoos on her forearms. She rubs her thumb over the names there. "Proof these people existed. Proof I carry with me everywhere." She is haughty. Performative in her grief. Yet I can see why Fitchner chose her to helm the Daughters. There is calm charisma and power in her, a certitude wrought from hardship.

"These poor souls believed in Ares. They all believed in Eo. They all believed in you. *I* believed in you," she says. "The hope I felt when you led us to victory against Fabii . . ." She laughs at herself. "Well, I forgot Helldivers are used to plunging headlong into the dark, outracing the debris they leave behind." She tosses the holocube to me. "We are your debris, Darrow, and we matter. You're so good at memorizing, learn the names of those you betrayed."

She heads for the door, then stops and pulls out my neck chain and Pax's key.

"What is this?" she asks.

"It's from my son. He made me a bike."

She tosses it back to me, then slams the door.

In her absence I rage at her intransigence, at Aurae's betrayal, at this consummate inanity of my own people killing me. I should have struggled when I saw Cheon's tell, moments before Lyria shouted a warning. I should have ripped my seat from the bolts that fastened it to the deck—I had even chosen that seat because I noticed that rust had corroded the metal. I should have put on the Twilight Helm, killed them all, and stormed the Deep, taken Athena prisoner and had her march me to the ships she stole from the Raa. I should have left these fools to die, and gone home to save my planet.

The rage passes. In its wake, I'm left sick to my stomach. I pick up Pax's key and put the chain around my neck. Then I pick up the cube Athena left behind. Turning it over and over in my hands, I feel it gaining weight. The mass of guilt has weighed down on my soul for so long that holding it, facing it, is harder than charging through any breach.

I activate the cube. Holograms emerge.

A thousand little horrors grow and infest my cell. They are the interrogations and executions of the Sons of Ares I betrayed. All the things I've run from for so many years. But it was not the moments of brutality recorded in the cube that would make me rove the rooms and halls Virginia and I shared whenever I made it home, not really. I could handle the violence, the death. It was the lives I'd cut short that would make me insane with guilt. It's the unimaginable complexity and love and hope in those lives that I could never understand, never witness, that made me feel as if I had invited an abyss between Virginia and me as we laid in bed. A writhing, black, stinking hole that would always stand between me and my son.

I gave over lowColors like me—like Eo—to Romulus.

Why?

Because I was afraid I could not win if I didn't. So many died for me so I could lay by my wife, cradle my son, win my war, have my peace.

I watch the executions with dry, sober eyes. Not one of the Reds, Oranges, Browns, or Pinks executed had my training or my teachers or a Mickey to make them into a god of war. Yet not one of them begged or recanted. Some died quiet. Some screamed. But most shouted a name.

I thought it would be Ares's name that they shouted before death. Or Eo's name. But no.

It was mine.

60

DARROW

The Weight of Guilt

THE DAUGHTERS OF ARES have assembled for my trial.

I shuffle through the old nickel mine draped in chains. The gold cape a few Black Owls hung around my shoulders in mockery sways. A dozen guards lead me forward. I search for Sevro in the crowd but do not find him or Lyria. My grubby prisoner's shift itches. It feels familiar, the shift, the chains, the fear. How many different kinds of shackles have I worn over the years?

My judges are far more numerous than the guards. There must be seven thousand of the armed rebels, as many as the chamber will hold. They watch from the suspended cable walkways, dangle their feet from the circular jumpways that link the levels of the mine township, and perch atop landed skimmer hulls. They crowd the bottom level to either side of my route to the dais where I will be judged. They are equal parts women and men. In their ranks, I see what I recognize as Reds, Browns, Yellows, Pinks, and Oranges. All cover their sigils in black wraps.

"They are the original Daughters. All lost kin in Romulus's purge," Aurae says. Their faces may be soft from lifetimes spent far from the sun, but their eyes are harder than any miner's hands.

On Luna, I strode before senators with contempt in my every step. It got me nowhere. So, I look these judges in their eyes, as humble as a seven-foot-tall man of war can be amongst those bred for service and toil. I take on their contempt, their anger, their resentment, just as I took in the love of my Free Legions. If I deserved one, I certainly deserve the other.

Most fearsome of all are the young. Callous youths who've never known me as a hero, puffing their burners, polishing their guns, picking their teeth, swaying their boots. They glare at me in silence from the jumpwalks that string across the cavern to link its levels. My eyes chance on a slim Brown girl above. She looks no older than Eo was when she died. Her hair is shaved, half of her pale face smeared in grease or war paint. A big weapon meant for a Gray lies in her lap. She sees me looking at her and she makes a gun of her hand, points it at me, and pulls the trigger.

"You said Athena preached forgiveness," I say.

Aurae seems sad. "She did once. Now she carries a gun."

I turn on Aurae as we reach the stage. She tried to take the gold cape from my shoulders when I entered, but had her hands swatted away by the Owls. Athena waits atop the stage wearing her helmet, a gun, and Pyrphoros. Behind her, Diomedes stands chained. Aurae watches him with pained eyes. "It's love then?" I ask.

"He once told me that love which obstructs duty is not love. It is an addiction that must be denied." She smiles, sad. "Maybe he was right."

"No. He's a noble idiot who was brainwashed by a military cult, and somehow still turned out to be a decent man. Aurae. Two-thirds of Europa's population is still on the surface. If Diomedes and Athena can be brought to reason, then we could evacuate many of them down here. I think I can convince the Raa, but Athena will listen to you. If you—"

"She has listened to me. And to Sevro and Lyria. But Diomedes's life is not in her hands. Neither is yours. It is in theirs." She nods out to the Daughters and their sea of vengeful eyes.

Well. Shit.

She turns my head to look into her eyes. They are filled with acceptance and fierce love. "I expected you to be an arrogant tyrant. That is what they see. Show them what you showed me. Show them who you are. A traveler on a path," she says softly.

The guards push me up the stairs to join Athena. My mind races as I ponder Aurae's words. A few chants of Athena's name echo through the chamber, until Athena marches up to me, yanks off the golden cloak in disgust, and hurls it off the stage. She holds up her hand. Silence falls like night, slowly then all at once. Her voice echoes through the chamber.

"Darrow of Mars! You stand accused of collaboration with the enemy,

Romulus au Raa, resulting in the liquidation of thirteen thousand four hundred twelve Sons of Ares from Jupiter to Pluto. You stand accused of mass homicide in your assault upon the Dockyards of Ganymede, which resulted in the fatalities of more than one hundred and fifty thousand Reds, Greens, Browns, and Oranges."

As she recites several more accusations, I find Sevro in the crowd. It is hard to meet his eyes. They are angry. They should be. I brought us here despite his warnings. How many times have I ignored him? Placated him? Told him I would get him home only to somehow drag him further and further away? He just wants to be a husband and father. So did I.

I remember the purity of that feeling. It was clean. To love and be loved, to guide and be guided. This is dirty, this life I lead instead. I am dirty, as Dancer promised. Sevro said he had to keep me shiny, that was his job. It's time to tell them I haven't done mine. It's the only chance to complete my mission. And my mission is not to get ships, not to slay Fá, not even to save Mars, it is to make sure that the light does not go out.

When Athena has levied all her charges, she asks how I plead. Aurae nods up at me from the crowd. I see Lyria standing beside Sevro, and think of Camp 121. One of many I could not protect. Then I smile at Sevro, thinking of the time he saved Cassius's life long ago when the Obsidians tried to hang him, and say: "Years ago, a friend stood before a court much like this one." I lift my chin. "I plead now as he did then: I am guilty."

The response is mixed. The Daughters murmur, some in confusion, many in vindication, others in fury that I would make a mockery of them. Sevro hangs his head. Aurae smiles. Lyria leans forward, her face open. She is my audience. Those I uplifted only to abandon.

"You know the sentence is death?" Athena asks.

"I do. I have no defense. I did sell your kin to Romulus au Raa." I glance back at Diomedes and say to him, "I am guilty of destroying the Dockyards of Ganymede, of murdering its workers and caretakers." I turn back to the Daughters and raise my voice so even those in the back can hear me. "I am guilty of enough crimes for a thousand men. Torture, kidnapping, blackmail, murder, bombings, Rains. All of it. I have broken nearly every oath I have taken. I have flattened cities, set fire to generations, raised oceans, broken worlds. I've killed men, women, children, if not with my own hands, then with ships under my command.

I have betrayed mentors and friends and led them to their deaths. I have left my legions to die to save myself.

"In my name, if not by my consent or orders, prisoners have been slaughtered, populations displaced, ice caps melted, Iron Rains hurled down on the just and unjust alike. I *am* guilty. I reek of blood and shame. I am sorry for what I've done, but I will not apologize for why I did it.

"I believe in the dream of Eo, the dream of Ares, the dream of Ragnar. That we are all born with the right to choose our own destinies. To live in peace. To pass down that same freedom to our children.

"I will not apologize for that. For doing all I can to give this dream to my son. Even if in doing it I lost my right to walk the path to the Vale, to pass the Old Man who guards it, and join my father, my friends, Eo. But if I could, I would take back my crime against you. It is the great regret of my life. I did not betray you because I sought your misery. I did not turn you over to Romulus because I delighted in your suffering. I did it because I was young, blind, but most of all, I was afraid. So I strayed from the path of Fitchner, of Eo, and I took a shortcut.

"I began like many of you. Born to drill and die. I was given power, but that power never made me less afraid. That power made me desperate. Arrogant. And far too willing to sacrifice others. After the Battle of Ilium, I feared the Raa would fall upon our flanks. I was afraid that I could not save my people and your people at the same time. So I chose mine. That was the folly, pretending we were separate.

"We are one people. We always have been. I know that now. My betrayal of you betrayed the dream I claimed to fight for. Eo did not even know these worlds of yours existed, but she would have believed, as Ares did, that this dream has no boundaries. It is open to all. It includes all of those brave enough to stand when the Golds tell us to kneel. And it includes those who are perhaps not brave enough, not yet. My mistake was in thinking I was alone. That if I fell, if I lost, there'd be no one left to fight. I know that is not true. Because Ares fell, and look at all of you."

I look down at Sevro.

"Alone we are weak, at the mercy of fear. Alone we are too willing to compromise our morality. Our courage comes from the belief that we are not alone. That we cannot be divided. That is why I beg you: learn from my mistakes. Let my death have a greater purpose: saving as many lives as it can. I am not here to petition for myself, but for those Europans stranded on the surface. For the Ganymedes hiding behind their shields, or the Ionians still holding out in their crypts. I beseech you all, do not turn your back on the Core, on those living free on Mars, or those fighting to regain freedom on Mercury, on Earth. We are all one people. None of us is alone.

"Here, now, you believe you are alone against Fá and his Horde. Your fear will tell you that you must protect your own. That you must keep the sealifts closed, even if it means the civilians on the surface will be slaughtered, enslaved. You believe you have no choice. But you do." I nod to Diomedes. "That is the prince of Sungrave. You can judge him for the sins of his ancestors. You can kill him. Or you can let him tell you of Kalyke. Let him tell you of Sungrave and the slaughter he has witnessed. You want change? Now is the time to make it. To show this Gold, all Golds, the quality of your dream. You want progress? Unity? Make it. Here and now, and for the future."

I pause until the echoes of my voice recede. No one jeers any longer. My hands tremble behind my back. Bound as they are, I cannot reach for Pax's key. But I feel it pressed against my chest, and hope he would be proud of this speech, overwrought as it is. In my head, I wrote it as if he stood beside Sevro. Even if I die, maybe he will hear it one day and know I found myself in the end.

"When I was sixteen, Dancer O'Faran, one of the great heroes of my life, told me that I was a good man who would have to do bad things. That is why Ares chose me: he knew I could be the dirty hand of the Rising. I could be the man who does the bad things. For most of my life I have thought that was a curse. Now I see it was a blessing. If you look at where we started, we are a thousand times stronger now.

"I do not ask for your forgiveness or your mercy. I ask only that you succeed where I failed. Do not surrender your dream to fear. Do not take the short route through shadow. You know your path. If you think you are alone on it, just look to your right, look to your left, look across the solar system, and see what I see. A tide of one people who want only one thing: liberty."

I am done. The eyes judge and the eyes hate. There is no cheering or pumping of fists, only a shuffle of feet, a clatter of chains as the guards exchange Diomedes and me. Athena reads the hulking man his charges.

When it comes time for him to speak, he looks around without any contrition and glowers out as if facing a firing squad.

"Civilization is based on exchange and social contracts. I was taught that the lowColors exchanged liberty for security and stability. We have failed to provide security. We have failed to provide stability. We have failed you. The contract is broken. Take your due."

61

DARROW

The Three Masters

IOMEDES AND I ARE escorted into a nearby cell to await the
verdict of our sham trial. The cell is stone. The metal door is the
cell's only hint of modernity. Another man occupies it. A handsome
man with a black eye and a burn from a stun weapon on the left side of
his neck.

"Oh, it's you," I say to Cassius.

"Hello." He waves politely, both hands shackled together. I sit next
to him.

"What are you doing here?" I ask.

"I'm in the middle of a rescue, actually. While it is taking longer than
expected, I'm optimistic with regards to its outcome." I don't laugh. "All
right, I'm lying. They left some Black Owls on the *Archimedes* and now
I have a black spot on my pride and a very black eye." He winces. "The
Owls are far better at sneaking than fighting Obsidians, I'll tell you that."
He scratches his beard and ponders for a moment. "Are we all going to
die?"

A cheer from the Daughters in the cavern rattles the cell.

"Yes," Diomedes says.

"Probably," I correct, annoyed at the man's pessimism.

"You talked forever," Diomedes mutters at me. "And looked weak."

"You basically told them to slag off and shoot you," I snap.

The Daughters cheer in the cavern again.

"Apparently you both were terrible." Cassius leans back. "What a
waste of talent. Honestly, it's like a bad joke. We might be the best three

razormasters to share a room in the last sixty years, and it's a prison! *And* not one of us was taken in a straight fight." Diomedes and I look at each other, each wondering about the other's claim to the title of master. "Oh, that's right. You two haven't seen each other fight—"

"Cassius?" I say.

He perks up. "Yes?"

"Shut up," Diomedes says.

"My goodmen, it's uncivilized to do anything but laugh in the face of death. Why do you think I'm always so jaunty these days?" Cassius grins when a third cheer comes, the loudest of all. "That must have been for my sentence." I roll my eyes. "Come, come, Darrow, am I not allowed to be the best at anything?"

"Fine. You can be the most despised," I say.

"Thank you, contrition at last."

Even Cassius's false bravado thins and he goes silent after a while. He doesn't ask, but we all wonder what's taking the Daughters so long.

It's Diomedes who breaks the silence. "I did not need you to speak for me," he says.

"What?"

"You impugned my honor," he says.

I stare at him. After a moment of anger at the man's unbelievable pride, I shake my head and look away. "Why did you?" he asks.

"Lives. Saved," I reply, mocking his laconism.

Cassius snorts a laugh. Diomedes is not amused.

I take Pax's key from under my shirt and hold it between my hands. "It's not for the cell," Cassius says when Diomedes perks up at the key. I close my eyes and send a prayer to Pax across the void. I'll not get my book or letter, whatever it is, to him now. But maybe Sevro will, and maybe he'll hear this prayer and know that I thought of him in the end.

"It was the Cestus," Diomedes says. I look up from my prayer. He's staring at the floor. "Kalyke."

I sit straighter and glance at Cassius. "Go on," Cassius says.

"Helios had only just returned from a scouting mission," Diomedes says as if sharing the information is causing him physical pain. "He boarded and I transferred the Cestus to him. Only it was not Helios. It was an imposter with Helios's limbs carved onto him. The imposter must have used the Cestus to fire on our own fleet."

"An imposter?" I ask.

"Yes." Diomedes's eyes narrow, troubled by the memory. "His speech patterns and body mimicry were nearly perfect. Yet . . . I sensed something was amiss. The way he apportioned his weight as he walked . . . I could have stopped it. But I second-guessed myself. Was afraid I was wrong." He snorts at himself. "That is why our armada is gone. I did not trust my instincts. You seem to have learned from your mistakes. So I will trust my instincts now." He looks up with dark conviction. "I believe my uncle was that imposter. I believe Atlas au Raa is the Allfather of the Obsidians and that Fá is his creature. I believe this is repayment for our rebellion and that Atlas will not stop until all of the Rim is burning." He considers. "Or starving."

I stare at him.

Tension coils in my belly. It fits. It all fits. The unseen hand I felt. "Atlas was on the bridge of the *Dustmaker*? In person? He's in Ilium?"

Diomedes nods. "I did not see his face. I have no evidence. But yes."

I laugh and laugh. "You chose a damn fine time to tell us," I say and wipe my eyes.

"I did not trust you before," he says, petulant.

I bolt upright and bang on the cell door. "Athena, if you're listening, you need to let us out. Athena! Fá will not let you live. Athena!"

Another cheer trembles through the stone, and a chant I can't quite make out.

Cassius turns to Diomedes. "Say you're right. And Atlas is the devil himself—as everyone keeps telling me. Why would he do this now?" he asks. "Why not wait for the Republic to fall? Mars could have been theirs."

"Inertia," I reply, abandoning my efforts on the door. "Atlas would have had to put this plan in motion years ago." Diomedes nods his agreement. "Not even he could stop the boulder once it started rolling downhill. And . . . because he knows the Republic has already lost," I admit. Cassius stares at me. "It's true. As things stand. Atlas is preparing for the future. It's not just about punishing you, Diomedes. That's not how he works. He's all about closed loops. He'll make the Rim remember fear, and pave the way for a savior named Lune."

"Not Grimmus?" Diomedes asks.

"No," Cassius says at the same moment.

"Lysander's fleet was still on its way out here last we saw," I say. "They missed the ambush, Cassius. But they'll arrive in time to play the hero.

I know Atlas. All this horror he's spread has been under the name of Atalantia—the impalements, the burnings, the pacifications. It makes sense now. He's not a sociopath. He's a student of history. He'll pin all the evil on the Republic and on Atalantia, then take this war to the abyss so a snow-white savior can pull the worlds out into a shining dawn." I laugh. Even the name of the ship is too rich. "Silenius the Light Bringer. Lysander the Light Bringer. That son of a bitch."

Cassius shakes his head. "Lysander is many things, but he's not a monster. Men like Atlas disgust him. He'd never be able to quiet his conscience. The slaughter in Sungrave alone . . . look what Lysander did at Heliopolis. The lengths he went to in order to save lives!"

"He's a Lune," I contend. "They're capable of anything, especially when backed into a corner."

"Oh, so everything is hereditary?" Cassius asks.

"No. What I'm saying is Octavia had him from the start."

"And then I had him for ten years," Cassius snaps. "He was never like that. Not even when I took him from Luna. He gave Virginia the scepter. He was a sweet little boy."

"How was that sweet little boy the last time you were on Io?" I ask.

Cassius looks like he wants to hit me.

Diomedes, who had been watching us in silence, interrupts. "Cassius is right, Darrow." Cassius relaxes, but still glares at me. "Lysander is not a part of this. I saw his face on the *Dustmaker*. When the ambush was sprung. He did not know. He recognized something was amiss as I did. Something about the imposter's short-sword."

"Wait." Cassius turns on him with a frown. "On the bridge of the *Dustmaker*? Lysander isn't . . . with his fleet? He isn't on the *Lightbringer* crossing the Gulf?"

"No," Diomedes says heavily. "His ships were too slow to match our pace, and had repairs to do. So he traveled with our navy at my invitation, along with a decade of Praetorians. He was with me on the *Dustmaker*'s bridge when it fell."

Cassius's face falls and he sinks back against the wall. "Is he dead?"

"I don't know. I would imagine so. Atlas put a void contraption on my face. I could neither hear nor see. There was just darkness and pain." He pauses, remembering that pain. "Then I felt someone grab me. I could not smell either. This someone dragged me. And fell themselves. I felt their body on mine. No armor, but a strong build. It had to have been Lysander. There was no other Gold on the bridge without armor. They put me in the lifepod and then I felt them grasp at my leg as they got pulled out."

"If Lysander was on the bridge, was he not struck by the spines you were? The paralytics," I say to Cassius's umbrage.

"He was."

"Then how could he move?"

"I have thought of this. My mother gave him a toxin leech after he was poisoned on Phobos by Atalantia. He was in a coma. He nearly died. It must have drained or neutralized the paralytic Atlas employed." His tone softens for Cassius. "I am sorry that he was aboard. He wept when he thought you died on Io, and I know you had your differences, but he was the only Gold of the Core who gained my trust, and my mother's, and even, I think, Helios's. He honored his word and was truly a noble man. Had I to grant the credit for that, it would not be to Octavia." He touches Cassius's knee. "I mourn the loss of his light."

It is the only eulogy that could have given Cassius reprieve from the guilt that's been eating him alive, and it is even a redemption in a way. He slumps back against the wall, overwhelmed with conflicting emotions. Whatever animus I have for Lysander, I feel compassion for my friend, so I shut my mouth, and hope Diomedes's words are true.

62

DARROW

The Tyrants' Debris

A TROUPE OF BLACK OWLS shoves Diomedes, Cassius, and me into a war room aglow with a map of Ilium. Dozens of techs turn from their work in the shadowy room. Athena stands with Aurae beneath the constellation of information. One by one the moons and cities wink out until a single image hangs over her. The Obsidian armada creeps across the face of Jupiter toward Europa.

Aurae turns and gives me a smile before moving to the side to watch Diomedes. Athena rolls tension from her neck and sits down on a stool. The black hasta, Pyrphoros, lies in her lap.

"I was fifteen when my clan decided to seize control of our mine," she says without preamble. "A long time ago now. The uprising was beautiful at first. But when I watched my elders execute our hostages, I knew we were doomed. Still. When my favorite elder put the gun in my hand and asked if I was a gasfly or a warrior of Red, my finger pulled the trigger. Eleven times. I took eleven lives. My clan proved to the Rim that Reds are bloodthirsty animals who must be kept in check."

She activates Pyrphoros and scratches eleven marks in the floor in front of Cassius's feet without leaving her stool.

"I escaped when the Raa soldiers came. Few others managed that. I fell in with pirates and sunk into my own shame. I learned to believe I was never a freedom fighter. That I was a terrorist. An animal. Then Ares found me and showed me that the elder who put the gun in my hand was alive. Alive and far from the gas mine where he sparked our uprising. Living in peace, luxury. He confessed that the uprising was a Krypteia operation from the start. Even in revolt, we were their tools.

"Thanks to Ares, I learned the truth, that Gold control is an illusion comprising fear, guilt, and distrust." She looks back at the ships creeping over the swirling storms of Jupiter. "Atlas au Raa. Is this . . . genocide truly his work?"

So she was listening to us in the cell. "Yes," Diomedes says.

"You don't have proof."

"No, but that is only a testament to my uncle's skill. Nothing more."

Athena chews on her lip before turning on me. "Ares says you can shatter Atlas's illusion. Can you, Darrow?"

"Ares?" I ask with a frown.

Someone moves in the shadows of the war room. Then everything turns to black. Sound and light, even my own hands disappear. Then the voice of Ares, destroyer of men, stormer of ramparts, growls. *"I am the kneeling son. I am the broken daughter. I am the widow and her trembling fist. I am the sum of the tyrants' debris. I am the whipped, the bent, the broken, the enslaved. I am the meek, the gentle, the humble, and all their silent rage. By taking your voice, Gold has given me mine. I am you. I am we. I am Ares, breaker of chains."*

I know the speech. It is an old one given before I left the mines. I found it years later echoing around the holonet. I believe it is still cherished by many because it is what Ares was. Not a hero, not really. He was a consequence of empire, an empowering reflection of the shadow the Golds had cast over all our small and divided hearts.

A pupil of blinding light devours the darkness until I see Sevro standing in front of us wearing the Twilight Helm. It shimmers like a star then fades molten red. So *that's* what it does.

"Neptune's prick. I thought I just died," Cassius mutters.

Sevro takes off the helmet and it fades to black. He's shaved his beard and has his old goatee back. He grins at his little drama. "Savage, right? Thank Hades it has a manual in its software."

"Sevro, what's what?" I ask.

He hops onto a console and dangles his feet. "Well. It's like this. After they put you idiots away, I thought I should have my own little speech. It's easy to make Da shiny in death. But we forget Da was a mess of a man. More broken than any of us. That's why he chose Athena here. Why he chose Dancer, Harmony, Darrow." He pokes the helmet at me.

"He took the broken people because he knew he could reforge them stronger.

"He was a dreamer, Da, but he wasn't an idealist. Naw. He woulda chosen a sweeter god to play if he was. Ares is the bloody truth behind the shine of the Golds. He is the shadow of their glory, and that shadow belongs to us. It is the trauma that made us mad enough to not just go along.

"Da chose you all for different reasons. Dancer was a builder, like Athena here. She's showed me what she's done these last years—the network she's built." He casts her a look of unreserved admiration. "You, Darrow, he chose to be his breaker. But you're more than that. He told me that before he died. You could be both, if only he could keep you on the right path. He died too soon, I think. Left us to our own wicked devices. We weren't ready, but we did what we could."

He nods to Athena and the Daughters in the room.

"That's what I told the Daughters when I marched up there with his helmet. Da slagged up too. Athena cited me half a dozen times just off the top of her head. But he always got back up, dusted himself off, and stuck with it. I told the Daughters no one's done that more than you, boss, maybe not even Da, and each time you try to change. Try to be better."

It's the first time he's called me *boss* in a long time. The Daughters and even Athena herself listen to him with pride in their eyes, as if they'd all watched him grow up. I feel, maybe for the first time, that he has found the same conviction in this part of his life as he does in being a father. It is like both sides of him, Sevro Barca and the Goblin, have finally melded together. I watch him with so much pride.

"You got messy, you know," he says to me with a sigh. "Said it yourself. You cut corners because you wanted that light at the end of the dark. You forgot your own words. That's what's pissed me off the most." I cock my head at him. "Years ago, was twelve? Thirteen? We were standing over Ragnar's body and you told me we gotta stop waiting for the light, because we're it." He looks around the room. "We're it. But our light is fading. Why, I asked them."

He holds up a finger and glares around the room.

"Da was one person. One pissed-off human being whose only power was realizing he could unlock the tide. He gave us permission to fight our way out of the cell they made us." He nods to Athena. "Then he was two. Then three. Now he is Mars. He is the Daughters. He is billions. So why are we fading? Because we don't wanna be here. We wanna be on the other side of this shit. We're waiting to live. But this is it. This is our life until we change it. That's all right. Like Darrow said, it's a blessing. It is our privilege to fight. So let's stop eating ourselves, chewing on each other's legs. It's stupid. It's endless. We got more to do."

He pats the helmet. "We need Ares. We need our builders." He looks at Athena. "We need our shields." He points to the Daughters. "We need putrid, spoiled allies late to the fray." He glares at Cassius. "And we need our Reaper to tell us all how we're gonna break this ugly-ass army, because that's his job." He looks over at Athena. "Right?"

Athena darkens as she turns to me. "Your plan?"

I glance between her and Sevro. "Your ships—"

"Off moon," she says. "And too far away."

The hard path then. "Fá's horde is a wheel that will roll over anything in front of it," I say. "But the axle of any Obsidian wheel is its champion. Kill Fá, the wheel breaks. I can kill Fá—if I have the right people."

Athena crosses her arms, wary.

"Fá is surrounded by an army. Do you have a plan to reach him? To deal with his army after it breaks apart?" she asks. "Hundreds of thousands of marauders loose in Ilium isn't exactly a victory."

"Judging by Sevro's face, he has an idea about that," I say.

"A real classic. You're gonna hate it," he says.

"What's to stop Fá from just killing you if you do reach him?" Athena asks.

"I challenged him to an *ashvar*. A duel of honor. Gossip like that goes through an army faster than the clap." Aurae, Cassius, and Athena wrinkle their noses, but Diomedes nods along like it's common wisdom. "The Ascomanni are a warrior culture. They'll have heard of me. And I still have sway with the Obsidians."

"You make it sound so easy," she says.

"He always does," Sevro says. "It's part of his charm."

"It won't be easy," I say. "But it's the only way. That navy is dangerous, but that army is a terror. Atlas and Fá hit all the right nerves to make it dance to their tune, but so can we. I know Obsidians, and they know me. Do you have chemists? Anyone versed in poisons?"

"Both," Aurae says.

"Good. I'll need them to get to work on those spines we found in Diomedes."

Aurae nods but waits on Athena.

Athena looks back at the Obsidian fleet and sighs in surrender. "After Sevro's speech, and reviewing your . . . conversation about Atlas, I have recommended to the Daughters that we commute your sentence. They have agreed." Aurae uncuffs me herself and squeezes my hand. "We will not be made to betray our convictions. We will not abandon the people of the surface. The sealifts will be opened. Refuge will be given to all. But that refuge means nothing if the enemy is not beaten." Athena tosses over Pyrphoros. "So, you will be our spear as you should have been from the start." I catch the blade by its leather hilt. Its balance is perfect for such a long blade. I turn it in admiration. Then brush my finger on the shape-toggle to form the shape of a slingBlade.

Athena and the Daughters stare at its shape with deep, mixed emotions. After a moment, she says, "It is not a gift. It is a reminder of your oath. Once Fá is dead, you will return it to me and you will kneel and face your sentence. Swear it, by your kin."

I glance at Sevro. He nods.

I touch the key on my chest. "In the name of my son, Pax, I swear it."

"And Diomedes and Cassius?" I ask.

"Already told her the Chin's with me," Sevro says. "It's how Da would want it."

Hearing this, Cassius gives Sevro a hard nod of solidarity. Aurae unlocks his cuffs and whispers something in his ear.

"And Diomedes?" I ask.

Athena nods to Aurae. Aurae brings around a tablet to hold before Diomedes. He is a slow reader. Bit by bit his eyes widen. "Abolition of the hierarchy . . ." He keeps reading. "Self-determination of vocation? What is this?"

"The future, Raa," Athena says.

"You cannot believe the Moon Lords would ever agree to this—"

"*We* believe in holding someone to their word," Athena says. "You say you have failed us. You have. But we do not accept your head as repayment. We will take your service instead. If you are a shepherd, as all Raa believe, prove it. Lead us to a new and better future. If we are to risk our lives, our cause, we refuse to return to the same chains we have lived in for centuries."

Diomedes reads the document further. "Even if I wished to honor this . . ." He almost says *absurdity*. "This . . . treatise, I cannot. I am no consul or Sovereign. I am only an Olympic Knight. It would be false to pretend I have the power to institute even one of these—"

Athena laughs at him. "Do you know the efforts it took to install a Daughter amongst your hetaerae?" she asks. "Akin to Ares's efforts with Darrow. Do you know what Aurae's tasks were? Tell him, Aurae."

Aurae looks nervous. "My tasks were to gather and pass information, particularly regarding Krypteian or naval matters. My . . . primary function was to ensure that no true tyrant ascended to lead House Raa. Fortunately, I found none lying in wait."

Diomedes tilts his head. "And if you had?"

"I would have killed them. For the people."

He's startled.

"Aurae said long ago that you would be a fair but stern ruler, Diomedes. We have known your character for some time," Athena says. "You are also the son of Romulus au Raa. That matters. Your voice will carry from here to Pluto. We are not fools. We know the Moon Lords will resist this. Things always move slower in the Rim. So we do not ask for you to dismantle the hierarchy in a day. All we ask is that you swear an oath to make abolition your personal cause until the day it passes in the Decagon. If we are to be allies in war, we must know we will be peers in peace."

Diomedes swallows. "You want me to become your . . . kept Gold . . . your agent?"

"No. We'd have you be our Virginia Augustus, Diomedes," Aurae says. "Not a 'kept Gold.' A visionary. A champion for the downtrodden."

"And . . . what is to stop me from betraying you at my convenience?"

Aurae smiles. "Your character. Your honor. Your heart. Your oath."

"You forget, I already swore an oath to protect the hierarchy . . ."

Aurae grips his arm. "You also swore an oath to protect the people of the Rim. Look me in the eye, Diomedes, and tell me I should serve you." She raises her eyebrows. "Tell me you matter more because of the sigils on your hands. Tell me I am less than you."

She guides his chin so he has to look her in the eye. His stare is as intense as a particle cannon until she flicks his nose. He explodes with a laugh that makes even me jump. He follows it with a smile I didn't think his face capable of making.

"If you can't do that, then maybe it's time you took a new oath," she says.

Diomedes turns to Athena, dour again. "If I give my oath, the sealifts open? The people can take refuge and I am free to take up arms with Darrow against Fá?" His voice darkens. "Against Atlas?"

Athena smiles. "We don't hold the sins of the ancestors against their descendants, Raa. Give me your oath and I'll put the blade in your hand myself."

63

LYRIA

Mashed Taters

THE OBSIDIANS ARE ON their way. The sealifts haven't stopped for two days. Up they take newly made soldiers with newly made rifles. Down they bring the civilians of the surface to the deeper levels of the undercity where the Daughters break their backs to build camps for incoming refugees. Except for the uniforms and rifles, the two groups don't look so different. Determination, fear, dignity—whatever expression the "soldiers" wear, they all look like children compared to the Obsidian frontliners I saw on Io.

The Daughters won't be able to hold back the Obsidians if they breach the undercity. Even I know that. Which means Darrow must be planning something. Not that they've told me. Daughters didn't even bother locking me up. Said I was an "innocent." Told me to make myself useful. So I have by sneaking into one of their barracks and stealing a uniform.

Cutting my way through the staging area where haulers trundle past laden with supplies, I climb the stairs to the hulking door into the command center. The Daughters guarding it hold up their hands. One's a Green man, the other a Yellow woman.

"Pass card," the woman demands.

"Pass card?" I say.

"No admittance without a pass card."

"Shit. Shit. No one said nothing about a card. Barca's gonna skin me alive. Don't you recognize me?" I ask. They look at each other. "I'm a bloodydamn Martian. Darrow's niece, Rhonna. Barca's adjunct. You know?" I hold up a can of gun polish I nabbed from the barracks. "Needed polish for his helm."

"You need a card."

"Listen to my vowels," I say with a nervous expression. "Look how short I am. I'm obviously from Mars." They believe that. "Listen, he'll kill me if he knows I slagged up. Can't one of you take me to him? Throw cuffs on me if you need. Have you met him yet, the Son of Ares? Do you want to?"

"I can take her," the Yellow says. The Green bickers. He wants to meet Sevro too. In the end, the Yellow wins and escorts me in. They lead me through a complex of halls to a big door that Greens are filing through. "Wait here—"

I dart right on past on the heels of the Greens.

I follow them into a room glowing with screens and buzzing with activity. Its epicenter is Darrow. Swarmed with Daughters, he stands at the holographic main display locked in an argument with Athena and Diomedes. The moon of Europa glows above them. A red dot travels through the sea. Then someone grabs my ear loud enough that I yelp. Darrow, Diomedes, and Athena all turn to stare at me as I'm dragged out of the room back into the hall pinned to the wall by Sevro.

"What are you doing?" he snarls in my face.

"You shaved your beard." He shakes me. "I didn't come all this way to be left in the cold. I need to talk to Darrow."

"How did you—" He stops and turns his head to look at the Yellow, who stares at him in awe and terror. "Get," he snaps. The Yellow bolts like a hare. "All the competent guards are off," he mutters. "What are you doing here?"

"I need to talk to Darrow."

"What did you see?"

"Nothing."

He flicks my ear. "Opsec mean shit to you? What did you see?"

"What's opsec?"

"What. Did. You. See."

"Nothing, just a few displays." His eyes narrow, but he seems to believe me. "Sevro, I need to talk to Darrow. Tell him he gave his word."

Hours later, I'm dozing in the command center's commissary when I feel the bench beside me sigh in protest. I sit up. Wiping sleep from my eyes, I glance over to see Darrow hunched above a pile of chow. Unlike Sevro, he still has his beard. He seems a different creature than the commander I saw in the war room. Tired, smaller somehow. His left hand has a tremor. His neck's stooped, body contracted. I almost feel bad for interrupting his moment of respite.

"Heard you wanted to talk," he says. "We've a lot of plates in the air. I've a hard out in five minutes."

Sevro slides in on the other side of me and digs into his chow. "That means talk."

"We had a deal," I say.

"That's why you have minutes," Darrow says.

"I can help you."

Darrow grimaces as he chews. "Listen. Lyria, I'm sure you think you can but—"

"Condescension? After that speech?" I ask. "This is my fight too, or were those words just to make sure you didn't swing?" Annoyed that he won't look at me, I pull his tray away from him. He spears a potato with his fork and pulls the tray back as he chews.

Doubt plays tricks on me. Tells me to just let him go. Don't slow him down. I'm out of my depth. War is his game. But I ain't gonna sleep sound in the barracks huddled with the children and the tender Colors as the Obsidians batter down the gates.

"I never loved Mars till I left it," I try. "Mars wasn't my home. The mines were my home. I loved them. Probably because I was a Gamma, but I loved them and you destroyed them." Sevro's eyes dart to Darrow. "You destroyed my world. It's gone and never coming back. Part of me will always hate you for that. But the farther and farther I go from Mars, the more I miss it. The more I want to fight for it. Lads and lasses younger than me will be shouldering rifles against Atalantia soon if they aren't already. Lads and lasses that lasted the assimilation camps like me. It wasn't their choice either, to leave the mines. You chose for us. But they ain't hiding or whining like I've done. They're fighting. This is my choice. I want to help." I lean closer to the man. "And between you and me, my value in the fray ain't in a Drachenjäger or manning an artillery piece or hauling freight. My value's in my social standing with a certain Obsidian."

Darrow sets his fork down and looks at me. Finally, I'm more interesting than his food. Sevro keeps eating.

"I know you think Volga's gone over to Fá lock and stock," I press.

"She leads a division now according to Sigurd," he replies. "Fá calls her 'daughter.'"

"But does she call him 'father'?" I plow on. "You don't know Volga like I do. She is a good person, Darrow. She's just never had a fair shake. So she adapts. It's what she does. Right now, she's lost. Like you said to those Obsidians on Io. I can guide her home. Deep down, Volga loves the Republic. She gave herself up to Fá to protect its people. Send me up top. Send me into the Obsidians. I'll bring her back to her senses."

His eyes narrow. "Send you into the Obisidans? How?"

"Use Sigurd," I say. "Have him take me to Volga."

"We don't know where she is. Neither will he. It's an invasion, Lyria. It'll be madness soon as they hit atmosphere." Darrow shakes his head. "You don't even speak Nagal."

"Ja ig syn fal tanga," I reply. He frowns. Sevro grins.

"You knew?" Darrow asks him.

Sevro shrugs. "May have heard her practicing every night on the *Archi*." I scoot a little away from him, bringing me closer to Darrow.

"You been tall so long you forgot what it looks like down here," I say to him. "How a Red like me can slip under a big man's gaze. From what I hear, ain't many bigger than Fá. I know you're planning something. Let me help turn Volga's heart. For Mars."

"You're afraid I'm going to kill her," he says.

"I don't know what you're going to do. But Ragnar was your friend. Don't you owe it to him to save his daughter?" I ask.

"She never met Ragnar," Sevro says.

"Is that her fault?" I ask. "She was bred in a lab, then moved freight in Echo City, then she was a freelancer, then a prisoner, then . . ."

"Warlord," Sevro says, unhelpful.

"She *is* the Republic," I say, and Darrow's frown deepens but it seems like a good thing. Am I getting traction? "It's not her fault that she became what she had to. But I know if I came to her and told her she could help you two . . . she would."

"She stole our kids," Sevro says. "Unlike you, she was an active participant. She shot Kavax. I like Kavax."

"And then she defended Victra against the Red Hand. Please, please trust me."

Darrow just prods his potatoes until they come apart under his fork.

He twirls the skin around one of the prongs. "Have you considered what will happen if you're caught? Or if you are wrong about her?"

I look at his now-mashed taters. "Yeah."

"And you know if you go in, we can't protect you? You're secondary to our mission."

"Yeah."

He sighs. "What do you think, Sev?"

"Hmm." He strokes his goatee. "I think you ain't as popular with the Volk as you think you are. I think if Lyria can get Volga to play ball, it doubles our chances when we do the Thing. I think if anyone can get us the evidence we need on Atlas, it's Volga. If Lyria is wrong and Volga won't play ball, then Lyria will probably die or be tortured. But she don't know shit, so she can't compromise the Thing. So the only real risk is her life, which is a risk I'm certainly willing to accept. More important, I think Cassius will hate it even more than he hates the Thing. So. What do I say? I say give Truffle Pig her shot. She's earned it."

64

LYSANDER

The Noble Lie

"**D**USTBORN THIRTY-THREE, YOU ARE CLEARED *for approach.*" Hearing Pytha's voice is like coming home. The battered Rim shuttle, one of the *Dustmaker's* own, coasts out from its hiding place in an impact crater on the moon of Valetudo toward my newly arrived expeditionary fleet.

Atlas cast my ten Praetorians and me as survivors of the massacre at Kalyke. The cramped confines and spartan creature comforts of the shuttle have left us looking the part. Bearded, exhausted, with our uniforms doctored by his Gorgons and wounds administered by Atlas himself, my Praetorians queue up to depart. I linger in the cockpit watching our approach.

"The *Lightbringer* has never looked nobler," Rhone says from behind my chair.

He's partly right. Additional repairs to the damage she received in the Battle of Phobos were completed en route by the Votum builders—an incredible achievement. Not only are most of the *Lightbringer's* guns finally operational, but the Lune crescent—black, for war—has been painted inside a gold pyramid along her port and starboard. Beyond that the rest of her hull is still patched, heterogenous, and unpainted.

I nod as if it looked fresh off the line. I will show no more reticence in front of Rhone. Gods know what he'll tell Atlas. I miss the total security in him I felt before he poisoned me. I mourn that loss of trust. It can never be as it once was. Nothing can.

"What of all this will you share with the ranks?" I ask him.

"The ranks are best treated like mushrooms: spoiled with shit and kept in the dark," he replies. "I recommend you treat your ranks the same, august though they are. Lysander may be good and noble to his friends, but a Sovereign must be a clinical operator." His eyes trace the house ships that attend the *Lightbringer*. They belong to Reformers who came out here for the unity I preached that day in Rome. "So many have honored your call. It would be a shame to stain this noble enterprise."

The full might of my Dracones XIII greets me in the main hangar of the *Lightbringer* along with my Reformer allies. Thirty-three thousand Praetorians snap to attention. I lost a fourth in the battle for Phobos. They are nearly as relieved to see me as they are distraught by my state. Limping into the hangar, I look back at their hard faces with far more wariness than I once did. If forced to choose, how many of them would follow Rhone or Atlas over me?

How many already do? Two hundred and twenty-one Gorgons aboard my ship, Atlas said.

I'm crushed into a hug by Cicero. "When we saw the atomic signatures, we feared you were dead at Kalyke. I feared—" He clears his throat, remembering himself and the eyes of the Reformers and Gold knights waiting behind him. Some of the knights have the dual scar of the New Shepherds, but there are several hundred new men and women. He swelled their ranks.

"Dido, Helios, Diomedes . . . what a waste," Cicero murmurs.

"They will be avenged," I say.

His eyes glisten as he nods. His grief is real, as is his righteous anger. He seizes Rhone's arm and works his way to Drusilla, Markus, and Demetrius. "Well done, Praetorians. You are a credit to your legion. House Votum—nay, all of the Society is in your debt."

"Any trouble from home?" I ask.

"Siege and stasis on Mars and Luna," he replies. "Though that doesn't stop Lady Bellona from playing Cassandra. She thinks Atalantia will sail on Mars any day."

"Then we must be quick."

Cicero pulls the command sceptre from its holster on his back. It was commissioned for the campaign to denote his imperium over the assembled factions. It is a bundle of iron rods that leads to a lightning bolt. "Your fleet stands ready, Lysander."

"To return home," Pallas adds. She stands with Lady Bellona's clients. I don't take the sceptre yet. I greet Pallas warmly.

"Pleased to see you retain all your parts, Lune," Pallas says. Her smile dissembles her wariness. Meanwhile her eyes collect and catalogue evidence to report back to Julia. To her, something's not adding up. "After seeing Kalyke, even I must admit you are indeed blessed by fortune. My Bellona ships are prepared to make for Mars as soon as you give the order, as are those of our clients."

I raise an eyebrow. "Mars?"

"Yes. This side venture was already ill-advised. The Lady Bellona would not have you risk our main endeavor on this . . . catastrophe that has nothing to do with our efforts anymore."

I smile and stride past her to remove my jacket and shirt. I bare my chest and back to my Praetorians and walk down the line. They might hate Moonies, so I'll play to their pride instead of their virtue. I tear off the bandages one by one to show the wounds Atlas gave me to lend credit to my harrowing story of survival.

"Look upon your Imperator," I call. "Look what Fá and his horde have done to me. Will you let this stand? Can Obsidians and Far Ink reptiles now brutalize a Peerless son of Luna with impunity? What say you, Praetorians? Shall we retreat? Or shall we hunt?"

The result is predictable. Shamed for a decade by the death of Octavia on their watch, the Praetorians respond with: "Hunt! Hunt! Hunt!"

I clothe myself and address the New Shepherds next. "Most of you are new men, new women. Your families are not yet storied. Many hold that in contempt. I do not. You wrote the first chapter of your family's legend on Phobos. Write its second with me now, and show all that you are the true keepers of the virtues the Conquerors held dear. You defend the weak. You shelter the low. Should the oceans rise, the sky fall, the darkness creep—you keep the wolves from the flock."

They pull their razors and salute.

With my foundation shored up, I return to the ficklest of my allies and change tack yet again. "My friends, you have risked personal fortune and our cause itself by following me here. The safe route is retreat. The bold route is forward. In days like this, with enemies like ours, boldness is prudence and retreat is folly. Now is the time to show the Rim that we are worth a thousand Atalantias."

They glance at one another, nervous to face the horde that humbled the Rim Armada.

"What good is an ally without a navy?" Pallas contends. "Shall we risk our lives, our ships, our soldiers, for those who can no longer aid us in our war? Who may not help us if they could?"

"My goodlady, Ilium is but a part of the Rim. Their domain is vast and slow to cross. They have more fleets. I assure you. Though they will not arrive in time. What we do here Neptune, Uranus, and Saturn will see, and they will remember."

Light kindles in the eyes of a few. Cicero herds the rest.

"The Raa cannot stand with us to defend their worlds," he says. "So we will stand for them. Yes?" He glares at his clients. "Yes?"

They nod in twos or threes, but in the end they all nod. Except Pallas. I thank them and return to her. "Lady Bellona didn't invest in an endeavor. She invested in me. Remember that, Pallas." She watches me with a thoughtful smile, but does not press the issue. I button my jacket back up and extend my hand to Cicero. "I'll take my fleet now."

Grinning, he hands me the sceptre of command.

I twist the sceptre's lightning bolt. My image streams onto the bridges of the fleet and my voice into the ears of all the sailors, legionnaires, and crew of the fleet.

"This is Lysander au Lune. I have reclaimed imperium over the fleet from Praetor Votum. You have sailed past Kalyke and seen the slaughter there. But the situation is more dire than you know. Not only has the enemy sacked Io, they have razed Callisto with atomics. Soon they will have Europa in their clutches. They have enslaved millions of our fellow citizens. And they have seized Demeter's Garter. They hold its destruction hostage over the Rim. Their war, their crime, is not just against our allies, it is against civilization itself! In his madness, the warlord known as Volsung Fá wishes to drag us back to the bitter pit of chaos from which mankind barely escaped."

As I orate I begin to pace. Walking with increasing speed and intensity past Praetorians whose eyes follow my every step. Past excited young Golds, eager to make their mark. Eventually, I come to Rhone and his eyes narrow with intensity. He is pleased with my performance. I pour on the gravitas.

"Fá is a cunning and brutal adversary. He has trampled all in his path. He does not yet know the taste of defeat. In his arrogance he thinks himself the lone power left in Ilium. He has divided his forces and so made a fatal error. One we will exploit by reclaiming the Garter with utmost haste. Once the threat of famine is removed, we will hunt the beast himself and teach his horde that civilization has teeth."

After meeting with my officers to explain my escape from Kalyke and dictate the plan Rhone and I created during our wait on Valetudo, I retire to my stateroom and summon Pytha. My stateroom is a heavily secured network of chambers not far from the bridge. The metallic nature of warships is softened by wood paneling chosen by Horatia au Votum. The engravings of my family history in the wood were not yet complete when we left Mercury. They are now. A pleasant surprise followed by another as I'm greeted by Exeter in the atrium.

I'd almost forgotten I'd commissioned him as my valet before my poisoning. I feel a pang of longing for Glirastes. Exeter's presence, more than the luxuries of the rooms, makes the stateroom feel more like home.

"May I recommend Debussy and a clean shave now that you're back from the wild, *dominus*? It always put Master Glirastes at ease."

Washed, clean-shaven, and dressed in my formal whites, I wait for Pytha in my library. Amidst the classic texts that line the walls, I recline on a chair examining the completed painting on the ceiling. It is a scene of the Conquering. My oldest ancestor is not alone in any of the images. Akari accompanies him—sometimes standing beside him, sometimes behind. I thought such images would impress Diomedes when he stood here with me. Instead, it is to be a different Raa beside me. A shadow that no portrait will ever render.

But if future generations do etch or paint us together, how will my distant descendants judge me for Atlas's presence? Will they revere him as I revere Akari, his evil deeds scrubbed clean by the brush of history?

Pytha greets me with a warm hug when she arrives, and doesn't let go until I surrender to the embrace. She clings to me like I'm her brother, and I feel like I am. "I'm sorry about Diomedes," she says after we take a seat on the couch. "I know you thought you had found a friend in him."

"More than that," I murmur.

"We both watched silence eat Cassius up," she says. "Tell me what happened."

With Rhone no longer in my trust, I told myself I would confide everything in Pytha, but as she holds my hand I realize that while she very well might understand why I accepted Atlas's offer, she will never look at me the same way ever again. Not with that protective love of an older sister. Lysander will cease to exist. She will look at me then only as her Sovereign. In time I will look at her as only my captain, and it will be as if our lives on the *Archimedes* never happened.

To preserve that, I lie to her. I tell her the tale I told Cicero and Pallas and my officers.

"The ambush came out of nowhere," I say. It's not hard to look haunted. "I don't know what happened. I woke in the barracks to Ascomanni in the halls. I tried to repel the boarders, but the *Dustmaker* was overrun. I wanted to stay and fight to the end, but my Praetorians forced me to evacuate."

"And you feel guilty for that?" she asks. I nod. "It wasn't your fault. You were a passenger." Her hand settles on my knee. "I saw the rubble. I heard your speech. You can be brave for them. You don't have to be brave for me."

"I know. I'd rather not relive it anymore," I say.

"But you don't have to live with it alone," she says. "Whatever happened. Whatever you saw—" She pauses. "You don't have to tell me. But I've never seen you like this, I can carry it with you. Whatever it is."

I want to tell her. I know I need someone else to trust. I feel that aching in my heart to share this burden. Glirastes is gone. Ajax too. I want to tell her I am afraid. That my Praetorians are not my protectors. That I am a fool. That there are strings inside me I don't know if I'll ever be able to cut. Instead, I deflect, shame binds my mouth from telling the truth.

"It's just how cold it all was—Kalyke," I say. "How cold it all is."

That truth, though not the truth, makes me crack. The tears stream out, and she takes me in her arms. I cry into her uniform and hold on to her warmth. She knows I've not said it all, but Pytha—sweet and dear as she is—accepts the deflection and whispers that it will be all right. It can't be, I know, because it never was.

65

LYRIA

Into the Maelstrom

W
ITH DARROW'S MESSAGE FOR Volga burning a hole in my
mission pack, I follow six Black Owls through the bustle outside the main pedestrian sealift to Heraklion. The sealift doors groan
like old men going down stairs. They open to release thousands of refugees from the surface. In the robes of their Colors, the refugees stream
out between the statues of Poseidon and Aphrodite like migrating but-
terflies. Not just on the ground but by means of lines strung in the air.
Gray soldiers floating about in leviathan-marked cuirasses of House
Kalibar herd them toward the magnetic trams where Daughter militia
load them into cars to take them to refugee cities nearer the core. The
tension between the groups of soldiers is enough that everyone expects
a firefight to break out at any moment. Yet everyone is keeping their
tempers, sensing that feeling that hangs in the air. The feeling I had as a
girl in 121 when storms would wrack the Cimmerian plains and the
clans would abandon the camp and huddle together in the mines, even
with us Gammas.

It is strange. Couple years ago it'd be me filing along clutching my
siblings' hands, making sure we all stick together as we flee the storm.
Now, I trudge toward the maelstrom, and I'm surprised that I don't feel
unprepared. Darrow himself handed me off to the Owls. I will not let
him down. I will win Volga back to the Republic.

"Wrong way, squibs!" a Gray shouts to the Black Owls in an accent
so thick I can barely understand him. He sets down in front of us in

beautiful blue armor. The leviathan on his chest is golden. An officer then. "Follow the lanes and get with the others."

"We're going up top," I say.

The Gray snorts. His bluff face is half hidden in his helmet. Hard eyes peer out at us from the dark blue steel. "Naw, ya ain't, little rusty. Them reptiles will make a meal of ya."

"It'll be the crows," a second Gray says. "Reptiles are sacking the Dryads."

The first Gray shrugs. "Either, neither. Yar going nowhere, lass."

"Let us through," a voice booms behind us and the Owls and I spin around.

Two giants in armor enter the doorway. Cassius and Sigurd. The former is unexpected. "What you doin' here?" I ask Cassius with a smile.

"You didn't think I'd let strangers drop you off, did you?" he asks. "I thought I'd come along in case you met trouble."

The Gray who'd blocked us is as surprised to see a Core Gold as he is the Obsidian brave standing next to him.

"D-Dominus," the Gray stammers and steps aside.

Cassius sweeps me into the lift along with Sigurd, leaving the Owls outside. The door closes and the motors hum to life.

"I have a warrant badge," I say as the lift begins to rise. "I would have used it to get past that tinpot. Truth is you just can't stay away from me, Bellona."

"Psh. Any Golds left in Heraklion aren't very happy with Diomedes or the Raa right now. That badge won't mean much." He falls in beside me. "Sorry I missed your briefing. I was playing ambassador for Diomedes."

"Ambassador?"

"He might have convinced the Kalibar to take Athena's offer, but some of the sealords—those who haven't fled to Ganymede like the rest of the cowards—would rather die than 'collude with terrorists.' My father was friends with a few of them. Though I don't see why. They're stubborn as mountains. Their people will pay the price of their pride, as always."

Haunted, he looks out the glass of the lift. The lights of the Deep shrink in the darkness as we rise. A river of bioluminescent fish illuminates his face with pearly light. I touch his vambrace. He gives me a brave smile. "I'll escort you and Sigurd to the shuttle, but that's as far as

I can go. I'd come with you into the Obsidians wearing prosthetics, but Sigurd says I'd blow your cover."

Sigurd nods. "You would. Krypteia tried to assassinate Fá in the Garter. Their guises were without flaw. But Fá sniffed them out. He skinned them, castrated them, and keeps them leashed to his throne."

Cassius and I stare at him. "You sure your friends will find us first, Sigurd?" Cassius asks. "And that they won't turn Lyria over to Fá?"

"Fenrir and Gudmund were there on Io," Sigurd reminds him. "They wanted to come with me when I surrendered to Darrow. I begged them to stay behind in case they were needed. He has spoken to them himself on the frequency I provided." Sigurd looks at me now. "They have no love of Fá, Lyria, and unlike my father, they are not too cowardly to act. Gudmund yearns to redeem his honor in Darrow's eyes. Fenrir . . . less so, but he owes a blood-debt to Sevro and misses Attica, his favorite city in all the worlds. We will take the shuttle to them, and they will take you to Volga. On my honor, such as it remains."

Cassius eyes Sigurd with little trust. He lowers his voice. "What's rule number one, Lyria?"

"Don't get caught by Ascomanni and shipped off to the far dark," I say.

"Rule number two?"

"There is no rule number two."

The lift begins to slow. Cassius's anxiety mounts. I grab his massive hand. He holds mine and together we wait for the lift doors to open.

The pounding of waves and the distant thunder of the bombardment flow into the lift as the doors part with a groan. Outside, a floating gunship hovers over a sea of refugees. It blares orders and they move in military-like blocks toward the lift. I let go of Cassius's hand and we head out.

The station is a grand stone crescent out over the water with an open face to a massive courtyard filled with humanity. The city looms, connected to the station by several pedestrian bridges. The sky throbs from distant bombardments. Grays in gun installations peer up or out over the water where warships patrol the perimeter.

"That's us." Cassius points across the station's courtyard to the shuttle that will take us to the rendezvous with Gudmund and Fenrir. It waits past the refugees and a slew of military vehicles. Four Black Owls guard it. We head for the shuttle through the crowd.

We haven't taken thirty paces when I see something—a shadow crawling on one of the gun installations looking out over the water. I tell Cassius but by the time he looks, the shadow is gone.

He picks up our pace. A faint whistle followed by a warble comes from my left.

A few dozen paces off, a giant shimmering figure stands amidst the refugees as if he'd always been there. His ghostly guise dissolves to reveal a towering warrior. He is lean and nearly eight feet tall, and naked except for a shark-head helmet. Water drips from leathery, orangish skin. His feet are clad in curious boots with twin fans on either heel. He looks around as if admiring a school of sleeping fish. Stunned refugees back away, too startled to scream or cry out at his sudden appearance.

Then he starts to kill. He does it with two blades, each as long as my legs.

With his first swing, lowColor bodies and limbs geyser up in the low gravity. He swings again and again as if sweeping rubbish with a giant broom. A young Yellow finally has the wits to scream. Then more are screaming and pushing to get away from the butcher. Laughing, the giant disappears.

The scene may not even have lasted ten seconds.

The Grays of Heraklion mobilize, shout commands. Anxiety spreads through the refugees. They stir like confused cattle. Grays make a battle line on the steps leading to the lift.

Cassius draws his razor and activates his aegis. "What was that, Sigurd?"

Sigurd peers out to the sea. "That was a Harbinger." He sounds frightened. "They swam in past the sonar. I did not know they could swim."

"More are coming?" Cassius asks.

"Likely they are already here."

66

LYRIA

The Fall of Heraklion

CASSIUS TAKES CONTROL. "SIGURD, let's plow a path. Lyria, grab my belt and don't let go."

We rush toward the shuttle. Cassius and Sigurd batter their way through the crowd. More shadows flit through the courtyard. The lights above go out. A Gray fires in the distance. Another Ascomanni berserker appears ahead of us and kills three Blues before she's gunned down. Another appears to the left. A Gold knight descends to fight him.

Then hundreds of throats roar: *"GAAAANFAAAAGH."*

The Heraklions may have impressed me with the discipline of their evacuation, but the roar flips a switch. In an instant, they disintegrate into a mob of animals. Silent at first, they surge against us, against the battle line of Grays holding the half-filled lift. Then, once the Grays are swamped, do the berserkers attack everywhere all at once. Only the animals begin to bay. Screams and bodies clamor all around. Pressing in on me like a vise.

I can see nothing but flashes of insanity—panic-struck faces, clenched fists, falling bodies, barbarian butchers clad in darkness, children losing the hands of their mothers or fathers, boots on their backs. I clench Cassius's belt for all I'm worth, terrified I'll fall and be trampled. He plows through the madness with Sigurd. I can see the transport through them. We're close. Twenty paces off. Then something slithers overhead. The transport and the Owls guarding it disappear in a flash of white light. Heat washes over me. I fly back like a ragdoll.

My head spins. My brain aches. I gasp. I'm on the stone ground. My ears wail. I retch as I try to stand. A knee knocks me flat. A boot steps on the back of my head. Another presses on my hand. I use a man's body to crawl to my knees. His elbow glances off my nose but I gain my feet only to be trampled under a trio of back-pedaling Silvers. Two of them spill down and we scramble at one another. Someone else falls on me. Fingernails rake my face. A knee falls on my stomach. A shoe steps on my right breast. I wheeze and punch the Silver. I'm tangled in his balls until he stops squirming and untangles from me. I scramble up.

Cassius is nowhere to be found. I'm too short to see anything through the chaos.

Disoriented, I take cover at the base of a monument to some famous Gold holding a pyramid over his head. My ears ring as I clutch the stone of the statue's base. I climb up to its waist to see over the havoc. The shuttle is a fiery wreck. Refugees swamp the sealift. Its doors try to close only to be jammed with bodies. Then a ragged cheer goes up.

People turn and point. A flight of shining Golds descends from the acropolis of Heraklion. The cheers die as glowing brands slither up from the sea. Missiles. White light flashes in the sky, and when the light dims, the Golds are twirling debris.

The station is turning into a bloodbath. Horror greets me everywhere I look. I can't stay here. I don't know what to do. I search for Cassius and find him twenty paces off fighting a taller berserker. Sparks shower as spear meets razor. Cassius turns the spear up and sticks his razor in the berserker's chest. Sigurd appears, and slams his axe into the berserker's back. I climb higher up the statue and wave at Cassius. Cassius raises his razor when he sees me. He levitates over the crowd with his gravBoots to meet me at the base of the statue. Sigurd joins us, shouting into his com.

"Sigurd!" Cassius shouts when he sees the chaos at the lift. "We can't stay here."

Sigurd motions him to wait and ducks his head to listen to his com. Cassius is not having it and grabs my hand and drags me after him away from the courtyard. Sigurd rushes after. "My friends. They say they will come to us."

"Where?" Cassius shouts.

Sigurd points up to the acropolis in the distance, the highest place in the tiered city. Cassius's expression falls. "Anywhere but here!" I shout.

"I'll fly you," he says.

"Did you not see the Golds?" I ask. His face hardens and his eyes settle on the pedestrian bridge that links the sealift station to the city.

He leans down to say over the noise: "I am your shield. Stay in my shadow." Sigurd fires at something behind us. "Move."

The two armored men and I set off at a run.

Soon the sounds of the station are lost in the *tick tick tick* of our loping gait and the panting of my breath in my ears. At first there are others on foot like us but after we clear the bridge, the crowd thins, and we run alone into the low city, bound for the jump pads.

Jupiter stains the glass and stone buildings in bronze light. The meandering stone ways are abandoned but for long-legged cats with bones as thin as birds that watch us from windowsills. One hunts a shadow on the ground. I don't need to look up to know the shadow belongs to an Ascomanni ship. It roars past overhead firing at something before disappearing behind a great library complex. Two more ships follow it. Armored figures stream out their sides to fall onto the city.

Fear fuels my legs.

We turn right onto a shopping agora and see its pedestrian jump pad is still active. We take it at a run, and I feel myself go light and my stomach lurch a little as I sail up in a parabola maybe eighty meters before arching back down toward another jump pad set in a public water garden. Its gravity field slows me just as I land. I stumble, Cassius steadies me, and we run on to the next, ascending each ring of the city a jump at a time.

Wind whistles past. The sea roils in the distance and emits a deep groan. Only it's not the sea. I look up. The great shield that protected Heraklion from the sky is gone. A moment later, four molten fists begin their descent from orbit. Ships. Big ones.

A smaller gunship flies past overhead. It catches us in its wake and hurls us off the aerial path. All three of us crash down onto a rooftop garden. The plants below absorb most of my fall but pain jolts through my left shoulder as I hit the turf. Scrambling through flowers to the edge of the garden where Cassius stands, I see the gunship drawing up a half-klick away. Its guns wink as it fires down at the city's defenders in the high-rise bunkers.

There's movement in a higher garden on the level above. Cassius jerks his pulseFist upward. Three Grays look down at us. They're young. Maybe my age. They nod their heads. Two carry long metal rods. The third some sort of launcher. Cassius shouts at them to stop as they aim the launcher at the gunship. I don't know why.

The Grays fire. The only evidence of the missile leaving their launcher is a faint thread of distortion in the air. They score a hit. The gunship belches fire. Sigurd shouts he's found a way down. Cassius pulls me along, and we run before the Grays start loading the second missile. I hurl myself off the garden after Cassius and Sigurd, then down to the next, and the next below that. We're halfway down the block when heat washes through my bones from behind. In the reflection of a carver's store window, I see a pillar of light tethering the building we just abandoned to a warship so high above it looks like a splinter. Then the light is gone, and the building crumbles.

I'm choking and spitting dust out of my mouth by the time we land in the acropolis of Heraklion. I wipe tears from my eyes and turn to see Sigurd looking down. The lower city has begun to rattle and groan with war machines beneath a shroud of dust and smoke. Anger swells in me, an anger I see on Cassius's dust-caked face too. "Where are your friends?" I ask Sigurd.

He looks up at the sky. "On their way, they said. They said to meet them in the relic garden."

Cassius is wary. "Where's that?" I ask.

"I've been here before," Cassius says. "Follow me."

The acropolis has been abandoned, mostly. Its high gardens lie untouched by the invasion below. Sigurd watches the sky as we pass through the gardens. Fountains as tall as ten men babble water. Birds chirp on the shoulders of stone tyrants and in the boughs of fat olive trees. And there's music.

Through a squall of dust, I see a Violet woman in a grove of silver-leafed trees. Her eyes are closed as she plays a harp. She is pale with long, elegant limbs. She wears a maroon silk tunic and headscarf. In her lap lies a long, dark knife.

We push on, accompanied for a little while by her song. The stone grottos and parks of the acropolis seem deposited from an older, grander age. Except for the music of birds and the shuffle of alien creatures in the trees, they are lifeless. The Brown growers have fled. So too have the guards of the acropolis, likely to help with the evacuation or the defense.

We pass a black stone building with ten sides. Its sides are open. Through the black columns, I glimpse a dozen white-bearded Golds sitting on the stone benches in its center. They are silent and still as statues. They watch the sky through the open roof, their razors in their laps, their dolphin rods leaning in the nooks between their shoulders and necks. Their white hair stirs in the breeze.

Then we are past and entering a grove of trees amidst which lie black stone shrines shaped like pyramids. Sigurd is still watching the sky. Cassius peers around. I pant for breath. "Where are they, Sigurd?" Cassius says.

In his Obsidian armor Sigurd no longer feels like a friend, but when he turns, his eyes are hard and focused. "Cassius, they are close. But you must leave now."

Cassius pulls out his razor. "I think not."

"Ascomanni have landed on the acropolis," Sigurd says and taps his communication link. "Your armor. They will want it. They will know you are Gold. You will ruin the mission. They will not attack me. Go."

Cassius looks at me in fear. "Your friends are close?" I ask Sigurd.

"Very."

"Cassius, go," I say. "Go."

He strides to me, kisses the top of my head, and his armor turns dark as the night. Wind whips around us, and he's gone into the sky. Sigurd sees something back near the black building with ten sides. I see it too, shadows descending through its open roof. He motions me back, and searches the sky. "Brothers, hurry," he whispers into his com. Then to me, "Go to your knees. Say nothing. They come."

His helmet slithers up to hide his face. He's already cut off his Helm's beautiful horns to hide his identity. He pulls the axe from the mag holster on his back. I go to my knees, trembling in fear. The leaves rustle. Thunder rumbles. Metal clinks toward us through the grove. I sense eyes on me. I twist my head. A small, almost childish figure watches me from the top of one of the black shrines. It wears light armor that drinks in the light and pulls something from its back to mark the pyramid with a symbol in white paint.

"They're claiming loot," Sigurd murmurs. "You are mine. Do not run. Do not speak. And whatever happens, do not look them in the eyes or they have to kill you."

Lean warriors stride through the trees. They are tall, lanky, with long spears. Their skin and armor are painted dark red. I dart my eyes to the ground.

A frigid voice calls in broken Nagal. "You are lost . . . warm brave. Alone. Tribe? Name?"

"That's for my brothers. My sisters. My jarl. Not for you."

"You . . . Fifth Ring. We . . . First Ring. This city . . . claimed. Leave all treasure. Slave too. Or lose skin."

"You can go have sex with a goat."

"Skin it will be."

Feet crunch dried leaves. Metal rasps.

"Sixteen on one? Fight me with honor," Sigurd growls.

I resist the urge to glance up. My eyes almost meet one as he sniffs the ground where Cassius took off.

"Names fight Names. You have none . . . but thief."

The sky whistles. I look up just as two mounds of metal land with a bang that almost knocks me over. "Oy, reptiles! You found our lost brother!" a big, happy voice bellows. He is a wide man and plants an axe on the stone. "Name's Gudmund the Jolly. We'll be taking our brother now. Unless you want to make a thing of it? What do you think, Fenrir? Should we make a thing of it?"

The Ascomanni turn to peer at the thinner, shorter Obsidian. Fenrir's face is covered, but he wears a black Pegasus Legion helmet. The horse head slithers into his collar to reveal a long face bearing the skull tattoo of a Stained. The Ascomanni tap their spears on the ground. Respect?

Fenrir asks something softly in a strange language. No one replies. He says something again, and the Ascomanni melt away to loot the shrines. The Obsidians stare after them, their guard still up.

"What did you say?" I whisper in Nagal.

Fenrir looks down at me with little affection. One of his eyes is black, the other a green-hued techjob. His nose is flat. His lips scarred. He is terrifyingly calm.

"I asked if there was a Name here, or if anyone would like to make one," he replies in Common. He looks to his brothers. "They'll pass the word. We should flee, before one shows up."

Gudmund bends to help me up with a jolly smile as a lean corvette approaches above. "Arms or back, lass," he offers politely. I clamber onto his back, and he takes off toward the corvette.

I sit in the back of the corvette's garage with my legs out the open door. The sea rolls beneath. Heraklion is already lost in the distance. At times I see the light of a passing ship on the horizon, a flare of atmospheric descent, or a flash from a bomb. I wonder about my friends. I don't see how they can possibly stop this.

Sigurd approaches and squats beside me. "I must leave now. I thought my absence would not be noticed, but there is a mark on my head. Fá knows I surrendered to Darrow. Gudmund and Fenrir will take you straight to Volga's ship. She is not far." He sees me looking back at them in worry. "You can trust them."

"It's not them I'm worried about," I say. "Thank you for helping."

He cocks his head. "You help us," he says. "It is our people who should thank you. Unnatural or not, Volga is the blood of Ragnar. The longer she is under Fá's sway, the deeper we fall away from Ragnar's dream. We must return to the sun, and the smiles of our mothers. We must have a queen. I tire of kings."

"For the Republic," I say and stick out my hand. He takes it.

"For the Volk too. Good luck, Lyria of Lagalos." He says farewell to his brothers and flies out the back. I don't know these men. They could deliver me wherever they want, or just dump me into the sea. Fenrir glares at me like I spat on his boots. Gudmund pops down beside me eating a sausage. He hands one to me. I pass, nauseous with dread.

"How long till Volga?" I ask.

"Forty minutes. She leads a hunting party." I nod like I know what that means. "Cimmeria, huh?" he asks with his mouth full of sausage.

"South pole, huh?" I reply.

He thinks that's funny. "This place is terrible. I cannot wait to go home."

"What do you miss most from Mars?" I ask.

He scratches his beard and his plump face lights up. "The parades! I look so glamourous with ribbons in my hair." He pulls out a long wire and winces. "I'm sorry, but we must deliver you like loot."

"Of course you bloody do."

67

LYRIA

Volga

Fenrir and Gudmund fly out from the corvette into fog. I dangle beneath the duo hogtied to Gudmund by a wire. Wind gnaws through me. I flinch as a cliff of gray metal appears in front of us out of the fog. It takes a moment to realize it's no cliff. It's a warship, and a grand one at that. It flies low with its main lights off. Strange umbilicals connect it to the sea beneath.

Gudmund and Fenrir glide toward a hangar lit with red mission lights. Several hundred Gray captives stand at the hangar's edge, all connected to a great chain with a hook at the end. A dozen wounded Golds stand to their left, also chained and guarded by Ascomanni.

Deeper in the hangar, Core Obsidians sprawl on looted purple couches. Their helmets are off, and like their armor, their faces are smeared with sweat and soot from battle. Passing around huge skeins of wine, they watch as a green globe floats over an Ascommani and a short Obsidian in brilliant black armor studded with gemstones.

Both seem important.

My eyes fix on the back of the short Obsidian. Their honortail is stubby. Their cape made of dragonscale. A dozen Ascomanni guards come to investigate our landing. Fenrir slips them a small pouch of gems and Gudmund eats a sausage while they assess the gems. Once the gems are approved, one of the guards returns with a very prim, very serious-looking Copper woman. Her head is shaved. She is branded with a winged symbol on her forehead.

"Lord Fenrir, you are out of position," the Copper says in Nagal and references her datapad.

"Speak your own language, slave," Fenrir replies in Common.

The Copper obliges. "Your assignment is north of the equator. What are you doing here?"

"We found something," Gudmund says and waves down to me. "Lost property of your mistress. So she claims to be. We were going to sell her for labor, but we are conscientious men."

"Ask your mistress if she's missing a slave from Mars," Fenrir demands.

The Copper scurries off toward the short Obsidian standing beneath the green globe. She whispers in the Obsidian's ear, and the Obsidian turns.

For a moment I don't recognize Volga. Her face is covered in war paint and her neck is tattooed with wings, but I know those eyes that follow the Copper's finger. Though they are bitter and hard, they flinch when they see me. A shout of excitement comes from the Ascomanni at Volga's side. A contact blinks on their sensor globe. The Ascomanni issue a low chant and somewhere in the hangar, drums begin to beat. Rolling their eyes, the Core Obsidians drink on.

Volga's eyes harden as the Ascomanni beside her runs to the hangar's edge toward the Gray and Gold captives. The Golds salute the Grays.

"Akari!" one of the Grays, a grizzled woman with a missing right eye shouts.

"Bear witness!" roar her men and salute the chained Golds as the Ascomanni reaches the edge of the hangar and kicks a huge metal hook over the side. Attached to the chain, the weight of the hook pulls the Grays along with it toward the sea. Long after they've disappeared, the Golds continue to salute in silence. Then the Ascomanni kicks their chain and they disappear one by one. Gleeful Ascomanni gather in droves to look down into the sea.

"What are they doing?" I murmur.

"Chumming the water for leviathan," Fenrir replies. "Fá never lets a victory pass without a feast."

"Nor do I," Gudmund says and eats another sausage.

I am taken from the hangar by what seem to be Volga's slaves—three heavyset Reds with collars on their necks. More slaves fill the innards of the ship. Blues, Oranges, Greens, Reds. All shuffling along in their collars to maintain the warship. Beneath the winged brands on their foreheads, their eyes are blank and refuse to meet mine. I wonder how long it would take here for my eyes to go blank like theirs.

I'm dumped in a stateroom. Inside is a trophy wall filled with a dozen razors and dragon's teeth. The stress of the day has left me exhausted. I sit on one of the room's couches and without meaning to, I fall fast asleep.

I dream of dark water and deep creatures until I hear a voice.

Sevro's.

"—you don't know me. I don't know you. But the real tragedy is that you didn't know your father."

I wake to find a blanket has been draped over me. A voice comes from the table where, beside two leather sacks, Volga hunches over the holocube Darrow gave me. The message for Volga is not from him. It's from Sevro. Volga focuses so intensely on the message that she does not see I am awake.

"You didn't know him, so you have to listen to others tell you about him. You have to see him through their eyes. It's a tainted picture. I'd know something about having a da like that." He chews his lip. "I knew your father. Fought beside him as brothers. Volsung Fá didn't. He knew Ragnar as well as you knew him. I was Ragnar's family. His friend. So, figured I owed it to Ragnar to tell you who he was.

"Don't buy the myth. He wasn't a god. He wasn't a messiah. Shit, he wasn't even a good man for most of his life. He was a gladiator and slave-knight. A prized possession to one of the worst families out there. He did what he was made to do. He fought. He killed. He was a Stained. The butcher they send for the other butchers. And butcher he did, right up until Darrow chose to trust him. Darrow revealed his secret—the fact that he was a Red—to your father. Something he didn't even do with me until I forced him into it. I was always raw about that. Darrow saw something in Ragnar. A latent goodness. A potential to lead. I don't know. Whatever it was, he put his life in Ragnar's hands long before that famous razor. It was the best bet he ever made.

"So, what did that butcher's butcher do when his chains were broken? Did Ragnar make himself a crown from the shards? Try his hand at empire? Naw. That was beneath him. Your father built shields for the old, the small, *the gentle, the low. That's what he chose to be. A shield. Your da believed his people were part of a greater whole.*

"Fá's campaign spits on Ragnar's name. Using power to enslave is the way of the Golds, Volga. Your father wasn't great because he could kill. He was great because he dared to try and make a world where he didn't have to. He was a protector, Volga. A builder."

He stares awhile, away from the camera. I watch Volga. Her eyes are unreadable.

"I know Ragnar would be very sad to see the path his father has chosen for the Volk. Because it isn't his father who has chosen it. It is Atlas au Raa. I'm sure you know the name. Your grandfather serves him. Maybe this is news to you. Maybe it is not. But either way, if you think you are making a kingdom for your people, you're wrong. You're just a tool of the Golds." Volga frowns. *"I know Ragnar would want this stopped. He'd want the Volk to return home to Mars and build something good. He'd have the Volk protect Mars. He'd have them led by a queen.* You, *Volga. Volsung has no right to lead, you do. You must throw off Atlas's yoke. You must take your place as Queen of the Volk in the name of your father and protect the Republic."*

He sighs and scratches his goatee. *"The Republic has not been good to you. I know it's clumsy and ugly. I know you don't trust Darrow. He's a sinister shit at times. You've every right to be wary of him. But he was a better friend to your father than even I was. Bet on him, Volga. Bet on us. You stole our kids, and we're willing to forgive. My wife made you an oath when she swam for Ulysses."* Volga swallows. *"In the gens Barca, an oath given by one is an oath shared by the pack. If you choose to walk in your father's footsteps, I've got your back till Vale come. But if you decide to walk in Fá's shadow, Atlas's shadow, it won't just be Darrow you'll have to worry about. The choice is yours.*

"And, Lyria, if you're listening to this before giving it to Volga, you're a nosy little shit but I hope you don't die. Barca out."

Volga turns off the hologram and sits, pensive, until I clear my throat. She starts up from the table, and comes over with a smile to sit beside me on the couch. She knows I saw her listening to the message, but for a moment we both pretend I didn't. Her large hand strokes my cheek. Four gold bands clink on her wrists. Her voice is tender.

"You're far from home, Lyria."

"So are you," I reply. After a moment of searching my eyes, her own soften and she smiles and traces the surgery scars on my head.

"You are free of the parasite. How?"

"It's a long story. But sorry. It cost me the *Snowball*." Though happy for me, she looks older than I remember. For some reason we always felt the same age. Her face has more lines now. The ones on her forehead are deep grooves. "How goes your hunt?" I ask. Dumb question.

"Poorly. We hooked a calfling. Another has taken the sigil beast. An Ascomanni."

Neither of us says anything for a long time.

"I didn't know if I'd ever see you again," I say. I take her hand. She rubs a callused finger over mine. Silence stretches. There are so many things to tell her. To ask. To say.

"Lyria, why are you here?"

"I came for you. To bring you home."

"Home." She pulls her hand back. I feel a distance form between us. There has always been a dark part of her. A part only too willing to use the guns she so fancied. "I am where I should be. Back with my people. I am home, Lyria."

"Your people?" I ask. "I'm your people, Volga. That's why I came all this way for you."

Her eyes go cagey and she nods to the holocube. "Did you come for me? Or did you come for Darrow?"

"It's not like that. This was my idea. He didn't want me to come. I had to stow away on his ship to get here. He thinks I'm mad for coming to see you. Mad to think you're not like Fá. I came here for you, Volga."

Her eyes narrow. "Why?"

I'm hurt that she'd even ask like that.

"Why? I told you. Because you're my friend." She grimaces. "Aren't you?"

"I am, yes. I am. But I am . . . more than that now. My grandfather has opened my eyes."

"Volga. He serves a Gold. Didn't you hear?"

"He *served* a Gold, long ago. He broke his chains in the Kuiper Belt. He has not seen Atlas since, and if he does he has sworn to kill him."

I stare at her, barely able to contain my frustration. "He's lying. This is all Atlas's plan. He is Fá's Allfather!"

"You have evidence?" she asks like a lawyer.

I hesitate. "No, but Diomedes saw him on the *Dustmaker*."

"Diomedes? A Gold." She smirks. "When Fá learned Darrow was here, he told me he would use tricks. Lies to turn me against him. Anything to reclaim his hold over the Volk. But the Volk are not Darrow's to claim. They . . . we have our own destiny now. These worlds are meant for us, Lyria. With the Garter, we can feed ourselves. With the Deep, we will have technology to defend ourselves. With Ganymede, we will have a homeland with trees, mountains, seas. Soon enough the Republic will fall. When the Core Golds come, and they will come, we must be ready, strong. We will either win our freedom or we will die."

I shake my head, unable to believe the words coming from her mouth, the excuses she uses to forgive herself. "Volga. Fá ate Ephraim's heart."

She pauses. "Yes."

"He *ate* Ephraim's *heart*."

"It was a sign of respect."

I pull my hands back from her and stand. Even sitting she is taller than I am. She peers down at me as if I were a child. "You swore to kill him."

She licks her lips. "I meant to. I was filled with hate. Eleven days after Mars he put a blade in my hand. I put it to his throat. He told me to kill him for what he did to Ephraim. But he warned me. He said that if I killed him, his bloodguard would kill me. I could sacrifice my life for a Gray who sacrificed nothing for me. Or I could stay my hand and help him build a kingdom for our people." She does not avoid my eyes. She is proud of her choice. "I chose my people."

I'm bewildered. "Ephraim was like a father to you."

"Ephraim?" She sighs. "You did not know him. He was a killer. A user. Ephraim treated everyone like a tool. That was his way. He used me from the day he met me. If I were not useful, he would have discarded me." She picks her stubby nails. "I do miss him. Sometimes, I do. But he is in the past. My duty takes me elsewhere."

"And that duty includes sacking cities? Enslaving people? That's not the Volga I know."

"You do not know me either," she says. "You never did."

That pisses me off. "Oh. Must have been talking to myself in that cell on the *Pandora* then. Must have just been Victra and me who fled the Red Hand across the snow. Just me and her when Ulysses was born. You must have never cried and told me it was because you could never have children, because they spayed you." She grows angry, and I can't stop pushing. "Must have not freed you from chains when the Red Hand had you working the mines like a Red. Must have been alone when Victra swam to mourn Ulysses." She says nothing. "Volga, I don't know what you've seen. What Fá's told you. But I know this ain't you. That you're sick inside about all this. The Volk don't belong out here, on the leash of a monster. They belong with the Republic."

"The Republic." She scoffs.

"The Republic stands for people like you, like me. It *freed* us for Vale's sake. Not Fá. The Republic."

"Freed us? How?" she asks, passionate. "By pulling your people up from the mines only to forget you and give your mines to Silvers. By pulling my people from the ice to die in their wars or as freelancers and mercenaries. Serving not just highColors, but Coppers. Greens and Reds. What has changed in the ten years since the Rising? A Gold still sits atop a throne and sends the lowColors to die for others who will not die for us. That is what Darrow wants. He has come here to kill my grandfather and take his Volk axe back. Nothing more. I will not be used to depose my grandfather only for Darrow to discard me and crown himself."

"Did you get that from the old monster? It's rubbish. Darrow didn't come here for that. He came here for ships to save Mars. But when he saw what was happening to the lowColors he couldn't let it pass. Now he's helping the Daughters of Ares. You should see them. It's all the Colors. He has even united them with the Raa to stop this massacre."

"Of course. When we do it, it is a massacre."

"When the Fear Knight is pulling the strings, yes. It is. Fá nuked Callisto. I saw Io!"

She waves off my mention of Atlas as another lie. Her disillusionment puts dread in my bones. She even talks like a warlord now. Where is the innocence I saw in her? Where is the friend I made?

"I am not a monster," she says.

"Must be your conscience you heard, because I didn't call you one."

"Your eyes accuse." She leans forward like a child excited to share a new discovery. "Lyria, you have no grasp of these matters."

"And you do?" I snap.

"Yes. I used to slouch, then I began to read. All my life I indicted my own size, my own power. You know I did. That shame was taught to me. To limit me. Have you not read the histories of man? Of course not. My grandfather gave them to me. I read on our journey from Mars, as we hid in wait in the asteroids. Alexander of Macedon. Caesar of Rome. Genghis of Mongolia. Ayaz of the Turks. These are the names that were hailed before Gold fell on Earth. Silenius au Lune, Akari au Raa, Lorn au Arcos, the Reaper. These are the names hailed today. Butchers of millions. Human history is proof of one thing: violence builds empires. Violence is worshiped, respected, heeded. Why are we monsters for embracing this truth? Why am I a villain? Every great people has done it!

"After so long fighting the wars of masters and conmen, are we not due our own war? Our own land? Golds have their games. Silvers have their contracts. We have our axes. Why not use them for ourselves?" She watches me and sees that I will never agree. "You will not understand. You had power in there." She taps my head. "And you feared it. So, you gave it up. That is your choice. I have learned to stop fearing what's inside me. That is my choice."

I am crestfallen. I see in her what I saw in Harmony. Bitterness breeding entitlement. It's a bitterness I know. For years it filled my mouth with ashes. My time with her, Victra, Ulysses, taught me I could not keep that bitterness. Better to die than live with it in my veins and let it poison me like Harmony. To be better, like Aurae, Sevro, Darrow, Athena, and even Cassius. Surely it's not too late for Volga.

"I will not play the Reaper's game," Volga says. "I am deaf to his lies. But you are my friend. You were kind to me, so I will be kind to you. Go back to Mars, Lyria. Go back to your own people."

"Aren't you listening? You are my people, Volga. I came here for you and I'm not leaving without you. I already lost one sister. I won't lose you too."

"Your sister was a victim. I am not. I do not need saving."

Anger flushes my face. "When did you become a Gold with black eyes?" I ask. "Polish it all you like. Read all the histories till you forget your own. Tattoo your face till you can't see yourself. Will you kill babies, Volga? Like Harmony? You gonna send women and boys to your braves? We both know if Ephraim were here you wouldn't be able to look him in the eye. Will you take slaves, and bed them against their will like some middling Gold?"

She rises in a fury and towers over me.

"Who are you to judge me?" She shoves a finger in my face. "We were slaves. You were *never* a slave. You were a fat rat Gamma." Her voice becomes nasty. "I know more about them now. About your mine. Your clan. Informers. You were bred to lord the scraps of the master over those more lowly than yourself. Bred to be their rats in the mines. Bartering secrets for cheese from the masters. Traitors to your own people." She leans in. "And you are still their rat, Lyria. Coming here as Darrow's tool. Asking me to betray a man who has given me everything. No, rat, I am not like you. I am a warrior of the Volk. If you will not leave, my duty is clear. I will deliver you to my king."

"Then do it," I say. "Because I ain't leaving without you."

"You think this a game? Are you not afraid? Look what my guards have done."

She walks to the table and retrieves the sacks. She returns and empties them. The heads of Gudmund and Fenrir fall into my lap. Nauseous and sick, I feel a stubborn strength swell within.

"You afraid now, Lyria?"

"I been afraid since I can remember. But I ain't giving up."

68

LYRIA

The King and His Court

JUPITER PEERS OVER THE eastern horizon of Europa. In the twilight between the day and night, a chain of archipelagos stretches westward. Volga's dreadnaught creeps over the water just as surely as dread creeps over my heart.

Thirteen islands pulse with the light of bonfires. High above, torch-Ships patrol the sky over the half-dome shields that protect the archipelagos and writhe with the muted color of soap bubbles. I've seen Hyperion. I've seen warships. But even I am awed at the sight of Europa's famed Nixian Isles as Volga's ship comes to a halt beyond the shields.

Each of the islands is host to a black stone statue of a Greek god. Like the statues, no two islands are alike. Some bear dramatic waterfalls and mysterious woods. Others are riven with fjords, like the north coast of Cimmeria. Some are spotted with wildflowers that drift into the sea like tattered shawls. The warriors who came to conquer the Rim gather on the plateaus of the islands around stolen acropolises that dance with firelight. I am too far away to distinguish their shapes, but the gems and gold the warriors wear must catch the light of their fires because it is as if the islands were sprinkled with multi-hued frost.

"A sight, are they not?" Volga's *actarius* says from my side at the edge of the open-faced hangar. The Copper's black and white robes have not a spot of dirt on them. "Volk for the most part. Fá could not leave too many to guard the Garter. Fá knows many still love Darrow. He could not trust them to watch after that great prize."

I don't know why she's telling me this. I've learned her name is Nicator. A slave since the sacking of Olympia, she was once the vice-tertiary administrator of helium management in Cassius's home city. Whatever that all means.

It's been three days since Volga decided to give me over to Fá. Three days for the surface of Europa to be pacified. Apparently it's ahead of schedule. I wonder if Darrow's already tried his plan. I sigh. Not knowing is good, I guess. Means they can't torture it from me.

"How many are there?" I ask the Copper, hoping to take my mind off what awaits me.

"Volk on the moon? Many. At the feast? Enough to require a requisition of one thousand auroch, four hundred thousand liters of mead, six hundred thousand liters of wine, fifty tons of bread, cheese, butter, five thousand drums of olives, one hundred thousand fowl." The Copper spares a look back at my guards. "The great Fá knows his Core braves are restless out here in the dark, especially with the gossip that spreads through the ranks. He will tell them to take the Deep soon. A great demand. So he bribes them with riches, and sedates them with mysticism."

"The new gossip? Darrow," I say.

Nicator looks over at me, with interest. "Were you on Io when he fought Skarde? Of course you were. Sigurd's friends brought you." I say nothing. "Is he here? On Europa?"

"If I knew, why would I tell you?" I say. I glance behind us. The hangar is busy with preparations for departure. My Ascomanni guards smoke tobacco a few paces away while hundreds of Volga's household braves load onto flatbed skiffs. They look glorious. The four gold torcs on each of their right arms are polished. They wear bright cloaks made from exotic furs or dread scale. Like Nicator, they are clean. Unlike Nicator, they are already drunk and laughing.

"They don't look troubled."

Nicator shrugs in a mixture of surrender and resentment. "Humans are a herd animal. We do as our fellows do, for few can bear the shame of doing otherwise. Why else war? Why else traditions? Look below. How many islands with fires do you count?"

"Thirteen."

"And how many torcs upon the arms of Volga's braves?"

"Four."

Nicator points a finger toward an island, the fourth from the left.

"The heir's household guard will feast there upon the island of Apollo. They belong to the Fourth Band. Fourth from Fá's favor. Do you understand?"

I feel the sickness of it creep through me. "The hierarchy. It's happening all over again," I murmur. "Can't they see it?"

"If you are raised in a house that is square, what shape do you think you will build your house when you are grown?" Nicator asks.

I say nothing. The beauty I saw in the Daughters of Ares—all the Colors working together to escape the hierarchy—seems such a frail thing before the might of this ordered host. I thought they were just barbarians. I shake from fear of what's to come. Then Nicator slides something into my hand. A pill. "A small mercy for a fellow child of Mars," she says.

On principle, I flip the pill out to sea. She watches it disappear with a growing smile. "Do not fear, Lyria. You are not to die today. My mistress plays politics. Fá's spies would have told him of your arrival the moment that those young fools brought you aboard. She will ask him to spare you, and he will because he craves her love. Fá fathered many children but raised none. He thinks of Volga as his daughter."

"Then why did you give me a suicide pill?"

"It was a breath mint. The muzzle you'll be wearing when you meet the Great Fá will taste . . . unpleasant. Easier to bear with a mint."

The muzzle tastes like rust and a cow's spit. Bitter sea wind gnaws through my thin prisoner kit as Volga's skiff coasts beneath the rim of the shields toward the islands. Flanked by the skiffs of her new household warriors, it is not a small procession. The wind carries music and laughter and cursing and the clatter of dishes and the screeches of slaves. Volga stares into the clamor like an old sailor heading toward a storm. The skiffs carrying her men bank away to the right toward the island of Apollo, where the Fourth Band feasts. Volga's carries on alone toward the isle of Zeus, where Fá awaits.

The isle of Zeus is not large, but it is beautiful—a family of snow-covered peaks floating above the deep sea. Between the two highest peaks, each a pedestal for the statue of Zeus's feet, a black acropolis hangs suspended over a frosted valley. My eyes are drawn up toward Zeus as we land. Carrion birds churn around his legs and torso. Golds have been nailed to the statue. Many are still alive.

I look away and see Volga watching the bodies with an expression that doesn't match the iron she put in her hard words.

Volga leads her small entourage off the skiff when we arrive at the acropolis of Zeus. I'm dragged behind to the acropolis's courtyard where amidst shrines and tall pines the great Fá and several hundred ornamented jarls feast, drink, wrestle, and rut. Our procession grinds to a halt as Volga stops to stare at the scene. Just for a moment, but it makes me wonder: did my words find some purchase after all?

I'm again pushed forward. To keep up with Obsidians I have to go at a trot. Squadrons of Pinks nearly as thick as the birds above flock to a vast piece of debris serving as a table for the jarls. It seems to have been taken from a Raa ship's hull. Part of a blue dragon's head can still be seen on the charred metal.

The sight of the jarls is gross and absurd. In furs, scale capes, spider silk jackets, they glitter with gold and drip with jewels. They don't mingle, the Ascomanni and the Core jarls. Even here, at the high feast, they cluster in factions within factions like Red clans at a Laureltide dance. The most curious to me is a group of about twenty Core Obsidians in great fur cloaks. They sit far away from the rest drinking heavily and glaring at the line of Obsidians that queues before the man anyone could tell is their king. Fá sits above them all on a pitch-black chair encrusted with melted gold, diamonds, and skull trophies. Pinks surround him like the feathers of a peacock.

I can't help but stare at the beast. It's not Fá's size that terrifies me, though he is a giant. It's not the metal grafted onto his body. It's the calmness that emanates from him. He is the pupil in this eye of insanity. Cold, aware, watching, and sober.

His eyes flick to Volga and then to me before tossing a glass orb that glows from within to an Ascomanni leader on his right. He yawns as the next warleader scampers forward to unveil a trident. It is the most beautiful weapon I've ever seen. Polished platinum flashes in the firelight. Its killing tips are flanged and shaped like dolphins.

The jarls stir. Fá sheds his Pinks to stride across the top of the table and hop down to seize the trident with greedy hands.

"**Daughter!**" he calls to Volga as he measures the trident's balance. "**This brave of the Twelfth has brought us a treasure. The Trident of Ignaeus.**" Then with the trident's edge, he cuts several torcs off the right arm of the Obsidian until only five remain. **"Rise to the Fifth Ring, son of the Volk. The Allfather wills it."**

The Ascomanni keen in approval. So do the Volk but with less enthusiasm.

A half hour later, Fá motions Volga forward. She drags me along with her by a chain linked to a collar around my neck. The wind moans as if in pain.

"Jarl Volarus! Hunter of Dragons. You come at the Allfather's hour of hunger. The Slaying is almost upon us. Truly his fire burns in you, daughter." For her he's a jolly giant with clever, smiling eyes. **"But your catch is smaller than Jarl Gherala's! I'd hoped you would have the honor of catching mighty Cyaxares, not a minnow."**

"Great Fá, this is—"

"Lyria of Lagalos," Fá finishes. **"The companion you've told me so much about. We have another guest worthy of note."**

Volga and I follow his gaze to see Sigurd half naked and standing in chains beside a pile of presents given to Fá. My heart grows heavy. Sigurd has been beaten badly, but tries to look so proud. They caught him after all.

Fá calls back to a miserable-looking Obsidian in mockery. **"Jarl Skarde, you pout. I told you to rejoice for your son and his liberation from his _imprisonment_ under Darrow."**

Sigurd stares at his father with his head held high. Slumped, Skarde says nothing.

They're all so afraid of Fá.

Fá's eyes fall on me. They are no longer smiling. They are pits of evil in a face that looks like a piece of steak dragged by a truck and then repaired with titanium. I look away and feel ashamed. The shame is replaced by horror when I see a small gap between the hunk of metal serving as their table and the ground. Gold eyes look back at me. It was not the wind moaning. Golds lie crushed beneath the massive table.

Volga has noticed. Her eyes linger then dart away.

"You are frightened, Lyria," Fá murmurs. **"Do not be. I know a debt is due. My granddaughter has told me how you saved her from the mines of the Red Hand. For this, I shall spare you the pain you deserve for coming to turn her against me."** His metal fingers caress the scars through the hair on my head. **"After all, nothing of interest**

resides in your head any longer." He tilts my face up to look at his. **"Darrow would not send you unto us with secrets. Would he?"**

Fá begins removing the muzzle.

"She may blaspheme the Allfather," Volga warns and shoots me a look that says, *Don't get yourself killed.*

"Did I break Ilium only to fear the voice of a silly Red girl?" he says and finishes removing the muzzle. I'd spit at him if my mouth was not chalk dry from fear. **"Darrow has fallen far. Once, I admired him. But what sort of warrior sends such a fragile thing to do his dirty work?"** he asks. **"Defeat has made him a coward."**

"He issued you a challenge, didn't he?" I reply. "You're the coward. Hiding behind your army."

"I am here," Fá says. **"Under the open sky. Where is he? Hiding in the Deep."** He smiles as I try to hide my surprise. **"Yes. I know he awaits me there, girl. Just as I know he let me take two of the sealifts, both leading to an obvious trap. But there are other routes down, down, down."** He chuckles. **"Do you know what a Moses Column is? A pillar of force that parts the very sea."**

Oh gods. Does Darrow know Fá's plan?

I sneer because it's all I can do. "Did Atlas show those routes to you?" I ask in Nagal and shout to the jarls. "Fá is a puppet of the Fear Knight. You are tools of Gold." Then in Common, "Do you hear? The Fear Knight is the Allfather! You are puppets of the Society!"

The party is loud and Fá has not called for their attention. Few pay me any mind. Their diversions are more interesting than a babbling Red girl. Fá smiles down at me. **"Your Nagal appalls. Darrow must be desperate if the only weapons he has are lies."** He returns his attention to Volga. **"I am told she carried a message too?"**

Volga proffers up the holocube.

Fá rolls the cube between his fingers. **"More lies?"**

"They say you serve Atlas," Volga says.

"I have told you of my time with Atlas."

"They say you serve him still."

Fá watches her a moment before chuckling. **"They would. Would they not? So many lies to tear us apart."** Fá crushes the cube. **"Your loyalty brightens my heart, daughter."**

"I am glad, for I must ask a boon of you. I owe Lyria a debt. She is dear to me. Aside from you, she is all that is dear to me. I would ask for your mercy, my King. Allow me to add her to my retinue or send her back to Mars."

"Is she a friend of our people?"

"Yes."

"Did she not come for Darrow?"

"No. She came for me." I know deep down she believes that. "She was a slave like us, and the Republic has mistreated her too. Her eyes are not open, but her heart is brave."

For a moment, I see great sadness in Fá's eyes. He opens his mouth to speak, and then seems to change his mind. His eyes harden, and he waves to the partying jarls. **"You know what they say of you, my kin. The Volk claim you are impure. Unnaturally born. The Ascomanni whisper of your mercies. They think you are weak, with Republic sympathies, and worse. A woman. Look at them. Beasts, all. They follow us like desert creatures follow a man without water. Waiting. Waiting."**

"We are the blood of Ragnar," Volga says. "Let them wait."

Fá smiles. **"The power of blood is like the power of a crown. It is an illusion. There are deeper truths you do not yet grasp. Sacrifices I have made to become what I am."** Again, he looks sad, and he touches her face. **"You have led in war, but you are still like snow. Now is not the time for mercy, granddaughter. Now is the time for you to prove what you are. To them. To me. To yourself."** He pauses. **"To the Allfather, most of all."**

Volga frowns in worry. "I don't understand."

A gong sounds, followed by several more. Ascomanni with strange helmets begin to drone from their place atop the acropolis's roof. Fá glances up at them in annoyance. **"Shamans. Ugh."** Jarls playing in the garden begin to find their way back to the table. The Ascomanni move with excitement, the Volk in annoyance. **"First, another mythic feat for the small minded. The Holy Kill is upon us. To your seat, daughter. All will be made clear."**

Fá's bodyguards take custody of me and drag me toward Sigurd as Volga takes a seat at the high table. When the jarls have all returned to their seats, Fá jumps onto the table. The added weight from all the jarls leaning forward on it has ended the misery of the Golds beneath it.

"My jarls of war! Invincible brothers! Sons of Kuthul! Brothers of Ragnar! For three hours we have feasted, ten more lie before us!"

The Ascomanni roar. Some of the Core Obsidian join them. **"Now the Allfather, who has delivered Europa's bounty unto us, hungers for our sacrifice!"** Ascomanni shamans drift down from the acropolis's roof to cry out a song and fall to their knees shrieking prayers. Slaves file out carrying entire trees, which are stacked before the shamans. When their chanting reaches a crescendo, fire leaps up from the stacked trees. Like magic. The shamans' chanting subsides, and a hush falls over the crowd. Fá has raised his palms, calling for quiet.

"On Io, Jarl Volarus claimed the honor of the hunt! We feasted on Abraxes, mightiest drake of the Raa herd. Yes, we ate of his heart and flesh, and pitched his organs in the volcano Prometheus in offering to the Allfather."

He flourishes his scale cape and then thrusts the trident at a flat-nosed Ascomanni.

"On Callisto, the honor of the hunt was claimed by Ramanar the Ice Blood. And we feasted on the mighty ghost raptor Fenoracius and ate his heart and flesh and burned his organs in offering to the Allfather. On Europa, the honor has been claimed by Jarl Gherala of the Third Band."

He turns to a lean Ascomanni of his own height.

"Jarl Gherala, I starve like a slave. But you, my most loyal jarl, you have brought me the fallen King of Europa to feast upon! You have wrested him from his ocean throne, dragged him up from his watery lair. Where is he? Where is Cyaxares?"

69

LYRIA

Hour of Hunger

I FEEL LIKE I AM watching a Violet drama.

Jarl Gherala points his spear at the sea. Engines rumble and a gravskiff rises up from the sea, up and up toward the acropolis. It is an immense machine, maybe two hundred meters long and just as many wide. Its edges are gilded in gold and silver. Maybe the surface is too, but it's hard to tell because a beast covers it end to end.

A leviathan thrashes beneath chains. Its body is black and gold and nearly too large for the altar. Its central face is like that of a shark. About ten meters behind its neck sprout fin-like appendages, each with their own eyes and mouths at the end—smaller than its central face and the mouths more like the beaks of squid. Its midsection is swollen like a whale's and tapers to a long, thick tail with three dorsal fins. Lidless milky eyes stare out.

Even Sigurd flinches at the power of its thrashing.

Jarl Gherala watches it with cool satisfaction. He cries out in Nagal: "Only kings may kill kings. My lord Fá, the honor is yours."

Fá twirls his new trident and heads for the gravskiff. As the shamans chant, he jumps the gap between the acropolis and the skiff. He may be old, but he's as nimble as an acrobat. Using the chains that bind the beast, Fá climbs until he stands just behind its main head. He laughs and rides its bucking muscled body. Its smaller mouths snap at him. **"Allfather! I offer you this stain!"** Fá cries and brings the trident down.

The beast struggles so hard against its chains Fá nearly falls off. A link of chain snaps and hits the acropolis with a crack. Stone showers and the Ascomanni bay. Fá plunges the trident down again and again in a terrible frenzy.

The leviathan wails so loudly even the carrion birds flee. It gives one last thrash and falls still. Its last sound is lonely and filled with three hundred years of sorrow. I look at Volga. She's looking away. What is wrong with her? How can this be right to her?

I want to scream.

There are tears in my eyes. I don't know why. Sevro told me Cyaxares was three centuries old and I thought it scary and horrible back in the ship, but part of me feels like Europa's soul has died today. Fá doesn't give a shit. Life doesn't matter to him, only the taking.

Slick with ichor and blood, Fá slides down the dead beast's side and returns to join his jarls. Anything that was kingly about him is gone for me. He took what he wanted, both the credit and the high of the kill. He doesn't even harvest the meat himself. Coming from smaller secondary skiffs, hundreds of enslaved Reds rush onto the altar with spiked shoes, saws, and cleavers. Several Brown butchers direct their works. The Ascomanni shamans join them to oversee the butchering.

I feel ashamed even for watching.

Fá walks back across the table dripping blood and ichor behind him. He does not return to his throne. Instead, he stops in front of Volga as a dozen figures are led out from one of the acropolis's buildings by his bodyguards. Captives. There are twelve. One from each Color, except Red and Obsidian. Sigurd and I look at each other at the same time.

"Shit," he murmurs.

"What's happening," I say.

The bodyguards array the twelve captives before the high table. Sigurd and I are shoved out to join them. The heat of the bonfire sends sweat trickling down my spine.

"What's happening?" I ask Sigurd.

"My father has forsaken me. Volga has forsaken you," he replies, his eyes sad and fixed on his father, Jarl Skarde. "And we are about to die. Badly."

"In a world of chaos, where it is all against all, strength is not measured in the power of a body nor the numbers of your host. Strength is measured only in what the heart can bear to attain its goal." He peers around at his jarls. **"What we are willing to sacrifice is the test of our worth. I have sacrificed *everything*!"** He glares at them as if he hates them. His voice quiets. **"That is why you follow me. That is why I am favored by the Allfather. That is why my son Ragnar awoke the spirit of the Volk. As I anointed myself with stains, so did he, so will you."** He turns to Volga. **"Volga Volarus. Tonight, you take *your* Passage of the Stains."**

He motions Volga to meet him before the captives, where two Pinks wait with an onyx box.

He pulls out a horrible gauntlet crusted brown with old blood. Twice the size of his own hand, its fingertips end in sharp talons. He pushes it into Volga's hands.

"Now is the time to prove your lineage, to wash away the taint of weakness upon you. Anoint yourself with their lifeblood. For the Allfather, take their hearts."

My heart pounds in terror. I try to retreat, but someone holds me from behind.

Stunned, Volga stares at the gauntlet in her hands, then at the captives, then at me. Her eyes flee mine. "Who are they?" she murmurs.

Fá walks before our line to touch us one by one on the head, starting with the Gold and carrying on down the hierarchy. **"Slaver, war profiteer, murderer, arms manufacturer, rapist, murderer, child lover, liar for the state."** On and on he goes down the line until he comes to Sigurd. **"Traitor to his people."** Then me. **"Rat."**

His hand drips ichor down my forehead. I recoil from his touch.

Volga's voice is quiet. "Grandfather . . . I have proven my loyalty. Is my vow not enough?"

"No. It is not."

Her voice grows harsh. "She's my only friend."

"She and the Republic are your past. I am your future. Choose." Her shoulders sag and all life seems to drain out of her. Gentle, he grips her head between his hands. **"You have killed in battle, it is true. But there is another kind of killing. A difficult but necessary kind. The killing of a captive or a foe who is at your mercy. There is no honor in it. That is the point: to take an honorless, necessary action. One that helps your people, but blackens your heart. Your sacrifice to your people is bearing the guilt of what must be done."**

"My father did this?" she whispers.

"And more. Are you above this? Above him?" His voice grows wounded. **"Are you above me?"**

He fits her right hand into the gauntlet. Its motor wheezes alive. The powered finger joints twitch like the limbs of an awakening spider and the hand of the gauntlet ratchets back over its wrist. Cocked and loaded. **"Do it upward, to your right of their sternum. Grasp, wait for the click, then pull."**

Fá steps back from Volga. My knees shake. Or maybe they've been shaking the whole time. I'm numb with fear. Dark stains spread down the pants of several captives. Not Sigurd's, though. He stares straight ahead. I find strength in that and mimic him. Volga is still. Pinned under the gaze of Fá, the expectant silence of the jarls, the crackle of the flames, and the cutting of the leviathan's meat. She swallows, then closes her eyes as if to find her strength.

When she opens them, I know I'm well and truly slagged.

70

LYRIA

Passage of the Stains

As the Reds behind her carve up the leviathan atop the altar, Volga punches the Gold sacrifice in the chest, just to her right of their sternum. The gauntlet disappears up to its cuff. The Gold gasps and jerks. Volga's face contorts from the effort and she pulls the gauntlet free with a sucking sound. A heart the size of a grapefruit beats out from between the mechanized fingers. She gives it to a shaman and the Gold crumples to the stone. Golden flames leap from the fire when the shaman casts the still-beating heart into it. The Ascomanni sing like coyote.

I think I'm gonna shit myself.

Volga approaches a dark-skinned Silver man with a widow's peak and narrow eyes.

I look the other way. On the altar far behind Fá, a team of Reds saws off the fins of the leviathan. Another works on its tail with ion cleavers. Others load the meat onto sleighs or harvest its eyes and teeth. I'm trapped in the violence. Everywhere I look: sawing and hacking and slicing and sorting. The Silver screams. I feel one welling in my own chest. Volga hands the heart to the shaman and the flames leap silver. The Ascomanni chant deepens. Volga moves to the White and then the flames leap white. Fá's smile grows as Volga moves down the line. Volga stares straight ahead as she works.

Reds laboring on the leviathan's middle plunge in ion blades and split open one of the leviathan's stomachs. White scales, black flesh, and yellow fat peel back. The altar tilts. The Reds hold fast. Offal and chains of half-digested bodies spill from the stomach into the gap between the acropolis and the altar. Down out of sight into the sea. The altar flattens out and the Reds go back to work.

My eyes return to Volga to see her jerk the gauntlet from the Copper's chest. He wavers there and his grunt becomes a whimper as she hands his small heart to the shaman. She moves on to the Blue before the Copper even crumples down. Four of the leviathan's fins are already gone. Something has made the Reds around the leviathan's second stomach stop. Their blades lower and they lean forward, washed in the blue light that dances out from the bonfire. Soon it turns yellow, then green. When the light becomes violet, several of the workers step back. One drops his saw. The other crews work on in the orange light. But when the light turns pale gray, the Reds at the stomach turn and flee. The shaman supervising the harvesting atop the beast slides down its flank to investigate.

The firelight turns muddy pink and the leviathan twitches. Volga's so close now I can smell the iron in the blood as it dribbles on the stone. I look up at Sigurd. There's fear in his eyes now. "Brothers! Can you not see! We are slaves now yet again! Atlas's chains are upon us! Are you blind! Father! Father, look at me!" Skarde looks at his son as Volga takes his heart. Sigurd falls to his knees where he rasps: "Hail . . ." and tips over.

My hands shake. I can't look up at Volga. The belly of the leviathan moves again. Swelling locally just beneath its chest. Like a blister's forming.

Volga's heavy boots clomp on the stone as she comes to the bottom of the hierarchy, me. She blocks my view of the leviathan and the forming blister. I look up into her black eyes and see tears there. Hesitation. She turns back to Fá, reopening my view to the leviathan. "Please. Not her. Not this. I can't. I can't." The blister has taken on a new form. An angular distension. Like something inside is making its way out.

"Kill your weakness."

"For you?" Volga asks.

"For the Allfather."

She stares at him for a long time.

Volga turns back to me. Tears stream down her face. She raises the gauntlet. It ratchets back. Blood and bone drip from its clawed fingers. It hangs there in the air for what seems an eternity. Volga's shaking. Her eyes meet mine and I see not just pain there but doubt . . .

"Y-You d-don't have to be broken l-like him," I say through chattering teeth. "Eph-phraim's d-daughter . . ."

A small breath escapes her chest and her will to kill me crumbles like rusted iron.

The gauntlet sinks to her side. Then someone screams.

Volga turns. One of the Ascomanni shamans is running away from the leviathan's belly even as another stumbles back from it holding a bloody stump for an arm. Red work crews run in terror.

A demon is born forth from the viscera.

There's no other way to describe the figure that bursts from the blister in the leviathan's belly in a spume of dark liquid. A gristly black thing with two flashing blades. The screaming shaman soon has no head. Then the one with the stump for an arm has no legs. Two more demons follow after the first. A flash comes from a short rifle in one of their hands.

The first demon leaps from the altar and lands behind the last shaman just as the shaman clears the gap between altar and acropolis. The shaman stops and collapses in two pieces, cut from the crown of his tattooed head straight through the groin. The demon lifts a black, curved blade, dripping gore and effluence. His helmet slithers back.

Firelight bathes Darrow's face as he cocks back his head and howls.

71

DARROW

Ashvar

I DO NOT BELIEVE IN gods, but that didn't stop me from praying during my time in the belly of the leviathan. I prayed for Lyria. I prayed for her safety to relieve my own guilt for sending her. I prayed for her success because it would mean that the spirit of Ragnar might still live on in Volga. And I prayed to not be met with a barrage of gunfire as soon as I exited the stomach that has been my home since Diomedes convinced the Kalibar to let their sigil beast swallow my friends and me whole in the acid-resistant pods we've lived in for three terrible days.

All that prayer calmed the mind, but if I've learned anything by now, it's that only a fool relies on prayer alone.

Dripping with gastric acid and blood, I march toward the high table with Sevro and Cassius on my flanks. They are as heavily armed and armored as I am. In Godkiller, all.

Behind us, the Reds who carved at the leviathan howl like maniacs. Pinks scatter. LowColor servers and slaves evaporate, leaving only the actors in my play—Fá, Volga, the jarls, Lyria—I thank the fates she is alive—and bodyguards. Lots of bodyguards. They swarm in from the fringes of the garden to kill us. Fá roars for them to hold because Sevro's rifle shot was true.

"Halt or the ugly bastard dies!" Sevro screams and holds up a detonator.

A dart protrudes from the Fá's bare chest. He reaches for it and a red light glows from the end of its explosive payload. He freezes and lowers his hands, and resigned to watch me approach, like a pitviper watches a drillboy draw closer—swollen with poison and discontent, eyes seething a possessive hatred out from his lair in the rocks. Yet Fá's lair is not made of rock. It is made of men, and men have ears.

"Volsung Fá! King of All Liars! I am Darrow of Mars, ArchImperator of the Republic, Tyr Morga of the Volk, and I have been wronged! *You* have waged war on my planet. *You* have enslaved my Red people. *You* have sullied the name of my brother Ragnar. *You* have killed my sister Sefi. *You* have taken my army like a thief in the night to corrupt their honor. I claim holy vendetta against YOU! I claim *ashvar!*"

I stop ten paces from Fá and thrust up my left gauntlet. In it, I clutch a chunk of coal that I wipe on my brow in the mark of the Norse wargod Tyr. In the old Obsidian way, any wanderer so marked abdicates any worldly concerns except the resolution of their vendetta. They are to be given hospitality and immunity by all, for they have set their life on a mission to rectify their honor in one-on-one violence to the death.

No one speaks.

The bodyguards slow and encircle us. As many as fifty in the black armor with the blood crescent—all Ascomanni, I note.

At the table behind Fá, my old warlords are frozen in existential confusion. None have so much as stood, but various mouths hang agape. The Ascomanni are a different story. Dissuaded by distance and pirates, ships may seldom travel to the Kuiper Belt, but radio and light waves are not similarly constrained. A decade's worth of broadcasts has heralded my slingBlade, my face, my great war against the hated Golds. To a warrior race banished from the sun by Gold, I am a natural celebrity, and my arrival via the leviathan is a religious experience.

They throw up their hands in gratitude to their Allfather, praising the darkness between the stars for giving them this gift. What more worthy foe could the Allfather summon to face their invincible Fá? Surely it is a miracle I have emerged from their sacrifice bringing not the awkward grinding of armies, but a clean fight. A test of Fá's divine favor.

I rolled the dice and they came up sixes.

Even Fá looks surprised by the exultation and the joy on the Ascomanni faces. His surprise turns to anger as he realizes the bind he is in. Volga has shed the gauntlet. She pulls Lyria to the side, distancing herself from Fá. He frowns after her and lifts his hand. His bodyguards shout for silence. It does not fall at once. Many of the Ascomanni finish their prayers to their Allfather before heeding their mortal ruler.

"Only an Obsidian can claim *ashvar*," Fá says. "You are no Obsidian. You are not even a Red any longer, Darrow. The Gold in your eyes has leaked into your heart. False prophet. Even your tongue is rotted. I know why you are here. *You* are the thief. Come here to steal the power of the Volk for your own selfish aims." He gestures to the dart. "You are lower than an assassin. Ragnar would weep to see how far you have fallen."

"Glumnar, Fjod, Skarde!" I call to jarls I recognize. "You were there when I was made a son of the Volk beneath the Valkyrie Spires and the high stables. You saw the blood of Sefi meet mine. You saw the blood the griffin offered to stain the snow. You called me brother and gave me the touch of life. Do you deny me now?"

I thought they would rise up and support my claim. Fjod because his conservative bloc must be chafing against Fá's decadence. Glumnar because he served as my personal attaché for years. Skarde because Sigurd lies dead on the ground. To my dismay, they remain silent, even Skarde. The shame on his face is total. Is their fear of Fá so deep? Or is it their distrust of me? Have I fallen so far in their eyes?

I have.

Not one speaks for me. They look down at their plates or into their wine. Fear holds them in its grip. Sevro sneers. "Cowards! Does not one of you have any balls?"

"Should we run?" Cassius asks. "That's always an option. I can snag Lyria and—"

"No," I whisper, eyes on Skarde.

"Come now," Fá coos, emboldened. "If there is a man here who claims the false prophet as their brother, let them speak. Let your voice ring clear so that I might hear you, and may you stand tall so that I might see your face and know you speak not just for yourself but for your kin and tribe down to the children amongst them."

I seek Lyria's eyes and see in them fear for me. Volga is unreadable. And then a man stands. Though he is a fine warrior, the only thing he is more famous for than his greed or his cleverness is his cowardice.

It is Skarde and his face is calm, his temper even.

"I have no kin left to speak for, but I will stand tall so you might see my face, great King. I will let my voice ring clear so that you might hear me, great King. When you sentenced my son to death, I did not object. When your granddaughter delivered the sentence, I did not object. For my son—whom I adored—broke the laws of our people and went against his king. But when I see that king disregard those very laws, the laws that bound a father to silence as his son had his heart ripped out, not five minutes later. To that, I fear I must object."

Every single Obsidian jarl turns to look at Skarde. "A warrior must say what he knows to be true. Every jarl of the Volk here bore witness to or has heard of Darrow's acceptance into the tribe of the Valkyrie Spires. We did call him brother for many years. And according to the laws we follow"—he points to his son's body—"Darrow is afforded the same rights as any brave of the Volk. And *any* brave of the Volk, even if they be our enemy, may declare *ashvar*. You may choose a champion, my King. But you may not say no and keep your throne. And if your champion is beaten, we must kill you ourselves." He splays out his hands as if he's sorry, but it cannot be helped. "That is the law of the ice. That is the way of the Volk. You are above us, but not our people's law."

Then the man's eyes twinkle, and I know he hates Fá with all his cunning heart. He's not done yet.

"I am no shaman, but surely, my invincible King, this is a propitious sign. Tyr Morga came from the sacrifice. Is this not a sign that the Allfather blesses this fight? Surely his death at your hand will wash away all doubt held by your Volk as to the dangers of the attack on the Deep. Kill the past." His lips twist and he spares a glance to Volga. "For the Allfather."

To make sure the stiletto really goes in, he translates the last part in the Ascomanni tongue. At least I think so, because the Ascomanni go wild.

Skarde faced several courts-martial in my legions. He escaped every one without having to hire a Copper lawyer. His argument to the jarls is as shrewd and cynical as it is effective. He cannot betray Fá outright without losing face and undermining his own conclusion, so he used the very traditions that bind the Volk and the very weapon Fá uses to uphold his throne: religion.

Obsidians do not think it right to criticize their ruler unless they are willing to fight their ruler. It creates a cult of silence. By the heads nodding, I see to my joy that the Obsidians are not all lost in the darkness. Skarde speaks for many of them. Volga watches from the side with shame on her face, fear for Fá, and fear of me.

Fjod is the second to find his courage. The hirsute, semi-deranged jarl slams the heft of his hammer into the ground twice, and roars for Fá to fight. Then the whole bloc of conservative jarls joins the famous madman. Then Glumnar and Uther and many of the rest. The Ascomanni were just waiting to take up the call, cheering for their king to embrace the Allfather's gift.

Trapped by the religion he fed to his subjects and the martial code he used to seize the throne, Fá has no choice but to acquiesce. The Ascomanni sing in joy. **"I accept your *ashvar*,"** Fá rumbles.

I nod to Sevro and the dart's payload deactivates. Fá plucks out the dart and picks his teeth with it. **"Since I have honored your right, you must honor mine."**

All quiet. The danger to a challenger is severe. It comes when the challenged chooses the terms of the fight. They always favor their strengths. "Weapons?" I ask.

"Honorable."

"Field?"

"Dome."

"Panoply?"

He smiles with freshly picked teeth. **"Full-metal."**

72

DARROW

Full-Metal Panoply

T HE JARLS FORM A large circle and clear the ground before the high table. A world apart, Volsung Fá and I study one another as his Orange slaves equip him in his war gear. The spiked pulseArmor is the thickest kit I've ever seen. As soon as I saw it in person I knew my God-killer armor wouldn't win this for me. Cassius prattles in my ear while clearing my armor's joints of leviathan guts, half-digested chum, and assorted gore. It wasn't as clean an exit from our pod as the Kalibar's marine biologist promised.

"In this gravity Fá's mass won't slow him much. He'll use that mass to crowd you, especially under a dome. His armor is as thick as Sevro's head. He'll come close to put you on those spikes. It'll be hard to get through his armor, so avoid the temptation to counter without power behind your blows. Don't even bother slashing. Thrusts only."

"He knows," Sevro says.

"He's stronger than you are, so don't get pinned down."

"He knows," Sevro says.

"And whatever you do, don't use your boots."

I turn and look at him. "Why not? My boots are quicker."

"It's a trap. Whatever angle you take skyward, all he has to do is ac-celerate into you, then you hit the shield, and he smashes you until you are a stain. *Do not go into the air.* You are a razormaster. Not an acrobat." He nods at me and I nod back.

Even in Europa's paltry gravity, it takes three Oranges to ferry Fá's giant weapon from his throne. The blade is almost as tall as I am. Skarde needs both his hands to take it from the Oranges. He waits by his warlord, along with a cadre of Obsidian jarls I don't recognize. Nine of them wearing ruby amulets shaped like shields. Gorgons, no doubt. They peer daggers into the back of Skarde's head, and I know he will not live long after backing my challenge. Cassius is agog at Fá's weapon.

"A warsaw? Gods. That saw will eat your razor if it catches the whip. Reel you to the spikes—"

I turn on him. Cassius quiets when he sees the look in my eyes. "Remember, a circle is unlimited ground. Don't get pinned down. Don't go into the air." I nod. He slaps me on the shoulder and lets Sevro pull him away to join the circle. Oranges finish securing Fá's cuirass and move on to his legs and arms. He is big. He'll be the biggest man I've ever fought. A full head taller than Apollonius. At least a hundred kilograms of solid muscle and steel heavier. That warsaw is unlike any weapon I've ever faced. One good sweep will take a limb or my life despite my armor. Godkiller is built for range, speed, flexible use. His warsaw is meant to break things.

"I admired you in your early years, Slave King," Fá calls to me and lifts his metal hand. **"I too know the importance of taking more than nature gave me."** The Oranges finish fitting his legs and lock on his gravBoots—another armament he insisted upon. **"Unlike you, I know nature cannot be changed. The strong will always prosper. The mighty will always conquer."**

I do not answer. Shamans come forward to paint our armor in the ritual bright blue of an *ashvar* duel. They glaze it with paint wands, drawing runes in the leviathan's blood.

I draw Bad Lass to duel-wield with Pyrphoros in my off-hand. I mean to keep Fá at a distance until I can deliver a sure blow.

"Here is my offer, dog," I taunt. "Confess your crimes. Tell your jarls whom you serve, tell your 'daughter' there, and I'll let you leave with your heart."

He smiles, wily and confident within his castle-like armor. I summon my helmet up and bring my two blades together.

Clang. Clang. Clang.

"Confess," I call.

Fá has no doubt killed too many men to count. For all those he's killed, even more have tried to kill him and failed. But no man is the predator all the time. Even the best know there will come a day when they are the prey. I have been Atlas's prey for years. I was Apollonius's prey over Venus, and it terrified me. I will make Fá feel that same feeling for what he did to Sefi. For the perversion he has made of Ragnar's dream.

"You serve Atlas au Raa. Confess."

Clang. Clang. Clang.

"It will take more than your lies and needles to kill me."

His armor powers on with a lion's roar. He seizes his warsaw from Skarde and shoves him away. He hefts it with one hand and twirls its mass as if it were no heavier than a walking stick. The serrated edge of the warsaw becomes a liquid blur of vibrating teeth. He lifts his blade to the heavens and bellows, **"In the name of my son Ragnar, Allfather, accept these stains!"**

The Ascomanni roar. So do some of the Volk.

Fá and I watch the drone float between us and cast its shield. An iridescent dome glides down to meet the nexuses a few handspans from the ground. Fá wants it so we don't end up dancing in the sky, and so that I can't flee if the duel doesn't go my way. A shaman shouts. The jarls outside beat on the dome with the flat of their axes. The Ascomanni slam the hafts of their spears. It thunders inside, and the duel is on.

Neither of us move.

Clang. Clang. Clang.

He circles to the right, measuring me, and then leaps into the air. Fueled by his gravBoots, he brushes the top of the dome, and accelerates down to bring a huge overhand onto the crown of my head. Only I am no longer there. I moved forward under the trajectory of his arc. He lands with a tremendous bang and accelerates straight back at me with startling speed.

I move out of the way of his charge. Only it's not a charge. He *is* wily. He swings after me as he turns, a sweeping horizontal blow. Instinctively, I rely on the Willow Way.

I block with both blades, intending to deflect it upward and lash back at him under it. Instead, the force is so strong I am sent reeling. I counterattack and land half a dozen slashes on his armor in the Summer Lash of the Way. None even come close to penetrating, and they cost me. Four more of his attacks pound my guard. Reverberations rattle my bones.

I knew I wouldn't be able to meet his strength when I saw the size of his armor, but I didn't know he'd also be so bloodydamn fast. I should have fought him in heavy gravity. He has all the advantages here and he knows it. Pounding me back, he herds me toward the edge of the circle where the dome leaves no room for retreat. I'm running out of ground. His last sideways chop slams against my razors with so much force the blades are pushed back toward my helmet. His warsaw follows them, maintaining just enough momentum to take my head off if I don't give ground. I can't—the pulseShield is already pushing at my shoulders. There's only one place to retreat. Up.

Gods I almost do it, but I listen to Cassius. Instead of using my boots, I lever the warsaw upward as I intended to the first time, slip underneath, and go for the kill.

Already shown the futility of slashes against his armor, I thrust for his head with Pyrphoros and his stomach with Bad Lass and follow through with my body. Bad Lass bites home but Pyrphoros glances off his helmet. Then his mass crunches into me with bewildering force. I thought I was the one hitting him. I feel a pinch in my left thigh and spin right.

Despite the quality of my armor, the collision is hard enough to send me stumbling around him. I got free, but shit it hurt. I retreat to the center of the circle. I lost hold of Bad Lass. The razor is embedded in his stomach armor. By his laughter I know it did not bite deep enough to penetrate. Damn that armor.

The pinch in my left thigh evolves into a throbbing pain and a racing itch. One of his spikes penetrated the armor enough to draw blood but not pierce the muscle. I'm surprised.

My eyes dart to the tips of the spikes on his armor. Onyxium metal. They'll be poisoned too. The man's a walking death trap.

A low chuckle comes from Fá as the poison races through my veins. **"And now you are dead. The rest is all theater. I'll chew your meat slow."**

73

DARROW

The Breath of Stone

I PRESUMED FÁ'S SPIKES WOULD be poisoned, which is why I took tissue samples from the wounds of the fallen Golds in the Raa grotto. I wanted to see if the poison matched that on the spines in Diomedes's body when we found him in the pod. They did.

I only hope the blood leech Athena gave me and the anti-toxins they fit into the applicator in my suit will counteract Fá's poison. I feel nauseous already, a little slower, and a burn spreads down my leg, but I'm not paralyzed yet.

Fá's Ascomanni pound their spears on the dome. Thunder rattles and shakes. Fá does not let me recover. With Bad Lass still stuck in his armor, he closes in on me and unleashes an onslaught of downward blows, each strong enough to cleave through three men. My arms go numb taking the impacts. I land a dozen blows myself, but none come close to penetrating. Twice I try to grab Bad Lass, but that's why he left it buried in his armor. Each time he lunges for me, his spikes hungry.

He issues another horizontal chop. I retreat, and he flows into the same spin maneuver he used before. The one that leaves his back exposed. A mistake. I see the opening and instinctively spring toward him, ready to flow into the Winter Storm counterattack of the Willow Way and spear him as his back presents itself.

But then I remember who Volsung Fá's mentor is and bail out of the manuever. Atlas is the type to feign a weakness to bait an attacker, and I bet Fá is doing the same. No way he leaves his back open to me twice.

Sure enough, Fá never completes his spin. His maneuver and brutish style alter as he arrests his movement and flows into an elegant razor maneuver called the Horse Bane. His knees sink. With his back still to me, his warsaw comes at me off his hip like a pike rising to spear a horse in its chest.

If I'd followed through with my initial attack, it would have sheathed itself through my guts and ripped out my innards. It still almost does. Its teeth chew through a millimeter of chest armor before I shift my weight around it to the right.

I whip Pyrphoros at his leg. It snares his calf armor. He jerks his leg away from me to either pull me onto his warsaw or tear the handle from my grasp. I have a Helldiver's grip and my power armor is not letting go, so I twist right and the saw chews a wedge from my cuirass. I retract the blade and sparks spit as it tries to cut through his leg armor. He brings his warsaw's hungry teeth toward the whip. I give up my attempt to take his limb and pull the whip back, twist again, and deliver a two-handed chop aimed for his neck.

He just straight-lines for me and hits me in the ribs with his massive, spiked shoulder. I fly back and slam into the dome wall. Only instinct saves me, and I roll left. I don't even see him, just a metallic blur as he slams into where I once was.

I stumble back to the center, armor dented along my left rib cage, the left breastplate sheared off down to its last protective layer. At least one rib is broken.

Fá stalks after me.

"I see Atlas taught you more than genocide and toxicology," I call.

He hears the pain in my voice, but he is clearly confused why I have not yet been perceptibly slowed down by the poison on his spikes.

"You will not be the first Willow branch I have broken. I have your measure. You are not as fast as they claim. You are not as strong as my weakest Kinshield. The *Morning Star* has fallen from the sky. Fear not. Tonight, I will give you wings."

He knows how to fight Lorn's style. I didn't go into this fight intending to use the Willow Way, but in panic we rely on our oldest mechanisms, and being bulldozed by a giant in spiked armor is enough to make any man panic. The puncture in my thigh aches, but only the puncture. I felt a little sluggish from the poison at first, but it's fading and barely burns anymore. The leech and anti-toxin are doing their job.

My turn to do mine. I will not feign weakness to bait him. No tricks. No devices. This will be a clean kill.

I glance at Cassius. Sure enough, he's forming a circle with his hands. It's so easy to forget the lessons we learn. I breathe in and out, centering myself, and find the smallest of Europan breezes making its way into the dome. I realize after a beat that the cold air must be coming up from a crack in the ground, from the hollow core of the island itself. It is, just where Fá's first strike hit and broke the marble. The stone breathes as it always has.

"The path directs itself to the Vale." The words escape my mouth before I realize I've recalled them. *"Same as our breath rejoins the deepmine wind."*

As Fá reaches to pluck Bad Lass from his armor like an inconvenient toothpick, I whip Pyrphoros out and draw the razor out by its pommel. I snatch Bad Lass from the air as it comes back toward me and I assume one of the stances I tested out in my training with Cassius—a nameless hybrid of Lorn's way, Cassius's, and my own. I crouch and I hold Thraxa's razor like a dagger and Pyrphoros like a javelin.

"Atlas is your master." *Clang. Clang. Clang.* "Confess."

Fá tilts his head, amused by my strange form. He comes for me again with confidence and supreme competence. Just like before, he baits me to take to the air. He uses his warsaw to batter at my guard and his body as a ram. I am nimbler, but that advantage in counterattack is mitigated by the weight of his armor. This is what the heavy gear was made for. Closer-quarters meatstraws in ship halls. So this time, instead of bending back and countering with the Way or trying to match his strength as my armor tempts and my ego demands, I simply receive what he gives.

No teeth-chattering blocks. No counterattacks. No lusting for the air.

I deflect and move, always sideways. Never backward. Always at an angle so that I begin to make a wide circle around him, forcing him to constantly turn his hips to face me, upsetting his charges by switching my rotation. Time and again Fá tries to close. It worked against the Willow Way, which depends on maintaining a central axis for movement, like a tree trunk. But in this new form of mine, the center moves along with my target. I exhale and try to find the moving air once again. The path spreads itself out before me; all I need to do is feel the wind and follow it.

For two minutes, I decline any invitation to attack or close. I maneuver. I study. I learn. Fá is the best armored Obsidian fighter I have ever faced. Full stop. He relies on his strength and mass in the attack. An attack so overwhelming he's never needed to develop his defense. Not with his seemingly invulnerable armor that can soak up slashes and trap thrusts long enough for him to cleave his enemies in half.

I doubt he's ever had a fight last this long. In fact, I doubt anyone has ever survived more than a minute with him. I barely did. But past our second minute, I see the way to win.

His relentless assault is unsustainable. Even in the armor, his pace has begun to slow, his decisions become more judicious. He's saving energy. Waiting for me to make a mistake. Preying on that, I set a lure and let him break my circle and push me back toward the dome wall. When he rushes forward to crush me against it, I swim right and hack not at his body or his head but at the spike on his left shoulder. The spike shears off. I slash with my other blade and I take a spike off the elbow. I don't get greedy. He clears me off with a backswing and I dance away.

Clang. Clang. Clang. "Confess."

I lure him back to the center, retreating until he tries to charge me again. I take another spike off, and feel myself sinking into the shallows of a flow. He expects me to back off again. I don't. I accept the flow and strike off another spike. I begin to move around him faster and faster like a vortex of wind, my current shifting directions whenever his balance is uneven. Spike by spike I denude his monstrous armor. When spikes litter the ground, I shout again: "Confess!"

He roars in frustration. To me the sound is ambrosia. I am beyond him now, beyond this plane, submerged in the depths of a battle-flow unlike any I've ever felt. My body is not flesh and bone, not a clawDrill, but the wind I sought to emulate. My will is pure current. Pyrphoros and Bad Lass become a rain, state-changing between whip and blade with musical fluidity. The blades whittle the armor, the whips tease the wrists and ankles, forcing Fá to dedicate all his focus to preventing his limbs from being snared lest I sever them.

He starts to curl inward, no longer daring to attack.

I retract my helmet, realizing it's in my way from feeling the movement of air around me. I laugh like a boy, but not at Fá. It's because I feel the ascendent rushing through me. It's swelling inside me. He cannot stop it. For years I've used Lorn's art to make my name. Somewhere along the way, I began to think of him as a god, the custodian of some unimpeachable magic. I thought there was no potential beyond mastery of the Willow Way. Even training with Cassius in the pinched confines of his dueling room I felt as though we were only refining that craft.

No. We were sharpening my fundamentals—so I could then find *my* art form.

And this is where that art is found: where my breath meets the wind my blades make, the wind up from the stone, the wind of Fá as he flees my attacks.

My worries come and go, easy as an exhalation.

It is beautiful, natural, this movement I've stumbled upon. I feel part of nature and part of my past, full and empty, unable to falter or make a mistake because even when I misplace my blade—which I do—or my foot, or my weight, or my intentions, I can flow it into a new movement as if it was the original design. My mistakes become new opportunities, each flowing together like a drunken dance with Eo on the dirt-packed Laureltide floor.

It is that same joy as in a dance. That same reckless fun.

No longer concerned with overanalyzing my opponent or my own movement, my mind is free to wander and stumble upon a realization. All my life I've had the Helldiver's mentality: smashing through obstacles fast enough will gain the laurel for my clan. But now, after breaking a million drills and myself, I can see the flaws in that mentality. I'm done forcing my way through rock like a hungry claw until I break. Now I know to shift around obstacles, flow through gaps, like those same deepmine winds that the path referenced, the same winds that filled the old tunnels around Lykos.

I feel transported to a memory from my past. As children in the mine we played a game called Tempt the Dark. We'd gather and shout down into the abyss of an old tunnel to wake what slumbered therein. Then we'd turn our backs to see who could stand there the longest. Who could conquer the fear growing in their own chests.

Eo won that game, every time.

Some called her daft or dumb in the head. Others snickered and said she was mad standing there with her weird little smile. I thought her brave and beautiful, darkness all about her, red hair whipping my heart into tangles. It's taken me all this time to understand that smile.

She was not afraid because she was not thinking of the dark. She was enjoying her moment alone with the deepmine wind.

That wind becomes sacred to me with that realization. It finds its way through the smallest cracks and the biggest gaps. Darkness cannot stop it nor alter its journey. It cannot be chained nor held in the palm. It is movement unending. It is the sound of my childhood and Mars's song to my people. It is my path to the Vale, back to Eo one day, back to Da, and Fitchner, Dancer, and Ragnar, Theodora, and Orion, Alexandar, Ulysses, and Uncle Narrol too. When I die, whenever that day comes, I will hear the wind that howls like a wolf and know I am home.

No magical force overtakes my body, but the memories, my lessons learned through Aurae's little book, and my training with Cassius coalesce together. I can't be a Helldiver gnawing my way forward. I must flow like the breath of Mars's stone.

My eyes find a vulnerability in Fá's armor. One of his pauldrons is a little bit looser than the other from the force of his charges.

Gently, like wind guiding a kite, I guide his warsaw down and to his left. Still busying the warsaw with Pyrphoros in my right hand, I reverse directions with Bad Lass in my left and deliver three neat strikes to dislodge his right pauldron. His shoulder lies exposed. I cross my arms, pinning his warsaw down with Bad Lass, and hack off a chunk of meat from the top of his shoulder with Pyrphoros.

Fá grunts in pain, and I spin around to his right and deliver a double-slash to the back of his right knee that sends him stumbling away. The mood changes. He recovers from his stumble and stares at the blood pouring from his shoulder, then the chunk of metal missing behind his right knee. The Ascomanni and Obsidians no longer chant. They must never have seen their king bleed like this in single combat.

There's a blur to my right as the shield flickers off and a figure enters the fighting circle. I don't let it draw all of my attention, and catch Fá nodding at someone behind me. Two people have entered the sacred fight, it seems. Two interlopers. I don't bother with the one on the right. Instead, I flash Pyrphoros back in whip form underhanded as I turn, and throw Bad Lass like a spear.

Behind me is one of the Obsidians I suspected of being a Gorgon. He has a rifle pointed at my back and is about to fire just as Pyrphoros lashes across his eyes. He screams and Bad Lass takes him in the chest with a *thunk*. Without thinking, I form Pyrphoros into a blade and fling it sideways at the other Gorgon, the one I first saw entering the circle on my right. I turn to watch the blade pinwheel toward him and cut him in half just above his hips.

Seeing me without a weapon, Fá charges with a roar. I don't rush for my blades. That gap isn't open yet. Instead, I wait for him to swing, and bend away from the warsaw. I wanted to retrieve Pyrphoros first, but his attacks guide me away, and I find my path back to Bad Lass instead. I pull it from the downed man almost casually as I pass. With it in hand, I slowly turn Fá around and work toward Pyrphoros. Soon both blades are back in my hands, and only then do I resume my attack.

I guide Fá's blade when I can, and get out of the way when I can't. My breath is rhythmic, and the clarity I've found feels semi-divine. Fá almost seems to move in slow motion. No longer a machine I cannot oppose, he is a puzzle I'm excited to deconstruct. I do it piece by piece, guiding his blade, weakening his armor in multiple places, only to return when the opportunity arises.

Between flashes of metal, idle thoughts still come and go.

Cassius will be mad that I'm using my boots a little bit.

Why were there people in the circle? Has the dome gone down?

Should I kill Fá here? Should I draw it out?

Then I'm punched in the back and reality crashes down on me.

Clarity shatters. Sound rushes in. I fall to a knee and smell my skin burning. Many of the Volk are chanting my name. The dome is down. Two bodies wearing ruby amulets lie in the circle. The Gorgons, Fá's inner circle, old friends of the king. Given reprieve from my attacks, Fá stumbles to one of the dead men and falls to a knee.

"Darrow!" I follow the shout. It's Cassius. He's staring at me like I'm on fire or something. I check my arms. My suit tells me the shot I took in the back isn't mortal. "Stop toying with your meal. Kill him!"

I thought I was doing just that.

Fá stands up from kneeling beside one of the bodies baying like a wounded animal. He rushes at me. He must have cared deeply about that Gorgon.

I baffle his charge by continuing my circle around him. This time I whip at his eyeshields a few dozen times with both Bad Lass and Pyrphoros. He tries to tangle them in his warsaw, so I just switch Pyrphoros to its longest spear setting and poke at the weaknesses I've made in his armor as I whip him repeatedly in the helmet with Bad Lass. It's almost funny how off-kilter he is now. When a wild slash overextends him and presents his flank where I've worked on the armor a bit, I close and thrust Thraxa's razor into the underside of his extended left arm. The armor gives, the blade passes in and comes out the other side red with his blood. I retract it, see him try to grapple with me, so I swim right and back off while inhaling a fresh breath. The flow state is gone, but I still wade in its shallows. I bang my blades together.

Clang. Clang. Clang.

"Confess," a dozen people yell.

It's the first time they pick up the call.

Having Sevro and Cassius both out there has freed me to focus. I know they have my back, but it's no longer all about the duel. There are other factors at play outside the circle. Fá is beyond exhausted now. I go at him again, circling like before, striking only at his helmet's eyeholes with the tips of my whips until they're so mauled he can't possibly see out of them. As I'm doing it, I'm glancing around. The Ascomanni have fallen silent, but many of the Volk scream and cheer. Those Gorgons that have not rushed in are almost surrounded by Skarde and his friendly jarls. They look nervous. I'm beginning to see why. There is no question to any watching, I can kill Fá at will.

I can't, not at will. Not truly. I won't be tempted by hubris. Even wounded he's dangerous and waiting for his chance. But he and I both know eventually I will kill him.

So I back off, and slam my weapons together again to give him time to think.

Clang. Clang. Clang. This time more blades join mine in slamming together. Volk blades.

Sinister. The sound of judgment. "Confess!"

Fá can no longer see out of his helmet. He has no choice but to remove it. It reveals a face flushed and soaked in sweat and even tears. He pants steam into the cool air and leans on his warsaw. The look of fear in his eyes is total. It's a fear you can only know if there's ever been a man who wants to kill you more than he wants anything else in all the worlds, a man relentless and without pity, a man you are too tired to stop.

"Atlas au Raa is your master. Confess!" I whip him in the face and leave a bloody gash. "Tell them how he stole the *Dustmaker*. How he gave you the keys to Ilium. How he helped you master the Ascomanni. Turned you from their hunter into their king. Confess."

Someone is shouting translations in the Ascomanni tongue. The Ascomanni know the name of Atlas au Raa all too well. They stare in absolute silence at Fá.

Skarde and others beat their axes together. *Clang. Clang. Clang.*

I wait for Fá to speak.

The circle waits with me. The wind howls around the acropolis. It carries laughter from the other islands. The smell of roasted meat, the iron tang of the slaughtered leviathan, the rich scent of burning wood, and the sighing of the sea. **"Shoot him,"** Fá whispers. He looks over at his Ascomanni bodyguards. Those with their helmets down look horrified at Fá's distress. **"Shoot him now."**

Before they can obey, an Ascomanni shaman with emeralds embedded in his forehead shouts something I can't understand. More shamans enter the fighting circle and put their bodies between me and the bodyguards as shields. None of the Ascomanni bodyguards move. The horror on their faces becomes shame. Shame at what Fá has asked them to do, and confusion. He has not yet answered my accusations. His shamans yell at him in their alien tongue.

Clang. Clang. Clang.

Enraged, Fá turns to the richly dressed Gorgons. There are only four left. Two lie dead in the circle, where have the others gone? **"Brothers. Kill the Gold."**

Only one of the four is stupid enough to try. He raises a pulseFist but Skarde throws an axe end over end to cleave his head in two. The others sense the conservative jarls waiting to kill them should they dare intervene.

"You are blessed by the Allfather. Kill him yourself, Great Fá," Skarde calls.

Fá just waits, heaving for air, smiling at me. A scream comes from atop the acropolis. I hear metal on metal and the sound of men dying. A howl goes up. Sevro. He slipped away during the fight to search for snipers and the like. Cassius hasn't. He monitors the circle for threats.

Fá's smile dies in the wake of Sevro's howl. **"Fergaras . . . no . . ."** He tears his eyes from the top of the acropolis to glare out at the Volk jarls.

"Oathbreakers! Sheep! Before me you were slaves to him!" He raves at the Ascomanni to attack me. **"Before me you were worms! Half a millennia squelching under the Raa boot. I have given you their riches! Their worldly delights! If not for me, you'd be as I found you. Maggots digging tunnels in dead stone."**

· "Stone breathes too," I tell him.

He looks at me as if I'm mad.

"Confess!" Skarde calls. More pick up the call.

Lyria watches from behind Volga, but the big woman only has eyes for Fá. She glares at him until his panicked gaze lands upon her. When their eyes meet, Volga turns her back, ushering Lyria away. In my own periphery, I see Cassius move off to shadow them.

Watching Volga turn her back on him sends Fá into a rage. He screams something primal to the sky, and then shudders with an almost tragic fury.

I realize only too late: his armor must have just injected him with stims. When he decides to move, he moves fast as a snake. He hefts his warsaw, but rushes away from me after Volga. A shot from Sevro atop the acropolis slams into his back. He stumbles but only picks up speed. Lyria steps in front of Volga. The jarls around them shrink away from the onrushing giant and his whirling blade. Then Cassius hits Fá's flank. Fá saw him coming at the last moment, and bats his razor to the side. They tumble down. The warsaw flies from Fá's grip and falls amongst several of Skarde's jarls. It chews them apart. Lyria rushes for the warsaw as it rattles amongst the ruins of bodies and tries to lift it to strike at the downed warlord.

It's too heavy.

One of the jarls kicks her off and then loses his head to Sevro's sniper fire. The three remaining Gorgons pull razors and shimmer as their pulseShields activate. As a trio, they rush to help Fá from the ground and fend off his attackers. More Fá loyalists leap at Skarde. He's defended by the conservative jarls and ushered away.

It's bedlam—my old friend.

Lyria is about to be trampled between the two groups, when Volga swoops in, picks her up and leaps into the air, gravBoots whining. I didn't even see her put them on. I feel Cassius breathing a sigh of relief as Lyria is carried away from the field of battle.

The Truffle Pig did well. I chide myself for having doubted her.

With his warsaw finally reclaimed, Fá gains his feet amidst the carnage his three Gorgons have made about him. And what carnage! The trio are glorious butchers—dauntless and blood-spattered—who've dissuaded even the bravest jarls from making an attempt on Fá's life. Roaring, they dare any and all to come forward and die on their stained blades. My eyes lock on those of the old warlord, and he knows no matter how blessed by the gods of battle his bodyguards may be, they will not stand against me should I charge. Not today.

I don't charge. Instead, I smile and bash my blades together.

Clang. Clang. Clang.

"Confess," I taunt.

Instead, Fá flees.

Fá's gravBoots whine and he bursts into the sky, heading south toward the *Pandora*. The three surviving Gorgons follow behind. The rest of Fá's loyalists did not wear their gravBoots to the feast. Abandoned by their king, they are set upon by Skarde and the other jarls. Some fight back nobly. Some beg for mercy only to be hacked apart. Others escape into the garden to be pursued and killed amongst the trees.

I cannot stop this bloodshed, so I do not try.

The Ascomanni watch Fá shrink in the sky. They have not yet recovered from their stupor. Many have fallen to their knees. They believed their Fá a messiah. Invincible. Yet he fled before my blade, my accusations. He fled because he was afraid to die. Their religion crumbles before their eyes.

I stalk toward them, lift Pyrphoros, beat my chest, and howl at them in challenge. "You have seen your king bleed. You have seen him run. Come, witness him confess."

As a shaman translates, I feel a hand on my low back and know it's Cassius. "You used your boots."

"Sorry."

"No. That was . . . What *was* that?"

Skarde stumbles to his feet, cradling a bloody left arm. He points after Fá and shouts to me. "Tyr Morga! If he makes it to the *Pandora* he will nuke this entire island!"

"Cassius, summon the Raa and the Owls." I see the heart-seeker gauntlet lying on the ground, snatch it up, and toss it to Cassius to carry. Sevro howls as he flies past overhead, already after Fá. Cassius and I lift off and fall in on his flanks.

74

DARROW

The Hunt

"**G**OT TWO OF THE GORGONS *atop the acropolis. But you know, if Diomedes left us hanging out to dry, we're well and truly slagged,*" Sevro says. "*You know that, right?*"

I don't answer. There is no point. My bloodlust is on, and what will be will be.

Wind whistles through a crack in my helmet as we eat into Fá's lead. He was a speck in the sky before I set off. As he passes over a complex of blue-painted domes on the edge of the island, he is now large as a coin. Our boots are faster, but I'm not sure we'll catch him before he reaches the *Pandora*. That's fine. If Diomedes plays his part, we shouldn't have to.

If.

The *Pandora* hangs low over the sea only a few clicks out from the islands. It is the only warship within the security cordon. If he lands and cocoons himself within that fortress, it will take an army to pry him out. He will glass the witnesses of our fight. I will lose and all the people in the Deep will die.

If.

Black thoughts race through my mind. Was I a fool to trust Diomedes? Athena? Were the submarines not as stealthy as the Kalibar promised? Were they spotted after all? Are my allies dead on the bottom of the sea?

I laugh at my spiraling brain.

"*Boss, do we break off pursuit?*" Sevro asks.

In reply, I accelerate past him to take point. A moment later a pupil of light winks along the shadowy topography of the *Pandora*'s green hull. Sevro, Cassius, and I break in separate directions as a particle beam meant for us cleaves through the gloom.

"Boss?" Sevro asks as we come back together.

Just over a kilometer separates Fá from his onrushing reinforcements. Already the air fills with toroids of superheated plasma. Rail slugs scream toward Sevro and me, leaving behind blue-tinged contrails. We weave through the incoming fire but the fusillade does not last long.

Diomedes has come as he said he would, and so has Athena.

From a distance, their arrival is a peaceful sight, one that could almost be authored by nature herself. A flight of pods fired from deep-sea submarines slips up from the water. Unnoticed, they blossom to disperse their payloads. Hundreds of tiny pollen-like specks float outward. Only when the specks form up together and streak toward Fá's reinforcements do they hint at the menace they bring.

Manmade thunder peals as Diomedes, three-dozen crack Peerless Golds of Europa, and several hundred Black Owls in mech-suits and power armor hit Fá's reinforcements from beneath.

The chaos is immediate. A dogfight swirls to block Fá's path back to the *Pandora*. Fá still intends to push through it. Then Diomedes and four Golds peel off the dogfight and race directly toward Fá. When he sees them coming, Fá abandons his route back to his ship and swerves away toward the nearest island to seek refuge amongst the tribe feasting there. To buy himself time, he leaves behind the three Gorgons who accompanied him on his flight from the duel.

Diomedes and his four Golds streak for the Gorgons.

Sevro, Cassius, and I follow Fá.

We push our gravBoots for all they're worth, closing to within twenty meters by the time Fá crosses over the seawall of the island. We pass low enough to see the expressions of confusion on the faces of two Ascomanni pissing off the edge of the wall as they stare at the nascent firefight in the distance. They nearly topple over as we rocket past.

Libraries and shrines blur beneath. Fá lowers altitude, weaving through blackstone buildings to try and shake us, heading for a plateau aglow with fires and striated with ranks of long tables. The feast here is in full swing, and the din tremendous. Bonfires glow and crackle. Slaves ferry huge platters of meat and flagons of drink to their violent masters.

The Ascomanni gorge themselves under totems to their tribe and sub-tribe, many sitting at long tables, others sprawled out in the parklands beneath the great statue to Hera.

I fall upon Fá just as he reaches the feast. We crash down onto a table. Wood splinters. Wine spills. Meat cascades around us as we beat at one another. His elbow slams into my head and I lose my grip. He stumbles away, desperate to be free of me. I gain my feet. Tattooed faces stare at us. Every way I turn—coarse black hair, glittering gems, and snarling mouths. Fá stumbles from the wreckage and roars: **"Assassins! Assassins! Defend your king!"**

The Ascomanni gape. Two of the least drunk uncoil their long bodies, grab their spears, and come for me. But they are unsteady, unprepared, and I am the breath of stone. I flow through them instead of chewing into them. I turn a spear thrust up with Pyrphoros and disembowel the brave with Bad Lass as I pass. The second I dodge and disarm to leave for Sevro or Cassius. Three more try to arrest my progress. I weave through them without slowing down to kill. My friends follow behind, guarding my back.

Fá leaps to another part of the feast. I follow and land on a table hard enough to split the wood. Ascomanni fall back from me. I crash into Fá and send him stumbling through a bonfire. Flaming logs roll in every direction.

"Confess!" I roar. "You are a pet to a Gold! You are the hand of Atlas au Raa!"

Fá shoves men in my path to use as human shields, hoping to tangle my blades in their bodies. It almost works. With Pyrphoros buried in the chest of one, I take a huge blow from his warsaw to my left shoulder that knocks me sideways and into the table and a mess of bodies. Fá levers down with all his strength, trying to press his warsaw through my armor. The saw gnaws through Ascomanni in the way, through my armor, and into the flesh of my left triceps before I slide underneath and battle him back.

We smash through great spits of meat and over drunken braves, like lions fighting in the midst of startled oxen. Fá knows he can't win, not even fueled by stims, so he pushes a giant Ascomanni into my path, roars a laugh of triumph, and takes off into the sky.

The Ascomanni is as tall as Fá and freakish with muscle and scars. An unbound mane of black hair falls to his low back. He is unarmored, like the rest, but he carries a terrible spear and shield with a massive snake skull surmounted on the front.

The Ascomanni chant the warrior's name. "Ur! Ur!"

Ur's eyes flick to the slingBlade shape of Pyrphoros. To the blue paint and blood ruins glazed on my armor. *"Ashvar?"* he asks in a thick accent.

I nod. He glances after Fá, snorts, and sits back down at the table where he brushes aside a disembodied limb and returns to his drinking. I return to the air and leave the second island in my wake.

Jarls and other spectators with gravBoots are following us now to watch. It is a spectacle, our hunt. They make a trail of laughter and toasts across the sky. The Ascomanni come too, just as interested in the great bloodsport. On troop barges and gravskiffs and air sleds, they toss out coarse jests.

I catch Fá just as he reaches the next island of the archipelago. The island of Artemis is larger than that of Hera and shaped like a crescent, with high cliff walls and an interior dominated by a statue to the goddess Artemis. The statue stands flanked by woodland effigies half a kilometer in height. Drawn by the fight around the *Pandora,* braves have left their tables to gather on the edge of the island's cliffs. Fá lands amongst them and has only a few moments to exhort them to attack me before Sevro and I send him fleeing to the heart of the island. We catch him there over the feast around Artemis's feet.

Familiar standards wave there above the long tables—Volk standards. Braves scatter as I pursue Fá into their fire-lit feast grounds. Their moon-pale faces blur together in a sea of stained beards, agape mouths. I hound Fá through their ranks.

I am no stranger here. For ten years I led these tribes and these men. On Luna, Earth, Mars, and Mercury. For ten years they trudged with me through the ruins of Gold cities. Through rain and sleet and mud and desert heat and mining tunnels, we marched together toward victory. They do not mistake me now as I battle Fá from one end of their feast to the other, whipping him before me like a beast of burden. He stumbles. He roars for aid. None comes. They see the paint of *ashvar* on our armor. They see the curve of my blade. Tyr Morga has come, and the Volk seem ashamed of being found here by me like this.

This time, I let Fá go when he realizes there is no shelter here under the protection of the Volk. He takes to the air yet again and mistakes the spectators trailing my hunt for allies in his fight. He flies to them, and they shoo him away and shout, *"Ashvar."* Sevro and Cassius kill those few who try to intervene, but most have just come to watch the hunt.

In his desperation, Fá heads for the next island on the archipelago chain. The braves on the ground stare at me in awe and bewilderment. I pitch my head back and howl again. Amplified by the speakers in my armor, joined by Sevro's and Cassius's, the howl resounds over the feast and is picked up by many of the spectators in the sky. I follow after Fá and give the man no respite.

By the time he makes it to the next island, I am in his shadow. He steals a pulseFist and fires to no avail. Across the feast, I pursue him. His death is already written. All he can do is draw it out.

I harry him island to island, over rock-built citadels and elegant moon-lit shrines, through dark upland groves and fire-lit plateaus where standards of Volk tribes wag in the evening breeze, hunting him, mocking him, whittling away the warlord's myth until he becomes a disgusting, limping grotesquerie so all can see the craven heart of the man who killed Queen Sefi just to call himself king.

75

LYRIA

Prove It

V OLGA FLIES LOW OVER the sea to the island farthest from Fá's
favor. There, she sets us down on a beach beside strange contrap-
tions aimed at the sky. They look like railguns. She pulls me along as she
heads for them.

"Stop pulling on me!" I yell at her.

"It's not safe here," she says and drags me toward a pod fit into the
firing chamber of a railgun. "The crews must have gone to watch. We
can still use the guns, I think. They will fire at us between the gaps in
the shield and out into space. Fá keeps escape vehicles on autopilot in
orbit—"

"Stop it!" I shout and wrench my arm free.

She turns back in anger. "Lyria, get in the pod."

I stare at her. "You ain't saving me. You're trying to run away," I say,
shocked. "Oh, is that the freelancer in you? Or is that Fá? Society special
forces always have a way out?" I ask.

"He did not confess—"

"But you know the truth. They do too. He played you all like fools."

"Fá is all that protected me. The braves may revere my blood, but the
jarls call me unnatural. A lab freak. They will kill me."

"Then they kill you." She looks so afraid, but I'm spitting mad. "You
don't get to run away anymore, Volga. I'm glad you didn't tear out my
heart and throw it in a fire. Really. Thanks. I'm glad you didn't have *that*
in you. But you killed thirteen people before me. Thirteen, woman!
What the fuck?" She looks at the pod. "Look at me!" I throw a handful

of sand at her. "Look at me!" She does. "You killed Sigurd. *He* was trying to help his people get free of a liar, a Gold tool. You might not be broken, but you got stains on your hands. If you run away now, you always will. Don't you think that's what Ephraim would tell you?" I point back behind us where tiny shapes make a trail over the islands. "You have to face what you've done. You said your people are here. Prove it."

"This is insane," she protests with wide eyes. "He hid in a leviathan. Darrow—"

"Is apparently a werewolf who eats warlords and shits nightmares. But he likes me. He trusts me. I should be nothing to him. A rat. But he saw my worth. He let me come after you because I *begged* him. I told him you were brave. I told him you were kind. I told him you were my friend!"

I find power in realizing I have convictions. Deep ones. My voice finds its edge.

"If you go in that pod, you go on your own. You'll have no people, Volga. Not me, not the Obsidians, not the Republic. I ain't friends with rats who jump ship after they dined on all the cheese." I point behind me as a roar of the crowd rolls in across the sea. "Or you go back. You face the fathers whose kids you kidnapped. The jarl whose son you killed. You face the stains you put on your hands. You choose accountability. You choose your people. You choose me. That's the kinda person worthy of *my* friendship. Ephraim, Ragnar, Fá. Don't pin it on all the daddies. This is it. Who are you, Volga?"

Even now, her every instinct is to run. To survive. It's what the worlds taught her. Frightened, she looks out at the *Pandora* beneath which more pods are bursting up from the sea. It looks like the Daughters and Diomedes are storming the low-flying ship. Then she looks at the crowd of flying lunatics following Darrow and Fá to the next island on the chain, and makes her decision to face her mistakes.

"I will go back. You stay here," she says.

"Negative, dumbass."

"You are tiny. This is insanity. You will get hurt. The Ascomanni, the Obsidians . . ."

"Then protect me from the giants, and I'll protect you from the wolves," I say. A single laugh escapes her, and she looks at me like I'm ten feet tall. That doesn't last long. She comes to pick me up. I shove her hands away. "I'm not a child. I fly on your back."

76

DARROW

By the Laws of the Ice

The throng gathering in the wake of my hunt grows island by island. Thousands trail us now. On and on I chase Fá over the archipelagos until we reach the island of Hades, a rocky home to the feast for the braves farthest from Fá's favor. I chase him through groves of wild fig trees bent inland by the wind. To my left and right, Sevro and Cassius shatter gnarled boughs laden heavily with swollen fruit. Pulp and splinters smear our armor until the grove gives way to slate rock formations covered with orange moss. Fá winds through them and emerges on a headland where hot bubbling wellsprings belch steam. He sets down there at the terminus of a spring. There is nowhere left to run. The sea is all that lies ahead.

He looks out at it as Sevro and Cassius find perches on the rock behind me. Fá's tattered armor rises and falls with his breath. Blood weeps from the many punctures and gashes. It stains the blue paint his shaman applied to his armor and trickles into a puddle around his boots. His warsaw is now a millstone too heavy to even lift.

"I've called Diomedes. He's leaving Athena the battle. He's on his way," Cassius says.

Clang. Clang. Clang.

Fá flinches at the sound, as if he had forgotten I was there. Slowly, he turns. The spirit is gone from the doom-struck man. **"What do you want from me?"** he asks. His voice warbles. **"Why won't you just leave me alone? What do you *want*?"**

Our audience has not caught up, but the wind carries their demand.

Clang. Clang. Clang.

"**I have he**lium. Weap**ons. Ship**ssss." His voice warbles again. Sparks spurt from his metal throat. He digs at something there with his sharp fingers and discards it. "Hundreds of thousands of lowColors, Darrow!" His voice no longer carries the same baritone as Ragnar's. It is softer, more intelligent, and more afraid. "A million innocents on the Ascomanni ships. In the Garter, more! I will free them. I will give you back your precious Volk killing machine. Take them. Good riddance. I will leave Europa." He waits for me to reply. I don't. "Tell me what you want!"

Again, the wind makes its demand.

Clang. Clang. Clang.

His eyes creep up. I turn to see the island's braves gathering on the cliffs. The laughter drifts in the wind as the throng in the air arrives, banging their axes on their boots or their skiffs. Hundreds. Thousands. *"Volga spotted. And Lyria. Three o'clock,"* Cassius says. *"Diomedes thirty seconds."* Volga curves around a giant slate of rock with the mad little Red riding on her back. As the two set down, I look back to Fá.

Clang. Clang. Clang.

"Then you will let me leave?" he asks.

I see him clearly now. Beneath the mountain of the man lies a venal, quaking spirit. A greedy little man. Or am I choosing to see him as small, to ease the dread in knowing there are servants of the enemy with the sort of conviction his mission would take? I doubt it is his fault that Atlas made Fá his tool. Fá went along with the worlds, as do most of us. Had he been born one generation later, who knows what side he'd be on.

Diomedes coasts in low to the water. He hesitates when he sees the audience I've gathered behind me, but settles down beside Cassius to watch.

"Answer me, Darrow! If I confess, you will let me leave?" Fá asks.

"I give you my word. Confess your crimes and I will not kill you."

The Obsidians watch in silence, a silence made all the deeper when several hundred Ascomanni arrive. The wind whooshes against their strange armor. The sea sighs. Fá looks down at the blood around his feet. It has started to draw crabs from the tide pools of the headland.

"Fine. *Fine.* Atlas is my master," he says. "Are you satisfied?"

Clang. Clang. Clang. From the Volk above.

"Shut up!" He shouts like a man pestered by wasps. "I . . . was born Vagnar Hefga of the Valkyrie Spires. As I claim. To the gens Grimmus stables. I was a slaveknight and rewarded. I enjoyed the life of a gladiator and all its attendant spoils. It came with a price and expiration date. I died. Then I began my second service. I served *in cohors nihil* under the greatest mind of his generation, Atlas au Raa. A man who knows duty, as do none of you. I was banished along with him to exterminate the Ascomanni *vermin*. We tried for years. After Luna fell, Atlas raised me amongst the Ascomanni to unite them to use against the Dominion and the Rising. To remind the traitors that beyond the Society lies only the abyss, only chaos."

"And to give the Rim a savior from the Core," I say.

"Yes," he says. "Atalantia. My reign was to last three years, then Atalantia would sail to bring order to these spheres. Without order, chaos rushes in. Kill me. Find out." He grins at the Volk and the Ascomanni. "They will eat each other unless you claim the throne, Tyr Morga. Unless you prove me right—you came to get your axe back. Go on, Gold. They were designed to be used. An ouroboros. Unless you feed them enemies, they are a serpent eating their own tail."

He chuckles and spits blood.

"Where is Atlas?" I ask.

He grunts. "You asked me to confess. Not give up my brother."

"Atlas thinks of you as a loyal dog, at best. Where is he?"

"You do not know him. That is why you cannot fight him."

"Where is he?"

"But he knows you. He knows all of you."

"*Where?*" I shout.

He does not reply. His eyes change, like he knows now whatever vision he had of his future is no longer in reach. He says farewell to it with a heavy sigh and a small smile. He lets go of his warsaw. It clangs against the ground.

"Where is Atlas?" he asks and pats his chest over his heart. "Here. There." He nods to me then up at the audience. "In all our hearts. He may be mortal, but his work is not. My Gorgon brothers you butchered were patriots, Darrow. Their sacrifice will live on in the works of our brother, our teacher, our Allfather. Before only him, I kneel." He closes his eyes and goes to his knees. He no longer speaks to me. "Without darkness, there could not be light. Forgive me, brother, for seeking a little more for myself before the end."

He unfastens his armor. His huge body is rent and dark with blood. The armor clangs to the ground a piece at a time. From the smile on his face, I know he's sown poison in his truths.

"Did you kill the Raá in their family vestibule?" Diomedes asks. "The children, was it you?"

Cassius stays Diomedes with a hand on his chest. We had agreed beforehand: Fá is the Volk's to kill.

Fá does not answer anyway.

Diomedes relents and Cassius throws me the heatseeker gauntlet he carried from the isle of Zeus. It is heavy with sharp fingers. I walk toward Fá and see Skarde floating above, surrounded by jarls. No doubt already spreading dissent against my pending reign. "You saw how he used my boy, my Sigurd," he will say. "You saw how he let him die."

"He wants the throne. I told you!" Fá calls. "Did I kill your son, Darrow? Skarde, should not you deliver the blow? Avenge Sigurd?"

The Volk hand that kills a king or queen takes the crown. That is often the Obsidians' way.

If I take Fá's life, I am king. If Skarde takes it, then he is. Both are a problem.

Skarde will not cross me. Not today. None will. If I kill Fá, the Obsidians will cheer. They will kneel. They will hail me as king. They will follow me to Mars and be my axe. But their actions speak for the thoughts they will not voice. Already some of them are floating to join the orbit of the strongest who are not me.

This is the problem. The Obsidians' is a cult of silence that follows strength. That silence is called honor, but it is really fear. The seeds of resentment sown here will grow to yield more destruction. The Obsidians will rebel again or, when I die, start the cycle all over. I cannot decide their fate either by sitting on the throne myself or installing a puppet. Yet if I leave the throne empty, they will destroy each other in their rush to fill it.

Nothing will change. So I will try to get them to tread the thin line between chaos and tyranny: that fragile experiment we call demokracy. Not now, though. First, Fá must die. And then I must give my candidate a chance.

"I'm not going to kill you," I say to Fá. "That's up to her." I look over at Volga and motion her to join me. The Volk jarls roar in protest, especially Skarde. I raise my blade for silence, and call out. "A servant of the Fear Knight cannot be King of the Volk, can he?" They quiet. They see what I'm doing. If Fá is not really their king, I am declaring his murder will not serve as a coronation for their new monarch.

"No. He cannot," Skarde says, sly, sacrificing the day to win tomorrow.

"This man is no king then! He is just a man! Just a father! It is known by the Volk that a father's shame is his family's. So by the laws of the ice, let blood judge blood," I say.

The jarls let it pass.

I toss the gauntlet to Volga as she approaches. Lyria follows. Volga is shorter than I am, and shy to meet my gaze. Eventually she does, and the shame in her expression is eclipsed only by her anger at Fá. She slips on the gauntlet and faces Fá. I take Lyria by the shoulder and guide her off to the side.

Whatever peace or malice Fá had left drains from him as he looks up at Volga.

"If not for the Volk . . . why did you do this?" she asks him.

"For a brother, and my deserved peace," he replies.

"But the Passage . . ."

He seems to shrink a little. "This farce was not to last. I thought . . . if you were like me, you could not hate me. You could understand me. You could love—" He jerks as she plunges the gauntlet into his chest, up to the wrist, and gives a twist. Their faces draw close together. For the first time I see his features in her, hers in him, and Ragnar's in both. Then Volga pulls out Fá's heart and holds it before his eyes.

"Unworthy."

She throws it over her shoulder and soon after, he teeters down to the ground to the delight of the crabs. Silence presides but for the sounds of the dwindling battle beneath the *Pandora* in the distance. No Obsidians cheer, because for the first time in years, they have no ruler. Seeing the chaos coming and the factions already forming, the Ascomanni look one last time at the corpse of the man they thought blessed by god and slip away into the dark.

I motion to Sevro.

He jogs over with his helmet off to become the scariest town crier the worlds have ever seen. "Hello. Sorry!" He steps up onto Fá's corpse. "That's better. Can you hear me now? Good. Great to be back. Lots of favorite faces here. We've shared a lot of good times. And now, a few bad ones. Let's not make it worse. You know it could get really shitty really fast. You know what you're like . . . come on. You do."

The jarls all look at those with whom they have a grudge. For a moment, no one is looking at Sevro except Volga.

"So! With your consent, we will be your mediators in this transition period. Twenty-four hours from now you will meet on this island—furthest from my step stool's favor—where you will vote on your new monarch. Each jarl will have two votes. Two! One for themselves. One decided by their braves. The braves cannot, I repeat, cannot vote for their own jarl. Recall your men. Bring your ships above these islands. If anyone leaves without a Howler escort, if anyone steals, if anyone kills, if anyone cheats, if anyone intimidates, they break Tyr Morga's peace, and will earn his *ashvar*." He gestures to me like I'm a show pony. "As you have seen, he's gotten a lot scarier since you last saw him. *But. He. Will. Not. Be. Your. King.* He is not on the ballot and will not interfere." Diomedes looks my way. "*If* you do not like these rules, let's have it now."

I walk to a flat spot and draw both of my blades and wait in the silence.

"Good," Sevro calls after half a minute passes. "Now sober up! Wash your beards! You've campaigning to do. If you have *any* questions, I'm going to be on my wife's ship testing out my new knives."

He takes off. I offer Lyria a lift, but she turns me down. I follow Sevro into the air. We land a few minutes later in a hangar of the *Pandora* that Athena and Diomedes secured. Diomedes and Cassius land behind me. Gunfire rattles from deeper in the ship.

"Ascomanni are dug in throughout the ship," one of the Kalibar Gold knights reports to Diomedes. "Resistance is stiff."

Sevro gasps at the arcane symbols and religious totems erected by the Ascomanni in the hangar. "Jove's putrid cock, this place is filthy."

"Oh, now you care about a ship being clean?" Cassius says. "That's rich."

Athena rushes over from tending the wounded. "Is it done?" she asks.

"Fá is dead, but the menace remains," Diomedes says. "Darrow has seen fit to experiment with demokracy for his Obsidians at the expense of our people."

Athena is torn at hearing that. "We agreed you'd get them off Europa, Darrow."

"I will, and I'm trying to make sure they don't nuke the place as they go, or steal millions of your citizens," I reply, more than a little peeved by their pedantry.

Diomedes gets very close to my face. "We agreed: they would surrender all the people they have enslaved, all the loot they have taken, and leave. Now you will have chaos. Now the Ascomanni will flee and infest the Garter. You have put *everything* at stake."

I take a deep breath. "They already infest the Garter. Do you have an army to cleanse that infestation? Do you have an army to smash the Volk? No. So your only hope is that that Volk army out there chooses to let shine the better angels of their nature. Your only hope, Diomedes, is that they help you. So please get out of my face."

He is furious, and whips around when Sevro clears his throat.

Sevro and Cassius have their weapons out. "Victra's employees are in slavery on this ship and have been for a year. My employees," Sevro says and takes the Twilight Helm from, of all people, Cheon. Four dozen Black Owls await his orders. "So we gonna whine or we gonna go—"

"Sweep your halls?" Cassius drawls. "Waiting on you, Ares."

"Idiot," Sevro mutters, puts on the helm, and runs toward the gunfire with Cassius at his flank. Diomedes and I exchange another glare and follow with the Black Owls. We can argue later. For now, there's killing to be done.

PART IV

BROTHERS

For a friend with an understanding heart
is worth no less than a brother.

—HOMER

77

DARROW

Old Stoneside

TWENTY-THREE HOURS AFTER WE left the Volk jarls to begin their campaigning, I set down on an island in the northern Discordia Sea with Cassius. The light is a bruised blue. The water restless dark. There is not another island to be seen in any direction. Even in my armor, without its heater on it is cold this far north of Europa's equator. I shiver. Cassius doesn't. I wrap my thermal cloak tighter.

"So should I let you go in alone?" he asks.

"You're the one who insisted on coming," I say.

"Well, you're injured and need a bodyguard," he replies. "Savages about, not to mention Atlas."

"If he's not already back in the Core," I reply. "Walk with me."

"As long as you promise not to bring up the gala," he says and touches his arm.

"Only if you don't mention again how you don't have a scratch on you." Somehow he wasn't injured at all in our fighting.

"I swear," he says, and we walk together toward the keep.

The waves have not yet claimed the wandering island of Harmonia or the castle upon it that Lorn once called home. They will soon enough. The Discordia Sea is violent here in the north, and without its caretakers Harmonia cannot help but lose its war against the elements. Breakers thunder against its seawalls. Lichen grows on the castle's towers. Coral and barnacles creep on ramparts that once sheltered the hills and forests that comprised the heart of the estate.

Maybe because Cassius is with me, I find its dereliction less tragic than I expected. Time marches on. Nothing we build lasts forever, not without others to keep it. That was one of the many reasons I did not take the throne of the Volk for myself. Fá's words haunt me. Ouroboros. It reminded me of what Lorn once told me: *Death begets death begets death.*

Crabs skitter from our boots as we walk along the bridge from the landing pads to the keep. I am sore, and not just from my fight with Fá. Even with Diomedes and the Daughters, Sevro needed help taking the *Pandora* back from the Ascomanni who wanted to keep it. This time Cassius and I guarded Sevro's flank as he led the fight to free his wife's ship wearing his father's helmet.

I have broken ribs, three punctures in my right thigh, a wound on my upper chest from a spear that went through me, and countless bruises, sprains, and superficial lacerations. Not to mention, Fá's poison lingers in my system, still giving me boughts of nausea. Lorn would laugh and say I walk like him now.

The fight on the *Pandora* turned when we freed the enslaved crew— many of Julii's old sailors, techs, janitors even. They helped us use the ship's systems against the holdouts and flushed them into the sea to feed the gathering leviathans. The lowColors cried and kissed Sevro afterward, and he fell to his knees with them when they heard they were going home. Not yet, though. There's still more to do.

Cassius pauses before we enter the keep between the stone hippogriffs that guard the doors. He looks out to sea. "You'd almost think the moon is sleeping," he says.

"It does seem eerie," I say. "Not a ship in the sky."

The surface of Europa is quiet. Its cities dim. But its people are not gone. They are safe in the Deep with Athena protecting them, waiting to hear if they will get their moon back and can emerge like spring flowers from the winter snow. The Ascomanni may have fled the stronger Volk ships in droves—streaming back to the Garter to seek strength in numbers with their own people—so the Volk remain the only power on Europa.

"If the wrong person wins your election, will the Europans get their moon back?" Cassius asks.

"I don't know," I say. "I really don't."

So much rests on the Volk vote that I had to leave to resist the temptation to interfere any more than I already have. Athena begged and

Diomedes demanded for me to pick a ruler, but I can't just think about their moons, their people. I have to think of us all.

"You promised Diomedes we'd help free the Garter," Cassius says, watching a gull coast past. "If the wrong person wins, how are we doing that without the Volk? If Atlas didn't go back to the Core, then—"

"Cassius."

"Sorry. Anxiety spiral. Yes, yes. But also, what if Athena does actually take your head, or doesn't take you to the ships once Europa is free of the Volk like she promised?"

I leave him to worry without me.

"Darrow!" He rushes after me through the doors. "No need to be rude."

"Can we just walk?" I ask and put an arm over his shoulders. "Please?" He smiles grandly and wraps his arm back behind my waist, ready to saunter. "Stop it."

"Fine. A dour trudge down memory lane it is."

The keep is as cold inside as it is outside. The place was abandoned when Lorn's household followed him into the war I sparked between House Augustus and House Bellona almost a decade and a half ago. Its hundreds of lamps lie dark. Its halls, once filled with summer midnight dances and the laughter of his many grandchildren, lie mute. I pass room after room, each as unfamiliar as the next. I have no memories of this place except for the ones I made on that day I brought Lorn out of his retirement and into my war. He fell before he could return.

We descend the stairs to where Tactus died on the edge of Lorn's knife, and stand in that room to honor my dead friend. Tactus hinted he might have lived for more than himself just before he died. I remember it as one of the sadder moments of my life.

Cassius lets me go into Lorn's room alone. It is emptier than I imagined it would be. There are no trophies, no razors, no mementos from his wars. Only pictures of his family, books, and rings by the bedside. One for each of his sons, and one for his wife. He left them here. He did not bring them to war. The Kalibar said they kept the place exactly as he left it, and protected it from looters.

I believe them now.

I catch myself in one of the room's mirrors. I look like his ghost. But I'm not. In his bathroom I search for a razor. Then I laugh, because I remember one of the old stories about him. When he was a lancer, his

Praetor told him to go shave because *Peerless are beardless, boy*. Lorn pulled out his razor and did it right there. I shave my beard with Bad Lass in his bathroom mirror. In this way I say goodbye to him and Ragnar both. I do a sloppy job and cut myself a few times.

"Wait. Who are you and what did you do with the ancient mariner?" Cassius says when I exit without a beard.

I scratch my bare chin. "Remembered an old story."

"Oh yes. The 'Peerless Beardless.' Love that one. Think it's true?" he asks.

"Definitely. Why do we even buy laser trimmers anyway?"

He scoffs at the knicks on my chin, and begins to shave his beard right in front of me. "Social conditioning," he says and continues both chattering and shaving as we descend to the training grotto. "Pervasive marketing. It's the companies really. They get you when you're young."

I tune him out and eventually he runs out of opinions on the topic. Unlike me, he doesn't cut himself shaving once.

The seawall that once sheltered the grotto lies only a few paces above the waterline now. The statues of the gods that surrounded the grotto were too weak to face the ocean's storms, and many of the gods who watched Lorn practice the Willow Way lie broken. I clear barnacles and seaweed from the training floor with Pyrphoros to reveal the willow tree inlaid into the stone. It is identical to the one in his old estate on Mars. I feel another deep pang of nostalgia.

Several disembodied fingers from one of the statues lie on the training floor. Setting my knee on the outsized digits, I kneel, about to say a silent prayer to Lorn. I feel Cassius watching me. "You know, when Lorn left Mars for Europa, he wanted me to withdraw from my position as Nero's lancer and come with him to finish my training," I say.

"You regret not going?" Cassius asks.

"No. But I always wonder what if I had."

"Well, you'd have missed the gala." I look up at him and he's pointing at me like I said it. I laugh. "I think you've finished your training at this point. So why are we here?" he asks.

I look around. "I came to say I was sorry to him. About Alexandar."

Cassius looks down. "Ah." He hesitates.

"What?"

"Well, do you think that's right?" he asks.

"What? Praying to a dead atheist?"

"Well, yes. That. But also apologizing?"

"Alexandar died as my lancer," I say. "Lorn lost all his sons to war. He didn't want their daughters or sons to go the same way."

"Yes. Well. From what I hear, Alexandar died being a bit more than a lancer," Cassius says. "Don't give me that shrug as if I don't know. Sevro told me some things about him. More than just the Tyche bit." I frown. "Yes, Sevro and I are capable of exchanging information when you're not around. Gods. You really are so arrogant. Anyway." He sits on a god's face. "I only knew Lorn from afar, but I think he would be flattered if people said you were a reflection of him."

I wince at that.

"Even without the beard?" I ask.

"Even in the asteroid belt we heard stories about you. Not all worldbreaker ones either. That time you had Pax whip you at the Institute? I was pouting in Castle Mars at the time. Then eight years later some pirate in an asteroid cantina tells me about it in the middle of an unbidden lecture on leadership. Gods, she rambled on. Point is, students are always a reflection of the teacher, Darrow. Fá was for Atlas. You are for Lorn. Alexandar was for you."

I nod. Seeing his point. "Colloway is that for Orion. And Lysander is for you," I say, knowing he needs someone to say it and clear that last ledger for him. "In the end." He leans back and breathes out. "Does Diomedes strike you as a man in the habit of giving compliments?" I ask.

"Gods. Not even with a gun to his head. Whatever does Aurae see in him?"

"Truth," I say. "I've never met a man who means what he says more than that one. So when he says Lysander was a man of honor, that he cared about the Rim, that he saved Diomedes's life and sacrificed his own, do you think that's a reflection of Octavia or you?"

He grins. "Well, me, obviously. I'm famously selfless."

"You're actually getting that way," I say. "It's not unnoticed."

"What? Did somebody compliment me?" he asks. "It's the jawline. Isn't it selfless, really. I take the pressure off everyone else. They don't have to worry about being the most handsome in the room. They can just *be*. Ah. Heavy is the chin that sets the bar." He tilts his head. "Do you hear that?"

"A ship," I say.

Our radios squawk a moment later. It's Lyria. Cassius brightens up.

"*. . . this is Lyria. Howler One, Eagle One, do you read?*"

Cassius holds up a hand to me. "Who?"

"*Lyria. Requesting—*"

"Who?"

Her radio crackles. "*Truffle Pig to Eagle One, requesting hot drop and perimeter cruise—*"

She's hilariously formal on the radio. "Oh, Truffles! Come on in." He smiles as the roar of the ship grows louder. "Oh. Darrow. I remembered. No more Truffle Pig. She hates it. Says it's demeaning to her other contributions and athletic stature."

"Uh-huh. Well. She doesn't get to choose her own callsign."

"Of course not. I was thinking Strawberry Lass. No? Crow Whisperer? Red Rabbit?"

"We'll figure it out later." I have a thought. "What do they call baby eagles?"

He acts like he's just seen a puppy. "*Eaglet*. Oh gods. She'll die."

We wait in the grotto as Lyria performs a dramatic arrest overhead to impress Cassius. She almost hits the building. "*Shit,*" she mutters over the radio.

"Still on janitorial, Eaglet One," he says into his com.

"*What?*"

"Nothing. Yet."

He literally acts like he's twelve around her.

Volga jumps out the back of the ship and makes a beeline toward me. Her head is down under the wash of the ship's engines. She glances at Cassius. She does a double take. He's staring dramatically out to sea now, either thinking about Lysander or posing for a coin. She's so captivated by him her foot clips an uneven stone. He doesn't look over at me, but draws a finger along his jaw. Idiot.

Volga blushes as she comes to a stop. "You shouldn't be off the islands," I say.

"Sevro said Lyria's a Howler," Volga says. "Counts as my escort."

"Did he?" I say. "You should be campaigning."

"That is done. The votes are being cast. Can we talk? Alone?"

"Cassius," I say.

He sighs. "Are the services of a hero required?"

"Go up these stairs, around to the left. There's a garden. I saw some tide pools there." He stands and checks his razor. "Admire your reflection for ten minutes, and come back."

"Funny. I think I'll hop up and talk to the young eaglet instead. I hope I don't open any wounds in my exertions. Oh wait. I have none." He jumps upward after Lyria's shuttle. Volga watches him go. When he's gone, she wheels on me, angry.

"Why did you let me kill Fá?" she asks.

"Is there a problem?"

"People are trying to make me queen."

"And you're telling them not to?" I ask.

"Yes, I am telling them not to."

"Oh, that *is* a problem," I say. "Skarde and Fjod must not know what to do."

"Braves keep seeking me out to tell me they will vote for me. The jarls are angry. I cannot escape them. I do not want to be your puppet queen. I do not want to be your Fá, but you made me that when you had me kill him."

"That was your choice. Did you not want to kill him?"

"He had to die. And yes. I wanted to kill him," she says. "That's not the point."

I sit down on the stone with a wince. I wave for her to join. She doesn't, then grows awkward standing over me, and sits. For the first time I really look at her. She is not as callused in the face as most Obsidians. She has deep lines on her forehead, scabs from a few cuts, a nose that's been recently broken. But it's her eyes that are the most captivating. They seem too young for her face, and can't meet mine without glancing away. "We're not gonna talk about Ephraim or Ragnar or Fá. We're going to talk about the future. Fá said something before he died that made think about this place. My mentor once told me, 'Death begets death begets death.' That's the sickness that eats the Golds. It's the sickness that ate the Red Hand.

"Fá said your people were an ouroboros. Do you know what that is?" She shakes her head. "It's a circular symbol of a snake eating its own tale. It represents infinity. The Golds created for your culture a cycle of violence that can never be escaped, Volga. I think you see that in the Ascomanni. How deep a culture can sink if it gets trapped in that loop." She nods. "We're seeing it with this war everywhere now.

"Part of that is the fault of our enemy, and part of that is my fault.

Especially when it comes to the Volk. I promised your father I would build a future for the Obsidian. I didn't. I just took the handle the Golds made on their Obsidian axe and used it like they did. Sefi saw that, so did others, like Atlas and Fá. Sefi began to resent it and look at me the same way you're looking at me now. With suspicion. Resentment.

"Sefi really was a great woman, Volga. A visionary, I think, who will never get the credit she deserves. She knew that to have a future, the Obsidians must escape the ouroboros that is war. She tried to change how others saw them, how they saw themselves, to give them an identity beyond war. She thought she could make education a bridge to the modern world.

"She wasn't wrong. She just didn't get a chance to see it through before Atlas swooped down and grabbed the axe by its handle. I let you kill Fá because I think you can see it through. I think you are the bridge Sefi was looking for."

She snorts. "Ephraim was smoother at greasing a mark."

"You think I am patronizing you. Do you think any of the other jarls would be mad at me for giving them my endorsement?" That lands. "You are skeptical because you know the modern world in a way Sefi never could. Your teacher was a Gray. You found a way to thrive in the city jungle that is Luna. It's a pitiless place, I know. Most important, you never served anyone as a weapon of war. You know what it's like to live in the Republic. The struggle of the lowColors in its cities, the mundanity of just being a citizen without the privilege or the weight of a uniform. You know what the Republic promises Obsidians and how it falls short better than Sefi could. Better than I could. Atop a throne, everything beneath it seems so small.

"The Golds made your people to be weapons to be wielded. Your warrior culture, the Volk religion, your superstitions are the handle. There will always be a hand reaching for it."

"Like yours."

"Is that what you think?" I ask.

"You want me to sail back to Mars and fight for you. And when we have, you will remember what we did out here. What I did. And you will discard us like you did Fá."

"My hands are dirty too," I say. "If the Daughters of Athena can forgive me, the Republic can forgive the Volk. At the end of today, Sevro will hand whoever sits on that throne an olive branch. That branch will be an offer of amnesty for the Volk braves from the Republic, and a blank slate with me. A chance to start fresh, and yes, an offer to return with me to fight for Mars. But it's not just my family or people trapped on Mars. It is the heart of the Volk people too. This army is just the Volk's fists, its feet, throwing a tantrum, while the children, the old, many of the women of the Volk, are back on Mars fighting for their lives. I would like this army to redeem itself, to unite the Volk and stand with the rest of the Republic against the Society, but it is not my choice to make."

"And if . . . whoever sits on the throne says no?" she asks.

I lift my hands. "You are in hostile territory without the Gold strategist who made this campaign so easy or the strongman who bound you all together. You have mostly men, many of whom hate each other. You no longer have the Ascomanni as allies. The Rim may be vast, but sooner or later, the Shadow Armada will arrive. Until then you will be facing endless attacks from guerilla fighters. And if you outlast all that, when Atalantia is done with Mars, she will come out here at her leisure and annihilate you. So I will wish you good luck, and I will go home."

She leans back. "This is what the braves are saying. They know we have no options. They know you are our only hope out of here. Fjod says we can take Ganymede, then keep raiding out to Titan. Uther says we should take the Garter and rule the Rim. Skarde says we should go back with you. But you didn't let Skarde kill Fá. You let your choice be known. Why not just make me queen yesterday? Why manipulate us?"

"Because otherwise they would have felt you had been imposed upon them. You think you're dirty, Volga. But to them, you are clean. You are literally the only Obsidian here who didn't commit treason against the Republic and attack it with the Alltribe. You didn't stand by and watch Sefi get butchered by Fá. You didn't sack Martian cities. In fact, you gave yourself up to spare Mars more bloodshed. To protect the Republic.

"And yes, because you are a woman, and it is that half of their people they betrayed the most. Their mothers, their sisters, their queen. Not only that. A Red came for you, and they know Reds and Obsidians are a terrifying power when they are united. If they pick you, they believe they can come back from the dark to a home that just might forgive them. You are not a puppet queen, Volga. You are hope. I can't give that to them. The Volk must choose hope as we do in the Republic. With a vote."

She looks overwhelmed. Terrified, even, by the weight suddenly thrust on her. "I called Fá unworthy," she says. "I know nothing about leading a people. He made it look so easy. They are insane, many of the braves. Terrifying people."

"Who will have voted for you," I say. "You will not have the power of Fá over them. You should never want to. They will bitch, they will moan, that's a demokracy. It will not be fun. It will not be easy. But you will have help, if you want it."

She rocks a little, the weight of her people on her. It's not fair, the responsibility she's been given. She still feels like an outsider, and probably will for a long time. But it is what it is.

"I promised I wouldn't talk about your da, but I have to. Everyone calls him the Shield back home. But I remember him mostly for what he said to me once: 'A man thinks he can fly, but he is afraid to jump. A poor friend pushes him from behind. A good friend jumps with.' He was that friend for me. You have that friend already in Lyria. But if you want, you will have me and Sevro too."

She considers that and nods. "Be honest then. Do we sail to death? Atalantia is so strong, everyone says. If we lose again, we will be nothing."

"You've only seen your people fight for greed, Volga. I have seen them fight for hope. It is another thing entirely. And you will not be fighting alone. Virginia is gathering her power. Storing it up for one last effort. When I return, Mars will rise and the Golds will fall."

"If we win, you must not forget us," she says, and plows on as if I don't understand. "This is what they fear more than anything. To be made fools of twice. That we will be used and spat out. We have seen the Raa with you. We know you want peace with them. The Rim will never forgive us for what we have done here. What will happen when they ask for our heads from the Republic?"

"They won't forgive, no. But you can start making amends."

"How?"

"This is not my home. So before your coronation, perhaps you should meet with Diomedes, meet with Athena, and ask them."

Her eyes rise as Lyria's shuttle banks back around far more elegantly than the first time and performs a perfect hot drop. Only it must be Cassius flying, because it is Lyria who jumps down.

"We just got a call from Sevro. The vote's been tallied."

She looks at Volga with a mixture of pride and terrible worry. Then she goes to a knee. Volga hangs her head for a long moment, then looks back and says, "I would like to be your friend. But if you mean what you say, when I am crowned, you should not be there."

78

DARROW

The Monster in the Storm

"How'd it go?" I ask Sevro as I wait for the caf to process. Diomedes pretends not to be listening across the *Archimedes*'s mess.

Back on Europa, Sevro's face is fuzzy from the interference our proximity to Jupiter has on our coms. *"Bloody brilliant. Volga, man. I mean, awkward as a duck learning to walk at first. She came out in so much gold and jewels and stuff. But then she picked up Fá's warsaw. Right, and I'm thinking—oh shit, she's gonna cut her own arm off. But she chopped up Fá's throne for like five minutes. Then I was thinking—shit, Obsidians love thrones. This is bad. But then, she said the Golds dream of being atop the hierarchy. Ragnar dreamed of breaking it. She gave this speech about how they were all stained. All dirty. So is all their loot, their slaves. Then she tore off the gold, the jewels. The jarls hated that. They love their gold and jewels. But then, man, then she cut off her valor tail. And the jarls were all like, 'what,' but the braves went ape. Next thing you know, the braves are ditching all their shiny shit and I'm staring at a sea of pale, bald heads. And the jarls were like, 'shit, let's not get beaten to death.' So off their hair went too."*

"So—"

"I'm not done," he says, cold, and waits, then: *"My favorite part was when she said Red was the blood in all our veins. Unnoticed, unseen beneath our skin, filling us with strength. She could hear Red beating the Obsidian war drums. Fading, like the dirge. Calling them home before light is lost forever. She closed her eyes. Said she could feel the sun on her face. She said she was going home to find her honor, to fight with Red, to fight for*

Mars. Then she asked who is coming with her. Pandemonium. Bloody great day."

"So, it went well."

"It was fine. Gotta go. Athena and I are helping them unload all the captives. She's being a hard-ass. Won't take me to her ships until all the people are free. There's relics and stuff too. Want me to steal you anything?"

"No."

"That was a test," he lies. *"Don't die, bye."*

I look at Diomedes sitting hunched over the breakfast table. He only trusts Aurae to send him updates. "Volga is keeping her word," I say.

Diomedes nods and goes back to making sure she keeps doing that. I set down a caf for him. "I don't drink caffeine," he says.

"Of course you don't."

I take Cassius a cup in the cockpit. He thanks me as I slide into the co-pilot seat of the *Archimedes* with a sigh. Jupiter rolls beneath. We are so close to the Gas Giant that it feels like we are riding a sea made of marbled storms. Our destination is still hidden by the planet's horizon.

"How's the laconic one, talking your ear off and spreading rubbish about?"

"Rest easy. Diomedes swore the same oath of cleanliness you did." I wince and recline in the chair. Feels good to relax. Even caught a few hours' sleep. "He's in the lounge hunched over his datapad."

"Reading love letters from Aurae?" he asks with only a hint of annoyance and sips his coffee.

"Been meaning to say . . . sorry about all that."

"It's fine," he says. I know it's not fine, because I swivel the chair and put my feet up on the wall and he doesn't say a thing. "I know that it wasn't meant to be. With Aurae. She's a dream, that one. But it's all right."

I swivel back. "Yeah?"

"Yeah. I project."

He seems more at peace than usual. I feel that way too. I stifle a yawn.

"How long to Io?" I ask.

"Two hours, going tight over Jupiter's pole this time. More magnetic interference."

"Scared of Ascomanni seeing us?" I ask with a small smile.

"Obviously. Even Sevro will be shitting his bed when he's old thinking about those things."

"Still no sign of any?" I ask.

"No. Probably all packing their wagons full of Garter beans to feed their evil little broods of children back home. A souvenir from the Gas Giants," Cassius says. "Really makes you wonder. What type of nightmares do Ascomanni children have? Do they have monsters? Or do they just dream of daddy coming home with gas beans?" He shivers.

The Ascomanni had no interest sticking around Europa after Fá died. Cassius is probably right. Most will be busy stuffing their ships full as they can for the journey home. But quite a few will probably dig in and try to stay. With Diomedes terrified they'll destroy the place and take as much of the population as they can with them, Cassius and I agreed to go with the man to contact the Ionian fighters he thinks are in bunkers hidden across Io.

"You really think this is a good idea?" he asks.

"What? Popping open the bunkers of a bunch of pissed-off Moonies who hate me to try and stop the people whose god king I killed?" I ask.

"Yes. That. Amongst other things."

"I dunno." I swivel my chair around and pat the box containing Fá's head. It sits strapped into one of the fold-down seats. Cassius has drawn a face on the box with fangs. "Hey, *Dominus* Portobello has a friend."

"*Dominus* Stinkhorn. It was the ugliest mushroom I could think of. Honestly, Darrow, atomics, warlord heads. I thought our honeymoon would be more romantic."

"Honeymoon."

"Yes. Apparently we're a couple till Virginia fights me for you."

I laugh, and think about helping Dustwalkers out of their cubbyholes. Honestly, the path just seems to be guiding me on detour after detour. But I'm alive. So are my friends. I have a fleet, and will have another soon. I have an army of brutes, and an army of specialists. And I have a Raa in the boot. All in all, not a bad trip. I touch Pax's key and shoot a prayer out to Mars for him, for Virginia, for all my friends and loved ones there.

"We need Diomedes," I say when I'm done with my prayer. "That's why we'll help him get the Garter back. But this is for Athena and the Daughters too. The Garter feeds everyone out here. Anyway, it was best that I wasn't on Europa during the coronation."

"You heard from Sevro then? It shook out?"

"It shook out."

"Do we blame it on the Red?" he asks.

"I think she might've contributed," I reply. "Certainly paid us back for those hams. Thanks for making her feel welcome. Honestly I think it made all the difference."

"Like sees like, I think. She just wanted people." He chews his lip, pondering something. "You think she'll go with Volga then? On the trip back."

"Probably. But Volga will likely take the *Rage of the Valkyrie* as her flagship. It is big enough to park the *Archimedes,* and Volk queens lead from the front." He frowns, not understanding. "Volga will need a razormaster. She should have the best. To be honest, it'd really make my day seeing Ragnar's daughter learn it from you."

He seems fond of that idea, and touched. His eyes go a bit distant.

"Julian." I sit a little straighter. He never mentions Julian. "He'd say I judged my own worth too much by the people I kept around me. I was poor in those days. I'm quite rich now, I think." He means it even if he knows it sounds silly. He looks me right in the eyes. "Really, Darrow. I don't know many people as long as I've known you. I just want to say that I really appreciate you. As a person. We've had our spots. We really have. We brought out a lot of the bad in each other, but a lot more good. I think it's like that because we speak a common language, you know? We've always understood each other deep down."

I nod. He looks out the window.

"I'm not really blessed at keeping friends. But you are. I truly respect that. I know how special your friends are to you, how protective you are of them. And it means . . . quite a bit to me that you've invited me into your pack and made me feel welcome. No . . . it means everything, really. Without this, without your friends, I'm very much alone. You've put a lot of faith in me. Faith that I don't think I've always deserved. I just want to say . . . thank you, Darrow."

He looks over after I don't say anything.

"Hey, why you crying?" he asks with a laugh.

I wave for him to give me a minute. I wipe my eyes and with tears on the back of my hand, then clap his shoulder and just squeeze. My composure doesn't return very quickly, but when it does I say, "Without you on this journey I would have fallen apart. You're my brother, Cassius."

He thinks I speak in hyperbole. "What's next then, when this journey ends?" he asks.

"Cassius. I wasn't just talking about this trip. By journey, I meant my life." He looks over at me, touched and more than a bit surprised. "You're my brother. We let ten years slip past. Ten years we should have fought side by side. I won't make that mistake again. Whether you like it or not, you're with me to the end."

A very small "Oh," is all he can manage. He thinks for a long moment. "I mean that's a lot of commitment, Darrow."

I knew the sarcasm was coming but I still almost burst a stitch laughing.

"Brothers," he murmurs. "It does feel like it fits. We'll try it on."

He smiles and leans back like a dog that's had a perfect meal and is happy to sit in the sun. His thoughts must wander, because a few minutes later he asks, "Have you thought of a name for it? That blade form you found with Fá?"

"I just found a flow is all."

He looks over. "Lorn would say it's far too serious a flow to not have a name."

"You can't laugh." He makes no promises. "Breath of Stone."

"Why?" he asks in the voice he gets when he puts on his blademaster cap, solemn.

"In the mines there's always a wind flowing. No sky, no sun, no seas, no rivers, no grass. It's the only thing that keeps you sane down there. It felt like it belonged to that part of me I'd forgotten. It felt holy."

He considers and gives a nod of approval. "I like it."

I'm actually relieved at his approval. "When we get back, I'll take you down if you like. You can feel it for yourself."

"I'd like that too. Nothing like a bit of spelunking—" He jolts up in his seat. "What is that?"

"What?"

Cassius shuts down the *Archimedes*'s engines and kills everything but emergency power. The last thing I see on the sensor screen is a ghost flickering out. A big ghost. Diomedes bursts in like he's invading New Sparta.

"Problem?" he asks.

Cassius points out the viewport. "Nine o'clock, eighty degrees south of our horizon. Against the orange band."

I lean forward and a cold hand squeezes my heart. "They didn't turn around."

"I don't see anything," Diomedes says. Then his breath stops as he spots the flicker of a scout torchShip. "They're hiding their burn in the magnetosphere too. By Akari . . . that's close."

Cassius's voice is a whisper. "No. That's a minnow." Cassius summons the camera feeds from the *Archi*'s belly. We all stare in dread. "My goodmen, we are swimming with leviathans."

Core warships move directly beneath us. Tough hulls. Immense firepower. Passing close enough below for us to see the hammers, crescents, and eagles on their topsides. A powerful strike force moving fast around Jupiter, bound for Io. Then, amidst all that sleek, killing mass, a monster.

The emotions awoken by seeing eight kilometers of warship depends entirely on its paint job. With the white stars of the Republic replaced by black Lune crescents and golden pyramids, my old ship moves through the storms below like doom itself.

"That's the *Morning Star*," I murmur.

Cassius seems less surprised than he'd hoped he'd be. "Was," he reminds me. "It has a new name now."

79

LYSANDER

Teeth of Civilization

"WE HAVE CAUGHT THE REPTILES *flat-footed*," Cicero says to our New Shepherds as we're fired out of the tubes. *"Maintain discipline. Maintain your hydras. We kill them all."*

Ascomanni warships garland the orbit of Io with fireballs as I emerge from the spitTube in armor burnished to a golden sheen.

Intending to use my Rain as the centerpiece of my propaganda campaign for years to come, I've staged it for maximum visual and allegorical effect.

My Gold knights form a spear, with me at the tip and Cicero on my right flank. Behind us two hundred and fifty-three New Shepherds, their ranks swollen with new volunteers. Waves of Praetorians and two House Lune legions follow my Gold vanguard. To the east, Votum and the Reformers. To the west, the Bellona clients.

In our wake, the Ascomanni fleet burns. They thought they were the lone power left in Ilium. They never stood a chance. All goes according to Atlas's plan except one thing.

The Volk are where they should be, on conquered Europa. But there were far more Ascomanni ships in orbit over Io than Atlas said there would be. Not that it matters. In fact, it's preferred. Rhone described my feelings best as the infantry loaded up.

"The roaches are all in one bucket, and the lads are in the mood to stomp!"

This first fight will be sloppier, the men and women of our fleet filled with rage. Better to vent it now before the serious business with the vaunted Volk infantry and their nasty dreadnaughts.

Shorn of the Allfather's blessing, the Volk, and the element of surprise that allowed the savages to taste victory at Kalyke and Sungrave, the Ascomanni are introduced to the Core school of warfare, and unmitigated slaughter.

Their response to my fleet whipping toward them around the curve of Jupiter was ridden with doctrinal flaws and hamstrung by their lack of a unified command structure. It only shows the depth of Atlas's genius and Fá's skill to have made them part of a force that could maul Ilium's best.

At the sight of the onrushing *Lightbringer*, the largest ship any of them will have ever seen, their fleet broke before a shot was even fired. Some fled toward space, as if we would leave paths of retreat, some stood to fight, some even rushed toward us to close in and board our ships.

They were the first to learn the awesome power of my flagship.

Pytha smashed them at ranges of fifty thousand kilometers. Exactly the treatment their Allfather went to such lengths to spare them from at Kalyke. They are deadly, yes, but not when they're the ones taken by surprise. Racing closer, my Praetors and captains vivisected their fleet with calm, professional contempt. Even the enemy's cynical strategy of hiding their charge behind cosmosHaulers filled with civilians was nothing more than a bleak demonstration to all of Ascomanni cruelty and ignorance. RipWing pilots and dashing Bellona and Votum corvettes made mincemeat of them without even scratching their human shields. My boarding ships leapt after cosmosHaulers like flying spiders to pump in Praetorians and Gold melee brawlers trained in hostage rescue.

With the fleet in Pallas's steady hands, my concerns lie on the surface. The emerald Garter awaits to be liberated like a maiden from a dragon.

The Rain is clockwork in its precision, and it reflects the vast doctrinal gulf that separates savages from civilization. Even on the ground, the Ascomanni are caught with their hand in the cookie jar. They thought their Allfather gave them the Garter to be the heart of their new kingdom. Now they stare up at the sky and see it raining golden death.

Lonely strands of gunfire lick up toward us by the time I can make out the individual shapes of the Ascomanni flowing onto the battlements of Plutus. They will be discovering that many of the air batteries have been sabotaged and the blessing the Allfather bestowed upon them by tearing down the kinetic shields over Plutus has now become a curse.

Nothing protects them from my Rain, not even their prayers.

I am the first to pierce the atmospheric pulseDome over the city. Cicero is second. A flight of Ascomanni on gravBoots serve as an example to the garrison Fá left behind. More than two hundred surge up toward us from the Arbor of Akari. Cicero and I bank in opposite directions. Behind us, my spear parts. Into the gap descends a column of light from the *Lightbringer* to gore the center of the Ascomanni formation.

Cicero and I come back together to fall upon the dazed survivors. I kill my first with my razor out before me like a lance. I take a second with a backswing that cleaves his bestial helmet in half, and my third in his spine just above the shoulders. Cicero kills twice as many with half the effort. He did not joke as we loaded up. Righteous wrath becomes my friend, the courtier. The rest are slaughtered by the New Shepherds.

Cicero and I pair up again, and surge downward to land hard on an anti-ship gun firing at Rhone's assault shuttle. Cicero shoots open the door with his pulseFist. I follow into the firing control chamber to see a collared Green sitting in the firing chair. His torso is perforated with a shard of shrapnel. He'll be dead in a minute. A pity. I kill the two Ascomanni monitoring him and exit to a nod from Cicero. We peer over the city. My Shepherds fall on Plutus to sow chaos in the Ascomanni defenders. Hugely outnumbered, but not for long, the Shepherds do their job and pave the way for the Grays. A curtain of dropships falls across the curve of the horizon.

War has never looked so glamourous, nor so tidy.

I cross the city as it falls to my army. All over Plutus, the Ascomanni are in flight or clustering together in knots, only to be targeted by roving gunships or picked apart by rooftop snipers or drones. Only those who retreat into Plutus's buildings or down to the subterranean levels of the Garter buy themselves reprieve. But their coms are jammed. They are isolated. And Praetorian killsquads aided by New Shepherds are already clearing buildings block by block.

By the time I reach the spaceport with Cicero the fighting there has migrated toward the citrus groves east of the tarmacs. Thousands of

Ascomanni litter the durocrete already—rather pieces of them do. Rhone's century, joined by a cohort of New Shepherds, hit the tribes there as they rushed to their ships. Many of those ships are now on fire from bombs detonated by the Ascomanni. Spiteful cretins.

I land with Cicero beside thirty New Shepherds gathering outside a cosmosHauler. Smoke seeps from the ship's topside. Fenixa, a fellow Lunese of thirty, salutes me. She has the honor scar I gave out on Phobos. She's thick as a bull, fond of mathematics, and zealous in her loyalty to me.

"Imperator, we broke their defense of the spaceport in the first thirteen minutes, most fled north. Into the groves. I held here on your directives. Shall we pursue with the Grays and lend support to their fireteams?"

Rhone, directing his men from a mobile headquarters nearby, needs no help in prosecuting the massacre. He's already ordering ammunition dumps. Fenixa itches for action. Understandable, but that's not the impression my Golds must leave behind.

"We're here to save lives, Fenixa," I say. "These ships are loaded with citizens of the Society. Help them. Prioritize by the severity of the fires."

Cicero sets the example and blasts through the cargo bay of the cosmosHauler with a plasma charge. He breaches alone. Gunfire flashes from within. I follow. By the time I make it into the hold, he's slain the four Ascomanni waiting inside. Pulling his blade out of the belly of one, he activates his helmet lights. They illuminate a vile scene. Cages have been stacked as far as the hold stretches. They are filled with lowColors. Thousands meant for the asteroid homes of the Ascomanni.

Cicero has a spearhead sticking through his thigh. He calls out in a voice trembling with emotion. "Fear not, citizens. House Lune has come. Lysander has come! You are safe."

To the sounds of weeping, we begin to free the lowColors.

I am exhausted when at last I stumble away from the smoking haulers to collapse with my Shepherds around a Praetorian medical tank. Soot scores my armor. My air filter is so clogged I can't draw oxygen into my helmet anymore. I hack out black phlegm and take water from the tank's hose as Fenixa passes it on. Cicero's standing in front of the rest of us staring off. With effort, I join him in standing to set an active tone.

"The barbarity," he murmurs to me. "We must investigate how this came to happen, and punish all found derelict in their duty and all collaborators."

"Your leg, Cicero." The spearhead is still through his thigh. Blood covers his entire boot. I motion over an early drop medicus. "Cicero. I think it's compressing the artery you—"

"Damn my leg. I can get a new one." He grabs the medicus and stabs a finger at a Green girl with terrible burns carried by a woman who looks to be her mother and pushes the medicus on. "Triage, goodman. We are made to last." Cicero returns to barking at his Grays over the com.

The resting New Shepherds watch Cicero for a moment. I wait to see what they'll do. Without looking at each other, they all get up and go back to helping the relief efforts.

Above, waves of hearthcraft—slow-moving support ships packed with water, rations, and medical supplies—descend from the *Lightbringer*'s hangars to the spaceport to tend to our wounded and the thousands of civilians who huddle in various states of infirmity.

It looks impossibly clumsy, all the corpses, all the refugees, all the ships, gunfire still crackling in the distance, Golds barking orders at centurions who bark orders at legionnaires, who bark again at civilians, but from the awkwardness comes industry, and from the industry a feeling of order.

Cicero's Grays must finally be performing to his liking. He shuts down his com and peers up at the sky. RipWings pass overhead.

"A long trip for such a short battle," he says.

"The next one will be the real fight," I reply.

"I look forward to it, as do my legions. The last time we saw Darrow's painted ravagers, they were splashing Mercury red with its sons and daughters. Not this time, I think." He rips the spearhead out of his thigh and flings it away, jams a paste cauterizing gun into the wound, injects, listens to his flesh sizzle, and glares across the tarmac. "Missed the artery," he says without looking over. "One can feel these things. Let us go see if the Grays need us."

We cross the spaceport to Rhone's command control. Demetrius and Drusilla land as well a few moments later. Fully kitted up in exo-armor they are neck and neck on the day for the legion's kill tally. It's kept on the legion's cloud, and updated automatically by their helmet cams.

Drusilla salutes me. "*Dominus,* Kyber and Markus have freed a cache of high-value prisoners in the Arbor of Akari. Moon Lords and a Raa. Gaia."

Cicero turns.

"Gaia's alive?" I ask as if surprised.

"Yes, *dominus*. Battered but healthy."

Cicero breathes out in relief. "Thank Jove, a Raa survived. If their line dies out in this . . ."

"Why don't I have a visual?" I ask.

"Signals are slagged in the city proper," Demetrius drawls. "Ascomanni have tech. Had to rabbit this down the line." That means the Praetorians are annoyed, privately, at delivering news I already knew. They want to get back to the hunt and get the legion bonus for slaughter-monger of the day. I didn't know they had the bonus or the competition until two days ago, but recently I've been looking at the guard a little more thoroughly. I was glad to learn that Kyber, amongst a few others, doesn't play their indecorous kill game.

"I'll accompany you, *dominus*," Rhone says, and passes his duties to a subordinate.

"You coming too?" I ask Cicero.

"No." He turns toward the rifle-fire that still comes from the distant groves. "Less Grays will die if I'm in the field. Where do you need me, Flavinius?"

"Seventh Cohort is having trouble with a tribe holed up in an olive oil refinery. I'll mark it on your HUD now," Rhone says. Cicero nods to me and bursts into the sky. Rhone, Drusilla, and Demetrius watch him go like a pack of wolves, admiring, but no less feral.

"I like that one," Drusilla says. "Hope he comes back."

"Me too," Demetrius replies. "Phobos, though. Shame if he slagged up our fine work again."

"I think he's learned. Olive oil and not even one masturbation joke."

"Centurion Demetrius, Decurion Drusilla, open your mouths," Rhone says. They snap to attention. "B-knives on tongues. Now." They both stomp their right boot and knives pop up to waist height, they catch the knives and put them to their own tongues. "*Dominus,* your dragoons stand by to apologize for their insolence. Orders?"

I wave a hand. "Put them to use."

Rhone turns on them. "Rarity gains privilege, it does not assure it. Respect the hierarchy. Prime?"

"Prime, Dux!"

He steps closer, and whispers. "Flex on your *dominus* again, I will fuck you to death with your own knives. Now go make sure our Sovereign's friend and valuable ally comes back in one piece." They replace their knives, salute him, me, then take off. "That will not happen again, *dominus,* I apologize. And for my language."

Strange thing is he actually means it. A man with a code, Flavinius. Sadly not one I understand. "Thank you for handling it, Rhone."

"Markus has relayed your alibi to the Moon Lords. Stick to the script, all will be well. Now to Gaia, *dominus*? The drags are just dying to see a Raa kiss your feet."

I arrive at the Arbor of Akari to the sound of the enemy's lamentations. The Arbor where Fá kept Gaia and a choice selection of Moon Lords for me has been liberated by my Praetorians and house legions. Hundreds of injured Ascomanni and Volk prisoners have been herded into the courtyard beneath the Arbor. They wail like hounds to their god.

Markus and Kyber lead out a procession of Golds. The Moon Lords are in a deplorable state from their captivity, a far cry from the haughty figures they cast when they declared war on the Republic. They are beaten, bald, and barefoot as they limp into the silver sunlight.

To Rhone this is just punishment for their hubris and mercy considering their treason. To me it is a tragedy, even if they did lord my own exiled state over me the last time I saw them. Many even called me a snake. Sadly true, but I became a snake only for their protection.

I soften my eyes as I greet them at the top of the Arbor's steps. "My friends . . ." I pause, letting them see that I mourn their sorrows but respect them enough to not condescend with pity or condolences. They would never forgive that. Instead, I offer hard facts.

"The enemy fleet in orbit is annihilated. Rescue efforts are being made on every cosmosHauler. My army and allies are deployed hunting down the savages across the Garter and saving as many of your citizens as we can. Our priority is to protect the Garter and restore it to your stewardship. All control established is temporary and for the protection of your citizens and infrastructure. We are not here to stay, only to aid our friends."

Their thanks are stoic, polite, and dignified.

"Where is Gaia? I'm told she is alive?" I ask.

They part to let a bent, wrinkled old woman shuffle through their ranks. I didn't even see her. She holds Thalia's hand. In the few weeks since I saw her in her cell, Gaia has aged decades. Her eyes are hollow. Her skin hangs loose and pale. When she reaches me, Gaia lets go Thalia's hand and extends it to me. At first, I think she means to embrace me. Instead, she says, "Gun."

All the Moon Lords extend their hands.

I nod to Rhone. He gives Gaia his pistol and has Markus's men arm the rest. The tattered pants of the Moon Lords rustle against the steps like the robes of judges as they follow Gaia down to the courtyard. Without ceremony or even a declamation, the Moon Lords open fire on the Ascomanni prisoners. My Praetorians watch from the steps without expression but I know they are smiling inside. Kyber, my eerie whisper, leans against a pillar watching Thalia. The young girl's face is blank. Her eyes flash with the flare of muzzles.

When the prisoners are dead, Gaia limps back up the steps and kisses me on the cheek. "Indebted," she says. One by one the surviving Moon Lords follow her and kiss my cheek and repeat the most precious phrase in all the Rim. "Indebted. Indebted. Indebted."

"Diomedes?" Gaia asks. The Moon Lords gather behind the old woman.

"I'm sorry. We did not see him as we escaped the *Dustmaker*. I fear the worst. We will avenge him together. We will avenge Io together."

"Next?" Gaia asks.

"I will rally Ganymede to sail on Europa, crush the Volk, and bring Fá's head to you on a pike."

"No pike," Gaia says. "Slow, and with fire."

80

DARROW

Stirring Stuff

We've been floating off the shoulder of Jupiter watching Lysander beat the living hell out of the Ascommani for not more than two hours before the powerful main coms array of the *Lightbringer* begins bombarding us with scenes of his heroism: the *Lightbringer* eradicating the best Ascommani ships like a kid killing sparrows with a flamethrower; Lysander's grand charge upon the Garter; Lysander rescuing the lows from flaming transports; Lysander liberating Gaia; Lysander kissing the heads of burned Browns; Lysander embracing freed captives.

I want to puke fire. It is undiluted propaganda and it is stirring stuff.

I've already got Sevro to convince Athena to take him to her ships by the time Lysander greets the Rim in battle-charred armor backed by the Moon Lords on the steps of a building with trees growing out of it.

"To the citizens of the Rim Dominion. This is Lysander au Lune. In these dark days you could not be blamed for believing yourselves forgotten by your friends in the Core. We are proof you have not been forgotten. My forces have won a great victory on Io and the Garter has been restored to the keeping of the Raa. The enemy's vile garrison has been slaughtered to a man. Many of your countrymen, taken as slaves by Fá and his barbaric host, have been liberated. But Ilium is not yet saved. Fá and the iron heart of his fleet and host remain upon Europa. I call upon all brave children of Akari to join me over Io to form a joint force to bring this dark king and his evil brood to justice. For Kalyke. For Sungrave. For Ilium." His voice darkens. *"And to the warlord who calls himself Volsung Fá. Your life is already forfeit. If you*

sail out and meet us as warriors upon the field of battle, we will allow you—"

I have only one thing to say.

"That motherfucker's gonna burn."

Cassius and Diomedes both turn on me. "Darrow—"

"No, Cassius. I love you, but no. He is Atlas's Good Tyrant. Don't look at me like that. I'm gonna lather him in honey and feed him to the berserkers. I swear to Hades."

"Are you done?" Diomedes says.

"Talking? Yeah."

Cassius has gone very introspective. "Do we know for a fact Lysander's working with—"

"For," I say.

"*With* Atlas?" Cassius asks.

"He was surprised on the bridge. I know that. He saved my life," Diomedes says. "That he lives suggests there is a new arrangement. Perhaps he surrendered to a fait accompli. Darrow, I know you are angry. But this is a good thing."

"For you," I say very slowly. "Not for the Volk. Their ships are slower than Lysander's. And I know what that moonBreaker can do. The Volk are dead. The Daughters too. You'll have your justice."

I can't help the petulance. This false summit is close to breaking me.

"No. I will not have my justice. Not if this is Atlas's plan. Not if those Volk do not become a weapon against Atalantia." Diomedes pauses. "I do not want to see the Daughters slaughtered either. I am not stingy with my oaths. The only hope the Volk have is to unite their fleet with Athena's. That is in motion. It will take time."

Even then. We can't outrun the Core ships. This battle will eat Mars's reinforcements. So what now, I kill a Lune? Atlas switches back to Atalantia, and acts like it was his plan all along? Bloodydamn. Why can I never be a step ahead of that man?

"For now, I recommend you suggest to the Volk that they stay on Europa," Diomedes says.

That's ridiculous. Breathe in, out.

"Why?" I ask.

"Atlas has planned this. That feast you interrupted was part of the plan. But we know the next step after that was to take the Deep. Massacre the Daughters. Casualties didn't matter, because that monster was coming to smash anything left." He points out at the *Lightbringer* in the distance. "They know they're faster. They know the Volk can't run."

A thought comes to me. "Atlas functions best in the dark. Perfect coms discipline. We've almost never intercepted a signal. He trusts his operatives."

Diomedes nods. "Eventually they will know their plan has gone awry. Why let them know until we've made our move?"

Maybe it takes a Raa to beat a Raa. "They won't be in a rush," I realize.

"How fair is Lysander? Is he greedy with glory?" Diomedes asks Cassius.

"Very fair, in his way. And no. He's not greedy with glory."

"Then he will wait for Ganymede's soldiers. To make this a joint operation so as not to offend Rim dignity."

"So we have time," I say. He nods.

"Not much, but a little. Whatever you think of him, Darrow, Lysander came out here to protect the Rim," Diomedes says. "To reawaken the idea of unity. We know now my grandmother is alive. We know Lysander craves a lasting alliance with us. We also know we have a ship that can get to the surface. And I know how to get into the Garter. So I suggest we go down, find my grandmother, and show her the truth behind Lysander's theater." He points at the *Lightbringer*. "That is a monster that cannot be dueled. So let's tie it down, and find some leverage."

"What is the one thing Lysander is afraid of losing?" I ask Cassius. "A person, a—"

"His reputation," Cassius says, already accelerating the *Archimedes* toward Io.

81

LYSANDER

Parting of the Shadow

FOUR-HUNDRED-AND-SIX PEERLESS KNIGHTS OF the Rim kneel in the wheat fields west of Plutus.

The knights are as old as a hundred and twenty, and as young as sixteen. Some came from bunkers burrowed across Io, or from the cells beneath Plutus, or from smaller moons—having fled Fá's army—but most came from Ganymede. They left behind the safety of its orbital shields to honor my call to arms. Eleven hundred knights of the Core join them in the sacred rite. After the ritual, we will flow up into the ships that wait beyond Plutus's life-abiding pulseBubble. Then on to Europa and battle against the crème of Fá's host.

The climax to Atlas's play draws near, and I ache to be done with it.

An ancient Ganymedean with a face like a mallet stands from his knee and bellows, "I fear that I shall never banish my shame. I fear that when I die, all my granddaughters will remember of me is that I hid behind Ganymede's shields while Io and Callisto burned!"

He sinks back to his knee.

The Rim dwellers call the ritual the Parting of the Shadow, or the Expiation of Fear. First performed by Akari and his bosom companions before they put themselves into tubes and launched themselves down at Earth.

Since we do not believe in gods, the confession is dedicated to our ancestors. Though I know they do not hear us in the Void and that we speak only to make ourselves brave and hone our intentions before battle, the importance of Gaia's invitation to partake in the rite is impossible to ignore. No knights of the Core have taken part in the ritual since the Dark Revolt.

Atlas was right. Nothing makes people fall apart like fear, or come together like hope. That hope for the Rim is me. My fleet, my knights who sailed here with the virtues of the Conquerors in their hearts. I feel heady with momentum.

I am impatient to send the Obsidians reeling from the Rim and out of my life. I shudder to think of what might be happening back home. Yet I allow myself this moment of satisfaction. The battle will be a formality, though I am the only one in the field today who knows that.

A nineteen-year-old Olympic athlete from Ganymede famous for her prowess in the javelin and the pankration rises with severe dignity and shouts, "I fear I will run if death is certain. That I will break before the common Gray falls back in retreat. That my body is greater than my will. And my station greater than I deserve."

She sinks back to her knee. Cicero stands to my direct right, a look of profound importance gripping his face. Kneeling at the head of the ceremony with me, Gaia, the legates of Ganymede and my own army, he scans the ranks of Peerless, tears in his eyes.

"Though this cause is worthy, I fear that I will perish out here in the dark! That I will never feel the kiss of Sol upon my face again!"

He falls to a knee. Lit by the light of the Garter's artificial suns, his armor burnished to a mirrorlike sheen, he is the picture of a holy warrior. Gaia rises. Her wizened face would be comical peeking out from her armor, were it not so twisted by hate. "I fear that even in victory, we have lost the future. I fear our people already sailing into darkness will never be found nor liberated. I fear they will endure forever in bondage."

She sinks back to a knee.

There's a pause. The longest of the ritual before another stands.

A half hour and nearly a hundred admissions later, a silence falls on the gathering. It is not mandatory to speak, but it is seen as bad form for a commander of my stature to not participate. It reeks of pride. I stand and stare at the faces of my people and wish I could speak honestly.

I fear Atalantia. I fear crossing Cassius again one day. I fear Darrow causing mischief back home. I fear my own weakness. I fear Atlas and his wrath. I fear his presence almost as much as I feared his absence. He is due back today before we sail. I fear he failed in his mission. I fear he will have succeeded. That a weapon powerful enough to make Mars surrender in a week will fall into his terrible hands. I fear that I will never be anything more than his puppet. Most of all, I fear my own concessions will come back to haunt me. That I will be laid bare before these people as a fraud.

"I fear the chaos of these ten years will leak from this decade to stain the centuries to come. I fear Pandora's box has opened. I fear Gold division," I say instead. It is true enough at any rate. "I fear that this unity, so hard in coming, will last only so long as the threat to your people exists. I fear we will forget this moment and—"

A few dozen of the Rim Knights turn their heads to look back toward the city. A smudge appears in the distance. It seems to be a lone man flying our way at breakneck pace. How did he pass through the Gray cordon without molestation?

I clear my throat. "I fear—"

More knights are turning now. Not just turning, murmuring to one another. Furious at the ritual's interruption, Gaia signals two of her enforcers. They bellow for silence. No one listens. Some of the knights go so far as to stand and point. The onrushing man is close enough now to see the color of his flapping cloak and armor.

They are gray. Storm gray.

My Core Knights frown in confusion and finally turn to follow the gaze of the Rim Knights.

Shouts of, "Storm! Storm!" come from the Rim Knights. Soon they are not alone. My own knights of the Core join the rising chorus as the man flies over their ranks. They rise with a roar.

It is Diomedes.

I can barely believe my eyes. His black and gold hair streams behind him in the wind. His broad face is pale and hard. He's survived! Somehow his escape pod made it through. He's alive. My heart swells with relief and joy.

"By Jove. He's alive," Cicero crows. "The mad bastard survived Kalyke somehow!"

The knights, solemn and fixed on the battle to come only moments ago, erupt into mania as Diomedes lands in their ranks. The Ganymedeans and Ionians swarm him with so many kisses and embraces that Diomedes has to shove his way through the throng. Only Gaia remains on her knee. She stays there until Diomedes trudges up. He glances at me with a hard smile, and then back to his grandmother. His eyes soften when he sees she is sobbing. He falls to his knees and wraps his big arms around the old woman. Together the two weep and I stand there elated, but wondering.

I am at a loss for words.

"Smile, man," Cicero says and jostles me. "Look at the Rim. Their champion's back. They'll fight like dauntless gods."

"Yes," Pallas says from his side, far more thoughtful. "Smile, Lysander."

I wait for Diomedes to pull back from his grandmother's embrace. He doesn't seem eager to do so. It's the old woman who finally pulls away. Cupping his face in her hands, she kisses him on the brow. "You live. My darling. My little storm."

"Thanks entirely to Lysander," Diomedes says and nods to me.

I return the nod, still baffled.

He lifts his voice so the commanders can hear him. "Apologies. I am late. I answered Lune's summons with all haste. I did not want to miss the battle."

He turns to me, stern, and shakes my hand. His armor is standard Dominion kit and, like his cloak, recently painted gray. "*Salve,* Lysander. I thought you dead at Kalyke."

"And I you. Your pod made it through the battle. A miracle."

"Apparently we're both hard men to kill," he says.

"How did you survive?" I ask, and realize our stories will not match up. Those discrepancies may prove troublesome.

"Impacted on a hull. Floated in space. Nearly froze to death. Enslaved by scavengers. Chased by Obsidian. Boring stuff until I saw your broadcast," he says. "Grandmother, I wish we had more time, but battle is near and I don't wish to slow the army." He grips my arm. "Something is wrong."

"Wrong?"

"Your kit. You saved my life. You have kept your word and protected the Garter. When you fight our foe, you should be carrying the Shield of Akari." He grins. I am stunned. "Come."

My Praetorians follow along as Diomedes and I fly east of Plutus. He touches down in the high gardens etched into the side of a dormant volcano. I land next to him in the grass before a discreet door in the stone. He removes his helmet and breathes in the air. It still smells of smoke, but notes of cherry blossoms and citrus cut through the lingering stench of battle.

We head for the shrine and my Praetorians follow. He turns with a frown. "Only Golds are allowed inside."

"Of course. Kyber, Markus. Wait here."

Kyber obeys, but Markus's eyes narrow.

I fall in with Diomedes. "I feared many of your relics would be stolen in the sack of Io," I say.

"It is not always good to draw attention to precious things," he replies and spits on the door. He smiles at my expression. The door does not open, but another one does ten meters to the right. I follow Diomedes through.

The sanctum is cold and lit with green globes. Somewhere water rushes. Diomedes leads me through an antechamber and down a stairwell. "I did not think it proper to ask for the shield until after the threat was gone," I say, growing a little uneasy.

"Lysander, I have always treated you with respect. Do me that same courtesy," he says.

I stop on the stairs. Diomedes has played me. "The shield is not here."

"Are you calling me a liar?" he replies. He has stopped as well, beneath me on the stairs, but has not turned around. I have my razor. I could strike him down.

"Whatever you heard, I didn't know about Kalyke. About any of this," I say.

"Any of what?" he asks softly.

"Diomedes—"

"Say his name."

"Atlas."

"You know how I knew it was him, in the end? Back on Mercury. When he met us at the theater. He couldn't resist mocking us. 'Had I a moonBreaker in my palm, I'd shake even the devil's hand with a grin.' He is only a mortal man, Lysander. He errs, too." He looks up at me. His eyes glint in the low light, measuring me. "I know you came out here for unity. That much is clear. You honored our alliance, and you had no knowledge of my uncle's attack on the *Dustmaker*. After Kalyke it must have been either Atlas's version of unity or death. If it was not you, he would hand the Morning Chair to Atalantia. I believe I understand why you chose what you chose."

I feel ashamed, but there's some relief in his words. The incisive fairness.

"It's not what you would have chosen," I say.

He smiles. "I would never have been given that choice. I'm not known as a man to compromise. I am working on that."

"Have you told anyone else?" I ask.

"No. It can remain that way. It depends on the outcome of this conversation." He walks on down. I frown, not understanding. "Honor does not mean I am absent discretion."

I could run. I am very fast, but so is Diomedes. I doubt he would chase me, even then. He does not need to. He knows I have to follow, so I do. The stairs even lead out to a subterranean garden. Shafts of sunlight lance through the gloom and gather on strange chunks of stone which glow to spread the light evenly. The room pulses with a bluish white light. Several indigo rose trees reach for the nearest shafts. The air is fragrant, kind. In the center of the garden lies a stone shrine.

"You've had my back. Now I have yours," Diomedes says and motions me to lead into the shrine. I walk up the steps. He follows. The walls of the shrine are composed of ionic columns and open. Passing through them into the dimmer light of the shrine I become aware of a scent. It is a heavy scent. A nostalgic scent. Wet fur. I'm taken back to that night on the Palatine when I saw a wolf floating outside my window. I step backward. Diomedes forms a wall behind me. Gently, he pushes me forward. Then I see the shrine's lone occupant sitting on a bench by a white rose tree with a twirling trunk that spears its way through the shrine's roof. Light lances in from many directions.

A broad-shouldered man sits on one of several benches surrounding a central pool before an altar where the Shield of Akari lies with a box set atop it. The man sits hunched, his back to us, a black hasta around his right arm, a razor around his left. Hearing our approach, he half turns. A pale scar runs down the right side of his hard face. My heart thunders in my chest. My feet slow. My hand grips my razor, and I know how it is Diomedes performed his miracle and survived Kalyke.

The man on the bench is Darrow of Lykos.

82

DARROW

Civil Discourse

Diomedes has betrayed me. Seeing him enter the shrine with Lysander instead of his grandmother, I bolt to my feet and draw my hasta. Lysander's razor is already in his hand. At first I did not recognize the young man. War has that effect on the face and eyes. It's reassuring that it touches even the shiniest boy on the Palatine. His face has been thinned out by anxiety, his eyes made brittle by concession and sacrifice.

I glance through the columns out into the garden for signs of Praetorians or Gorgons. The only thing that moves are the weird lizards eating thorns from the rose trees. That doesn't mean Atlas isn't out there.

Shit.

I level Pyrphoros at Lysander. He's taken a fighter's stance and searches the recesses of the shrine just as I search the trees outside it for enemies. He didn't know I'd be here either. What game is Diomedes playing?

"Diomedes, if that's Gaia, compliments to your carvers," I say.

"Diomedes, what is this?" Lysander asks.

"Civility." Diomedes walks over to one of the benches and takes a seat. My fear dissipates a little, but the confusion remains. "Goodmen, enough. I'll not have my guests shed each other's blood."

"Guests?" Lysander asks.

"This is my moon. You are my guests," Diomedes replies. "Please. Rest your blades. They've had their say. Now I'll have mine. We are alone here. I've made sure of it." His gesture to the benches is gentle, but his voice is not. "Sit."

"So much for never lying," I say. "Atlas could be just outside."

"Lysander," Diomedes says. "Let us not play games. Where is Atlas?"

"I don't know," he replies. His eyes dart toward the box.

"Wouldn't be his first lie either," I say, still watching the garden beyond the columns.

"Darrow, stop," Diomedes says.

Lysander looks embarrassed. "Diomedes—"

"No. It is not your time to speak. It is mine." The authority in Diomedes's voice goes unchallenged by Lysander. "Darrow, you've implored me to trust you and in return you have trusted me this far . . ."

Recalling my blade, I take a seat. Wary, Lysander stays on guard, his blade pointed at me until he reaches the bench opposite me on the other side of the pool. He sits but keeps his blade in his lap. I yearn to take it from him and shove it down his throat. My eyes drift to his sidearm, my thoughts to Alexandar.

Diomedes must see the machinations taking place in my mind.

"Our fight is not with him," Diomedes says.

Lysander's eyebrows float up. "Our?"

Diomedes walks to the box atop the Shield of Akari and pulls out Fá's head. Lysander blanches. "You chose the twisted path we find ourselves upon, Lune." Diomedes stuffs the head back in the box. "Darrow straightened part of it."

"I—did not know what Atlas had planned. Not until it was too late."

"That is why you are still alive," Diomedes says. "And I am still alive thanks to the both of you. That is why we are here today."

Lysander and I stare at each other across the pool. He keeps glancing at the box, and I keep searching for Atlas in the Garden. Diomedes rubs his hands together in thought. "After today, I will likely be appointed Hegemon. A post that has not existed since Akari retired it. Ilium may be on its knees, but the Rim is not bereft of strength. Though most of it is not here yet. When I hold the Spear of Akari, I will be in total command of the Shadow Armada, and the local garrisons of Uranus, Neptune, and Saturn. Unfortunately, even then, I will be the weakest party in this shrine. Yet even with the strength we three represent, there is one who eclipses our combined strength. Not Atlas. Atalantia au Grimmus. Many of the evils that have befallen us have been on her orders via her schemes and her agents. She has used Atlas to outplay us. I imagine, Lysander, that Atlas has given you her role in this little play?"

Lysander nods. "To spare further loss of life—"

"Three years. Yes. We know." He nods to Fá's box. "While we have torn each other apart, she has only grown stronger. As I see it, we have two choices before us. Either we can continue as we have and you two can pound each other apart over Io or Europa—"

"Happy to," I say. "The last time we met, I was on my knees due to the efforts of your betters, boy. This time, you'll have my full attention."

"Agreed. I welcome the contest," Lysander says. He is not afraid, and that makes me happy. It's less fun killing people who are afraid. "But I have the advantage in mass and firepower, Darrow. And I have the *Lightbringer*. You will lose."

It's a taunt. He believes it a fact.

"Maybe. But either way, I'll still kill you," I say.

"No matter who wins, you both lose," Diomedes says. "The victor will limp home and Atalantia will open her jaws and chew the remains. Both of you pride yourselves on your logic and cold reason, tell me I am wrong in my assessment."

Neither Lysander nor I say anything.

"Common ground," Diomedes says with a sigh. "Good. There it is: we are outplayed . . . unless we form an arrangement."

Lysander and I both scoff, then glare at one another. Diomedes says nothing.

"What sort of arrangement?" I ask eventually.

"A military alliance with me," Diomedes says. "A triumvirate against Atalantia." Silence reigns until I break it with laughter. "Why not?" Diomedes asks. "You both want it from me and don't want the other to have it. I won't give it up, unless it's to both of you."

"Diomedes, this man is Atlas's puppet," I say.

Lysander has his own charges to levy. "Have you forgotten the Dockyards of Ganymede? Darrow's litany of transgressions?"

Diomedes is a hard man to discourage. He smiles, patient. "Lysander." He motions to the box. "Darrow . . . your new bloodsoaked queen?" I grunt. "I think we can all agree that today, I am the most aggrieved party. I have lost my mother, my father, my sisters, my brothers, my mentor, and my home. This war has cost me all that I love except two people. There is a voice inside that demands revenge. It tells me revenge will fill the holes torn in my heart."

He goes quiet and stares at the pool, and I wonder if he sees their faces in the water.

He goes on. "But I know that is a lie. Arcos, a man known to all of us, said it best: 'Death begets death begets death.'"

I hang my head back in frustration. When did he get so chatty?

"If we demand restitution for all the evils that have been done to us, there will be no end to this war. It will consume us and the people we claim to lead. The future is more important than our wounds." He looks straight at me. "The purpose of war must not be vengeance. It cannot be to kill your enemies until none are left. That is barbarism. That's how Earth and its multitude of nations strangled itself." He looks at Lysander. "The purpose of war must be to find the road back to peace. I am not a politician. Nor a philosopher. I do not know the peace we three might find when the dust settles, but I know this: all Atalantia and Atlas—and those like them—will accept is either subjugation or annihilation."

He leans back.

"I do not see a tyrant in either of you. I see two humans who want to leave the worlds a better place than they found them. Let us start here, now. From each of you, I request an act of humility and service. Darrow, you will present the head of Volsung Fá to the Moon Lords and ask for their mercy as your boon for the service you have rendered. Lysander, you will bring the head of Atlas to the Moon Lords and ask for their mercy as your boon. If you do not, then slag off."

And like that, Diomedes returns to his usual stony silence to wait for us to speak.

Neither of us do.

The passions within me war. I want this fight with Lysander. I want it more than I wanted Nero's death, but I remember all too well the hollowness I felt when he lay dead before me slain by his own son. Nero's death did not fill the holes torn in my life. It was his daughter who did that. From the day Virginia stayed my hand at Octavia's gala and stopped me from killing Cassius, she kept me from falling into the shadow within myself.

Today, I think of what she would say to this.

I study Lysander. Behind his petulance and the scars of war, behind even his awesome entitlement, I see the same conflict that rages in me. It is hard to put down the blade when you are afraid.

"Virginia treated with you at Phobos," I say, halting. He looks over at me. "You let her withdraw to Mars, when you did not have to. Why?"

"I wanted her to know that there were options other than fighting to the death."

"Why?"

"Mercury," he says. "Your army. What Atalantia and Atlas did to them. The impalements. The massacres. How could Virginia ever surrender Mars if she thought that was all that awaited your people? How could they do anything but fight to the last?" He frowns. "I wanted her to know that I was not Atalantia or Octavia. That I was not Atlas."

I can understand that. But I don't know if I believe it.

"Then what are you?" I ask.

"A shepherd," he replies. "That is all I want to be. To use the gifts given to me to make lasting peace. But this . . . this is a fantasy, Diomedes. Even if I agreed. Even if we did turn together on Atalantia, Darrow will never put down the sword until our people are dust. There would be no peace. Only a delayed end to what we can finish here."

Diomedes turns to examine me. "We do not see the same man, Lysander. You have forgotten that Darrow let you live when you were a boy. That his son is half Gold. That his wife is Gold, born of the family who killed his first wife."

"Lysander is right. There would be no peace," I admit. "Not if there was no change. Not if the hierarchy remained. Not if my people continued on in slavery. Not if a Lune sat upon the Morning Chair. But . . . if there was a middle path, if there was a way forward without tyranny. For that, I could put down my sword. I could find compromise."

I can't believe the words coming out of my own mouth.

"Spheres of influence then?" Lysander shakes his head, adamant. "This won't work. He has you around his finger, Diomedes. The last time he made peace with your father, he stabbed him in the back."

"If a man cannot learn from his mistakes, then what hope is there but to kill us all at first sin?" he replies. More Stoneside.

"Diomedes, for a decade, he has given mankind nothing but war."

Diomedes nods. "And if you were born a Red on Mars what would you have done?" Lysander flinches at the question in revulsion, unable to imagine such a thing. "When I was a boy, my father asked me that question. I said 'rise up' and he smiled.

"Darrow is not to blame for this war. Gold is. The hierarchy gave humanity the stars, but the decadence and cruelty of our rulers gave us this rebellion. You told me once that we have forgotten who we are, Lysander. You were right. We are not kings. We never were meant to be. We are shepherds. Shepherds do not rule. They guide. They nurture. They protect. Because they know it is not the shepherd who produces. It is the flock. Without the flock, we are just beggars with sticks and esoteric rites. It is our time to find humility. To show we are more than autocrats. I need you to be the man you claim to be, Lysander."

Diomedes's words seem to find Lysander's heart. "I hear you, Diomedes. I do. But I have compromised once at the point of a sword. If I say no—"

"There is no sword to your throat. You may leave and consider our proposal aboard your ships if you wish," Diomedes replies. "I am not my uncle any more than you are."

I stand up. "Diomedes, you cannot just let him leave."

"A man's word may no longer matter in the Core, but it is all that matters in the Rim. Lysander came to help my people because I asked him to. He saved my life aboard the *Dustmaker*. He came to this garden without his guards as my guest. As my guest, he may come and go as he pleases. Seek to harm him, you are at war with me."

He means that.

"Not to mention, I'm your only hope of catching your uncle," Lysander says. "He's run circles around Darrow for years."

Diomedes smiles. "That too."

I admire Diomedes's consistency, but at any other time in my life, I'd leap across the pool and hack Lysander's head off. That would cost me Diomedes today, forever. There's a friendship between these two men.

Lysander stands to leave. He pauses, conflicted. "Darrow, you would really consider this? Even though I killed Alexandar?"

I tame the anger. Instead, I look down into the reflecting pool. "We were on a hill overlooking Tyche as the waves came in when Alexandar asked to go down to save people who called him the enemy. I know what he'd want if he were here today."

Diomedes says, "Your fleets will remain where they are. Io and Europa. At nivalnight the Moon Lords will meet in the House of Bounty. *Acta non verba,* goodmen. I will have your answer there."

"I need the shield as an alibi for this meeting," Lysander says.

"The shield is for a true friend of the Rim. It will be waiting for you, I hope," Diomedes replies. Lysander nods and departs.

When he's gone I grimace at Diomedes. "You may regret that."

"Come. You should wait on your ship. You have your own decision to make."

With Diomedes as escort, I follow the tunnel from the shrine back to the grain warehouse where I left Cassius behind with the *Archimedes.* He does not wait outside where I left him. And when I call into the ship, he does not answer. My stomach sinks when I find a holodrop waiting for me on his captain's chair.

I don't need to listen to it to know where he's gone. I rush out of the *Archimedes.* Diomedes turns with a frown and follows me to the open doors of the warehouse. I peer up to where the *Lightbringer* forms a dagger in the sky. I frisk myself. Diomedes finds it for me. A listening device as small as a ladybug.

"Bloodydamn Bellona," I mutter.

"Darrow." Diomedes squeezes my arm. "Do not draw your weapon."

Something whispers behind us. I step back from the doors to see a dozen shadows falling from the ceiling of the warehouse. They land quieter than cats. One already has a blade at my throat. More appear outside the warehouse. Dustwalkers.

Diomedes's eyes narrow. "Grandmother?"

A woman clucks her tongue from the shadows. "My little storm, what in the worlds have you been up to?"

83

LYSANDER

A Way Out

My Praetorians in front of my command shuttle salute as I land at the spaceport of Plutus. Demetrius is the first to greet me. "*Dominus,* you had your Dux worried. You disappeared with the Raa prince back from the dead." His eyes flick to Markus behind me. "Flavinius feared the worst."

"Are you my keeper or my bodyguard, Centurion?" I ask Demetrius.

He smiles. "We guard the Blood, *dominus.*" He obstructs my path forward for an insolent second. Kyber is there immediately. "Where's the Shield of Akari?"

"Move, sir. Your *dominus* is walking," Kyber says to her superior.

Her voice is strange. It sounds almost like anger. Markus must have done something off when I was inside the shrine with Diomedes. Demetrius glares at Kyber like he could break her in half, but steps aside. He is not scared of Kyber. Maybe familiarity with whispers dulls the general anxiety most people get when Kyber gives them attention, or maybe Demetrius is not scared because his reign as slaughter-monger in the secret kill pool is entirely justified.

I let Kyber see the situation a little more clearly and explain far more than I should to a centurion meat mallet like Demetrius. "Diomedes and I had much to catch up on. In the end I told him I would not take the shield until I earned it. He also had reports of strange behavior on Europa."

I pause. "Kyber, the attack is on hold until we have better intel. Go tell the knights."

She does not turn her head, but I sense her glancing at Demetrius and Markus from behind the blacked-out lenses of her goggles. She salutes and skips up into the sky.

I motion Demetrius and Markus to follow me into my shuttle. When we're alone and a jamField's active, I say, "Is there a way of contacting our friend? He should be made aware of this intel."

"We'll pass it on," Markus says.

"I think not. Not this time," I reply.

"You can tell him in person soon enough," Demetrius says. "He radioed in not thirty minutes ago. He's black till approach. Should be a few hours, but you never know. The transmission. Dead silence, seven seconds."

I tense. Seven seconds. "He already called off the attack on Europa then?" Demetrius nods as the shuttle accelerates. "Was his mission a success?"

"Dead silence, seven seconds." He cocks his head at me. "The Raa prince. Do we need to send a few lads?"

"I don't think so. But I don't know. So, we should talk to our friend."

"Quick study," Demetrius says and leans back, takes out his boot knife, and trims his nails on my boots. Markus just watches me like a spooky crocodile.

Markus and five others—all part of the kill pool—escort me from the hangar to my quarters. The last thing I need is the business of the bridge buzzing in my ear and Pytha's questioning looks as I contemplate Diomedes's offer and Atlas's arrival. Darrow might be desperate enough to bear the shame of compromise. But I can barely stand the thought of humbling myself before the haughty Moon Lords and begging for their forgiveness. If I do that, I will lose Bellona, and Votum, and Rath, and I will lose my reputation. Then again, all will be lost anyway if I don't.

"Let me know when Atlas arrives," I tell Markus as the door guards— kill pool, all four—part to allow me into my chambers. "And send me Flavinius."

"Flavinius is escorting in our friend, my liege." Markus snaps a crisp salute. I close the door and call for Exeter. He doesn't answer. I slump toward the sitting room off which the halls to the other rooms branch out.

"Exeter, are you knitting again?" I call. "I need something to drink. Exeter?"

"Oh, fetch it yourself, you spoiled brat," a familiar voice says from the sitting room. I stop and almost summon my Praetorians. Almost. Wary, I press on to find a large man sitting on one of the couches. He smiles at me. "Exeter is just taking a little nap."

"Is he dead?" I ask.

"Well, that would be a very long nap, wouldn't it?"

"How did you get in here?" I demand.

"Is that any way to greet an old friend?"

It's been over a year since I've seen Cassius. He looks like he's been through hell, and made all the healthier and handsomer for it. His face is leaner, like he's been on the hunt and not hunted. His body is more relaxed. Though naturally an athlete of rare form, he's a coiled spring now. I imagine he's been fencing with Darrow. His hair is still all golden curls, but shorn shorter. There's not a spot of stubble on his chin. I imagined him out there with the famous Ragnar beard that's all the fashion in the Rising. The drinking bags under his eyes are not nearly as inflated. Instantly I know he has changed. What once was rusting iron has been infused with carbon. He's steel and smiling and happy to see me.

It almost feels like a purposeful insult.

The tiger-styled armor he wears is not his. It belongs to a man named Strabo from Earth, one of my New Shepherds.

"And Strabo?"

"Of course, you know their names," he says. "Strabo . . . well, he's taking a long nap. I tried to make it short, but he was very tough and not very likable. Honestly, you can't imagine what he was doing, or to whom." Cassius's eyes flare. "Let's just say his life was the second thing he lost."

Armor alone doesn't explain how he accessed my quarters without my Praetorians noticing. How he can sit here without the security teams seeing him on the feeds, or how he could have gotten on the ship at all. Of course, there are secondary entrances built into my rooms. Two that the Praetorians know and guard. And one only two other people know about: Horatia and Pytha.

"Pytha," I mutter. "You told her about Atlas."

"I did."

I close my eyes in anger. "Rather presumptuous of her to let you in."

"She only wants to help you. I only want to help you. You're no Strabo after all."

I keep my distance. My hand rests on my razor. "So that's why you're traipsing around the system with Darrow, why you saved him on Mercury, helped him over Venus. To help me."

Cassius watches my hand on my razor.

"Lysander, I am here to help you. If I wanted to kill you, I'd have hidden in a closet and burst out while you were meditating upside down practicing Mithridatism—or whatever new strange hobby you have. At any rate, do you think Pytha would have let me aboard if she thought I meant you any harm?"

He's making an effort for it to feel like old times. Only it isn't. Not just because of all the deeds between us, but because he is far more dangerous than he ever was.

"No," I confess. "Though the fact that she left that decision in your hands is . . . troubling. If you aren't going to kill me, why not ditch the armor?"

"Your drags. I imagine I'm the only person the Praetorians hate more than they hate Darrow. He is the enemy, so there is a measure of professional respect for him, no doubt. Me? Well, I betrayed the company. Shamed them by getting the Sovereign."

"History is not kind to Olympic Knights who break their oaths, is it? Most get the Kiss of a Thousand," I say. I wouldn't want that for my worst enemy, much less Cassius.

He pats his armor. "I like my skin where it is. Thank you." He smiles. "Now, can we talk?"

"If you wanted to talk, why didn't you come—"

"To the meeting? Wasn't invited. Diomedes wouldn't let me attend. Apparently it was for Imperators only, and no one's rallied behind my banner in a long time. But I did hear what was said, for what it's worth." He raises his eyebrows. "Not going to sit. All right. I'll stand." He stands, feigning ease as he strides away from the couch to admire the room. "You redecorated. It's quite stately now. Far less spartan."

"I nearly forgot. You've been here before."

He nods at the leading question. "Darrow brought me up from the brig when he was sailing on Luna. We spent the night watching old videos of ourselves at the Institute, drinking scotch. Or was it bourbon?

Scotch. It was smoky. Regardless, I remember Darrow hadn't had a chance to adjust the decor. Fabii's blood was still wet on the bridge deck. These are nice." He strokes the wooden walls and peers down some of the hallways. "A library too. Knowing you, I suppose there's a garden somewhere."

"Three doors down to the left. If they notice Pytha is hijacking the feeds of the cameras, this will end very badly for you," I say.

"I trust her competence. Obviously you do too. This ship is a monster. The *Archimedes* must have felt like a very small prison for you. This is quite a home, one fit for a Lune."

I shrug. It's hard to keep my guard up around Cassius. "Truthfully, I haven't spent much time here. The *Archimedes*. Well, that was home."

"Not a prison like you said?"

"No. Not all the time," I confess. "I often miss it."

"It could be home again," he says. "After this."

I smile. "You haven't changed. Ever the romantic, at the expense of any kind of realism. It's your charm."

"I do that. Don't I?" he says, a little dark. "Suppose that's natural for a man who makes so many mistakes." He spots the display case that dominates the far wall. "Is that what I think it is?" He approaches the case. "May I?"

"It won't bite."

"Unlike its owner." He picks up the spiked helmet of Ares from the case. He turns it in his hands. "I haven't seen this in a long time."

"I lost three men salvaging that from Sevro's room. The whole place was booby-trapped."

"Far less than Aja and I lost taking it from its first owner," he says.

It's easy to forget he killed Ares when he wore the cloak.

"Is he here?" I ask. "Sevro?"

"You mean did I bring him? Gods no. That wouldn't go well at all. Have you ever put it on?" he asks of the helmet.

"Why would I?"

"Curiosity. Just for a lark?"

"It wouldn't fit."

He grins. "No. I suppose your head is too large. Not that I'm one to talk." He sets the helmet back down on the shelf with incredible reverence. That reverence says everything. "What did you feel when you saw the *Archimedes* at Mercury? When you knew I was alive?" he asks.

"Are we Violets now?" I ask, still staring at the helmet.

"I know it's terribly common, emotions. But still . . . I've wondered. Humor an old friend who's risking life and limb to see you."

I really do believe he means my body no harm, so I sit down on one of the leather couches to decide if I mean his any. I've both feared and yearned to speak to Cassius since I learned he was alive. Now that I can, I find myself at a loss for words. I consider his question.

"Shock. Confusion. Rage. Then relief. Then betrayal. Then a distant numb sadness," I answer. "I didn't want you to die in a Raa dueling pit, Cassius. I didn't. I was trying to do what I thought to be right. But when I saw you there, saving Darrow, I felt . . . well I suppose I felt traded in. Like you'd chosen him over me. Like you'd been waiting to."

He leans on the edge of the couch. "Do you still feel that way?"

"What room did Darrow bunk in? On the *Archi*," I ask.

He grimaces. "He wanted yours. Nothing weird, mind you. Said he wanted to wake up every day and be reminded of his failure." He pauses. "He's very dramatic."

"There's your answer then," I reply, more wounded than I thought I'd be. The idea of Darrow in my bunk falling asleep beneath my childhood scrawlings is a violation.

"How does he feel about me having this ship?" I ask.

"Did that factor into salvaging it?" Cassius asks.

"A little." I shrug. "Even Lunes can be petty."

He sighs and slips down onto the couch. "Have you ever wondered where we'd be if we didn't have these last names?" he asks.

"No. What's the point," I say.

"Liar."

"We'd be mangled in some ditch to be cleared off a battlefield by a plow with the other nameless dead," I say.

"Life's not all war, Lysander," he says softly. "I've always wondered the people we'd be if we weren't born with these names. Bellona. Lune. They've given us such . . . horrible choices to make. Choices we never asked for. I know we got the riches too, but it's not fair, this inheritance of yours. Silenius squatting on your back since you were born. Everyone else thinks being born a Lune is a blessing. But I know it's a curse."

"Do you?" I ask.

He nods. "I saw it in you every day for a decade. Since your parents were killed, you've been under siege. Haven't you? Magnus, Octavia,

Aja, Atalantia, now Atlas and your Praetorians, all jockeying to harness the power of your name. Shape you in their image. That pressure. I can't imagine it. It's required you to shift your shape to survive. It's not your fault. It's kept you safe over all these years, shape-shifting. It's the only thing that has kept you safe—being what Octavia wanted you to be, what your guards expect you to be, what Atlas needs you to be. What I needed you to be."

He looks down at his gauntlets, rueful.

"Since I woke up on Europa after being cut to ribbons by those Raa cousins, I've thought about what I'd say when I saw you again. I was angry at first. Angry that you wanted this war. That you didn't obey me, didn't heed the lessons I'd tried to teach you. I saw that as a betrayal. But now I know I was angry because I was always asking you to be someone you weren't. Someone you could never be."

I look down. "Julian."

He sighs, frustrated at himself.

"He was my twin, but he always felt like my younger, sweeter brother. He made me feel like a better person, because I had his love. Made me feel a like leader, because he always followed my lead. When he died, it punched a hole in me. I tried to whittle you down to fit that hole. When you did, I retreated and left you reaching out and confused because I felt dirty for replacing him, angry at you for trying to—even though it's what I taught you I wanted.

"I know that . . . inconsistency on my part made you feel you were not enough. I know it bred contempt in you for me. I was selfish, then cowardly, then cruel." He meets my eyes. "I'm sorry for it, Lys. I am. I'm sorry I couldn't be the teacher you deserved. That I poisoned you with neglect. Suffocated you with judgment. I know when you looked at me you just wanted me to be happy. But I couldn't be happy. I've . . . always had trouble with that. Without distractions . . . well. If I could do it all again, I wouldn't try to shape you. I'd try to let you shape me into what you needed. I think we'd both have been better off for it."

I look away.

I did not know how long I was waiting to hear him apologize until this moment. His words slip past the armor I've built around my heart. The emotions of childhood rush back. All the loss, the loneliness, the fear and instability. The need for him to be happy, and when he wasn't, feeling like it was my fault.

I don't know if I'll see him again after this. I think of Ajax and the words we never got to speak. I think of Glirastes, and all the nights we could have spent surrounded by his trinkets talking in detail about nothing but how to capture magic.

"In my head, you were a giant," I say slowly. "But now I'm the age you were when we set off from Luna. I don't blame you, Cassius. I don't know how I'd have raised me either." I sigh. But more won't come out. Fear and pressure have me too wound in knots.

"But now we get a second chance," he says. "That is, if you take Diomedes's offer, Lysander."

I darken inside. "Ah."

"We have to talk about it."

"It's why you're really here. Why not? Let's talk about it."

"I'll tell you why I'm really here when we get to that part. You know I care about you. But I'm afraid too, brother. You are surrounded by people who terrify me, Lysander. They don't know me. What we have here." He motions between us. "And even if they did, they'd tear me to shreds. Respect the risk, if not the reason."

"Fair," I say. "Very fair."

"Diomedes told me what he'd propose. Asked my opinion. I told him he had the right of it. You are a man of honor. You'd do the right thing. You'd give them Atlas."

"Honor. It sounds so silly when you say it enough," I reply. "It can excuse anything. But we only pretend it protects. Yet it is there. A feeling of what is true and what is slippery and false. But you're right. I do have it. That inclination, maybe more of a desperation, to have honor. But time and again, I've found that it's like opening a vein while swimming with sharks."

"Am I a shark?"

"No. Sharks don't have such good hair," I say. He laughs. My smile fades. "I can't, Cassius. I can't accept the offer."

"You are Lysander au Lune. If you can't, who can?"

"You don't understand," I snap. "At every turn, I try to take the right action."

My heart is beating fast, but I can't stop talking.

"I acted like the hero of the Rim, Cassius. But I'm not. I am called Imperator, but I am not. I could be. I really could help people, I think." I swallow, seeing the truth of my condition. "I . . . I am just a puppet.

That's all I have ever been. A puppet or a prisoner or a pet. Octavia's, Atalantia's. Atlas's. That meeting . . . Atlas may already know . . . my jailers were sniffing. Demetrius . . . Markus . . ."

The more I think of Atlas, the harder it becomes to breathe. I feel hot. My hands start to shake. This has never happened before, except once with Octavia. Once was enough for the Pandemonium Chair. *It'll get rid of the shakes.* That's what she said. When I got out of the chair, I was calm. It was a while after the chair before I realized I couldn't remember my parents. I clench my fists but the shaking won't stop.

"Atlas is coming back. If he does know . . . if he suspects anything, he'll enslave me," I say. "With chemicals. Pain. He can do that. If I'm lucky, he'll just kill me and put a doppelgänger in my place. But no, he'll take his time. He'll peel me apart one layer at a time. He'll kill Pytha. Cicero. Exeter. Horatia. Anyone I care about. My Praetorians can't protect me. The ones who came with me on the *Dustmaker,* they are sociopaths. They kill hundreds of people and keep a running tally. They make bets about it. They serve *him.* Not me. They worship him. Call him a patriot. Me? I'm just a spoiled Palatine brat. He'll skin me in front of them and they'll just salute."

His hand grasps my shoulder and I feel the strength in it.

"Then let's kill him together. You asked me why I came here. Let's kill that piece of shit." Tears stream down my cheeks. "I told you I came here to help you. Let's do it soon as he lands, Lysander. Let's set you free. Enough shifting shapes. Enough compromises. Finally you can be the man you want to be."

I jerk when a door hisses open in the distance. Cassius holds me steady. "Lysander?" It's Pytha's voice.

"It might not be her," I say quickly.

Cassius looks at me with so much love I feel the shakes leave me. "In the sitting room," he calls without even looking back. His hand slides to the razor and his face hardens.

"Is all prime?" Pytha says. He takes his hand off his blade when he sees her reflection in my eyes, but he doesn't go to her till I give him a nod.

Cassius picks Pytha up and twirls her like a big brother, then pulls her into a hug. In his arms, my captain, once his captain, looks no larger than a child. She pulls back and beams at me. "Thank gods you haven't killed each other. Did you ask him, Cassius?"

"Only just."

She bends on a knee and cups my head. "Moonboy, tell me you said yes."

"You're not angry with me?" I ask her.

"I just wish you would have told me," she says. "I could have helped. If I had known . . . But it doesn't matter. We can end this now. We can do this, Lysander. Together."

Anxiety claws at me. Atlas was a tool I needed to set things right, but there are other tools now. "It would have to be Rhone too. If we fail . . ."

"We won't," she says. "The three of us together. How can we?"

84

LYSANDER

Hangar 17B

T HE THREE BLACK NIGHTRAPTORS coast in from space. They broadcast no radio signals or light except the red range-finders on the tips of their wings. Even those are turned on only at the last possible moment.

To me, standing in the abandoned hangar flanked by Markus, Drusilla, and four more kill-pool dragoons, the range-finders seem like the eyes of Atlas himself. Nocturnal, omniscient. As the bait in the jaws of my own trap, I have never felt more like prey.

Pytha knew the hangar Atlas would use. It was cut from her systems by someone earlier in the day. Power outage supposedly. It is filled with war machines too damaged to repair and awaiting the attention of Oranges to be harvested for parts.

My razor hangs on my hip. My aegis-cuff on my left vambrace is dormant. I wear a sidearm, which is not too unusual. I wish I could've come in my pulseArmor, but Atlas will be suspicious enough to find me waiting for him in the hangar. He told me to meet him in the barracks, where he'd be untouchable. Only bullying Markus and Drusilla with my "intel" got me here where he can finally be killed.

Instead of pulseArmor, scarabSkin guards my body, concealed beneath my white uniform and cape. My hands sweat in my lambskin gloves. Only the Mind's Eye keeps the sweat from my brow. It's all I can do not to search the hangar for Cassius.

He is here.

Somewhere in the ranks of damaged ripWings and mechs. Or perhaps above, in the shadows of the high ceiling. It's better I don't know. I'm afraid Atlas will read my face immediately.

The nightRaptors hiss as they pass through the pulseField that hems in the hangar's atmosphere. Their bulk is alienating. Battered and carbon-scored, they hover over me in a line, their engines groaning, their guns big as men. They stay there, floating as if waiting for me to kneel. When they set down, they do so in unison. Ramps unfurl from beneath their reinforced cockpits like tongues to disgorge their human cargo.

Only none comes.

An invisible jamField extends with a pop.

He knows.

No. He's careful. Making sure no one records him.

I counted on this.

A few minutes pass. I resist the urge to flee. I wish I'd just had Pytha blast Atlas the moment his ships came in to land. But I had to be cautious. I was right to be. A fourth nightRaptor glides through space toward the hangar, far delayed behind the others.

A cautious man indeed.

As it lands, the Gorgons disembark. A Gray long-arms specialist trudges down the ramp of the rightmost ship with her rifle. Her face is half-covered with a bandage. She is hairless, her scalp bright red and peeling. She smiles at me like a ghoul—half monster, half militarist fantasy. More Gorgons follow with their gear and their wounded. Around thirty, all told. Whatever they faced on the moon of Orpheus, Atlas did not exaggerate its dangers.

Few are uninjured. Many are missing limbs and wear cautCuffs from their battle with Orpheus's defenders. Unless some are remaining on the nightRaptors, their numbers have been depleted by eighty percent. Witnessing the state of Atlas's dread force fills me with a measure of confidence. He's not invulnerable.

I search their ranks for their leader, hoping to find him as wounded as his men. I am disappointed. He exits the fourth ship with all his limbs, but he is not in armor.

He is not in armor.

Clad in black fatigues, with only a pulseShield generator on his belt, he helps a bulky Gray woman bear out a man on a stretcher. Over Atlas's shoulder is slung a reinforced pack. My eyes ache to stare at it, but it must be like the sun to them: forbidden. Atlas feels my eyes on him, and his head turns like an owl's to meet my gaze. He calls back into the nightRaptor. My heart sinks at the heavy bootsteps. Rhone trudges out in his full Praetorian field armor. Like Atlas, the man appears uninjured.

Of course he is. He just went out to escort Atlas in. His eyes sweep the ranks of machines in the hangar.

Do they know? No. He looks at everything like that.

Rhone told me when I was younger to always have a plan to kill everyone you meet, and any deviation in a pattern is a sign of someone preparing a trap. He's just as big of a threat as Atlas is, especially in that armor.

Atlas passes off the stretcher to a Gorgon. Together, he and Rhone make their way toward me. "You're late," I call.

Be entitled, but reasonable. A Palatine brat who's learned his lesson.

Neither man replies. Rhone stops a few meters from me and nods to Markus, Drusilla, and the others. They salute him and hold the salute for Atlas. Flavinius's eyes bore into me. He smiles, pleasant. "Heard you had a visitor." I nod.

Atlas strides up to me with his pack on his shoulder and stops about a foot away. His eyes are everywhere, collecting data, except meeting mine.

"I told you to meet me in the barracks. Did Markus confuse my orders?" he asks.

"I told him," Markus says.

"There's been a problem. It couldn't wait," I say.

He sighs. "I left you the pig trussed, gutted, and cooked. All you had to do was eat it."

"Diomedes is alive."

"Yes. Markus already told me."

He's still not looked into my eyes.

He knows. Or he doesn't. The man looks absolutely smashed with exhaustion.

"The feast is ruined." Atlas's eyes finally meet mine. "Fá is dead." His Gorgons within earshot—which, due to their augmented hearing, is all of them—turn or stop dead in their tracks.

"Talking business in front of the ranks? Pull yourself together," Atlas says.

Rhone takes the hint. "Clear the deck. On the double! Wounded to sick bay. Showers, grub, and comfort flesh for the rest. You've earned it, nils. You've earned it for the rest of your lives. On the double, I said!"

The mission must have been a success then. Is *Eidmi* in the pack on Atlas's shoulder?

The Gorgons flow past me to either side. Atlas keeps looking at me. In time he will discover me. My only defense is his exhaustion and the magnitude of the mission he was on, and telling him the truth before he suspects it. I have to unravel it slowly but not so slowly I lose his interest. Most of all, I have to keep him here until I get the green light from Pytha.

When the last of his men have cleared the hangar, he steps back and hangs his head. He is exhausted but the act is also one of respect and profound sadness.

"You knew about Fá. That's why you stopped the assault," I say.

"Correct. The Kinshield is also gone. Certain patterns have been broken."

"I'm sorry. I know they were close to you."

"Do you have anything else?" he asks.

I glance back at Markus, Drusilla, and the other four. "Give us the deck."

Markus looks to Atlas, who shakes his head for him to stay. "They're in the Zero," Atlas says. "What else, Lysander? I want to take off my boots."

"Darrow killed Fá."

He sighs back at Rhone. "And I thought I'd get a shower before they piled more shit on my shoulders again."

Rhone grimaces in sympathy. "At least we have confirmation now."

"You were aware of this?" I ask.

"Suspected. When Obsidians see a curved blade they shout 'wolf.' Why am I just hearing this, Markus?" Atlas asks. I think he's lying. I think he knew of Darrow's involvement for fact.

"I was not aware of the information," Markus says, worried at displeasing Atlas and accusing me of withholding with the same tone.

"How did you come by it, Lysander?" Atlas asks me.

"Diomedes told me after he arrived at the Parting of the Shadow."

"You were right. Raa *was* with them on the Nixian Isles," Rhone says.

I resist the urge to look toward the exit. Pytha can't see into the hangar. No one can with the jamField. But she will let me know when the coast is clear with a green light over the hangar's pulseField. That light is hardwired. I picture her in the sync, watching the Gorgons filing through the halls to the lifts and then riding them deeper into the ship, their minds occupied with fantasies of hot water, food, and warm flesh. Why is it taking so long? Are some of them lingering? Has Pytha been frozen out?

Stay the course. Trust your team.

I need more time, and I need to get rid of the six Grays behind me.

Even with Pytha's green light, this will still get messy.

Atlas is about to leave.

"I saw Darrow," I say.

Atlas stops and turns. That he did not know.

Rhone takes a half step forward. "You saw Darrow in person?"

I nod. "Diomedes took me to meet him."

"Go on. Tell us," Atlas says. It's the first time I've gotten his full attention, and I'm worried I've turned on a machine that will gobble me up. Questions come at me with no logical order except to help Atlas form a private mental construct and to shake free information from me that I might not know is useful. It's like being hit, pulled, and twirled by a wave.

"Was it just the three of you? Who left first, you or him? Did you get the impression he was staying? Was there a green tinge on his lips? Describe the tone of his voice. You said there was mud on his boots, describe it. Did it come from the cave? Was it dust then mud, or mud with dust? More on the heels or the toes? A steep incline then. He came from the east."

His eyes snap to a Praetorian behind Drusilla. "My men are exhausted. Rhone, do you mind? Gratitude. Marcellus, rabbit to Flavius. Tell him to get Camillus and the Triad down to the surface. Darrow must have accessed the shrine through the granary three point one kilometers east-ish. If he's there, do not engage. I will lead the team. If he's not there, take samples of everything. Bring Janus too. Get him on all that grid's cameras. All I need is a direction or a metal sample. No radios." He flicks a hand and one more Praetorian is shed.

Five now. No green light. The anxiety is insane.

"They've sensed my involvement then?" Atlas asks me.

"They have. Diomedes and Darrow want an alliance with me against Atalantia. They sent me back here to kill you."

"Lysander, this is very important. What did you say to their offer?"

"I said maybe."

Rhone frowns. "And they let you leave? They didn't take you hostage?"

"He did it right. They wouldn't have believed you if you said yes, Lysander. And if you said no, we wouldn't have them by the nose. But they are still engaged." Atlas takes me by the shoulders. "Well done." He lets me go, smiling. Then, casually, "Do they know about my mission to Orpheus? Do they know about *Eidmi*?"

"Yes," I lie, and let him see the lie so he thinks I'm still playing a tricky game, but the game is up. He felt the scarabSkin under my clothes.

No green light. Oh well.

Double down, all the same.

I drop my hips and reach for my razor. In all my life I have never seen someone move as fast as Rhone except for Atlas when he slaps the pulse-Shield generator on his belt and draws his own blade. Knowing Atlas is easily good enough to parry my first stroke, I choose not to waste it on him. I go after the Grays behind me.

At the same moment, forty meters away and ten off the ground, Cassius pops up from the cockpit of a war titan with no engine and opens fire on Atlas with a heavy pulseRifle.

I activate the aegis on my left forearm as I turn on the Grays. A meter-wide blue shield flares to life, covering my flank. It takes Atlas's first stroke dead on. That first stroke is all he gets before Cassius's fire literally slaps him off his feet.

My first stroke takes Markus just under his eyes and passes through his unprotected skull to kill Drusilla beside him in the same manner. The three Praetorians behind them are amongst the best Gray soldiers alive, but the unexpected speed and ferocity of my attack catches them off guard. I spring at them and two precise strokes remove the three remaining Praetorians from the equation. It costs me.

The impact of a rail slug into the back of my left thigh buckles the leg and sends me spinning. Two more hit me in the right leg, just above the kneecap. I sprawl onto the deck and reach for my sidearm. A round from Rhone cuts the weapon almost in half. Only the scarabSkin and the low caliber of the pistol munitions keep the impact of his rounds from cutting my legs in half. Still, the pain is incredible. I'm on the ground a half breath before I push off amongst the ruins of the Praetorians. I glance up to see Atlas stumbling ten meters away, his shield crackling from Cassius's fusillade.

Seven near-perfect shots slam into Atlas's shield, wreathing him in a cocoon of blue and green fire. Atlas keeps the shield up even though his skin must be boiling inside it.

Rhone saves Atlas's life by firing at Cassius's sniper position with his pistol as he draws his rifle with his off-hand. He switches between the weapons like water flows to lower ground. His dragon helmet slithers up for combat.

"Kill clearance?" Rhone yells.

"Granted," Atlas calls. "Switch."

His shield cooling from the reprieve Rhone granted him, Atlas springs after Cassius.

Rhone shifts back to firing at me, this time with ammunition that will shred my scarabSkin. I rush my former Dux from behind my aegis and leap, leaving the crown of my head exposed as bait before shifting my aegis. He snaps two shots at my head. The aegis takes the rifle-fire at point-blank range. But he switches ammunition on the gun and fires a trick shot on the ground that bounces up under the shield and whizzes between my legs.

Rhone switches ammunition again, and a slow-moving slug pounds the left rim of my aegis. Still in the air, I'm spun around in a full revolution, coming out of it just in time to fall back toward him and plunge my razor through his pulseShield, through his armor, to take him in his bent right leg, midway up the thigh. Before I can withdraw it, Rhone deploys a buffer pulse from his armor. I'm smacked by an invisible, giant hand, stunning me and sending me sprawling backward.

I lose hold of my razor but not my aegis. I fend off a hail of gunfire and roll to my feet, dazed, to find Rhone with his leg still impaled by my razor. Instead of dropping his rifle to remove its tip from the floor, he pulls sideways against the blade, taking it through the meat of his thigh. Blood sprays from the wound and vaporizes against his pulseShield.

Crimson fog fills the space between his armor and the shield, obscuring his sight. He becomes a bloody shadow as he fires at me. I duck behind my aegis and take three more shots meant for my head. I try to close again, and launch myself toward my razor—still sticking upright in the deck. Grasping it on the roll, I come up and drive the blade toward his head. He deflects that strike and two more with his rifle.

The deflections must cost him his rifle because he shocks me by closing within my guard. No Gray ever tries to close on a Gold. It's suicide. Not for Rhone ti Flavinius. I feel a pinch in my right breast and glance down to see a dagger buried to the hilt in my chest. The ribs caught it before it reached my heart. Rhone's other hand punches toward my throat. I duck my head to take the punch on the chin and take his opposite elbow on the side of my head. At the same time, he tries a kravat move to sweep my legs. Instead of stepping out of the kravat move, I step in to him and drive my knee upward into his stomach armor. An electric thrill from his shield courses through my leg, deadening the limb. Still, the force of the blow lifts Rhone off his feet. He lands like a cat and hurls his broken rifle at me. I bat it aside and narrowly dodge an acid pack he throws to cover his retreat. Acid eats into the deck and hangs in the air in a fine mist between us.

I go around. Breath comes shallow and filled with blood. Fire spreads through my diaphragm. My left lung is punctured.

Knowing Rhone is a menace at a distance, I try to close and overwhelm him with my mass and speed. He keeps space between us, boosting backward and upward with his gravBoots. He reloads his pistol and fires down at me as he goes. I hide behind my aegis. The rounds affect my shield in a strange way. It's overheating too fast.

How many kinds of ammo does he have?

I don't know what's happening with Atlas and Cassius. My situation is turning desperate. I can't hide behind my aegis much longer. It's glowing red, melting the scarabSkin into the flesh of my left forearm. No time to go back for a Praetorian rifle. With a roar of pain, I lunge out from my aegis's cover and hurl my razor at Rhone like a javelin.

It takes him in the right shoulder and he spins in the air. His shield spits sparks and he careens into the side of a nightRaptor. He spills down its fuselage to crash onto its wing. I leap up to join him only to find him already recovered. He lost his pistol in the collision but his armor is an equalizer, and he extracts my razor from his shoulder to grip in his right fist. He stomps his boot and another knife pops up into his left hand.

Barking like a dog, he charges me.

He's a gorydamn terror.

Unarmed, I search for a weapon. I spot his pistol on the deck below and bail off the wing before he closes. I grab his pistol on the run, drop, turn, and fire just as he bears down on me. The shots finish his pulse-Shield and I roll under the sweep of my own razor as he swings it at my head. I spin around as I come out behind him and kick his legs. It's the legs you go for on an armored opponent because with their balance compromised, the weight of their armor becomes a liability. My shin-bone almost breaks, but he teeters off-balance and begins to fall. Still he manages to whip the razor back at me and tear the pistol from my hand.

It is not his first time handling a razor. Not in the least.

Stripped of the pistol, I back off from him. He cracks the whip at my eyes and underhand throws the boot knife. I track it and catch it and hurl it back at his face. He blocks it by raising his armored arm, and I sprint at him.

He's terrifying at any range, but up close I can overpower him. I hit him before he can bring the razor around on me and tackle him to the ground. I manage to pry free the razor as we roll. It bounces away. He's out of blades but ends up on top. He drives his right hand toward my neck. I raise my left forearm just in time to intercept the knife that emerges from his armor. Gorydamn. Another one? Unlike the first pistol rounds, the knife has a diamond edge. It goes through the scarab-Skin like paper and emerges through my forearm, nearly taking my left eye too.

I block a second stab with the same arm. This time the knife goes through the forearm into the side of my face. It goes into my mouth and cuts through a few teeth. Its tip just tickles the roof of my mouth. He's so close to killing me, but he's just not strong enough to pound the blade home. I push the blade back out of my mouth and I twist my arm and push down. I trap the blade against his chest and roll him till I'm on top. Keeping my gored arm tight to his chest, I use my left knee to pin his right arm. I reach blindly with my right hand for my discarded razor. I grab the blade instead of the hilt and lose the top third of my pinky and ring finger for the effort.

Rhone's resistance suddenly slackens. His hips push up against me with a boost from his gravBoots. I'm rocked off-balance. My momentum takes me over his head, freeing the knife from my impaled forearm. Fortunately, that momentum also pushes me toward my razor. Sprawling forward, I grasp the hilt with my mutilated hand and swing backward in a daisy-cutter stroke. Resistance jerks my arm. I scramble up to see Rhone standing behind me with a long black needle clutched in his steel fist. He tries to take a step. He cannot. My razor cut through both of his calves just above his gravBoots.

Grunting, he spills sideways and lands with a thump on the deck. I stumble toward him. He squirms like a crab on its back. Even now he's dangerous. He hurls the black needle at me. I slap it away with my razor. Gods know what it was coated with. I stomp on his chest.

"If I was born Gold, I'd eat you alive," he says with a chuckle. "No Blood. Of Silenius. No—"

I spike my razor through the crown of his dragon helmet and into his head three times. Knowing even Rhone ti Flavinius can't survive a trio of holes through his brain, I spit blood and broken teeth down on his body. Then I leave him to his death spasms and fetch his pistol from the bloodied deck. I load a new magazine from his thigh cache.

Numb and seeing double, I stumble toward Atlas and Cassius. With Rhone's opening shots on my legs, it's hard to walk. The wound in my face oozes blood. My left arm is badly punctured and a few ligaments severed. Each breath is frothy with blood. I couldn't keep up with the dance that lies ahead.

Atlas and Cassius are locked in a deadly game. Cassius's right hand is gone. He's fighting with his left. Three deep slashes score his chest plate. His armor bleeds electricity. Atlas's face is a crimson stain, half his scalp is hanging off the side of his head, his left leg drags behind him, and three long gashes flay his chest. Cassius's bright razor and Atlas's hasta blur like butterfly wings. I'm too far away. I raise the pistol but can't find an opening that doesn't put Cassius in the line of fire. I stumble closer. My left eye must be damaged. It can't focus.

Cassius is winning, though something is wrong with his armor. Acid or something has eaten through the back. His armor is quitting. The helmet stuttering up and down. He cuts it off completely and delivers a horizontal sweep that should take Atlas in half at the waist. Atlas handsprings over the blow, using Cassius's own shoulder for leverage.

He stabs down as he passes overhead, and pierces Cassius's armor just inside his left shoulder. The blade sinks two handbreadths deep and sticks as Cassius twists. Atlas abandons the weapon and dodges two of Cassius's return thrusts, darts back in, takes his blade, retreats, and sweeps at Cassius's armored head. It's a feint to draw Cassius's guard. Atlas pivots and drives his hasta underhand toward Cassius's heart.

Even wounded, Cassius keeps his defensive discipline. He redirects Atlas's blade into the deck, stomps on the tip with his boot, and backhands his razor toward Atlas's head with his left hand. At the last moment, he converts his razor into a whip.

The whip snakes around Atlas's neck with a snap.

Beautiful.

Atlas goes still. His hasta is stuck in the deck. Cassius holds him on a leash. The two fighters pant for breath. It's only then I see the blisters on Atlas's skin. He *was* boiling inside the shield when Cassius first opened fire on him. Cassius doesn't dare take his eyes off Atlas.

I turn, scan the hangar. It is quiet. The jamField is still up.

The light is green. I wish Pytha could see. We've won. We've won. I stumble toward Cassius, searching the deck for my prize.

"Drop your blade and get on your knees," Cassius orders. Atlas does not obey. "Lys?" Cassius calls when he hears me limping toward them. My legs give out and start to cramp. I fall to a knee. "You prime?"

"Prime," I say.

"Flavinius?"

"Dead. Kill Atlas."

I see my prize. Atlas's pack: it's halfway between Cassius and me.

"Kill him," I tell Cassius again.

Atlas looks over at me like I'm a worm that has crawled out from an apple he was eating. "Ask Lysander about the weapon," he says.

"What weapon?" Cassius asks.

"Silenius's. Biological. *Eidmi*. It can target a Color. Any Color. On any—"

I shoot Atlas au Raa in the head. Everything above his eyes turns to mist. He teeters, takes a step, and falls. His bored smile remains. Mocking me.

I wait for something terrible to transpire. For Gorgons to rush in. For the *Lightbringer* to break apart. For gas or snakes to hiss out from Atlas's corpse. Nothing happens. The man is quite simply dead. Part of me did not believe he could die. Watching his blood flow around the bits of his fragmented brain, I begin to accept it.

I push off the ground with the pistol and stumble up toward the pack. A weight slides off my chest, replaced by one far worse. Cassius turns on me with a strange expression.

"Lysander."

"You need to leave before anyone sees you," I say.

His eyes have fallen on the pack. I'm not far now. Only a few more steps.

"Lysander. *Stop.*"

My boots scrape forward.

"Take one of the nightRaptors . . . let Diomedes and Darrow know the deed is done." I spit blood. My vision is clearing a little. "I'll let you know when I have control of the ship. Then . . . we can talk accords."

The pack is at my feet. I bend down to unlatch its clasp. It opens a little, but I dare not give it any more attention. Not with how Cassius is looking at me. I straighten. My heart sinks, because even Atlas's last words have sown misery.

"Lysander, what did Atlas bring back?" Cassius asks.

"Peace."

"Is that what he told you?" he asks. "Lysander, what is that? *Eidmi.* My linguistic education was not as expansive as yours, but that sounds like 'I eat' to me." He takes a step forward, his razor bloody and straight in his left hand.

A loaded pistol can weigh twenty-four ounces or a lifetime of regret. At my side, Rhone's is heavy in my hand. The magazine is full with armor-piercing rounds. I let Cassius see it.

A small laugh of surprise escapes him. The betrayal in his eyes shakes me. I never wanted to hurt Cassius, just like I never wanted to hurt Glirastes. Not ever. But war is a game of double down. Once it starts, if you flinch, it's all for nothing.

He looks at the blood. The bodies. His disembodied right hand lying on the floor. The bag at my feet. Horror grips him.

"You used me? For that? For this?" he asks. "To cut your strings and pin it all on me. The Betrayer."

"Yes."

He sways and looks around as if mortally wounded. "Lysander . . . I thought we were . . . I . . . believed in you."

"You believed in your own reflection," I say. "We're not brothers. Let us go our separate ways. Take a nightRaptor. Fly away. Live. Escape this. I can't. I won't. I will be Sovereign. I will be a fair Sovereign. I will fix what is broken. But I must break what no longer works. Division." I toe the bag. "With this."

"That's a biological weapon," he concludes.

I nod. "I couldn't trust it in Atlas's hands."

"But it's safe in yours?"

"If I don't control it, someone else will. Why not me?" I ask. "I didn't start the war. I have only ever tried to do what is right! Why not me?"

"Because I don't trust you, Lysander," he says. "If you give it to me, I will take a nightRaptor and drive it straight into that monster." He jerks his head toward Jupiter. The Gas Giant swirls beyond the pulseField to the hangar. "Your strings are cut, Lysander. You're free. We can take on Atalantia. Is that not enough?"

"It's time for you to go, Cassius."

He watches me for a long moment.

"Say I don't?"

"Then you're choosing death."

He staggers, exasperated. "No, Lysander. *You* choose. That's the point of it all. Isn't it? *You* choose. The chair means this much to you? More than the people in your life who love you?"

"Go, Cassius."

"Not without that weapon."

"This is not a debate. You are thirteen meters away. Your armor has quit. My mind is made up. And my pistol has nineteen rounds."

"What happened to y—"

I point the gun at him. "Go."

He looks at the gun as if it were an interloper, goes very dark for a moment, and then laughs. "You're being ridiculous. In the end I'll be more famous than you anyway. Cassius Bellona, the Man Who Killed Fear."

"Leave. Cassius. Please."

"You won't kill me. You love me too much. The guilt will crush you."

"I will learn to bear it."

He looks me in the eye, sad. "No. You won't. But if it must be guilt that drags you down, brother, I will be your millstone." He smiles at me, forlorn. "Remember when you told me Octavia never allowed you sweets? First chance I got, I took you to that candy emporium on Eros and piled a stack of credits in your hand. That look on your face when I said you could buy as much as we could carry . . ."

He takes a deep breath and sighs it out. He adjusts his armor and gets a better grip on his razor.

"Cassius . . . don't—" I warn.

"I must. I am Cassius Bellona, son of Tiberius, son of Julia, brother of Darrow, Morning Knight of the Solar Republic, and my honor remains."

Then he rushes forward.

He is not fast. Not injured and in dead armor. But he is determined and he is brave and he is tough and he is clever and he is daring. He is only things I admire in him in that moment, and none of the things I don't. He covers his exposed head with his armored arms and runs at me for all he's worth. I fire methodically, breathing through my nose, both eyes open, like Rhone taught me. At first Cassius runs through my fire, then he plows, trudges, stumbles, until the gun is empty and he sways. But he does not fall. Not Cassius au Bellona.

The tip of his razor wobbles just two fingerbreadths from my heart.

Even though I have made a ruin of him, I cannot tell if he could not kill me or would not kill me. Nor can I tell if he opens his arms to embrace me or if he's simply teetering forward. A seizure wracks his once-powerful body. The blade falls out of his hands. I catch him and carry him to the ground, desperate for one last word from him. But Cassius is already dead and he is smiling.

The rest of the world vanishes. I see a black door. A hand pushing it. A chair waits for me between shafts of light. On that chair I see a boy whose feet don't touch the ground. In his hands he holds a candle and with a single breath, he blows it out, and with it go all the shafts of light.

The hangar is quiet. My broken scarabSkin creaks as I twist around. I am alone. I am in an agony in which the pain of wounds is a welcome distraction. It is quiet, but for the first time all the strings are cut.

Gentle now that I can afford to be, I strain and lift Cassius to the side. Beneath him lies the pack. The solution to disunity. The greatest fear of my life grips me and I look at Atlas and his bored smile, then back at the bag. What if it is empty? The gun is still in my hand. Odd. I thought I'd cleared the clip. There is one bullet left, in the chamber. I set the gun within reach and I open the pack.

I stumble through the halls smearing blood as I go. I depress Kyber's whisper beacon. "Kyber, need you." An Orange mechanic ahead in the hall stares at me and my mutilations in horror. Cassius's razor is in my chest now, just above the heart where I planted it. The Red fire team rushing down the hall to put out the evidence-destroying blaze in hangar 17B grinds to a halt as they see me dripping my way along.

"Assassins . . ." I hiss. Blood pulses through the wound in my cheek. The Reds form a human wall around me. Alarms begin to blare. "Get me . . . to safety." I stagger and fall. The Reds catch me and carry me. Others form around like legionnaires to escort me to safety. They run with me through the halls, roaring for others to clear a path until Praetorians finally arrive and order them to put me down.

The Reds refuse at first and shout at the Praetorians, demanding to know why they didn't protect me. I had to embarrass the guard. That was almost as important as burning Atlas's body beyond recognition. To bind them to me, I had to make the arrogant guard look like fools who failed me, again. The Reds relent only when I whisper to them to hand me over. I raise a hand in thanks as the Praetorians rush me away to safety.

Demetrius storms up and almost blocks the way into the medBay when my Praetorians arrive with me in their arms. He is a totem of terror, but he lets us pass into the bay. Coriolanus, and others of his cabal, form a cordon around us after I'm set on the medical bed.

"What happened?" Demetrius demands.

"Assassins. One dead. May be more. Had help." Each word is a misery with the wound in my mouth. "Find them, Demetrius. They killed them. They killed Rhone and Atlas. Markus and Drusilla too."

Death enters Demetrius's eyes. The suspicion toward me is there, but he'll investigate first then turn that death on me if I'm to blame. For now, he wants immediate retribution. "Who?"

"The Raa prince . . . Dustwalkers. Find them. Kill them."

He storms off with purpose, his cabal pounding after him. I will not see him again, I hope. Kyber comes to my side after the medici have removed Cassius's razor. I shoo the medici from the room. "You need me, *dominus*?" she asks.

I pull her close and whisper. "Kyber, my defender. A coup. Surely you have felt it? In the guard?" I feel the lean muscles of her shoulder stiffen.

She nods. "It was the cape on Phobos. Rhone poisoned me." Her eyes go flinty. No doubt thinking of the sniper who prevented her from joining us on the *Dustmaker*. "He was with the Fear Knight. They were trying to control me. I don't know if there is anyone I can trust."

"Me, *dominus*. I am your whisper."

"Thank you, Kyber. It will ruin the guard if this comes to light. You have your own circle of trust?"

She nods.

"Demetrius and all in his cohort are to be found dead. Killed by the same Rim assassins who did this to me. Yes?" She nods again. "There are Gorgons hidden in level thirty-one, block C . . . make them disappear. Arrest Captain Pytha, no harm is to come to her. Will you do this for me, for the guard?"

"Thirteen is *your* body," she says. "Demetrius. Slow or quick?"

"Quick, always. When we can."

She almost smiles at my nobility.

"One more thing, Kyber. I dumped a black bag down the hangar's waste chute. It will be in the recycling queue on level nineteen. Before anything else, retrieve that bag and hide it in my quarters."

"Your will be done." She salutes and slips way.

The medici drift in. "Patch only what you must to preserve my life," I tell them. "My allies and the crew must see my state. We cannot sanitize the truth any longer."

85

DARROW

Dusk and Dawn

NIVALNIGHT APPROACHES, AND STILL all I can think about is Cassius up on the *Lightbringer* with Lysander. A dozen of Gaia's Dustwalkers lead me across Plutus's skyway. I watch the *Lightbringer* as we walk. Its spear shape is distorted. They've gotten a shield back on over the city, but it will take years to repair the damage from Fá's attack.

Beyond the broken battlewalls, Io darkens as it slides into Jupiter's shadow. Only the Garter glows on. Its artificial suns cast light over the fragile world of orchards, grain fields, and silver mists. Refugee camps fill the distant spaceport and wind through the citrus groves all the way up to the stone folds of the goddess's robes. I hear the camps also cover the next level of the Garter beneath the surface.

Demeter of Plutus, the great statue that sits to the north of the city embedded in the side of a harnessed volcano, wears a passive expression. The goddess clutches a bundle of grain to her chest in her left arm. Her right arm is held out, the hand open, the palm up. In that palm, she cups a simple circular building of Europan nickel that emits a silvery light. Like moths, the dusky-robed Moon Lords rise from the city or descend from their ships to attend Diomedes's summit.

All the beauty seems so inconsequential when someone you love is in danger. Stone, states, philosophy, they feel so secondary to the fleeting preciousness of life.

Beneath the statue, in the agricultural offices in the heart of Plutus, the Dustwalkers deposit me in the room of an archGrower and depart, leaving two at the door in reserve. There, in a simple sitting room, Gaia waits with the man of the hour. Diomedes and his grandmother are both dressed in homespun vestments. Gaia's are brown and gold. Diomedes's the color of storm, a dragon pin and the lightning bolts of his office the only embellishments. Gaia, curled on a cushion by a window looking over grain fields toward the statue, does not turn as I enter.

The box containing Fá's head lies on a chair. Pyrphoros lies in Gaia's lap. I feel possessive of the blade, protective of the Daughters who made it and what they'd think of it lying on the lap of the woman who ran the Krypteia for half her life. To many, especially Athena, Gaia would be considered the architect of the Rim's subtler form of tyranny.

"Any word from Lysander or Cassius?" I ask Diomedes.

"Not yet."

My anxiety deepens. I glance at the House of Bounty. "We're going to be late to your own summit," I say. "We are still attending . . . yes?"

Diomedes does not answer.

Gaia nods out the window toward the building in Demeter's palm. "For five hundred and nineteen years the *ekklesia* have met in the House of Bounty before every cycle. I remember my mother taking me there when I was a girl. Sitting on the steps listening to the growers bicker about the next harvest, the rotation of the crops, the fertilization of the soil. This is the first time it'll host a conference of war. Diomedes has told me of the triumvirate he wants to make with Lune."

"It can be a conference of peace too," I say. "We could end war in our lifetimes. I assume Diomedes has explained his plans with Lune and me. Will you lend support?"

Gaia turns a little to look at me. Disgust fills her eyes. "No."

I glance at Diomedes. He already knew this. I'm baffled. "Diomedes gave me his word—"

"Diomedes is a servant of the Dominion. His personal guarantees and honor are subservient to his duties," she says. "My son Romulus knew this. He lied about your crime to keep us from war, Darrow. He shamed himself for the sake of his Dominion. So too will Diomedes."

I feel the world sinking out from under me. She's not going to let me go to the summit. "You're going to let Atlas get away with it," I whisper. "You're going to just swallow it all."

"The Volk will pay for their crimes. The Daughters are terrorists. Lune will destroy them. And I will destroy you," she says. I search Diomedes's face for signs of shame. There are none.

"Atlas is responsible for the deaths of millions of your people," I say.

"Yes," she says.

Oh no. No.

"You already knew," I say.

"I am cursed to be the mother of Fear. My boy is so much like me. He feels too much. He is tortured. But he has his duty. And I have mine. That is what my son told me when he visited me in my cell when I was held captive by his pet warlord. It was his last revenge, you see. When we sent him as hostage to Luna, I did not see him off. I couldn't bear it. The last words I spoke to him were, 'Do your duty.'"

I feel like I am drowning. All my allies, all my people out here will be undone by this woman who is so old she will not live to see the future she steals from them.

"You are the matron of House Raa," I say. "You are part of the Moon Council. You have a duty to your people. You would cast the moons into the shadow of another lie? Worse, you'll demand your grandson bear its weight? Tell me, Gaia, how will it feel to watch Diomedes march to the Dragon Tomb when this lie is uncovered? To watch him waste his life the same way Romulus, *your son,* wasted his own." I can't help but laugh.

"Are we amusing to you?"

"No. You are tragic." I look at Diomedes, unable to understand.

He just watches his grandmother.

Gaia hefts Pyrphoros. "What does it take to master one of these blades, Darrow?" Gaia rasps, but answers without giving me a chance to reply. "Pain. Discipline. Sacrifice. We of the Krypteia have a sacred charge separate from the edicts of the Moon Lords to keep order in these spheres. The hierarchy is essential to order."

"Flawed as it may be, the Republic has proven that is not always the case," I reply.

"Twelve years!" she cackles. "Twelve, all at war. We have secured contiguous government for more than a half a millennium, boy. Your frail experiment hasn't the legs for another year. You think Gold is the problem? *Pfff.* There has always been a human pyramid, in every civilization beneath the sun. It is human nature to crawl upward. But if there are not rigid ceilings, everyone will think they should have everything. Then what do you get? An unstable structure at war with itself. Ravenous resource consumption, the despoilment of natural habitats, beauty, worlds. Your Republic and your free market rape natural sanctuaries, poach rare beasts to extinction, consume, devour what took an epoch of order to build."

She glares at me. "I can speak twenty-one dead tongues, name every species of wildlife in our spheres, recite the caloric intake of at least one hundred and thirty cities in this Dominion. I have dedicated my life to the study of social engineering, to the history of humanity, and you tell me that a Red who can't name five moons of Ilium should have the same say in government? Demokracy gives humanity what it wants, boy. The hierarchy gives humanity what it needs. Structure, and hope to escape our own stupidity.

"My son Atlas knows that my duty to the hierarchy supersedes all others. Even my great love of Rim independence. That is why he told me of his work here face-to-face. He knows I will be trapped in silence. He knows I understand the chaos that will awaken if his work here seeps into the light of day. He even granted me a boon, and said Fá would solve the problem of the Daughters for me. His last words were, 'Do your duty, Mother.'"

I stare at Diomedes. His face is unreadable. "Diomedes, you can't really go along with this. You can't be that full of shit—"

Gaia looks at her grandson with absolute love. "Diomedes is a servant of the Dominion, of his ancestors, of the hierarchy." She extends Pyrphoros to him. He takes it. "The blood of Akari swirls in his veins, so he will do his sworn duty. He will keep his silence, he will bear this disgusting lie for the greater good. And he will kill you. Here and now."

"What of my guest rights?" I ask.

"Have you eaten bread?" she asks.

I almost laugh again. I'll die because of a bloodydamn technicality?

"So what does she make of your new oath, Diomedes?" I ask.

"I was waiting for the proper moment to tell her. It is now." He looks at the guards by the door. "Leave."

They wait for Gaia to nod before obeying.

When they have gone, Diomedes stares hard at me, then wraps Pyrphoros around his own neck, hands his grandmother the handle, and then goes to his knees. Gaia stares in shock. "What is this?"

I feel exultant and watch Diomedes in admiration. A true man of honor.

He looks up at his grandmother and says, "Gold has failed its duty, Grandmother. In the Core, and here. When we failed to protect the people even from our own blood, the Daughters of Ares had to for us. How then are they terrorists? On Europa, they saved millions, both by harboring refugees and taking part in the assault on Fá. When defense was needed, they offered it freely and paid with their lives. I have sworn to protect them, to take up their cause as my own. Tonight, when I become Hegemon, I will deal with the matters before us, but I will, in time, pursue the cause of dismantling the hierarchy. I will reform our laws. I will demolish the Krypteia. You've said it yourself. The Achilles' heel of the Core has always been greed, and ours has always been pride. I tire of both, so do the people. Gold has failed. We need order, yes. But not the same order that brought us here."

Horrified, Gaia looks about to reply, but Diomedes is on a roll. It is the most verbose I have ever seen the man.

"I will not swallow this monstrous lie of Atlas. I will not make nice with Atalantia, who treats the lives of millions as a game. Akari asked for Gold to be philosopher kings. Maybe we were that way once. Now we are just dragons guarding our treasure. We may be superior in intelligence, in our life spans, in our capacity for violence, but not in our humanity. We failed, Grandmother, long before Atlas set his warlord on us, long before Rhea. We are medieval. We are grotesque. I love you with all my heart. But you represent a past that fears the future. I will not accept that. So, if it is true that the young cannot teach the old, and the old must always teach the young: kill me, for I will learn no other way."

If anyone else had said such a thing to Gaia, she would laugh at them, but Diomedes is not a man fond of hyperbole. Gaia watches him with shock, then disbelief, then horror, then anger, and finally absolute misery. A burst of grief escapes her mouth. Tears stream. "No. Diomedes. No. *No*." She flings away the handle of the weapon and tries to pull him up but it's like moving an anvil. He pushes the weapon back into her hands.

"Diomedes stop this. It's because of her. Isn't it? That viper in our garden. *Aurae*. She's cast a spell on you." She slaps him. "Wake up." She slaps him again. "You betray all your ancestors. Our family has been devoured! You are our future!"

"I am," Diomedes says. "So believe in me. I will honor Akari. I will protect the people. I will bring order, but in my own way."

Gaia looks up to the ceiling as if to ask the heavens why they cursed her with this affliction. Then she hardens, looks at her grandson, wrests her thumb on the retraction toggle on the handle of Pyrphoros, as if she's about to take off his head. He watches her in sadness, but he will not yield, he will not bend, his convictions are iron, and when she realizes that, Gaia breaks. The weapon falls from her hand and she sinks to the floor in grief.

Diomedes unwraps Pyrphoros from his neck and wraps his arms around his grandmother. He whispers to her and she buries her head in his chest. All the grief from these last months, and maybe even this last decade, pours out of her. Her frail body shakes for some time before growing still. After a few minutes, Diomedes helps Gaia stand. "The summit is nigh. I will need your support, Grandmother. This family has more to do."

Her eyes are raw and red from crying. They fix on the floor. She is frozen.

"Grandmother?"

"I heard you."

"Will you help us?"

"I cannot . . . but I will not oppose you."

"That is not enough," he says and tilts her head up and looks her in the eyes. "When my brother died at the Battle of Ilium, you told me it was my duty to take his place as heir to the Dominion. You are the matron of House Raa. But you are more than that. You are our link to the generations who came before. Most of your contemporaries have faded into the mists of history. It is not yet your time to fade. Shine bright for me, Grandmother. Lend me the light of your wisdom, your cunning, your fame. Atlas claimed your duty is to keep his secret. Atlas is wrong. Your duty is not silence. Your duty is to use your voice."

The words and the conviction behind them animate Gaia.

She touches his cheek. "My little storm. I have waited so long for you to realize your strength is not in your arms. That it is like this . . ." She laughs. "I will never agree with you on this course of action. But . . . maybe that is natural. I am the dusk now. You are the dawn. I have lived. I have had my say. I will help you have yours. That is what your mother and father would have wanted."

I look out the window. The darkness beyond the Garter is now complete.

"It is nivalnight," I say. "It's time."

"Then we go," Diomedes says. "And we must trust Lysander and Cassius will meet us at the summit."

86

DARROW

Nivalnight

I WAIT IN THE SMALL chamber beneath the House of Bounty's speaking floor. Periodically I glance at the entrance, hoping to see it open and Cassius waltz in carrying a box and wearing his cocksure smile.

As time ticks on, anxiety starts to creep in. Diomedes's condemnation of his uncle and his wicked schemes is muffled through the walls. Now and then the stone rumbles with the anger of the Moon Lords. There is a pause that must mean they are voting for Hegemon. A cheer trembles through the stone, followed by Diomedes's voice and a grumble of anger, Diomedes's voice again, then silence. A moment later, Diomedes comes through the chamber's door.

He now wears a pure black cape and a ring with a black stone that swirls with motes of dust. "I am Hegemon. It is time."

I glance at the room's other door. "Lysander and Cassius are not here yet."

"No. I had wanted to present the lords the truth, then the heads of Atlas and Fá at the same time to show no favoritism. But Lysander is late, so you have the honor of going first."

"You told them about Lysander's involvement with Atlas?"

"Yes, I revealed to them its full nature, and the mission I have charged him with. They also know you saved my life, and of your heroism on Europa. They do not know what you carry, however." He nods to the box in my lap. "Come." He departs and leaves the door open behind him. I follow with a last glance at the other door.

I walk through the stone tunnel to the sound of Diomedes's voice.

"Should you draw blood from this man, you draw that blood from me."

Honoring the Rim ritual of not bringing the dirt of the external world into the sacred meeting, I remove my boots at the end of the tunnel and slide on a pair of slippers before stepping out to join Diomedes.

In his full power, he stands in the center of the speaking floor holding a plain black spear. The Spear of Akari. It is made of duroglass to show the dangers of war. I walk toward him under the gaze of the three Olympic Knights who stand to either side of the speaking floor. They must be the only members of their order to have survived Fá's invasion. Knees crackle in the risers and robes shift as the Moon Lords stand to watch me approach Diomedes. There is an emblem of a golden flower on the floor. When I join Diomedes atop the emblem, he breaks a piece of bread from a loaf and I eat it. After this guest rite, he nods for me to proceed.

Now, as a guest of all the Moon Lords, I turn to face them. War has pruned the legislative body of its numbers and many of its military-age members. But Atlas must have wanted an audience for his horrors, because they look as if they must have been in session when Fá attacked. Though their robes are identical, each of the lords carries a heavy iron staff.

The staffs are unremarkable except for the iron hand on the end of each. These iron hands clutch the sphere the lord represents. The depictions of their worlds are as beautiful and colorful as the staffs are austere.

The lords are despicable in so many ways, but there is dignity here in their cloudy gold eyes and hair shot through with white. Though not all are old—many are very young, and must be the only members left in their delegation who survived the invasion because the young ones sit alone. Silent, noble, they all watch me with contempt.

"You know me. I am Darrow of Mars, ArchImperator of the Republic, and I come to present a gift, ask a boon, and to beg your pardon. My gift first." I set the box on the floor and pull out the head of Volsung Fá by its valor tail. It shifts the wintry weather of the room like a Storm God.

There is no sound. The dignity the Moon Lords are obliged to retain before an enemy like me would not allow that. Yet they regard the head of Fá with relief in their eyes. Pure, sweet relief. Gaia is the first to bang her staff on the floor. The entire room follows her lead, even the Codovan of Ganymede whose dockyards I once destroyed. They recognize and affirm the gift and the worthiness of the act. The acclaim goes on for almost a minute.

When it ends, I go to a knee, the Moon Lords sit. Their slippers whisper against the stone, their knees crackle, their robes shift.

"I have slain your enemy, but I am the same man who turned the guns on the Dockyards of Ganymede after the Battle of Ilium. That battle secured your independence, but my act cost the lives of thousands of your citizens, and deprived the Rim of its best tool to secure a brighter future. We were allies. The act was dishonorable and a crime. I know I cannot hope to have your forgiveness as a man for that, but I hope to attain your formal pardon for the benefit of the peoples we represent."

No staffs recognize my apology. Not even Gaia's. The senators of the Republic would be awed by the expressions of the lords. They are models of rugged, impassive haughtiness.

"I have told you how this man saved my life after Kalyke, and his defense of the peoples of Europa, but now you wonder why I have asked him here," Diomedes says. "It was a reason important enough for him to risk coming here. I'm sure you think it was no risk. After all, *we* know his life is not in jeopardy. If we found him in the field, or if he'd entered this chamber as an interloper, his life would—of course—be forfeit. But as a guest of the Moon Council, who has now eaten of the same loaf that filled your mouths, *never*.

"But in his mind, it was dangerous for him to even walk in here, where any one of you could charge down and cut off his head. Because that is the world he comes from. That is the type of Gold he has long battled and has been conditioned to expect. He is a consequence and product of Core Gold tyranny. He does not know us very well. For us and for him, that is a good thing. He came and risked your wrath because I, as Hegemon, have offered to restore the military alliance my father made with the Rising."

The Moon Lords, silent so far, now erupt like a volcano. I glance back at Diomedes. He gives me an amused smile and motions me to stand. He tilts his head to Gaia.

She rises in a fury and raves with her staff at the other lords. "Now you roar? You, Pnyx? Who fled Europa and left your own people to die? You, Isegoras? Who cowered behind Ganymede's shields? *Now* you are brave? Now that Darrow has slain the beast and saved Europa? Now that my grandson has unveiled the master? Shame! Shame! Ungracious toads. You listened to the bombardments. You listened to the screams of your people. Listen now to your Hegemon who still bears the shadow of battle upon his body."

She sits and glowers. Diomedes forges ahead into the silence his grandmother carved.

"For almost twelve years we have known independence. Twelve years, out of the seven hundred of our existence. Twelve years, because we formed an alliance with a fledgling movement and a young warlord. Twelve years of independence purchased for the price of a dockyard. Who would not have paid that price?"

He peers around. In that moment, he's not an orator—he's a blacksmith eyeing a piece of iron that doesn't want to bend. Now he works the bellows.

"Our worlds are fragile, far apart. It is in our nature to be practical. Except when we don't want to be. We are furious because trading those dockyards was not our choice. We take pride in having a choice. But isolation is not a choice. It is a fate. If we do not pick a side, others will choose for us. Our history and this . . . fraudulent invasion prove that. Our enemy is and has always been the tyrannical nature of the Golds in the Core. Today they manifest as Atlas and Atalantia. That is why I have offered Darrow and Lysander to form a triumvirate against them."

"Then where is Lune?" a Codovan woman asks. "Atlas. Lysander. It is easy to throw around their names when they are not here. Why does Lune not come and face his shame like Darrow has?"

"Lune has been unwavering in his respect toward the Rim," Diomedes replies. "He sailed out here as a friend, as an ally. I have no doubt he will yet again prove himself to be a man of honor who seeks unity instead of division. When he joins us, he will bring the head of the puppet master to join that of the puppet." He gestures to Fá's head. "Then he will ask your pardon as Darrow has, for the concessions he made to Atlas."

"When?" the Codovan asks.

"Soon," Diomedes says with a glance at me.

I can barely think of anything but Cassius up there fighting the Fear Knight. He and Diomedes can't both be wrong about Lysander, can they?

A Callistan asks very softly: "I do not understand. Are we not to seek vengeance then against the braves who did the raping, the killing, the burning? My moon is not just broken. It is ash."

Diomedes considers. "An enemy sics a kuon hound on you. It rips out your liver, kills your friends. Do you spend your treasure, your life, hunting down the hound—or the enemy who unleashed it? Atalantia sponsored this attack. She helped lure us into the war. I would turn that kuon hound, the Volk, on her and watch with a smile as it rips her to shreds."

"Am I to simply forget the wound Darrow rent in my moon when our docks fell?" the Codovan asks.

"Yes, if you want to keep your moon," Gaia says. "Atalantia will come, not tomorrow, not the day after, but when she comes, she'll kill everyone in this room who does not kneel. Even if you kneel, she will probably kill you and install one of her creatures in your ancestral home. She does not need to compromise. We cannot beat her alone, so we *must* compromise."

Diomedes's attention has shifted to a Green attendant signaling him. He motions the attendant over. The Green whispers in his ear and Diomedes lifts a hand for silence.

"We are receiving a tightbeam from the bridge of the *Lightbringer,*" he announces with a smile and motions the Green to put it on. The hairs on the back of my neck rise.

"Why a tightbeam?" I ask Diomedes. "Why is Lysander not coming in person?"

87

DARROW

Casus Belli

T HE PYRAMIDAL HOLO CASTER glows to life. Hundreds of Golds
fill the bridge of the *Lightbringer* and stand arrayed behind Lysander. I recognize a few. Cicero au Votum stands at Lysander's right
wearing an expression of contempt. Lysander is covered in blood and
horrific wounds. His cheek has been punctured. His chest too. His left
arm is savaged and hangs limp. His face is swollen. Yet it is the darkness
of his eyes that haunts me.

All hope and warmth drain from my body. Something is terribly
wrong.

As Lysander speaks, the wound on his cheek reveals his molars.
"Salve, *brothers and sisters of the Rim. In the spirit of friendship, unity, and
honor, when you cried out for aid, I set sail without hesitation. I called on
my allies to set aside your past treasons. To forget that it was the Raa that
slaughtered the Sword Armada at Ilium with Darrow and the Rising. To
forgive the Raa who made the deal that sent the Rising to attack Luna and
set fire to the Society.*"

I look over at Diomedes. He is stricken with confusion, but Lune
isn't done.

"*My allies showed the strength of their character. They forgave. They forgot. They sailed. They risked their lives, their people, their treasure, and delayed the siege of Mars all to help you. Only to find Darrow—our great
enemy—once again a guest in your house drawing up schemes for war in the
Core. Only for me, who vouched for you, to be attacked by assassins sent up
from the Garter. I bear the marks of their efforts on my body. I live only*

because of the sacrifice of Rhone ti Flavinius, one of our greatest patriots. I am sick with grief and disgusted you would send a man after me whom I once considered a brother. Look on what you've done."

A body is dropped from above. It sways from a rope tied around its neck. His neck. I am gripped by a great stillness. My skin crawls. The world takes on a dreamlike quality. Words are muffled. Sight two-dimensional. I waver, struck dumb.

Cassius.

Pressure builds in my chest.

My beautiful, brave friend hangs like a carcass in a butcher's freezer. He is naked and brutalized. His arms broken. Blood leaks from dozens of bullet holes and stab wounds. His sword hand is missing. The hand that used to reach over and squeeze my shoulder as we sat in the cockpit of his ship. The hand that used to grip my wrist to correct my blade form. The hand he drank with and would gesture with like a trained orator as he spoke. Tears pour down my face. I hurt all over.

He is dead.

Cassius.

This is a nightmare. I'll wake up in my bunk on the *Archi* and find him yawning in the cockpit. I cover my mouth to stop myself from crying out in pain. Why did he go? Why did he have to go? Why didn't he just wait for me on his ship? It's such a waste. I just got him back. I can't think of anything but him smiling on the *Archimedes* when I told him we were brothers and he agreed and how he then just sat there in such contentment. So safe with me. Why did he go? I don't want to be here. I want to be home with Virginia's arms around me. Or back with him in the cockpit. We should have stayed on Europa. We should have fought. Dying at his side would have been better than this. I'd trade him for all the ships. All these Moon Lords. He was worth them all put together.

Diomedes is talking. I can't hear what he says. He's enraged. I've never heard him so angry. Then I look over and see the tears streaming down his face. He points at Lysander.

"Lune, you are a liar. And your empty words are evil. We spoke of Atlas. You confessed his involvement—"

"Who would not agree to a fiction to survive a meeting with Darrow? I only escaped as a child because I put the Dawn Scepter in Virginia's hand. But I ask you, where is the Fear Knight? Lurking in the shadows? So he must

be all around us all the time. Too often the Rising has blamed him for every evil that besets it. One man cannot be everywhere. I know for a fact he has been seen in operations in South America. Hundreds of witnesses can attest. As my allies can attest to my character. Darrow has poured poison in your ear and called it honey.

"I know you are a good man, Diomedes. But you have been manipulated. As have you, my noble Moon Lords. An enemy besets you, an enemy who has fought for years by Darrow's side, led by the father of the man Darrow still claims as brother. And then Darrow arrives, as if by magic, to deliver your Diomedes from the clutches of doom, and present himself as your savior."

I am too heartbroken and disgusted to speak. Gaia does for me.

"You wretched worm! Weasel," Gaia snaps. "Foul tyrant seed. I spoke to my son Atlas. I looked in his face. I heard from his own mouth the game he has been playing."

"Atlas did all this only to reveal himself to you and . . . let you live?" Lysander frowns. *"Strange. Gaia, you are a master spy. You know how ludicrous your story must sound. Is there any person in that room who hates the Core more than you? Your husband was killed by my grandmother's orders, as were some of your kin when they rose up in arms against their Sovereign. My lords, has she advocated for an alliance with Darrow?"*

The Moon Lords look at each other. I could kill them all. Diomedes motions me to stay silent. As if Lune was leaving room for anyone else to speak. I watch the man prattle with a heart full of hate.

"Romulus was tricked by Darrow. Diomedes has been tricked by Darrow. The Raa have failed you, my lords. I came out here to save Ilium because I believe in unity. I believe in reform, peace, prosperity for the high and low. I believe in order, and the sacrifice needed to achieve it. But I also believe in tolerance and forgiveness. My allies and I will still destroy the Volk threat and the insurgents on Europa and sail home at no cost to you. No cost—save proof that we are united in the pursuit of peace. That proof is simple. Render Darrow unto me, or face the consequences."

The Moon Lords, who have so far been entertaining Lysander's tower of lies and allowing him to cast the shadow of doubt over Diomedes's honor, show their true character. Without even looking at one another, they stand in unison against the ultimatum. Pride may be their folly, but it is also their beauty.

Diomedes speaks for them.

"Darrow has eaten the bread of this body. He is a guest. We decline your ultimatum. It is impossible. Lysander, I have offered you another path—"

"You say the Slave King has saved you. Very well. Let the Slave King feed you."

The signal dies. The Moon Lords, all standing, wonder what the hell just happened. I am still slowed by the loss of Cassius. Diomedes turns to me, absolutely astonished at the bald-faced lies.

"Lysander knows your ways," I say, numb. "He knows we have evidence. This call wasn't for the lords. It was to show his allies he has a *casus belli.* You need to get your people to safety. If you can."

I look at the slippers on my feet, everyone's feet, and I feel dread in my belly.

Diomedes is about to say something, and then his eyes widen. We need more people like Diomedes in the worlds. He is true. He is noble. But unfortunately, that also makes him naïve to the extremities evil will embrace. The Moon Lords are naïve as well, because they think Lysander came to them in earnest to win their approval. As if their approval means shit to a man with a MoonBreaker. None of them yet understand that Lysander was just covering his ass before committing a war crime. The realization comes to Diomedes as a bar of light in the distance divides the blackness of his pupils. I turn to follow his gaze in time to see the catacomb-like darkness of the nivalnight beyond the Garter become as bright as a Mercurian summer day.

Particle cannons.

A column of light links the *Lightbringer* to the golden horizon of Demeter's grain fields. The columns multiply, stemming from the *Lightbringer* and then from the Bellona and Votum ships. To the east, one of the atmosphere bubbles pops in slow motion, like a water balloon pierced with a needle. Orchards and grain fields flash burn as the superheated air ignites everything in its path.

The shieldDome of Plutus bangs like a gong struck by an avalanche as the particle beams hit the shield to form a cathedral of light and sound thunder over the city. The noise wakens me from my stupor of sorrow. I have faced many bombardments on three separate planets. They are the definition of hell. Far worse than anything else in war because of the helplessness they instill. Yet I have never been caught off guard like this. Like a civilian. No armor. No plan. No resources. No men. No gravBoots. Kilometers from my ship. The terror sweeps the humanity out of me, out of the Moon Lords, and we turn into mice scrambling for the exit.

"Order!" Diomedes calls, and the three other Olympic Knights rush from the side of the room to echo him. The authority in his voice is a tonic to our panic. "Evacuate by seniority."

Marveling at their near instantaneous reversion from chaos to discipline, I watch the Moon Lords file toward the main exit by rows.

I peer out from between the columns of the House of Bounty, scanning the air over the city, over the burning grain fields to the east, and the burning orchards to the west, and I see what I feared. They fly low, visible only because of the light that shines off their plating. Missiles. The recently restored defensive shield over Plutus is strong, nigh impenetrable due to its energy coming from the tidal shifting of the moon itself, but there are always gaps for missiles to slide in under.

The decapitation stroke is on its way.

The city's remaining defensive towers target the missiles and detonate the barrage shy of the House of Bounty. The missiles still tear a hole in the cityscape a kilometer wide. The House of Bounty shudders and lurches from the shockwave. I keep my feet. I'm one of the few who do. Diomedes and the Olympic Knights shout for the Moon Lords to move faster and carry the old. Something hits the building. A carving of a dryad breaks free of the ceiling and falls to crush a teenage Moon Lord who likely never held his world staff before today. Sticking out from under the statue, his hand twitches for the staff. It is out of reach. His hand takes on the same shape of the iron hand that grips the world he will never see again. His home, Triton.

Then hairline fractures race through the ceiling. I sidestep a piece of rubble before it crushes me. Gaia, who has stayed behind to help a colleague, sidesteps another dryad as it crashes down.

A shudder goes through the building as something slams into its roof. A crack races through the wall into one of the pillars holding up the exit arch. The pillar begins to lean inward. If it goes, the arch will collapse and we'll be trapped with a sheer drop to either side.

I shout a warning to Diomedes and race up the risers to jump over the Moon Lords who clog the exit artery. I shove my way through the leaner moon-born bodies just as the lower half of the pillar caves inward. I arrest its collapse, taking the weight on my shoulder. Something pops on impact, maybe my collarbone. My feet scrabble on the ground until they find a crack between the paving stones.

On Earth, with its punishing gravity, I could not hope to bear the burden of the pillar. On Io I can take five times the weight. I grunt and roar with effort, holding the pillar up and holding back the collapse of the exit. Moon Lords flow past me. My body is breaking. The weight compacting my vertebrae. I am losing my battle against the stone. Then Diomedes is with me. Then a woman, her face centimeters from my own. Grecca au Codovan, whose dockyards I destroyed. And then two more Olympic Knights. Together we push against the pillar. It feels like an eternity. It must be less than half a minute. Then a hand grabs my shoulder and all together we throw ourselves through the exit arch. It collapses behind us with a grumble of stone.

Something hits me in the back of the head. I trip and fall. My vision swims. The world groans and shakes all around me. I struggle to get up, my shoulder a ruin, to see a leathery hand extending down toward me. I grip it and Gaia pulls me up with surprising strength. Stumbling like drunks after the Moon Lords, we pass through the antechamber filled with washing pools where the lords doffed their skipBoots for their cer-emonial slippers, through another chamber where incense still burns in braziers. I feel the building tilting under my feet. Then we're through the antechambers. Out under the blazing, thundering sky.

Rock grumbles and cracks behind us. I glance over my slumped right shoulder. The House of Bounty is gone. The great hand of Demeter upon which it sat has broken off at the wrist. For a moment a single Moon Lord stands in its place, frozen in time, his hand outstretched, his mouth open. But there is no ground beneath his slippers, and he follows the building down into the abyss.

The Moon Lords ignore the landing pads and carry on along stone stairs cut into the statue. They disappear into an aperture beneath Demeter's right breast, one after the other. I must have been hit in the head harder than I thought, because I swoon on the stairs. Gaia's grip on my belt keeps me from tumbling over the side. There is nothing to do but follow the quickening current of bodies into the statue. By the time I realize we've made it to safety the statue seals the door behind us.

The affectations of antiquity do not grace its interior. A modern lift lies within. Not one of the Golds rejoices in surviving their near brush with death. Their faces are drawn, pale, lacerated by broken stones, and their eyes hopeless as Lysander's ships make their world shudder.

You really should think about changing the slipper policy, Cassius would say right now.

Crammed together with them, my right shoulder probably broken, blood slithering down the back of my neck, I think again of Cassius swaying on the end of that rope. I sink into my grief as we descend down and down through a chute into the metal and stone world of bunkers. A shudder goes through me. My heart weighs as much as a planet. It was all finally starting to go so well.

Medici greet us when we arrive in a bunker. They tend to us and start to usher away the wounded. Diomedes turns to face the others. His shoulder is fleeced of skin after his efforts with the pillar. The Moon Lords look no better. Their robes are tattered. Their skin flayed by stone.

Diomedes looks gutted, lost. Almost insane. "There are people on the surface. People in the second level. There are people everywhere . . ." He nods after the medici. "That way lies safety, shelter. The garages and tunnels to the surface are this way." He takes off at a jog toward the garages. All but the oldest of the Moon Lords follow.

"Carry me," Gaia says. I look down to see the old woman glaring up at me. Blood sluices down her left leg. "Carry me, *gahja.* I can't run but I can fly."

"Shoulder's shot. Get on my back," I say.

The old matron of House Raa clambers onto my back and I take off at a run.

88

LYSANDER

The Sack of Demeter

A LONE PIECE OF ASH twirls down from the sky. I catch it on my hand.

"The fire is spreading from the eastern Garter," Kyber reports. The air has started to smell like smoke. I rub the ash into my palm.

"No matter, we're almost done here." I watch a loader mech slowly pulling a giant plum tree from the ground. Thick as four Grays lined abreast with long, narrow leaves and huge blue plums, the trees are the culmination of centuries of horticultural splicing and research by the growers of House Raa. I turn from the excavation and walk, surrounded by Kyber's trusted Praetorians, toward the mobile command post where my house horticulturalists oversee the sack of the Garter. Industry bustles all around. Hundreds of mechs trundle with trees toward waiting transports. RipWings buzz in the sky. Praetorians land in curtains of dust, dragging trussed Raa growers behind them.

Three stories from the ground, Pallas stands with my growers atop the command post. She turns with a smile as I arrive. "Ah, Lysander. Lucilla here was just apprising me of the haul," she says. "Lady Bellona will be impressed."

"Not upset I'm going into the produce business?" I ask.

"As long as you stay clear of helium, she will revel in your success. You have creditors to pay after all. What a trove, Lysander. The value of the fruit trees alone rivals all the gold of Persepolis. I'll not lie, I told the lady this adventure was likely to be nothing more than an expensive lark. I couldn't have been more wrong." She points at two passing mechs. "What are those, Lucilla?"

"Ah, a prized pair. Those *Prunus domestica caeruleum* will be the first of their kind in the Core, *domina*," my archGrower, Lucilla, says.

Pallas sighs. "I feel like I'm watching Noah's ark load, but the animals are all made of money."

Lucilla was selected for my household by Glirastes, or rather by Exeter. She is a plain Brown woman with narrow, ochre eyes, a stout body, and ambition far beyond her thirty-six years. Until now, she has just been an expensive eccentricity on my household roster. I am grateful now for Exeter's foresight. In the sixteen hours since the bombardment's inception, she has earned her keep ten million times over.

"Lysander, might I borrow a Praetorian?" Pallas asks. I nod. She has more respect than to pick Kyber. Her eyes fall on Draconis, one of Kyber's favorites. I'm told he shot Demetrius in the head personally. He is a dark-skinned man, with bright eyes, a solemn face, and an optimistic disposition. He despised the kill-pool nonsense, and is apparently Kyber's best mate. "I'm lusting for some plums. Fetch me two, please."

Draconis pops into the air on his gravBoots and returns with two plums. Pallas eats one and tosses one back to Draconis. "What do you think?"

He tastes. "Just desserts, *domina*."

"Couldn't have said it better myself," Pallas says and pats my shoulder. "Well done."

"Fires are coming. What's the haul, Lucilla?" I ask.

"The majority of their western agricultural portfolio is now under our control," Lucilla says and begins to go into details. I listen and watch my troops. Below, caked in dust, ash, sweat, and occasionally blood, groups of Praetorians and house legionnaires flow in from looting seed banks and capturing valuable human assets.

"You are confident these trees can grow in the Core?" I ask Lucilla, interrupting her. "I've lost nearly a hundred Praetorians in this endeavor already."

"We have already begun preparing to adapt the cellular samples to Mercury's biome."

"Mercury?" Pallas asks with raised eyebrows.

"Rim horticulture outpaces the Core's by a century, at least. With the DNA sequences alone, we can close that gap within the year," I say. "In five years, I will make the Waste of Ladon a crop heartland fertile enough to feed the whole of Luna, and then some."

"I hear rebels make good fertilizer," Pallas says. "Cicero must be delighted. As you must be. The revenues will be . . . immense."

I nod. "It's about time my house diversified its portfolio."

"Yes, can't sell power alone." She glances up at our ships above. "Walk me to my craft, Lune?"

I walk with Pallas to her ship. She flew a custom ripWing down instead of a shuttle. One of the charioteer's many eccentricities. She appraises me in its shadow.

"I apologize. After your games on Mercury I told Lady Bellona you didn't have the stomach for this sort of enterprise."

"I didn't yet," I say.

"What changed?" she asks.

"I was taught how the worlds work," I say. "If you don't have the stomach to win, there's plenty of people who do, and will."

"Well said." She looks around and steps closer, her voice low. "The lady will appreciate how this was done, Lysander. We still have our hero narrative—thanks to Darrow and the perfidious Moonies—and now we have also bewildering profits. Some of the Reformers may blanche at this, but our clients are perfectly satisfied. None can even detect the smell of bullshit radiating from you. That's a compliment."

"Bullshit?" I ask, innocent.

"Flavinius isn't the only Praetorian missing. Kyber is the only one on your personal detail to survive your little purge, it seems."

"The assassins were very thorough," I say.

"How thorough?" She tilts her head. "Do I have to sleep with one eye open?"

"You have nothing to fear," I say.

An invisible weight falls off her shoulders. "My, my. Really?" She brushes ash from my hair. "Remind me to stay on your good side." She pulls herself onto the wing of her craft. "Cicero. He's valuable, and a sweetheart. Polish this up with him, and I'll polish up Cassius with the lady, yes?"

"That can be done."

She pauses. "It's best she does not see his body. Julia is a realist, but also a mother. You understand?"

I nod and back away as she takes off.

I find Cicero near the burn line watching the wall of fire creep across the grain fields. His eyes are red and his shoulders and hair covered with ash. I follow his gaze toward a huge grove of olive trees. Several dozen growers stand facing the oncoming fire holding hands.

"They give each individual tree a name," he says when he hears me approach. "They said they sing to them and it makes the trees happy, and a happy tree produces better fruit."

"Why aren't those growers in the sanctuary?" I ask. Three cities will be spared bombardment. I know not everyone will make it there, but it seemed decent to spare as many as possible. The infrastructure is the target not the civilians.

"They said the trees were their children, and they will die with them. Then they spat on me." He turns. He looks miserable. "I know the Raa and Darrow tried to kill you, but these growers, they just live here. What they said was beautiful. This place was beautiful."

"This place is military infrastructure, Cicero. It feeds sedition. Disunity. I know this act feels monstrous. I know it does not feel right. If it did, we would be monsters." I think of the pain I feel and will probably feel forever for killing Cassius. "When we lose something, we remember only the good and yearn for that. We forget the bad. We forget the Rim's transgressions. We forget the war back home started just up there." I point to the sky. "Half-measures only lengthen the road to peace, and make that peace all the more fragile. This was necessary."

He sighs and looks up at the falling ash. "They will call us Ash Lords."

"No, Cicero. A man once told me that the burning of Rhea was a mistake only because Octavia assumed the credit. That man was wrong. The burning of Rhea was a mistake only because it targeted the wrong organ—the heart of that rebellion. We have targeted the stomach. The Raa, if they survive, and the Moon Lords will either crawl to us for food or kiss our feet, and call us deliverers, or their people will rebel and we will sail and they will call us *domini*."

He says nothing.

"Look at me, Cicero."

He does. "You are what? Thirty-six? You and I will live for a hundred and fifty years more. I will end this war this year. And the hundred and fifty years that follow will be a time of unity, healing, and building. Those who die now do so so that billions more may live in peace. We will need your good heart then." I touch his chest. "Together, we will construct wonders, explore near stars, spread light further into the darkness than ever before. You and me. Now come. It's time we depart."

He smiles at my last words and lets me pull him away. But before we take off, he glances back to watch the growers burn.

The *Archimedes* idles in the hangar. Before I called down to Diomedes and Darrow, I had Kyber send a team to retrieve it. Thanks to Atlas, I knew right where it would be. It was bad enough to kill Cassius. I could not bring myself to also destroy his ship. It feels like it is part of him, and if it is destroyed, he will truly be gone.

Pytha stands over Cassius's corpse, which lies atop a gravSled. I approach and set down the helmet of Ares on the sled. He took it long ago when he knew his duty. Seems right he should keep it. Pytha does not look up. Cassius is dressed in a snow-white tunic and pants. I had Exeter sew a Morning Knight badge onto one of my cloaks for him. He does not look asleep or at peace in death. Too much damage was done to his corpse by my Praetorians after they saw Rhone's body. Knowing that this is not how I wish to remember him, I close my eyes and picture the first time we met in the halls of the Citadel of Light. How dashing he looked standing between pillars gripped by jasmine, his blue cape fluttering, the Bellona wings on the shoulders of his court armor catching the light like pearls. I hang my head in wordless sorrow. If only he had left when I asked.

I consider entering the *Archimedes* again, but there is nothing waiting for me inside except the past, and the past is dead.

Pytha's eyes are bloodshot. Her work of sneaking Cassius aboard was discovered not long after I relieved her of command. My Praetorians, except Kyber and her circle, think she already escaped. She speaks only when I free her from her manacles. "You're still sacking the Garter," she says, noting the faint tremble of the ship.

"Yes."

"Seventeen hours."

"Yes," I say heavily.

"If I ever see you again, I will kill you," she says. "So why not kill me now? Too good to punch down?"

"I'm not a monster, Pytha. Cassius was an enemy combatant. You are not a fighter. I cannot kill you in cold blood any more than I can bear to bring his body home to his mother. I know that is not what he would have wanted. In the end, he chose Darrow. The Republic. They killed him, so let them bury him."

She won't even look at me. "Did he kill Atlas?"

"Yes."

"Good. You didn't deserve to kill that dragon. Cassius did. He was a true knight. Can I go?"

Wounded that she has nothing more to say, I nod. She pushes Cassius along on the gravSled toward the *Archimedes* and disappears inside. She will go to the Republic, I know, and carry with her sensitive information. But I know what she knows, and that presents opportunities to lay traps.

The ship rumbles as it lifts off. I feel a little sad as she turns the cannons my way. When she discovers they do not work, she flies out of the hangar and soon disappears. Kyber waits for me by the exit.

"Kyber, I owe you a great thanks. Not merely for helping me stop the Fear Knight's coup, but for bringing honor back to the guards. I want no more of this kill-pool nonsense. No more cabals within cabals. There are still Gorgons amongst the ranks. We will sniff them out together."

"Thirteen is a sacred legion, *dominus*. It's part of the body of the Blood. It is a part of you, *dominus*. I will allow no corruption to gain a foothold." I touch her shoulder. The whisper has never spoken more than in these last twenty-four hours, but command suits her, and the men respect her.

"With Rhone dead, there are very few candidates to replace him as Dux. There are many Golds who have already solicited me for the post. But it is important for all to know how close Gray is to my heart. I need someone the Praetorians respect. The post is yours, Kyber."

Kyber salutes. "Gratitude, *dominus*. I will support you in every endeavor."

I pat her shoulder and my com trills with an urgent message from the bridge.

I stand with the holograms of Cicero and Pallas reviewing the sensor report from their scouts. "Do we have any idea where this second fleet came from?" I ask.

"No," Cicero says. *"They are mostly Rim-style designs, some decades old, but it looks like the* Pandora *is the flagship. Very strange."*

"We can't hit the Volk fleet before they unite," I say. "And it looks like combined they will cause us some problems, perhaps even have the edge. It'll almost certainly come down to boarding actions. We're faster than the Volk, so I'm of the mind to pass on this scrap. What do your clients think?"

Pallas laughs. *"When your transports dropped off their packages, their eyes started glowing."* I gave a few of the horticultural spoils to each of the houses that contributed ships. Nothing compared to my own personal share of the treasure, but the revenue from just a single breed of bean or tree will pay for their expedition and more, far more. *"I say we head home with the victory, the riches, and get back to the real war. If these mongrels want a fight, let them meet there where we outnumber them four to one."*

"I agree," Cicero says. *"My sister's held down the fort long enough. Mercury will bloom after this, and my clients have barely lost five hundred men and women all told. Enough shadows and dust. Let us go home. I long to feel the sun."*

"Home it is then," I say.

I take a seat in Pytha's chair as the pilot guides us away from Mercury.

I look at the world I leave behind. The green band that once circled Io's equator is gone, replaced by a conflagration that mirrors the hellish flames of Io's many volcanoes. I wish I could finish off the Volk and be certain Diomedes and Darrow are dead, but with the bounty of the Rim in my pocket, my Praetorians scourged of the disloyal, the Ascomanni purged, and the strings that made me a puppet excised from my limbs and heart, I give the order for my ships to sail back to the Core at full torch.

Later, I return to my room and sit in the quiet in the place where I sat when I spoke with Cassius. The imprint of his body still marks the sofa where he sat. I feel empty and melancholic, but also strangely at peace. I fetch Atlas's bag from where Kyber stored it and set it on the table. I open it. Inside, still stained with Cassius's blood, are fourteen golden cubes.

I think that's where I went wrong with Atlas. He might have needed Diomedes or Vela to open the vault, but I don't think Diomedes knew anything about Orpheus or *Eidmi*. Knowing the Rim there was probably some old blind White hierarch who held the secret, and would whisper it in the ear of a Raa should the dread weapon ever need to be used.

I pick out two cubes, one with the Red sigil, one with the Gold. The only question I have left to ponder is which, were he in my position, Silenius would use first.

89

DARROW

The Only Path

I T IS A CRIME how easy it is to forget home and those you love when you are at war. I used to feel guilty for how seldomly Pax would cross my mind. Usually it was only in a quiet moment before sleep or waiting for the shower water to grow hot. I would bring him mementos from distant battlefields as a way of proving he was in my thoughts. To him. To myself. To Virginia. Even to our household servants.

One of his favorite mementos was from the Himalayas on Earth. A Gold commando captain whose name I forget had a curious collection of glass globes that I discovered after relieving the man of his head. Inside the globes were tiny models of cities. Some had weather that shifted with the seasons. The one I brought home was a city trapped in perpetual winter.

I spent much of the idle hours in the Raa bunker recovering from my shoulder injury, finishing my memoirs to Pax, and telling him more and more about Cassius. That is probably why, as I emerge from the mouth of the Raa bunker three weeks after Lysander's attack on the Garter, I think of that globe city and its fantastical buildings. Most of the atmospheric generators that allowed the bounty of the Garter to blossom and flourish on this hellish moon were destroyed in the two-day bombardment. But not all of them. Not Plutus's. The atmogens were stationed beneath its everlasting defense shield, and though he could have, Lysander didn't bother to send men to destroy them. As a result, a new climate has emerged.

Ash snows down on the buildings, on the blackened trees, on the barren fields where it gathers in drifts that shift with the wind much like the sea. The air is cold and those who bundle themselves against it move hunched like mourners across a solemn winter landscape. The gold of wheat, the green of corn, the purple of plum, the red of pomegranate, the blue of berry bushes far as the eye can see has all been washed gray.

But not all is lost.

Overhead, dark ripWings perforate a cloud and bank toward the mass of a jade green warship that hovers over the dead city. More ships trundle to the east and west, along the ashen band Lune has made of the Garter. Their spotlights carve through the grimness, searching for more survivors. It is only a fragment of the efforts Volga has made to help the people of Io, and Volga's contributions are only a piece of the puzzle. Even though they might help spot survivors, Volga is wise enough to keep her Obsidians on their ships.

Instead, smaller figures skip across the landscape like hares. The Daughters are not freshly arrived. They came to help a day after Lysander departed. It's taken them weeks to find and uncover the collapsed bunker entrances. Until today, we were trapped beneath the surface of Io. At Plutus alone, I spot ten hearthcraft offering medical aide to refugees. These craft may be painted Raa black, but the hastily sprayed red owls on their wings mark the emergence of Athena and her Daughters as something far more important in the Rim's political landscape than rebels or terrorists.

Standing by my side, Diomedes watches the Daughters' hearthcraft with mixed feelings. His grandmother's face is far less conflicted. Sour and humbled, she scowls at the hearthcraft only to shoot a glare at an Athenian frigate parked on a hill where apples once grew. "Are we to kiss their feet now? And thank them for stealing our ships? Our ships that might've made the difference against Fá?" she says. "We'll see how long that lasts when the Shadow Armada arrives."

It's that sort of talk that makes me fear this moment of idealism will be washed away by realpolitik before too long. All my hopes rest on Diomedes and his fabled honor. It is precarious to put so much faith in one man, but no more precarious than putting my faith in Volga. So much balances on the good intentions of dangerous people. It's enough to give a man gray hair.

"I do not kiss feet," Diomedes says after a long moment. He scans the

Moon Lords, seeing similar sentiments in their ranks. "But I will clasp hands."

"I thought Lune didn't use any atomics," Gaia says.

"He didn't need to," I say.

"Then what is that mutant?" she says and points to a strange figure descending a building riven down its center by an orbital strike. The figure leaps from one side of the fissure to the other, before bounding our way.

I run toward him and he stops, takes off his helmet, and opens his arms for a hug. I slam into him and cling to him and Sevro hugs me back. "Cassius . . ." I say.

"I know."

I break down and Sevro holds me, hard, not humoring me, but clinging to me too. I know Cassius always rubbed him the wrong way, but when I pull back I see tears in his eyes. "I'll miss the prick," he admits. "I'll miss him a lot." Sevro smells terrible, and like home. He presses his forehead to mine. "We saw the bombardment from halfway across Ilium. I wanted to come straight off, but Athena and Volga wouldn't join their fleets. Lyria worked on Volga. I worked on Athena. Finally they agreed to move in concert, but Lune didn't stick around to give battle."

"He's more afraid of Atalantia than he is of us," I say. "We'll make him pay for that."

"Damn right."

I tousle his warhawk. When he finally pulls back, he glares at Diomedes. "You idiot. What do you think this is? The Middle bloody Ages? The only thing Lunes honor is themselves. You had that piece of shit in your grasp, Bellona. This. It's all on you, man."

Diomedes holds out his hand and closes it over the ash that falls on it. "It would appear the lesson is learned."

"Glad Bellona could pay for your education, fool," Sevro growls.

"This man is the Hegemon of the Dominion now," Gaia says. "The Moon Lords have resurrected Akari's post for him. Show due respect. He is to be referred to as—"

Sevro turns on Gaia: "Shut up, crone. I know all about you. Athena's educated me." He spies armored figures descending from the *Pandora* and stalks toward the frigate on the hill. "Best not keep your saviors waiting."

Gaia stares after him, then at Volga and her descending entourage the way Caesar might have regarded Gauls entering the Forum with weapons. "Is this why we lived? To ally with beasts?"

"If Mars does not feed us, we will starve or else crawl to Lune," Diomedes says. "So yes."

When we reach the hill, Volga and Athena wait on either side of a square table charred black during the bombardment. The two women are a study in opposites. Athena wears her helmet but also the oil-smeared jumpsuit of a laborer, and stands with a slouch. Volga has become a warrior queen in image if not yet in proof. A mane of blue feathers flows from her shining silver warhelm. I'm disgusted to see Fá's warsaw clings to the mag-holster on her back. Yet Volga's face, when she doffs her helmet, is covered in a mask of ash. She is bald too. I search for Lyria amongst the titans of her entourage and spot her soot-stained hands folded in front of her. It was not Volga's idea to wear the ashes and so come bearing her shame on her face, but the fact that Lyria thought of it and convinced her means far more to me. She looks at me in pain and her eyes start to well up.

Somewhere, maybe in the Void or the Vale, Cassius would smile to see his accidental protégé is yet again more than meets the eye.

Then Diomedes, of all people, starts the meeting off on a bad note.

"You were to come unarmed," he says.

Volga is unimpressed. "You live by my mercy."

"You rose by my aid," he says.

They glare at each other until Volga shrugs, draws the warsaw, and breaks it over her knee. An impossible act if it hadn't already been weakened by a laser. Premeditated then. She tosses the tip to Diomedes. "So you remember its edge." She returns the hilt to the holster. "And who holds the grip."

Athena curses under her breath and looks at me as if I made these giants in my personal laboratory. "Shall we get to it before we kill each other then?" she asks.

"Ideally," I reply. "Diomedes. The Covenant."

Four Dustwalkers bring the Covenant to the table. The document is laser-etched into a hunk of iron Sevro found in the rubble. It is a vague document and carries none of the reforms to the hierarchy that Diomedes agreed to in private, but it is consequential for five reasons. It provides Dominion amnesty without expiration for all Daughters of

Athena, as well as promises of due process in legal proceedings for all Colors. It pronounces the Volk's oath to never venture again beyond the asteroid belt. It formalizes a military alliance between the Republic and the Rim Dominion for a period of ten years. And it binds all parties to a declaration of war on the Society. Not Lysander, not Atalantia, not whomever rises if they fall, but the Society itself.

It does not solve all quarrels. The Dominion was refused a right to prosecute Volk braves and seek any restitution for their liberated Obsidians. The Volk were not allowed to keep any spoils of victory save the Rim Obsidians who wish to stay in the Volk host. Athena did not get the abolition of the hierarchy she desired or ownership of the Deep, yet.

In the end, no one is happy, which means it is probably the only document anyone could sign with even the slightest suspicion that it might actually be honored by the others. When drops of blood are taken from each signatory and sealed into the metal, Athena, Volga, and Diomedes stare at the iron tablet with an expression I know all too well.

What have I done? Will it matter in the end? No. One of them will break the agreement. I should be ready.

Those same thoughts play through my mind as the meeting threatens to dissolve with enough frigidity to make even an optimist fear the worst. Before each signatory can retreat to their people, I point to the iron tablet.

"This means nothing. Not to us. We all know it. But it will mean something to people who weren't here, if we let it. I don't know what we'll find when we return to the Core. Whether Mars stands or not. Whether there will even be a Republic navy left to rendezvous with us.

"But I do know this. One way or another, this war will not last the year. A reckoning is coming. Either for the tyrants or for us. We are weaker. We are fewer. The only advantage we have is that they can't afford to trust one another. We can't afford not to."

"May I say something?" We all turn to the interloper. It is Aurae. Standing with the Daughters behind Athena, she takes off her scarf and goggles. Diomedes smiles softly. I motion her forward. "In the Garden where I was raised, we are taught to study people like flowers. Many Pinks are not destined for high halls and must know how to sense dark intentions behind even the kindest eyes. When I look at you, I sense you are all growing toward the light. There is something sacred in that, because you all represent a people. People who yearn for something more. For something they've never had. Lune, Grimmus, they are trying to reclaim what they have lost: control. There is nothing sacred in that. They do not lead. They pull, they corral, they confine. Their path has only room for one. Your path has room for you all. Remember that, and from this ash freedom will grow."

On that note, the meeting adjourns. Volga returns to her jarls. Lyria jerks her head at Sevro and me to join. I nod at her dirty forehead. "The ash didn't go unnoticed by the Moonies. Well done."

Volga grimaces. "There is more to do before it is washed clean. Darrow, I am sorry about your friend. Cassius. He was the most handsome man I have ever seen." Lyria snorts. Sevro rolls his eyes. "He was. A warrior must tell the truth. And I hear he was very kind. I wish I could have known him better. Lune will die. He has broken Lyria's heart. Whatever you need. When the time comes . . ."

"Thank you, Volga."

I look at Lyria. She's wiping her eyes. "He was quite fond of you," I say. She doesn't let me console her. She bull-rushes me and hugs my hips. I peel her off and kneel and take a real hug.

"He was really pure," she says. "I'm so sorry, Darrow. He loved you. I'm sorry."

She pulls back and wipes her eyes. "Shit. This sucks."

Not long after, Volga returns to the *Pandora* with Lyria as Sevro and I say our goodbyes to Athena, Aurae, and Diomedes.

"The fleets of the giants are well under way," Diomedes says. "Uranus will try to hit the outbound Ascomanni ships and return our stolen peoples. Neptune is across the sun and will meet us in the Core. Once the Shadow Armada meets me here, we will meet you at the rendezvous."

"I won't be able to wait long," I say.

"Our ships are fast. Maybe we will beat you there." He grasps my hand and then surprises Sevro by extending his hand to him as well. Sevro looks at it in suspicion.

"Don't be late again," Sevro says.

"Don't torture me again."

Sevro shakes Diomedes's hand as quickly as possible. "I will see you in Sungrave?" Diomedes asks Aurae. I've seldom been able to look at people and realize they are in love. With Diomedes and Aurae it is so obvious even the ash knows. They are a strange, shadowy pair. One raw iron, the other a moonlit glen. But people probably think Virginia and I are an odd pair as well. Aurae squeezes Diomedes's hand. He nods to me and returns to his people.

"I'm functioning as his emissary to the Daughters before he sails for the Core," Aurae says.

"Of course you are," Sevro says.

Athena grimaces after Diomedes. "Since I'm sending our fleet with you, Darrow, if his people turn on us, they'll be able to wipe us out in a week," she says.

"But they won't," Aurae says. "They need us too now."

"You sure you don't want to come with?" Sevro asks Athena. "Just in case?"

"I am not a warrior, and this is my home. The people need me more now than ever. Cheon will have to do," she replies.

"If that's the case . . ." I unwrap Pyrphoros from my arm. Aurae laughs.

Athena ignores the blade and peers up at the falling ash. "The Garter will take decades to rebuild. Without the croplands of the Core, we'll starve out here. Maybe not this year. But the one after? Raa knows it. I know it. So you have to win, lads. Martian grain. Martian fruit. Martian cows and pigs. That's your sentence. Feed us, and don't break all my ships."

With a nod to Aurae, she turns to head back to the refugee camp.

Sevro bumps Aurae's shoulder with a fist. "Will miss your songs," he says. "For a while they were the only thing that could make me feel anything." Without waiting for a reply, he swivels away and heads for the *Pandora*.

I face Aurae. "It's been a journey," I mumble. "I wanted to say thank you. For bringing us here. For giving me *The Path to the Vale*. I was spiraling. People have saved my life before, but I think you saved my soul."

"And you saved Cassius's," she says. "It wasn't me that did it. I liked him very much. In another life, I might have loved him. But he didn't need a woman's love. He needed a brother's. The way he talked about you. Well . . ." Her eyes swim with tears. "Lysander was an obligation. You were an aspiration. He was so afraid on our journey to the Core. So nervous to see you and be rejected. But when he saw you respected him, valued him, he shined like a star. His path led back to you, because you made him feel loved. That is all that matters, Darrow. When he died, he knew he was loved. So when you think of him, when you feel sad, remember that." She kisses me on the cheek. "If we do not meet again, I will see you in the Vale with Cassius. You know the path."

It is a strange mismatched fleet that departs Io. Not just because the Obsidian ships are hulking juggernauts while the Athenian vessels are lean lightning. It is the people on the ships too. The ships the Daughters stole or built themselves are understaffed and, while rich with crafty specialists and brigades of Black Owls, are short of meaningful infantry that can challenge the Ash Legions. The Obsidian ships, while rich with quality infantry, are riven by animosity between the crews and the returning Volk. The Blues and Oranges and Reds on those ships will never forget the treatment they faced under Fá's rule, nor should they. Once they were hired contractors serving under Sefi's generous hand, then they were slaves again to the very braves who called them colleagues. Only my tearful petition, the threat to Mars, and Volga's immediate reforms keep the lowColor crews from using their newfound freedom to sabotage or abandon the ships. Still I imagine most of them will hate the Obsidians for the rest of their lives.

It is good Lysander did not want to fight our fleet. We have no cohesion yet and would have lost despite our advantage in numbers. I hope on the journey home Sevro and I can form the ragtag fleet into a fighting force that can combine with the Republic ships not grounded on Mars to help turn the tide. I know it will be an uphill struggle.

On a journey full of surprises, it seems the Rim has yet one more in store for us. Twelve hours out from Io, we receive a hail from a ship that the *Pandora*'s scanners cannot see.

It is the *Archimedes*.

My heart is heavy as I walk toward the ship with Sevro. Each step up the ramp reminds me of a friend I've lost. Eo. *Thunk*. Ragnar. *Thunk*. Orion. *Thunk*. Dancer. *Thunk*. There are less steps to reach the top of the ramp than I have dead friends to list. They all drift away when I enter the ship with Sevro. It is empty and quiet. The inspection teams have come and gone. If Lysander left a trap, it is in human form. Pytha, the former copilot of the *Archimedes* and former captain of the *Lightbringer*, waits for me in the *Pandora*'s brig.

Sevro lets me enter alone. I wander. I see Cassius everywhere I go—

hunched over its controls in the cockpit pretending not to be nervous, navigating its halls with his too-wide shoulders, giving his toast in the commissary, grinning down at me from the training room as he puts me on the floor again. But when I stand before the door to his room, the only room in the ship I've never been inside, I feel his absence. The cold of the ship. And I know I have to face him.

Cassius's body is stored in the cargo hold. He lies within a funeral torpedo stamped with the sigil of his house. Lysander's last grace for the man who became his surrogate father, brother, family. Cassius is dressed in his favorite pale blue tunic with the ink stain on the cuff and a storm cloak. His family razor lies spooled on his chest. His face and hands have been cleaned and dressed with preserving oils, but the wounds and contusions and the purple kiss of the rope cannot hide the violent way he met his end. He hardly looks like the same man I knew. My hand trembles as it touches his hair, the only part of him that escaped the brutality of Lysander. His hair is no less golden now that he is dead. A single sob comes out of me, followed by tears and silence. Cassius had a heart like Eo, though it took him longer to find it. I wish he'd found it sooner. I don't know how long I stand there thinking not of the past but all the life he had yet to live now that he'd become the man I always hoped he would be.

Footsteps bring me back into my body. I hurt all over. I wipe my face and look up to see Sevro. He looks at Cassius with the same annoyance he first looked at him sixteen years ago. "The Blue says he killed Atlas."

"A poor trade," I reply.

"Yut. Bloodydamn Bellona. The Man Who Killed Fear. Gods we're gonna hear that song in all the bars when we're fat and old. Shit. Is that . . ." He walks to the far wall and holds up a helmet. "Da's main helm." He shoves it on his head. "Fits like a glove. Man. Still stinks like Fitch too." He turns to me. "I just realized it could be booby-trapped."

"I had them check the helmet, Sevro."

"Good. Whew. Ugh, the thought of Lune snooping in my room. Disgusting." He goes quiet and takes the helmet off. He looks down at it, one of his only mementos of his father, then puts it with Cassius between his feet. He touches Cassius's leg and grows somber. I don't know if I've ever loved Sevro more than I do in the depths of his silence. We stand quiet for a few minutes before he closes the coffin's lid.

He nods for me to follow him. "Found something."

I follow Sevro to Cassius's room. The door is open. I feel anger toward Sevro for violating Cassius's sanctum, but then I see the cramped room into which Cassius fit his huge life. On one wall his childhood, filled with moving pictures of Eagle Rest, Julian, his father, his brothers, his sisters, even his mother—all curly-haired and smiling. There are a few swordsmanship badges and mementos whose meaning will never now be known. A purple stone with flecks of gold. A chunk of metal the size of an apple. A carved length of wood. A large knife with an eagle-shaped pommel. On another wall hangs a House Mars pendant, surrounded by printed news clippings of my pack. Not just me, but Sevro, Screwface, Clown, Pebble, Virginia, even Pax. They are all happy moments, and it makes me sad that he couldn't be there to share them with us. On the third wall are images of Lysander, Pytha, and Cassius through the years. But it's the holoprojector that makes me stare. A loch floats in the air filled with two shivering boys while a wolflike creature slinks around its edges.

"Looked through his deck to see what the creep liked to wank it to," Sevro says. He picks up the eagle knife and pockets it. "He's got hundreds of hours of Institute footage in here. Some people peak too early." He winces. "Sorry. He'd get that." He sighs and takes a seat in Cassius's lone chair and nods to the floor. I take a seat. He plops his hand on my shoulder. "It's a long trip home. Where should we start?"

"Wherever he left off," I say. Together, now at the age of many of the Proctors who watched our antics from Olympus, we watch the three boys ride their horses across a moonslit plain. The boys were us once. Drunk on victory, they carried an owl standard and howled like idiots at the moons. We were idiots. Trapped in a world of lies, maybe the howls were the truest things that came out of our mouths. We were all just lonely and in search of a pack.

I've already tried a tightbeam to Mars. I don't know if they received my message. So I take Pax's key in my hands and send a silent message to Virginia and my boy.

I love you. I am coming home. I have an army. I have an armada. We will win. For Eo, for Ragnar, for Fitchner, for Cassius. For them all.

ACKNOWLEDGMENTS

Of primary importance: I would like to extend my gratitude to my noble hound, Eo. You gave snuggles when I was low, with nary a complaint for all the hikes you sacrificed on the altar of creation. Without you, my sweaters would be dander-free but my heart barren as the moon. You are my Patronus even when you piddle in my bed.

Now, the humans.

In the writing of a book there's always two camps to thank. The first camp is comprised of the rugged legionnaires who stormed the walls of my writer's block at my side and the crafty engineers who labor to get this book into your hands.

Thank you to Mike Braff, a best friend, a fearless Samwise, a Virgil who helped guide me through the bramble of my own thoughts to journey's end. You are a peerless creative collaborator, and I couldn't have found the heart of this story without you. Thank you to my editor, Tricia Narwani, who—when the fist of deadline tightened around my neck—jumped into the fray like a Valkyrie of old to wheel her editorial scythe and separate the wheat from the chaff. Thank you to Joel Phillips for your cartographic and Lit Escalates brilliance. You're my brother in crime on this since before these books even hit shelves (and happy bloodydamn birthday). And thank you to Hannah Bowman, my agent, who took a chance on a young writer with a weird story to tell.

I owe a great debt to the team at Del Rey, who never once pressured me to rush the work and had faith that time was necessary for this tale to be told properly. Scott Shannon, Keith Clayton, David Moench,

Alex Larned, Ayesha Shibli, Jordan Pace, Ada Maduka, Ashleigh Heaton, Tori Henson, Sabrina Shen, Angela McNally, Caroline Cunningham, and Regina Flath, you are all Howlers and have made me feel at home with Del Rey since I was a baby writer with a fledgling goatee. Without your efforts and trust these books would be gathering dust in the corners of my mind.

Thank you as well to the army of translators across the globe—like Edoardo Rialti—who have helped the tale of Darrow spread, and to my august narrator, Tim Gerard Reynolds, for giving Darrow a voice that still sends chills up my spine.

The second camp to thank is comprised of the humans who kept me sane and tended my spark of creativity: Josh Crook, Max Carver, Kevin Sheridan, Casper Daugaard, Tamara Price Fernandez, Alexander the Great of Detroit, Willow Robinson, Jarrett Price, Evan Holtzman, and Velia soon to be Holtzman.

Thank you to my sister, Blair, for sharing my love of Greek myth as kids, and for always having my back. Thank you, as always, to Mom and Pops. Mom, for pouring gas on my creative fire, and Pops for making sure the fire didn't set the house ablaze. Without you two piling books into my arms I don't know what I'd be, but it sure as hell wouldn't be a writer.

There's more people to thank, I'm sure, but I'm jet-lagged and my brain is fried like an egg on an Arizona sidewalk. So I'll close with a thanks to you, the reader. Thank you for reading my books. Thank you for your letters, your enthusiasm, your tattoos, your cosplay, your patience, your attention, your time, your hard-earned cash, your trust, and your tears. They sustain me. Especially the tears.

With this book Darrow said farewell to worry, you said farewell to Cassius, but one book yet remains till we say farewell to this tale. So goodbye for now, *Red God* awaits.

PIERCE BROWN is the #1 *New York Times* bestselling author of *Red Rising, Golden Son, Morning Star, Iron Gold, Dark Age,* and *Light Bringer.* His work has been published in thirty-four languages and thirty-six territories. He lives in Los Angeles with his hound, Eo, and is currently scribbling book seven of the Red Rising Saga in his bathrobe and lucky slippers.

piercebrown.com
Facebook.com/PierceBrownAuthor
X: @Pierce_Brown
Instagram: @PierceBrownOfficial

To inquire about booking Pierce Brown for a speaking engagement, please contact the Penguin Random House Speakers Bureau at speakers@penguinrandomhouse.com.